SWORD & SHADOW

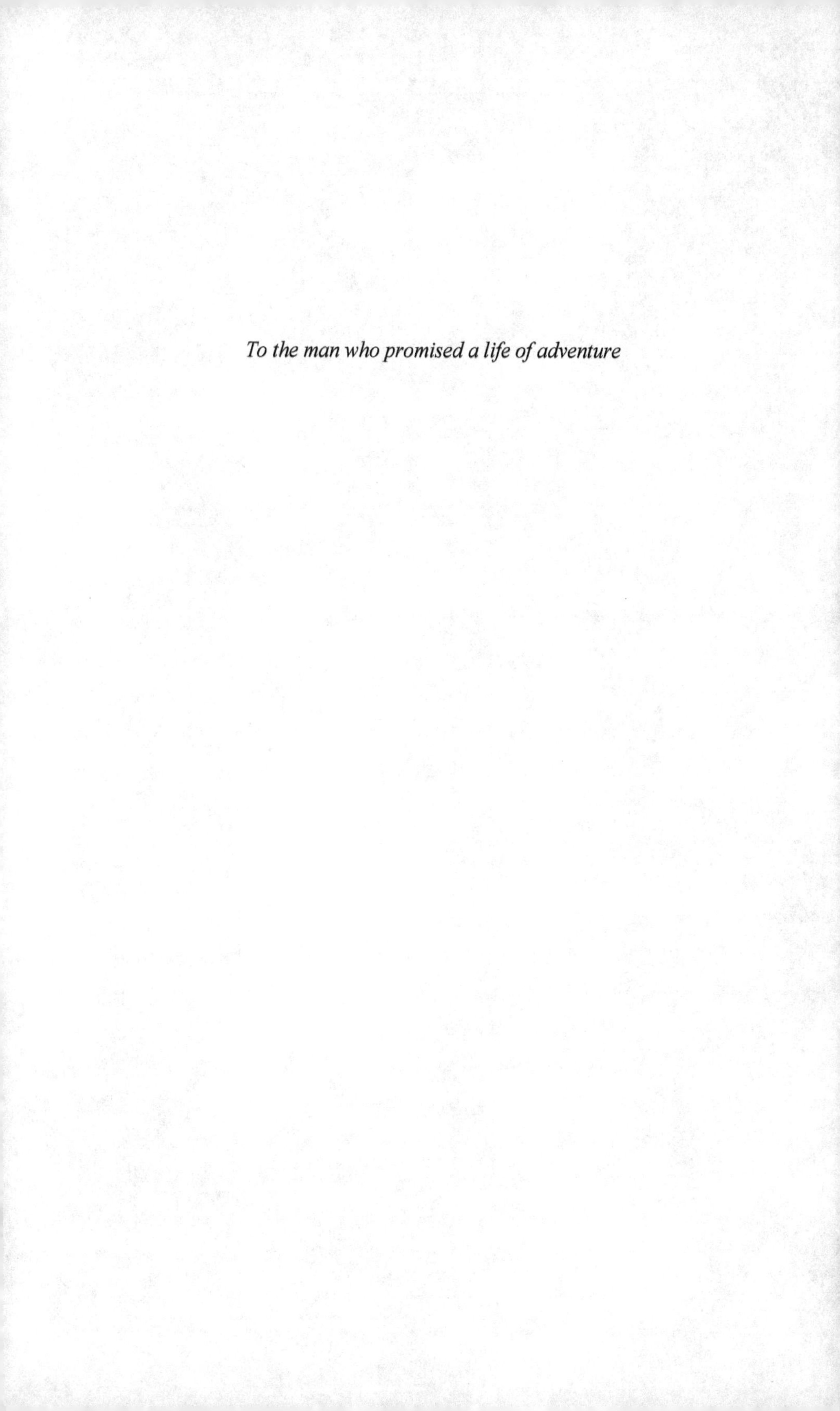

To the man who promised a life of adventure

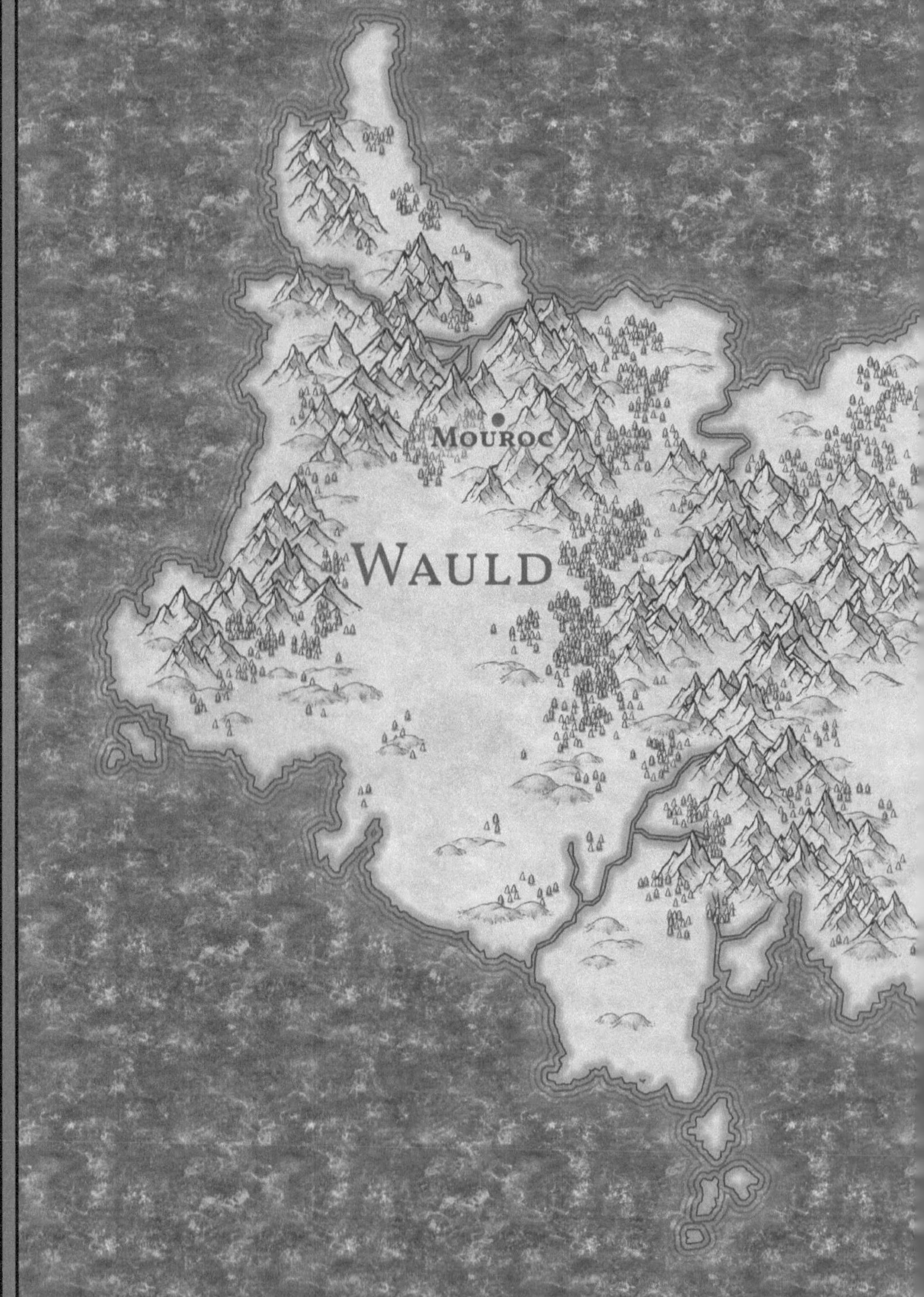

Mouroc
Wauld

KEVES ISLAND
ISLE OF
ALLUND
RIA

Part I: Shadow's Summons

I hear him. He whispers to me from the shadows.
I don't care what they say—I know in my heart, Verus is not dead. Not truly.
He whispers to me—my baby brother. I hear his voice as plain as my own. And
I will reclaim him even if I must descend into hell itself.
Excerpt from the diary of Maura Auldam, Magister in the Order of the Night,
entry date: 3rd of Chronos, 1552

ORDER OF THE NIGHT
VERLUND REACH
FLAMESEND CREST
BOUTON
PYRALUND
ORDER OF THE AGE
VAURA REACH
KEALE

CHAPTER ONE

32ND OF GALATAE, 1574

Fog drenched the stone walls of Norhels, awaiting their return. Evylin couldn't decide if the unchanged sight made her feel welcomed or threatened. She knew what lay ahead for them here.

Their troop had pressed hard that morning, knowing they couldn't take the horses with them on the continuation of their journey. Norhels was the end of the line, and the horses had handled the mere hour of hard riding with ease.

They'd done this for ten days, wearing on Evylin's already frayed emotions—ten days of walking, riding, hunting, and sleeping. The monotony of travel did little to distract her from the grief that hovered over her like that fog over the gray-blue ocean. The waves rolled beyond the city. They churned with the same agitation and coldness that enveloped her every mood.

Evylin turned her eyes to the craggy cliffside on the west side of the beach. Hidden amongst those rocks lay the entrance to the Day Keep. She tried to feel the spike of adrenaline lighting up her nerves, to anticipate the coming action with eagerness. They hadn't had a proper, pulse-pounding fight in over a week. Her Warrior's sensibilities should be thrilled to see battle once again.

Yet, all she could think as she stared at the jagged cliffs was that they were all flirting with death.

"Everyone knows what to do once we enter the city?" Deckard asked, his black mare carrying him into Evylin's sightline as he moved to the front of the group. Her heart gave a disgruntled patter. She couldn't determine whether its agitation was due to her guilt for accusing him of killing her uncle or bone-deep dread over the rising attachment she felt for him.

Though they'd reconciled after Hewitt's death and burial, she'd not regained her comfort with her husband. How could she when her whole being ached with her loss? So, while they maintained a companionable regard, it had grown more professional than marital, more that of officer and soldier than of husband and wife.

In the dim light of the morning, Deckard's hair looked more brown than red, its ends curling just over the tips of his ears. They'd traveled so long, he almost didn't look like the same man she'd met two months ago in Whickam Village. Like the other men, he wore a beard now, littered with bright copper strands. Though he had shaved daily while they traveled with the Ephrian Army, their fast-paced travel had disrupted his routine. He'd also grown more muscular, his lean frame firming up through his training with Hewitt.

Evylin tightened her jaw, forcing herself to pay attention as Deckard reminded them of their orders. "We'll have to travel light in Wauld," he said. "Once we make it through the Night Keep, we'll restock. Until then, sell what you can. We'll need the money."

Over the last several days, the Calder siblings had informed them of the intricacies of Waulden culture, mainly how regulated everything was. No weapons could be purchased without express written permission from each province's nobility. Merchants had to follow exacting laws and complicated practices on where and when to sell their goods, making the prices almost twice what they were in Ephria. Heavily armed guards monitored each settlement, even the villages.

And perhaps most concerning, they had to pass through checkpoints when entering and leaving the Reaches, the provinces that belonged to the Mages, bestowed upon them by the King of Wauld himself. These barricades were designed to prevent the Mages from usurping the non-magical king. Anyone wishing to enter or exit these territories needed an endorsement specifying their exact purpose for crossing the border.

"I still don't see why we have to sell the horses," Rafferty lamented, his ghostly complexion and white-blond hair making him look like a wraith in the fog. Even his dark gray coat helped him blend into the scenery.

Thom tossed him a dry grin as they rode toward the city. "Do you want to be on horse duty while we're in the Keeps?" he asked. "Keeping them alive will be the easiest part. It's getting them down those stairs that worries me."

"We can purchase new horses once we leave the borders of Verlund Reach," Auden said, his deep brown coat worn from their travels.

"And how long will it take to leave said Reach?" Rafferty countered.

Looking at his sister, Auden raised his dark red eyebrows. Ilain quickly calculated and said, "About two and a half days."

"Two and a half days of walking," Rafferty grumbled.

"At least we won't be carrying much," Ethenn offered from the back of the group. "That'll allow us to move quickly, won't it?"

Ilain passed a wry look over her shoulder at the young man. Her silken red hair cascaded down her back with the motion. "True, but speed only does us so much good. We must take caution everywhere in Wauld," her lilting accent made her words sound teasing rather than ominous, "even in the forests. It would behoove us not to enter any settlement unless we absolutely must."

"And even when we do," Auden added, "it would be best to keep the party small."

Rafferty frowned at Evylin, his horse keeping pace alongside hers. "Sounds like we'll be sleeping under the stars from here on out, then," he said with a dramatic sigh. "Life as a soldier in King Ephren's special Order isn't as rewarding as I'd hoped."

"Did you expect the lap of luxury, Raff?" Evylin asked, tossing him a half-felt smirk.

"I expected a bed, at the least," he returned. "No inns or taverns for however long we're trekking through that Allore-forsaken country. How will I ever survive?"

Evylin tipped her head in his direction, lowering her voice. "Let's just hope Auden's spice box doesn't run out."

"Heavens forbid!" Rafferty lifted a hand to his forehead, feigning a swoon.

Though Evylin would have normally laughed at his theatrics, she could only smile ruefully. She appreciated Rafferty's company, particularly these days. He never asked her questions or treated her in any special manner. He was, for good or ill, his wily, irreverent self. And he'd instituted himself as a personal companion for her ever since they'd left the forest near Virwoud and the grave that haunted her memories.

A twitch tugged Evylin's lips downward. Her mind retreated, crawling into the shadows that plagued her every thought. Back to the shock and pain. Back to Hewitt and his grave.

"Evylin," Deckard said, drawing her reluctant attention. As they approached the city, he'd pulled back from the front to ride at her side.

She kept her gaze drifting somewhere around his shoulders and where the high collar of his coat rose onto his neck. "Yes?"

"Due to the restrictions in Wauld," he began, his voice steady and calm as though speaking to a soldier rather than his wife, "I thought it would be a good idea to visit a smithy for repairs and possibly more weapons. Do you agree?"

Adjusting in her saddle, Evylin forced herself to shut off her emotions and focus on the question. Deckard had begun doing this days ago—seeking her advice on tactics and giving her strategic tasks. Usually, he'd have relied on Hewitt for such things. With him gone and her as the sole remaining Warrior of the troop, it was only logical that the charge of weaponry and strategy should fall to her. But Evylin knew the real reason he'd transferred the responsibility into her hands. He didn't care about her qualifications or her magical predisposition for strategy. He knew she needed the distraction.

As Rafferty had instated himself as Evylin's companion, it seemed that Deckard had become her guardian, always watching, always alert. The instant she began to feel the void of sorrow sucking on her thoughts, Deckard would notice. Before that void could leach her dry, he would step in and give her a job. Something more tangible and distracting than Rafferty's jests could provide.

Deckard's ability to read her pain annoyed her at first. Whenever despair attempted to latch onto her mind, he would inevitably be there, reminding her of his goodness. Each time, a surge of anger shot through her, desperate to wallow in her misery—to forget his very presence. Then, just as quickly, she'd find herself impossibly grateful to him for saving her from herself.

Her heart was in constant turmoil. After losing Hewitt and Ryen, she was broken beyond repair. Despite the feelings she'd begun to foster for her husband, despite the yearning that had grown within her, the soil of her soul was barren. It could nurture no more affection for any man, not when he would inevitably leave her too.

Yet, with the weight of her grief, Evylin had somehow come to require Deckard's help for the most basic of functions. Even rising from bed often required his order to get up, reminding her of their task to save their people. *"You are a Warrior, and the people of Ephria and Wauld need you. You're supposed to save them."* His charge didn't hold the same sway over her moral conscience the way he expected, but it did give her a sense of resolve, a goal. She'd already lost everything in the pursuit of Ryen's dream; she might as well see it through to the end.

Though Evylin hated to admit it, she'd begun to find herself relying on Deckard. She fought it the first few days after Hewitt's death. As members of the Order of the King, the personal soldiers of King Ephren, their status earned them lower rates everywhere they went, allowing them to survive more comfortably than the average traveler. At each inn, Evylin and Deckard acquired a separate room, which provided her the freedom to pull away from him to a degree she couldn't in the company of their troop. For the first several nights, she went nearly sleepless, curled away from him on the far side of the mattress. She'd grown so used to his arms around her while they slept that her body had forgotten what to do without him.

Deckard noticed. One night, as they got into bed and she moved to turn away from him, he gripped her arm loosely. She refused to meet his eyes but could feel his steady gaze scanning her as he whispered, "If you keep this up, you'll never sleep again."

"I don't know what else to do," she whispered back, feeling a sob welling up in her tense throat.

"I do." Gently, he pulled her closer. Evylin had grown weak in her resolve, too exhausted and distraught to maintain the distance. He'd carefully wrapped his arms around her as he always did, tucking her head under his chin. And she'd fallen asleep within minutes.

As the gates of Norhels loomed above their heads, Evylin forced herself to meet Deckard's stare. Patient and steady as ever, he watched her. "That seems wise," she agreed, her voice hollow to her own ears.

Deckard gave her a firm nod. "In that case, I'll leave that to your charge," he said with finality. But he didn't move away from her side even as they entered the city, as though knowing she needed him.

Tightening her hands on the reins so she wouldn't twist her wedding rings, Evylin stared at her horse's mane. Did she need him? She didn't think she should. The last two men she'd needed, she'd lost. The last two men who meant that much to her broke her. Could she risk needing someone that much again?

The city of Norhels hardly constituted the status in Evylin's mind. Its large populace granted its qualification, but compared to Loclight or even Virwoud, it lacked the grandeur she thought a city should require. Its walls were short, only about the average man's height, more for controlling the comings and goings than real protection. Its houses reminded her of the cottages in Estshire, and most of its streets were made of dirt with the occasional stone pathway worked into the wealthier areas. As a port city, everything smelled heavily of fish, dampness, and salt.

Coming to a stop in the main thoroughfare, shops located in a wide radius, the troop dismounted. Deckard gave his final orders, and they split off. Deckard and Auden went to sell the horses to the stablemaster. Thom, Rafferty, and Ilain went to sell whatever else they might and then purchase rations and other necessities for their time in Wauld. And Evylin and Ethenn went to the smith with the weapons.

The smoke of the forge singed Evylin's nose, calling forth memories of Hewitt and Whickam Village. Her skin warmed as they stepped into the interior. The tang of iron and soot filled the air. She could almost imagine her uncle, the bear of a man he'd been, laboring at that anvil.

Instead, a bald, barrel-chested smith looked up at their arrival. He scanned the pair of them warily, their arms laden with swords. "May I help you?"

Dumping their haul onto a clear-enough workbench, Evylin took the lead. "Yes, sir.

My comrades and I require repairs. We'd also be interested in seeing what you have in stock."

The smith looked at Ethenn with a frown. Apparently deciding that a man barely in his twenties held little more qualification than a woman, he turned back to Evylin. "That's a load of weapons there, lass. What sort of business are you in?"

Pushing back her braid, Evylin uncovered the insignia on the left breast of her gray coat. "The King's," she replied.

The smith's mangy eyebrows rose in shock as he gave her another scan. "My apologies, ma'am," he stammered, then glanced at Ethenn, taking in the patch on his coat as well, and added, "Sir. How soon do you need these done?"

"Immediately," Evylin said, clasping her hands behind her back as she'd seen Deckard do when he was addressing those under his command. "We need to leave as soon as possible."

The smith's brow furrowed nervously. "Yes, of course. One of my assistants is out on deliveries, and another is home with a cold—the youths are rather unreliable these days. My son and I will work as fast as we can, but as this is quite the order, it will take three hours, at the least."

Readily, Ethenn stepped forward, unbuttoning his coat. "I'll help," he offered.

The smith and Evylin both stared at him in surprise. "You will?" she asked.

Tipping up a shoulder in a shrug, Ethenn continued to work off his coat. "My uncle is a smith," he explained. "When I wasn't hunting, I was at the forge."

A subtle memory sprang from the recesses of Evylin's thoughts. Vernon Loxley was the smith in Trollenston, and though she hadn't known him then, Evylin had seen Ethenn working as an assistant when they'd said goodbye to his uncle. Remembering the smith brandishing a poker at his nephew during that occasion, she understood why Ethenn hadn't bothered to claim the relation before now.

"That explains the muscle," Evylin teased. Of a stocky, short build, Ethenn was the picture of a Shireman. "I always chalked it up to the fighting."

Carefully rolling up the cuffs of his tunic sleeves, he gave a dry grin. "That was just for fun."

"Mm." Evylin felt her mouth turn upward in humor even as she addressed Norhels's smith to determine the price of the labor.

With Ethenn's help, the smith and his son, a strapping lad of seventeen, completed their work within two hours. Every blade was sharpened to deadly precision, all nicks mended, and scrapes polished. When the rest of their troop arrived, they practically bought out the smith's stores. Ethenn was loaded with a full quiver and an extra bundle of arrows. He looked particularly fearsome with his sword hanging on his right hip, his hatchet and a large hunting knife on the left, and a leather band across his chest with a dozen small throwing knives.

"Look at you, kid," Thom said, straightening Ethenn's collar in jest, then fluffing up the front of his shaggy brown hair. "You're practically the whole Ephrian Army in one."

Brushing down his hair, Ethenn scowled at Thom. "Your things are over there," he grumbled, gesturing to the far bench.

Once they were all fully equipped, most looked as stocked as Ethenn. Rafferty carried a short sword on each hip along with his own bandolier of daggers. Evylin, Deckard, and Thom all wore broadswords and several knives. She'd had to purchase a new sword, having lost the one Hewitt made for her in the Water Keep. Her sensibilities grated at having to use a weapon forged by anyone else, but after the smith refined the weight and flex for her, she slid the blade into a scabbard at her side.

Only the Calders were weapon-free, though their bright green gazes held a dangerous glint. Ilain's rings glittered in the forge light anytime she moved, reminding them of the Elemental resources she wielded.

After paying a fair sum to the smith, they departed for the nearby tavern. "Auden suggested we eat before entering the Keep," Deckard explained. "We're not sure when our next meal will be."

"I didn't think it was wise to eat before a fight," Rafferty commented. "You know— stomach cramps and the like. Can't have Thommy here losing his lunch on his fair highlady's skirts."

Thom whacked the back of Rafferty's head, and Ilain chortled.

"Better that than any of us fainting due to hunger," Deckard said, ignoring their antics.

Over lunch, they reviewed all their supplies. They'd procured three packs full of dry goods and the barest necessities. They wouldn't even have bedrolls for the first several days of their journey. But Deckard insisted they replace any clothing with worn holes or fraying edges. "We need everything we carry with us to last the rest of the way through Wauld," he said.

"What about our coats?" Ethenn asked, then gestured to the insignia of the king's Order.

"I'm afraid we'll have to leave them behind," Deckard said. "We can't very well journey through the country wearing the sigil of their enemy."

Rafferty frowned down at the coat. "I suppose they'd fetch a pretty penny."

"I don't think the king would want other people having them." Thom tapped his patch. "Can't say I'm keen on some fisherman earning the rank of captain all at the cost of a coat either."

"We'll leave them with the farrier," Deckard said. "I've already arranged it with her."

"You have?" Evylin asked, surprised.

"Farriers board horses, Colonel," Rafferty mocked. "Not coats."

Deckard leveled a dry stare at him. "Yes, and she's boarding my horse," he explained. "She'll keep the coats in a small trunk in the stall with her."

"You're keeping your horse?" Thom asked with a somewhat incredulous air.

Evylin shared the sentiment. "Won't that cost a large sum?"

Deckard shook his head. "I worked out a deal with the farrier. In exchange for her board, she's allowed to rent her out for labor around the town. She readily agreed, as my mare is of strong, well-bred stock."

"You're *keeping* your horse?" Thom repeated.

Deckard shrugged. "She was gifted to me when I earned my captaincy, and I've gotten attached to her."

Once, Evylin would have teased Deckard about his attachment to a horse, but she merely smiled wryly. No matter how much she relied on him, she was struggling to return to their old banter. The schism in her mind between fear and reliance kept her from finding that middle ground of companionship with him. Sarcasm couldn't find a place amidst her unsteady feelings. Instead, she often found herself silent in his presence, simultaneously fearful of drawing him near and driving him away.

After changing into their new clothes and dropping off their coats, the troop made their way to the back gate of Norhels. Auden and Deckard took the lead. Their band, heavily armed and dressed primarily in black, garnered the stares of the citizens as they passed. They resembled mercenaries, Evylin thought. Or, with the Calders present, perhaps they appeared more like a noble escort.

The noontime sun cut through the dissipating fog, glinting off the sea. The waves lapped at the shore as they walked toward the beach. They climbed over the rocks, traversing the rugged terrain all the way back to the Day Keep, well out of sight of the city.

Rafferty turned to Ilain, who lingered near his and Evylin's side as they walked. "Last time we were here," he said, "Blount took the Relic, and the Keep went dark. What are we expecting this time?"

"I couldn't say for sure," Ilain admitted. "With the Relic returned, I'd imagine the magic will come to life again. And that may mean the Shades will fight to get it back."

"Does that mean we'll have to fight the Guardian too?" Ethenn asked on her other side.

"Probably."

At Ethenn's frown, Ilain laughed. "Don't worry, dear," she teased, reaching across to squeeze his bicep. "With the Day Relic in our possession, Auden is twice as powerful as usual. And the Fire Relic makes me three times as powerful. We'll keep you safe."

She said the last part with a wink that made Ethenn's cheeks turn pink. "Why does it make you more powerful than him?" he asked, studiously avoiding her gaze.

"Because I'm naturally more powerful than my brother," she said nonchalantly.

"How'd that happen?" Rafferty asked.

Ilain grinned. "Allore's grace, I suppose."

"Guess that's good for us," he replied. "And what about the Night Keep? What should we expect in there?"

At that, Ilain's bright mood dimmed. "That's a mystery, I'm afraid. As in all Keeps, we'll face Shades and a Guardian, and the structure will be more or less the same. However, as I'm sure you've come to notice with the two Keeps you've had the privilege to enter, they reflect the Relic that they house. And a Keep that reflects Night is a rather unsettling prospect."

"How so?" Rafferty prodded.

Ilain gave him a pained expression but didn't respond.

Having experienced Night magic as the captive of Prince Blount, Evylin answered for her. "It isn't a magic any sane man would deal in."

With an understanding nod, Rafferty let the subject go. They knew of Auden and Evylin's suffering at Prince Blount's hands. The heir to Wauld was after the Relics himself, and he'd been using their party to lead him to them. He'd ambushed them, leading to Hewitt's death and taking Ilain, Thom, Rafferty, and Ethenn captive. To learn the locations of the rest of the Keeps, Blount used Night magic to torture Auden. When Evylin attempted to rescue her comrade and escape, the prince kicked her across the face, then slapped her for her further disobedience. If it hadn't been for Deckard's rescue of the rest of their troop, Auden and Evylin would have died at the Night Mage's hands.

Night magic was horrible. Of that, Evylin had no doubt. Dark and cruel, just like the prince who wielded it. Its Keep would be no different.

With Auden and Deckard at the front of the group, they found the Day Keep's entrance at the base of the cliff. A large rock butted against the jagged face, its weatherworn surface crusted in lichen and mollusks. The faintest split in the cliffside revealed the narrow passage down into the Keep. One by one, they slipped into the darkness. The air grew cooler and damper in the cave, and they were shrouded in black for a moment.

Suddenly, bright golden light shot forth from the antechamber of the Keep, lighting up a pathway of stone columns and arched windows. At the far end, an iron door awaited them, with rays of light etched across its face.

As Deckard made to move for the hall, Auden stopped him. "May we have the Relics now?" he asked, a respectful tilt to his tone despite its pointed request.

Deckard paused, drawing back his shoulders. The golden glow on one side of the antechamber clashed with the darkness from the other, casting Deckard half in light and half in shadow. It gave him a stark, haggard look, showing the wear and stress their journey had placed on him. Tall, he nearly reached the hall's low, arched ceiling.

For a moment, Evylin thought he might refuse, their trust in the Calders still tremulous after their weeks of lies, but then he turned to Rafferty. "Go ahead," he ordered.

Digging a hand into his coat, Rafferty retrieved the two Relics from the inner recesses of his coat. Their golden chains and pendants shone in the light, but their gemstones—a yellow topaz and a scarlet ruby—refracted dimly as he held them up.

"I'll take the Fire Relic," Auden said, reaching for the red talisman.

Deckard held up a hand to stall him. "Isn't that wasting our best assets? If you're a Day Mage and Ilain is a Fire Mage, you should carry the appropriate Relics."

Though Ilain stared at the Fire Relic with excitement in her eyes, Auden's brow furrowed with worry. "That isn't a good idea," he objected. "You'd be giving us a taste of the complete sum of our powers. We won't want to give it up."

"We have to make it through these Keeps," Deckard said. "I'll risk your hunger for power if that means our safety."

"That sort of power can become an obsession, Jonn," Auden argued.

Deckard didn't back down. "If it becomes a problem, I'll trust Evylin to knock you out and pry the Relic from your hands."

Pressing her lips together around a dry smile, Evylin almost laughed. Though part of her doubted that she could best a pair of Mages at the height of their power, her pride appreciated the sentiment.

Auden looked reticent but nodded.

Rafferty proffered the ruby Relic to Ilain. "Milady," he crooned, then tossed the topaz Relic to Auden.

As soon as the Relics hit the Mages' hands, the gemstones lit up as though with an inner beacon. Once the chains hung around their necks, Ilain gestured to the hall. "Shall we?"

CHAPTER TWO

Passing into the sunshine-yellow beams of light in the antechamber, Evylin felt an immediate sense of warmth spread through her. The metalwork windows bore images of suns, and as they walked farther, the light grew brighter. Their boots thumped against the stone floor, each soldier cautiously drawing weapons. Auden hesitated momentarily before placing a hand on the iron door. An immediate *thunk* sounded the release of the Keep's lock, then a rolling *click-click-click* accompanied the door's opening.

The rooftop garden of the Day Keep awaited them, a heavy brown sky hanging above them. But the moment Auden set foot inside, the sky flared to life. Yellow pulsed all around the tower, causing Evylin's eyes to ache in its instant brightness. The sweet scent of flowers drifted to her nose as she moved along at the Mages' backs. Vibrant grass and a pebbled path stretched to the back of the Keep, flowered bushes and trees guiding their way.

With cautious steps forward, the troop scanned every inch of the garden. The path led to a tall obelisk at the back of the Keep, where the entrance to the Chamber lay. Shifting her grip on the leather hilt of her sword, Evylin moved to Ilain's side. Her heart started beating heavily in anticipation. She tried to grasp hold of the sensation, willing her magic to kick in. After their time in the Water Keep, she'd yet to lock onto her powers as a Warrior again. It seemed to elude her, held away by the mundane depression she fought.

She feared that she couldn't access it anymore and would fail her friends when they needed her most. But as the pebbles crunched beneath her feet and the golden light surrounded her there in the Keep, she found her senses coming alive with sharp relief.

Suddenly, Deckard moved to Evylin's flank. "I hear them," he said, sword raised in preparation.

Fanning out, Thom and Rafferty shifted before the Mages while Ethenn nocked an arrow, gazes keen on the roof's edges. They took position not a moment too soon, as hundreds of Shades rose over the sides. The humming pulse of their presence filled Evylin's ears, undulating with the creamy yellow light that fused their clay forms.

As though summoned by the magic itself, Evylin's Warrior senses sharpened, her skin prickling with ready power. Her muscles grew taut with eagerness for action. She could see every blade of grass, feel every pebble under her boots, and hear her companions' heightened breaths. The world slowed imperceptibly to allow her to take it in.

The *twang* of Ethenn's bowstring drawing back signaled Evylin that the fight was about to begin, and she readied herself when Auden suddenly cried out, "Wait!"

Body primed to strike, Evylin nearly stumbled forward, and Ethenn fought to hold the tension on the string.

The Shades stood still at the tower's edges, staring at the troop as their magical forms hummed.

Auden set a hand to the Day Relic. "It's warm," he said to Ilain.

Her hand flew to the Fire Relic at her breast. "Mine's not."

Red hair shining with a golden tint in the brightness, Auden took a step forward, surveying the Shades. "You," he pointed to a particular Shade, "come here."

As instructed, the Shade stepped forward while the rest remained still.

Though the threat seemed nonexistent, Evylin and Deckard exchanged a worried glance, weapons ready. Thom shifted uneasily on her other side.

Examining the Shade up close, Auden's green gaze swept over it excitedly. The Shade bore no facial features, only an oblong head. Its form mimicked humanity in the most rudimentary way, as though someone had shaped their clay but had not taken the time to put in the details.

"No one has ever. . . ." Auden paused as though remembering their business here in the Keep. He looked up to where the Shade's eyes should have been. "You are under my control?"

The Shade's glow winked once as if in answer, and Auden gasped. "I heard it," he murmured, then looked to Ilain. "I heard it in my head. They can speak through the Relic."

Mouth ajar, Ilain blinked rapidly. "We don't have time for study, Auden."

He nodded as though trying to convince himself, turning back to the Shade. "You will let us pass unharmed?"

Another wink of light.

"Will you join us below in the Chamber?"

This time, the light winked twice.

Auden frowned. "No," he translated for the troop. "I'd hoped we could take them with us into Night."

"Too good to be true," Ilain quipped.

Relaxing his stance, Deckard let his sword lower, and Evylin followed his lead. She could hear the other men easing beside them. Ethenn shook out his arm, taxed from holding the bow taut for so long.

Auden dismissed the Shades with a near-reluctant tilt to his voice. He was ever the magister, a scholar seeking new knowledge. His eyes carefully studied the Shades as they retreated down the sides of the tower and out of sight, their hum receding with them.

Rafferty clapped a hand onto Auden's shoulder. "Not to worry, Highlord," he teased. "With that Relic around your neck, I'm sure they'd happily let you come back and prod them to death in pursuit of academia."

As Ilain chuckled along with Rafferty, the Mages made for the path. Ethenn jogged around them to move to the front. He kept an arrow nocked as he ensured the way was clear. Evylin looked up at the Deckard brothers, one on either side. "Too good to be true?" she muttered to them.

Thom let out a huff.

Deckard shook his head dubiously but began to follow their team.

The false start caused Evylin's grip on her magic to stutter. Her skin didn't tingle with the same ferocity, and her senses returned to a natural awareness. The flowers didn't smell as sharp, her eyes didn't adjust to the light, and their footfalls now sounded rather muted, like she had a pillow pressed over both ears.

It worried her, yet they crossed the rooftop without incident. Evylin couldn't shake the feeling that it was all too easy. They should be fighting for their lives, yet they were about to enter the Chamber at full strength. She supposed she should be grateful for the blessing. But she worried this was lulling them into a false sense of security.

They reached the marble obelisk, its door a replica of the Keep's entrance. While Ethenn watched their backs, Rafferty took the lead, holding the door open for the Calders. The troop stepped into the obelisk's stone interior, a spiral staircase leading them into the Chamber. Winding down what Evylin imagined to be dozens of flights, she worked to maintain a touch of her magic. Even if the Guardian below allowed them to pass, they would enter the Night Keep in mere minutes. She had to be ready for whatever insanity it would throw at them.

The Day Chamber sprawled before them, creamy marble with golden veins covering every inch. The columns, the floors, and the ceilings—all of them shone with brilliance. No windows lined the space, but it radiated light as though the sun's rays beamed over it all. At the far end of the Chamber, the dais awaited with a pair of metal gates at its back. And stretched out in front of the dais lay a massive golden dragon.

Evylin's heart fluttered at the sight of the beast. The echo of Ryen's memory whispered to her. They'd dreamed of fighting a dragon as children. It was part of her vow to him when she left Whickam Village.

"Win dozens of duels, rescue a princess, fight a dragon . . . and become legends worthy of five hundred tales."

She'd fulfilled her promise, but it had come at the cost of Hewitt's life.

Evylin's fingers trembled against the grip of her sword. No matter how docile the Guardian seemed, the troop crept forward cautiously. When last they were in the Chamber, the dragon's talons had sliced open Deckard's stomach. If it hadn't been for Auden's Day magic, Deckard would have died.

Even weeks later, Evylin's body grew cold at the memory.

Leaning toward Auden, Rafferty motioned toward the Relic. "You think that thing'll let you control the Guardian too?" he asked.

"I hope so," Auden replied.

The dragon lay still as they approached. Its golden eyes watched them, though it never lifted its head. Nor did the creature seem surprised by their presence. It simply watched.

Cautiously, they moved around the Guardian for the dais. Stepping up and to the back, Evylin kept one eye on the dragon, sword at the ready. She couldn't fathom that it would be this simple, not even as they all crowded onto the platform before the gates.

Ilain hurried up to Auden's side before the pair of gold metalwork gates. A pulsing yellow light beckoned, so bright Evylin couldn't see what lay beyond it. The scrollwork of the gates twisted like vines and branches, coiling up to encircle a half-sun and two half-moons.

The gates whispered danger to Evylin—a warning of darkness and death on the other side.

She tightened her grip on her sword, shoving down her fear.

Stepping up to her side, Deckard stared at the gates with a narrowed gaze. His hand brushed over the marble pedestal where the Relic once lay. His jaw had clenched, and his brow pinched together in that way of his—a sure sign of his worry. "You said the Keeps are mirrors of one another?" he said.

The Calders turned back to him. "That's what our studies suggested," Auden confirmed. "The ancient Mages' accounts claim this as a back door between Day and Night."

"That seems like cheating," Ethenn remarked, watching the Guardian warily, arrow nocked securely.

"You got a problem with that?" Rafferty asked, twirling a short sword in his hand.

"No," the hunter returned, letting his arrow relax a little in his grip. "I'm simply saying that it doesn't make sense. If this is truly a back door, and if the Keeps truly mirror one another, then doesn't that mean we'll walk right onto the dais, right next to the Relic?"

"Theoretically," Auden said.

Ethenn nodded at his point proven. "Why would the makers of the Keeps do that?"

A slow grin worked across Ilain's face as she scanned him. "You're right. It's a trap."

"You're telling me we're willingly walking into a trap?" Thom demanded.

"We don't have a choice," Auden countered.

"To little Loxley's point," Rafferty said, "aren't we walking straight up to the Relic?"

"To the best of our knowledge."

"Then who cares if it's a bloody trap?" he returned. "We walk right in, you grab the Relic, Highlord Existential Mage, and poof! There goes the Night Guardian."

"It isn't that simple," Ilain said, despite her grin.

"It never is," Evylin muttered.

Ilain tossed her an amused glance. "It takes focus to kill a Guardian, like *all* magic. Walking through and grabbing the Relic will help, but Auden and I will need to focus on connecting with Night to destroy the Guardian. Then we'll have to fight our way out."

"Why couldn't he just control the Shades again?" Thom suggested.

Auden took over with a shake of his head. "I have two theories," he said. "First, we are returning with the Relic. There is nothing for the creatures to defend now. But with the Night Relic still in its Keep, the Shades will be tasked with reclaiming it. My second theory is that I could control them because I'm a Day Mage with the Day Relic. Neither may be true, but I think we should assume that we need to be on our guard."

"Very well," Deckard said, then motioned to the gates. "We made our plans last night. Let's not squabble about them any longer."

Rafferty and Thom stepped up behind Auden and Ilain as the Mages prepared to open the gates. Ethenn held the back, with Evylin and Deckard just before him. She didn't like the plan any more now than last night, but she didn't have any better suggestions either.

The plan was simple: The Ephrians would distract the Guardian while the Calders found the Relic and channeled their connection to Night. Not elegant, but hopefully successful enough to avoid death.

Evylin's throat tightened. Eyes locked on the metalwork of the gates before them, she tipped her head toward Deckard. "Do me a favor?" she said, voice low.

"Anything," he returned.

Auden and Ilain lifted their hands to the gates.

"Try not to get severely injured this time," Evylin said. "I'd rather not carry you out of another Keep."

The warm, breathy sound of Deckard's laugh seeped into Evylin's core, and her muscles instinctively relaxed. "I'll do my best," he promised.

The sun and moons on the gates began to glow, forming a radiant globe of light. Pure yellow light pulsed out from the sun, and deep purple beamed from the moons. The gates opened soundlessly as the light beyond grew brighter, and the metal doors swung inward.

"Quickly," Auden summoned before grabbing his sister's arm and disappearing into the light.

Thom and Rafferty disappeared next, Deckard and Ethenn hurrying at Evylin's side. Golden light enveloped them, covering every inch of her skin in warmth and blinding her entirely. For one terrifying second, she lost track of Deckard. For one heart-stopping moment, she thought she'd lost him too. But just as quickly, the awareness of his presence returned, and she could breathe again.

It only took four steps to pass from Day into Night: two to walk through the gates and two to leave it.

Evylin was no longer blinded by light beyond comprehension. Now, she lost her vision to an all-consuming darkness that smothered her.

CHAPTER THREE

"So," Rafferty remarked, his voice echoing somewhere to Evylin's left, "this is the Night Keep, huh? Seems a little on the nose, if you ask me."

Darkness wholly surrounded Evylin. She felt like she'd had a blanket thrown over her head, engulfing her in black. Then she realized it wasn't black at all.

The deepest, most saturated purple beamed around her. The shift from unfathomable brightness into the deepest depths of darkness felt like hitting a wall head-on. All her senses were out of order, trying to make sense of this collision.

Evylin tried to gather her bearings, working to form some concept of where she was and what surrounded her, but she struggled to trust her senses.

"I can't see a damn thing," Thom grumbled toward the front of the group.

A cautious step sounded to Evylin's immediate left. "The pedestal should be right before us," Deckard whispered.

"Don't move," Auden hissed. "I can sense the Guardian."

Ethenn's bow creaked as he drew it back. "Where?" he whispered.

"I'm not sure," Auden replied. "Its presence is here, but I can't pinpoint it."

Grappling for control of her magic, Evylin tried to reach out and sense the Guardian's location. Surely if Auden could feel it, she could too. But as she stared into the dark of Night, all she saw was more of that all-encompassing purple pitch.

"You know," Rafferty murmured, "you'll have to move at some point. If you want to get that Relic, I mean."

The lowest, ominous rumble rolled out from the Chamber in response.

Evylin went to raise her blade, but it knocked against something. "Careful," Deckard whispered, causing her to blanch.

"We have to spread out," she suggested quietly. "If that thing is about to attack, we can't fight all bunched up on this dais."

"Why *hasn't* it attacked yet?" Rafferty asked louder than Evylin would like. "Not that I'm complaining. It just seems to be its job."

As though offended by the suggestion of its lax security, a sudden thundering ricocheted through the room. Heavy impacts shook the floor, vibrating into Evylin's feet. Whatever the Guardian was, wherever it was coming from, its hesitation was over.

"Move!" Deckard commanded, eliciting an instant flurry of movement from the troop.

The plan was in motion—the Calders would get the Relic, and the Ephrians would defend. However, they hadn't accounted for doing it all in the dark. She heard the shuffle of her troop moving into defensive positions just before Thom collided with Ilain.

"Now is not the time, darling," she quipped through gritted teeth.

The Guardian's hammering steps were almost upon them, and from what Evylin could tell, none of them were any more prepared to defend the Calders than before.

As Evylin shifted to take up the front line, she ran straight into something very hard and *very* immovable. It hit her just above the hips, causing her to heave a grunt as she put out a hand to steady herself. Her palm fell on an unstable object that shifted under her touch. A sharp tingle sparked up her arm. The object slipped across the smooth surface beneath it, a flash of amethyst light filling her vision.

As Evylin realized what had happened, the object flew off the pedestal, and she rolled her eyes at the darkness. "I found the Relic," she called.

The roar of the Guardian—a guttural, almost growl-like sound—preceded the blind attacks of Deckard and Rafferty.

"Wonderful," Auden replied, several steps to her left. "Give it to me."

Evylin grimaced. "It's on the floor."

Before the Mage could respond, the ground under Evylin shook with even greater fury. The Guardian rammed into the dais, and all of them as a result. Thrown back, Evylin reached out to catch herself. Her sword clattered to the marble floor. Chaos erupted around her as they scrambled away from the beast's attack.

Senses still fuzzy from being sightless, Evylin closed her eyes. She had to stop fighting the darkness. When they went through the Day Keep and the Shades burst into blinding flashes of light, she could only rely on senses other than sight. Night was the mirror of Day. If it worked there, it would work here too.

Absorbing the harried sounds of her teammates around her, the cool marble beneath her hands, and the crisp scent of night, Evylin embraced it. All that Night was, she took into herself.

Terror. Panic. Pain.

Stillness. Rest. Security.

That was the dichotomy of Night. It was horrifying. It was restoring. And Evylin felt it down to her bones.

In the split second it took to tap into her powers, the Guardian—whatever it was—began its second assault. Evylin sensed it raise its giant feet, and she rolled away on instinct. The ground trembled as its feet crashed back down, and she was immensely grateful for her magically heightened speed. Someone else hadn't been so lucky.

One of the men cried out as something snapped.

Fearing it was Deckard, her eyes flew open. But now, Evylin found herself not wholly encompassed by the dark purple of night. She could see the rough shape of the Night Chamber, columned and towering. The marble took on color, a rich amethyst stone with veins of silver and gold like shooting stars. The shape of the pedestal was several feet from her now, and a hulking, monstrous figure hovered over it.

Evylin blanched, the Guardian taking form. A hound the size of her family's home in Whickam Village whipped its ginormous head back and forth, snapping and snarling at her comrades. Its deep fur looked like a shadow, veins of violet woven through its coat. Vibrant purple eyes beamed down at them, vicious and calculating.

It was a bloodwolf. A creature of myth that haunted children's nightmares, no matter their imaginary status. Said to hunt the souls of the damned, the wolves were demons of hell that bled in and out of the shadows. They survived not on flesh, but on blood, sucking it from the veins of their prey.

Ethenn let loose arrow after arrow, striking true yet failing to pierce the Guardian's impossibly thick hide. Deckard was on his feet, assuaging her fear of his injury, hacking at the beast's trunk-like legs. Rafferty chopped at its hindquarters while Auden was on his hands and knees searching for the Relic. Ilain pulled Thom to safety off the dais, his leg a misshapen mess.

As her Warrior magic kicked in, Evylin's mind stilled. Noise reverberated off the walls, helping form the shapes even more. She reached for her sword and rose to her feet. All her senses leaped to the forefront, ready for battle.

Evylin struck out with her sword, dragging it along the side of the Guardian's body. The blade merely swept past its furred hide, failing to penetrate. She slashed again, to no avail. Yet, at the same time, one of Ethenn's arrows finally embedded, and the Guardian released a fierce wail.

Evylin remembered how difficult it had been to damage the Day dragon. The

Guardians were too well-armored for basic attacks. You had to strike hard and with pointed aim.

Sheathing her sword, Evylin reached for the long-bladed dagger on her belt and pressed closer to the bloodwolf. She sprinted under its belly, slicing up with her dagger. The blade did nothing.

A spurt of flame burst out, heat searing through the air as Ilain called on her magic. Evylin turned away, closing her eyes to shield them from the sudden flash of light. Immediately, the hound howled in enraged pain, lashing out in fury. She heard it make contact with one of her teammates, and her gut twisted at the barely contained grunt of pain.

Sensing the heat from Ilain's magic dissipating, Evylin returned to her attacks. She fought to keep hold of her focus. She feared for Deckard. What if he were seriously injured again? What if they couldn't save him this time? How would she manage to go on without him?

The swell of uncertainty made Evylin's magic surge. She attacked with renewed vigor, slicing at the bloodwolf's coat. She still couldn't hit hard enough or precisely enough to cause damage. She needed better leverage.

Another arrow sank into the hound, this one striking high on its leg. A foolhardy idea came to Evylin, and she bolted forward. She sprang up, grabbing the arrow's shaft, letting her momentum carry her. Though the arrow snapped, it gave her enough leverage to swing up and press her foot against the other arrow embedded in its shoulder, her weight pushing the arrowhead deeper. The wood snapped, too, but Evylin thrust her knife down before the beast could fling her away. The knife connected, the hide barely giving enough for the blade to sink in.

The Guardian's roar shook the room. Evylin struggled to hold on to her knife as the bloodwolf flailed madly, trying to buck her off. She knotted her fingers in its fur with one hand, attempting to pull herself up by the blade with the other.

A bloodcurdling howl split the air as the knife sliced lower under her weight.

Just as she felt she was gaining enough leverage to launch a full-strength attack, Evylin's sweaty palm slipped on the handle of the blade, the Guardian's thrashing finally knocking her free.

Tumbling to the marble, Evylin's lungs lost all their air on impact. Her vision went spotty, but she had no time to recover as the bloodwolf raised its paw above her. With the Guardian's immense size, she knew only one hit could crush her. Instantly, Evylin rolled away, the paw missing her by a fraction. Its horrifying claws dug into the marble, causing it to crack.

Another arrow met its mark, drawing the Guardian's attention away from her to bellow at Ethenn. Evylin scrambled to her feet, drawing her sword once more. Then, all at once, an enraged howl ripped through the Chamber, and the Guardian vanished. The knife she'd embedded in its shoulder now clattered to the floor.

Evylin stared in shock, taking an instinctive step back. Her eyes darted around the space. With the disappearance of the Guardian, the Chamber now looked decidedly empty. Though the room remained a shadowscape of purple, she saw with far more clarity than before.

Whipping her head toward the dais, Evylin took stock of her team. Thom lay on the far side, Auden kneeling next to him. A flash of golden light marked his healing. Rafferty stood alone, his short swords searching the air.

"Is it gone?" he asked.

Evylin bolted for the final group. At the back of the dais, Ilain and Ethenn crouched next to Deckard, his head in his hands. She dropped to her knees beside Ethenn, panic rippling through her. "What happened?" she demanded.

"He's just fine," Ilain assured her.

Deckard dropped his hands and looked up at her. His eyes searched the darkness before finding hers. "I'm all right," he promised. "My head's just spinning a bit."

Evylin looked to Ethenn. "He took a hit for me," the hunter explained. "I still don't know how he managed it."

"What do you mean?" she asked, confused.

"I mean, it's bloody dark in here," Ethenn remarked. "I could hardly see well enough to focus on the Guardian. But when it struck out to hit me, the colonel was just . . . *there.*"

Ilain narrowed her eyes as Evylin glared at Deckard, but he waved a hand. "I saw its attack coming and found the speed to intervene."

"And you got hit in the process?" Evylin surmised.

"I was only knocked to the ground. No cuts or scrapes, I promise." He held out a hand to Ethenn. "Help me up, would you?"

Despite their notable height difference, Ethenn easily pulled Deckard to his feet. Auden and a freshly healed Thom ambled over, drawing Rafferty along.

"Is everyone all right?" Auden asked.

"Define 'all right,'" Rafferty said.

"We're all well," Deckard assured Auden before turning to the weasel. "You look perfectly fine, Rafferty. What's wrong?"

"Oh, I'm right as rain, Colonel," Rafferty returned. "It just seems you lot can see far better than I can."

"I doubt that," Thom grumbled. "I'm completely in the dark. Are we sure the Guardian's gone?"

"It's gone," Auden confirmed. Then he scanned Thom and Rafferty anew. "Neither of you can see?"

"Nope." Rafferty frowned, his eyes searching unseeingly.

Auden turned to the rest of them. "What about all of you?"

Evylin looked to Ilain, Deckard, and Ethenn. "It isn't perfect," she admitted. "Everything is still very dark, but I can make things out well enough."

"Same for me," Ethenn confirmed. "But I've always had good eyesight."

"Hunters," Rafferty grumbled.

Deckard nodded his agreement. "I can see shapes but no details."

Ilain looked toward Auden. "It seems by Allore's grace that we're only down two members," she remarked.

"Are you all right?" Deckard asked Thom, taking a step toward his brother. "It sounded like the Guardian broke something."

"It did," Thom said. "My whole left leg, according to Auden."

"I got him patched up," Auden assured them. "It'll be sore, but he can run out of here all the same."

"I can't run if I can't see," Thom argued.

Deckard frowned. "That is a problem. We have Shades to face upstairs. Can we defend Thom and Rafferty the whole way?"

"We don't have much choice," Evylin said. "They can't exactly stay down here."

Ethenn nocked an arrow. "I'll hold the back," he suggested. "If you, Auden, and Ilain clear the way, the colonel and I can defend Thom and Raff."

"It's as good a plan as any," Evylin lamented.

With their worrisome plan in place, Evylin reclaimed her knife from the floor and reset her grip on her sword. She jogged lightly to the front to walk alongside Auden and Ilain while Deckard and Ethenn herded Thom and Rafferty at the back. The long walk through the dark purple Chamber and up the stone staircase took several minutes, especially as their sight-impaired comrades struggled to gauge each step.

Evylin could feel her magic thrumming under her skin, begging her to return to the action. That was something she'd come to learn about her Warrior instincts. When they kicked in, she stopped thinking quite as rationally. Logic and strategy pervaded, but in a far more reactive fashion. She wanted to move, fight, run, jump, and slash. It made her feel discombobulated when she forced herself to slow her gait. Her skin tingled with unspent energy, and her head swirled with excitement even as her heart weighed heavily in her chest, each beat a reminder of how fearful she was of losing any of her teammates.

Finally, they reached the top of the staircase. Auden paused at the iron door that awaited them. "I'll go out first," he offered, the Day Relic's yellow pulse and the Night's purple beam resting on his coat. "If nothing else, I may be able to slow the first wave of Shades with the additional power."

All of them prepared as Auden cautiously opened the door. Evylin remained at his side, watchful. She lifted her sword, prepared to strike the second a Shade showed itself.

Emerging from the staircase, the team walked out into a tall but narrow stone enclosure. Twinkling violet gems glittered across the midnight purple stone ceiling, and veins of amethyst ran through the rock. It would have been beautiful if she hadn't been far more aware of the arching passage before them.

They were in a cave, Evylin realized. The home of the bloodwolf. She'd read about their habitats in her novels. Tight, enclosed spaces that often twisted and turned with numerous dark passages so winding you could easily get lost.

Cool, damp air tickled Evylin's skin as she and Auden moved for the passage, Ilain at their back. As they continued, the Shades' hum rose to Evylin's ears. The sound was pure, sharp, and piercing. The Shades of Night sang differently from those of Day and Water. The haunting minor refrain sent chills down her spine even as she admired its beauty.

The dichotomy of Night filled her once more: safety and anxiety, protection and betrayal, peace and terror.

Senses honing as the magic tugged at her, Evylin lifted her sword. Her focus refined while her heartbeat rose, a furious hammer against an anvil. The cave of Night grew clearer as her vision sharpened.

Evylin could see down the singular passage now. Rock pillars twisted out of the ground, keeping the path narrow and hard to maneuver. Out of their shadows rose the clay and magic forms of the Shades. Smoke-like shadows curled around the clay, holding their strange, amorphous figures together.

In an instant, Auden's hands flew forward. A stream of light burst out, causing Evylin to recoil, her eyes watering at the sudden brightness. "Don't!" she called even as the Day magic seared the Shades into oblivion. They burst apart into thick clouds of smoke, obscuring the hall.

Furiously blinking away the spots that now burned her retinas, Evylin attempted to glare at Auden. "You can't use Day in here. I was just getting used to the dark."

Auden held his hands up in apology, his eyes blinking wildly like the rest of their team. "My mistake," he assured her. "I wasn't thinking. I will use Time or Night from here on."

"And I," Ilain added with a sour tone, "will refrain from using Fire."

"Wait," Rafferty interjected. "Why don't you use Fire to make a light? Then Thom and I could see."

Ilain tossed him a disdainful look. "Even without Fire magic, I'd be of far more use fighting than as your magical lantern."

"Fine," Thom grumbled, rubbing his eyes. "Let's just *get out of here!*"

Moving for the passage, Evylin could feel her magic working to clear her vision rapidly. "Stay close," she warned Deckard and Ethenn. "The more of those Shades we bring down, the more difficult it will be to keep sight of each other."

Deckard strode forward with purpose, his every move primed for attack. "We'll be right behind you," he assured her.

His promise did little to assuage her concern, but Evylin pressed into the opening. The cave matched the descriptions she'd read in her novels. The passages were winding and narrow; the ceiling soared in some places and dropped low in others. They had to crouch, walk single file, and turn to the side to slip through some sections. In others, they had plenty of room to spread out.

As they traversed the difficult terrain, at each step of the way, they had to fight Shades. True to their promises, Auden and Ilain utilized their lesser forms of magic, which helped everyone grow more comfortable in the darkness. But it also meant their attacks weren't as strong as they might've otherwise been.

Auden struck out with invisible forces of Time magic, manipulating the Shades as they ran for them. He'd reverse their timeline, throwing them back on their tracks, or locking them in time, their forms freezing altogether.

Ilain brandished her Elemental magic with a flourish. As always, her magic carried a more dramatic, embellished flair. Wind sliced like a blade under her command. She drew pillars from the rock with Terrae magic, piercing into the Shades. And, more rarely, she summoned spiraling spears of water that disappeared in a spray of droplets after hitting their marks.

As the Mages worked their magic, Evylin channeled her own. Able to sink into her Warrior urges, she moved as Hewitt taught her. She cut through the Shades with precision and speed, returning them to vapor. Her whole body came alive, jubilant in the fight. Arrows sailed past her, their *hiss* through the air tingling acutely across her skin.

It felt so good to fight again.

For a moment, Evylin forgot anything but action. The world outside was gone, and their mission itself was forgotten. She was alive with the fight, and nothing else mattered.

Another wave of Shades joined the fray, the halls clouding with the shadows of their death knell. It was almost impossible to see anything but the Shades before her and Auden ahead of her. They continued forward, shifting into one of the narrower paths. She knew she wouldn't have the arm span to swing her sword in the passage, so she took her first opportunity to sheath it in exchange for two knives.

Twisting through the corridor, Evylin sliced down the Shades in her path. She could feel the sweat trickling down her back from the long exertion of their fight, but her Warrior magic compensated readily for whatever exhaustion she *should* have felt.

More Shades poured into the passage, and Evylin could hear the rest of the troop fighting as Deckard called from behind, "They've surrounded us." On instinct, Evylin began to turn back to help.

"Evylin!" Auden cried just before she heard a crash and a groan. She whirled around again to find him grappling with half a dozen Shades.

Evylin's body sprang into action before her mind caught up with what she was doing. She sent a throwing dagger flying toward one Shade. It connected, and a shadow burst out. She leaped around a pile of ragged rocks, kicking back another Shade. She landed as Hewitt taught her, rolling to her feet on the other side of Auden before she struck out at another Shade. However, she wasn't fast enough to take them all down, and the horde pressed in.

As the other Night Shades struggled with Auden, one of them managed to grab the Night Relic. It wrested it over his neck even as Auden fought back desperately. The Shade yanked the necklace free and retreated toward the Chamber.

Auden cried out, but Evylin was already on the move. She jumped, kicking off the side of the passageway and flipping over the Shade to land in its path. Her feet hit the stone, and she thrust her knife up, straight into the Shade's chest. It dissipated into shadow, and the Relic dropped.

Evylin reached out to catch the necklace. Cool metal hit her palm, a sharp spike of energy radiating across her skin: *peace and terror.*

In a flash of amethyst, the Relic beamed brighter in her hand. A vibration worked through her fingers as, in a split second, the necklace transformed into an elegant, angular sword in her grip. Violet light radiated off the dark purple blade, its grip and hilt formed of purple leather and metal. Lighter than any blade she'd ever held, she knew without having to swing it that it was already perfectly balanced to her.

Despite the shock that thrummed through her chest, Evylin heard the fight raging around her. She sprang back into action with her knife still in her dominant hand. Readily, she took down the remaining Shades that harried Auden before falling back to aid the rest of their troop. Somehow, she found that wielding this magical blade made everything easier, even using it with her nondominant hand. No feint or attack failed her as she tore through the Shades.

Shadow curled through the air, tendrils spiraling into nothing as she brought down the last Shade. Their team paused in the narrow passage, now freed from their attackers. Another wave would come, but they had a moment to breathe. And as Evylin drew in a full inhale, she noticed those who could see were staring straight at her.

"By Allore's might," Auden muttered, awe filling his tone. "It's true."

Ethenn gaped from the back as Ilain's gaze twinkled merrily in the darkness. And Deckard—he stared at her with something between fascination and confusion in his expression.

"Is that—?" Ilain asked.

"The Night Relic," Auden confirmed.

Ilain began to laugh ecstatically, and Deckard's brow furrowed.

Before anyone could ask for clarification, Auden hurried down the path without giving them time to consider the transformation. "Come on," he ordered. "We're nearly there."

Warrior senses thrumming, Evylin took off after him. In mid-stride, she slid her knife into her belt, switching the Night sword to her right hand. The Shades returned swiftly, another, larger horde attempting to block their path.

With her new weapon, the fight was even easier for Evylin. Nothing could stop her. No opponent or maneuver was too difficult. She spun and ducked, avoiding each Shade's attack. The world seemed to slow around her as though she were moving at twice her normal speed, or like the Shades were moving through water.

In the midst of the fight, she realized almost absentmindedly that with her newfound weapon and the Calders' magic, neither Deckard nor Ethenn had to do much more than guide Thom and Rafferty onward.

They entered a vaulted cavern, a giant rock spire spurting from the center of the room. Amethyst gemstones glittered overhead, lighting the space. Seven other passages branched off the circular cavern.

Auden called while they worked to bring down the remaining Shades, "We have to stop here. I can't sense the way forward."

As their party came to a halt, Deckard jumped into the fray. He ranged to the left, defending Ilain's side as Evylin worked with Auden. Ethenn picked off Shades from the back as Thom and Rafferty stood still, irritated that they were useless in the dark.

"Do we need to clear this wave?" Deckard asked.

"That'd be preferable," Auden confirmed.

It took them several minutes, but they managed it. Thick clouds of shadow hung around the room as Auden finally reached for his sister. "I'll need help," he said. "Night and I . . ."

Ilain took his hand without any more explanation. They stood together in the center of the room, their heads bowed and eyes closed as they concentrated.

The desire for action beat in Evylin's rib cage. She met Deckard's gaze across the cavern.

"We should watch for the next wave," he suggested.

Thankful for something to keep her moving, she turned to check the passages on her side while Deckard examined the others. Ethenn stood watchfully by Thom and Rafferty while they grumbled together about the disagreeable nature of being blind while battle raged around them.

Used to the darkness of Night, Evylin scanned each rocky corridor. A faint breeze drifted from them all, raising gooseflesh on her skin. She heard droplets of water down one path. The air smelled of dampness and metal.

Her ears strained for the telltale hum of the Shades as she stepped up to the next opening. It looked like the rest, with formations of rocks, curved walls, and dark shadows.

Evylin did a double take, blinking into the darkness. One of those shadows had moved.

She was about to call out a warning when she froze. Her palm tingled around the Night sword's grip. Her breath caught in her throat, and without thinking, she took a step forward, her chest straining with hope.

"I have it," Auden said, causing Evylin to whirl around in shock. The Calders were already leading Ethenn toward Deckard, who stood nearby at the head of the cavern.

Panic bound Evylin to the spot, and she spun back to peer down the passage again. But the shadow was gone.

"Evylin," Deckard called.

Blinking away what she was sure must have been a hallucination, Evylin forced herself to step away. She turned to the troop and hurried to follow. Deckard waited until she reached his side to join them down the path.

"Did you see something?" he asked.

Had she?

"No," she said, tightening her grip on the Night sword. "It was the shadow of a rock."

Forcing the vision from her mind, Evylin pushed to the front again. The Shades returned. She fought without hesitancy or thought. Every action came from impulse, allowing her mind to drift elsewhere.

Evylin could have sworn—for a moment, she would have staked her own life that she'd seen him. Burly shoulders, towering height, scraggly beard. Hewitt.

He couldn't be there. It was impossible. *But I saw him.*

The Night sword pulsed in her grip. Evylin knew it couldn't really be her uncle. No matter how deeply she wanted to believe it. She *knew* that she'd imagined his form, hidden in the rocks. What she didn't know was why. Why now? After ten days without him, why had she imagined him *now*? And why here, of all places? Could she blame the heat of the fight? Or was it the intensity of her Warrior magic drumming up strange visions? Could it do that?

The ground rumbled under Evylin's feet as Ilain used Terrae magic to summon a stone pillar to crush a whole section of Shades. Without missing a beat and swinging the Night sword with barely conscious effort, Evylin took down three more. Auden rushed past her, barreling straight for an iron door.

So focused on the fight and caught up in her thoughts, Evylin hadn't even realized they'd made it to the exit.

The troop chased after Auden. Given her speed, Evylin made it to him just as he set his hand on the metal, guarding his flank. The *thunk* of the lock caused the Shades to attack with renewed aggression. Ethenn sent arrow after arrow into them, losing precious weaponry to their defense. Deckard held the line with his blade, and Ilain reached through Thom and Rafferty to send a slice of wind through the horde.

The door opened behind Evylin, and she spun to get out with the Night sword in hand. The second she crossed the threshold, the Shades would have nothing to defend, and their attacks would cease. Or at least, that's how she *assumed* their instincts worked.

But when she turned, she found herself faced not by an empty antechamber but by two men. They wore dark coats emblazoned with two golden moons on a patch of amethyst over their breasts: the emblem of the Order of the Night. The unknown men presented an immediate threat.

The Night Mages raised their hands, deep purple shadows already eliciting from them. Their magic roiled viciously through the open entrance.

Immediately, Evylin dropped low to avoid the Night magic. Auden released a surge of light that protected him from their attack. However, the remaining shadows rolled to strike Ilain, Thom, and Rafferty in the back. All three of them collapsed, taking Ethenn down with them.

Evylin didn't hesitate. She sprang across the threshold into the antechamber hall. They'd left the purple-blackness behind, and violet light now flooded the path through the star-studded windows. Before either Mage could respond to her sudden advance, she swung the Night sword at the man on the right. It slashed straight through his gut with as little resistance as it might have a Shade, cutting through him like he was made of clay and magic, not sinew and bone.

Brandishing the sword, Evylin spun to the other Mage, stopping as the blade touched his neck. He tried to leap back, but she went with him.

"Stand down," she ordered.

The Night Mage's hands lifted in surrender rather than attack, his fingers trembling as he stared at her, wide-eyed.

As she held him in place, Ethenn and Deckard carried the moaning and groaning Thom and Rafferty into the hall. Auden coddled Ilain, though she insisted she was fine.

"It hardly stung," she assured him as the Keep's door shut behind them. "I didn't even have a horrifying vision."

Thom and Rafferty didn't appear to have gotten off so easily.

The Night sword's purple glow shaded the Mage's pale complexion as Deckard stepped to Evylin's side. "What's your name?" he asked.

The Mage glared at him, unwilling to answer.

"*Ahck*," Ilain grumbled, then stepped forward. She waved Deckard back, then used the same hand to summon a flame. "You'll tell us your name, or I'll burn you."

His nervous gaze flickered to Evylin. "She's already got a sword to my neck," he countered, his voice threaded with the same accent as the Calders. "Threats won't do you any good, traitorous wench."

Ilain rolled her eyes. "You lot are so predictable. Did Blount send you here?"

He pressed his lips together.

Ilain looked up at Deckard. "I'd say it's safe to assume he did," she surmised, then turned back to the Night Mage. "Are there more of you above?"

Still, he remained silent.

"I'd say," Thom mimicked, "it's safe to assume there is."

Ilain turned a dry smile his way. "Imitation truly *is* the sincerest form of flattery, darling."

"We don't have time for this," Auden interrupted. "We're still technically within the Keep's antechamber, but the moment we step outside, every single Night Mage on Terraeus will feel its removal, even if they can't pinpoint its location. But if Blount sent these two here, there's no doubt dozens of others are waiting above."

Panic swept through the room at the thought. Since the Keeps led to the world above by only narrow staircases, they would have to exit single file. That would put them at a severe disadvantage if Mages were waiting for them right outside.

"What do we do with him?" Ethenn asked.

Deckard hesitated, but Evylin knew the answer. "Sorry," she said coldly to the Night Mage, then immediately flicked her wrists, driving the blade down in a slash across his chest. He dropped to the stones in an instant. "Nothing personal."

A heavy sigh escaped Deckard. "Was that necessary?"

Evylin frowned at him. "Did you want to tie him up?"

"She's carrying the Night Relic," Auden remarked, bringing the potential argument to an effective halt. "Night tends to make its wielders more violent."

Evylin followed their gaze to the Night sword, hanging limply by her side. She lifted it, offering it pommel-first to Auden. "Here. You can have it back."

"No, no," Auden insisted, though he eyed the sword with awe. "You keep it."

"Auden, it's just like the drawings," Ilain whispered, a sense of wonder in her voice.

He nodded excitedly, some of his bright copper hair falling onto his forehead and obscuring his intense gaze. "We'll discuss this when we're free," he said, though it sounded very much like he wanted to discuss it now. "We should focus on our escape."

"Sounds like we'll have to sneak our way to freedom," Rafferty surmised, a wily grin on his lips. Now that he could see again, the weasel was back to his usual good nature. "I'm up for that."

"It won't be easy," Deckard warned. "We have no idea where they might be hiding or how many of them there will be. And we are now entering enemy territory."

The memory of entering the Water Keep flickered through Evylin's mind. She turned to Auden. "Can't you hide us? With Night magic, I mean."

Deckard caught on, nodding. "Yes, you became invisible in the woods outside of Virwoud."

Rafferty's silvery eyes went wide with excitement, but Auden's wary expression immediately cast doubt on the plan. "A shroud, yes. But it's Night magic, and I'm not particularly good at it," he admitted. "I could *possibly* shroud us with the Night Relic's help, but—"

"Do it," Evylin insisted, offering the sword to him again. "If it'll get us out of here, do it."

Auden looked reticent.

Ilain set her hand on her brother's shoulder. "We just traversed a Keep," she reminded him. "We're too tired to fight our way out."

"And after using Time and Night within, I've depleted much of my energy," he replied, a pained expression on his face. "I'm no good with Night to begin with."

"Can you try at least?" Deckard asked. "Even if it gets us a step farther from here, it's worth it."

Dropping his chin, Auden acquiesced. He reached up, but not to take the Night sword. "Here," he said, lifting the Day Relic from around his neck. "I won't be able to maintain a good grasp on Night if I wear this. And if we do have to fight, it would be wise for our Warrior to carry a weapon that will give us the best chance of success."

In exchanging Night for Day, Evylin watched with amazement as the purple sword turned back into an amethyst necklace while the topaz talisman transformed into a golden broadsword. She wanted to ask the siblings about this phenomenon, but by their bafflement, it seemed they were just as surprised as she was. Her fingers tingled with joy as they clutched the leather hilt—a gentle warmth radiating from the blade, the feeling of life flowing through her veins.

"Are we ready then?" Deckard asked, drawing her back to the moment.

They prepared their weapons as Auden gathered his focus. Then they moved up the staircase to take their first steps into Wauld.

CHAPTER FOUR

Deckard struggled to believe that they were truly invisible. Even though Auden assured them the shroud was in place, he could still see each troop member. Granted, the edges of their forms were less solid than normal, like they wore a hazy fog as a cloak.

Still, Deckard insisted that Ethenn ascend first with Auden, his bow at the ready.

They climbed the staircase together, leaving the Keep's antechamber. With their weapons drawn, the narrow steps forced them to rise one by one. Auden told them to stay close, as his grasp on Night magic was tenuous even with the Relic.

Deckard made sure to walk in front of Evylin in the procession. Even with the warm golden glow of the Day sword in her hand, he wanted to face whatever awaited them first. Perhaps it made him a fool. Evylin was more than capable of defending herself. He'd seen how the Relics enhanced her skills in the Keep. He did not doubt that she could also hold her own up above. But he would never forgive himself if she faced danger from which he could have protected her.

The moment they stepped out into the soft morning light, Deckard felt an immediate wave of exhaustion roll through him. He'd experienced this sensation before when they'd left the Day and Water Keeps. Each time, he'd felt fine while within the magical walls. But the energy he'd expended finally caught up to him the second they stepped free of the Keeps' influence.

Exiting the narrow slit in the cliff face, the troop came to an immediate halt. Twelve Mages whirled toward them, muttering to one another under their breaths, hands raised.

They'd felt it, Deckard realized, the Night Relic leaving the Keep. And they were prepared to attack whatever appeared.

Even in his exhaustion, Deckard held his sword ready. Their troop stood huddled together on the slick rock that abutted the sea. Auden lifted a forestalling hand to the soldiers. Immediately, Deckard understood why.

The Night Mages stood frozen, eyes wide and hands still raised, but with obvious uncertainty on their faces. "Where are they?" one of them grumbled.

"Hold steady," another commanded. "They'll emerge any moment."

Suddenly, Ilain flicked her wrist. A large crash sounded off to their left, and all the Mages turned, alert. Ilain grabbed Evylin's arm without warning and jerked her to the right in front of Deckard. The troop needed no more direction. They sprinted after the two women, barreling past the enemy Mages. Auden worked to stay in the middle of the group to keep his shroud over them all.

Mindful of their footing, they raced across the wet rocks of the coastline. Wherever they had emerged in Wauld, they were surrounded by moss-covered mountains and beaches of black sand. The sea foamed against the shore and the jagged rocks. With their weapons drawn, Deckard worried they would lose their footing and injure themselves in their desperate escape to safety. But they couldn't risk stowing them, not when they might need to defend themselves.

Just as he'd feared, the Mages heard their sprint away. They called out to each other, sending blind surges of Night Magic their way. The troop veered, and Auden screwed up his face in rigid concentration.

"I'm struggling to hold it," he warned.

Instantly, Ilain grabbed her brother's hand, offering her additional focus and power. Deckard couldn't tell if it helped, but he refused to slow their pace.

The team curved around the side of the mountain, heading straight toward another group of Mages. Deckard diverted their path, leading them around the group and across the beach, their footprints embedding in the black sand.

The evidence of their passage unhidden, the Mages charged in pursuit of their path. More deep purple shadows streaked across the sand, narrowly missing their targets. Without warning, the water began rushing up the shore with sudden violence, rising to form a massive wall, ready to crash over them.

Water Mages. Deckard remembered that the Order of the Night had absorbed the Order of the Sea when the Shepherd King's rebellion pushed the Mages of Auld back across the Allmar Mountains into what was now known as Wauld.

"This way," Ilain yelled, taking an abrupt right up the beach.

They were fast but not quite fast enough. The wave slammed into the sand, hitting Ethenn and Rafferty in the back. They were thrown forward, losing their footing. Evylin instantly adjusted her course, with Deckard and Thom at her side. By some magic he didn't comprehend, she turned the Day sword back into a Relic, haphazardly throwing its chain around her neck. Then she tugged Rafferty off the ground, wet sand clinging to his clothes and face and streaking his hair an ashy black.

Deckard and Thom reached Ethenn at the same time, helping the hunter to stand. But they'd been too slow while the Calders continued up the beach. Auden's shroud was too weak to cover the distance between them. The haze around their forms began to fade, sharpening their figures, and several Mages cried out excitedly.

The Ephrians bolted after their Mage comrades as their attackers pursued with renewed vigor. Purple shadows sent black sand spraying as they zigzagged up the coast. A thick line of trees awaited them: massive evergreens, elms, and alders in the deepest shades of emerald. When they reached it, the dark sand was marbled with the teeming underbrush. Lush ferns and moss filled the forest, making their sprint difficult. A thick mist obscured the depths of the trees.

They maintained their course with no assurances that they were truly running from and not toward more Mages. Ilain and Auden's fire-bright hair flared against the forest's dark green, the Ephrians' only beacon of direction. Wherever they were running toward, Deckard prayed it was to safety.

The troop ran until Ilain practically collapsed onto the forest floor. The rich greens and overcast sky lent themselves to the Wauldeners' visages. It gave their pale skin and sharp features an ethereal appearance even as they slumped against the trees, worn out from the Keep and the sprint for their lives.

With one hand on her rib cage, Ilain stared up at the team. "Can we walk now?" she begged, panting around each word.

With his pulse pounding and lungs gasping, Deckard surveyed the forest behind him. "I don't hear any sign of pursuit," he offered.

The whole troop sagged in relief. Evylin alone seemed to have some semblance of control over her breathing as they relaxed. Rafferty dropped to the mossy ground as Ethenn and Thom finally put away their weapons.

"We can't rest long," Deckard warned, sheathing his sword. "Only enough to catch our breaths."

Auden agreed. "It should be safe for us to turn south now."

Hands on his knees, Thom gaped incredulously at the Mage. "You mean we've been running in the wrong direction?"

"We've been running northeast toward Taulence," Auden confirmed. "If they believe we're headed for the nearest town, they'll search there first. Now that we've lost them, we can head for Colmar with less fear of interference."

"It'll take three days to get to Colmar, right?" Ethenn asked, his hunter's training aiding his fast recovery.

"So long as we keep going," Auden confirmed. He reached up then, removing the golden chain of the Night Relic. The amethyst stone beamed in the dim light as he held it out to Rafferty.

"You sure you don't need to keep us shrouded longer?" the weasel asked, still on the forest floor.

Auden shook his head. "I had to release the shroud nearly as soon as we entered the trees," he explained. "I don't have the energy to maintain one. Not even with the Relic's help."

As Rafferty tucked the now-dull necklace into his coat, Ilain readily handed over the Fire Relic. Deckard surveyed the exchange warily. The return of the Relics was a show of good faith on the Calders' part. And while Deckard wanted to trust them, he still held reservations regarding their true agenda.

While Deckard had agreed to work with them and their Alliance to overthrow Wauld and Ephria, he couldn't say he was entirely convinced of their cause. He had yet to fully understand what the Alliance hoped to achieve by recreating Allund. He could not offer them his true allegiance until he knew their true intentions. However, with Rouland Blount II, Crown Prince of Wauld, also hunting for the Relics, Deckard would place his faith in the Calders over the Waulden heir.

They resumed their journey, veering south under Auden and Ethenn's guidance. The Mage and the hunter took the lead, forging the path. The rest of the team ambled behind, exhausted.

They'd left Norhels in the morning and arrived in Wauld's Verlund Reach hours earlier. The change in time zones played games with Deckard's head. They'd spent at least an hour within the Day and Night Keeps only to gain more daylight. His muscles ached, his stomach was empty, and his energy was depleted.

After hours of traversing the forest, the heavy mist clung to the trees. Rafferty, energy slowly returning, chatted at the back, entertaining Evylin, Ilain, and Thom. Fighting his tiredness and the mindless task of slogging through the untamed terrain, Deckard allowed his thoughts to wander.

Since they'd left Hewitt's grave, Deckard took every silent moment to worry about Evylin. Her struggle was understandable, her depression pervading, and her self-isolation reflexive. Every day, he did what he could to be helpful to her.

Almost a month ago, Hewitt had told Deckard the story of how Ryen died—Hewitt's son and Evylin's best friend. The boy's death had broken both uncle and niece, and only together had they found any semblance of solace. However, neither of them had ever truly healed. *"We've both isolated ourselves in our grief, with only each other for company,"* Hewitt had said. *"I refuse to care, and she refuses to trust."*

Now that Evylin had lost the one man she *did* trust, Deckard knew she was floundering, drifting in the void of loss. When they buried Hewitt, Evylin had broken down in her grief. She'd admitted to Deckard that she wasn't happy—that she didn't want what she'd thought she wanted: adventure. She'd told him that she didn't know what to do. And since then, Deckard had done all he could to give her a purpose. Something to hold onto while she recovered from her pain.

He knew she didn't trust him, not yet. But he promised himself he would be there for her as Hewitt had been when they'd lost Ryen. Even if it took her years to recover and trust anyone again, he would stay by her side. He wouldn't let her isolate herself, not from him.

The sudden, incomprehensible sound of laughter struck Deckard in the back. It wasn't just anyone's laughter—it was Evylin's. Looking over his shoulder in shock, he saw the group sniggering at something Rafferty had said.

Evylin walked between the weasel and Thom, a hand to her mouth. Her dimples lightened her entire expression. It baffled Deckard. He hadn't heard her laugh like that since Hewitt's death. And yet, she seemed practically joyous, like her old self.

Was it possible that she was getting better? Had the distraction of the Keeps been enough to jolt her back to herself? Had she only needed the thrill of a fight to restore what had faded?

The drizzle of rain spattered through the treetops, startling them all into action. Swiftly, Deckard slipped the pack from his shoulders to procure their wool cloaks. He handed them out, and the whole team donned them, rapidly lifting the hoods. The Calders had warned them that rain persisted year-round in Wauld, so they'd tried to prepare adequately.

Dispersing once more, the troop found their previous groupings. Deckard wandered closer to the front with Ethenn and Auden. "What part of the country are we in?" he asked the Mage.

Droplets of rain trailed over the man's hood as his sharp nose stood out even against the shadows it cast. "Technically, we're not in the country," Auden explained. "The Reaches, being Mage land, don't count as Waulden territory. The Orders are the governing body within their boundaries. It's part of the deal between King Blount and the Orders."

"Why would the Mages make that deal?" Ethenn asked, his gaze affixed to the forest before him. "If they're as power-hungry as you say, wouldn't they want to control the country rather than small parcels of land?"

"I wouldn't call the Reaches small," Auden commented. "However, you aren't wrong either. The Mages *do* want to control Wauld. The bargain is largely a matter of mutual necessity. The Waulden Army is large enough to pose a serious threat to the Mages, while the Mages are powerful enough to pose a serious threat to the army. To keep the peace and not decimate one another in a civil war, the first king of Wauld offered the Mages a treaty: the Reaches in exchange for their compliance."

"Is that why there aren't many Mages fighting in the war?" Ethenn asked.

"That's precisely why," Auden confirmed. "While a handful of Mages live throughout the Waulden continent—noblemen and the like—they are only granted that freedom due to Blount's surety of their undying devotion. He does not, however, trust the majority of Mages."

"His son is a Mage," Deckard remarked.

Auden's expression turned wily. "And he trusts his son least of all."

"For good reason, it seems," he noted. "Is the prince's end goal with the Relics to overthrow his father?"

"To be honest, I'm not entirely certain of his intentions. I assume it resembles what you suggested, but with a more nefarious end in mind. Overthrow his father, then, with the Mages' support, take back Ephria."

Ethenn looked up from his inspection of the woods. "So the Mages want Ephria as well?"

"Indeed," the highlord confirmed. "They wish to reclaim the land with the same authority as the Mages of Auld. However, I doubt that's what Blount desires."

"No?" Deckard prompted.

"Of course, I can't know for sure," Auden said. "But I would assume that Blount intends to rule the whole continent himself. Without any fellow Mages by his side."

"Why would the Mages work with him then?"

"For the same reason they stay in the Reaches, I presume." Auden raised his brow. "They don't have a choice. It's either fight against Blount, giving Ephria the chance to truly win this war, or work with him, potentially gaining the opportunity to destroy him and reclaim their thrones at a later time."

Ethenn's attentive gaze paused his scan of the forest to glance at Auden. "But won't the Relics give Blount the ultimate power?" he noted. "How do they intend to wrest them from him later?"

"Which would you prefer?" Auden replied. "Being bound in the Reaches with no chance of taking back your 'rightful' place or risking an allegiance with a man who can expand your influence but may subjugate you until you find a way to defeat him?"

"Neither sounds good," Ethenn said.

Auden chuckled. "They are in quite a pickle. Of course, this is primarily speculation on my part. While many Mages, particularly the elders among us, regularly speak of their desires to retake Ephria, I was wholly unaware of Blount's goals. I imagine his alliance with the Orders is a reaction to our taking the Fire Relic."

"So," Deckard interjected, his thoughts spinning, "by taking back Ephria *with* Blount, the Mages hope to regain enough power to overthrow him? How?"

"Likely through the reintegration of the old Orders." Auden ducked beneath a rowan's branches as they continued through the forest. "Prior to Ephren's reign, the Day, Water, Terrae, and Space Orders were within Ephria's borders. If the Mages can rebuild them, they can raise and train more Mages to help them with the fight."

"But I thought Mages couldn't be born to Easterners," Ethenn said.

"It isn't that they can't be born there," Auden corrected. "It's that the magic doesn't flow in their veins."

Deckard and Ethenn exchanged a confused glance.

"Think of it this way—" Auden gestured to the hunter at his side. "Ethenn was born in Estshire, correct? Just like Evylin. However, they aren't Easterners because of the place of birth, but because of their bloodline. You, Jonn, are also a Shireman like Ethenn, but it is clear by your genetics that your bloodline is not pure Ephrian."

Deckard felt his brow pinch together at the suggestion. "I beg your pardon?"

Auden scanned him knowingly. "It's pretty obvious. You and your brother both show the signs."

"What signs?" he demanded.

"Ethenn is the pinnacle of an Ephrian, is he not? Short and stocky with dark features. He'd only appear *more* Eastern if he bore a darker complexion." Auden gestured to Deckard then. "You, on the other hand, are tall and trim with pale skin and red hair."

"My hair is brown," Deckard argued.

Auden and Ethenn both gave him a look that said they disagreed.

With a sigh, Deckard brushed off the comment. "I see your point," he admitted. "So the Mages intend to flood the eastern half of the continent with their people, repopulating it with their bloodline. Is that it? That sort of thing will take generations."

"Mages are inordinately patient," Auden said with a wry grin.

"And what about Blount?" Deckard pressed. "If you know the Mages' ultimate aims, surely, he does too. Doesn't he fear them stabbing him in the back?"

Auden raised his ginger eyebrows. "Why do you think he wants the Relics?"

Feeling the weight of their mission impressed even more heavily upon him, Deckard confirmed his faith in the Calders. Be the Alliance purehearted or not, it *had* to be better than the plans Blount and the Mages had for their continent.

"Do you really think the Alliance can overthrow both countries?" Deckard asked.

Auden gave him a confident smile. "I do."

"What if we fail in our mission?" he pressed. "If we don't obtain all the Relics, can they still win?"

"The Alliance *will* win with or without the Relics," he assured him. "Fail-safe after fail-safe has been put in place. We have members in the highest places, individuals devoted to our cause. Even if we fail, even if Blount obtains the Relics himself, our victory is inevitable, though it will be far more difficult. The question isn't if we'll win, but when."

"How can you be so sure?"

"Because we aren't seeking selfish ambition," Auden insisted. "Our cause is for the people, who will always stand with us."

Deckard studied the Mage, wondering at his certainty. Was it possible that any organization could be *that* unstoppable?

Thinking back to their assignment as the Order of the King—the special soldiers assigned to King Ephren's personal missions—Deckard began to understand. The Alliance's reach was far greater than he'd realized. King Ephren's most trusted advisor was Lord Carlile, a double agent for the Alliance. A man skilled enough in the study of Mages and Warriors that he'd recognized Evylin's magic upon a single meeting. A man who'd set them up, ensuring their eventual connection with his organization.

The duplicity of the Alliance worried Deckard. Could such an underhanded ploy ever speak well of an organization's intentions? But what else were they to do? In the overthrowing of kingdoms, was any behavior ever truly honorable?

Deckard didn't like where his thoughts took him. He didn't like the idea of being party to something dishonorable. But he didn't think he could go back either. Not when the alternative was living under the rule of a lackadaisical king who kept his citizens uninformed and his country locked in a never-ending war.

Yet, Deckard worried that Ephria as a whole would not accept the truth he'd learned. The country was staunchly opposed to magic in all its forms. The first King Ephren had seen to that, annihilating all references to magic within the country's boundaries. The Allorian church named it heretical. Though the Calders claimed that the true faith taught that magic came from Allore himself, even Deckard struggled with such notions from time to time.

How could he expect an entire nation to accept such an antithesis?

But if the Alliance failed to raise Allund again, what would happen to Evylin? As a Warrior, she carried magic. And while Ephren's Allorianism only declared the magic of Mages to be heresy, the magic of Warriors was long forgotten. Surely, the church wouldn't accept it any more readily.

Would that mean Evylin would have to go into hiding? Could she live in secret like that? Or would she have to flee, like the Warriors of old, across the sea to Schon?

Deckard would go with her, of course. He would follow her to the ends of Terraeus if she'd let him. He didn't want to leave his home or family. But he would abandon it all for her.

The only question truly was: Would she let him?

CHAPTER FIVE

Throughout the rest of the day, they walked, the rain drizzling constantly around them. It splattered on the vegetation, spraying little droplets onto their faces that even their hoods couldn't deter. Despite the wool cloaks, their boots and hems soaked up the dampness, brushing against the thick, wet flora around them.

The Ephrians' introduction to Wauld was unpleasant, to say the least. As far north as they were, the chill of winter laced the air with a sharp twinge. It didn't help that the canopy of leaves above them blocked what little sunlight filtered through the rain clouds.

Worn down and damp to the core, the troop finally made camp as the world grew too steeped in gray shadow to continue safely. Though "making camp" was too generous a term. They'd have to sleep on the wet ground without bedrolls or blankets. And with the chance of the Mages still pursuing them, they couldn't risk a fire either.

The troop found the most shaded clearing they could, backed up to a large outcropping of rocks. It would provide a comfortable, well-hidden place to rest.

"We should keep watch in shifts," Deckard suggested as they ate their meager rations. "I don't want to give anyone the chance to sneak up on us."

With their odd numbers, Deckard assigned Ethenn to watch with Ilain for the first shift, Thom and Auden to the second, and he would take the third with Evylin and Rafferty. He'd attempted to divide them into the most palatable groupings possible, and he also took care to separate those who might distract one another most. With Ilain and Rafferty's penchant for chatter, he paired them with those who wouldn't encourage such behavior.

"I've never been on watch duty before," Ilain remarked as she sat next to Ethenn near the entrance to their camp. She patted his knee playfully. "You'll have to teach me what to do."

Ethenn's whole neck burned scarlet. "It's pretty straightforward," he muttered, fidgeting with his cloak's hem. "You just watch and listen."

Thom stepped up to Deckard's side, several paces from the pair. After Auden's healing magic, his leg had recovered nicely, only the faintest of limps suggesting the toll the day had exacted on their bodies. "That," his brother remarked under his breath, "wasn't your finest idea."

"No?" Deckard inquired.

His gray-blue eyes flashed with an amused glint. "That boy's gonna be so distracted he wouldn't be able to hear a Guardian crashing through the trees."

Instantly, Ethenn whipped his head around, scowling at Thom. "I heard *that*," he returned.

"Heard what?" Ilain asked.

"Nothing," Ethenn grumbled, then turned back to the forest.

Deckard and Thom shared barely restrained laughter. "He's got sharp ears," Deckard noted.

The remaining five found what open ground they could to sleep on in the small clearing. Rafferty snored soundly, nestled under a fern to hide from the constant rain. Auden lay more comfortably near the entry, seemingly undisturbed by the weather conditions.

Thom dropped down near Evylin at a respectful distance. He rubbed his hands together beneath his cloak. "Are your fingers as numb as mine?"

Back pressed against the rock, Evylin shifted to give Deckard the room to take his seat next to her. "Actually," she countered, "they aren't that bad."

Unsure if she was being sarcastic, Deckard glanced down at her. "Then perhaps you'd graciously lend me some of your warmth." He curled and uncurled his frigid fingers. "I can't feel mine anymore."

A low, airy chuckle escaped Evylin, and Deckard froze. She'd not laughed at any of his jests in twelve days.

Even more surprisingly, she nudged his side and held out her hands. "Give them here," she instructed.

Deckard stared at her waiting palms, baffled. "What?"

She motioned toward him. "Your hands. I'll help you warm them."

In a stupor, Deckard found himself placing his hands in hers. Evylin gently rubbed her palms over them, her touch surprisingly warm as she massaged life into his skin. He couldn't help glancing up at Thom, who watched with equal shock. Since Hewitt's death,

Evylin had been altogether distant from Deckard. Their only physical interaction was due to the necessity of sleep. For her to willingly offer to touch him like this was unprecedented.

"Better?" Evylin asked, her gaze fixed upon her work.

Deckard found himself nodding mutely.

Finally, she looked at him with a dry grin, then squeezed his hands. "Good."

Thom held up his hands then, a teasing tilt to his lips. "I suppose I'm on my own?"

Evylin sniggered, beginning to lie down. "Goodnight, Thom," she said in response, then rolled onto her side, facing Deckard.

Still incredulous at what had just occurred, Deckard remained locked in his seat. He and Thom exchanged a silent, mystified conversation. Had the Mages somehow exchanged their Evylin with an impostor? That was the only explanation.

Forsaking comprehension, Deckard settled onto the ground next to his wife. Her head lifted in anticipation of his arm, which he extended in its usual fashion, propped under her neck. He lay facing her as he always did when it was especially frigid, using one of the packs for a pillow. Evylin had always struggled with the cold, and early in their relationship, his warmth made sleep bearable for her. At this point, they'd grown used to their snuggled positioning.

Despite their nightly closeness, there were clear lines that Deckard had never crossed. He was profusely aware of her shyness regarding physical relations and intended to honor it. Tonight, given the very public setting, he was even more cautious. Even when they'd slept in their shelter-halfs, they'd had far more privacy than this.

Now, Deckard's sense of propriety made him anxious. With no escape from the wind or the rain beyond their cloaks, Evylin huddled against him, her arms creating the semblance of a barrier between their bodies. It was a joke, Deckard often thought, to consider such a menial blockade an actual impediment to their physical contact. A bald-faced lie, he ventured, as most nights, Evylin's lower half wound up firmly pressed against his, their feet often intertwined. He'd never mentioned this to her. Whenever he woke in those conditions, he rose before her, as he didn't care to lose what little opportunity he had to enjoy the pleasure of his wife's affections, even if she were asleep.

Gently, Deckard laid his arm over Evylin's side, forcing himself to settle in and get some rest. His fingers were already growing numb once more, but he worked to ignore it.

"Jonn," Evylin whispered into his chest.

"Mm?" he murmured in reply.

She drew her head back, tipping up her chin to look at him. Her eyes took on a darker brown than usual in the shadow of her hood and the ever-growing night. "Your hand will freeze if you leave it out there."

Rather certain there was only one other option in their current sleeping arrangement and equally confident she would disapprove of it, Deckard lifted his shoulder with a shrug. "I'll be fine," he lied.

Evylin heaved an exasperated sigh, then knocked his arm off her side. She grabbed his wrist, tugging it under her cloak as she drew near again. "There," she said, satisfied.

His arm remained rigid around her back as Deckard tried to understand why Evylin was suddenly so comfortable with him. Over the last twelve days, she'd never relaxed so fully in his embrace. And she'd certainly never encouraged it.

"Are you sure?" he asked.

Evylin tucked her head down, her temple pressing into his chest. "Yes. Now, go to sleep."

With his hand resting against her back, Deckard tried to follow her command. He stared into the darkening forest around them, struggling to process how to behave. In the past, he'd grown into the habit of letting himself rub her arm or brush his thumb in small circles against her back. Since Hewitt's death, he'd stopped, knowing the action would not elicit his intended soothing sensation.

Evylin's breathing deepened, her muscles relaxing as she fell asleep. She was abnormally warm, Deckard realized, as she subconsciously burrowed deeper into him. Almost too warm for his comfort. But he didn't pull away, unsure if this moment would last if he moved.

Holding her as close as he dared, Deckard scanned the trees one final time. Their comrades were all either asleep, attempting to sleep, or on watch. He could hear the light murmur of Ilain's voice as she talked with Ethenn. The young man's deeper, steady voice occasionally joined the conversation. Deckard was sure his hunter's training would miss nothing in the forest around them.

Nothing . . . except for the singular shadow that Deckard alone could see.

A figure stood in the pines and alders, arms crossed and eyes on the camp. Massive. Burly. Bear-like.

With a self-deprecating smile, Deckard forced himself to close his eyes. He was going mad, he knew. Slowly sinking into insanity. The figure wasn't real but a simple figment of his imagination. But somehow, the vision gave him peace.

And resting with the knowledge that the ghost of his guilt watched over them, Deckard found his way into slumber. Darkness surrounded him in his dreams. A shadow of the deepest amethyst encircled him. He could see a horde of Shades rushing toward him. Yet, he stood steadily, absorbing them into his body.

The dichotomy of Night filled him with each Shade that became part of him. Bliss and fright. Pleasure and panic. Rest and violence.

Then, suddenly, he stood in the Night Chamber once again. His fingers brushed the pitch-dark pedestal where the Relic lay, veins of silver glowing in its marble. The amethyst pendant beamed with power. Its facets and golden setting were warm as his fingers brushed the necklace.

He'd had this dream before, after the Day Keep. It made sense, he supposed. The chaos of the fight, the heart-pounding sprint to freedom, the worry for Evylin's life—his brain needed some means of processing it all.

Deckard's eyes drifted up to the metalwork on the door behind the dais. The sun and moons glowed bright yellow and deep purple. The door began to open . . .

33RD OF GALATAE, 1574

Deckard woke with each changing of the watch. As Thom and Auden took Ethenn and Ilain's places, he immediately checked the trees, again spotting the figment that haunted him. He drifted back to sleep, assuring himself for the hundredth time that it wasn't a problem. So he was seeing things? It wasn't altogether surprising when one was grieving.

In his years with the Ephrian Army, Deckard had experienced far too many deaths. Ones with seemingly little purpose too. And while he'd never had this reaction before, he could honestly say that, except for his first kill, no death had ever rattled him as much as Hewitt's.

Seeing visions of his mentor and Evylin's beloved uncle made some semblance of sense even when he wasn't exhausted.

When Thom woke Deckard for the final shift, the sky remained deep gray. Rain splattered on the large ferns and pine branches around them. With Evylin tucked against him, he stayed warm, but he knew that would change in moments.

Rousing both Evylin and Rafferty was more difficult than Deckard had anticipated, but eventually, they took their place at the front of their camp. Since Evylin tended to be in a groggy and silent mood in the morning, she didn't take to Rafferty's low chatter like she normally would. Instead, she sat on Deckard's other side while he conversed with the weasel.

"I've had a thought," Rafferty began quietly.

Deckard raised an eyebrow at him. "You were asleep two minutes ago," he commented in a whisper.

"I've a quick mind, Colonel. Try to keep up." Rafferty angled toward him, but his eyes continually scanned the forest. "You're a reasonable swordsman these days, what with your secretive training. By the way, I am impressed that you managed to hide that from *me*. No one hides anything from me."

Tucking his hands underneath his cloak, Deckard settled in for an ambling discussion. "What's your point?"

"My point," Rafferty continued, "is that despite your improved skills, you're still not *that* great on the battlefield. Would you concur, Colonel?"

Deckard dipped his head in a nod, causing a droplet of rain to drip from his hood onto his cheek. He wiped it away as he admitted, "I would."

"Right. So that brings me to my thought—" Rafferty's silver-gray gaze landed on Deckard for half a second before drifting toward Evylin. "How's it possible you're so much better at fighting in the Keeps?"

At that, Evylin looked over, and Deckard furrowed his brow. "Pardon?" he asked.

Shifting their direction, Evylin held out her hand to stall Deckard. "I've been wondering the same thing. You saved my life with a precise knife throw in the Day Keep. If you had been off by an inch, it would have killed me instead of the Shade."

Rafferty took over for her. "Then, yesterday, in the Night Keep, you saved Ethenn from the Guardian's attack. Moving impossibly fast, if the kid's account is to be believed."

With a glance back and forth between them, Deckard returned to his inspection of the forest. "If you'll recall, I also wound up with a near-fatal injury in the Day Keep, a dislocated shoulder in the Water Keep, and yesterday, the Guardian knocked me flat on my back with that hit I took." He gave a self-derisive grin. "Should you be keeping count, my track record is currently three-to-one in favor of poor performance."

With a low chuckle, Evylin leaned against his side, yet again surprising him with her sudden comfort with their physical contact.

"Don't you want to hear my theory?" Rafferty lamented.

Distracted by Evylin's nearness, Deckard lamely replied, "What?"

"My theory," Rafferty repeated. "On why you're better in the Keeps."

Deckard scratched at his beard, grown thick from their weeks of travel. He wished he'd taken the opportunity to shave before they left Ephria. "What is your theory?"

With a happy waggle to his white-blond eyebrows, Rafferty grinned at the couple. "You're feeding off of Evylin."

The odd terminology made Deckard's face scrunch up in confusion while Evylin adjusted her seating to peer around him at the weasel. "Excuse me?" she protested.

"Think about it," Rafferty went on, his voice excited though still low enough not to disturb those sleeping in the camp. "Eve's a Warrior, which makes her magically inclined to be good at battle. Warriors seem to be in short supply these days, and the Calders aren't exactly experts on the subject, so we don't know what all that involves. But if we consider the legends and the concept of a master fighter, what does that suggest? A person who's not only skilled in combat but also a great tactician and leader as well."

The assessment brought the immediate thought of Euon Sergus to Deckard's mind. The King's Knight was a legend that he'd looked up to since his childhood. Sergus was the man Deckard always wished he could be. Hewitt had once said that there were old tales that marked Sergus as a Warrior, but he'd never heard them.

Evylin crossed her arms, a dubious lift to her brow. "What does that have to do with Jonn?"

"Nothing, directly," Rafferty said. "The idea is, maybe *you* give your teammates some sort of magical boost. You know, enhancing their skills with your magic."

Deckard continued to run a hand along his jaw, considering the possibility. But Evylin scoffed. "That isn't what's happening," she objected.

"How do you know?" Rafferty returned. "You just learned that you're a Warrior thirteen days ago."

"It's a good theory," Deckard said, then shook his head. "But is anyone else doing abnormal feats within the Keeps?"

"Ethenn is," Rafferty said. "He could see just as fine as both of you and the Calders yesterday. And I'm pretty sure he was doing better in the Day and Water Keeps as well; we just didn't notice because he's always a badass killer."

Evylin snorted at the description.

Deckard tried to stay on track. "So it's just me and Ethenn?"

"Seems like it."

"Which proves your theory wrong," Evylin concluded.

"Not at all." Rafferty's face lit up with excitement at the opportunity to explain his idea. "You're new to your Warrior powers. So new, in fact, you weren't even aware that you were tapping into them. But we know now that you were even before you knew anything about being a Warrior. And if that's the case, maybe you're tapping into other magical abilities yet unknown to you. Such as siphoning off your magic to your comrades."

"But why just Ethenn and me?" Deckard asked.

Rafferty cocked an eyebrow as though it should be obvious. "Loxley is our best fighter. Of course, she's gonna give him a boost. That's just reasonable. As for you, Colonel—" He flashed a wily grin. "You *are* her husband. Could it be she has some stake in you staying alive? It seems you need all the help you can get in that arena."

Turning back to the trees, Deckard let the concept sink in. It made a surprising amount of sense. Not even the Calders knew what a Warrior was fully capable of. When the

Auldan Mages eradicated them from the continent centuries ago, they also destroyed all documentation of them. Auden and Ilain had suggested that the Mages never valued the records of the Warriors, which meant that whatever little information the Mages' Orders held offered only vague descriptions. The rest of the information was supposedly held in the libraries of the old capital, Aulton, which Ephren razed at the start of his reign.

There was a viable chance that Rafferty's theory was correct. And while they might never have the chance to study the original texts on Warriors for confirmation, they could test it.

"You should try it," Deckard told Evylin. Her expression pulled down dubiously, but he pressed the notion. "I think he might be right. It's the only thing that makes sense. Heavens know I'm not magical, and Ethenn isn't either. But you are. So next time you practice, you should try . . . siphoning off that magic to those around you."

Evylin pulled at one of the leather clasps on her coat. "I wouldn't even know how to begin," she whispered.

"If you're already doing it subconsciously," he offered, "then I'd imagine it's as simple as making a conscious effort to control it."

Though Evylin didn't respond to the suggestion directly, she did turn to Rafferty and tip her head toward the forest around them. "Should we give it a go?"

His pale eyes grew wide. "What, now?"

"Why not?"

"Though I appreciate your enthusiasm," Deckard interrupted with a low chuckle, "we *are* supposed to be on watch. And others are sleeping."

"I'm not suggesting we spar," Evylin said. "There isn't room here for that anyway. I'm simply thinking that if I can pass my power to others, then perhaps I don't have to be in a fight to do it."

"What do you mean?"

She stood and unhooked her cloak, dropping it onto the log next to Deckard. With deft, swift movements, she unbuckled her weapons belt, removed her harness of throwing knives, and freed the clasps on her coat. Deckard attempted not to overtly appreciate her well-formed figure as she shrugged the coat off, leaving her only in her dark trousers, gray tunic, leather armor vest, and vambraces.

Rafferty, however, sniggered. "Don't stop on my account."

Deckard sent him a withering glare.

Evylin ignored the innuendo, beckoning Rafferty to join her. "Come on," she said, voice still hushed. "We don't have to duel. We'll just exercise."

"That's my least favorite part of life."

Evylin reached over and hauled the weasel to his feet. Then she looked down at

Deckard with one of her more charming smiles. "Can we leave you here for ten minutes while we run a mile?"

"You need ten minutes to run a mile?" Deckard returned. "I'd imagined you'd be faster than that."

"The ten minutes are for Rafferty's sake."

As the soldier in question grumbled through the removal of his cloak and weapons, Deckard found himself grinning. His initial reaction was to tell her no; splitting up wasn't a good idea, especially if she left her weapons behind. However, it was just a mile; she'd have Rafferty with her, and he knew perfectly well that Evylin was never without a weapon. If nothing else, she had the blade hidden in the ankle of her boot. But he imagined she'd concealed several others on her person as well.

And Deckard relished the opportunity to be alone for even ten minutes.

"Be careful," he charged.

Evylin dropped her chin in deference, a bright smile warming her expression. "As you wish," she replied sweetly, then grabbed Rafferty's arm and started off at a jog.

Watching until the pair ran out of sight, Deckard swallowed his instinctive nervousness. He didn't like being separated from Evylin these days. An anxiousness now swelled within him until he saw her again, and he was reassured that she was safe. But he shoved down the feeling to glance over his shoulder at his sleeping comrades.

With only four of them asleep at the moment, they each had more room than before. Auden and Ilain slept nearest one another. The brother and sister looked comfortable, despite the damp and chilly night. Ethenn curled up in Thom's old spot, having traded out when their watches switched, leaving Thom to huddle against the rock outcropping for shelter. A healthy ten feet away from the nearest member, Deckard didn't fear that their conversation had woken anyone.

Which gave him all the courage he needed to turn back to the shadow that lingered in the trees. "It's an interesting theory, isn't it?" he asked, voice even quieter than when Evylin and Rafferty had been with him.

The figment stepped out from the densely grown trees, wholly unchanged: dark brown beard unruly, massive forearms crossed, steel-gray eyes unyielding. "If you believe in magic," Hewitt's ghost said—Deckard's personal form of insanity manifested.

With some emotion between annoyance and amusement rising, Deckard shook his head at himself. Ever since he'd dug Hewitt's grave, he'd started seeing the vision. Out of desperation, he'd spoken to it. And even though he knew he was merely soothing his conscience, he couldn't help holding onto the apparition.

Deckard saw Hewitt's ghost everywhere. It had become his constant companion since they left the man's grave—a shadow always lingering in the trees, at his side, in the distance. Whenever Deckard looked for him, Hewitt was there. That's how he knew he was going mad—he only saw him when he *wanted* to see him.

"You know magic is real," Deckard said, feeling idiotic for arguing with his imagination. "You've seen it. You've fought it."

Hewitt's ghost leaned against the large, gnarled oak near Deckard's side. "It killed me."

The acknowledgment cut deep into Deckard's chest. "So you agree then?" he asked. "You think Rafferty's theory is correct?"

"No," Hewitt rasped, "I don't."

Deckard breathed out a humorless laugh. "Why am I not surprised? What's your theory then? Why am I better in the Keeps?"

Knowing he was asking himself these questions, Deckard wondered why he didn't believe Rafferty. What was within him that held such a cynical perspective on something reasonably put forth?

"I told you weeks ago," Hewitt grumbled. "You think too much. When you're in the Keeps, you act on instinct. It makes you better."

"And you think it's the same for Ethenn?"

"The boy was trained as a hunter since infancy," Hewitt said. "He's been fighting in the streets since he was thirteen. Magic doesn't play a role in it. His skills have been honed over two decades, and the Keeps give him a place to show it off."

This was why Deckard talked to the vision. Whether it was insanity or not, his subconscious managed to provide him with clarity of thought to process his challenges, most of which concerned Evylin. And who better to talk to about his wife than the one man she trusted above all else—even if he was actually talking to himself at the end of the day?

"I think something's wrong with Evylin," Deckard heard himself mutter.

Hewitt's ghost hovered menacingly in his peripheral vision. "Why?"

"Ever since we entered Wauld, she's been different," he said. "She's laughing and acting happy. She's even touching me as though she hasn't flinched away every time I've stepped near her the past twelve days."

Tugging on his scraggly beard, Hewitt let out a thoughtful hum.

"I considered that it might be the change of scenery," Deckard continued, knowing his subconscious would interject when it came up with a better idea. "Perhaps a place so new as Wauld is enough of a distraction. Or maybe the fight in the Keep gave her some life back."

Hewitt let out a grunt.

Deckard looked up at him. "You don't think that's it, do you?"

"It took her an entire month to smile again after Ryen died," the ghost said. "She wouldn't speak to anyone but me; she wouldn't leave the house without me at her side. Loss destroyed the girl she was. And even the woman she's become has never fully recovered from that."

Nodding, Deckard felt the truth in his gut. "She's not over you," he muttered to himself. "Whatever this is, it's a fluke. She isn't better. She's momentarily altered by her distraction."

"A fight isn't enough to distract Evylin."

Deckard stared up at Hewitt, confused. "Then what is?"

A rustle in the forest drew Deckard's attention back to the task at hand. His vision vanished, returning to the void of his insanity.

Hand on the hilt of his sword, Deckard stood. He scanned the trees, watching and listening. The steady, rapid gait informed him that Evylin and Rafferty were returning, but he remained ready until he caught a visual of their approaching forms.

Assured they weren't being chased nor was their camp under attack, Deckard resumed his seat on the mossy log. Rafferty staggered over, dropping unceremoniously at Deckard's feet, while Evylin easily reined in her jog to pace before them. Catching her breath, she smirked at Rafferty's melodramatic, languished display.

"How did it go?" Deckard asked.

"Invigoratingly," Evylin replied, her braid wet from the constant drizzle. "I don't think Raff enjoyed it much, though."

Deckard looked down at the weasel, his ghostly pale face coursing with sweat and rain. "Did she give you any magical assistance?" he asked.

Rafferty snarled. "If she did, it wasn't good enough."

Sitting at Deckard's side, Evylin tugged the leather tie free from her hair. She unfurled the dark brown plait, squeezing out the excess moisture. "I don't think it worked," she admitted. "But I don't know if that's due to a failure on my part or a failure of the theory itself."

After discussing with his subconscious, Deckard concluded internally that it was probably the latter. Instead of offering that thought, however, he said, "Then I suppose Rafferty will have to run another mile to prove it."

CHAPTER SIX

34TH OF GALATAE, 1574

The massive, ashen-gray walls bordering the Reach into Wauld stretched for miles. The cluster of forest trees had been cut back, creating a few hundred feet of distance, making it impossible for anyone to climb the giant trees and leap onto the stone parapets. Guards patrolled the top and the roadside. A garrison protruded near the gate.

In the heavily clouded midday, rain pummeled the stone wall and the dozens of guards and travelers lining the narrow, muddy road. Even in the dreary conditions, Evylin couldn't quite bring herself to worry about those guards or the weapons at their sides. A lightness had settled into her, a knowing that everything would turn out for the best. Despite the strangeness of such a carefree attitude after her weeks of sorrow, she was just so glad to feel like herself again that she didn't bother to question *why* she was experiencing this sensation.

The troop stood at the top of a hill, still a half mile's distance from the gates. They'd passed the small town of Colmar late that morning, giving its boundaries a wide berth. And now they scouted their path ahead.

"You know," Rafferty muttered to Evylin as they surveyed the land, "I'm rather disappointed so far."

She passed him an amused grin. "How so?"

"Well, aside from being a grandly depressing place, this half of the country doesn't seem all that different from our side," he remarked. "Granted, their forests are a lot denser than ours, but other than that."

Evylin thought he had a point. She'd also noted how similar it all felt to their homeland in the three days they'd journeyed through the northwest. Though the foliage was larger and greener, she'd not seen anything that made Wauld feel any different from Ephria.

Standing at the front of the group, Deckard spoke with Auden. "How strict is the border patrol?" he asked. Like the rest of them, he still wore his cloak with the hood up to keep the rain off his face.

"It depends," Auden replied, ginger beard turned cinnamon in the shadow of his hood. "Some guards are lax, and others are more susceptible to a spare silver or two thrown their way. But today, it shouldn't matter."

When Deckard gave him a questioning look, Auden patted one of the pouches on his belt. "I have the proper documentation to get us through," he assured. "The Alliance knew we'd have to come to Wauld eventually."

"That's all we need?" Thom asked, a hand on the pommel of his sword. "They won't be suspicious of five heavily armed Ephrians traveling with two Mages?"

"The endorsement makes provision for that."

"And if all else fails," Ilain added, the lilt of her accent exaggerated, "I'll bat my pretty eyes at them. I've yet to fail at bringing a man under my charms."

Rafferty sniggered. "I don't think you've met my friend Thommy."

A smug grin pulled at Ilain's lips as she scanned Thom. "If I wanted him," she turned to Rafferty, "I'd have him."

An exasperated sigh rolled out of Thom and Deckard, while Evylin fought to maintain her laughter. She didn't know who she'd bet on in a battle of wills: Thom or Ilain. But something told her that the woman was right—if she truly wanted Thom, then all his denials wouldn't stop her from achieving her conquest.

Eyes focused on the wall, Ethenn motioned at it. "Is this the only gate between here and Wauld?" he asked.

"No," Auden said. "There is another much farther west. Verlund Reach's border is rather small, so it only has the two."

"And we've chosen this one for what purpose?" Ethenn asked, a wary glint in his dark eyes.

"It's a direct path to Blacklion," Auden replied, then looked at his sister.

Ilain nodded in confirmation. "If we were to take the other gate, it'd add at least three, maybe even four days, onto our journey. Time we don't have to spare."

"Why do you ask?" Deckard interjected.

Ethenn tipped his chin toward the gate. "I think they're searching people."

"What?" Auden asked in shock.

"Look—" Ethenn motioned toward the line of people on the road, his keen hunter's eyes catching what the others hadn't seen. "They're moving slowly. And it seems too slow for the guards to be checking documentation alone. I can't make out the details this far away, but . . . it seems suspicious. Why would they be searching people?"

"They're looking for the Relic," Ilain guessed. "The Order of the Night must have sent word."

The panic in Auden's gaze made it clear that he agreed. "Which means that their Mages can't be far behind."

"How do we get through, then?" Evylin asked.

Rafferty drew a hand along his wiry, white-blond scruff. "Hm. It's a shame we don't know someone who was paid to move illegal contraband from one location to another. Oh, wait—" A bright smile spread across his face. "That was my job."

Evylin laughed, jabbing him in the ribs. "All right, Mr. Draaw," she teased, using the name of his favorite legend. "How would you smuggle three Relics across the border?"

"I'd ask for a lot of money," he replied, then held up a finger. "At which point, I'd keep ninety-eight percent for myself and give the other two percent to a very hungover-looking guard. If there weren't one of those gentlemen available, I'd seek out a different assistant. Perhaps a fellow traveler who had reason to want the guards' attention off them just as much as I wanted it off me."

"Or," Ethenn interjected dryly, "we could use magic."

Rafferty's wily eyebrows shot onto his large forehead, making him look even more like a weasel. "Take all the fun out of it, why don't you?"

"You mean a shroud?" Deckard surmised.

Auden frowned. "That's not a feasible idea."

"Why not?" Thom asked. "You did it when we ran from the Night Keep. With the Relic and your energy restored, surely you can do it again."

The Mage's expression grew tense. "I'm a Day Mage. We are at direct odds with Night magic. Yes, I can use it, but my hold on it is tenuous. With how slowly they're moving people through the gates, it will take us an hour to get through. I don't have that kind of strength."

Hesitantly, Ilain lifted a finger, drawing her brother's attention. "You *could* attempt to disguise them," she suggested.

Auden frowned. "I'd have to connect to Space for that."

Remembering their brief reference to that magical resource, Evylin furrowed her brow. "Why should that be a problem?" she asked.

His sharp green eyes turned to her, surprisingly bright amongst all the dark green around them. "Space is the most unknown resource," he explained. "To reach into it is . . . well, it's nearly impossible for a non-Space Mage. And there have existed only a handful of those in history. As far as I know, there are only two living today. Studies on Space are nearly as rare as they are on Warriors."

"Any particular reason for that?" Deckard prompted.

"Beyond the rarity of them?" Auden shook his head. "No. There are truly just too few of them in this world."

"And you can't connect with the resource at all?" Evylin asked.

"I can *try*," he replied. "But it isn't a guarantee."

Rafferty grinned. "Sounds like we're doing things my way."

"How long will it take you to devise a plan?" Deckard asked.

The weasel shrugged. "I'm fastest thinking on my feet. Let's say we get down there, head for the gate, and if all else fails, our highlord taps into that magic of his."

"I'm not leaving this up to chance, Rafferty," he protested. Then he turned to Auden. "It's either Night or Space. You choose."

Auden looked truly conflicted. His face screwed up in deep thought as though he were waging war with his thoughts.

Suddenly, Ilain stepped forward. "There's another option," she said, then turned to Rafferty. "Give me the Night Relic, please."

Auden jerked out of his internal debate. "You're not an Existential," he objected. "You won't have the strength for it."

She gave him a withering look. "I'm the most powerful Mage born in the last two centuries, Pyra's Heiress, and I've trained with all the elements *and* the existents. You've taught me how to connect with Day just as well as many of your contemporaries. Don't tell me I won't be strong enough."

Evylin felt her lips part in surprise at Ilain's credentials. She'd known the woman was powerful but hadn't realized she was *that* powerful.

"You're the most powerful Mage in two centuries?" Thom exclaimed, clearly baffled.

Ilain's smirk turned smug. "I told you," she crooned. "I can have any man I want." Then she turned to Deckard. "I can do this," she promised. "With your permission, I would like to shroud myself and Evylin with the Relics."

Deckard pressed his lips together in consideration, but Thom jumped in first to ask, "Why just you two?"

"The fewer people I have to conceal, the better," Ilain said. "I can't carry anything but Night, as Fire and Day will distract me from the resource. It will be an extremely tremulous connection. However, as Evylin is a Warrior, I can borrow her magic, and it will give me additional strength. Therefore, she'll carry the Day and Fire Relics, giving her even more power and focus to help me ensure we both make it through the border completely unseen."

Pinching the bridge of his nose, Deckard looked about ready to drop from exhaustion. Evylin understood. They'd been traveling for so long, pushing so hard. And they'd only just begun.

Stepping up to his side, Evylin set her hand on Deckard's arm, his cloak wet against her palm. He jerked in surprise, staring down at her. She rubbed his arm comfortingly. "We'll be safe," she said reassuringly. "I believe that Ilain can do this."

"Admittedly," Ilain interrupted, "I'll be out of commission afterward."

The Ephrians looked at her, confused. Auden just looked disappointed in himself.

Ilain clarified her statement. "At least, for the rest of the day. Touching a resource that isn't your primary always requires more energy. Since Night isn't even in my technical classification . . . well, I'll burn out quickly."

Deckard turned to Auden. "And you're sure you can't do this?"

With an apologetic lift of his shoulder, Auden opened his mouth to speak, but Ilain cut him off. "Not as well as me," she insisted.

"All right," Deckard sighed. Then he motioned to Rafferty to hand out the Relics. He offered the amethyst to Ilain and the ruby to Evylin under Auden's keen observation. The highlord shared a meaningful look with his sister but said nothing.

Tucking the flickering Fire Relic into her coat next to the Day Relic already hanging there, she felt heat tingle along her skin. It was a different sort of warmth than Day had already given off. That was really why she hadn't returned it to Rafferty in the first place. The subtle, comforting heat that emanated from the Day Relic felt like the sun's rays. It gave her body an immediate feeling of life. She felt a constant sense of renewal and serenity in her body. And in the cold rain that refused to cease, she didn't want to let go of such a luxury.

The heat from the Fire Relic felt different. It fused with Day, mellowing what she assumed Ilain must always feel—a sharp, blazing sensation deep in her heart. If the Day Relic made her feel alive, the Fire Relic empowered her. Suddenly, everything felt more intense. The urge within her to get moving, to march through that gate and see the other side, swelled. The desire to expend her energy on something—a duel, a run, a kiss— became an instinct she couldn't ignore.

Evylin found her gaze drifting to Deckard with that last thought. Her fingers sought her rings, twisting the metal bands in a comforting manner rather than her usual anxious ritual. He'd moved from her side to talk with Ethenn about the best path to the gate. They would take the main road, but from their hilltop, they'd have to backtrack to ensure the guards didn't notice their sudden arrival from the woods.

Deckard was a surprisingly handsome man, she'd come to discover. Not the immediately striking sort like the heroes in her novels. He had a sharper, more regal quality to his features. She knew he possessed plenty of muscle, conceptually from his skills in a fight and personally from her physical experience. It was hard not to notice the firmness of his chest and the strength of his arms when she slept so snuggled into him.

Over the past two months of their marriage, Evylin had become deeply aware of Deckard's attractive qualities. Yes, he was charming, amiable, and well-spoken. Those things had drawn her to him immediately. But she hadn't noticed just how striking his looks were until she'd come to know him better.

Evylin's conscience rose, reminding her she was mourning and probably shouldn't be ogling any man, not even her husband. But ever since she'd put the Day Relic around her neck, she'd found her depression elusive, almost as though it had drifted away like clouds to reveal the shining sun. Despite her previous discomfort, she, at last, felt free to return to who they were before the turmoil of Blount's ambush. Her heart urged her forward with new resolve to reach out to him and draw him close, to be the affectionate wife he'd always deserved.

Now, with the Fire Relic resting against her skin, a new sensation joined: the compulsion to feel, move, and live with the height of passion.

Fingers tingling with magic she hadn't realized she'd summoned, Evylin watched as Ilain carefully adjusted the high neck of her navy dress over the Night Relic. She'd only held the amethyst necklace as a sword for a short time. But even that brief experience caused her to wonder what feelings it might elicit within her. Did it impact the Calders the way it did her? Or were Warriors more susceptible to the Relics, wielding a more physical magic than Mages?

While the men waited, hands on their weapons as they prepared to leave, Ilain stepped over to Evylin's side. "Here," she said, holding out her pale, bejeweled hand. It looked pure white under the gray light of the cloudy skies. "It'll be easier for me to maintain focus if I have direct contact with you."

"Shouldn't we wait until we're closer to the road?" Evylin asked.

Ilain shook her head. "I can more easily find focus here, away from others and the immediacy of our challenge."

Understanding, Evylin took her hand, noting the depth of contrast between their skin tones. She'd never imagined herself to be particularly dark. The Glaas family bore a complexion of a lighter tan than most Shiremen, while her mother's side had a moderate, olive cast. Unlike other Ephrians with much richer brown or black skin, Evylin carried a softer, medium tone. Yet, next to Ilain, she appeared almost almond-brown by comparison.

Ilain took a deep breath, then closed her eyes. Her fingers tightened around Evylin's hand, a tremble of magic flowing through her arm. Then she saw their edges go hazy. "There," the highlady said, opening her eyes. They glowed bright green under the shroud.

"That's disconcerting," Thom muttered.

Evylin and Ilain turned to the men who stared at them unseeingly.

"Are you both ready?" Deckard asked, his gaze somewhere over Evylin's shoulder.

"We are," Ilain assured him, drawing Evylin to join the men.

"How are we supposed to know you're still with us?" Rafferty asked, eyes flashing in every direction as though to find them.

Ethenn pointed to the ground. "You can see their tracks. I'll keep an eye on their progress."

"But just to be sure," Evylin added, the men's heads whirling toward where she and Ilain stood near Deckard's side. Reaching over, she brushed her fingers along the back of his hand. He flinched in surprise but didn't move away, his gaze searching the air where he suspected her to be standing.

Smiling up at his bemused face, Evylin couldn't help enjoying the chance to tease him. "I'll find ways to remind you I'm still here, huh?" she said, then patted his cheek playfully.

Deckard jerked away upon instinct before letting out a self-deprecating laugh. "That is *highly* disconcerting," he remarked but gestured to the rest of the troop. "Let's go."

As they moved through the trees, carefully traversing the large roots and rocks that littered the forest floor, Ilain allowed Evylin to guide them. They stayed close to Deckard, only shifting away from him when the terrain called for it. Ethenn tracked their progress from the back, stopping to wait for them when they slowed down or altered their course. His sharp attention didn't lose the women's position for a second.

Still, Evylin took every opportunity to sneak playful jabs at Deckard's side or brush her fingers along his back, arm, or hand. Each time, he flinched at the sudden touch before relaxing once again. Eventually, his lips twisted into a smirk. "You're enjoying this too much," he whispered to her.

"I so seldom get to pick on you," she replied under her breath. "It's more fun than I remembered."

He shook his head. "It's about as enjoyable as I remembered."

Evylin snorted, drawing the attention of their troop. They'd spoken softly enough that up until now, they'd escaped notice. However, Ilain walked at her side, hand in hand, so the woman heard the whole exchange.

A dry grin had affixed itself on Ilain's face, and Evylin allowed herself to distance the two of them from the rest of the troop. "Sorry," she muttered quietly.

With a shake of her head, Ilain kept her eyes on the path ahead. "Oh, I don't mind," she replied. "We Wauldeners aren't as coy as you Ephrians. It'll take much more than simple flirting to embarrass me."

"I'm not flirting with him," Evylin objected good-naturedly.

"Dear," Ilain's tone held a knowing tilt, "you're wearing the Fire Relic. If you aren't flirting with him, you're the most controlled being on the face of Terraeus."

Evylin laughed softly. "Fire denotes flirtation?"

"Why do you think I'm the way I am?" She squeezed Evylin's hand. "We Mages reflect the resource to which we're most closely tied. I am impetuous, dangerous, fervent, and passionate. Flirting is a means of expressing those traits, most often when I'm bored. But also, when I find a man desirable."

"Hm." Evylin considered the explanation. She felt those things coursing through her now, though perhaps tempered by Day's steadier, calming presence. "I will admit," she said with a smirk, "this is somewhat boring."

Ilain gave her a sly glance. "Oh, yes. It has nothing to do with your attraction to him."

Evylin's instinct was to refute the claim. However, she felt reckless, so she said, "That's just a bonus."

A stifled giggle worked out of Ilain as a heavy sigh sounded behind them. "You two do realize I'm following you, don't you?" Ethenn asked.

Though Evylin had forgotten the young man's presence, Ilain shrugged and said, "That's part of the fun, dearest."

A pink flush spread up Ethenn's neck, and Evylin couldn't help laughing with Ilain. She felt she better understood the woman now that she wore the Fire Relic. Her whole being was lighthearted and impulsive. In her natural state, Evylin used sarcasm and humor reflexively. With the Relic, that reflex was heightened. No wonder Ilain came across so bold and irreverent; being in touch with that sort of magic day in and day out must fill her with a nearly uncontainable wildness.

The women fell silent when the troop broke out of the forest and onto the muddy road. Though they waited until no one was around to emerge from the trees, they couldn't risk any travelers hearing them. Careful to disguise their steps in the mud, Deckard, Auden, and Thom took the lead with Evylin and Ilain behind them. Rafferty and Ethenn followed closely, careful to step in the women's tracks.

The road squished unpleasantly beneath their boots, squelching as they walked. Their weapons rattled with their gait, disguising the sound of Evylin's. She reached out to tug on Deckard's cloak every few dozen feet. Each time, his shoulders eased downward as though being reminded of her presence soothed him.

Without Ilain's banter to distract her, Evylin chewed on her lip, the subtle reminder of her grief pressing against the magic that held it at bay. Over the past three days, she'd wondered if it was wrong to let go of her pain. She'd noticed the shock on Deckard's face when she offered to warm his hands. She could feel his lingering surprise at her continued comfort with him. She knew it wasn't natural, and she knew that if she took off the Relic, she wouldn't feel the same sense of contentment. But did that make it wrong to harbor the Relic and embrace this relief?

For the first time in nearly two weeks, Evylin could breathe. She felt alive again. She could laugh and enjoy the company of her friends. She could train and spar without the memories of her uncle plaguing her. She could be near Deckard, touching him and, yes, flirting with him, without feeling guilty or afraid. And she didn't want to lose that.

No, it wasn't real. But she didn't think she cared.

The giant stone wall loomed in the distance, the clouds growing darker overhead. A crowd of people stood between them and the gate. Guards patrolled the sides, keeping people orderly and in line. The travelers shifted impatiently, grumbling about the long wait.

"Are there usually so many people going in and out of the Reaches?" Deckard asked Auden in a low voice.

"They're mostly merchants and businessmen," Auden explained. "Some might be scholars as well. I'd imagine it only looks to be such a large number due to the thorough searches they're doing."

"Do you think it's a cavity search?" Rafferty mumbled to Ethenn in the back, and Evylin heard a muted *thump* just before the weasel squealed. She pressed her lips together to hold in her laughter.

Between the combined magic of Ilain and the Relics, magic thrummed through Evylin. She felt good, despite the steady drain on her power. The Fire magic suggested foolhardy action to her brain. Why didn't they just rush through the gate before any guards could notice? But the Day Relic's magic soothed her racing heartbeat, reminding her that such a course would put them at too great a risk.

Hand growing clammy in Ilain's, she adjusted her fingers. The woman tightened her grip, drawing Evylin's attention. Beneath her large hood, Ilain kept her chin tucked and her eyes tightly closed. The signs of fatigue worried Evylin. They were still far back in the line, and at the rate the guards were passing travelers through, it could be another half hour at the least.

Suddenly, a patrolling guard called over to them. Evylin could see that she and Ilain's figures still bore their hazy edges, marking their shroud. But while the troop turned to the guard, the highlady stayed frozen, concentrating.

"You lot," the guard said on his approach. He waved between Rafferty and Deckard. "Tighten up. This ain't some gallery. We've got dozens more waiting behind you."

Realizing that the gap between their rows looked grandly broad to outsiders, Evylin gently guided Ilain forward. Rafferty and Ethenn had stayed back to give the two of them space. But that left enough room for two people between the men.

What was more disconcerting was the heavy drizzle. It wouldn't be noticeable from a distance, but if the guard came any closer, he might see how the rain bowed around the women's figures.

Moving forward, Evylin pulled Ilain closer to her side. To make the space between the men look natural, they had to stand almost completely flush against the three men in the front. And even then, Ethenn and Rafferty brushed against the women's backs.

"Sorry," Ethenn murmured at Ilain's sharp inhale when he pressed into her.

Thankfully, the guard hadn't heard their exchange. He nodded, satisfied with his job completed, and moved on.

Practically flush against Deckard's back, Evylin kept a wary eye on Ilain. The muscles in her face had relaxed slightly, and she leaned into Evylin. "I'm all right," she whispered so quietly that Evylin was sure she'd only heard it because of her Warrior senses.

Magic seemed to float through the air around them now. Evylin felt her skin tingling and her mind cooling. The Relics tugged at her, urging her to use them. To sprint across the field and through the gate. She could take down a few guards if she needed to. How good it would feel to fight, her body alight with power. Fighting was like a dance for her—a beautiful, intoxicating release of energy.

Hand pressed upon the damp wool of Deckard's cloak, Evylin flexed her fingers against his back. She remembered what it was like to dance with him. They'd danced together twice: once after they rescued Prince Ephren and then again at the king's ball. Both times she'd felt alive, just like in a fight. Just like when he kissed her.

Deckard stretched his shoulders, his back pressing more firmly into her touch. She couldn't help smiling. Whether he was surprised by her renewed comfort with him or not, she knew he liked it. And she thought that was probably why he hadn't said anything to her about it yet. He was afraid that if he mentioned her strange behavior, it would stop.

When they paused briefly, Evylin rested her forehead against his back. It wouldn't stop so long as she had the Day Relic. With the restorative joy it gave, the fear of losing him seemed but a memory. She could be happy with him, letting their affection grow into a true love. And she needn't worry about facing the same devastation of Hewitt and Ryen's loss again.

At an achingly slow pace, they made it to the gate. Ilain's grip had grown almost painful around Evylin's hand, but she refused to let go of the woman. The feeling would return to her fingers once they got through that gate.

The ironwork portcullis hung halfway up the stone walls. Should anyone make a break for it, the gate could be released to halt their progress with plenty of time. Evylin counted twenty-nine guards before losing track of which men she'd already tallied. They all looked similar: pale skin, angular features, and narrow frames. Their uniforms were reminiscent of the Ephrian Army's, but with black boots, trousers, and dark purple coats. Their insignias also differed, featuring a fearsome hound with bloodred eyes above their rank. The symbol of King Blount, she supposed.

A captain stepped forward, requesting their endorsement with a bored tone. Auden handed over the paper to him. A thick wax insignia sealed the bottom. Evylin wondered what nobility the Alliance had managed to ally with here in Wauld. She knew noblemen in Ephria who worked with the organization, like Lord Tybaalt, who'd kidnapped the prince near Banbury. But she struggled to believe that many of Blount's gentry supported their own usurpation.

"Looks like everything's in order," the captain said, then gestured for his men to come forward. He returned the paper to Auden. "By the king's decree, we're to search every individual who enters the kingdom. With your cooperation, we won't detain you long."

"Of course," Auden replied, tucking the endorsement back into his pouch. He turned to Deckard. "Let them search the men."

Taking on their roles of hired arms, Deckard, Thom, Rafferty, and Ethenn followed orders. Evylin carefully guided Ilain out of the men's way, grateful for the cover of the walls shielding them from the rain's reach. The guards immediately requested that the men remove their cloaks for an easier search. Each man was unceremoniously patted down, their weapons examined, and their packs searched.

Ilain began to slump against Evylin. "I'm tired," she whispered. Then her head lolled forward.

A flash of panic coursed through Evylin. She tightened her grip on the highlady. "Hold on just a little longer."

There was no sign that Ilain heard her.

Though their forms retained the subtle haze marking the shroud, Evylin looked at Deckard. She needed to warn him. Though what did she expect any of the men to do? They couldn't get the guards to speed up their search. And Ilain was growing slack with fatigue.

Evylin had to get her out of there immediately.

Scanning the gate and guards, Evylin saw a narrow path clearing as some guards stepped aside. Ilain began to shake weakly. With no other options, Evylin wound her arm around the highlady's waist and took her chance.

CHAPTER SEVEN

With her arm tight around Ilain, Evylin practically carried her toward the gate. If they could make it to the forest on the other side, they'd be safe, hidden in its thick foliage.

Careful to step where the terrae was already disturbed by footprints, Evylin moved with purpose. Her sword jostled against her hip, and she grimaced whenever a guard came near. Ilain was getting heavier; her breathing was becoming shallower. They were about to pass under the portcullis when one of the men stepped too close and clipped Evylin's shoulder.

"What was that?" he gasped, whirling around.

Evylin froze for one second before deciding she couldn't wait to see what the guard would do. Tightening her hold on Ilain, she made a break for it. Doubling her stride, she almost dragged the woman, her shuffling feet struggling to keep up.

She could hear a terse debate beginning behind her—likely the guard's companion telling him that he was imagining things—but she refused to look back. There was another line on the Waulden side of the gate, travelers looking to enter the Reach. But the guardsmen on this side were far fewer in number.

Evylin veered to the right, guiding Ilain toward the trees. They'd hardly made it past the first branches when the highlady gasped, her knees buckling. Carried down by the woman's deadweight, Evylin dropped with her. They fell into the underbrush and bushes, water splattering their faces.

While Ilain lay there motionless, her eyes squeezed shut, Evylin checked their surroundings. With Allore's mercy, they were out of sight. However, she didn't like how close to the edge of the forest they were, so she tucked her arms under Ilain's shoulders and dragged her farther into the cover of the trees.

Setting her down again, Evylin placed a hand on Ilain's arm. "Are you all right?" she whispered.

Eyes still closed, Ilain's whole body trembled with exhaustion. "Yes," she murmured. "Just tired."

Not fully convinced, Evylin drew one of her knives, watchful in case the guard had grown suspicious enough to pursue their run-in. She couldn't see the gate through the thick trees. Only the faint rumble of conversation, the creaking of cart wheels, and the distant thump of footsteps kept her informed of the goings-on outside their hiding place.

She waited for several tense minutes. But no one came.

Evylin sat in the cold foliage, Ilain lying at her side, for several minutes before realizing her mistake. The men didn't know where they'd gone. They didn't even know that the women had left them. And they wouldn't be able to search for them until they were out of the guards' sight.

With Ilain in her present state, Evylin didn't think it wise to leave her. Not even to scout to see if the men had gotten through yet. She reminded herself that Ethenn would have noticed. He would know they were gone and be able to track them. All she needed to do was keep them safe until he found them.

Taking the time to rest, Evylin settled in. She reset her hood and straightened her coat. Then she made Ilain more comfortable, tucking the woman's cloak more securely around her and brushing slick fire-bright strands off her cheeks while the woman rested.

She waited in the forest for a quarter of an hour, listening for any sound of Ethenn's arrival. The braying of horses, the groans of wagons, and the chatter of travelers on the road were all she heard for a time. Ilain's breathing had steadied. Evylin wondered if she'd fallen asleep. Then she heard the soft crunch of leaves in the distance.

Whipping around, Evylin saw Deckard and Ethenn emerge from the dark woods. Immediately, she smiled. "About time," she lamented.

The men rushed forward upon seeing Ilain's prone figure. Evylin rose to meet them. "She's all right," she assured them, then furrowed her brow. "I think."

"I'm fine," Ilain muttered, though she didn't lift her head. "I'm just bloody exhausted."

Ethenn knelt next to the Mage with a gentle grin. "Would you like help?" he asked with a small chuckle and held out a hand.

Her sharp green eyes flashed open, peering up at him. "Are you laughing at my misery?"

"Just pleased to see that you're safe," he promised.

"Mm." Ilain pursed her lips, dubious, but she took his hand, letting him pull her up to a seated position. She eyed him with a wily expression. "I don't think I have the strength to walk."

Ethenn's neck and ears burned red, and Evylin suppressed a laugh. However, the young man graciously offered to carry the highlady, at which point Ilain patted his cheek and accepted. While Ethenn cautiously lifted the woman, Deckard placed his hand on Evylin's shoulder.

She looked up at him, finding his brows pinched together. She understood his worry. Their plan had come too close to failing. If she hadn't acted quickly enough, they would have been caught, and she didn't want to begin to think of what danger they would have faced.

Evylin set her hand over his. "I'm safe," she whispered to him. "The Relics are safe. That's what matters."

Though Deckard looked about to argue, he nodded. "Come on," he said, withdrawing from her. "Let's get back to the others."

After the long day of travel and the delay at the gates, they didn't arrive at Blacklion until nightfall. The introductory terrain and landscape of Wauld proved to be the same as in the Reach. Vast, thick forests stretched across the countryside, the rain clouds constantly shielding the sky. Rather than travel on the muddy roads, they kept to the trees. While it protected them from the rain, it made their journey equally difficult.

Given Ilain's exhaustion, Ethenn wound up carrying her not just to the team, but also for several miles. Rafferty and Thom teased him mercilessly, but Evylin wondered if the young man cared. After all, he got to be near the beautiful Mage, of whom he seemed to be growing ever fonder.

Once Ilain recovered enough, she walked with Auden's continued assistance. They traversed steadily through the trees nearly the entire day, the forest turning dark and alive with the chirping of insects. They'd found another alcove to shelter in for the night, mostly walled in by large, intertwining trees. In Ilain's exhausted state, they'd given her the night off watch to recuperate, which meant that Rafferty would take her place with Ethenn.

"We're a mile from Blacklion now," Auden informed them. "In the morning, we can restock and purchase horses."

"Oh, thank the Heavens," Rafferty exclaimed. "I could use a nice, soothing pint of ale."

"You won't be going in," Deckard said.

"Why not?"

"We're in Wauld now. We have to move with caution."

Rafferty frowned. "I thought that was why we weren't allowed fires."

"It's also why we need to take care in the settlements," Auden said. "We should only take a small party."

"So why can't I be part of that small party?" Rafferty demanded.

"You don't know Waulden customs, nor do you appear or sound Waulden. You wouldn't know how to interact, and you'd be bound to make us suspicious."

While Rafferty opened his mouth to counter, Deckard stepped in. "It'll just be me and Auden going."

Auden nodded approvingly.

Evylin smirked at Deckard, sharpening the blade of her boot knife. "I think you're forgetting something," she said.

"What's that?" he asked.

"You're not Waulden either," she reminded. "You don't know the customs, nor do you sound like them."

From her seat against a tree, Ilain waved her hand through the air. Her whole demeanor was far less vibrant than usual, dark circles tracing her eyes. "That's hardly a problem," she objected. "We'll teach him both the customs and the accent."

Deckard's brow furrowed. "Why do I need to learn the accent?"

"Ephrians are not common in Wauld," Auden explained. "Which means sightings of them are memorable. The guards at the gate are sure to remember us. The best way to ensure that we *aren't* remembered in the town is to make ourselves as unremarkable as possible."

"And that," Ilain added, "can only happen if you speak like all the rest of Wauld."

Deckard frowned but motioned toward the siblings. "Go on, then," he said in resignation. "How do I speak like a Wauldener?"

Seeing the decision made, Thom turned to Ethenn. "We're out of rations after tonight," he said. "Should we hunt?"

"I doubt we'll find much," Ethenn replied. "But it couldn't hurt to get a better feel for the wildlife in these forests."

"Raff," Thom turned to his friend, "care to join?"

"Nighttime hunting?" Rafferty returned. "No, I'd prefer to hear the colonel fumble his way through the Waulden accent over getting shot in the ass by an arrow, thanks."

Deckard sent the man a long-suffering frown as Thom chuckled. "Evie?" he then offered.

"I've had enough traipsing through the trees for one day," Evylin replied, perched next to Ilain on the roots of a massive elm.

With a shrug, the two men moved to the edge of the camp. Ethenn already had his bow ready despite his doubts about their success. The thick foliage folded around them, and droplets of water flung through the air as they passed into the darkness.

"Speaking of rations," Rafferty said, stepping back toward the packs. "I'm starving."

"Don't take more than your fair share," Evylin called.

His silver eyes sparkled mischievously. "Would I do a thing like that?" he asked, then sauntered closer to the packs where the rations waited.

Evylin rolled her eyes with a sigh. "I'd better go watch him."

As she began to rise, Ilain caught her elbow. "Wait." She fumbled with her collar. "Take this to him while you're at it, would you?"

The woman retrieved the Night Relic from around her neck, and Evylin suddenly remembered the two she carried. She'd grown so used to their warmth and comfort that she'd forgotten their very presence. Now, she realized that she'd be expected to give them away.

Evylin forced a smile on her face as she replied to Ilain. "Of course."

Taking a seat on the roots, Deckard ran a hand through his damp reddish-brown curls. "So where do we begin?" he prompted.

Auden and Ilain began to speak, passing sentences back and forth as they explained the lilting Waulden accent. Their rounded tones always sounded melodic to Evylin, but the accent carried a definite edge. While it was not very different from the Ephrian accent, it had a far more nasal and far less refined air. However, she also thought it suited storytelling and dramatics better than an Ephrian's more controlled tones.

Moving across the small camp, Evylin loosened her jacket and tunic collars. Her fingers brushed the twin chains of the Day and Fire Relics. She should give them back. There was no real reason for her to keep them. They'd served their purpose, and it was best that Rafferty kept them hidden on his person, safe from prying eyes or potential attackers.

But then, Evylin reasoned, *am I not the best defense against attackers?* She was the Warrior amongst the troop. She could utilize the Relics to their full potential if someone were to find them. Why shouldn't she keep them?

Rafferty dug through the packs, scrounging up the remaining rations. "Two strips of jerky and four dried apricots apiece," he lamented when Evylin reached his side. His white-blond eyebrows rose dubiously. "After a day like ours, that hardly seems enough."

"It's all we've got," Evylin replied.

"True enough."

She crouched next to him. "Here," she said, handing him the Night Relic first, then reaching up to lift the Fire Relic's chain over her head.

The amethyst and ruby necklaces sat with a dull luster in Rafferty's hand. He held the hand aloft in expectation. When Evylin didn't move to add the Day Relic to the stack, he cocked his brow.

"You gave out two Relics," she whispered to him. "And you're getting two back."

With a wink, Rafferty tucked the necklaces into his jacket. "Understood, Eve."

Whether he truly understood or if he assumed she was trying to keep one from the Mages in case they proved untrustworthy, Evylin didn't care. She couldn't give the Day Relic back. Not yet. Not while she was finally finding a way past the grief that had been so suffocating to her.

Once Rafferty had appropriately stowed the Relics, he handed Evylin her share of the rations. They watched Deckard attempt to master the Waulden accent as they ate, sniggering as he struggled to capture its lilting tone. He sent them a disparaging frown, then cleared his throat.

"It'd be much easier to practice if you two weren't hecklin' me," he said with a near-perfect Waulden cadence.

Ilain let out a cheer, reaching over to pat his arm. "There you are! You're a natural."

Deckard shrugged, seemingly unimpressed with his improvement. They continued practicing for a long while, even as they ate. Evylin found it strangely amusing to hear Deckard speak with a Waulden accent. She couldn't decide if it suited him or not. His sharper features and red-tinged hair certainly fit in with the Calders. Still, she couldn't quite imagine him saying her name or whispering to her in the night with his words swaying melodically like that.

Ethenn and Thom returned empty-handed. While the rest of them bedded down, Ethenn and Rafferty took their places on watch at the front of the camp. The cool night had grown cooler, and Wauld's drizzle never ended. While the trees provided a semblance of a canopy above them, droplets still broke through. They all pulled their hoods up, huddling to stay dry.

Tucked against the roots of a large tree, Evylin relaxed into Deckard's embrace. The warmth that radiated through her body was her confirmation that she'd been wise to keep the Day Relic. She couldn't fathom sleeping in this icy downpour without it. Even Deckard's typical warmth wouldn't be enough, confirmed by a sudden shiver that shook his body.

Head tucked under his chin, Evylin slipped her arm around his waist and scooted closer. Though one arm still rested between them, she angled so they were otherwise wholly pressed against one another. "Does that help?" she whispered.

Deckard lay rigid and unmoving. Even his breathing seemed to halt for a time. Then he softly cleared his throat and muttered, "Yes, but . . . it presents a different problem."

"What's that?"

"Evie. . . ."

The simple intonation of the way he said her name took a moment to sink through Evylin's naivety. Then she blanched, realizing just *how* she'd pressed herself against him—how she was leaning *into* him—their arms, chests, hips, and legs closer than ever before. "Oh," she murmured, loosening her grip to ease back. "I'm . . . sorry."

"No, you—it's fine. I appreciate, uh. . . ."

Evylin snorted at his discomfort. "We *are* married," she reminded him. "It's probably a good thing. You being attracted to me."

Deckard hesitated. "That has never been in question."

Feeling emboldened by the cheery comfort of the Day Relic's warmth, Evylin tipped her head back to look up at him. The hood of his cloak cast such heavy shadows that she struggled to catch his cool, green-blue gaze in the darkness. "Is that so?" she teased. "Did you work up an infatuation for me?"

"Admittedly, yes." Deckard's voice was low and, surprisingly, reluctant. "I . . . Well, truth be told, I had considered asking to write to you."

Evylin fought to comprehend what he was telling her. "You mean in Whickam Village? Before our marriage?"

"There would be little cause to write to you after our marriage."

"You liked me?" Evylin surmised. "All the way back then?"

His eyes flashed between hers. "I did."

A bashful smile pulled at her lips. Deckard had liked her after a mere three days of knowing her. What a lovely thought. "I suppose it was my pretty face that won your favor?" she quipped.

There was a cautious pinch between Deckard's eyebrows as he stared down at her. "Your beauty played its role," he confirmed judiciously. "But it'd be more accurate to grant the accolades to your charming personality and snide remarks."

"When have I ever been snide?"

"Constantly."

They were smiling now, faces close together to allow for their hushed exchange. Fondly, Evylin regarded the pleasant slope of his nose—a strong, almost regal nose, with its sharp bridge and narrow tip. An impulsive voice within her suggested that she ought to kiss it.

Before she got the chance to enact the impetuous plan, Deckard shifted, drawing back. "Are you all right, Evylin?" he asked, a thread of worry in his voice.

Confused at the shift in his demeanor, she frowned. "I'm fine. You seem to be colder than I am."

Deckard shook his head. "No, I don't mean the cold," he whispered. "Are *you* all right? After what happened to . . . what happened in Ephria?"

Realizing that he meant Hewitt's death, Evylin paused. Was she all right? Strangely, she hadn't been thinking much about Hewitt for the last two days, not more than in passing. And while she still sensed the sorrow of his absence deep within her, she couldn't quite *feel* it, not since the soothing presence of Day had been with her.

Evylin placed her hand on Deckard's arm, rubbing reassuringly. "I promise, I'm just fine. I'm still grieving, of course, but . . . I think I'm ready to live again."

The pinch returned to his brows, unsure if he should believe her.

Endeared by his concern, Evylin planted a small, quick kiss on his bristly chin. Then she tucked her head back against his chest and snuggled close. "Thank you for taking care of me," she whispered.

Several seconds passed before Deckard relaxed, his embrace drawing her closer. "Always."

Of that, Evylin had no question. Deckard would always be there with her. He would always care for her. And so long as she had him, she could be happy.

CHAPTER EIGHT

35TH OF GALATAE, 1574

Wauld had officially made Thom's list of worst places to visit. In his five years of being a soldier, he'd journeyed across the greater land of Ephria, finding only small settlement after small settlement. That had made his life feel immeasurably less grand than he'd hoped. How could such a vast world hold so little excitement? But at least those towns and villages had pleasing scenery or semi-comfortable taverns to kick back in after a long day.

From his minimal experience, Wauld was one great rainforest filled with power-hungry Mages, greedy nobility, and suppressed countrymen.

In the gray dawn light, Thom leaned against a dew-damp oak, watching his brother and the Day Mage disappear into the fog clinging to the pines, hazels, and ferns surrounding them, on their way to the town. His curiosity plucked at the jealousy that rested endlessly in his chest. Once again, Deckard got to go off and have an adventure while Thom sat back and babysat.

"Blacklion," Rafferty said wistfully, sitting in the low fork of a hazel. "Bet there's a pretty barmaid in that town just waiting for a weary traveler to brighten her day."

"Well, you certainly are wearying," Thom said.

Rafferty ignored him. "Neither the colonel nor the highlord is gonna put their time to good use."

"One of them *is* married after all," Evylin said with a smirk, the image of her old self.

"And the other is an impossible bore," Ilain added. Her dark skirt swirled as she spun to the low-burning fire in the camp. They only risked the campfire because it would be hidden in the daylight, and they needed to boil fresh water for their journey. "Now, we've got at least four hours without those two making things dull. What shall we do?"

"I have a pleasant diversion for us," Evylin replied, voice chipper.

Thom eyed her, caught between worry and gratitude at her improved mood. This sudden turnaround bothered him. She'd begun acting so carefree. It was as though Hewitt had simply chosen to return to Whickam Village. If that wasn't concerning enough, she'd resumed flirting with Deckard again. A sure sign that she was moving on far too quickly.

"What sort of diversion?" Rafferty asked, gray eyes sparkling with mischief.

Evylin tapped the hilt of her sword. "It's been weeks since we've properly trained," she explained. "Now that we're in Wauld, that needs to change."

Hunched against the oak, Thom frowned. "We just woke up," he lamented. A large drop of rainwater from the leaves above took the opportunity to splatter the hood of his cloak, leaking down onto his nose.

He scowled up at the tree as Ilain laughed outrageously. "And," he added, "where this forest isn't covered in dangerous tangles of roots the size of Raff's whole body, it's slick with mud."

"You're a pansy," Evylin said, then turned to Ethenn for support.

The young soldier sat at the fire, poking the embers with a stick. His tired expression showed even less excitement than Thom's.

Evylin let out a disapproving hum. "Some soldiers you are."

"We've defected," Thom noted.

"You're still soldiers," she said. "Only for the Alliance, now."

"Technically," Ilain cut in, "the Alliance doesn't have an army." She sat beside Ethenn, and the boy glanced nervously at her from the corner of his eye. "It's more of a militia."

"So we're militiamen," Rafferty surmised.

"I suppose so. Though we do have officers."

Evylin waved off the formality. "Either way—" She turned back to Thom and Ethenn. "We need to keep up our strength and skills. That means running every drill Hewitt taught us."

Thom watched Evylin's face, looking for any sign or flash of grief at her uncle's name. He found none. Another sign that something was up. Even he felt a tremor of disappointment and loss at the thought of Hewitt.

Rafferty hopped up from the hazel. "I'm for it," the weasel announced. "Not that I'm any more a fan of Hewitt's exercise regimen now than before. That part's downright torturous. It's the sparring that interests me. I've been itching to duel for weeks."

Evylin smiled, and Thom sighed. "All right," he said. "Let's get this over with."

"Excellent!" Evylin moved toward the entrance to the camp. "There's a reasonable clearing a few hundred feet that way. We can run our paces first and spar there afterward."

"Shouldn't someone stay with Highlady Calder?" Ethenn suggested.

Ilain brushed a dismissive hand through the air. "Nonsense," she insisted. "I'll be just fine with my sketchbook for company."

"Besides," Evylin added, "we'll be within sight. We can even take breaks here at the fire."

With the kid's strange protectiveness of the highlady taken care of, Ethenn rose.

Under Evylin's instructions, they gathered the two training swords they'd deemed to bring into Wauld and headed for the clearing. "We'll start with a quick warm-up," she said. "Then a quarter-mile jog before we go one-on-one."

Thom nudged her arm. "Try not to wear us out *before* we get to the real work, eh, Evie?"

She held out her arms in a dramatic sweep. "Try not to be such a girl, Thom."

Rafferty and Ethenn snickered.

The insult rankled at the edges of Thom's ego, but he paid it no attention. Of all the people in the world, Evylin was the only one who could insult him without damaging his pride. He'd wondered at that peculiar phenomenon dozens of times. He felt sure that her opinion of him *should* be the one that mattered most. Yet, he could always sense her regard for him in every jest and taunt. No matter how flippant or blunt she was, she spoke with a fondness that he rarely heard from those in his life. And he loved her for it.

Still, the curiosity of her good humor kept his smile from fullness.

"How's this, then?" he offered. "I challenge you first. And whoever strikes the first hit gets bragging rights for the day."

"For the rest of the week," Evylin countered, grinning ear to ear.

"You're on."

They wore through the first hour of their morning with the warm-up, run, and the first couple of bouts. Much to his disappointment, no matter how unsurprising it was, Evylin landed the first hit in their duel. They'd set up, her in her usual stance, perfected by Hewitt over more than a decade, and him in his still-improving one. He was prouder of his swordplay these days, but going up against Evylin didn't do much for a man's confidence.

Rafferty had called the start of their bout, and Evylin feinted upward before slashing at his hands. The strike left his fingers stinging and his pride bruised.

She didn't gloat *too* much, but Rafferty and Ethenn jeered at Thom from the sidelines.

"Ah, Thommy, what a shame!"

"It's not much of a loss, though, is it?" Ethenn said.

"Whyever not, little Lox?"

The kid smirked. "When's he ever had anything worth bragging about?"

Their baiting proved successful. Thom's muscles tightened, and his jaw tensed. If he wasn't so focused on holding his own against Evylin in the duel, he might've found the wit to make a retort. Instead, he put his frustrations into the spar, finding his movements more sloppy than usual.

Evylin knocked him off his feet, sending him sprawling in the mud. The men laughed even more vigorously at his demise.

Thom took Evylin's offered hand, and she helped him up. "You can't let them get to you like that," she said, her voice low and her gaze knowing. "A level head is the key to winning any fight."

"It's not the only key," he grumbled. He attempted to brush off his back but only covered his hand in mud. "Strength, skill, and magic help."

Evylin raised her brow. "I wasn't using magic."

"You *are* magic," he said, and he meant it. "Everyone else is a mere mortal compared to you."

She breathed out an incredulous laugh. "And you say that Jonn's dramatic."

Thom held his tongue, backing away to give Ethenn his blade. Rafferty took Evylin's spot, and she called the start for them. Then she stepped over to Thom's side, where he was wiping the mud from his hand with the back of his cloak, draped over the branches of a rowan.

"What do you think it's like?" she asked. He raised his brow, and she clarified, "The town."

"Ah. Probably just as wet and muddy as the rest of this Allore-forsaken country."

"You're in a fine mood."

He gave her one of his more cynical smirks. "When am I not?"

"That's an excellent point. Is anything in particular the cause of this radiant countenance, or are you just feeling adequately hydrated?"

He snorted but didn't feel the humor it held. What caused his sour mood today? Yes, it could be the damp and the cold. It could be the urge to get out of these perpetual forests. A good night's rest would likely offer improvement. But then, his ill-tempered demeanor might be tied to the fact that his brother still had everything, while Thom had nothing.

Wiping the last remnant of dirt from between his fingers, Thom offered a half-felt grin. "Turns out I have a taste for waterlogged fowl."

"Mm, yes." Evylin leaned back against the tree, watching Ethenn lazily defend Rafferty's wild attacks. "Waulden geese are quite the delicacy, aren't they? I believe I caught a hint of loam in its flavor profile."

Thom shook his head as she chuckled. He rested against the tree at her side, bumping her shoulder. "What's gotten into you?"

"What do you mean?"

He stared down at her, the dim forest turning her dark eyes a silty brown. He hesitated, seeing the joy they held. "Evie, I don't want to upset you," he murmured.

Evylin's brow wrinkled, but her smile remained. "Are you going to tell me that you let me win?"

"*This* is what I'm talking about." He gestured to her smile, then the rest of her relaxed demeanor. "You're acting *happy*."

"Why shouldn't I?"

He stared at her, incredulous.

A beat passed before Evylin sucked in an understanding breath. "Because of Hewitt."

Her words weren't as heartbroken as Thom thought they should be.

Suddenly, Rafferty cried out in exasperation. "Stop playing with me, Loxley!"

Twirling the practice blade in his hand, Ethenn gave the weasel an innocent expression. "I just wanted to make you feel good about yourself."

"I don't want to feel good about myself. I want to win!"

Evylin sniggered at their banter before turning back to Thom. Her voice was soft with peace. "It doesn't hurt anymore, Thom," she said. "I miss him. Desperately. But I can't live in the past."

Thom tried to hear the lie in her words. He stared deeply into her eyes and studied the rounds and angles of her face. But he couldn't find deception anywhere. Not in the weight of her brow or the curve of her lips.

He drew in a long breath. "You're sure?"

"Quite."

Thom's brow furrowed so tightly that it began to ache. He didn't believe her. He couldn't. Not when he knew how much her uncle meant to her. Not when he'd seen sorrow leach all the life from her soul over the past few weeks.

A loud *crack* and Rafferty's howl of pain startled Thom out of his thoughts. He looked over to find Ethenn holding up his hands and backing away, even as he laughed. Rafferty hopped on one leg as he gripped his shin. Evylin pressed her hands to her mouth to quell her amusement.

"What've you lot done now?" Ilain called across the way, her lilting voice carrying only the most minor concern.

Face contorted with pain, Rafferty lowered his leg, glaring at Ethenn.

The kid held up a finger. "You said not to make you feel good."

"I'm gonna kill you!" Rafferty bolted for Ethenn, setting them off on a chase. They leaped over roots, ducked under branches, slid on the mud, and trampled over moss. It all ended when Rafferty sprinted around a tree, cutting Ethenn off before whacking him on the face with the flat of the training blade.

"Ha-ha!" Rafferty exclaimed proudly. "Now, we're even."

"Men," Ilain said with a huff. Then, spotting the welling red stripe on Ethenn's cheek, she marched over, still grumbling under her breath, to grab the young man's jacket and tug him toward the firepit.

Evylin scooped Ethenn's discarded training sword from the mud. "All right, Rafferty," she said. "How about you and I have a go?"

"I'm in a right foul mood, Eve," he declared. "So you'd best watch yourself."

While the two prepared to spar, Thom moved back to the camp. The mud caking the back of his coat had begun to clump, and he wanted to get it off before it could stain the wool. He began to shrug it off as he approached the fire.

Ethenn sat patiently while Ilain dipped a cloth in a bowl of water. Though the cut on his cheek wasn't deep, a thin trickle of blood welled at the corners.

Thom smirked. "That's not going to do you any favors with the ladies if it scars, kid."

Ilain dabbed at the cut, and Ethenn grimaced. "You do realize I'm only two years younger than Rafferty, right?" he said.

"Don't listen to him," Ilain said, eyes on her task. "He wouldn't know what a woman wanted if she handed him a notarized letter detailing her desires."

"Oh, I have experience to the contrary," Thom noted.

Ilain sent him a bland stare. "You sure she wasn't protecting your ego?"

He held her glimmering green gaze like a dare. "I have stories that would make you blush, my lady."

With a disbelieving snort, Ilain turned back to Ethenn. "I think it'll bruise," she said, studying the skin. "That was a solid wallop he gave you."

"That's all right," Ethenn said. "I felt bad."

Ilain drew back, appraising him. "You mean, you let him hit you?"

He shrugged.

"Don't tell Raff that," Thom warned.

"Wasn't planning on it," Ethenn replied.

Ilain dabbed the wet cloth to his cheek again, then dropped it into the bowl. "Either way, I think it'd be best not to leave a reminder on your face, hm?"

She moved to take his face in her hands, but Ethenn jerked back. "What are you doing?" he asked, his voice shaky.

Thom held in his urge to laugh. Ethenn's crush on the Fire Mage had been blatant from the start, his youth making him impossibly bad at concealing his nerves around the highlady. Thom couldn't exactly blame him for his attraction. Ilain was a beautiful woman—her fiery hair, lithe figure, and sharp features gave her a distinctly regal elegance that was practically unseen amongst the Ephrian women—if one could look past her obnoxious personality.

Ethenn's panicked reaction to her more intimate touch made sense.

The worry that flashed across Ilain's face did not.

But then she smirked, all trace of distress gone. "Well, we could wait for Auden to get back," she replied, a teasing melody to her raspy voice. "*Or* I could heal you."

"I thought healing was a Day magic thing," Thom interjected.

Ilain and Ethenn looked over, eyes wide as though they'd forgotten he was there.

"It is," she said.

"Aren't Elemental and Existential magic mutually exclusive?" Thom pressed.

With a haughty lift to her chin, she said, "For the normal Mage, yes, they are. But I'm special."

"And what makes you so special?"

"Beyond my dazzling personality?" She winked. "I'm the most powerful Mage—"

"Born in two centuries," Thom completed with annoyance. "I get it."

"Mm." Ilain turned back to Ethenn. "Auden taught me enough Day magic to heal myself should I ever be in a dire situation. I'm not great at it, but a cut like this and a little light bruising is child's play."

The wariness still creased Ethenn's brow, but he nodded, accepting her touch. Ilain placed her hands on either side of his face, the right resting more gently over his wounded cheek. Her thumb twitched in the smallest caress, and a flame-like burst of orange light licked between his skin and her palm.

Thom had begun to grow somewhat numb to the effects of magic, but he found himself continually surprised by the woman's power. She drew back her hand, revealing Ethenn's now blemish-free cheek. It looked as though Rafferty had never hit him at all.

Drawing in a deep breath, Thom was about to let out a low, impressed whistle, but it dissipated into a puff of breath as he watched her brush a finger tenderly over Ethenn's healed flesh. Her eyes regarded him with baffling affection.

Then she dropped her hand into her lap.

"There," she said haughtily, leveling a superior look in Thom's direction. "If you're ever so injured, don't bother coming to me. I'm not sure you could handle a touch as potent as mine."

Any retort died before inception. Her snide quip carried a new resonance in Thom's ears. It didn't matter how flirtatious she was with him; he'd witnessed the softness in her expression while her hands lingered on the young man's face.

By the way Ethenn sat slumped away from her, the kid was ignorant of it.

"Loxley," Rafferty called, all sins forgiven. "Come help me teach Evie a lesson."

Ethenn excused himself, thanking Ilain for her help, then jogged over to the others, saying, "We only have two training swords, idiot."

Rafferty hoisted two thick branches. "I've fashioned my own blades."

Shaking his head at their antics, Thom turned back to find Ilain returned to her sketches. He'd often wondered what she drew in there. If anyone but Auden got close enough to find out, she'd flip it shut. Now, he had an idea of one of her subjects.

"Make sure you capture the shading of his blush just right," he quipped. "Wouldn't want him appearing too heroic. Realism and all."

A sharp eyebrow rose on her porcelain skin. "Whatever are you talking about?"

"The kid." He tipped his chin in the direction of her page. "Your drawings."

She shut the book with a *snap*. Her lips lifted mockingly. "Don't be jealous, dear. If you want your likeness captured, I will happily oblige."

"Mm-hm. And how many times have you captured our young friend's likeness?"

"I'm afraid your envious insinuation holds no ground. I've drawn each of you with equity."

"Have you?"

She gave him a bland stare before returning to her work. But Thom noticed the subtle shift of her eyes toward the trio sparring a handful of yards away.

He grunted in bafflement. "Are you boffing the boy?"

That made Ilain's charcoal slice up the page in a startled jerk.

Suddenly, her gemlike eyes were on him, a blazing green fire. "How dare you?" she snarled. "I may be flirtatious, but my honor is above reproach. Should you like proof of it, I'd be happy to jilt your own sordid desires."

Thom laughed. "Sordid desires, eh? Yes, I've had many of those. None of them involving you."

Her rosy lips pursed with sarcasm. "My heart aches at your rejection."

He motioned toward Ethenn. "And here I thought I was the object of your affection."

Languidly, Ilain stretched out her legs, crossing them demurely at the ankles. She wore a contemplative expression as she eyed him. "Don't be too heartbroken. It takes a certain finesse to hold a flame."

The admission made Thom's mouth drop open in surprise. "You like the kid?" He scoffed. "What a future that would be. You'd burn him up in ten seconds flat."

"Why do you think I've chosen to flirt with *you*?"

"Wait—what?"

Ilain rolled her eyes. "You don't think I'm foolish enough to intentionally seek out the company of a man who's not wise enough to recognize my worth, do you?"

His face scrunched in confusion. "You've been flirting with me to make him jealous?"

"Not at all," she said with a huff. "I've been flirting with you because I'm trying to dissuade him, and you don't pose a threat."

"Dissuade him? I thought you liked him."

"I'm attracted to him. There's a difference. But he *does* like me, and I don't care to hurt his feelings."

"What *do* you care to do to him?" Thom couldn't help teasing her. He enjoyed the way it made her eyes narrow and her jaw twitch.

Ilain set her sketchbook to the side. "Even your indelicate mind couldn't handle my aspirations."

"Can't say I'm not intrigued."

"I'm afraid you'll remain unsatisfied."

"You're awfully good at this."

"At what?"

"Baiting a man."

She smiled, cunning and arrogant. "You spend thirty-two years in an Order with tedious Mages twice your age, and you'd find yourself rather excited at the attention of handsome young suitors too."

Thom's expression fell into shock. "You're thirty-two?" He'd pegged her for being closer to his sister Meria's age at twenty-five.

"I spent thirty-two years in the Order," Ilain corrected. "I lived at home a decade before that."

Thom gaped at her.

She smirked. "Magic has its benefits."

"Almighty," he mumbled. "I'm flirting with a woman fifteen years my senior."

Her copper brows lifted in delight. "You've decided to return my coquetry?"

"What's life without playful banter with a pretty woman?"

She set a hand to her chest, mockingly coy. "You find me pretty?"

Thom raised his brow. "Why didn't you tell me of your disinterest in the first place? I would have happily assisted your discouragement of Loxley from the start."

"Hm." Ilain considered him. "I suppose I could use some assistance. He doesn't seem to be getting the idea."

"You're not doing a very good job rejecting him."

Her green eyes sparkled. "You'll oblige me then?"

"It'd be my pleasure."

CHAPTER NINE

Built into a valley between the rocky hillsides dotted with emerald trees, the city of Blacklion greeted them like a ghost. The fog sapped all color from its stone walls and buildings. A jagged, muddy path wove its way to the rusty iron gate. It was as though the moment they'd exited the forest, the world had turned a gradient of grays and browns.

The guards at the gate eyed them suspiciously, asking far too many questions about their visit, only allowing them through once Auden slipped a dozen strange copper coins their way. When Deckard asked about the currency, the Mage brushed it off.

"With a millennium of Auldan coins floating around, neither Wauld nor Ephria deemed it worth curating a completely new royal mint," he explained. "However, there are copper mines aplenty in the southwest, and the managers decided to take their overabundance of copper, cut it with tin, and create these—" He held up one of the coins, its once-shiny face dulled with age. It bore the symbol of a goat's head wearing a crown of twigs. "They're called nanny farthings, or nannies for short."

Deckard tipped up a brow. "A regal name," he said in the Waulden lilt.

Auden grinned. "They're viewed as somewhat traitorous in the eyes of the king, since they're a currency created without his approval or the backing of his treasury. However, by the time he'd learned of their existence, it was too late. They'd spread throughout the whole of the South and even up into central Wauld. Now, they're viewed as a commoner's coin. You couldn't pay a reputable man with them, but they'll work just fine for daily provisions or simple bribes."

He tucked the coin back in his pocket. "I brought a bagful on our journey, knowing we'd likely need them."

"Why the goat?" Deckard asked.

"The copper mines are located within the Vaulgan Mountains, notably rife with Vaulgus goats. They overpopulate the area so much that they're more of a nuisance than a resource. Granted, their fur makes for quite soft knits."

Moving through the dirt streets of Blacklion, Deckard stuck close to Auden's side, warily taking in the foreign sights and people. Learning about the goats and the coins of their name left him keenly aware of just how little he knew of the Waulden people's lives. And how easily he could be identified as an outsider. Had someone mentioned something as ordinary as "nannies" to him, he would have readily made a fool of himself.

Deckard vowed to keep his mouth shut in the settlements of Wauld from then on.

The city was a maze of corridors and moss-covered buildings. Everything was built close together with only minimal dried patches of grass or spindly, barren trees. The citizens wore weary and haggard expressions, the majority of them in plain, well-worn garments of charcoal gray or terrae brown. Men patrolled the streets, hands on their weapons and embroidered patches on their breasts.

"Who are those men?" Deckard whispered.

"In the plum-colored coats?"

"Yes."

"Liege officers," Auden said. "They're appointed by the nobility to police their fief. You don't want them to catch you paying with nannies."

"What about the guards at the gate?"

"They aren't liege officers. They're Cityguard, and they take their jobs less seriously. Probably due to their lower pay."

Deckard watched as two liege officers walked into a shop, several customers vacating within seconds of their arrival. "I take it they're not well-liked," he remarked.

Auden scratched his beard, tempering his smile. "Certainly not."

They entered a general store, its windows less grimy than many others. A chipper voice greeted them from the back. The interior was more refined than Deckard had expected, with plastered walls and polished floors. Dozens of shelves lined the shop, each one decorated with organized symmetry. Dry goods, basic groceries, toiletries, home supplies, and even finer luxuries filled the shelves and bins.

While Auden bartered with the shop clerk, a tall, spindly blond man with the thickest Waulden accent he'd yet heard, Deckard perused the nearest shelf. He was surprised to find it covered in paintings, wood carvings, ceramic sculptures, and other handmade decorative pieces. A porcelain tea set dominated the display, featuring intricate yellow flowers painted on each cup and the pot. Deckard didn't recognize the variety, wondering if the flora was unique to the western half of the continent. He glanced at the price tag, and his brow rose. Who could afford such a frilly luxury?

The door opened, and it seemed his thoughts had summoned one such man. He wore a scarlet brocade waistcoat, his dark hair neatly swept back from his lightly aged face. With his shoulders back and chin held high, he approached the counter even as Auden spoke with the clerk.

The newcomer cleared his throat, bringing their exchange to a halt. Unconcerned with his rudeness, the man ignored Auden as he slid a slip of paper to the shop clerk. It bore a short note and a wax seal on its bottom edge.

"Ah, yessir," the clerk said, his voice taking on a stuttering quality. "Righ' away, sir." He turned, paper in hand, and departed behind a curtain to the back of the building.

Quiet descended in the room. Auden and the well-dressed man waited side by side at the counter. Deckard expected some small talk to engage between them, but Auden took a deferential step back as though abdicating his right to service.

The clerk reappeared, a square parcel in his hands. "'Ere yeh are, sir," he said, gently placing the brown paper-wrapped package on the counter. "An' please tell Duke Obel, tha' anytime he needs anythin', I'll get it for 'im."

At the mention of the nobleman's name, Auden stiffened but remained silent.

The man, whom Deckard now assumed to be a steward of the duke's, gave the clerk a disparaging glance. "You'll carry the package to my carriage," he instructed, his accent far smoother than even the Calders'.

The clerk nodded as though he should have thought of it first. "O' course I will." He scooped up the parcel once again, which was barely large enough to hold a teapot.

Deckard marveled as the clerk hastily followed the steward out. Once the door was shut behind them, he turned to Auden. "Are all noblemen and their staff so condescending?"

"Huh?" Auden blinked as though clearing away his thoughts. "Oh, yes. It's expected."

Though Deckard had experienced his fair share of haughty nobility in Ephria, they weren't so high and mighty that their *stewards* couldn't carry a package that weighed less than five pounds.

Returning to his examination of the shelf, Deckard found himself more disenchanted with Wauld than he'd anticipated. Between the dreary weather, despondent citizens, and tyrannical ruling class, he wasn't altogether sure who would want to live in such a place. The Calders' defection and the Alliance's rebellion made all the more sense.

As he scanned the shop, a trio of small vignettes on the display caught Deckard's eye.

He leaned closer, all qualms forgotten. The delicate, detailed landscapes in oil paint sat within daintily carved wooden frames. But it was the image on the far right that swept the breath out of his lungs.

The clerk reentered, grumbling under his breath. By the time he reached the counter, all Deckard heard was, ". . . wi' their pompous 'airdos."

Setting his hands on the counter, the clerk surveyed Auden. "My apologies, mucker. Livin' wi' those shite noble lackeys ain't easy, is it? Now, where were we?"

As the men resumed their haggling through Auden's list, Deckard carefully lifted the painting. It was lovely with beautiful craftsmanship, though he didn't recognize the artist's signature in the bottom corner. Not a great artwork, but with a vastly meaningful image. It looked uncannily like the Ephrian countryside of Wayford in winter: frost-tipped grasses, pine-green copse of trees, and an iced-over lake. A soft yellow sun reflected with a lifelike glow off the water's surface, downy clouds filling the sky.

The only thing missing was a blanket, a bag of books, and two strangers-turned-spouses searching for their perfect adventure on a map.

"Yer companion find somethin' he likes?"

Upon the clerk's direction, Auden turned, seeing Deckard with the vignette. "That's nice," he noted disinterestedly as he glanced at it.

Working to remember his accent, Deckard cautiously addressed the clerk. "How much for this?" he asked.

"There's a price tag, ain't there?"

Deckard stepped closer. "It's for all three. I just want the one."

"Well, it's a set, ya see," the clerk said. "Can' go sellin' bits of a set on their own, can I?"

Hearing the tone of a salesman in his voice, Deckard set the vignette on the counter. "How much?"

Auden drew his shoulders back, his brow furrowing.

Deckard kept his stare on the clerk.

Tapping his chin, the shopman scanned Deckard and then the painting. "It's a valuable piece, ya see. Over a hundred years ol'. Paint'd by the legend Fortinne Graas, an Easterner by birth. He paint'd this triplet from memory, 'tis said, of the travels of his youth."

No matter how unknown Graas's work was to Deckard, he was even more convinced that this was the very lakeside where he and Evylin had shared their afternoon in Wayford. He leaned forward, holding the clerk's gaze. "How. Much?"

Greed sparkled in the sharp blue Waulden stare. "Ten crowns."

Auden scoffed. "That's outrageous. The triplet is twelve altogether."

"An' I'm takin' a loss, splittin' a collection so fine."

Deckard fished the coins from the pouch on his belt. "I'll give you seventeen, and you'll include everythin' else on our list with it."

The hungry glimmer in the clerk's eyes grew brighter. The supplies should have cost closer to ten on their own, prices in Wauld being higher than in Ephria naturally. But he knew that Deckard was desperate for the painting.

"Nah." He shook his head. "Can' do that. Full price for the goods on the list, and an upcharge on the broken triplet."

Deckard knew the value of the painting wasn't near what the clerk claimed. He'd lived in Ephria's capital for years, and the name Fortinne Graas had never reached his ears. The potential merit of the tale of Graas's travels and emigration notwithstanding, whoever the painter was, he hadn't been a legend. But the average Wauldener wouldn't know that.

"Listen," Deckard rested his hands on the counter, "we passed a grocer, a baker, a chandler, and all other varieties of shops on the way here. There was even another general store down the way."

The clerk drew his shoulders back. "Morty ain't got all I got."

"But I'll bet that Morty would be downright chuffed if we'd do business with him rather than you."

The clerk tapped the list. "He can' give yeh the deal I'm givin' yeh."

"You're not giving us a deal," Deckard countered. "You're cheating us."

Offense colored his face red, and Auden set a hand on Deckard's shoulder, but he waved the Mage off.

"This triplet has been here quite a while." Deckard brushed a finger over the vignette's frame, revealing a streak of now-clean wood. "No one has even glanced at it but me, leaving a thick layer of dust to accumulate. Wouldn't that be damaging to such a valuable heirloom?"

The clerk's lips pursed at his lie uncovered.

"So," Deckard held his stare, "how's that seventeen gold sound?"

They left the shop with their bags full and their list complete. All they had left to find were horses for purchase.

"That cost us nearly twice what it should have," Auden grumbled.

"It only cost us seven gold," Deckard corrected as they wound through the streets toward the sound of metal on metal and the smell of manure. "The other ten were my own expense."

"We share the same Alliance-funded purse, Jonn."

"Should I live through this, I'm sure I can find some way to pay them back."

Auden shook his head, unsatisfied. "Why did you want it so badly anyway? Ten gold for any painting so small is theft."

Reasoning there was no point in hiding his intent, Deckard tightened the strap on his pack. "Evylin's birthday is in a couple of weeks."

His copper eyebrows drew low. "You're buying gifts while on a mission to save the world?"

"She'll appreciate it."

"A painting? Evylin doesn't strike me as a purveyor of the arts."

"It's the subject of the painting that she'll appreciate."

"I suppose you'd know better than I."

The conversation ended as they entered the farrier's stables. Gentle nickers filled the air from the paddock and stalls. The owner was a stout man, tall with arms toned by pounding steel into horseshoes. His accent was even thicker than the shop clerk's, and Deckard settled for understanding only one side of the conversation. The one word he regularly picked up from the farrier was "mucker," the same term the clerk had used.

"Yes, very well," Auden finally concluded. "That will have to do."

With that, the farrier grunted and headed toward the paddock, yelling at his stable boy while gesticulating wildly.

"I take it we're getting our horses," Deckard said.

Auden sighed. "Five of them. We're short on the funds for the other two." He said the last bit with a disgruntled glare.

"Ah." Deckard made sure his expression was adequately penitent. They'd only brought enough coins with them to procure what they absolutely needed, not wanting to risk drawing the eye of a back-alley thief by flashing around too much gold. "We could retrieve more and come back for the others."

"We can't return," he said. "Best not to give them a reason to remember us."

"Right."

The fire crackled in the small forge, bars of steel sticking out of a barrel beside it. Despite the cultural differences, the stables looked the same as any in Ephria. Granted, the prices were higher, and he couldn't understand the owner well enough to attempt lowering the price.

Deckard turned back to Auden, brow furrowed. "What was that he kept calling you?"

After a moment of consideration, the highlord understood. "Mucker. Means friend."

"Then why not call you 'friend'?"

"There's nearly a thousand miles of land between our two countries, Jonn," he said. "So much separation and space are bound to create some differences."

"But we speak the same language."

"Yet, our accents are different. So is our colloquial speech."

Deckard found himself growing curious to discover the roots of the Waulden accent and turns of phrases. He wondered if there might be a book on the subject. Regardless, if he were to continue going in and out of the settlements with Auden, he'd need to learn their everyday expressions and slang.

The farrier and his stable boy returned with their fully saddled horses. Most of them resembled any standard Ephrian horse, with short brown and black coats. However, there was a smaller one of a heartier build, with large white patches splotched over its black coat and a silk-like mane.

Once the horses and coins were exchanged, and they'd begun their journey back to camp, Deckard asked about the unique breed.

"A Brounes Gypsy," Auden said. "They're mostly used for pulling carts or wagons, making them excellent traveling horses. I'd have liked to have more, but he gave me a deal on the others."

Upon their return to camp, there was a general confusion as to why they'd only brought back five horses when they'd taken enough money for seven. Graciously, Auden kept Deckard's secret, telling them that the supplies had cost more than expected.

"We'll get two more when we arrive near Vaulley," he announced.

Ilain quirked one of her sharp eyebrows. "That's three days away. Why don't we stop in Jourdan tomorrow?"

"I'd rather put more distance between us and Blount's Night Mages before we stop again."

Everyone agreed with the sentiment, leaving Rafferty to ask the inevitable question that remained. "So who's doubling up?"

A collective silence fell, no one wanting to volunteer.

Evylin rolled her eyes. "I'll ride with Jonn."

"It won't be comfortable," Deckard warned.

"We've done it twice before."

Thom piped up then. "Ethenn and Raff are short enough that they could probably share."

Both men sent him scathing looks.

Evylin grinned at their reaction but shook her head. "With all his muscle, I'd imagine Ethenn weighs as much as you."

Ilain sighed. "Very well, I'll volunteer. Whom shall I ride with?"

The four remaining men considered it. Rafferty and Ethenn looked ready to offer, but Thom spoke first. "I'd be honored to escort you, milady."

Everyone stared at him in shock.

Folding her hands on her lap, Ilain batted her lashes at him. "Are you certain that you can bear being so close to me?"

"I think I'll manage for three days," he said, with a suggestiveness to his tone that made Deckard's brow pinch.

Was his brother *flirting* with Ilain?

"With that all sorted," Rafferty said, distracting from the strange moment, "which horse is mine?"

Within an hour, they rode out, old and new belongings packed into the saddlebags. Rafferty wound up with the gypsy horse whom he'd affectionately begun calling Betsy. Ilain sat behind Thom, full skirts splayed out behind her.

"Try not to get too attached to me," Thom said as she adjusted the fabric.

She settled her chin on his shoulder teasingly. "Wouldn't dream of it, darling."

Watching the exchange suspiciously, Deckard startled when Evylin's arms threaded through his to clasp around his waist.

"Did you forget I was back here?" she asked with amusement.

"Momentarily," he admitted.

She scooted closer, legs pressing against him on both sides. "I'm rather offended. Am I so forgettable?"

They swayed with the gait of the horse, its hooves clomping and squelching on the dirt and mud road beneath them. Deckard's suspicions shifted from his brother to his wife. He still couldn't pin down what was causing this return to normalcy. He wanted to be grateful for it and lavish in the comfortable way she leaned against his back. But he couldn't. Not when she seemed to have moved on from Hewitt's death so suddenly and completely.

Still, he would take whatever closeness to her that he could get.

Resting his hand on hers, Deckard glanced over his shoulder. "In a million lifetimes, I couldn't forget you."

She released a soft laugh. "What a charming sentiment."

"I'm a charming man," he quipped.

Evylin slipped one hand free to reach up and tug the hood of his cloak from his head. He began to protest, turning to scold her when the sudden presence of her lips on his bearded cheek halted him. He gaped at her, baffled.

Her smile sparkled in her amber eyes. "More than any other."

Unsure how to respond, Deckard let out a small puff of a laugh. He didn't feel the humor of it, though, confusion clouding his head. Evylin had grown increasingly casual with her flirtation and touch since they'd entered Wauld. And while it initially made his chest fill with the warmth of hope, now it twisted like a knot.

Something was wrong. He just couldn't puzzle out what.

Staring at the path ahead, Deckard scanned the tree line. His subconscious formed into Hewitt's phantom, standing there with his arms crossed as they neared. His gray eyes summoned Deckard, a call to walk through the forest and think through this problem.

He just needed an excuse to go out alone.

CHAPTER TEN

38TH OF GALATAE, 1574

"I'd forgotten what a joy it is to have your own horse," Ilain said, patting the newly purchased mare.

Rain sleeted through the tree cover. They'd taken to traveling the roads, the forests too densely grown to allow for travel on horseback. Deckard and Auden had returned from Vaulley that morning with two more mares, one for each woman.

Thom reached over and took her hand playfully. "Just when I thought we were closer than ever."

Evylin spurred her speckled gray horse to ride through the gap between Ilain and Thom, forcing him to release her. "The day you two start getting along is the day I'll relinquish my sword," she said.

Settling back into his saddle, Thom smirked. "You may have to give it up sooner than you'd think."

"Hogwash," she replied. "Whatever nonsense this is, it isn't real."

Ilain twirled a lock of her red curls thoughtfully under her heavy gray hood. "She's awfully insightful, isn't she?"

A curious frown came to Thom's face, cast in shadow from his own cloak.

"What can we say, Evylin?" Ilain said. "You've caught us."

"I knew it," Evylin declared. Then she tapped her saddle hesitantly. "What exactly have I caught you in?"

Sharing a look with Thom, the fire-haired highlady smiled. "For the betterment of the troop, we've called a truce. No more nasty remarks on either side."

Thom sighed. "It's a difficult burden, but I'm man enough to bear it."

"Hm." Evylin questioned their sincerity, yet they had been quite civil to one another. In fact, she'd almost call their behavior flirtatious. The scruples of such actions she'd yet to determine, but she'd not heard a cross word between them since they left Blacklion.

"You doubt me?" Thom asked.

"I doubt most of what you say," Evylin replied. The Day Relic warmed around her neck, adding to her sunny disposition. Even in the rainy, endless travel, she found herself uncomprehendingly happy. "Though I am inclined to believe Ilain."

"You believe a Mage over your own friend?" Thom tutted. "I thought you had better judgment than that."

Ilain snorted on Evylin's other side. "Those words veer dangerously close to an insult, darling."

"Forgive me, milady," he returned.

"I'll consider it."

For the rest of the day, rain continued to pour, and they traveled on. Evylin took comfort in the banter of her companions. They spoke of nothing consequential and of many things silly, and it filled her head with memories of what life was like at the start of their journey. This was what she and Ryen had always hoped to experience—blissful moments of friendship with exciting battles on the horizon.

"I've been wondering something," Thom said.

"How you got so lucky as to win my companionship?" Ilain jibed.

"No. Though only Allore knows how I came to deserve such a . . . blessing." Thom gave her a sly grin before continuing, "I'm curious as to how you and your brother came across the Fire Relic."

Evylin perked up even more, having wondered the same thing herself.

"We didn't come across it," Ilain replied casually. "We retrieved it in the same manner as the Relics we're seeking out now."

"You went through the Fire Keep, then," Thom said.

"Obviously."

"Just the two of you?"

"Even with all my impressive abilities, not even Auden and I could make it through alone." Ilain flicked a leaf off her skirt. "The Alliance sent us help."

"Why didn't they come with you to Ephria in that case?" Evylin asked.

"They had other tasks," Ilain explained. "Both were Warriors. You'll meet them eventually, I'm sure."

This statement drew Evylin's mouth to fall into a gape.

Thom leaned forward in his saddle to get a better look at Ilain. "I thought you said that Warriors were eradicated."

"Did I?" Ilain furrowed her brow, considered it, then said, "Ah, yes, I did, didn't I? Well, that was a lie."

"Splendid," Thom grumbled.

"Don't be upset. We lied about whatever we thought was necessary. If the wrong people learned that Warriors still existed, they'd want to hunt them down. Either to kill them or to enslave them. And at the time, we still didn't trust you."

"Your past secrecy makes sense," Evylin said judiciously. "Why didn't they come here with you? We could have used their help with the rest of our journey."

"Our entrance into Ephria was difficult enough with two," Ilain explained. "And while I did lie when I said that Warriors are eradicated, it isn't far from the truth. There are very few in the world these days, and even fewer still in the Alliance. With our limited numbers, we couldn't risk them accompanying us on the rest of our journey."

Remembering the simple tale of how the Calder siblings snuck into their country, Evylin didn't bother asking more about it. From all accounts, it sounded rather dull, the brother and sister often traveling in a similar state to their current situation, only with even less excitement as they dashed for the border.

"And what was it like?" Evylin asked instead. "The Fire Keep, I mean."

"It was a desert," Ilain replied.

"A what?" Thom said.

"Desert," the highlady repeated. "A sandy place with little water. Have you never heard of the red sands of Rhazim?"

Thom and Evylin shared a glance. "No," they said in unison.

"Ah, well." Ilain sighed in disappointment. "Rhazim is just below Jal'Khoyan, on Giyda. While it runs along the shore, most of the land is one great desert. In fact, I believe that's its namesake. Its sands are crimson red, almost like blood. And they're only populated by the *lehavran*. Or flamehorns, as said in the Allundan tongue."

That last name sparked a memory in Evylin. "I think I read about those in a novel once. They have literal flaming horns, don't they?"

"They did," Ilain corrected. "Before the Ateri Relics were locked away. Now, they're just red-horned, and though they do still spit, it isn't fire any longer either. Though I've heard their saliva is acidic enough to burn through flesh."

"That sounds terrifying," Thom said.

"Yes, though I took care of the flamehorn fairly easily in the Keep, so I can't say that *I* fear them overmuch."

"You fought one?" Thom gasped.

"The Guardian," Evylin realized. "They all take different forms of mythical creatures."

"They're not mythical," Ilain returned. "Like I said, flamehorns live in Rhazim. They used to populate more of Giyda, but they've been driven back to the desert by the loss of their magic. They're not nearly as effective at fighting off hunters anymore. Did you know they have some of the most tender meat? Even more than lamb."

"People *eat* flamehorns?" Thom said incredulously.

"Not much anymore," Ilain replied.

Bemused by this information about a country she'd never heard of before, Evylin focused on the part of the conversation she most cared about. "What else was in the Keep? What were the Shades like?"

"Fire and clay," Ilain said, and Evylin supposed she should have guessed that. "You know how the Day Shades burst into flares of light, the Water Shades into spurts of water, and the Night Shades into shadow? The Fire Shades, aptly, became great plumes of flame. Olsen almost lost his eyebrows at one point." Ilain chortled at the memory.

Evylin presumed that Olsen was one of the Warriors she'd mentioned but didn't interrupt, eager to hear more of the story.

"We had to run through great red dunes to get to the obelisk," Ilain continued. "It was rather harrowing. We hadn't known what to expect, any of us. And while Olsen and Breata defended us well, they struggled to fight the Guardian flamehorn. Their weapons could hardly damage the beast. And though they managed to get in a slice or two, it emitted sloughs of flame-hot blood with each wound. Auden had to heal several burns on them both."

Ilain took a deep breath. "But we all came out alive, and that's all that matters."

Thom blew a raspberry. "I'm glad I wasn't there."

"How chivalrous of you."

"I'm no Mage or Warrior," he returned. "My life is constantly in far greater danger than yours. Besides, sand is the worst."

Evylin laughed at his brooding. After the story, her muscles suddenly ached for the chance to work themselves. "How far is it to the next Keep?" she asked hopefully.

Ilain wrinkled her nose. "Are you already antsy? It's another week and a half, at a minimum. And that's if we're careful about our number of stops."

"So long?"

"It is on the other side of the country, after all."

Evylin sighed. She stared at the muddy path ahead. The rest of their troop spread out before them in comfortable pairs on the narrow road.

Thom nudged her elbow. "Is our company not entertaining enough for you?"

She gave him a disparaging smirk, but Ilain replied before she got a chance. "It's the plight of a Warrior," she said, absentmindedly braiding her horse's black mane. "They can't help but seek out the next thrill."

Though it more than adequately described how Evylin was feeling, she pursed her lips. "And how do you know that?"

"I just told you." Ilain grinned. "I'm well acquainted with Warriors."

The thought gave Evylin a strange sense of hope. Ilain *knew* Warriors. That meant she could help her better understand herself and her magic. "What else do you know about them?"

"Not much." A few copper strands drifted free from Ilain's hood. "There are only fourteen within the Alliance, including you."

"But you know them all?"

"Oh, no." The woman's jade eyes were bright even in the dim light. "Most of them are on secret assignments throughout the continent. One is even in Schon, working to develop allies in the empire. Many of the others, I've never met."

"How many do you know?" Thom asked.

Ilain did a quick count in her head. "Six."

"Including me?" Evylin asked.

"Including you."

"So few?"

"As I said, they're spread throughout the continent. And fourteen isn't a great number in itself."

Evylin supposed that was true. "Are you friends with any of them?"

A wry tilt lifted the corner of Ilain's lips. "Not in the strictest definition. We're friend*ly*, but I wouldn't consider myself close with any of them. Particularly the woman."

Though Thom looked amused by this idea, Evylin frowned. "Is there only one other female Warrior?"

"No, no." Ilain waved a hand through the air. "There are two. But I only know the one."

Evylin furrowed her brow. "Three women out of fourteen Warriors? Is that common?"

"We don't really know what's common among Warriors anymore. Nearly all the literature on their history was either destroyed by the Mages of Auld or the records are missing." Ilain undid the braid in her horse's mane and began again. "The control of information was originally a ploy by the Auldan Mages to keep the Warriors submissive."

Thom gave Evylin a mocking grin. "I should have thought it impossible for a Warrior to submit to anyone."

Evylin rolled her eyes.

"Not impossible but highly difficult," Ilain said. "And don't bother asking me the methods they used. That information is held within the missing texts I mentioned."

"Were they stolen?" Evylin asked.

"I couldn't say. It isn't really discussed in the Orders. Mostly because the majority of Mages don't care."

"Why wouldn't they?" Thom asked. "Aren't they still concerned about controlling Warriors?"

"What Warriors?" Ilain replied dryly. "They're eradicated, remember?"

"But you *lied.*"

"I gave you the common truth. The Orders aren't worried because why would they be? What few Warriors *are* born, like Evylin and Hewitt—" She stopped herself immediately, sharp green eyes flashing to Evylin in apology.

Knowing that such a casual mention of Hewitt's name *should* cause her heart to stutter with sadness, Evylin didn't feel an ounce of pain. The Day Relic warmed her skin, keeping her safe from such spontaneous emotion.

Evylin reached over to pat Ilain's arm. "I'm fine. What were you saying?"

"Well . . ." Ilain eyed her warily, almost suspiciously, then continued, "What few Warriors *are* born, they're like you: completely unaware of magic. If you'd never met Carlile and been brought into the Alliance, you would never have accessed it. At least, not enough to make you aware."

"So there could be other Warriors in Ephria?" Evylin asked.

"I'm certain there are. And once the Alliance has successfully rebuilt Allund, they'll go through the whole continent testing for both Warriors *and* Mages to help train them properly."

Another surge of excitement and hope filled Evylin. "How many do you think are out there?"

"We have no way of knowing. But the ratio for Mages is about one in five thousand. Which means there are a little over three hundred Mages somewhere on the continent. I'd assume the same is true of Warriors."

Evylin and Thom exchanged a look.

"There are roughly a million people in Ephria," he said.

Evylin struggled to do the math, but Ilain did it for her. "That would mean there are about two hundred Warriors, give or take a few. And nearly all of them are unknown."

The number initially felt large, but as Evylin compared it to the overall population, it seemed impossibly small. Only one in five thousand children would be born a Warrior. A sense of isolation crept into her mind before the Day Relic twisted the thought. One in five thousand. Evylin truly was unique.

Cautiously, Ilain added, "It's what makes finding two Warriors in the same band of soldiers so incredible. Though you share a bloodline, so that makes it less shocking."

Realizing that she meant her and Hewitt, Evylin perked up. "You mean it's inherited?"

"It appears that way. While it doesn't necessarily follow a direct lineage, the odds are greater when one or more members of a family were magical before." Ilain motioned toward her brother at the front of the line. "Take Auden and me, for example. Our great-great-grandfather on our mother's side was a Mage too."

Evylin didn't know what to think about that. "But Hewitt was my uncle, not my father. It isn't as though I inherited magic from him."

"No, but perhaps it came from another ancestor of yours," Ilain suggested. "Or perhaps it was just a coincidence. While magic *can* be hereditary, it is truly a gift. A higher calling, given by Allore himself."

Thom narrowed his gaze. "Don't tell me you're religious."

"You already know that I am," the highlady said. "Over the past thousand years, Auld became polytheistic, regarding the Mages as divine incarnations of the gods themselves. When Ephren drove the Mages into the West, they took the Faith of Eight with them. But there are some of us in Wauld who still worship Allore. Those of us in the Alliance, chief among them."

"And magic is part of your religion?" Evylin asked.

"It's the same as your religion," Ilain replied. "Ephren just twisted it to remove the magical parts."

Evylin kept the truth of her lackadaisical faith quiet, not wanting to upset the woman. She considered herself an Allorian, but she couldn't say she practiced her religion. Oh, she'd gone to mass and said grace at dinner, but she'd given up her nightly prayers after Ryen died. It seemed pointless to waste time on vespers when life could be so cruelly fleeting.

Attributing her magic to a divine calling made Evylin uncomfortable. She didn't want to be some pious priestess dedicated to proclaiming the faith. She wanted to travel and enjoy all that life had to offer, to be free of anything that might inhibit her adventures.

Her gaze drifted toward Deckard, riding at the front with Auden under the emerald green canopy of trees. What would he think about this claim that the Alliance made about their religion? She'd known him to be devout since their first meeting. She could still remember the heartfelt "by your grace" he'd given after her father blessed the meal. And while traveling had precluded any traditional religious observances, she could tell he took his faith far more seriously than she, if only due to his impeccable moral compass.

If he found out that her magic was considered a sign of a "higher vocation," would he want her to become some grand instrument of the Alliance and the church?

A comforting warmth flowed into Evylin's hands, and she discovered that she was playing with the Day Relic's chain.

Quickly, she released it back under her collar. She glanced first at Thom and then Ilain, worried that they'd noticed. She realized they were still bantering about religion, both of their faces set with dry grins. However, as Evylin's eyes turned to Ilain, the highlady's keen gaze flicked up and away.

Evylin kept herself from gritting her teeth.

Ilain had noticed. Now, all she could do was hope that the woman had not seen the color of the chain and assumed it'd been the silver necklace Hewitt gave her, rather than the golden links of the Relic.

To distract from her error, Evylin grasped for another question. At the first break in their raillery, she said, "Will I ever meet these Warriors?"

"Yes, of course," Ilain replied. "I can't say when, but likely after we've completed our mission. We'll have to return the Relics to the Administration, and there are typically two or three Warriors assigned to them for safety."

"The Administration?"

"Our governing body at the moment," Ilain clarified. "Once we have a singular country again, that will change, but for now, there are two groups of Ministers, eight in Wauld and eight in Ephria, and they preside over all the decisions within our organization."

With little interest in politics, neither Thom nor Evylin pursued the subject. Instead, she returned to the previous question. "And will these Warriors train me?"

Ilain tipped her head to the side, her hood casting deep shadows along the angles of her face. "Whatever training you require, yes," she confirmed. "Though you are already highly skilled."

Evylin frowned. "But there's so much I don't know about being a Warrior."

"There's a lot they don't know either." Ilain raised her eyebrows. "Missing literature, remember?"

"So they're as untrained as I?"

"I wouldn't call you untrained. Hewitt did a fantastic job preparing you for the role of Warrior."

"He taught me how to fight," Evylin said. "Not how to use magic."

Ilain brushed her hand through the air. "Fighting is more than half the battle for

Warriors. If you can fight, the skill frees up your instincts to tap into your magic. Just as you've already done dozens of times."

Before Evylin could argue, Ilain kept speaking. "Yes, it would be preferable for you and all Warriors to have more specific instructions. Yes, knowing the particulars of your magic would be ideal. But without the texts, there's no way for you to learn without practical application."

"We're just to find our way blindly in that case?"

"For now," Ilain admitted. "And perhaps when this is all over, you can search out those missing texts and help the Warriors become all they were meant to be."

Evylin thought about that. It seemed like a dull task to undergo. What could that sort of mission involve but researching and studying history? She had no interest in sitting in a library, day after day, reading dusty tomes. If a book had no adventure, it held no allure.

Still, Evylin wished there was some way she could better understand her magic. She felt sure that talking to another Warrior would help. Someone with whom she could compare experiences and gain insights. Surely that would make her a better Warrior.

And being a better Warrior would lead her to more exciting adventures.

"I'd like to meet them," Evylin determined. "As soon as I can."

Ilain let out a doubtful hum. "Gathering the Relics will take us another two months. And that's if things go smoothly. The likelihood of meeting with the Alliance before then is slim. We can't risk letting Blount get ahead of us."

"But wouldn't it be better if I were a stronger Warrior now? Or even having a secondary Warrior to help. Wouldn't our mission be more likely to succeed?"

"Of course, it would. But as I said, there are only thirteen other Warriors, and they're all assigned to other important tasks. The Alliance can't spare them."

Thom met Evylin's disappointed stare. "Don't fret," he said. "We're already doing well with a bright young Warrior such as yourself. Now that we've got three Relics for you to wield, things can only get easier, right?"

Ilain gave a caustic chuckle. "Your optimism is foolish."

He smirked at her. "I believe the word you're looking for is 'inspiring.'"

Her eyes twinkled. "I'm inspired by how foolish you are."

"You think it'll be so difficult?" Evylin asked, amused by their quips. "We know what to expect now, and as Thom said, we have three Relics. Won't that make a difference?"

"It will make all the difference," Ilain replied. "But this journey will still be incredibly difficult. The ancient texts state that every Keep increases in complexity and challenge, which is why we're pursuing them in their designated order. And we *don't* know what to expect beyond Shades and a Guardian. No two Keeps are alike, remember? We're going into the Wind Keep with nothing more than our imagination as a guide."

Evylin and Thom listened warily as she continued, "Do not think that our prior modicum of success guarantees anything. Making it through the Keeps with our lives will take every skill and trick we have. Even Blount, with his host of Mages, struggled through the Water Keep. We have two Mages and one Warrior. Our odds are good, but not great. And any one of us could lose our lives at any time."

A deep shadow hovered over Evylin's heart as the highlady's words concluded. It threatened to wrap itself around her, suffocating all hope and joy, attempting to leach into her veins and turn them black with fear.

"Any one of us could lose our lives."

Her eyes rose to Deckard's back, his thick gray cloak enshrouding him like the shadow in her chest. She could lose him like she'd lost Hewitt and Ryen. This mission of theirs was fraught with danger, not only in the Keeps but here on the road. Blount's men had to be searching for them. Just because they'd made it six days without an incident didn't mean they weren't one moment away from being found or attacked. It could happen any time. Death could come for them—it could take *him*. . . .

The Day Relic pulsed on Evylin's skin, radiating its cheery glow into her body. Her muscles relaxed as she basked in the peace coursing through her. Her breath came clearly, and she smiled. It felt like sitting under the sun's rays on a winter day.

And her fear faded completely.

"Well, then," she said good-naturedly, "I suppose we'd better train to improve our odds."

CHAPTER ELEVEN

3RD OF CHRONOS, 1574

Finding an excuse to walk through the woods alone was more difficult than it seemed. They'd all agreed that, given the potential of Mages hunting them, no one should go out on their own. And Deckard didn't have the luxury of offering to hunt. Aside from the Calders, he had the fewest skills in that arena.

Part of him questioned the value of trying to sneak off at all.

Deckard knew it was ridiculous, thinking that he could glean wisdom from his subconscious. But it helped. Somehow, his mad visions helped him sort through the stress and fear, allowing him to focus on the issues at hand.

Like why Evylin was suddenly so happy all the time.

But thinking around camp was like trying to talk underwater. You might get a few words out, but the pressure in your ears and the air escaping your lungs would suffocate any rational thought before long.

It took him a full four days to come up with a solution.

"Evie," Deckard said, crouching down beside her at the campfire. They'd all finished their meal a few moments before, Ilain and Ethenn settling in to start their watch while the rest of them prepared to sleep.

Evylin looked up at him, steady fingers rebraiding her hair. "Jonn," she replied, giving him a teasing smile.

Deckard hated to use her newfound joviality against her, but he couldn't figure out another means of slipping away. "You know how I'm boring?"

"Intimately."

"Mm-hm." He'd anticipated the jocular reply and took it as proof that his plan would succeed. "Well, boring people like myself have the occasional desire to be alone."

She held a hand to her chest in feigned offense. "Are you saying that you don't want to spend your every waking second with me?"

"Believe it or not."

She tied off the braid, still smiling. "Why are you telling me this?"

Deckard intentionally gave a slow scan over the rest of their companions. "Because I plan to take a walk, and I need you to cover for my absence."

"A walk?" Evylin quirked her brow. "In the woods? Alone?"

"Yes."

She narrowed her eyes. They glowed like embers in the firelight. "I thought we agreed not to split up."

"We did."

"And you're breaking that agreement because you're a boring sap who likes to spend time alone?"

"Precisely."

She shrugged. "Fine. How can I help?"

"Come with me."

Evylin looked at him like he'd lost his mind. "I hate to tell you this, Jonn, but if I come with you, you can't be alone."

"I'm aware of that," he said with a chuckle. "We'll tell them that we're taking a walk, but instead of you coming with me, you'll stay right on the other side of the trees over there."

"And what am I supposed to do in the trees over there, hm?"

"Think. Sleep. Eat." He held up his dinner ration of the bread they'd purchased in Vaulley. Bread didn't keep long enough to carry enough for more than a few days, and to Evylin, every piece was sacred. "Do whatever it is you'd be doing if we were in camp."

She eyed the slice of bread greedily. "I'd be talking to you if we were in camp."

"Then pretend you're talking to me over there."

"My imagination of you isn't as entertaining as the real you. He doesn't respond when I make fun of him."

"Do you want the bread or not?"

She took it and stood, hiding her hand under her cloak. "Jonn and I are going on a walk," she announced.

"A walk?" Auden asked warily. "At night?"

"Auden," Ilain chided.

"What?"

Rafferty sniggered. "I believe 'walk' is married people's code for 'time alone.'"

"Shut up," Evylin said, but she grabbed Deckard's hand and started for the trees.

The ruddy light of the fire faded behind their backs as they stepped farther into the foliage. In the night, the forest looked like an emerald shadow. Though the rain had stopped, remnants of its deluge dripped from the tree leaves and pine needles.

When they were thoroughly out of sight, Evylin dropped his hand. "You owe me," she said, then took a vicious bite out of her bread.

Deckard motioned to the mutilated slice. "I've already paid you."

Her jawline grew taut with irritation. "They think we're out here . . . kissing."

He found her disgruntlement rather cute. "Evylin, we're married. They think we're out here doing much more than that."

"You owe me more than a slice of bread."

Deckard set his hands on her shoulders. "Tell you what: While I'm gone, think of what you'd like in payment, and I'll give it to you."

"Anything?" she asked.

"Anything."

She scanned him. "Hm. Good enough."

Backing away, Deckard dipped his head in thanks. "I'll be back shortly."

"Don't take too long," she called.

He waved in acknowledgment before heading deeper into the trees.

In the darkness, it was harder to see the overgrown roots and tangled underbrush. Deckard moved carefully onward, searching for a good spot to sit and think. Or pace and think, as he was more apt to do. Somewhere clear and open, with plenty of space to spar. The sort of place that Hewitt would have taken him to train. A rather large request for the thick Waulden forest.

After several minutes of searching with no luck, Deckard allowed himself to stop. He couldn't stay out too long, and he didn't want to waste precious time working his way back to camp. Nor did he want to walk so far out that he lost his way. He'd come just far enough that no one would hear him talking to himself, and he'd intentionally checked behind him regularly to ensure that Evylin hadn't followed him.

Secure in his solitude, Deckard slumped against a densely rooted oak. "I'm not sure what to do," he muttered to himself.

"What's happening now?" Hewitt asked, the vision appearing across from him by a tree.

"Nothing new," he said. "Something is just off. Evylin can't have gotten over you so quickly."

"She's still acting happy?"

Deckard nodded.

"It's a farce," Hewitt growled. When did that deep grumble of the man's voice become so reassuring? "She holds onto people too fiercely for that. It's why she's so selective. She can't risk choosing them for them to disappear."

"She's not that good at pretending," Deckard said. "Or at lying."

"Maybe you just don't want to see the truth."

"But I'm actively seeking it," he argued. "I'm genuinely trying to tell if she's moved on or if she's faking it. And I can't see any way that this return to her good-humored self is a façade. Not when she hasn't broken one single time."

Hewitt stroked his scraggly beard.

"The only answer is that she's moved on."

"Not possible."

"Why not?" Deckard threw his hands up, exasperated. "What if she really has let go? Am I holding her back by expecting her to cling to her grief?"

Hewitt eyed him. "I told you, she's yet to recover from Ryen's death. Mine will hit her twice as hard."

"But she's flirting with me," Deckard said. "Intentionally."

That caused the ghost of his subconscious to frown. "You're sure?"

Deckard ran back through the memories of their days in Wauld. He thought of how she'd warmed his hands and scooted closer to him, how she'd wrapped her arm around his waist, pressing herself to him, and teasing him about his attraction to her. He remembered the kiss she'd planted on his cheek. Even tonight, he'd seen the twinkle in her eye as she'd said, *"You owe me."* She pretended to be perturbed by the others thinking they'd gone off to be alone together. But he'd recognized the tilt in her voice and the lift to her lips.

"She wanted me to kiss her just now," he admitted. "She was disappointed when I didn't."

"That's not surprising," Hewitt said. "Wives take comfort in their husbands."

He scoffed at the idea that Evylin would ever see him that way. "She doesn't want that sort of relationship with me."

"You just said she wanted you to kiss her."

"That doesn't mean she wants to take solace in me." He rose to begin pacing. "She's not interested in my husbandly affection. Not like that. Not anymore."

"This isn't a conversation I relish," Hewitt complained.

"I can't say I care for it myself." Deckard ran a hand through his hair, annoyed at its growing length. "But the thing is, she's starting to touch me more openly. Not in a way that begs for reciprocation but simply in a manner of familiarity. And then, this."

"If you came out here to determine the ethics of your attraction to my niece, congratulations, it's justifiable." Hewitt crossed his arms. "Now, go back, kiss your wife, and give her a good life."

"I don't know if she wants me to."

Hewitt glared at him. "You just said that she did."

"No." Deckard brushed the thought away. "I mean, she hasn't decided about us yet."

"What is there to decide? You're married. Even if she's still working through her loss of me, she'll come to trust you. Whether that takes a year or ten, she will let go and choose you."

"If she gives me that long," Deckard said through a sigh.

Hewitt's gray eyes narrowed on him. "I beg your pardon?"

"Well, I promised her that she wouldn't have to decide about her future until after our mission." Deckard ran a hand over his face, reliving that foolish promise. "I can't go back on that."

"Are you telling me," Hewitt began, each word a sharp cut, "that there's a chance she could leave you?"

Deckard glanced at the ghost his madness had summoned. "Well . . ." He shrugged. "Yes."

"I'm going to kill that girl," Hewitt snarled. He took a step in the direction of the camp before turning on Deckard, evidently remembering that he was a figment of imagination.

Hewitt's fury gave him the wild look of a bear charging an unwelcome intruder. "I told her to finalize it," he nearly shouted. "Did she not listen?"

Had the man not been a vision that only Deckard could see and hear, he'd be bothered by the loudness of his voice. Instead, he stared at the ghost, dumbfounded. "You told her to do what?"

"I told her to consummate the damn thing."

Slightly embarrassed by the bluntness of Hewitt's delivery, Deckard found the ability to overcome the awkward conversation within the irritation he felt that the man had meddled in the intimacies of their relationship. "Why would you do that?" he demanded.

"Because it needed to happen," Hewitt said matter-of-factly. "To ensure you'd never send her home, she needed to let you bed her and make the marriage unbreakable. When I saw you two with your hands all over each other after that party at the palace, I took it as a confirmation that she'd listened."

The discomfort of discussing the topic—even with himself and his own deranged manifestation—made Deckard's throat tighten.

Hewitt scanned him, bushy eyebrows pulled low. His mouth held a disbelieving frown. "So you haven't, then?"

Deckard blinked a few times, disappointed with himself for letting the conversation devolve to this subject. "No, we haven't."

"Allore's might, man," Hewitt said, his face twisted in shock. "Why the bloody hell not? She's an attractive woman, you two clearly like one another, and from all accounts, she's not opposed to your affections. What's stopping you?"

Pacing away, Deckard sighed. That was a question he'd asked himself many times. They slept in each other's arms nightly. They'd shared more than one passionate kiss. They'd nearly concluded the matter twice—first in Loclight, then on their journey. The only reason things came to an end was due to Hewitt and Thom's presence upon their return home and their lack of privacy at the camp. But there had been other opportunities. There were nights in his tent with the Volunteer Company or at inns once they'd begun traveling with the Calders. Privacy hadn't been impossible to come by. Even tonight, had he not taken the time to come out here and talk with himself, they'd have found a way they could be alone.

So what was stopping them?

"I've always left it up to her," Deckard said. "I didn't want to pressure her."

A heartbeat passed, and Deckard realized that wasn't wholly true. "I wanted her to want me," he admitted, "the way that I want her. I wanted her to *trust* me. And I don't believe she ever has."

He let a long pause pass before turning back to face his unconscious mind, given life in Hewitt's form. "I'm worried that she never will."

The ghost wasn't impressed by his dramatics. "If it's between losing her or keeping her, you may have to give up your romantic notions."

Deckard frowned. "I couldn't do that to her. It has to be her choice."

"She's a soldier, Deckard," Hewitt said. "She follows orders. She doesn't want to be controlled, but neither does she want to be in charge. If you wait for her to make a decision, you'll be waiting your entire lifetime."

He shook his head, rejecting the sentiment. "I don't believe that."

"You doubt me? The sole man she trusted?"

"I doubt my baser instincts," he countered. "I doubt the darkest parts of me that would advise me to force myself on my wife."

"I'm not suggesting anything of the kind," Hewitt spat, obviously offended. "She wants you. You said it yourself. But she's too afraid to give herself to you, to trust you. You wait for her to figure that out, and you run the risk of losing your chance."

Annoyed with himself, Deckard held up his hands to end the conversation. "This isn't helping. I wanted to figure out why she's acting strangely, not to waste time thinking about why I'm not enough for her."

"Perhaps that's your answer," Hewitt replied.

Deckard froze, staring at him in shock.

A gentle breeze cut through the forest, rustling the bushes and leaves around him. The air turned damp with the chill. Shafts of moonlight glittered in the darkness, with Hewitt standing in their midst.

"While waiting for her to fall in love with you," the ghost said, "perhaps she already has, and you refuse to see it."

Deckard drew in a sharp breath, the cold air burning his lungs. "Why would I—?"

"Because if she loves you, then you have to do something about it. And you're afraid that you'll fail her again."

Deckard stared at the man, stunned into silence. Could it be that simple? Could it be that *wonderful*? Had he been blinded by his fear, blatantly missing that Evylin *had* come to trust him after all? Was that why she was so different, so joyful and carefree? Had he done his job, comforting her through her grief and helping her come out the other side? Was he truly enough for her now?

Hope grew around his heart like the ivy of Estshire.

And yet, his gut felt unsettled.

A soft pelting sound echoed around him just before the rain began anew. Even with the great canopy of trees above him, it flooded through, readily drenching him and completely ignoring the figment of Hewitt.

Deckard jerked his hood up, then wiped the water from his face. "I have to go back," he said, unsure why he felt the need to explain himself to his imagination.

"I'll be here," Hewitt's ghost said.

Darting through the thick forest and deluge, Deckard had little chance to wonder about his conclusions. The night was almost pitch-black now, and the treacherous growth and muddy terrae required his whole attention. He'd been gone too long. Evylin wouldn't be pleased with him for leaving her to wait in the cold rain.

When he finally arrived back at the place he'd left her, Deckard found it empty. He frowned, scanning the darkness. His heart sped up, fear lancing through him. Memories of Blount's ambush plagued his mind. Had she been discovered?

A flash of movement caught Deckard's attention, and he spun toward it, hand on his sword.

"Careful," Evylin said, landing on the ground in front of him. "It isn't good manners to kill your wife."

Deckard sighed, releasing the hilt. "Where were you?"

"In the tree. I didn't feel like sitting in mud."

"You couldn't have warned me before popping up like a ghost?" he said, then bit his tongue at the term.

Evylin's eyes grew playfully wide. "Do you believe in ghosts? I would have thought that was too pagan for you."

"It's a figure of speech."

Her teasing grin made his heart swell in its cage of ivy.

Another frigid gust tossed the rain in their faces. They hunched away from it, huddling under the boughs of the large tree she'd climbed. "We should get back," he said, raising his voice over the hum of rain.

Evylin caught his hand. "But I've decided on my payment."

"And it has to be discussed here?"

"It'll be raining there as much as it is here," she said. "We don't have tents, remember?"

Seeing her point, Deckard pressed farther under the tree's cover. "Let's hear it."

Evylin's eyes gleamed even in the darkness. "Two things," she said. "First, I want the rest of your bread rations for the remainder of our journey."

Deckard scoffed amusedly. "You can have my bread rations for the rest of our lives, should you so desire."

She shook her head in a mockingly business-like manner. "That isn't what I asked for. And you haven't heard my second compensation."

"Pray tell."

A sly smile worked its way across her lips. She sidled closer to him, her arms slowly working around his waist. Deckard grew rigid, wary yet intrigued by this forward display.

Evylin held his gaze as her hands settled against his lower back. Then he felt something jerk free, and her hands were back between them, a shining blade in her grip. "I want this knife," she said.

"You already have a dozen knives," he replied.

"Yes, but this one is prettier than any of mine."

He glanced at the pommel, etched in rosettes. He'd chosen it for that design specifically—a symbol of her: Evylin Rosette. "I see the appeal."

She flipped the blade, stashing it in her belt. He could see in her stare that she was aware of the advance she'd made and his instinctual reaction to it. It had been a deliberate tease.

She still wanted him to kiss her.

Deckard studied her for a moment longer, their gazes locked together. Had his subconscious been correct? Had she truly moved on because of her love for him? Did she trust him at last?

He supposed there couldn't be any harm in testing it.

Cautiously, Deckard leaned down toward her, slowly enough that she could pull away should he have misread her.

She stayed.

Inches separated them. He relished their closeness and the chance to examine her beautiful countenance in such detail. Her delicately tanned skin glowed warm in the coldness of Wauld. There was something so soft yet strong about her features. Rounded but striking.

As he dipped his head, Evylin's lips parted in a sharp inhale, as though anticipating his kiss.

The tip of his nose brushed her cheek just as she whispered, "That will cost you extra."

Deckard paused. He'd heard the jest in her tone, but he couldn't help wondering if she meant it on some level. He pulled back, brow raised. "Forget it, then," he said.

Her face scrunched in confusion and, he thought, disappointment. "What?"

"I'm afraid you've bled me dry. I have nothing left to give." He stepped back, turning toward camp.

Evylin caught his wrist and tugged, pulling him around to face her. She grabbed the collar of his coat. Then her lips were on his. His thoughts fell away as he instinctively took her in his arms.

Heat trickled along Deckard's spine. How he'd missed kissing her! The last few weeks had felt like ages, his desire for her never waning as he patiently waited for her to recover. The experience didn't disappoint his memory. The warmth grew, spreading into his chest. It always felt like this when he kissed her, like she was slowly filling him with sunlight until he radiated with a fever that tingled under his skin.

Breaking apart, Deckard and Evylin stared at one another. His arm was still draped around her waist as her fingers clung to his collar. It felt as though neither of them was quite done, yet neither was prepared to go any further.

"There," she said, her breath warm between their lips. "I've satisfied your integrity."

The kiss still misted over Deckard's mind like the fog that obscured Wauld. "Hm?"

Evylin smiled, the dimples appearing on her cheeks. "We told them we wanted time alone with one another. Now, you can hold your head high, knowing that you didn't lie."

The laugh that trickled out of him hardly registered under the patter of rain around them. "I'm indebted to you," he whispered. "Yet again."

Evylin gave him a pleased smirk. "After *that*, we can call it even."

CHAPTER TWELVE

4TH OF CHRONOS, 1574

Deckard woke with a nagging feeling at the back of his brain, as though he'd forgotten or overlooked something important. It lingered through his early morning watch with Evylin and Rafferty. It persisted as he ate a meager and hasty breakfast of porridge. And it followed him as he and Auden rode into the city of Carrickbrack to restock.

According to the Calders, they were making good time across the western half of the continent. It scarcely felt possible in the dreary mist-covered landscape filled with perpetual moss and pine-riddled forest. Deckard was growing tired of riding, eating, and sleeping in the rain. And while the siblings promised that it was only the impending springtime that made it rain so profusely, the continual drizzle made every day feel the same.

Even the three settlements they'd entered in the span of nearly two hundred miles all looked the same. So much so that Deckard found himself quietly absorbed in that nagging sensation as Auden handled the shopping. *What am I forgetting?* he wondered.

Had there been an extra supply he'd needed to add to the list? Perhaps a piece of Auden and Ilain's tutelage on Waulden culture had slipped his mind. He felt sure that he'd remembered the date of Evylin's birthday correctly, and he took her giving no sign of being upset with him as a confirmation. Should their kiss last night be of any indication, she felt quite the opposite of vexation toward him.

No, it was something else. Something critical.

Deckard helped Auden load up the packs and saddlebags with the replenishment of hardtack, barley, and other rations. He'd remembered to purchase another supply of bread—a luxury but a cheap one—so that couldn't be what was troubling him. Had one of their comrades said something to him on the road? He didn't want to forget anything in the town. They couldn't afford to waste time on another stop so soon.

Stepping out onto the street, Deckard ran back through the previous day. It bled into the others so much that it was no wonder he'd forgotten something. He couldn't even remember whether they'd had goose or rabbit last night.

Rabbit, he recalled. Auden had been cleaning off the final spit they'd skewered the coneys on when Deckard and Evylin announced they were going for their walk.

Deckard smiled to himself at the thought of the previous night. The ivy around his heart grew at the memory, knowing that she'd come to trust him at last—that she loved him, even if she wasn't ready to say it yet. He was quite thankful to Estshire for the unexpected blessing it had given him in Evylin. He was even more grateful to Hewitt. After all, he was the reason Deckard had even had the chance to marry her.

A cold tingle pricked the back of Deckard's neck.

Hewitt.

That was what was bothering him. His conversation with his subconsciously induced vision of Hewitt niggled at his mind. Something hadn't been quite right. But what?

Deckard couldn't deny that he'd been embarrassed by how he'd allowed his thoughts to devolve into contemplating the frustration he felt toward his and Evylin's physical relationship. That wasn't a conversation he cared to entertain with anyone, even a figment. But then, he couldn't exactly consider it unexpected. He might pride himself on his honor and gentility, but that didn't negate the fact that he was a man. His attraction to Evylin had never been in question, and even a gentleman had desires that weren't to be spoken of in polite society.

No, while the topic had been awkward, that particular portion of his contemplations with Hewitt wasn't what plagued his brain. It was something more important. Something specific. Something that made him feel as though he stood in the middle of the forest, attempting to find one very particular tree. . . .

"Jonn—"

Auden's voice jolted Deckard out of his thoughts. He whipped his head to look at the Mage. He could only see the tip of the man's knife-sharp nose peeking out from under his hood as they rode toward the city gate.

Promising himself that he'd return to his contemplations later, Deckard cleared his mind to focus on Auden's words.

"I have a question to ask you," the highlord said. "One that may . . . well, it may come across as an accusation, but I swear to you, it isn't."

Furrowing his brow, Deckard kept his voice low as they passed through the gate, the guards alert to their exit. "All right," he said cautiously.

Waiting until they'd put several dozen feet between themselves and the guards, Auden asked, "Why does Evylin still have the Day Relic?"

Deckard blinked. *Does Evylin still have the Day Relic?* He hadn't realized that was the case. As he didn't want to appear such an unaware leader, he said, "No reason. She simply does."

"You're sure?" Auden asked, his words clipped.

Deckard raised an eyebrow. "That certainly sounds like an accusation."

"Only voicing a concern."

"A concern that we're keeping the Relics from you?"

"Not at all," Auden assured him. "My sister and I are more than happy to relinquish the Relics after our time in the Keeps. We understand how dangerous they can be, and we don't want to become liabilities to our mission."

Deckard found that statement to be rather pointed. "What exactly are you getting at?"

"I'm worried about Evylin's sanity."

That caused Deckard's heart to stutter, the ivy rustling with shock. "Her sanity? What could possibly lead you to believe—?" He broke off as understanding flooded him. Evylin's sudden change in demeanor, her unexpected joyousness. Somehow, it had to do with the Relic.

Auden's downturned mouth and softened expression radiated a sense of compassion. "I'm sure you've noticed it too. She's not the same as before we left the Night Keep. She's begun to laugh, joke, and live as she did before Hewitt's death. The change was immediate. I didn't expect that you'd let her keep the Relic, so I didn't think to speak up. However, Ilain noticed her playing with its chain while they rode together yesterday, and we felt it imperative we warn you."

Deckard had no means to deny the highlord's words. His mind worked to comprehend the issue as their horses plodded through the mud. How had he completely overlooked the tie between Evylin's access to a Relic and her emotional adjustment? But then, he hadn't known the Relic could cause such a dramatic change.

"Warn me of what exactly?" Deckard asked.

Cautiously, as though approaching a sleeping wolf, Auden said, "Day magic is life-giving. It is healing. And Evylin underwent a deeply wounding experience."

That is an understatement, Deckard thought.

"As a general rule," Auden continued, "Mages are studious and creative beings. We are the balance to the Warriors' more strategic and aggressive nature. As such, we tend to seek ways to make things with our magic."

"What does that have to do with Evylin?" Deckard asked.

Auden wet his lips, his eyes downcast. "Centuries ago, some Day Mages discovered the ability to infuse their magic into physical substances. Through the right methods, they could synthesize an elixir made of honey or heated sugar water. Originally, it was intended to be for medicinal use, but it was discovered that in higher concentrations, the magic within could provide amplified feelings of joy and peace. Nobles like to purchase these elixirs and mix them into various beverages, often tea or spirits, resulting in a drink imbued with Day's essence. It helps them to lose their inhibitions or clear their minds of fear and doubt, and in high doses even results in lifelike hallucinations."

The Mage met Deckard's gaze then, his verdant eyes impressing solemnity. "Do you understand what I'm telling you?" he asked.

Deckard drew in a tight breath. "It's a narcotic."

Auden dipped his head in confirmation.

Thinking back to Auden's warning about the power gifted to him and Ilain by their magic's corresponding Relic, Deckard now realized his concern. "You said that the power granted by the Relics can become an obsession."

"It amplifies our magic," Auden said, "and along with it, the side of us that connects with the resource's essence. While the Relics are very fragments of Allore himself, their raw power can cause dramatic, potentially dangerous effects upon humans. As such, when I wore the Fire Relic, it made me more reckless, more violent. It amplified my zeal for our quest and turned me into a fighter when the time came. Ilain and I shared the load on our journey into Ephria, and once we arrived, we left it under Carlile's care. But once we began our mission, I alone carried it. It was a daily struggle not to give in to its pull upon my emotions. And I still feel the effects from time to time."

Auden shifted to face him more fully. "That is why it's dangerous for those of us with magic to carry them. The longer we hold them, the more influence they have over us. And the more we desire to feel that side of ourselves and the power that comes with it."

Deckard ran a hand over his beard. "And that's what's happening to Evylin?"

He nodded. "The power of Day is making her feel happy and whole. Something I'm sure she desperately desires."

"Something she desperately *needs*," Deckard retorted.

"It isn't real, Jonn. Whatever she feels when she wears the Relic, it's not real. She hasn't recovered from her grief; she's covered it up."

"Perhaps that's what she requires for a time, to help her heal."

Auden's fiery brows rose. "If she asked you to procure a hallucinogenic drug to help her heal from the loss of her uncle, would you do it?"

Deckard stared at the Mage. "That's not what this is."

"It's the magical equivalent."

The ivy shuddered around his heart. "What do you expect me to do?" he asked, already sure he knew the answer.

"I'm not telling you to do anything," Auden assured him. "Nor am I blaming you for the situation. However, I *am* warning you of the truth: It is dangerous for Evylin to carry the Relic. She may be capable of ignoring her grief with its power, but eventually, it will overtake her. Magic naturally alters every magical individual. Mages become more like the resource they connect with most deeply. Warriors become stronger, more agile, and more cunning.

"But what's happening to Evylin *isn't* natural," he warned. "Carrying a Relic for an extended period of time will taint her soul, making her dependent on its power. And should she lose it—*when* she loses it, she will fall into a despair far greater than if she'd lost Hewitt a dozen times over."

If Auden had wanted to scare Deckard, he'd succeeded.

"I have to take it from her," Deckard realized.

Auden's expression radiated the greatest sympathy. "If you don't do it now, it will be taken from her at the end of our mission."

That information diverted his thoughts long enough to ask, "What does the Alliance intend to do with the Relics? If no magical person can carry them without losing their sanity, will they return them to the Keeps?"

Auden stared at the road ahead for several seconds before replying. "The Relics are too valuable to return to the Keeps. Terraeus has suffered from their confinement. Allore gave the Relics to his people to use, not to hide, and over the last millennium, we've seen the degradation of the resources because of it."

"How do you mean?"

"Not only are our powers as Mages more volatile and difficult to master, but you can see it in the terrae around us." Auden motioned to the sky. "The constant rain of Wauld isn't natural. It is a result of Water magic weakening and becoming unwieldy. The overgrown forests are the consequence of Terrae magic running unchecked. Even in Ephria, you experience the resources out of harmony through the extremity of summer and winter with little autumn or spring to regulate them, due to the battle between Day and Night. Or you can see it in the sudden, turbulent wind that sweeps across the plains. These things could be brought back into balance with the Relics present in our world."

Deckard had never realized that their world's weather and seasons *were* unbalanced. Growing up with scorchingly hot summers and bitingly cold winters was as natural as looking up at the butter-yellow sun. But then, was that the sun's natural color?

"Balancing the resources is all well and good," Deckard said, "but how can they retain possession of them if no Mage or Warrior is safe to carry them? I assume they wouldn't work if a non-magical person wore them."

"You're correct," Auden said. "Their magic is rendered ineffective when held by non-magical individuals, as witnessed while in Rafferty's possession. However, it is incorrect to say that *no* Mage or Warrior is safe to carry them. Allore would not have given us power without giving us the means to use it."

"And by what means is that?"

"Bonding." Auden said the word with a strange lift, as though in reverence. "A venerable practice that the ancient Mages locked away along with the locations of the Relics."

"I take it the Alliance unlocked that secret along with the instructions for recovering the Keeps?"

"Not the Alliance." Auden passed him a smirk. "Ilain."

"Your sister discovered the secret to carrying the Relics?"

"Why do you think they sent us on this mission?"

"Hm." Deckard wiped a wily raindrop that had outwitted his hood from his cheek. "What is this ancient practice?"

"Magic is all about balance," Auden said. "Day and Night, Fire and Water." He gave Deckard a meaningful look. "Mage and Warrior. Two opposing forces that keep each other in check. Once Bonded, a Warrior and a Mage are the embodiment of perfect balance. As such, they can carry a Relic without fear."

A sharp pressure rankled the center of Deckard's face, and he discovered his brows had pinched themselves together. He tried to ease them, unsure of how long he'd held his expression that way.

"At least," Auden went on, "that's what Ilain says. She's the foremost expert on the subject, being the one to discover the truth of it all."

"So the Alliance wants Bonded Warriors and Mages," Deckard surmised.

"Indeed. Though that's easier said than done."

"How so?"

"The requirements are quite specific. It's a perfect balance given flesh. Therefore, it must have perfect balance to be obtained. One a Warrior, one a Mage. One a male, the other a female."

"That doesn't sound so difficult."

"Tell that to the male Mages of the Alliance."

"I don't understand."

"For some reason," Auden said, sounding somewhat irritated, though more at the subject than at Deckard, "magic favors men. From what we know, it equals out to roughly eighty percent male. Ilain has a theory that it has something to do with Bonding, but no one knows for sure. Regardless, it puts us in a bit of a predicament, as we need eight Bonded couples to carry the Relics, and we only have two female Warriors eligible for the task."

"I'm afraid I still don't see the problem."

"Well, it puts us male Mages at a disadvantage, you see? If any of us hope to be chosen to help carry the Relic, we'll have to convince one of the two female Warriors to marry us."

Deckard blinked. "Why?"

"Bonding is a very intimate connection, even more so than marriage. To ask unmarried individuals to accept such a connection would be illogical."

While Deckard didn't pretend to comprehend the suggestion fully, neither did he care to follow this divergence. "All right," he said. "I'll tell Evylin to give the Relic back to Rafferty."

Auden gave him a pained expression. "It won't be that simple, Jonn. She'll want to keep it."

"Yes, but I'll explain the dangers to her, and she'll do the right thing."

"She's addicted to it. She won't give it up without a fight."

Deckard grimaced. He'd been worried about that. But she trusted him now, didn't she? He could help her see that releasing the Relic was in her best interest.

"I will warn you," Auden continued, his tone cautious once more. "She may take it as another betrayal."

Deckard bristled. "I've never—"

"I know you haven't," he insisted. "But I was there when she accused you after Hewitt's death. Whatever level of comfort she's regained with you, you have to know it isn't real. It's the Relic. And when you take it from her, she will revert to the pain she felt before. She'll blame you, and not just for his death this time."

A cold wash of worry spread over Deckard's scalp. His body went numb as his mind reconciled this new information. Evylin's comfort wasn't real. Her trust wasn't real. And as for her love . . .

Deckard clenched his jaw, thinking back to the previous night. The ivy encasing his heart withered, crumbling away to ash.

Evylin hadn't kissed him because she loved him. She'd done it because she was intoxicated. It'd meant nothing more than momentary entertainment. And after he took the Relic from her, she'd feel nothing but anger and betrayal toward him.

For a moment, Deckard considered asking Auden to do it himself. Let the Mage challenge her for the Relic. He stood to lose nothing from garnering Evylin's wrath.

But Deckard knew he couldn't do that. It was his job to protect her. He was her husband; no matter the difficulty it might place him in, he'd vowed to care for her. And up until now, he'd failed.

She'd lost her uncle. She'd fallen into depression. And he'd completely missed the fact that she'd held onto the Relic to ease her pain, instead rationalizing that she'd fallen in love with him to explain her behavior change.

No, he couldn't put this burden on Auden. He had to face it himself.

"I'll do it tonight," Deckard said, "when we reach our next stop."

Auden was silent for a time, accepting his decision. Then he offered a simple, "I'm sorry, Jonn."

Shaking his head, Deckard knew the man couldn't understand the full consequences he'd face from this task. He couldn't know that by taking the Relic from Evylin, Deckard would drive her even farther away from ever wanting him. By protecting her, he risked losing what little trust he'd earned.

CHAPTER THIRTEEN

Evylin

They rode from the moment Deckard and Auden returned from Carrickbrack until dusk, arriving on the outskirts of a village. They veered off the road before it became anything more than a shadow of buildings, going deep enough into the forest to avoid any prying travelers.

"Why is it," Rafferty asked, "that we have to stop by every bloody settlement? It's as frustrating as a corset."

"What do you know about corsets?" Evylin laughed.

The weasel waggled his white-blond eyebrows. "Wouldn't you like to know?"

"It gives us a bearing," Thom explained, then leaned in. "Though I *am* curious about your corset knowledge as well. I'd thought they'd gone out of fashion amongst all but the most salacious society. What types of women are you spending time around, Rafferty?"

"Not completely out of fashion, unfortunately," Ilain interjected. "It's still deemed proper amongst the gentry in Ephria. Thus, my backaches during our time around the palace."

Thom eyed her wickedly. "I seem to recall a white dress with a neckline too low for a corset upon our meeting."

"You noticed?" Ilain said with a smirk.

"Wasn't that the point?"

Clearing his throat, Ethenn rose from where he worked at trimming new fletching for his arrows. Without a word, he walked to the far side of the camp by the horses to complete his task.

"Seems our little Loxley hasn't taken to your and Thommy's banter, Highlady," Rafferty teased.

A flicker of tension pulled down Ilain's expression before it returned to amusement. "Can't say I blame him," she replied lightheartedly. Then she patted Thom's knee where he sat beside her. "Now, do tell me, dear, what did you think of my dress?"

"I thought it was improper, unladylike, and downright lascivious," Thom said, then affectionately tugged on one of her red curls. "In other words, I loved it."

While Rafferty snickered along with the pair, Evylin pursed her lips. She'd watched Thom and Ilain for days now, trying to work out this new relationship of theirs. Part of her reveled in their dalliance, glad to see them getting along rather than bickering so often. She even questioned if such a romance would be good for the pair. Ilain's wild and brash demeanor might help channel Thom's need for attention into a passionate love.

But the longer she studied their brazen act, the more she realized that was all it was: an act.

Evylin was about to comment on her deduction when she felt Deckard's hand on her shoulder. She could always tell when it was him these days. Her pulse would rise, and her head would cool, the first signs of her Warrior magic revealing itself. She craved the feeling. It filled her up and made her want to move. To fight, to run, to dance, to kiss—to experience everything the world could offer.

For days, the urge had grown within her, like a kettle over the fire, ready to boil. When Deckard had requested her help last night, she'd been embarrassed at first to think their troop assumed they'd gone out to take pleasure in one another. But the more she thought about it, the more she remembered the way it felt when Deckard kissed her. Her senses lit up, and the world became clearer under his touch. She'd wanted to kiss him before he left her there by the tree. She'd spent her whole time waiting, coming up with a ploy to make it happen. And she'd been quite proud of her success.

What she hadn't counted on was wanting more.

Now, Deckard crouched by her side again, and she found her blood thrumming with anticipation.

Hand falling away, Deckard's gaze was steady, more blue than green in the dimming forest light. "Would you come with me for a moment, Evylin?" he asked. "I want to talk with you about something."

The tight set of his brow told Evylin of his nervousness. His eyes darted to the rest of the troop as though worried they'd notice their departure. It caused her heart rate to spike.

Had Deckard been thinking of their kiss too? Was he as anxious as she to again experience the coursing rush in his veins? She knew he couldn't feel the fullness that her

Warrior magic brought on, the heightening of her senses until everything became sharp colors, sounds, and feelings. But that didn't mean he enjoyed it any less.

"Of course," Evylin said, smiling at the idea. She stood with him, feeling no need to announce their "walk" this time.

They slipped out of the camp, if not unseen, at least uncontested. The pines and rowan trees grew thicker as they left the small clearing. Raindrops clung to the needles and branches, a remnant of the afternoon deluge. The sky was still a dreary gray, but the rain granted them a momentary reprieve.

Following Deckard through the forest, Evylin began to step into the indentations of his footprints. Heel to toe, his feet were quite a bit larger than hers. She supposed it had to do with his height. He needed something to keep that towering, slender frame of his from toppling over.

Evylin grinned, happily hopping from footprint to footprint. She liked how tall Deckard was. She'd always been tall for a typical Ephrian female, but standing next to him made her feel dainty and ladylike. Neither word was a description she'd ever heard said of herself.

Deckard came to a stop next to an alcove of trees. "This will do," he said, then looked at her over his shoulder. Instantly, his brow furrowed. "What *are* you doing?"

Leaping across the final distance between his long strides, Evylin landed before him, her left boot solidly in the print he'd left. She peered up at him with a cheerful shrug. "Following in your footsteps."

He looked faintly amused. "I don't think that's what that saying means."

"Perhaps it should," she said, then reached over to take his hand. "It was awfully fun, pretending to be you."

Deckard's jaw flexed with something that resembled discomfort. He slipped out of her grasp, moving to the far side of the alcove. "Is that so?" he muttered.

Sure that he was only being coy because he feared her rejection, Evylin leaned against the soaring trunk of a pine. She crossed her legs at the ankles, giving him one of her most teasing looks. "Indeed. It was rather eye-opening as well."

He frowned but said, "Do tell."

She played with the end of her braid. "I realized how difficult it must be, standing so high among your peers. You're always so above the rest of the world. It's no wonder you have a martyr complex, trying to save us all."

Those words didn't have quite the effect Evylin expected.

Instead of laughing off her teasing compliment, Deckard stared back at her, clearly unamused. His expression grew tense, his back rigid. And suddenly, Evylin realized she might have misread the situation.

"Jonn," she stepped toward him, crossing half the distance in the narrow enclosure of trees, "what's wrong?"

Gaze dropping away from hers, Deckard raised a hand to run it through his hair. The action left the reddish-brown curls disheveled and drooping onto his forehead. "I want you to know, Evylin, that I'm sorry. If I could, I would ignore this."

Uncertain of what was to come, Evylin reached out to rest her hand on his arm. She couldn't deduce what was bothering him. Had he taken offense to her remark about his self-sacrificing tendencies? Or was there a chance she was right, and he brought her out here to confess his desire for her? Though she thought she'd made her willingness clear to him in the past, Deckard was a romantic. He surely didn't envision their consummation taking place in the muddy forest of Wauld. Perhaps this was merely his way of apologizing for not having the strength to wait any longer. Whatever the case, she attempted to ease his discomfort through her touch.

Deckard glanced down at her hand on his arm as if disappointed. Then he met her gaze, his eyes now a sharp green. "You have to give the Day Relic back to Rafferty."

The order didn't sink into Evylin's mind at first. It was so unexpected that she wasn't entirely certain she'd heard him correctly. But the determination in his stare confirmed that she had.

Dropping her hand away, Evylin kept her expression neutral even as her pulse began to race. "What?"

"When we get back to camp, you need to give the Day Relic to Rafferty."

No. The thought came unbidden and violently. A tight laugh slipped out of Evylin. "I don't have the Relic," she lied.

"You don't?"

"No." She didn't feel the dry grin that twisted up her lips. "Why would I?"

"That's an excellent question." He continued to stare at her, his blank gaze accusing.

Evylin crossed her arms, drawing back. "Well, I wouldn't—I don't."

Before she could react, Deckard hooked a finger under her open coat. He grazed her collarbone, sending a tingle across her skin as he tugged up the golden chain. "In that case, what's this?"

Glaring at him now, Evylin held firm. "A necklace."

He scoffed, letting the warm chain fall back in place.

Evylin sighed. "Yes, all right. I kept the Day Relic. So what? I thought it would be better this way."

"Better than what?" His tone said he didn't believe her.

"It wasn't safe, leaving all three Relics with Rafferty. He can't use them. What if we're ambushed again? Wouldn't it be better if I already had a Relic, ready to defend us? Hewitt might not have died if—"

"Are you serious?" Deckard gaped at her incredulously. "You're using Hewitt's death as part of your excuse—your *lie* to try and keep it?"

A thread of sorrow and horror bled through the strength of the Day Relic's hold upon her emotions. Evylin tamped it down, gripping onto whatever shred of joy she could find. "Why are you making such a fuss about this?" she asked through a feigned laugh. "I'm not grieving anymore. I've learned that life goes on, and so must I. The fact that I have the Relic has nothing to do with it."

"So you'd be happy to give it back to Rafferty then?" he challenged.

Panic flashed into her heart, searing in her veins like ice, but Evylin attempted a lazy grin. "Jonn," she said his name playfully, "I'd have no problem giving him the Relic. But I don't see why I would. It's illogical and dangerous."

"It's dangerous in your hands."

"Don't be ridiculous." She knew it came out more brusquely than she'd wanted, but she played off its tenor with a smirk. "You do remember that Rafferty only obtained the Relics because Blount was stupid enough to hold them all himself, don't you? If we do the same, letting Raff carry them all, it's asking for trouble. We're much safer divvying them up."

Deckard capitalized on her suggestion. "Why didn't you say so before? That's an excellent idea. We'll let Thom and Ethenn each carry one while Rafferty carries the other."

Evylin huffed. "That doesn't solve the problem at all."

"Why not?"

"Because then I can't protect us with them."

"So I'll carry one. If we're attacked, I can pass it to you in less than a second. Problem solved."

Seeing her argument failing, Evylin shook her head. "Every second is vital in a fight like that. We can't risk it."

"You're telling me that half a second is going to make or break a fight?"

"It happens all the time." She sucked in a sharp breath, attempting to slow her breathing. "Think about when I—when I sparred with Ethenn just the other day. He won because I was a fraction slower than him on his parry. If I'd have paid more attention, he wouldn't have gotten that chance."

"Evylin—" His voice was thick with emotion, ragged as though *he* were the one on the cusp of losing something. "You can't keep it."

"Why not?" It came out hushed and broken.

He raised a hand to comfort her before thinking better of it. "I'm not trying to hurt you, Evie. But the longer you keep the Relic, the harder it will be when you have to give it up. And I want to protect you from that."

"Why would I have to give it up?" She already knew that she would, but she'd reasoned with herself that during their mission, she could keep it. And by the time they were done, she'd have enough distance from Hewitt's death not to need it anymore. For now, she just needed it for a little while longer. Long enough to help her forget.

Seeing Deckard's knowing stare, Evylin shook her head again, trying to deny it. "I'll be fine," she promised. "I just—I'll carry it a little longer, and I'll be fine."

"This isn't you, Evylin."

"Yes, it is. It's more me than I've been in weeks."

Deckard's look was almost pitying.

Evylin hated it.

"Jonn, I'm fine," she swore. "I'm myself again. Don't you want that?"

"Of course, I do."

"Then let me keep it."

"I can't." He took a step forward, seeming too caught up in emotion to hold himself back. He set his hands on her shoulders. "Don't you realize what it's doing to you? You may feel happy, but it's a lie. And the moment you take that Relic off, you're going to wind up feeling every bit of pain you've been locking away."

"Then why would you take it from me?"

"Because you either feel it now, or you feel it a month from now. And I'd rather save you from a month's worth of added heartache if I can."

Evylin stared up at him, feeling a conflict of fear and comfort within her. She was angry with him, but she also felt drawn to him. She wanted to yell at him, yet she wanted to wrap her arms around his waist and press herself into his embrace. Her grief warred with the pull of the Day Relic, the truth fighting to emerge victorious under the lies.

Feeling herself beginning to shake from the thought of losing what had become so precious to her, Evylin knew she couldn't do it. She couldn't face the pain yet. She needed more time. Even a day would be better than a minute. She just needed a little more time.

"Jonn," she whispered his name, trying to smile, trying to convince him with a single word that he was wrong.

His hands slid down her arms before dropping away. "I'm sorry, Evylin. You have to give it back."

"No," she said flatly.

"Don't make me do this."

Her heart thumped with anger. "You don't have to do anything."

He looked heartbroken. "Please, Evylin."

Shaking her head even more vehemently, Evylin couldn't give up. She had to find a way to convince him. She had to keep the Relic.

Looking up into the softness and care in Deckard's eyes, Evylin knew there was one final chance—one last feint she could employ.

Evylin stepped closer, resting her hands on Deckard's chest. "Jonn, don't you see?" she whispered, her raspy tone inviting. Her hands slid up to rest on his neck.

He grew rigid beneath her touch as she threaded her fingers through the curls that brushed the nape of his neck. A thrill of magic tingled in her hands. Her heart leaped, the comfort of the Day Relic weaving through her veins, melting the icy dread. Even with the simple touch, she could feel the excitement rising within her at the anticipation of kissing him again.

The whisper of magic within her urged her for more. She rolled onto the balls of her feet, lifting her chin. *Not just a kiss,* her instincts told her. That wasn't enough anymore. After months of marriage and weeks of coming to know him and care for him, she wanted all of her husband—and to know what effect *that* could have upon her Warrior's senses.

Evylin could hear Deckard's breath coming out in a staggered exhale. He desired this as much as she did. His chin dipped subconsciously. Running her thumb along the corner of his jaw, just below his ear, Evylin whispered, "We can be together this way."

With a sudden jerk, Deckard knocked her hands off him, rapidly backing away. He glared at her, hurt flashing in his eyes. "Don't you dare," he hissed. "Not when you know—"

Evylin did know. She knew exactly how Deckard felt about her. But she was too desperate, too afraid of falling back into the despair of Hewitt's death to care.

"You want me," she said with an accusing tone. "*That's* what I know. You want me to be your wife in full. You've wanted it for months now. Well, you can have it."

She stepped closer. "Just let me keep the Relic."

Deckard immediately sidestepped her. "Absolutely not."

"I won't offer myself again, Jonn," she said, anger overcoming her rationale. How could he claim to care for her and still take away the one thing keeping her sane? How dare he reject her after all this time to protect his bloody ethics? "Let me keep the Relic, and I'll give you what you want."

"That is *not* what I want," he replied sharply. "Do you even hear yourself? Do you understand what you're offering?"

Evylin refused to be ashamed. Not when the alternative was an aching and inescapable pain. If it kept her from falling back into despair, she'd happily prostitute herself to him. After all, she'd begun to desire their union herself for the last month, purely for enjoyment's sake. It would only be a formality, finally taking him to her bed in exchange for keeping the Relic.

Seeing her determination, Deckard's face twisted in disappointment. "I won't entertain this conversation any longer. Give the Relic back to Rafferty."

Her hands curled into fists. "You can't make me."

His eyes went wide. "Perhaps I can't. But if you don't do it of your own volition, I will allow Auden and Ilain to use whatever force necessary."

She laughed with empty, caustic mirth. "You wouldn't let them hurt me. And with the Relic, I could do far more damage than they'd be willing to risk."

"Not if I give them the other two Relics," he countered. Slowly, he took a step forward. "Whatever it takes, Evylin, I will protect you—even from yourself."

The shaking had taken over Evylin's whole body now. Tears of fury filled her eyes as she backed away. If she thought it would do any good, she'd attack, forcing him to submit under violence. But she knew such a recourse would only convince him of the justification of his decision even more.

"You'll lose me," she warned. "If you make me do this, I won't ever forgive you."

Deckard's pinched brow and dejected frown gave his sharp features a stricken, resigned cast. "That's a risk I'm going to have to take."

Evylin glared at him. "Altruistic bastard," she spat.

He simply ducked his head, shoulders hunched as though he carried the weight of Terraeus alone.

She wanted to yell at him, to tell him that his disappointment was his own damn fault. She finally understood Thom's dislike for his brother. While Deckard did everything for the sake of morality and goodness, he made the rest of the world into his inferiors. He made it seem as though she was being selfish and weak by doing what she had to do to protect herself. And she hated him for it.

Just as her anger reached its crest, the warm pulse of the Day Relic began to defuse Evylin's fear. It swept over her body, soothing her trembling muscles. The anguish and fury in her heart eased even as a tear dropped over her lashes. It coursed a path down her cheek. Yet, she didn't feel the sorrow it held, succumbing to the Day magic's calming effect.

Evylin took the first clear breath she'd managed since the start of the conversation. Why had she been so upset? Yes, Deckard was self-sacrificing. That was part of what made him so wonderful. He might be trying to take the Relic from her, but it was out of concern for her. And she'd cursed him for it.

Evylin put her hands on her cheeks as a small, embarrassed laugh slipped out of her.

Deckard's head snapped up in shock.

"I'm sorry," she said around her laughter. "That was uncalled for. I quite appreciate your altruism. It makes you all the more charming."

He didn't speak as he continued to study her, doubt evident in his darkening gaze.

Evylin took a step closer, the Day magic curling contentedly around her limbs. "I know you're trying to take care of me," she promised. "But it isn't necessary."

He stood there, unmoved by her words.

"I'm all right, Jonn. I can carry it."

"No," he said firmly. "You can't."

Evylin chewed on her bottom lip. "You're going to make me give it back no matter what I say, aren't you?" she realized, hoping her fear didn't wend into her voice.

"Yes," he said.

Evylin nodded. "All right. What if—what if we make a deal?"

His eyes narrowed.

She held up a hand to beg his indulgence. "I'll give the Relic back to Rafferty," she said, then added, "for a day. And then, when I prove to you that you're wrong—that it won't hurt me to be parted from it—you let me have it back."

Deckard drew in a long, deep breath. "And if I deem that I was right, and you can't handle its inevitable removal?"

"Then you can keep it from me," she assured him.

As Deckard considered her proposal, Evylin steeled herself for his refusal. She needed this. One day. She could make it one day without the Relic. She *had* to make it one day. But he had to give her the chance first.

"Please, Jonn," she begged.

Slowly, Deckard released a sigh. Then, with a great deal of reluctance, he nodded.

"Thank you," she whispered, relief and anxiety coursing through her.

"I won't let you hurt yourself, Evylin," he replied, determination and compassion mixed in his words. "Even if you're convinced you aren't."

"I know," she said, forcing herself to smile. "I'll be fine. You'll see."

The disbelief plain on his face hurt her, knowing it was *her* he didn't believe in.

"I'll give it to you now if you'd like," she offered.

"I trust that you'll hold up your end of the bargain," he said. "When we get back to camp, I'll pull Rafferty to the side. We won't tell anyone else about this. They don't need to know."

Evylin nodded, appreciating his discretion.

They walked back to the camp, an uncomfortable distance and awkward silence in the chasm between them. *One day,* Evylin told herself. She only had to make it one day. And then she could have the Relic back for good.

CHAPTER FOURTEEN

5TH OF CHRONOS, 1574

The world had never been so cold.

After nearly a fortnight under the Day Relic's warming touch, the cold dampness of Wauld permeated deep into Evylin. It didn't matter that she wore two shirts, leather armor, a wool coat, and a thick travel cloak. The frigid rain and frosted breeze bit at her skin, slicing through to her bones, leaving her brittle and shivering.

Her memory of lying in the snow after Hewitt's death, freezing in her sorrow, tortured her with every shake of her body. Over and over, she felt the same hollowed-out sensation that came with knowing she'd never again see the person she loved most. Somehow, the ache was as intense as if she were experiencing that loss for the first time.

Hewitt was gone.

Gone.

Just like Ryen.

Evylin sat hunched in her saddle, attempting to keep a grip on her sanity. One day. She just had to make it through this day. If she could prove that she could bear the weight of this grief, she could have the Relic back, and she'd be free of the pain for good.

Or however long it'd be until she had to give it to the Alliance. But she'd be recovered by then. Surely, in the time it took for their troop to finish their task, she would have processed through her grief.

One day.

The words were a mantra in Evylin's head.

One day.

Only one day.

A fierce wind tore across the road, ripping her hood back and tossing the misting rain into her face. Evylin flinched, shivers coursing over her.

"Are you all right?" Deckard asked, riding at her side. He'd been beside her constantly since she'd given the Relic to Rafferty, keeping an eye on her, she knew. She couldn't tell if his watchfulness was so he'd be there if she needed comfort or simply to watch and see if she'd crumble.

Replacing her hood, Evylin refused to let him see her struggle. "I'm fine," she said, though her voice sounded frail to her own ears.

"Evie—"

"I'm *fine*," she repeated, stronger this time.

Deckard watched her but said no more.

His attentive presence was suffocating. Why couldn't he leave her alone? She wouldn't have to work so hard to pretend without him watching her every move.

But Evylin knew why he stayed at her side. He'd explained it to her last night as they lay next to the embers of the dying campfire. *"Don't do this alone, Evylin,"* he'd said. *"This is going to be hard, I know. But you don't have to do it alone."*

She'd tucked her head under his chin, burrowing into his warmth for the night. The full effects of the Relic hadn't worn off quite yet in those late-night hours, keeping her comfortable with him. Even if they had, due to the cold and the need to prove herself stable, she wouldn't have been able to abandon his arms.

Today, Deckard's constant presence was meant to remove any impediment between her need for help and her fear of asking for it. But she couldn't find it within herself to be grateful.

Evylin stared at the road ahead, focusing on her breath. Perhaps if she could regulate each inhale and exhale, she could fool her heart into believing that it wasn't aching. She closed her eyes, attempting to distract herself. Instead, her mind conjured the brutal image of Hewitt's face, sunken and blue from death.

Her eyes flew open.

The hours crept on at an unbearable trickle of time. Unshed tears stung, burgeoning on her lashes. Her throat burned with unspent emotion. Her body spasmed with the need for relief. Evylin needed a break from the never-ending road. She needed to be free of Deckard's hovering attention. And yet, they plodded along at a slow, steady pace.

By the time they finally stopped to make camp, Evylin was ready to run for the trees and hide. She wanted to crawl beneath a thicket of bushes and lose herself to the pain within her. But she feared that if she began to cry, she'd never stop.

"Only six more days," Ilain announced as they dismounted. "Then we'll be at the Wind Keep."

Rafferty hopped up from hobbling his horse. "Only six days, eh?" he said sardonically. "I've been soaked to the bone for nearly two weeks. I'm not sure I can last six more days."

"I'll say a prayer for your endurance," Ilain mocked.

Feeling somewhat mollified to hear that Evylin wasn't the only one struggling, she grabbed hold of the one sprig of hope within her. "Perhaps some sparring will ease the monotony," she suggested.

Rafferty's gray eyes scanned her thoughtfully for a mere second. He was checking on her, just as Deckard had done the whole day. Thankfully, only the two of them knew of her situation. But she was tired of being treated with caution.

"Yeah, that could do the trick," the weasel agreed. "Thommy, Loxley, Colonel, you in?"

"We're low on meat," Ethenn said. "I should do some hunting while it's still light."

Deckard glanced at Evylin, then shook his head. "You three go. I'll join Ethenn."

Evylin gave him an appreciative smile she didn't quite feel. He must have felt her irritation with him constantly at her side, and now, he was giving her space.

With no setup necessary in their barren camp, the groups split off, leaving Auden and Ilain with the horses. Evylin, Thom, and Rafferty struggled to find a clear spot for their practice. If the trees weren't densely packed, the ground would be littered with rocks.

"I swear," Thom said, "Wauld may be the worst place on Terraeus."

"Your ladylove seems to enjoy it well enough," Rafferty teased.

"Ilain grew up here," Thom replied. "And trust me, it isn't love. She's fun to flirt with, that's all."

Evylin sidestepped a rain-spotted fern. "I'll never understand that sort of behavior."

He scoffed. "What are you talking about? You flirt with people all the time. Hell, you've flirted with me."

"I have not!" she exclaimed.

"You've flirted with all of us," Rafferty said. "Well, maybe not Auden. But I'm not sure that man would know a flirt if a woman lifted her skirts and flashed her knickers at him."

While Thom laughed, Evylin glowered at them. "You're both disgusting."

The reprimand exerted no effect on Rafferty. "I will grant that in Estshire, banter is the conversation of choice, so you may not be aware of your wiles, Eve. However, even poor little Ethenn has blushed clear up to his scalp from your attention."

"Have you ever noticed what a feat that is?" Thom remarked. "Ethenn's tanner than all the rest of us combined, and yet he turns redder than a tomato anytime a woman looks his way."

"Ridiculous," Evylin said. However, she worried that they might be right. She'd mistakenly encouraged the crown prince of Ephria once, thinking they were merely having a pleasant conversation. Oftentimes, she didn't realize how flirtatiously her comments could be received.

Seeing what appeared to be a clearing ahead, Evylin dashed away from the subject. Though not large, there was an opening amongst the trees. Big enough for the three of them to spar, at least.

Evylin began some light stretching, attempting to ignore the aching hollow in her chest. If she could get moving, she could tap into her focus. She could feel the rush of magic and forget her pain. "What do we think?" she asked. "Two on one?"

Thom and Rafferty exchanged a look, then shrugged.

"Good thing I brought these," Rafferty said, brandishing the short swords he'd made of wood. They didn't stand up well against the dull edge of the training swords, but there was no shortage of supplies to make more.

Thom tossed the second training sword to Evylin. "You take the right," he told Rafferty.

"Sure, give me the easy side," Rafferty grumbled.

Evylin set her stance, failing to smirk as she normally would. "Either way, you're going to lose."

Neither man bothered to reply.

Rafferty and Thom charged, attempting to flank her. She ducked under Rafferty's swift jab, sliding away from the men. The muddy terrae aided her flight, but she knew she'd have to watch her footing carefully over its slick tread.

Evylin brought her sword up to meet Thom's attack, parrying it away before slashing out and knocking one of Rafferty's short swords out of his grip. Her mind began to cool with the first vestiges of magic, her fingers tingling on the leather hilt. She made an internal grab for the feeling, desperate for the escape.

While Rafferty recovered his fallen blade, Thom kept Evylin's attention. He relied on his strength, distracting her. Each hit sent tremors along her arms. Her muscles trembled, then flexed, her vision centering.

The slapping footfalls of Rafferty's approach from behind drew Evylin down to a crouch. The men's attacks struck one another's blades instead of her.

As she rose, she tilted her shoulder up, ramming it into Rafferty's gut. He let out an "oof," but she couldn't relax. Her sword met Thom's with a resounding clang.

Evylin's heart thudded wildly. The magic raced through her body, twisting and alive.

She felt like she was back in the Keep, surrounded by Shades. She could hear their humming in her head—pulsing, crashing, and piercing.

Fighting became effortless for Evylin. She thrust, parried, and blocked without thought. One attacker was in front of her, and the other was behind. Her head filled with the sound of battle: swords crashing together, grunts of exertion and pain, and the sharp staccato of breathing. Sweat beaded on her forehead, at the nape of her neck, and down her spine. Her lungs burned with the strain, fighting as though for her life.

Someone said her name, but Evylin didn't stop. She disarmed one opponent, dropping the Shade with a smack to the side of the head with the pommel of her sword. Then she spun back to the other, striking out with her foot. She hooked it around the Shade's leg and jerked back. It fell into the mud with a splat. But she wasn't safe yet.

Evylin slipped a dagger from her belt. She dropped to her knees, straddling the Shade, poised to drive the blade into its throat.

The Shade gripped her wrists, holding her attack at bay. She leaned harder against it, the blade sinking an inch closer to the Shade's neck. It said her name like a plea, begging for its life. But she couldn't give it mercy.

Ilain's words rang through her head. *"Any one of us could lose our lives at any time."*

She couldn't let that happen. She couldn't go through it again.

Evylin pressed harder, forcing the blade down.

A weight slammed into her side, yanking her off the Shade. She rolled, breaking free and regaining her footing. She'd lost her dagger in the scuffle, but she had others. Her fingers readily found the rosette pommel, drawing the blade from her belt.

"Eve!" The yell was harsh and loud, jarring her senses.

Evylin shook her head, mind clearing. Rafferty stood in front of her, his hands held up and body primed to pounce. His gray eyes were fierce, jaw set with consternation. A bloom of dark pink flesh showed at his temple. She blinked. Why was he staring at her like that? And why did she have a dagger in her hand?

Slowly, Thom rose to his feet. He wiped a hand along his throat, fingers coming away crimson.

Evylin dropped the dagger. She muttered a curse, her hands shaking as the world cleared around her. In the haze of her magic, she'd lost track of reality. She'd fallen into a stupor, attacking her friends as though they were Shades. She'd nearly killed Thom.

"Thom, I—I'm so sorry," she eked out.

Though his steely blue gaze showed fear, Thom stepped closer. "It's all right, Evie. You didn't hurt me. I'm fine."

"No," she whispered, the trembling spreading up her arms and into her shoulders. "No, you're not. You're bleeding."

"It was just a scratch."

"I could have killed you!" Her voice broke, her chest constricting.

Rafferty still stood to the side, watching her warily. Thom approached, rubbing his fingers clean on his coat. "But you didn't. I'm fine."

Evylin couldn't tear her eyes from the blood staining the gray wool. "I would have," she said, breath catching in her throat. "If Rafferty hadn't stopped me, I would have."

"Evie, look at me," Thom instructed.

She did, but all she could see was the nick on his neck, blood beading to trickle out.

"I'm fine," he repeated once more.

The shaking was in her chest, collapsing her lungs. Evylin felt like she was back in the Water Keep, slowly drowning in the massive blue pool. Her eyes filled, and she couldn't stop the tears from falling. The emotion crashed in on her, the pressure of it filling her lungs. She couldn't breathe.

Evylin's knees buckled, and both men jolted in surprise. Thom caught her arm, but her weight carried them down. Rafferty knelt by her side, open-mouthed in concern.

On all fours, Evylin gasped for air. Her vision grew spotty, her fingers curling in the mud. She could feel the weight of Thom's arm around her and hear him telling her to breathe, that it would all be all right, she just had to breathe. But she didn't believe him.

It wouldn't be all right. She knew that now. Without the warmth of the Day Relic, nothing would ever be all right again. Hewitt was gone; he'd died on this foolish mission of theirs. What chance did the rest of them stand? If Hewitt could be conquered, they'd all die. And why shouldn't they? There was nothing to live for if he weren't there to see them to victory. Evylin choked, her lungs burning with the need for relief.

Vaguely, she heard Rafferty speaking in a panic. "What do we do?"

"I—I don't know," Thom stuttered, his voice shaky. "Get help, maybe?"

"Right." Rafferty sprinted off, yelling at the top of his lungs, "COLONEL!"

Thom sighed, tightening his hold on Evylin. "I meant the Day Mage, you stupid git," he grumbled. Then he slid in front of Evylin, taking hold of her face in both hands. His sharp gray-blue eyes bored into hers. "Evylin, I want you to listen to me," he said. "You need to breathe. So let's do it together, all right? Take a breath in and hold it."

He demonstrated, and Evylin attempted a shallow breath. It caught, causing her to cough repeatedly. Bile rose in her throat, and the acid burned her tongue.

Thom swore under his breath, seeing that his attempts were failing. "Come on, Evie." He stroked the side of her face, desperation in his voice. "You can do this. I'm right here. You didn't hurt me, I promise. Please, just breathe."

Evylin couldn't comply. Her head was beginning to spin. All she wanted was to set her head in the dirt and sink out of existence. No more pain, no more loneliness, no more fear. She could fade away just as Hewitt had and finally find peace.

Rest. That's what Evylin needed. She could lie down and fall into oblivion, resting with Hewitt and Ryen for eternity.

As Evylin began to lower herself to the terrae, Thom quickly slipped his arms under hers. "No, no, no," he muttered, pulling her to his chest. He held her awkwardly, brushing the hair away from her face. He kept whispering for her to breathe. She started getting agitated. Why wouldn't he just let her sleep, allow her to slip from consciousness to rest with the men she loved?

Suddenly, there was a rapid pounding, startling both Thom and her. Her vision was too spotty with sorrow and hyperventilation to see properly, but she heard Deckard's voice. "What happened?"

Evylin's heart leaped. She caught her breath, and the tears fell free.

"I don't know," Thom was saying as his brother crashed to the terrae, kneeling before them. "We were just sparring and—"

Reason fled Evylin, seeing Deckard there. She sobbed, jerking free of Thom to throw herself into Deckard's chest and waiting arms. He embraced her willingly, drawing her closer to him. He was warm and solid, secure and tender.

Evylin couldn't stop crying. She thought she might have even wailed in her grief. Deckard said nothing but cradled her against him. Her head rested against his chest, blocking out the rest of the world. It all faded into darkness and the gentleness of his embrace.

Time fell away as Evylin wept in Deckard's arms. He stroked her hair, silent and reassuring as he patiently comforted her. He smelled of the forest, of sweat and dirt and pine. And though Evylin's heart continued to ache, though she wanted to fall into the nothingness of never-ending sleep to escape the pain of her loss, she found her sorrow lifting.

She burrowed deeper into Deckard. It was as though he'd jumped into the water and pulled her to safety. The tears had stopped, and she could breathe again. She didn't feel quite so hollow as before, the death of Hewitt not so potent.

Perhaps she didn't need the Day Relic, after all.

Just the thought caused Evylin to go rigid.

"Any one of us could lose our lives at any time."

What was she doing, taking comfort in Deckard this way? This was the role she'd granted Hewitt, the role he'd inherited from Ryen. And she'd lost both of them. She couldn't let someone else become that for her. Not when their lives were on so precarious a ground.

Evylin couldn't risk relying on Deckard this way. She couldn't allow him to be her safety. Her reaction to him, to his presence—it was illogical. Thom should have been able to comfort her. She shouldn't have needed Deckard to save her. Not if she was going to survive the inevitable loss of him.

Pulling back, Evylin drew in a shaky breath. Deckard let her part from him completely, his hands resting at his sides in the mud. She could see the caution in his expression, the concern for her stability and recovery. The light had faded, marking a great passage of time as she overcame her grief.

In the dimness, Deckard's hair was cast more brown than red. His features were almost severe in the shadows. Yet, he was as handsome to her as ever.

Evylin hardened herself. No, she wouldn't feel that way toward him. Not when he could leave her—not when she might have to face a world alone if he died too.

"Thank you," she murmured emptily, not meeting his gaze.

"Always," he promised.

Wetting her dry, cracking lips, Evylin scanned the empty clearing. "Where are—?"

"They went back to camp," he said, not needing to explain why.

Evylin nodded. Her cheeks felt tight from her dried tears. A self-derisive smirk came to her lips. "I suppose I'm not getting the Relic back, am I?" she joked irreverently.

Deckard didn't reply.

Waving a hand, Evylin sat back in the mud. "Don't worry. I—I agree with you now. After that. . . ."

She stared at her hands, unwilling to finish the thought. Her fingers absentmindedly tugged at her rings. She pressed her lips together and released the rings, not liking the way they made her think about her husband and the men she'd lost.

Evylin forced herself to meet Deckard's gaze. "It still hurts," she admitted.

"It always will," he said.

Yes, Evylin thought, *it* always *will.* And she couldn't bear to wound herself further.

"I need time, Jonn," she whispered.

His brow furrowed as though trying to understand what she meant.

Evylin worked to explain without being too blunt. "You were right. My time with the Day Relic . . . that wasn't me. Everything that happened wasn't real."

Deckard's chin rose, her meaning becoming clear. Their kiss, her affection, her comfort with him—she wasn't ready to be that person with him again. "I told you," his deep voice was steady, "we can figure out the future later. I will never rush you or require you to choose before you're ready. That's a promise, Evylin. Take all the time you need."

His sincerity almost made his kindness cruel.

Evylin whispered her thanks, but the words felt empty. Guilt tore at her already ragged throat. She shouldn't do this to him. He was everything good, generous, and understanding, and she could only offer him rejection and hurt. No matter what came, whether they survived their mission with the Calders or not, they would never be safe. There was no safety. And one day, Evylin would lose him too.

Better to protect what was left of her scarred heart.

Better to learn to live without him now.

Better to never love him at all.

CHAPTER FIFTEEN

Inferiority clung to Thom like a leech, sucking all the life from his veins. For twenty-seven years, it'd been like this. No matter what he did, no matter how hard he tried, it was never enough. Today was just another reminder of that fact.

He couldn't stop thinking about Evylin's breakdown in the woods. He'd tried so hard to help her through it. He'd had soldiers go through similar bouts of panic after their first time in battle, struggling with the weight of death dealt at their hands and the threat of their own immortality.

Seeing Evylin face a similar crisis wasn't completely unfathomable, nor was it even unexpected after her improved mood over the last several days. It seemed she'd been shoving down her grief over Hewitt, and it had finally caught up to her. Thom didn't judge her for it, nor was he surprised by it. Everyone dealt with grief uniquely. Helping Evylin through her panic was the natural course of action.

But all his heartfelt efforts failed.

Thom would never forget that feeling of inadequacy, watching her tremble and fight for every breath. He'd wanted to take her in his arms, to comfort her every pain. He would have given her the very breath from his lungs if he could.

Calling for help was a gut punch in and of itself. But Thom figured that if anyone could help Evylin, it would be Auden and his ability to heal through Day magic.

It turned out that Rafferty had made the right choice.

When Deckard showed up, Evylin had practically shoved Thom aside to leap into his brother's arms. She'd clung to him like he was the shore and she, the sea, desperate to become one with the sand. Deckard hadn't said a word. He hadn't done a thing. His presence alone seemed to be enough to soothe Evylin's aching heart.

Thom envied that most of all. How did Deckard do it? How was he so blessed that his mere existence made people feel cared for and secure? It was yet another proof in the comparison of his life that he could never meet the standard established by his older brother.

The small campfire sat in a heap of embers as they ate their meal. They took caution with all their fires, not wanting to risk being spotted by random travelers. Though they camped well off the road, there was no telling if Blount had Mages or even the army out looking for them.

Thom picked at his meager bowl of roasted hare and steamed barley. Despondent and embittered, he'd returned to camp with Rafferty, leaving Evylin in Deckard's care. He'd hated leaving; it felt like admitting defeat. But he'd hated watching them entwined in one another's arms more.

He knew it was wrong, feeling the way he did about Evylin. No man should want his brother's wife as his own. What sort of scum did that make him, wishing she would choose him over Deckard? Yet, he always reminded himself that it wasn't exactly his fault.

From the moment he'd first seen her, Thom knew Evylin was special. Beautiful, quick-witted, strangely comfortable in a smithy, and the valued niece of a military legend—what woman could boast all those accolades? She wasn't some tedious girl whose only aspirations were the accumulation of pretty dresses and a husband. Those things were nice, but Evylin wanted more.

Then Thom had seen the way his brother looked at her and spoke to her. And the way she looked and spoke back. He'd been disappointed, to say the least. But he hadn't been dissuaded.

What recommendations did Deckard have that he didn't? In fact, given all of Deckard's merits, Thom had them in heaps more. Perhaps Thom was shorter by four inches; he was built more muscular and broad and, therefore, stronger. He had hair so dark that it was almost black, contrasting with his subtle tan and sharp blue eyes—a quality many women had told him made him devilishly handsome. He felt more deeply, lived with greater passion, laughed more readily, and sought out more daring experiences. What more could a woman desire from a lover?

Deckard lived lightly. He didn't seek adventure or feel with zealous fury. Fun wasn't a word in his vocabulary. His whole existence was dedicated to service and implacable perfection. No flaws, no mistakes, no fervor. And who could love a man so dull?

No, whatever Evylin thought she saw in his brother, Thom hadn't been concerned. Once she got to know *him*, she'd forget all about Deckard.

On their final night in Whickam Village, Thom decided to ask to write to Evylin. He'd been planning it out since he discovered his brother's interest. If he asked her first, he'd ensure Deckard never got the chance. Then Hewitt had gone and ruined it all.

Why had he picked Deckard? That was what Thom never could figure out. Hewitt hadn't liked Deckard to begin with, yet he'd treated Thom with a nearly mentor-like hand from the start. So why Deckard? His captaincy wasn't that much more impressive than Thom's rank as a lieutenant. And Thom showed more military promise than his brother, so his future was clearly brighter. Why wouldn't Hewitt want to attach his niece to someone who could actually be her match? Someone whose path ensured lifelong adventure and whose temperament exuded passion.

While they still traveled with the Third Volunteer Company, Thom had been brave enough—or, more accurately, drunk enough—to once ask Hewitt that very question. "Why Deckard?"

Hewitt hadn't even needed clarification. He'd already known. "Because it was her only chance."

"No, it wasn't," Thom argued. "You could have chosen any number of men. You could have—*should* have—chosen me."

The flat gaze Hewitt gave him then showed equal parts repudiation and, shockingly, pity. He took several seconds before saying, "You weren't the one she wanted."

Thom couldn't accept that. Not when it didn't make any sense. She trusted Thom more than she did Deckard. It was plain for everyone with eyes to see. She spent her days in Thom's company, sought him out at every opportunity, and readily took him into her confidence. It wasn't her fault that her uncle had chosen the wrong man. Nor was it Thom's.

There had been a moment on their journey to Loclight that granted Thom one last flare of foolish hope. Evylin had unintentionally revealed that her marriage to Deckard had yet to be consummated, that the union could still be dissolved. And for weeks after, Thom's hopes were renewed. He was determined to win Evylin's heart and convince her to break free of his brother.

But then Evylin and Deckard returned from that damn Annaltide party at the palace, twisted up in one another's arms, locked in a kiss that inevitably set flames to the future he'd been planning. She might not have been Deckard's in full before, but she sure as hell was now.

And what could Thom do? He couldn't just scratch out his feelings like a line on paper. Even if he tried, they'd still be there, inked into his soul, forever stained.

"You weren't the one she wanted."

How true that proved to be today. And how insignificant it made him feel.

Deckard and Evylin returned to camp while the rest of them finished their meals. To Thom's surprise, the couple walked with a telling distance between them. He might have soothed her pain, but the damage of Hewitt's death still kept them apart.

No one asked where they'd been or if Evylin was all right. Only Ethenn was aware that anything was wrong, having been with Deckard when Rafferty found him. And the boy was smart enough not to bring attention to it.

Now, Evylin sat at the base of a boulder near the back of the camp, staring apathetically into the bowl of food she held. Rafferty had enlightened Thom to the situation on their walk back to camp. He'd told him how Evylin had kept the Day Relic since they'd left the Night Keep and that it must have been the reason she'd been so chipper for the near-fortnight. Then Rafferty explained how Deckard had pulled him aside last night and stood there like a disappointed parent as he made Evylin return the Relic.

Turning his gaze from Evylin's huddled form, Thom glared at his brother across the dim campfire embers. Deckard's shoulders were rigid as he slowly ate his meal and talked quietly with Auden. While the two men discussed the politics and cultures of Wauld, Rafferty had Ethenn and Ilain laughing. All of them acted as though nothing was amiss.

Thom was too annoyed to join in on the revelry. He wanted to sit with Evylin and ask why she didn't tell him about the Relic and promise he'd help her get it back if she'd like. He wanted to promise that he'd do anything—absolutely anything on Terraeus—if it would make her happy.

But Thom couldn't make her happy. She'd made that clear an hour ago.

Deckard rose from his seat and checked on Evylin. Their conversation was short and obviously tense. He came away carrying her still mostly full bowl. After offering the leftovers to Ethenn, he cleaned both his and Evylin's bowls and then took them to the packs by the horses.

Quickly, Thom got up to follow him. Perhaps he couldn't comfort Evylin, but he could see to it that she wasn't left so dejected.

He approached his brother casually, calling his name under his breath. Deckard looked up from the pack. He finished tying off the laces before standing to meet Thom's gaze.

"Could I talk with you for a moment?" Thom asked. "Privately."

Deckard hesitated, glancing over his shoulder at the others. "All right."

They walked a handful of paces out of the camp, though keeping it still in sight. They'd have to speak in low voices to ensure they weren't overheard, which wasn't preferable, but hopefully, the conversation wouldn't escalate.

Thom nearly scoffed at the thought. Of course, it would escalate. What serious conversation of theirs didn't?

Settling his stance, Thom did his best to approach the discussion like a fellow soldier rather than a brother. "Rafferty explained everything to me," he began, "about the Day Relic."

Deckard pressed his lips together around a sigh. "I told him to keep it quiet."

"Why?"

"Because I didn't want Evylin to feel ashamed."

"What does she have to be ashamed of? She's grieving."

Deckard gave him a disappointed frown. "Yes, she's grieving. But if everyone knew that she'd anesthetized herself, they might begin to treat her differently. That won't help her heal."

"And will this?" Thom demanded.

His brother's brow furrowed.

Thom motioned back toward the camp, where Evylin sat isolated from the rest of the troop. "How is *this* helping her?"

"It will take time—"

"She had a panic attack today, Jonn," he spat. "Because you took the Relic from her. What happens if she has another in the Keeps, huh? You're going to risk her life to help her 'heal'?"

Deckard's gaze grew sharp. "The Relic wasn't helping, Thom. It was masking the pain she felt. She couldn't keep the Relic forever. This would have happened eventually, and the longer we waited, the worse it would have been. Now, she has six days to recover before we enter another Keep."

"You think she can heal from Hewitt's death in six days?"

"I wouldn't begin to presume that she could fully heal from that in six lifetimes."

"Then why would you take away the one thing holding her together?"

"It was hindering her," Deckard insisted. "The Relic made her forget that she had anything to heal from. She wasn't getting better. She never would have. In order for her to ever find some semblance of peace with his death, she had to give it up."

"So she just has to endure this alone?" Thom raised his brow knowingly, accusingly. "Or is it that you want her to be reliant on *you*?"

Deckard's shoulders drew back as if Thom had shoved him. "Excuse me?"

"I know how you are. You like people to be dependent on you. It makes you feel important—special. The Relic took that from you, so you took it from her."

Deckard's mouth hung ajar in disbelief. "Do you really think I could do something so cruel?"

"Why else would you do this to her?"

"It isn't as though I *wanted* to. I *had* to."

"I know her better than you." Thom pointed to his chest. "*I'm* her friend. What are you? The man she was forced to marry?"

Deckard scoffed. "If you know her so much better, please, enlighten me: Why did she tell me that she doesn't want the Relic back?"

That surprised Thom, but he shrugged it off. "Because she knew that's what you wanted to hear."

"Evylin never withholds her true opinion. That's one of the things I've always—" Deckard stopped himself before he said aloud the damning truth they all knew: He loved her.

Thom clenched his jaw.

"Always appreciated about her," Deckard concluded.

Ignoring the accuracy of his brother's assessment, Thom glared at him. "She can't fight like this, Jonn. She almost killed me today because she was lost in some . . . mania. I don't know who she thought she was fighting, but it wasn't me or Raff. Without the Relic, we risk her turning on us, or worse, having another attack in the heat of battle. We could lose her. Are you willing to take that chance?"

"Today was a mistake," Deckard said. "It was the result of the Relic's repression of her emotions. She has the next six days to process her grief and train to strengthen her control of her senses, ensuring that she's capable of entering the Keep."

"How can you be so careless with her?" Thom demanded. "She needs more time."

"And what would you have me do?"

"Give her the Relic."

"To face another breakdown like today's, a week from now?"

"She needs relief, Jonn."

"She needs to heal," he countered. "And she won't do that if she has the Relic."

Thom ground his teeth. He heard the logic in the argument. But he couldn't help thinking that Evylin needed something—*anything*—to help her through her grief. If *he* were her husband, he wouldn't leave her side until she felt so safe and cared for that her pain melted away like the last of winter's remnants on a sunny spring day.

Hands curled into fists at his sides, Thom held Deckard's stare. "I won't let her hurt like this, Jonn. I won't stand idly by while you abandon her to agony."

"That's not what I'm doing."

"Then what *are* you doing?" he demanded. "'Cause from where I stand, it looks like nothing."

They glared at each other, their old resentments and animosity charging the air.

Thom took a confrontational step closer. "I don't care about your sanctimonious ethics. I will do *whatever* it takes to protect her."

Deckard's expression shifted into one that was deadly and emotionless as he looked down his nose at his brother. He leaned forward, his deep voice flat as he said, "She's not your wife."

Without another word, Deckard walked away, leaving Thom alone in the trees. His hands shook from holding them curled tightly for so long. His muscles protested as he flexed them at his sides.

Thom didn't watch his brother leave. Instead, he glared into the forest's depths and whispered, "But she should be."

CHAPTER SIXTEEN

6TH OF CHRONOS, 1574

There was one good thing that came of Evylin's time with the Relic: It seemed to give her a new resolve. Despite her descent back into the well of depression, she'd gained a strength that wasn't there before. And Deckard was proud of her for that, even if she did exercise it by facing away from him in her sleep *without* his arms around her.

She'd made her request when he'd returned from that absurd conversation with Thom. Ilain and Ethenn were already at their post for the night, while Auden and Rafferty were bedding down in separate alcoves for safety from the rain. When Deckard moved to take his place at Evylin's side, she set a hand on his arm before he could get settled.

"Could you—" She paused then, taking a deep breath to steel herself. "Could you let me sleep on my own?"

The rejection twisted Deckard's gut. "If that's what you want," he whispered back. "But . . . do you mean you'd like me not to hold you or that you'd like me to sleep elsewhere?"

Evylin considered that. "The others will be suspicious if we sleep separately," she concluded. "You can lie next to me, but . . . I need space."

Though Deckard doubted her ability to rest well without his warmth or the closeness they'd grown used to, he would honor her request. "Of course," he said, then lay down facing away from her. He wrapped his cloak tightly around himself, knowing it could only provide so much comfort on the rain-soaked ground.

And while he hadn't expected her to lie awake all night, he heard more than felt

Evylin's breathing steady into sleep long before him. In fact, though she managed to capture her rest within half an hour, he stared into the darkness for half the night.

But he could only attribute her shutting him out to part of his restlessness.

In the course of his day, Deckard had been so focused on Evylin that he'd altogether forgotten about the nagging sensation of the other day. The one that told him something was wrong in his conversation with his vision of Hewitt. Once he bedded down, the solitude of the night provided ample time for consideration.

And as he lay there for what felt like endless hours, Deckard finally figured out the truth that whispered in the back of his brain. A truth he wasn't entirely sure how to process.

The following day passed in the same plodding through rain and mud. The troop's usually cheerful mood was fully tempered by the torrent of bead-sized hail that journeyed with them. It wasn't dangerous enough for them to stop, but the horses snorted unhappily as they were pelted over and over, and the troop huddled, grimacing with each stinging strike of solid ice.

The weather put everyone on edge. When they arrived to make camp, several disgruntled arguments broke out. Deckard managed to set them all to rights, but Ethenn sulked as he prepared the meal, and Ilain refused to assist Auden with the fire on the grounds that he was "being a tedious crag-hag."

Deckard wasn't sure what a crag-hag was, but after every impossible thing the Mages had brought into their lives, he decided he didn't care to find out.

While Thom and Ilain sat side by side, passing flirtatious insults at one another, Deckard decided he'd had enough. "I'm going for a walk," he said, not caring that they'd all agreed to avoid going out alone.

Gratefully, no one questioned him. Rafferty and Evylin sat together under the boughs of a hazel; he appeared to be teaching her how to make a coin disappear. She wasn't smiling, but she wore a faintly amused expression. It gave Deckard enough security to leave her for an extended period.

Deckard moved through the trees, his hood as far over his head as it would reach. The hail that made it through the thick tree cover pecked at his shoulders like a hen at its feed. With the heavy, charcoal gray clouds that filled the sky, the forest was already dark, as somber as the mood in his heart.

Satisfied that he'd gone far enough, he came to an unceremonious stop between two pines. Hewitt was there, his burly frame filling the enclosed space. His iron-gray eyes scanned Deckard, mouth pulled taut in a disgruntled manner.

"Something's wrong," he surmised.

Deckard allowed several seconds to pass as he surveyed the man. His dark brown hair and beard were as unruly as ever, silver streaks showing the early signs of aging at fifty-five, according to his army contract. He still wore the gray coat given to them by King Ephren, marking them as members of the Order of the King. Weapons hung from his thick belt, and a hand rested on the sword there.

"This is exactly how you looked before you died," Deckard noted.

Hewitt's brow creased. "Is that important?" he asked.

Deckard shook his head. "Not particularly."

"Then why mention it?"

Hewitt's gruff growl struck Deckard differently now. It was a sound he'd never thought he'd hear again. A sound he'd thought he'd imagined over the last several weeks.

"I couldn't have known that you told Evylin to consummate our marriage," Deckard said.

Hewitt lifted his broad shoulders in a shrug. "I didn't expect you would."

"You also told me that it took a month after Ryen's death for her to smile. I couldn't have known that either."

"Believe it or not," Hewitt quipped, "I know many things that you don't."

"That's just it," Deckard replied. "You shouldn't be able to tell me *anything* I didn't already know."

"How arrogant of you."

Deckard took a step closer. "You're real."

Hewitt's left eyebrow rose derisively. "Of course, I'm real. What, did you think you were talking to yourself this whole time?"

"Yes!" Deckard exclaimed. "But you're a *real* ghost."

"Seems that way," he said casually. "One minute I was dead, and the next I was in those woods, talking to you. Which, might I add, if given the choice of people I'd like to spend my afterlife with, *you* would be at the bottom of the list."

Deckard laughed at the ridiculous comfort of having Hewitt insult him. "How are you here?" he asked in bafflement.

"How should I know? In a world of Warriors and Mages, it seems that ghosthood isn't as far-fetched as one would like to believe."

"This is incredible," Deckard muttered. He couldn't believe his good fortune. "You can help me care for Evylin *and* win her back."

"Win her back?" Hewitt scoffed. "I thought we'd already determined that she was in love with you."

Deckard grimaced. "We were wrong. Now that I realize you aren't a figment of my imagination, I suppose I have some things to explain to you." He went through the past several days, the discovery of Evylin's dependence on the Day Relic, his insistence that she gave it up, how strongly she fought against it (though he kept out the bit about her offering herself to him), her breakdown the previous day, and her newly established separation from him.

Hewitt took it all in with a bland expression as he stroked his unruly beard. "She was self-medicating with a Relic?" he commented, a layer of incredulity in his tone. "Just when I thought I couldn't hate magic more."

"It appears there's a great deal we don't understand about magic," Deckard replied, gesturing to the ghost himself as proof.

Hewitt grunted. "While it would give me no greater pleasure than to help Evylin out of this mess, I fail to see what I can do. It isn't as though I can chat with her to convince her how wonderful you are. You're the only one who can see or hear me."

"I did consider that, but that's not the help I need."

"Then what assistance are you hoping for?"

"She needs to heal," Deckard said. "Your death broke Evylin, as Ryen's did thirteen years ago. You helped her through that time. You helped her to heal. Tell me how to help her now."

A cool breeze cut through the trees, and the hail lightened, returning to a regular rainstorm. Despite his seeming corporeality, none of the weather affected Hewitt. He stood there, his clothes and hair as dry as on a sunny day.

"I don't know how to help you with that," Hewitt said regretfully.

Deckard frowned. "You did it before."

"I was *with* her before," the ghost said. "She didn't heal from Ryen's death. Neither did I. We remained broken in our mutual grief, finding solace in one another because it felt like being with him. I imagined Evylin to be mine because she was the closest thing I could get to having my son back. She attached herself to me, trusting me more than anyone else on Terraeus because I was the closest thing she could get to her best friend. We didn't move on. We only pretended to."

Deckard's instinct was to apologize. The grief they both must have felt and the way they'd let it linger for over a decade must have tainted even their happiest memories together. He thought back through all the times when Evylin chose Hewitt over him, the jealousy and rejection he'd felt. He now realized that it wasn't Hewitt she was choosing. It was the past. It was Ryen.

"I beg your forgiveness if this is insensitive," Deckard began, desperate to understand. "But why was Ryen so important to her? I know they were like siblings, but . . . even if one of my siblings died, I can't fathom it so irrevocably ending my happiness."

"Ryen wasn't just like her brother," Hewitt replied. "It was as if he were her twin. They were born barely a month apart. She didn't remember a day without him. And he was the only one who understood her. While her sisters played house with their dolls, she played pirates with Ryen by the stream. They built up dreams together. They made a vow to travel the world, experiencing one adventure after the next."

Sorrowful clarity came to Deckard at his words. "It wasn't only her dream you were fulfilling with our marriage. It was Ryen's too."

Hewitt shrugged dismissively. "They are inseparable in my mind. Ryen, Evylin. Doesn't matter what name you use, they are the same to me."

Rather certain that wasn't appropriate, Deckard didn't bother pointing it out to the man. "Does she even want it?" he asked instead. "Adventure. Is it really what *she* wants, or is it just what *they* wanted?"

"I'm sure she doesn't know. His dreams were her dreams, and the same for him. When he died, she never took the time to question what she wanted. Their dream remained because she couldn't bear to let him go."

"And you didn't think to help her find her own dreams after all this time?"

Hewitt laughed, gruff and callous. "Don't you understand yet? Our relationship was never healthy, Deckard. She used me as a link to him, as I used her. I love her more than I can say, but I doubt I'd have felt that way if she hadn't been so closely tied to my son."

Deckard supposed there was some bravery in the man's admission. It shed light on many of the nuances of their relationship that he hadn't understood. And it made Evylin's despair even clearer. She wasn't just mourning Hewitt; she was mourning Ryen for a second time too.

That thought brought another insight along with it. "I can't do what you did for her," Deckard said. "I can't help her move on because I have no link to Ryen. Whatever I try, it won't do any good because she's still not over her loss of him."

"Now, you're getting it."

Deckard sighed, tossing his hands to the side. "Then what am I supposed to do? Stand by while she aimlessly suffers through her misery? Wait for her to miraculously find a reason to live outside of him?"

"She's still living, isn't she?"

"She's surviving."

Hewitt shook his head. "If Evylin were done with this world, she would crawl into a hole and let herself die there. As she's actively working to save the world, I'd say she hasn't quite given up yet."

"So you're saying there's hope?"

"I'm saying," his sharp gray eyes cut through the darkness, "that she's already found a reason to live. She's just too afraid to admit it."

Deckard narrowed his gaze, sure he'd understood but equally sure that Hewitt couldn't be correct. "She told me she wants space," he said. "That she needs time."

"Like I said," Hewitt replied. "She's afraid."

"Of what? My willingness to comply?" He scoffed. "I'm fairly certain I've made my desire to be her husband explicitly clear."

Hewitt heaved a disgruntled sigh. "How many layers of idiocy do I have to peel back before I finally discover some common sense in that brain of yours?" He stepped forward to emphasize his next words. "She's afraid of loving you. Of trusting you."

Deckard listened warily as Hewitt continued. "Evylin has only ever allowed two people to see her heart: me and Ryen. We were the only ones she truly trusted because we were the only ones who didn't ask her to be anything but herself."

"Neither have I," Deckard said.

Hewitt raised a scraggly eyebrow. "You want to get in her trousers. That's the most blatant and untrustworthy agenda a man can have."

Abashed, Deckard muttered, "I would never act on that desire without her consent."

"But it is your ultimate aim. And she can sense that."

"That's not true. Even if I never—if we never had that sort of relationship, I would accept it. Having her in my bed is not an objective for me to reach."

"Then what is your objective?"

"Her," he said honestly. "Just her."

The ghost stared back at him.

"All I want," Deckard said, ready to bare his heart, "is to give her the life I promised: to love her, no matter what that looks like. I swore to take her across Ephria and help her find the place she loves the most, to give her the future she deserves. I want to see her happy. Whether that's with me or . . . or not."

Hewitt crossed his arms. "She'd take offense to that."

"I'd do anything for her. How is that offensive?"

"Because she'd feel indebted to you."

"I want nothing in return."

"You want her. You just admitted that."

Deckard sighed. "Fine. I want her. But only if she'll have me."

"A compensation she'd feel obligated to provide," Hewitt said.

"So what are you saying?" Deckard asked with exasperation. "Because I care for her, she'll feel compelled to return the favor?"

Hewitt raised a hand to point toward the camp. "I'm saying she can't trust you because she knows you love her. And those feelings of yours will influence her decisions if she allows herself to love you back. You are dangerous to her. You can control her. Therefore, she cannot trust you, and she cannot love you."

Deckard stared back at him, open-mouthed and in a daze. What a convoluted fear the ghost described. Was that truly how Evylin felt? Was she afraid of losing herself to him? Did she think he'd require her to sacrifice her dreams for him? He would never ask that of her.

But perhaps she'd feel obliged to as repayment for a debt she incorrectly presumed herself to owe.

"Then I'll make it clear to her," he said. "She's never obligated to me in any way. If she wanted to live here in Wauld, I'd do it. If she asked me to tear down every tree in this forest, I'd do it. If she told me to leave her side and never come back, I'd do it."

Hewitt's expression showed marked contempt. "Your goodness is oppressive," he said.

Deckard had never felt so insulted.

"Do you think that's what she wants?" Hewitt demanded. "To have some vassal to cater to her every whim? That's not a husband. It's a servant."

An old refrain came to Deckard's mind. *A servant, through and through.* One of his lieutenants had said that the first night he'd met Evylin. It wasn't the first time he'd heard the sentiment. Many of his fellow officers had said the same thing, particularly in their recommendations on his behalf. But for the first time in his life, Deckard wondered whether or not it was a compliment.

Thirty-two years of training told him that Hewitt was wrong. He wasn't simply bowing to Evylin's fancies; he was caring for her. Love required sacrifice, always. His dedication to her happiness wasn't a weakness, nor was it oppressive. It was selfless devotion.

Shaking his head, Deckard chose to deny the ghost's conclusion. Hewitt had proven he was incapable of being impartial when it came to his niece. He'd admitted to the malignant condition of their relationship itself. They reinforced one another's grief. Together, they'd ensured that they'd never have to let go of the past. Whatever Hewitt thought he knew about Evylin, it was tainted with his memories of Ryen.

That didn't negate his usefulness, though.

"If that's the case," Deckard allowed, "how do I get her to trust me?"

Hewitt surveyed him thoughtfully before replying. "First, don't pledge your undying love and loyalty to her. She'll feel pressured. Then . . . be there. Plain and simple. Evylin needs to know that you aren't after something. Don't promise her the world, and don't offer yourself as a living sacrifice. Stand by her side, and when she asks for your help, only then are you to come to her aid.

"Until that moment," the man concluded, "live as though you'd never met her. She needs to feel independent of you to know that her feelings for you aren't brought on by a need to return some favor."

The instruction gave Deckard pause. "I can't stand by and watch her drown in the despair of her loss."

"That's not what I'm suggesting," Hewitt said. "When you see her drowning, you pull her to safety. Then you leave her there. Don't coddle her, and don't hover. Trust her to take care of herself."

"In other words," Deckard raised his brow, "be like you."

Hewitt considered it, then smirked. "Precisely."

"Should I begin insulting people while I'm at it?"

"It couldn't hurt."

Deckard let himself chuckle. The rain eased, the storm calming as though lifting with his mood. "I'd hate for her to come to think of me as her uncle," he remarked.

"Well, she would trust you more quickly, but it wouldn't do much for your odds of seduction, I'll tell you that."

"I should hope not." Deckard scanned the ghost before him, letting the truth hit him fully for the first time. "I never thought I'd see you again," he said.

"Can't say I thought I'd see anyone again once that branch split me in two."

Hanging his head, Deckard let himself feel the sorrow of Hewitt's loss once more. "We're not the same without you."

Hewitt's expression remained steady, though his eyes glimmered with something like gratitude. "You're probably better off."

"Never."

"Don't try to charm me, Colonel. I still don't like you."

Deckard smiled. "Regardless, I'm grateful for this chance. However it happened, for whatever reason I'm the only one who can see you—it doesn't matter. Because it allowed me to thank you and to promise you that I will do it: I will do whatever it takes to give Evylin the life she deserves."

Hewitt didn't respond at first. He stood there, studying Deckard. What he was looking for, Deckard didn't know. But he remained steady under his scrutiny.

Finally, Hewitt took a step back. "You should return," he said. "You've been gone too long."

Knowing that was as much approval as he'd ever get from the man, Deckard accepted it. "I'll come to see you again."

"I know."

With one last nod, Deckard turned, letting the ghost fade away, knowing that if he were ever to have a chance at helping Evylin heal, it would be with Hewitt's help.

CHAPTER SEVENTEEN

The rain let up on the way back to camp. Deckard removed his hood, grateful for the reprieve. Though his conversation with the ghost hadn't entirely alleviated his worries, knowing that he was the real Hewitt, not simply a figment of imagination, gave him hope.

Still, a sprig of doubt lingered within his head. When he thought he was only speaking to his subconscious, there was no real cause for alarm. It was an odd coping method, perhaps, but everyone went a little mad when they grieved. However, the revelation that Hewit was truly a ghost brought more questions with it. Such as: How had Hewitt become a ghost in the first place? And why was Deckard the only one who could see him?

Deckard had considered these things during their travel that day as he waited to visit Hewitt. He supposed that if Day represented life, then Night, as its mirror, must represent death. Perhaps Night magic held power over the souls of the dead, providing the opportunity to summon a ghost. The disturbing consideration led to a worrisome connection to Blount. Yet, Deckard couldn't imagine the answer lay with the Waulden prince either. What reason could Blount have to bring Hewitt's spirit back as a ghost?

Deckard thought to ask Auden or Ilain. Surely one of them would know these things. He didn't doubt that magic had more implications on life than he could currently comprehend.

Yes, he would ask the Calders if they knew about ghosts in an offhanded manner so they wouldn't be suspicious. After all, he still wasn't sure why only *he* could see Hewitt, and he didn't want Evylin to find out. Not when she had no way of seeing him too.

Laughter met Deckard as he neared the camp. The troop's disgruntled moods had evidently cleared away with the rain. Sitting in the meager light of the forest, Rafferty regaled them with a story about a noblewoman who'd asked him to procure a rare, illegal fur stole of a Schonese mountain cat. Evylin remained at his side, nibbling on the remains of her dinner. Ilain perched on the fork of a hawthorn, braiding her long curls as Thom sat by her feet. Auden scrubbed the pots, and Ethenn sharpened his knives, listening to Rafferty describing the chaotic process of securing the piece.

In their small camp, Deckard took the clearest, driest space he could find. He reached for the bowl of now lukewarm dinner left for him by the cold firepit. A slice of bread rested on the side.

Deckard picked it up. "Evie," he interrupted.

Across from him, Rafferty paused, and Evylin looked up. Deckard tossed her the slice, and with her reflexes, she caught it easily. Their eyes held for a lingering second. Then he went back to his meal without a word.

"You have a nice walk, Colonel?" Rafferty asked.

"I did," he said, scooping a spoonful of the barley and meat stew. "Please, return to your story."

The weasel-like man grinned. "Nah, it was finished, more or less. There're more interesting conversations to be had. Such as," he raised his white-blond eyebrows, "where'd you go off to?"

Deckard raised his chin, unsure of the reason for Rafferty's interest.

"Leave the poor man alone," Ilain said, tying off the end of her braid. She smiled teasingly at Deckard. "Some people just don't understand the need for solitude."

"Since when have you liked solitude?" Thom asked.

"Oh, never," she replied. "I'm just used to Auden."

Her brother raised his head. "It helps one to think more clearly," he said, then looked to Deckard. "Though I'm not sure it's the wisest course to go out alone."

"I'll take that under advisement," Deckard said, returning to his meal.

A beat of uncomfortable silence filled the camp before Rafferty nudged Evylin's side. "I've been thinking," he said.

"Here we go," Thom said.

Ilain jabbed his side with the toe of her boot, though she chuckled.

Rafferty ignored them both. "With Eve's discovery of the Relics' ability to turn into a sword and all that, do you think they could turn into other weapons?"

Ethenn looked up, intrigued.

"Hm." Auden pursed his lips in thought. "The *Almanac of Elgur* does depict them in various weapon forms. Though his writings are debated."

"Because he was crazy," Ilain muttered.

Auden sent her a disparaging look. "While I've not studied his work extensively," he continued. "He is one of the few ancient Mages whose works survive today. From what I understand, his experiments as a Time Mage were the foundation for passageways like the one we used to pass through the Day Keep into Night."

"So that's how that works?" Ethenn asked. "I was wondering."

"It's a combination of Time and Space magic," Auden confirmed. "I'm not well-versed in either, so I couldn't tell you exactly how it's done. But it's impressively detailed work, I can say that."

"Anyway," Rafferty drawled, "back to my question. Can the Relics turn into, say, a dagger? Or a bow? Maybe a hatchet. That could be fun."

Auden shrugged. "I don't know."

A mischievous glint lit Rafferty's silver eyes. "We could find out," he said, the amethyst pendant of the Night Relic suddenly dangling from his hand. Its dull gemstone hung with no sign of the magic hidden within its core.

Immediately, Evylin met Deckard's stare. He could feel her fear across the camp. His instinct was anger with Rafferty for suggesting it in the first place. The weasel knew of Evylin's struggle with the Day Relic. But then, Deckard realized, this was Night that the man offered. The one Relic Evylin would have absolutely no interest in keeping.

"I don't think that's necessary," Auden said.

"Necessary? No," Rafferty said, making the Relic spin in the air. "Fun, yes."

The highlord gave him an imperious glare. "Relics are not for *fun*. They are sacred artifacts from Allore's own hand."

Rafferty ignored him. "Colonel?"

Seeing the barest flicker of interest in Evylin's expression, Deckard decided to take Hewitt's advice and trust her to take care of herself. "I'm not the Warrior. Let Evylin decide."

Rafferty swayed the Night Relic temptingly in front of her face. "What'll it be, Eve?"

Evylin stared at the pendant, emotionless. Whatever thoughts were going through her mind, Deckard imagined they must be quite at war. It took several seconds before she jerked up from her seat, snagging the Relic as she stood.

An instant glow of deep violet light radiated from the Relic as it morphed into an elegant, curved short sword. The blade appeared to be crafted from a vibrant purple metal, with the cross guard, hilt, and pommel all of a darker amethyst hue. From his distance, Deckard couldn't see all the fine detail, but he could tell that the weapon was far more intricate than any smith could design.

They all stared at it in awe, Evylin most reverently of all. She slashed up, slicing clean through the branch above Rafferty. Thin and primarily leafy, it crashed on his head with a gentle *whoomp,* causing them all to laugh.

Rafferty shoved the branch off, his wily grin wide. "Try another," he said.

Evylin flicked her wrist, and the amethyst light of the short sword beamed brightly before shifting into a slender, metallic bow. Ethenn sat up straight, mouth ajar as gemstones shimmered in the bow's limbs.

Thom sniggered. "I think Ethenn's met the love of his life."

"Unfortunately," Rafferty quipped, "it's unrequited."

"Mm. Star-crossed lovers." Thom clucked his tongue. "Devastating."

Ethenn sent them both scathing glares.

Thoughtfully, Evylin ran her fingers along the bowstring. "I've never trained in archery," she admitted. Then she gave Ethenn an apologetic look. "It feels like a waste."

With a good-natured shrug, Ethenn tapped the fletching of the arrows beside him. "I'll teach you," he offered.

"She'll be a quick study," Ilain said. "Warriors are notoriously good with *all* weapons."

Of that, Deckard had no doubt.

The bow beamed again, and Evylin returned it to its Relic form. The gem radiated with power as she handed it back to Rafferty. It went dull the moment it left her touch.

"Why do they do that?" Rafferty asked as Evylin sat beside him once more.

"Go dim?" Ilain said. "Because non-magical individuals can't use them. Magic responds to magic. When a Relic senses a magical person, it lights up, connecting to their power."

Rafferty held the necklace before him, frowning in thought. "But aren't they magical storehouses or something? Shouldn't that mean that non-magical people can use them too?"

Ilain smirked drolly. "You have to *be* magical to access magic. Just like you have to *be* a woman to be this stunningly beautiful." She said the last while framing her face with a demure hand, batting her lashes dramatically.

Thom snorted, and she slapped the back of his head. "Ow! Yes, you're stunning, and I'm constantly in awe," he grumbled, rubbing the spot.

Eyeing the two of them, Deckard once again questioned their newfound flirtations. He couldn't decide whether or not he approved of the idea of their dalliance. While Ilain was strong-willed and wild, she was also dedicated and clever. He'd grown to appreciate the woman's presence. But he didn't know if she'd do well for his brother.

Or—a more important matter—if his brother would do well for her.

"So," Rafferty said contemplatively, "what you're saying is that someone *has* to be magical to use a Relic."

Ilain raised her brow. "That's exactly what I'm saying."

"And," he continued, "if someone is magical, then the Relic lights up all pretty-like when they hold it?"

A curious glimmer came into Ilain's eyes. "Yes."

Rafferty leaned forward, gaze locked with the woman. "Which follows, if a magical individual who didn't know they were magical held the Relic, the Relic would inform them that they're magical purely by the fact that it's glowing. Yes?"

Deckard wasn't sure he followed the convoluted question.

However, Ilain's smile grew. "I think you must have some theory."

"Ilain," Auden warned.

She ignored her brother, holding Rafferty's challenging stare.

Deckard narrowed his eyes, confused. The two were engaged in a silent conversation, challenging one another. He attempted to puzzle through the weasel's earlier question but found his mind too baffled by the twisting words to remember them all. His conclusion was that whatever theory Rafferty had, he believed someone in their party had magic that they didn't know about. And that sounded downright preposterous.

"Put the Relic away, Rafferty," Deckard ordered.

Eyes still locked with Ilain's, Rafferty spun the Relic's chain around his finger, letting it flip into his palm. "Sure thing, Colonel," he said. Then he flung the necklace through the air straight at Deckard's face.

On instinct, Deckard raised his hand, catching it.

"What are you—?" Deckard cut himself off, finding the Night Relic a vibrant purple in his grasp. The facets of the amethyst stone beamed like moonlight as he turned it over in his hand.

He blinked, looking down at the glowing gemstone. He'd never seen one so closely before. A strangely familiar heat raced across his skin as he studied the etching along the gold pendant. It reminded him of his dreams after the Day and Night Keep. He realized the Relic in the second dream was identical to the one now in his hand. He wondered if the Day Relic would match too.

"Why is it glowing?" Thom asked, bringing Deckard back to the present.

The revelation hit Deckard suddenly: The Night Relic was glowing.

In *his* hand.

Deckard's eyes met Evylin's, confused. She stared back at him, her lips parted in shock. He turned to the Calders. "What is this?" He raised the Relic toward them. "Why is it glowing?"

Slowly and almost hysterically, Ilain began to laugh. She leaped out of the hawthorn and pointed at Auden. "I *told* you!" She cheered. "I told you back in Loclight, and you didn't believe me!"

Auden looked as though he'd been handed a sack full of potatoes and been told they were made of gold. He scratched his copper beard and mumbled, "Seems you were right."

Wishing that someone would show a shred of sanity, Deckard rose from his seat. "I don't understand what's going on," he said, brandishing the Relic at the two of them. "Why would this be glowing?"

"I think it's rather obvious, Jonn," Ilain said wryly.

Though he knew—he understood the truth and *knew* the answer—Deckard shook his head. His eyes found Evylin's once more across the camp. He couldn't read her expression, restrained and thoughtful as it was. The tight set of her mouth and narrowed slant of her eyes could convey a multitude of emotions. However, he wasn't sure that any of them were positive.

He turned back to Ilain. "No," he said decisively. "It's not possible. There's been some mistake."

"Relics don't make mistakes," Auden said.

Deckard shook his head even more furiously, holding the Relic out to Rafferty. The weasel just stared at him with a knowing smile. "Take it back," he ordered.

Rafferty shrugged. "Won't change the facts, Colonel."

Deckard stepped forward, thrusting the Relic at him. "Take—it—back," he commanded. He wasn't sure why he was so desperate to be free of the thing. But his mind couldn't reconcile the beaming stone in his hand. He couldn't accept the truth it offered. He wanted it as far from him as possible.

When it was clear Rafferty wouldn't do as requested, Deckard scanned the rest of his companions. They all stared at him: Auden and Ethenn with awe, Ilain and Rafferty with smug satisfaction, and Evylin and Thom with disbelief. And all of it made his skin crawl with panic.

"No," Deckard said again, now emitting a nervous chuckle. He thrust the Relic into Rafferty's lap, the purple gem falling instantly lifeless. Then he turned to Ilain, sure to show his determination in his expression. "No."

Ilain practically bounced with her uncontainable joy. "You can't run from it, Jonn. No matter what, you know now. And the magic will work its way out, however it must."

"I am not magical!" he exclaimed.

"You are!"

"Lain," Auden said cautiously. "Be careful. If you get him too riled, he may lose control."

Deckard glared at him. "Control of what? I don't have magic."

The Mages gave him a look that said he was behaving like a petulant child. *Which,* Deckard's most mature self told him, *you are.*

"I don't understand," Evylin said, her voice thin. "How is this possible? Is Jonn a . . . a Warrior?"

Though Ilain began to speak, Auden shot her a fierce glare. The woman pressed her lips together and sat down. Then the highlord turned to Rafferty. "Would you give the Relic back to Jonn, please?"

Rafferty held it aloft.

Begrudgingly and only to prove them wrong, Deckard took it. The amethyst light beamed accusingly once more.

"Try to turn it into a weapon," Auden instructed.

"How?" Deckard asked.

"Think about what you want it to become," Evylin said. "Any weapon. It'll listen."

Deckard sighed and thought about the short sword she'd summoned earlier. He flicked his wrist as he'd seen her do. Nothing happened.

Auden nodded. "As I suspected," he said.

"What?" Evylin asked.

"Jonn is a Mage."

The statement struck Deckard like the Day Guardian's talons, slicing open his gut. He looked down at the Relic. The impossibility of it all sapped the rest of his strength to argue anymore.

He looked up at Auden. "I thought you said that Ephrians can't be Mages."

"We've already established that you aren't wholly Ephrian," he replied.

"When did we establish that?" Thom demanded.

"Just after we arrived in Wauld," Ethenn said, turning one of his knives thoughtfully. "We were discussing why Blount wants the Relics, and Auden suggested that it's because he wants to control the whole continent so that he controls all magic along with it. Mages *and* Warriors."

Auden gave the hunter a nod. "Exactly. Ilain and I have recognized the signs of the West in both Deckard brothers. Though more predominantly in Jonn."

Thom shook his head. "That's not possible. The war put a stop to cross-border dalliances almost two centuries ago."

"Unless," Deckard frowned, "they snuck in like some other Wauldeners we know."

The group glanced at the Calders. Deckard considered Auden's previous point about the signature Waulden characteristics: red hair, lean figure, pale complexion, excessive height, and sharp features. He could admit that, aside from Thom, he looked far more like the Calders than any of the rest of their troop.

Thom opened his mouth to argue, then paused. "Grandfather," he said.

With a sigh, Deckard shrugged. "It was one of Father's favorite stories," he said. "No one knew Grandfather's family. He showed up one day, seeking work. Said he'd chosen to make a better life for himself away from the border. He even had a strange accent."

Reluctantly, Thom nodded. "Mother got her red hair from him."

Deckard sighed. "And she passed it down to me."

Their grandfather's story replayed through his memories. Marc Reid, a twenty-something traveler, arrived in Stocburrough with nothing but the clothes on his back and a handful of coins in his pocket. He sought trade as a day laborer around the farms in exchange for meals and a place to sleep, impressing the village with his efficient work and steady character. Soon, he met the Duncaan family and fell in love with their only daughter, Lizelle. They married shortly after and began a family of their own. Their youngest, Serah, grew to wed Mathes Deckard, and thus Jonn, Thom, and their sister, Meria, were born.

Throughout his entire childhood, Deckard remembered their father telling the story of the red-haired stranger who won the whole village's loyalty. But now, he wondered if they knew who their grandfather had been at all. Marc was a common name; Reid, an even more common surname in Ephria. Was it possible that he'd fabricated his entire identity to hide his Waulden heritage?

"It doesn't prove anything," Deckard said, unwilling to concede. "He said he was from the border. It could have been the Ephrian side."

"Does it matter?" Ilain asked. "Whether it was your grandfather or *his* grandfather, you're a Mage. Which means someone in your ancestry was Waulden."

"Which means . . ." Rafferty raised his brows, turning to Thom.

Lips parting, Thom sucked in a sharp breath. "I have Waulden blood too."

Ilain folded her hands demurely on her lap. "Your most desirable quality."

"So," Ethenn said, "Thom could be a Mage too?"

"Technically," Rafferty said, "he's more Ephrian than he is Waulden. So he could be either, right? Mage or Warrior. Or . . . both?"

"Either or neither," Auden said. "Never both."

"Ah, well." Rafferty shrugged, then sent another Relic flying across the camp toward Thom. "Heads up, Thommy-boy."

Deckard watched nervously. The determination of Thom's magical status would impact more than their chances at success. Their entire lives, Thom had been desperate to prove his worth. Proving to have magic would finally validate that worth. But if it were discovered that Deckard was magical and Thom was not, it would be another barrier between them. Another chance for Thom to see himself as the lesser brother and Deckard as the golden child.

With almost frantic anticipation, Thom sprang forward to catch the Fire Relic. It landed securely in his grasp, and they all leaned forward to see . . . nothing. The ruby remained dull and lifeless as it had in Rafferty's hands.

Thom's gaze locked with Deckard's, a flatness in their icy gray-blue depths. "Guess not," he muttered.

Ilain sighed dramatically. "Well, your value to me just decreased exponentially."

Thom glowered at her.

"Don't get yourself in a tizzy," she said. "I'm a precious commodity. I can't go marrying a non-Warrior."

"Whoever said I want to marry you?" Thom replied sourly, then tossed the Relic back to Rafferty.

"Can we not throw sacred magical artifacts around, please?" Auden said incredulously.

Seeing the disappointment in Thom's hardened expression, Deckard attempted to move the conversation forward. Night Relic still in hand, he held Auden's gaze. "Are you sure about this?" he asked.

"Quite sure," he confirmed. "As Ilain said, she's suspected for a while now. I was skeptical, but there were always signs."

"Like what?"

"Your time in the Keeps," Evylin muttered.

Rafferty nudged her arm. "My thinking exactly, Eve. After our failed trials with my previous theory, I thought: Why *is* the Colonel so much better in the Keeps? It's not like Ethenn's skills are that much improved during our mad dashes. He's always been obnoxiously impressive."

Ethenn's thick eyebrows rose, but he didn't reply.

"That was just one of the signs," Ilain interjected. "Other notable instances: You discovered the Keeps and heard the Shades early along with Auden and me, which is supposed to be nearly impossible, and you heal far too rapidly. Beyond that and your uncanny improvement in the Keeps, what more evidence do you need?"

Deckard pinched the bridge of his nose. It was becoming more and more difficult to deny it. He couldn't say exactly why the idea bothered him so much. Perhaps it was because he'd grown up his whole life hearing that Mages were evil incarnate, that they staunchly opposed the Allorian faith. And while he knew the Calders contradicted that dogma, it stuck in his brain.

What was more, he didn't like the weight that came with being magical. It was fine for Evylin. He'd always known she was special, a step above every other woman he'd met. Magic explained why. But for him . . . ?

Deckard was a soldier. He was a servant. That was all he aspired to be. If he became a Mage, that meant his entire identity would change. No longer an officer following the orders of his superiors, but a magical being, revered and dominant.

Yet, there was no way to contest the truth. Not with this Relic still glowing in his hand.

Deckard handed it back to Rafferty, telling him to put them all away. He turned to Auden once more. "What does this mean?" he asked.

"First," Auden said, "it means that our mission's chance of success has greatly increased. The Alliance will certainly want to continue working with you in the future as well. And it means you will have to train."

"And what if I choose not to work with the Alliance?" Deckard asked.

Auden looked disappointed but didn't challenge him. "Then they'll allow you to go your separate way. However, I wouldn't advise it. Once you begin to use magic, it starts to impact the rest of your life. You'd be hard-pressed to return to a normal one."

"More importantly," Ilain said, a twinkle in her eyes, "you're a Mage who's married to a Warrior."

Deckard's expression went slack. He glanced at Evylin, her shoulders ramrod straight. "What does that have to do—" He paused, remembering his conversation with Auden two days ago. "Bonding," he whispered.

Ilain nodded enthusiastically.

"What's that?" Evylin demanded. "What does that mean?"

Deckard saw the disaster coming before he could stop it. This was exactly what Hewitt had warned him against. Evylin wouldn't see Bonding as anything but a shackle— one more link in the chain that fixed her to him. She'd see it as a means of his control over her.

But he couldn't stop Ilain from answering.

"Warriors and Mages are meant to be together," the woman said with reverence. "Our powers are designed to be in balance. They strengthen and enhance each other. And that's when they're not even Bonded."

Ilain gripped a branch of the hawthorn, leaning forward in her passion. "When a Warrior and a Mage Bond, they take an oath of complete and total trust. They fuse their souls, becoming of one power, one mind, and one heart. It is an unbreakable vow, even more hallowed than the sacrament of marriage."

A cold breeze rustled through the trees, sending a shiver down Deckard's spine. Insects chirruped in the night, filling the silence. He didn't bother assessing the men's reactions. He only cared to see Evylin's response.

She sat there, face blank and shoulders back. The only sign of her discontent was her fingers, locked on her rings. "Why can't it be broken?" she asked flatly.

"It's magically induced," Auden explained. "To break the Bond would be literal suicide."

"Not that anyone would want to break their Bond," Ilain said flippantly. "As I said, it's a binding of hearts. If the pair weren't already in love, they would be shortly after. Which," she grinned knowingly, "obviously doesn't change anything between the two of you."

Slowly, Evylin met Deckard's stare. He hoped she could see the disapproval in his gaze. He would not ask her to make any such vows to him.

Deckard met Ilain's gleaming stare. "Nor does it mean anything to us," he replied with resolve. "As it doesn't apply to our situation."

"Of course, it applies," Ilain retorted. "You're a Mage, and she's a Warrior. *Not* Bonding would be ridiculous."

"That's out of the question. I've no interest in living my life as a Mage."

She scoffed. "Too bad. You are one."

"That doesn't mean I have to act as one."

Ilain pursed her lips as though he were being foolish. However, Auden spoke for her. "I would hope," he said calmly, "that you'd care to act as one in our present circumstance. As I said, our odds of securing the Relics and saving our countries become far more achievable with your power, whatever it may be."

Auden glanced at Evylin thoughtfully before continuing. "And there is no reason to rush a decision regarding the Bond. Even if you should desire it, it isn't something that could be accomplished during our travels. Such a sacred ceremony requires a specific set of rituals. Be that as it may," his tone lightened, "even not Bonded, a Warrior and a Mage joined in the holy sacrament of marriage carry a great deal more power than those of us who remain single. Together, your and Evylin's powers will be significantly more potent."

Despite himself, Deckard felt his heart stir at the thought. The way the Calders spoke, it sounded as though he and Evylin were meant for each other. Almost as though Allore had designed them specifically for each other. Even if that wasn't true, it felt like a confirmation—providence telling them they were destined for one another.

And yet, Deckard needed to reject every word to ensure his wife wouldn't see their unique union as a cage.

He looked at Evylin, tension filling his whole body. He had to fix this before it was too late. He had to prove to her that he wouldn't use this as a means of confining her. Hewitt said she needed to feel independent, free to make her own choices. So he had to make sure she understood: This would change nothing between them.

Deckard turned to the Calders. "This isn't fate," he said decisively, even if he wasn't sure about it himself. "Evylin's and my relationship isn't because of our magic."

"Certainly not," Ilain confirmed. "Love isn't destiny. It's a choice. But magic certainly helps *foster* that choice."

Raising his chin, Deckard directed his next words specifically to Auden. "I take it, this means you'll want to train me."

"Absolutely," Auden said. "It'd be best to start immediately. We only have five more days until we reach the Wind Keep. Getting your power under control should be our primary focus."

Deckard nodded. "Tomorrow. In the meantime," he said, meeting Evylin's hard stare, "could I speak with you privately?"

Slowly and silently, Evylin rose.

"We'll be back shortly," Deckard said. He pointed a finger at Rafferty. "No more playing with Relics."

The weasel saluted. "As you say, Highlord Colonel."

Pulling in a deep breath, Deckard moved out of the camp. He didn't bother checking to be sure Evylin followed. He knew she would. Deckard curled his hands into fists under his cloak, determined to mitigate this disaster before he lost his wife for good.

CHAPTER EIGHTEEN

Evylin could practically hear Hewitt's voice in her head. *"Rubbish,"* he'd say. *"Deckard's no more magical than I am."*

And yet, there was no denying the bright glow of the Night Relic when it touched Deckard's hand. Not when it had filled the whole camp with its radiant amethyst glow. Evylin wasn't even sure if he'd noticed that detail, just how strongly the magical glow had been projected. He was so focused on refusing the revelation that she doubted he saw the luminous beams that cast a purple tint over each of their comrades and the forest around them.

It was as though the Night had grown stronger simply by Deckard's touch upon the Relic.

No, the truth could not be denied: By the hand of Allore, Deckard had been born a Mage.

And it made her chest squeeze like a vise.

Evylin's hands trembled as she rose from her seat beside Rafferty. She followed Deckard into the trees, her mind roiling with confusion, and . . . was that fear? She didn't know why she should be afraid of this discovery. If anything, it should bring her relief. Deckard was a Mage, and their mission was sure to succeed.

"A Mage who's married to a Warrior." Ilain's words repeated like a warning bell. *"Warriors and Mages are meant to be together."*

Meant to be. As though Evylin had never had any say in the matter at all. She had been unknowingly born a Warrior and he a Mage. Of course, they'd meet and marry. Of course, they'd fall in love. Of course, they'd want to enter that sacred Bond, tying themselves together so intimately that parting would bring literal death.

Why wouldn't they want that?

She remembered Auden's words when they'd gone into the Water Keep, just the two of them. He'd told her about the tie between Warrior and Mage, that they sometimes chose to be a binding force, dedicated to one another by an oath. While he'd assured her that *they* would never choose to make such an oath with each other, she now knew that even if the Calders wouldn't make them Bond, the Alliance would.

"They fuse their souls, becoming of one power, one mind, and one heart," Ilain said. *". . . it's a binding of hearts. If the pair weren't already in love, they would be shortly after."*

Evylin glared at the dirt, following the depressions of Deckard's boots. But she felt no joy in it this time. Intentionally, she stepped around his footprints.

The Calders clearly didn't understand the nature of their relationship. They couldn't know their marriage was in name only or that she intended to keep it that way. Only yesterday, she'd completely given him up. She couldn't lose herself to him through something as irrevocable as a magical Bond. She was beginning to wonder if she could be with him, or even be around him, at all.

Evylin's eyes drifted to the hem of Deckard's cloak. It flapped around his ankles heavily, splattered with dirt. Though he'd vehemently rejected the idea of Bonding, her heart clenched with worry. Why had he wanted to speak with her so immediately? Was he already intending to use his newfound magical status as a lever to ensure their marriage? Would he try to appeal to her sense of religious duty as divinely gifted individuals?

She didn't think she could bear that. Even if Deckard didn't mean to manipulate her, there was a chance his altruism would feel a compulsion toward their cause.

All too soon, Deckard came to a stop. Gray shadows crept around the forest, coloring the trees and foliage with a soot-like appearance. Under the thick canopy and cloudy sky, not even the light of the two moons seeped through. It seemed the night chose to mimic their heavy mood.

Drawing back his shoulders, Deckard turned to face her. His eyes were piercing, and his pale skin contrasted sharply with the darkness all around them. With his hood down, his hair had a deep brown cast. He looked like a haunted version of himself, devoid of his usual optimism.

Deckard opened his mouth to speak, but nothing came out. He shook his head, pacing the moss-and-mud-covered forest floor.

Evylin watched silently. Whatever he had to say, she wasn't in any rush to hear it. She crossed her arms against the frigid air and waited.

"This is impossible," Deckard muttered at last.

When she didn't respond, he looked up. "Isn't it?" he asked as though in need of her validation.

"What do you want me to say?" Evylin asked. "Based on the evidence, I can't refute it."

He scoffed brokenly. "I can't . . . be *that*."

Something in his voice struck Evylin. Its lifted pitch, almost as if he were questioning her—begging her to confirm it wasn't true—drew her a step closer. She didn't think she'd ever seen him so undone. Even after Hewitt's death, when he'd been on the verge of tears, he'd remained solid and steady. Now, he was unraveling, becoming a version of himself that she hadn't known existed.

Unable to give him the confirmation he sought, Evylin let sympathy fill her voice. "Whatever we thought we knew before," she said, holding his gaze, "it's changed now. The Relic can't be wrong."

"I'm not like you, Evylin," he said falteringly. "I'm not magical or special. I'm only a soldier."

"Clearly, that's not all you are." Seeing his disappointment, she shook her head. "I don't understand this any better than you. But the Calders are right. Looking back, you have shown signs since the start of our time with them."

"That's—" He cut off his own argument with a frustrated sigh.

Evylin tossed her arms to the side, irritated as well. "Why did you bring me out here? To complain that you're magical? To refuse the obvious truth?"

"It doesn't make sense," he insisted.

"No, it doesn't. It's too convenient. Yet, however it happened, it's true. So why are we out here?"

Deckard ran both hands through his overgrown curls. "Because," he mumbled.

"Because what?"

"Because I don't know what to do, Evylin!" he exclaimed. His eyes searched the forest frantically, as if looking for an escape. "This shouldn't be happening. You're supposed to be the magical one, and I'm only here to stand by your side. That was why Hewitt chose me. I'm not the one who matters; you are. It's my job to protect you, not to become some—some . . . magical *legend*."

Evylin drew back, one of Hewitt's earliest assessments of Deckard returning to her. After his speech in Whickam Village, Hewitt had concluded that the then-captain had left his home village to do just that—become a legend. In the face of reality, her uncle said, the soldier had told himself that his greatest desire was to be a servant, making his inability to achieve such a lofty dream easier to bear.

As Evylin and Ryen had vowed to become legends worth five hundred tales themselves, she could understand such a dubious hope. Yes, she wanted to follow her and her cousin's dreams. But they, too, had seemed impossible. She, too, had mitigated her expectations by telling herself that she was happy enough with the independence life in Whickam Village offered her. Until she met Deckard, and he offered her a chance at her and Ryen's dreams.

Though Evylin had never decided whether or not she agreed with her uncle's assessment of Deckard's personal goals, she considered it anew. Was that why Deckard was so opposed to being a Mage? In the sudden realization of his dreams coming to life, did he fear it? When you relegated your ambition to fantasy, its reality was sometimes too frightening to accept.

Whatever the case, Evylin knew that the truth wouldn't help in the moment at hand. Not when Deckard was so frantic and irrational.

Instead, she looked up at him with a steady gaze. "I still don't know what you want me to say."

Pleadingly, Deckard held out his hands. "I want you to tell me what to do."

Evylin furrowed her brow. "I fail to see how that's my responsibility."

"This—all of this," he said, voice thick and insistent, "is for *you*. I lost the bet, remember? The whole point of our marriage was to get you out of Whickam Village and to give you the life you wanted. So I need you to tell me: What do you want?"

Evylin gaped at him, her pulse spiking. "You promised that I wouldn't have to make a decision yet."

"That's not what I'm asking."

"Then what *are* you asking?"

He stepped closer, a fierceness in his stare that frightened her. "Do you want me to be a Mage?"

Her lips parted before she even knew what she wanted to say. "No," she breathed.

His expression eased.

"But I don't think we have a choice," she concluded.

Once more, Deckard's jaw tensed. "I don't have to train. If this is all true, then I lived thirty-two years without using magic. That doesn't have to change."

Though sure he meant well, Evylin couldn't help feeling annoyed. He was too ready to sacrifice himself for her. Too willing to give up something of great benefit to him and the rest of the world, all to make her happy. There were bigger futures at play than simply their own.

"We are fighting a war, Jonn. One that's lasted for more than a century. Whether we like it or not, the discovery of your powers, whatever they may be, can help us *win*. You can't ignore it because you want to convince me to stay with you."

He flinched as though she'd hit him. Then he drew himself up, his gaze growing flat. "That's not what this is," he said without emotion.

"Then what is it?"

He scoffed; whether at himself or her, she didn't know. "I'm tired, Evylin. And I don't particularly enjoy trying to persuade my wife to stay married to me. So, no, this is not about convincing you. If you told me you wanted to go home today, I'd happily escort you back to your father and tell him to annul the damn thing."

Evylin's brow twitched at his harsh words.

"I only have one objective—" Deckard pressed his hands together before him like an adamant prayer. "I want to keep my word to your uncle. He made me promise to make you happy. Well, here I am, trying to make you happy. So what do you want me to do?"

"Don't put this on me," she shot back. "If you don't want to be a Mage, then fine. But don't blame me when you're the one being selfish."

"So you'd be fine with all of it then?" He tossed a hand toward the camp. "If I start training tomorrow, if I become a Mage, you won't care?"

Evylin blinked, wanting to say no but feeling the immediate weight of the Calders' expectations, of the Alliance's expectations. If Deckard accepted his role as a Mage, it could lead to them being forced to Bond as a matter of course.

Deckard recognized her hesitation. "*This* is why I want to be selfish, Evie," he said. "Yes, I know that having another Mage would make our quest easier. Yes, it could end the war in weeks or months, rather than years. But it will also make you uncomfortable."

"So my comfort is worth the continuation of a war?" she asked dejectedly.

Now, it was his turn to hesitate.

Evylin shook her head. "You're not that selfish."

"Perhaps I am," he said sharply. "Perhaps your comfort is an excuse."

"And you'll let the continent fall to Blount to placate your fear? I don't believe it."

"Then what will you believe?"

"Why are we arguing about this? Do you want to be a Mage?" she demanded.

"No," he said instantly.

"Then don't be one. Let the world fall to rubble. Who cares if people die?"

"Who's to say my becoming a Mage will stop that?"

Evylin let out an exasperated huff. "If you're convinced that remaining as merely a normal soldier won't ruin the world, then why are we still talking about it?"

He clamped his jaw shut, and she knew the answer.

"You can't help being a martyr, can you?" she said coldly. "You want me to tell you not to be a Mage simply so you don't have to feel guilty for rejecting the responsibility. I won't do that, Jonn. This is not a decision that we have to make together because it's not a decision that's relevant to me."

"That's where you're wrong," Deckard said. He took a step closer, pointing between the two of them. "The Calders believe this is real. They think that you and I love one another. And the Alliance is desperate for Warriors and Mages who can be Bonded together."

Evylin frowned, her worries realized. "Do you know that for sure?"

He began to nod, slowly and damningly. "Auden told me that they need eight Bonded couples to carry the Relics at the end of all this. And they are in drastically short supply of female Warriors."

A horrible suspicion crept up Evylin's spine.

"Married," Deckard continued, "you and I are a valuable asset. Single, we are *two* valuable assets."

Evylin instantly understood. "If they find out we aren't truly married, they'll make us marry someone else."

Deckard's sharp stare confirmed it.

She pressed her lips together, considering. "So . . . it's Bond with you or Bond with another stranger."

His eyes narrowed at her choice of words, but he didn't comment on her equating him with a stranger. "It seems probable," he admitted. "However, if I don't become a Mage, then this isn't an issue. We can continue with our lives as before, and neither the Calders nor the Alliance ever have to discover the status of our marriage."

A small fragment of hope eased Evylin's worry. Deckard was right. If he didn't train as a Mage, then the Alliance couldn't hope to make them Bond. They could make it through this mission the same as they always had, pretending to be a true couple. No one would question them, and no one would force her to marry someone else.

The thought gave Evylin pause. "So that's what this is about," she realized. "You're worried that I'd choose another Mage over you."

Deckard pinched the bridge of his nose. But instead of looking guilty, he just looked more annoyed. "Evylin," he said her name with a long-suffering sigh. "When will you realize that I'm not trying to control you? I'm presenting you with the information and giving you a choice. I can accept the fact that I'm a Mage, take Auden and Ilain's training, and give us greater odds of success. Or I can reject it and ensure that the Alliance never asks us to do anything we don't want to. Either way, at the end of this, whether you ask for an annulment or to spend the rest of our lives together, I will not hesitate to give you whatever you request."

His words fell on Evylin with such deep exhaustion, a weariness that spoke of such prolonged strain, that it almost hurt. She could see it in the lines of his face, in the furrow of his brow, in the downturn of his lips. He was sincere . . . and he was done.

Deckard had given up attempting to woo her. He was done with hoping for her love. No matter her past affection for him or their fledgling romance prior to Hewitt's death, her prolonged indecision and brokenhearted rejection had driven him to such fatigue that he wasn't merely on the verge of giving up: He had already.

Evylin tried to tell herself that it was good. That was what she wanted, what they needed. If she was going to put space between them, if she was going to protect herself and ensure she never had to endure the pain of his loss, she couldn't hope for a better outcome. If Deckard gave up, she wouldn't have to fight him—or her feelings—anymore.

Yet, her heart clenched, aching at the thought that she'd driven him away.

Spurning the feeling, Evylin pressed her hands against her thighs rather than twisting her rings. She returned to the matter at hand, accepting the gift of his detachment. "What if the Alliance doesn't care what we want?" she asked. "Like Ilain said, you're a Mage, and the magic will eventually find a way out, now that it's begun to reveal itself. The Alliance may force you to train; they may insist you accept the role and our future Bond."

"I'd like to believe we're working for a better organization than that," Deckard said, though she could hear the skepticism in his tone. "Unfortunately, I fear that you may be right. They may give us no alternative. But that wouldn't happen until after we complete our mission with the Calders."

"Giving me time to make a decision," she surmised.

He raised his chin in reluctant confirmation.

Evylin's fingers twitched. She settled them on the hilt of the dagger at her hip. It was the one she'd taken from Deckard that night in the rain. The one with rosettes etched onto the pommel. She'd never told him her middle name; he couldn't know the design's significance to her.

Yet, when she was wearing the Day Relic, she'd liked to imagine that he did know. That he'd chosen the dagger specifically because of her: Evylin Rosette. Now, holding his serious green-blue gaze in the night, she was glad he hadn't.

She'd known for a while. Deckard had confessed his attraction and romantic interest to her long ago. In response, she had felt a budding affection within her own heart. Throughout their short marriage, they'd both succumbed to the early stages of romance. But while Evylin hadn't allowed herself to feel more than a passing fancy, she knew that Deckard's desire for her had grown beyond mere attraction, whether he would admit it aloud or not.

When it had happened, Evylin didn't know. When in the course of their mutually beneficial arrangement did it turn into a true romance? How had he come to harbor deep feelings for her? She knew she had both inadvertently and intentionally encouraged his feelings. She felt guilty now for retracting her previous invitations and expressions of regard.

Despite her deepening attachment to him, despite her intent to be his true wife only weeks ago, at last she knew the truth: She could not love him. Should they make it through this dangerous journey unscathed, she might reconsider. If they went somewhere peaceful and safe, where she never had to fear what loving him would do to her, she might be able to entrust her heart to his care then.

However, the chance for that future seemed slim. As a Warrior, the Alliance wouldn't want her to go off to live a simple life. And Evylin didn't think she'd like that either. The urge for something "more" was why she'd left Whickam Village in the first place. Simplicity didn't suit her. She—and Ryen, before his death—was meant for wild adventure, not for rote mundanity.

So what was she to choose? A life of pain with Deckard or a chance of emotionless safety with someone else.

Either way, for her to make the decision, they'd all have to make it through this mission.

"We're being foolish," Evylin muttered. "This isn't something you can simply ignore, Jonn. You're a Mage. You've always been one, even if you didn't realize it until the Keeps drew it out of you. And if we want to succeed, you need to accept that."

Deckard looked crestfallen. "So you want me to train?"

"I don't see another choice."

His shoulders drooped, and he stared out into the forest for several aching seconds. Finally, he spoke again with a tone of hollow acceptance. "I didn't ask for this, Evylin," he said, almost as though begging her to understand. "If given the choice, I would have lived the rest of my life never knowing."

At first, Evylin didn't understand why he felt the need to tell her this. She frowned, slowly realizing that this was his way of assuring her that he didn't want to Bond any more than she did. A fact that she doubted but chose to believe.

Still, it didn't change their greater problem.

"We can't let the Calders find out about the status of our marriage," she said. "I will be honest with you, Jonn, I . . . I would like to stay with you. But I'm not ready to make that choice when my heart is still broken."

Deckard watched her, lips parted as though surprised by her admission.

"Regardless of our future choices," she continued, "the Calders can't know that our marriage can be dissolved—that we aren't in love."

Though he hesitated, Deckard nodded.

Evylin clenched her jaw, facing the unwelcome truth. "Which means that we'll have to make them believe that it's real."

Cautiously, he watched her as if she were a wild animal that could be easily startled if he moved or spoke too suddenly.

She ignored the agitation his careful movements stirred within her and went on, "We have to return to the couple we were before."

"You're still in mourning," he said gently. "They wouldn't expect that to change overnight."

"It's been weeks."

"And Auden knows what you went through with the Relic." He stepped forward in a near-comforting manner. "Nothing has to change. I promised you time, and I meant it. They don't have to understand what the distance between us means, because they'll believe it's only a reflection of your recovery."

Though Evylin was grateful for his surprising willingness to give her space, she shook her head. "It can't go on forever, Jonn. If I'm to play the role, I can't push you away. A woman who loves her husband would take solace in him."

"Not if the woman blamed her husband," he argued. "Auden was there, remember? He heard you blame me. And he knows that I took the Relic from you. Which is yet another reason for your distance. He'll believe it if you hold me at arm's length for a time."

"And you think that will convince them?"

"They don't know the purpose of our marriage." He raised his brow encouragingly. "They have no reason to doubt us."

Evylin should have felt lightened by his offer. It should have eased her fears. She could keep the distance between them without the worry of alerting the Calders. Deckard would become a Mage, their chances of survival would rise, and she could protect what little of her heart remained intact.

So why did she feel so disappointed?

"All right," she murmured, then took a restoring breath that fell woefully short. "You will train, and in the meantime, we'll remain as we are."

"This will change nothing," he promised.

But Evylin knew that wasn't true.

As they walked back to camp, a detached distance between them, she knew that everything had changed. No matter if they duped the Calders with their act, no matter if the Alliance never forced their hand, in the playful toss of a Relic, Deckard himself had changed. He wasn't the captain she'd married; he wasn't the friend she'd come to know. He was a Mage now. And according to Ilain, that meant he was all but made for Evylin.

The thought rankled in her chest like a wound improperly stitched together. She didn't want to be destined for Deckard. Her life was already filled with devastation and bone-deep pain. She'd lost Ryen. She'd lost Hewitt. If her heart were bound to Deckard's, if their very existence was drawing them together, then the loss of him would be beyond compare.

The rain began again as they walked back to camp. They pulled their hoods over their heads, and Evylin sank into her resolve. If she wasn't going to stay with Deckard, then she had to be certain she wasn't damning herself to a life of misery. Destiny, fate, serendipity, Allore's divine influence—whatever the Mages wanted to call it. She would not be beholden to their dictates. Not when she'd already lost too much.

CHAPTER NINETEEN

7TH OF CHRONOS, 1574

When they returned to the camp the previous night, Ethenn and Ilain were already on watch, while the rest of the troop attempted to slumber in the downpour of rain. Good to his word, Deckard allowed Evylin to sleep facing away from him again, their backs still pressed together. He'd done all he could to follow Hewitt's advice, easing her anxieties while giving her the space and independence she desired.

But even in the newness of morning, Deckard felt that he'd failed. The conversation with Evylin nearly turned to disaster. He could never have anticipated how unsettled he would be by the revelation of his magic. Seeing the Night Relic glow, lighting the circle of the camp, and knowing what that glow meant frightened him like few things did. And while he'd intended to alleviate her fears, he'd fallen apart before her.

Yet, she'd shown no surprise, as though his breakdown was expected. How had she known? How had she called out his fear so blatantly? He *had* wanted her to refuse his magical nature to save him from the responsibility. She'd seen his selfishness and refused to let him hide from it.

Deckard wasn't the sort to run from duty. He'd always taken on tasks with his steady dedication, no matter their difficulty. But this was different.

Discovering that he was a Mage felt wrong. He couldn't explain it, not when he had come to appreciate magic over the course of their time with the Calders. Perhaps Ephren's annihilation of all things magical was too deeply embedded in Deckard's psyche. After all, he'd been taught his whole life that Mages were evil incarnate. Even though they were meant to be creatures of myth, the church itself denounced them as demons, creatures from hell.

Maybe that was what bothered Deckard so much. He'd always taken his faith seriously, more than even his parents had. When it came down to it, he felt that if religion were true, it ought to dictate one's lifestyle. And while life as a soldier didn't lend itself to a devout routine, he did his best to stay attuned to his faith.

Now, the Calders were teaching him that the church was wrong, their truths tainted by Ephren's propaganda. He had decided he could believe that without letting it alter his convictions because the inclusion of magic didn't change the foundation of their religion: Their creator was Allore, and all life was meant for him.

Evylin's magic inspired him. Ilain and Auden's magic awed him. He could easily regard their powers as a gift from Allore.

Then why did he fear magic in himself?

Riding through the misty morning, Deckard struggled with the hollow feeling in his stomach. He rode at the front of the line in silence. Evylin was with the three soldiers, evidently enjoying their company. He'd intentionally allowed her distance, doing all he could to abide by Hewitt's guidelines, no matter how much it hurt him. And after how clearly she'd seen to the core of his fear, he had to admit he was grateful for the time without her insight.

The Calders either read his desire to be alone, or they'd decided horseback was not the place to begin their training. The siblings rode together, neither having mentioned his status as a Mage the whole morning. Whether or not they too could sense his fear, he wasn't sure, but he was grateful for the time to himself, all the same. Even if his thoughts did whirl around and around the same two subjects.

Was he *really* a Mage? And would he lose Evylin because of it?

The day plodded on in time with the horses' steady gait. They rode at a casual pace to keep the beasts hale and hearty. Horses were notoriously difficult to keep alive. They couldn't risk riding their steeds into the ground, spending countless golden crowns replacing them.

As the late morning sun peeked from behind the gray clouds to glint in the foggy day, Deckard's solitude came to an end. Ilain drew up alongside him. Despite the lightly misting rain, she let her hood hang around her shoulders, her fire-bright hair freely cascading down her back. "Might I speak with you, Jonn?"

Deckard attempted not to tense too noticeably. He wasn't ready to give up his ruminations for the cajoling of his Magehood. Yet, no matter his irritability, he dipped his head in acquiescence. "Of course," he said.

Ilain's smile didn't hold its usual luster. "I have a favor to ask." She bit the inside of her cheek demurely. "Would it be possible for me to change watch partners?"

Deckard blinked, not having expected the request. At first, he was surprised. Ilain and Ethenn got along splendidly. Why should she care to part with the young man? Then his mind returned to the darkness of the camp last night. He'd lain awake well after the rest of the troop had fallen asleep. And in the stillness of the night, he'd overheard Ethenn and Ilain's hushed conversation.

Deckard didn't mean to eavesdrop. It wasn't polite, but there wasn't much he could do in the silence. The whole troop knew that while at camp, they were never alone. Anything said *could* be overheard.

Still, it didn't make it any less awkward when Ethenn cleared his throat and asked, "Earlier, when you told Thom that you couldn't marry him . . . ?"

Ilain hesitated. "It was a joke. I never intended . . ." Her words fell off with a nervous laugh. "Our . . . relationship has never been headed for that."

"Because you have to marry a Warrior?" Ethenn asked cautiously. "Because of the . . . the Bonding thing?"

"I *want* to marry a Warrior," she corrected. "Because of the Bonding thing."

"Mm." Ethenn gave a dry sniffle in the rain. "Makes sense. It sounds like it's, uh—rather significant."

"It is."

There was an uncomfortable pause before Ethenn said, "Do you know many Warriors?"

"Only a few," she replied.

"And are they . . . eligible?"

Her voice was tinged with humor when she replied. "Some. Though I can't say I'm particularly drawn to any of them."

"Then you're still looking?"

"I suppose you could say that."

"Hm."

She let a few moments pass before adding, "I'll have to choose one at the end of our mission, though."

"Why?" Ethenn sounded almost worried.

"Because the Alliance highly values my abilities," she said. "They've offered me an important position, and I want to accept it. But I can only take the job if I'm Bonded."

From his conversation with Auden, Deckard surmised that the Alliance wanted Ilain to carry the Fire Relic after the war ended.

"Then," Ethenn said, "you'd marry a Warrior even if you didn't . . ."

"Love him?" Ilain said when he didn't complete his question. "Yes, I would."

Deckard heard the young man's weapons jostle as he shifted uncomfortably.

Ilain continued as though oblivious. "I don't have the luxury of romance," she admitted. "Not if I want to be of use in this world. The good news is that Bonding produces love, so no matter who I marry, I will come to love him as he will come to love me."

An expectant silence hung between them before Ethenn said, "I hope you're wrong."

A tight chuckle escaped her. "You hope I don't fall in love with my husband?"

"I—" Ethenn broke off, shifting again. "I hope you don't need to, that whoever you marry, you'll love one another *before* the wedding."

When Ilain didn't reply, Deckard grimaced internally. He'd known the young man liked the highlady, but he hadn't realized how much.

At last, Ethenn added, "You deserve that."

Then they'd both fallen silent for the rest of the time Deckard lay awake.

Now, in the early morning rain, Deckard understood Ilain's request. The hours spent during their watches provided too much opportunity for individual connection. It allowed Ethenn too much time to deepen his affection for the woman. And her discomfort made sense.

But if Deckard allowed Ilain to switch partners, he wasn't sure how to realign the rest. Placing the Calder siblings together wouldn't work, as neither was particularly skilled in the work. He couldn't have Rafferty join Ilain—the two would wind up too engrossed in one another's chatter to pay attention to their task. He *could* pair her with either Evylin or himself, but he didn't want to split up in case Evylin had another bout of anxiety and needed him.

After considering the options, he felt most assured of one solution that would suit them all. But first, he needed confirmation that Ilain's words last night were true.

"May I ask you a question?" Deckard said.

Ilain nodded, her sharp green eyes alert.

"Your relationship with my brother," he began. "It's not serious, is it?"

She let out an amused scoff. "Not remotely."

Deckard gave her a relieved smile. "Excellent. I'll have him join you for the first shift. Ethenn can work with Auden from here on out."

"Thank you," she said, then added, "And thank you for your discretion."

Deckard furrowed his brow.

"I may not be a Warrior," she said, "but I have trained myself to be quite adept at being aware of my surroundings."

He raised his chin, surprised. "You knew I was—"

"You held your breath from the moment he asked about the 'Bonding thing.'"

Deckard breathed out a laugh. "I apologize. I didn't mean to listen."

"We were conversing in public. It isn't as though you had much choice."

"Still. . . ."

She smirked playfully at him. "You're too much of a prude, Jonn. I've no qualms about discussing my love life with anyone. And that's not just because it's nonexistent."

"I can appreciate your candor, but my mother raised me to respect people's privacy," he said good-naturedly. "So I'll beg your forgiveness anyway."

Ilain shrugged. "It isn't needed, but I'll grant it to make you feel better."

Deckard found himself smiling. "I accept it wholeheartedly."

Her usually jovial countenance returned. A teasing glint lit her jade green eyes. "Do you want to know more about Bonding?" she asked slyly.

Deckard's jaw tightened instantly. A part of him *did* want to know more. If they had more information, they might feel better about their almost certain future, be it together or apart. But he feared that showing even the most remote sign of interest would give the Calders hope he couldn't afford to offer.

"No," he said decisively. "As Evylin and I told you, we've no interest in the subject."

"That's not what your reaction last night indicated," she remarked.

"Pardon me?"

Ilain met his gaze knowingly. "When you held your breath, it was because of the word 'Bonding.' You didn't care to discover more about Ethenn's feelings for me. You cared to learn what I had to say about Bonding."

Though she was correct, Deckard kept his expression placid. "You're mistaken," he said.

She smirked. "So you were simply keen on hearing Ethenn all but proclaim his affections to me?"

"Of course not. I was merely . . . uncomfortable."

Ilain allowed his lie to pass. "That makes two of us."

Having more knowledge than he wanted on the subject, Deckard chose to distract from Ethenn's interest in Ilain. "How can we be sure you're correct?" he asked. "About my . . . my magic."

"I thought we already proved that to you last night," she said incredulously. "Jonn, when a Relic lights up all glowing and bright like that, the facts are what they are. And as I said, I suspected all along. There was just something about you . . . The only reason I didn't suggest it sooner was because Auden talked me out of it. He's dreadfully cautious."

Deckard frowned inwardly. "But I've never used magic. What if I'm not a Mage but something else?"

Ilain leveled a bored glare at him. "Do you live on the continent of Allund?"

"Of course, I do."

"Then you have three options," she said, holding up a finger at each item on the list.

"One, you can be a Mage. Two, you can be a Warrior. Or three, you can be neither without a speck of magic in you. As you have magic, it'll be one of the first two."

"And if I didn't live in Allund?" he asked ruefully.

Ilain shrugged. "Technically, you'd still be one of the three. However, magic gets funny the farther it goes from the Relics."

"It does?"

"Mm. You know the Warriors who defected to Schon?"

"There are Warriors in Schon?"

"Didn't we tell you that?" Ilain pursed her lips in thought, then shrugged. "Well, yes. When the Mages turned on the Warriors in the late twelfth century, determined to kill them all to shore up power and establish the tyrannical rule of Auld, the few remaining Warriors had a decision to make: stay and be slaughtered or defect. Nearly all of them left the continent for the Empire, though I believe they've spread across the continent by now. I've even heard that some traveled to the islands surrounding Matteire."

Deckard nodded slowly, taking that in. "And what happened to their magic?" he asked.

"Not much," she admitted. "But they aren't quite as impressive as those here on Allund. If they return, they *may* regain their full power. However, magic tends to get twisted when it's away from its source. Mages who have left the continent have seen their powers strangely and irrecoverably altered."

"But they're still Mages?" he asked.

"They aren't called that, but all in all, yes. Their magic flows from a connection to the resources. It's just not as strong of a connection."

Deckard didn't know what to make of that information. He had little intention of leaving Allund unless Evylin asked it of him, which he didn't foresee. But knowing that magic could change in such a way that it could get weaker made him wonder if it wouldn't be better to leave after all.

"As we're sure you're not a Warrior," Ilain continued, oblivious to his internal debate, "you must be a Mage. And if you'd like definitive proof, you needn't worry. You'll have it tonight."

Deckard's heart stuttered in his chest. "I will?"

Ilain nodded. "The first step in your training is to determine your classification: Elemental or Existential. If the first, you'll train more closely with me. If the second," she gave him an apologetic grin, "it'll be with Auden."

He raised his brow. "And Auden is less preferred because . . . ?"

"Because he's tedious," she said with playful seriousness. "I love my brother, but he's a magister for a reason. And that reason is that he'd rather spend his life studying musty old tomes and talking about theories rather than actually *living*. Being his student would mean listening to him lecture for hours on the entire history of Mages and the finer points of hand gestures, as well as whether they're helpful or not. And Heavens help you if you're a Night Mage. He'd treat you like a bloody child the entire time."

Thinking of Prince Blount, Deckard shook his head. "I wouldn't want to be a Night Mage," he said.

Ilain snorted. "You wouldn't exactly have a choice. Your primary resource is your primary resource, and that's that. All the others will be harder for you to access— *especially* for a Mage as inexperienced as yourself, so don't bother trying to bypass it, whatever it is."

"But Night magic is bad," Deckard argued. "We wouldn't want me to use it."

"First of all," Ilain said emphatically, "no magic is *bad*. Magic is like that sword on your belt: a tool. *You* choose how you use it. And second, this is a highly theoretical conversation. Even if you are an Existential Mage, there's a chance you could connect to Day or Time more. But Elemental Mages are more common anyway. It's far more likely you're a . . . Oh, I don't know. A Terrae Mage. That'd be helpful. I have a horrendous connection with Terrae. Granted, it's better than most due to my unmitigated power, but it's abysmal compared to the rest of my connections."

"So," Deckard concluded, "the odds of my being an Elemental Mage are higher."

"And more preferable," she said. "Both for you and for the Alliance."

"Why?"

"We already have two male Existential Mages lined up to Bond," she explained, then pulled a face. "That's *if* Auden can convince Breata to work with him. We'd like to have at least one Bonded Elemental male as well."

"I've told you—"

Ilain waved off his comment. "I know, I know. Regardless," she gave him a weighty look, "being an Existential is more dangerous, to you and to others. It's more challenging to learn, and the resources are less predictable. Elements are straightforward. Existents are chaotic, at best."

She gave a decisive nod. "No, it'd be best for us all if you prove to be an Elemental Mage, and I could teach you."

Deciding she was right, Deckard allowed the conversation to lapse into silence. His mind was too full, his heart too unsettled. He didn't want to consider his classification as a Mage. It felt like a distraction from the more important problem in his life: helping Evylin heal.

When it became clear to Ilain that Deckard was through with the conversation, she excused herself to rejoin her brother.

For the rest of the journey, Deckard rode in silence. The sun drifted lazily behind the clouds once more, casting them into the shadows of the trees. No one bothered to approach him again, either because they read his agitation or were uninterested in pursuing a conversation. He was grateful. It gave him time to consider how to sneak away again to talk to Hewitt. He needed the ghost's advice more now than ever.

But finding an excuse was harder than Deckard expected.

He couldn't keep walking out into the forest alone. After breaking their agreement to pair up for safety once, he risked giving others permission to do the same should he repeat his offense. His only ally was Evylin, and now he'd lost her. He didn't trust any of the others not to ask him questions if he were to recruit their help. All this left him grasping at straws for a reason to be alone long enough to receive the advice he desperately needed.

At a loss, Deckard resigned himself to another night without Hewitt's aid. And as the Calders broached the topic of Deckard's classification during dinner, it seemed Allore's will was set against him that night.

"How *do* you find out what kind of Mage someone is?" Rafferty asked. "Is it some special rite? Or do the Relics tell you?"

"The Relics have been hidden away for centuries," Ethenn noted. "There would have to be another way."

"The Relics are of no use in this situation," Auden confirmed. "Holding the Water Relic, even *I* could access its power. But there is a basic technique used to determine what classification a child is once their magic reveals itself."

"And that is . . . ?" Rafferty prodded.

"It's a rudimentary form of tapping into the individual's connection to the resources," Auden said. "If an individual is an Elemental, they'll be more drawn to *all* of the elements, and so forth with an Existential and the existents. To determine the individual's classification, you only need to test their affinity via the push and pull of the two classes simultaneously."

Deckard furrowed his brow.

Rafferty blinked and said, "Huh?"

Ilain gave Deckard a pointed look as though to emphasize her earlier point about Auden's teaching style. "What he means is," she said, "you offer a choice: an element or an existent."

"Could you just choose what you wanted?" Evylin asked skeptically, sitting between Deckard and Rafferty.

"Not without tutelage," Auden said. "You see, without the proper incitement, magic can lie dormant an entire lifetime. It's likely why Jonn never realized his powers until our time in the Keeps. He needed its magic to prompt the magic within him."

"Same with Hewitt," Rafferty surmised.

Deckard glanced at Evylin, catching the way her jaw tightened.

"That would be our assumption," Auden confirmed. "It's why they both aged at a natural rate as well. Without knowledge of their power, it was like an old pair of shoes at the back of a wardrobe, unused and forgotten. But direct contact with magic sparks awareness of the resources themselves."

Ethenn fidgeted with one of his knives, flipping it end over end through the air. "Then . . ." he began thoughtfully, "is it possible to use magic without knowing it? Like you said before, Evie and Hewitt experienced that—that sensation when they fought. That was magic, right? But they didn't realize it."

"Exactly," Auden said. "Warriors are particularly notorious for this. While all magic is innate, theirs is even more so than Mages'. It's tied to their physical form, affecting their mind and body. Whereas a Mage's power is more abstract, so it requires a more intentional effort."

"Sounds like more work," Rafferty said with a tinge of disappointment.

"It is," Ilain said. "Magic requires focus, Warrior or Mage. But as the Warriors' magic is so intrinsically tied to their physical person, it is easier to tap into. A Mage can only access their magic through the resources. That kind of deep focus is highly conscious. You have to *know* what you're trying to do in order to do it."

"So how do I know what resource to choose?" Deckard asked. "If I have to make a deliberate connection, how am I supposed to make an uneducated choice?"

"That's the point of the test," Ilain said, a sparkle in her eyes. "I hold out a flame, representing the elements, and Auden will hold out a flare of light, representing the existents. Then we overwhelm you with magic until your instinct overrides your reason, and you connect to the resource that calls to you the most."

Deckard's stomach clenched around the hare stew he'd eaten. He set his bowl aside. "What do you mean by overwhelming me with magic?"

"It isn't as thrilling as it sounds," Auden assured him. "We surround you with our magic while you tap into your focus and let the magic guide you to a choice. Simple as that."

Deckard didn't think it sounded so simple. "And what if nothing happens?"

"*Something* will happen," Ilain said, adjusting her skirts. "How long it takes depends on how well you focus."

Scanning the troop, Deckard caught the expectant looks on their faces. Even Thom, sitting next to Ilain, looked more intrigued than annoyed for the first time since they'd discovered Deckard's connection to magic.

With a sigh, Deckard sat up straighter. "All right," he said. "Let's get this over with."

"Don't sound so excited," Ilain teased. "It's only one of the most important days of your life."

Without waiting for his response, Ilain turned to Auden. "Shall we?"

Auden dipped his chin, but his expression radiated caution. "Carefully," he said. "Jonn's power is unknown, and it's been repressed for over thirty years. It's bound to erupt if we push him too hard."

Ilain rose unceremoniously. "He's not a volcano, Auden. He'll be fine."

Ethenn leaned toward Rafferty, whispering, "What's a volcano?"

"An exploding mountain," the weasel said. "I've heard the Keves Island has one."

Ethenn frowned, clearly confused by the concept.

"Move, Rafferty," Ilain instructed as she and Auden came to stand in front of Deckard. "You're in the way."

Screwing up his face, Rafferty grumbled as he obeyed. "What about Eve? She's right next to him."

"As she should be," Ilain said.

Deckard and Evylin frowned.

"What? 'Cause they're married?" Rafferty asked.

"Only partially for that reason," Auden said. "As we said last night, Warriors and Mages are meant to be a team. They can aid one another, lending their focus." He turned to Evylin then. "If you tap into your magic while Jonn works to access his, it will help speed up the process."

Though she tugged on her rings, Evylin accepted the task.

Deckard could feel her tension as she sat at his side. She hadn't so much chosen her seat for dinner as it'd been the only one that remained. It was evident by her uncomfortable posture throughout the meal and into the present moment that she wished she could escape with Rafferty.

Deckard worked not to take offense at the small rejection. "Shouldn't I do it on my own?" he asked. "If the power could be volatile, wouldn't accessing it too quickly be dangerous?"

"Yes, *if* you didn't have good control over it," Ilain said, then gestured toward Evylin. "But with additional focus, your control will be stronger. Evylin's assistance will be beneficial in more ways than one."

Deckard and Evylin shared a reluctant look. Neither of them wanted to take part in this test. However, it seemed they didn't have much of a choice.

He shrugged in acceptance, and Ilain dropped to her knees before them, a bright smile on her face. "Now," she said excitedly, "the best way to prepare your mind for connection is to focus on the resources. While focusing *sounds* simple, it's anything but. It can take years of dedication to truly prime your mind for instinctive magical use. One way to accomplish that is by repeating the 'Poem of Life.' You don't have to recite it aloud, but you should constantly replay it in your mind."

"From memory?" Deckard asked incredulously.

Ilain furrowed her brow in confusion. "Of course, from memory. How else would you do it?"

"You forget, milady," Thom called, jaw tense. "We Ephrians weren't taught that poem in primary school like you Wauldeners. It was considered sacrilegious."

Her face scrunched even more. "It's the foundation of our religion."

"Not for us," he said flatly.

Ilain huffed, then turned back. "I'll recite it for you then. Are you ready?"

The urge to dash into the forest caused Deckard's foot to twitch. He resettled in his seat, reminding himself there was nowhere to run. One way or another, the magic would find him, according to the Calders.

"As I'll ever be," Deckard said, trying to convince himself to accept his fate.

Ilain clasped her hands before her while Auden hovered in the background. "Excellent," she said, her melodic voice softening. "Now, close your eyes and listen. As I recite the poem, try to visualize it in your mind. Imagine the resources, alive and tangible, right in front of you. Let the magic speak to you, and respond when it calls your name."

Though every part of his being recoiled, Deckard gritted his teeth and closed his eyes. He didn't know what to expect, but he shut out the world, only the dim amber haze of the campfire lighting his blacked-out view.

Slowly and lyrically, Ilain spoke. "First came Fire, the burst of Day. A tidal of Water doused the flame, Terraeus cast into the shadow of Night. Wind rolled in, a churning vortex of Time, to cool the molten Terrae. The Creator's grandest design, forever suspended in Space."

It sounded like a ballad, sweet and gentle—a song of devotion and adoration. Ilain repeated the poem, the words summoning a magic all their own. It swept through the air like a breeze, soft as a mother's goodnight kiss.

Deckard found the poem playing behind his closed eyes. A ball of fire erupted, flickering cheerily and radiating through the darkness like daylight. He imagined a wave as if from the sea, sweeping up to crash over the flames, smothering them into ash, leaving a shadow of the deepest night in its wake. He could almost feel the wind, soft at first, then a fierce gale, whirling round and round the hardened ball of terrae, creating time itself. All of it passed before his mind's eye, isolated and suspended in the infinity of space.

The scene played itself through his head, over and over. As Ilain recited, so Deckard's imagination followed. He could feel his brow furrowing, his body tense with concentration. A wash of warmth spread over his skin. Light erupted beyond his closed eyes, golden yellow on the left and ruby red on the right.

Heat crept up his spine, seeping into his muscles. It felt as though the warmth was trying to fill him, pushing its way in. His hands flexed subconsciously. He didn't know whether he wanted to grab hold of this feeling or shove it away. It prodded him, urging him to do . . . *something*.

Deckard's head pulsed painfully, an eerie whisper thrumming at the back of his skull. It was too much. The vision of the resources swirled before him, again and again. A ball of flame. A flash of light. The surge of water. A looming shadow. A spiral of wind. A stretching eon. A cooling land. The vastness of the Heavens. And with it all, a buzzing tingled across his neck and into his ears as the indistinct whisper grew louder.

He grimaced, his mind overly full from the vision and the sound. They tugged at him, each and every resource, as though testing him, asking him, *"Are you worthy of my power?"*

It grew too strong, the push and pull. He wanted to jerk away and grasp on all at the same time. Fire. Day. Water. Night. Power surged through him, begging for him to take hold. Wind. Time. Terrae. Space. It pressed in, a heavy burden, a potent responsibility waiting for him to don its mantle.

It was too much. He couldn't focus, couldn't find the connection, couldn't control the power. He feared that Auden was right, and it would erupt out of him in a dangerous outburst, desperate for relief.

Then, beside him, Deckard sensed the smallest thread of stillness. He reached for it, grasping urgently.

Evylin gasped, and beyond the world of his mind, Deckard realized that his hand had shot out, latching onto her forearm. He could feel his fingers clinging to her. At any other time, he would have worried he'd grabbed her too tightly or forcefully. But in the instant that his palm met her arm, clarity shot through his mind.

The focus came, the heat on his skin coating him, tight like leather armor. The vision of the resources slowed, and the buzzing became a whisper. He heard the call, the gentle prodding on his soul, claiming him like a second self, a half he hadn't known was missing.

And he heeded, reaching internally for the one source that was closest to him.

"The resources have spoken," Auden said from beyond Deckard's concentrated thoughts. It startled him enough to remind him of the world beyond, of reality.

His eyes flew open, finding his one hand still tight on Evylin while he held the other raised, a blaze of light shining brightly before him.

Deckard blinked away the lingering lure of his imagination. The whisper was gone, leaving the world in an abrupt silence. His vision shifted as he stared at his hand. He turned the palm to face him, and the light moved with it.

A flare of white-yellow Day lit the camp as though the sun shone down on them all.

The Calder siblings exchanged a look.

"We have another Existential Mage," Auden said with awe.

"Ah, well." Ilain sighed good-naturedly. "I never was much of a teacher anyway."

Deckard frowned, curling his fingers into a fist. The light extinguished within his grasp. The revelation felt anti-climactic and empty. A small part of him had held out hope that they were wrong, that he was no Mage. Without any proof of his abilities, he could deny it, pretending the Relics *could* make mistakes.

This put an end to every doubt in his mind.

He was an Existential Mage. And he'd liked it. The warmth and clarity. The release of power. The connection and control. He finally understood what made Auden and Ilain so enthusiastic about their magic. He felt an inexplicable desire to summon forth that flare of light again, just so he could feel that burgeoning, brilliant energy once more.

Deckard's gaze flickered past the Calders, past Thom, Rafferty, and Ethenn, past the trees, and to the shadow hovering in the darkness. This revelation came with another horrifying truth.

Yes, he was an Existential Mage. He felt it with more confidence than anything in his life. Because he knew now that *he'd* been the one to summon Hewitt's ghost. Day magic represented life, and Night, as its mirror, represented death.

No matter Ilain's protestations earlier, Deckard knew the truth.

He was a Night Mage, burdened with unholy power.

Part II: Writ of Attachment

The great consecration of their union is an unmatched drawing together of magic.

The Warrior feels it first, more in tune with their flesh as a natural course of their gifting.

Yet, the Mage responds, offering a grander display of power and passion to the Bond.

Excerpt from Attachments of the Soul,
author unknown

Cold is the Night, its darkness frenzied with ferity. Marrow-deep inquietude unsettles even the holiest of souls. We should extirpate them, every last demon, lest they drag us all to hell in their monstrous grasp.

Excerpt from a letter penned by Alphias Stenn, Aterian in the Order of the Day, to his fellow Mage, Restras Lew, Attendant in the Order of the Age, dated 12th of Terraen, 1125, shortly before his death at the hands of Obrus Eegon, ArchMage in the Order of the Night, and Father of the Eight, the first Mage King of Auld

FELSTON EDGE
AUCHROLM
CAULTO
SUTTERLUND REACH
ORDER OF THE WIND
FAURAMERS

CHAPTER TWENTY

Dropping under the numerous branches of a hawthorn, Thom glanced at Ilain. "Thanks for getting me off the second shift," he said half-heartedly. "I'm indebted to you."

Ilain flicked her fingers, sending up small spurts of flame with a bored flare. "Any time."

After dinner and the show (the testing of Deckard's classification), Deckard had pulled Thom and Ethenn aside, informing them of the switch in watch pairings. He said it was because, in thinking it over, it made more sense for Ethenn to have the later shift with his keen hunter's eyesight. But the true reason was evident to both soldiers: Ilain had made a request.

Thom glanced over his shoulder, catching as Ethenn settled uncomfortably on the ground, preparing for sleep. "I take it the kid isn't getting the idea?" he said, turning back to Ilain. She'd selected their spot on the rise of a hill. It was farther away from the camp than usual, but the vantage was better.

Unemotionally, Ilain continued to play with Fire magic. "He all but told me he loves me."

Thom snorted. "Idiot. Every man knows that's the *last* thing you tell a woman unless you're sure she loves you back."

Ilain raised a coppery eyebrow at him. "I didn't realize you were an expert in romance."

"Not an expert, no." He propped his arms on his knees. "But I've learned a thing or two over the years."

"Spare me the details," she said with a grimace.

"Oh, I don't know," he said teasingly. "You might find them enlightening."

"I've no interest in hearing about your illicit affairs."

"Illicit?" He scoffed. "My love affairs have all been aboveboard, I promise you."

Ilain eyed him. "How many women have you dallied with?"

He smirked. "Not *that* many. But enough to be well informed."

"Mm. I'll take your word for it." Ilain returned to her Fireplay, the flames glittering in the gem-encrusted rings she wore.

Thom gestured to them. "What are all those?" he asked.

She looked at her hands. "My rings?"

"Yes."

"They represent the elements." She spread her fingers, the varied gemstones casting a subtle sheen in the dim light of night. She pointed to each gold ring as she explained. "Ruby for Fire, sapphire for Water, diamond for Wind," she switched, pointing to her left hand, "and emerald for Terrae. I've spent the last thirty years imbuing each gemstone with extra stores of the resources, allowing me to access each one more easily. Though I never touch them. I'm saving their power for something . . . special."

"Oh." He pressed his lips together in consideration. "They actually have a purpose. I always thought they were simply ostentatious."

Her smile turned sly. "They are ostentatious. That's the point."

"I thought the point was making you a better Mage," he replied dryly.

She flipped a hand through the air. "That's a byproduct. But I could wear them as a necklace or something far less showy. I chose the rings because they make people think I'm flippant and garish. They underestimate me because of it, and that's how I like it."

"You *want* to be underestimated?"

"Of course. When they think I'm a foolish young woman, they don't expect me to be so strong and cunning. It gives me the upper hand in practically every situation."

Thom could see the merit in the idea but not the appeal. "Don't people treat you as a lesser that way? If they think you're a fool, they won't respect you."

"Respect is like sex," she said bluntly. "Nice if you can get it, but not necessary for personal survival."

Thom stared at her, baffled to hear a woman say something so crass. In Ephria, no woman of good repute would dare say something that suggestive. "Are all Waulden women as lewd as you?" he asked in a tone somewhere between good-humored and perplexed.

Ilain's jade eyes sparkled like her gemstones. "When you're forty-two and have only just begun to experience real life, you realize there's very little use in holding back for the sake of propriety."

With a shake of his head, Thom marveled at the oddity of Ilain Calder. Mages were a strange breed.

The thought made Thom frown, reminding him that his brother was a Mage now. He'd done his best to ignore the fact, to forget that Deckard had yet again surpassed him. But it seemed a truth he couldn't escape.

Clearing his throat, Thom stared out into the night. "Do all Mages, uh . . . never grow old?" he asked.

Ilain's light laugh rankled. "If you're worried about watching your brother grow old, don't be," she said. "You'll be dead long before he is."

Thom's head whipped toward her.

She met his stare steadily. "Mages live for centuries," she said, then paused. "Well, most of us do. The more powerful we are, the longer we live. The weakest have perhaps a century and a half, while the rest can go on for at least two to three."

His mind couldn't fathom such a thing. "You mean that . . . Jonn will live for centuries?"

"Most likely. Especially if he and Evylin Bond."

Thom couldn't hide his scowl.

Ilain rolled her eyes. "What is it about you and your brother? Why can't you ever be happy for him?"

He shifted uncomfortably, clasping his hands between his knees. "As the most powerful Mage in two centuries and a goddess incarnate, you wouldn't understand."

"Is that so? Hm." Ilain tapped a finger to her chin, mockingly thoughtful. "Could that mean that darling Thom Deckard is jealous of his brother's power and esteem? Oh, as someone who's vastly more special than everyone else, how will I ever know?"

Thom gave her a chastising glare.

With a speed he hadn't known she possessed, Ilain reached over and smacked the side of his head. "Don't be an idiot," she chided. "You're a grown man. Get over your petty jealousies and recognize that what your brother does or doesn't have isn't a reflection on you."

Rubbing the side of his head where her emerald ring had most assuredly left a mark, Thom glowered. "You don't know what it's like," he spat.

"Don't I?"

"How could you?" he said confidently. "You're an incredible, fearless woman who's never had to stand in anyone's shadow. How could you possibly understand what it feels like to grow up with *him* as your brother?"

Ilain's gaze was fiery, though she remained silent.

Thom leaned toward her, keeping his voice hushed so that it wouldn't carry back to the camp. "He's *perfect*. That's what I've heard my entire life. 'Oh, look at Jonn, how brilliant he is.' 'What an impressive young man you are, Jonn.' 'You're so wonderful, Jonn, I've named my bloody son after you.'"

He shook his head, the irritation of twenty-seven years festering. "And now—" He glared out into the darkness, staring into the dripping pines and rain-splattered ferns. "Now, he's a damn Mage, and I'm *still* nothing."

The chirrup of night insects filled his ears. A long, charged pause echoed in the space between them. He stared at his hands, somewhat embarrassed. He'd never expected to find himself confiding in Ilain. From the outset, he'd seen her as vapid and annoying. Just what she'd intended, he now realized. And somehow, over the last week and a half, he'd come to trust her enough to reveal his darkest secrets to her.

Ilain sighed, resting her hands on her lap. "Well," she said softly, "I stand by my earlier statement."

Thom felt as though she'd slapped him again. He gaped at her, unsure what to say. He'd expected her pity, not her derision. "Are you heartless?"

She scoffed. "What do you want me to say? I'm sorry you weren't chosen by Allore himself to be one of his most powerful servants, but at least you can live your life however you want."

Thom's brows pulled together, unsure how to respond to that.

"Meanwhile," Ilain continued sourly, "the rest of us have to go about our lives *hoping* to be as lucky as Jonn and Evylin, miraculously falling in love with our magical equal."

Thom grimaced. Though he sympathized with her sentiment, she wasn't privy to the full information regarding Deckard and Evylin's relationship. "I wouldn't consider them lucky," he said.

"Well, I would," she returned sharply. "*You* don't know what it's like, watching two people get everything you've dreamed of since you were a little girl. *You* don't know how it feels to be constantly in the light, with every one of your actions scrutinized by those around you. *You* couldn't comprehend how it feels when a man tells you that you deserve every happiness, expecting nothing in return—when he's lovely and kind and handsome and everything you *wish* you could have—you couldn't begin to know what it feels like to ignore every urge within you and have to reject that love even if it's the first and likely only time it will ever be offered."

With his breath caught somewhere between his chest and his throat, Thom stared at Ilain. "You love him?" he muttered. "Ethenn?"

"No." Her head whipped forward to survey the forest around them, jaw set. "I only wish I could."

Thom scratched his head, trying to comprehend everything she'd said. No, he didn't know what any of that was like. As the inferior second-born son, no one expected anything of him. He was granted freedom to do as he pleased. But it was that lack of expectation that made him feel so second-rate and unwanted.

Following her gaze, Thom sighed. "We're quite the pair. An all-powerful Mage and a covetous wretch."

"Don't think so poorly of yourself," Ilain said. "People like you; you're just not willing to see it."

"You don't think I *want* to be liked?"

"No, because if you were—if you weren't so wretched as you claim—then you'd have to let go of your bitterness."

Thom thought he should be angry with her. It should hurt to hear such a demoralizing truth. Yet, he found himself studying her anew. "You're a strange woman, my Highlady Calder," he said.

She smiled, eyes still on the forest even as she took his hand. After a solitary squeeze, she let go. "Don't fall in love with me, Thom," she warned. "I can't be with you either."

A rueful grin came to his lips. "Doesn't mean you couldn't have some fun," he quipped.

"I'm not in the habit of deceiving myself," she replied, then her eyes met his at last. "And I'm under no illusions about your worth."

Thom blinked, instantly unsettled.

Ilain didn't back down. "I won't risk losing myself to you or Ethenn. No matter how wonderful cither of you may be."

"I'm—" Thom hesitated, then cleared his throat. "I'm not interested in—"

"I know," she interrupted. "And I'd like to keep it that way."

They were silent after that, neither willing to he any more vulnerable than they already had.

Thom picked at the hem of his coat sleeve. In his head, he knew that Ilain was correct. He had friends, of course. His officers and fellow soldiers liked him. Hewitt had even chosen him to train on his exclusive team. Rafferty, Evylin, and Ethenn all sought out his company. So he couldn't deny that he was liked.

Yet, deep down, his heart didn't accept it. Not when, at every opportunity, his brother was chosen over him. No matter how much he knew the truth, he didn't feel it. And with the comparison of Deckard to live up to, Thom wasn't sure if he ever would.

CHAPTER TWENTY-ONE

9TH OF CHRONOS, 1574

The rain couldn't make up its mind. One minute it was a downpour, and the next a gentle mist. The wind whipped it up, splattering their faces and slipping under their cloaks. By the time they stopped to make camp near the village of Dunneshead, each member of the troop was soaked to the bone.

Evylin flexed her hand, refusing to let it drift toward her wedding rings. Over the past few days, she'd hardly stopped tugging on them. It wasn't only the weight of her depression that clouded her mind, begging for distraction. It was the discovery of Deckard's magic and his constant tutelage too.

From the moment they'd discovered his status as an Existential Mage, Auden hadn't let up for a moment. If he wasn't walking Deckard through the finer points of focus and connection to the resources, he was lecturing on the history of magic, listing the greatest Mages of the past millennium, or orating about the vast potential each existent held.

Except for Night magic. Any time Auden mentioned that resource, he inevitably began a short diatribe about how it warped the minds of every Night Mage, twisting them into villainous madmen.

Evylin would have sympathized with Deckard if her thoughts weren't already mangled with anxiety. It felt as though the terrae was collapsing beneath her feet. Everything she'd believed was wrong. Everything she'd feared was coming true.

Helping Ethenn hobble the horses, Evylin's hands trembled around the rope. She couldn't escape the memories of Deckard's test. Despite her desire to escape the moment, she'd sat at his side and did as Ilain suggested—she focused. She drew in a breath and let the "Poem of Life" guide her into a nearly trancelike state.

It was a soothing experience considering the last month of her life. Easily, she'd found her magic, that cool sensation tracing across her veins and into her head. The world came to life with clarity, and her heart settled.

Then Deckard touched her.

His grip on her arm sent an immediate jolt racing through her body. Every past experience she'd had with magic paled in comparison. In the moment of his touch, her senses lit up, taking in everything with shocking detail. It was as though the world slowed down as her perception increased. The steady chill calmed her thoughts, giving her a heightened awareness. Her skin prickled, and her muscles tensed, ready for action.

Evylin recognized the response intimately. It was the feeling she experienced both in a fight *and* when Deckard kissed her. It was her magic responding, her focus engaging, and her very being connecting with the foundation of Terraeus. And she finally understood.

She'd always questioned her reaction to Deckard—to his touch, to his kiss. Before she realized she was a Warrior and thereby connected the sensation to her magic, she'd asked Hewitt if he'd ever experienced it outside of a fight. He'd said no. Then she'd asked Thom's advice, questioning if kissing anyone would feel the same. She'd concluded that it must.

Now, she knew, it wouldn't because the experience wasn't coming from Evylin alone. It was Deckard's magic that hers responded to.

"Warriors and Mages are meant to be together."

Evylin ran her hand over her horse's smooth coat, avoiding the company of her troop. While she longed for the distraction of conversation, she struggled to find words these days. And with Auden's constant training, she couldn't forget the unbearable truth it brought.

Evylin refused to believe in fate. No greater power than King Ephren had brought Deckard to Whickam Village and into her life. They weren't written in the stars or destined by Allore above. But that didn't change the fact that Ilain was right: Warriors and Mages *were* meant to be together.

She felt it in her innermost being, this truth. She'd even tested her theory, intentionally bumping into Auden the previous evening, grabbing hold of his arm, and seeking the stirring of magic within her. And sure enough, it was there. Not as potent as with Deckard, but still shifting under the surface as though waking from a deep sleep.

So now Evylin knew—if she wanted to experience that rush, that feeling of being wholly alive, she had to be with a Mage.

She knew it should make her happy. After all, life as a Warrior married to a Mage *must* be the grandest adventure possible, just as she and Ryen had imagined. And she'd bet her future to ensure that their dream didn't die in Whickam Village with him. Surely, this revelation meant she'd succeeded.

But Evylin trembled at the thought of that life. Here she was, standing in a wet, muddy forest with a band of rebel soldiers and two Waulden Mages attempting to overthrow two countries. This was "adventure"—the fulfillment of her and Ryen's dreams. And the price was vastly too high.

Without warning, thunder erupted, startling the troop and the horses just as a fresh deluge came down. They all broke for the densest tree cover. Even under the thick leaves, they were soaked in an instant.

"That's it!" Deckard exclaimed, ducking under the short branches of two rowans. He looked straight at Auden, his expression tense. "Tomorrow, we're going into town to buy tents."

"Dunneshead is a village," Auden objected. "It's too small to risk—"

"We've spent two whole weeks sleeping soaked to the bone," Deckard said sharply. "It's a wonder we aren't ill."

Rafferty sniffled, hunched beneath the boughs despite his short stature. His eyes and nose were red, and his voice was crackly. "Speak for yourself," he grumbled.

Auden gave the sick man an apologetic glance before turning back to Deckard. "It's too dangerous," he said.

"No more dangerous than freezing to death," Thom said in agitation.

"Don't be dramatic," Ilain retorted, but set a hand on her brother's arm to stall his rebuttal. "They're right. We're pushing too hard as it is. We can't risk entering the Keep with so much as a head cold."

Auden sighed, then waved a hand in beleaguered acceptance. "Fine. We'll go first thing in the morning."

Deckard nodded but didn't say a word. He stood several feet away from Evylin, his shoulders slumped and his head ducked as he attempted to hold his rain cover. Though his hood shadowed most of his face, she could see the pinch between his brows. It'd been locked there since he'd held the Night Relic, unveiling his magic. She felt sorry for him, her heart's attachment fighting to resurface.

She shoved it down with all her internal might.

Rafferty shivered next to Evylin. "Think they'd pick up some ale while they're at it?" he asked.

She gave him a half-felt grin. "I've never heard of ale curing a cold."

"It's not for medicinal purposes," he said dryly, his tone even more nasal than usual.

Evylin granted him a stifled chuckle.

Under their rowan, Evylin leaned against the spindly branches. Rain splashed against the leaves, springing up into her face. She closed her eyes, flinching away. Behind her closed lids, she saw a flash of deep blue water, the undulations of the waves closing in on her. Her ears filled with pressure, the humming of Shades drawing nearer. She was going to drown.

Evylin sucked in a sharp breath, eyes flying open.

"You all right?" Rafferty asked, silver-gray gaze keen.

Curling her hands into fists, she replied honestly. "No."

Then she darted from under their tree and over to where Deckard huddled a few steps away. He looked over as she approached, alert. Neither of them bothered with pleasantries.

"Could I speak with you?" she asked quietly.

Readily, he shifted out from under the branches. "Thom," he called.

His brother turned, standing close to Ilain's side.

"We'll be back shortly," Deckard said, passing command to him.

Hurrying through the forest, Evylin and Deckard sought cover a short distance from the others. Not so far that they were out of earshot, but far enough that they wouldn't have to worry about being overheard.

The foggy grayness of Wauld clung to the trees around them, making Evylin feel caged in. She couldn't take a clear breath with her mind clouded with fear and sorrow.

Deckard stared down at her, eyes bright despite the darkness. Compassion and worry threaded together in his low brow and taut mouth. "What is it?" he asked.

"I—" The words stuck to Evylin's tongue. She couldn't meet his gaze, too uncomfortable with the knowledge that what she'd once thought was unique to them was now nothing but magic. His touch wasn't special. *He* didn't make her feel alive. His magic did.

Shaking the thought off, Evylin sucked in a frigid breath. "I want to go with Auden tomorrow," she said.

He was silent for several seconds. Then he sighed. "No."

Evylin bit the inside of her lip to keep from grimacing. "Jonn," she tried to look up at him but couldn't, "please, I—I need to go with him."

Deckard ran a hand over his mouth and beard as though holding in his response. His booted feet shifted in the soggy terrae. "It's too dangerous," he said at last.

"Don't do that," she said, her voice hollow and tired. "Don't pretend you're protecting me when you know I can defend myself. It's less dangerous for me to go than for you."

"You're more valuable than I am," he argued.

"Not anymore."

"Warriors are in shorter supply than Mages."

Evylin had anticipated difficulty in convincing Deckard, but now faced with it, she felt ill-prepared for the task. Her eyes burned with welling emotion, and she forced herself to take a long breath before trying another approach. "Try to understand," she murmured, desperation stealing her voice. "I *need* to go."

Deckard stepped forward instinctively. His hand slipped out from under his cloak to reach for her, but he stopped himself. She didn't know whether to be grateful or disappointed.

"Evylin," he said gently, "I can't risk you."

That carved a hole in Evylin's heart. He couldn't risk her, and she couldn't risk him. But they meant it in two entirely different ways. His affection tugged at hers. She'd begun to feel for him all those weeks ago, something beyond camaraderie but without a proper term. Over the course of their marriage, she'd come to find herself desirous of him beyond companionship. If Hewitt hadn't died . . .

Setting a hand to her head, Evylin tried to stave off the ache that shot across her temples. Her chest compressed, her limbs shaking. "I can't—" She cut herself off, trying to breathe.

Now, Deckard did reach for her.

He took hold of her arms, dipping his head to hold her gaze. "Stop," he said brusquely, not out of anger but instruction. "Whatever you're thinking about, stop."

"I can't," she muttered again.

Every time she blinked, it was like she was back under the water, her body thrashing helplessly. She could taste the salt. Her lungs tensed. She was drowning, and she couldn't get out.

"Evylin—" Deckard's tone was forceful as his hands cupped her face. The cold of his palms nipped at her cheeks, drawing her eyes to his. "Stop."

Staring back at him, Evylin's heart lurched. Her lips parted, and her breath caught. His eyes were so green in this light, his expression so adamant. Her skin tingled where he touched her, the magic within her rousing to him. Every muscle relaxed, and the panic receded as her senses came alive.

"Warriors and Mages are meant to be together."

Evylin jerked back. "I can't do this anymore," she said, words coming freely at last.

Deckard's hands dropped back to his sides as he studied her. He didn't seem hurt so much as surprised. "Do what?"

Desperate to be rid of him, to be safe from the mesmerizing pull he had on her magic—on her heart—she found herself reacting wildly. "Any of this," she exclaimed, throwing her arms out to encompass the whole world. "Since the moment I gave the Relic back to Rafferty, I've been crumbling. Haven't you seen that?"

His downcast expression confirmed that he had.

"Every moment, I feel like I'm drowning," she admitted, the tears burning behind her eyes. "I can't stop thinking about him. I can't stop thinking about death and the fact that every single one of us is moments away from losing our lives too."

Taking a step back, Evylin bumped into a tree. She recoiled, the world pressing in, the mist oppressive, the fog smothering. "I can't take it anymore," she said raggedly. "These trees are maddening. This infernal rain is—is—I can't do this."

The first tear escaped her, and Evylin drew in a painful breath. "I *need* to go with him," she pleaded.

Deckard stood still, sorrow etched in his features. His shoulders sagged as he scanned her. She could see how it hurt him to watch her in this state. He wanted to help. He desired to comfort her. But he simply listened, giving her the space she'd requested.

Evylin almost hated him for his goodness. Part of her wished that he wouldn't respect her decisions so much. She wished he'd throw aside his decency and pull her into his arms, forcing her hand. She longed for the choice to be taken from her. If only he weren't so noble and virtuous, then she wouldn't have to deny herself.

But Deckard *was* good. And for that very reason, she *had* to protect herself from him.

"I have to go," Evylin said one last time, determination lacing her every word.

They stared at one another. He tested her resolve while she clung to it.

Deckard sighed. "Auden won't like it."

"He's not in charge," she said tightly.

Deckard gave her a disapproving frown. "I can't do whatever I please, Evylin. King Ephren may have put me in charge, but his authority carries a little less weight now that we decided to defect. And I risk losing whatever role of leadership the Calders grant me if I push them too far."

Evylin rejected his sound reasoning, finding her own. "Then tell him. Tell Auden why I need to go. He'll understand. He'll *want* to help."

"It isn't that simple," Deckard argued. "If I let you go, then I have to let the others go too. Auden will know that, and he'll say no because we can't take those chances."

"We won't have to take chances if they don't ask."

"Do you think they're any less tired of these forests than you?"

"They didn't lose the only man they ever loved," she shot back, more tears threatening to drop.

Deckard flinched. His eyes drifted to the trees beyond her shoulder, hovering there. After a deep breath, he dropped his gaze guiltily to the mud.

Knowing what she'd implied—that she didn't love *him*—Evylin pressed her advantage on his emotions. "Jonn," she whispered, "*please*."

At her imploring words, compassion drew his countenance down. His eyes, his mouth, his shoulders, his head—all of him drooped like she'd settled the world on his back. She hated herself for manipulating him this way.

"All right," he murmured. "I'll talk with Auden."

"Thank you," Evylin replied weakly.

An uneasy distance remained between them as they returned to their companions. With each moment that passed, Evylin's chest expanded like an overfilled trunk, straining ever more wildly against its binds. The tears clung to her throat. With everything in her, she longed to remove this impediment that poisoned the space between herself and Deckard. She knew he thought she blamed him for Hewitt's death. But that wasn't what kept her from taking comfort in him. It was the knowledge that, should she allow him to become that comfort, she would put herself at risk of damning herself to desolation.

She'd survived Ryen. She'd survived Hewitt. She wouldn't survive Deckard. Not when he was the perfect equal to her soul.

Warriors and Mages—they were meant for one another.

Evylin couldn't bear that. And she wouldn't let herself give in to it.

Curse destiny. She would find her own solace, free of the certain devastation that such an attachment would wreak on her heart, mind, and body. She wouldn't be bound to Deckard in any fashion. Not so long as she might risk losing herself to him.

CHAPTER TWENTY-TWO

Thick, gray fog obscured the skies. The village of Dunneshead was a haze of buildings in the distance. Evylin and Auden rode casually down the road, hoods up. The softest misting of rain filled the air, less of a nuisance than usual. But that might have had to do with the growing lightness of Evylin's heart.

The tension had eased with each *clomp* of the horses' hooves, as though the greater the distance from Deckard, the calmer she grew. By the time they neared the village, she found herself smiling, taking in the world around her with interest. Rodents skittered from tree to tree, rustling the leaves, which tossed a spray of droplets into the air. The gentle crooning of mourning doves rang above their heads.

Evylin turned to Auden, his usually stoic demeanor in place as expected. Without his student around, he hadn't bothered to strike up a conversation. But with her improved mood, Evylin decided to engage his company.

"The last time we went on a mission, just the two of us," she said playfully, "things didn't quite go as planned."

Auden glanced at her, coppery eyebrows raised. "Nor were the circumstances quite as favorable. Though I'd say entering a settlement in enemy territory isn't the most promising situation either."

Evylin shifted with her horse as she guided it around a large depression in the road. "True, but I'd take it over facing a maniacal prince any day."

"As would I," Auden agreed pleasantly.

They lapsed into silence once more. Evylin furrowed her brow, trying to figure out what to say. She realized that it was surprisingly difficult to talk with the highlord. In their travels with the Calders, she'd only been alone with Auden once, and conversation hadn't exactly been a priority while fighting for their lives in the Water Keep. Thinking up something engaging to discuss was harder than she anticipated.

Evylin considered what she knew about the Mage. She hadn't learned much, aside from his academic and straitlaced conduct. He was nearly as prudish as Deckard, though his conservative leanings seemed borne of personality and indifference rather than religious or moral sentiments. This reserved manner of his made him difficult for Evylin to understand, and as he didn't show interest in pursuing more than a working relationship with any of the Ephrians, she had never thought to befriend him.

Grimacing internally, Evylin wondered if this trip into Dunneshead was destined to be as dull as a day on the road. She hadn't considered that when she'd asked to accompany him. And while the novelty and distance from Deckard would be a boon, she couldn't help being disappointed with the excursion's projected experience.

In the taciturn air between them, Evylin considered how she could goad him into entertaining conversation. She didn't want to discuss magic since she was uninterested in thinking about Deckard or encouraging Auden to bring up Bonding. Though she would like to learn about Warriors, she doubted that he knew any more than Ilain. And as that was the sole extent of her understanding of his interests, she was at a loss.

As the last topic of discussion, Evylin's thoughts reverted to their time in the Water Keep. Her throat tightened as the memories of falling into the water threatened. She pushed them down instantly and latched onto the one subject she could think of.

"Had you ever met Blount?" she asked suddenly. "Before the Keep, I mean."

Auden turned to her, emerald eyes wide. "No. Despite our position as Mages, Ilain and I aren't nobility. And with the king's paranoia, he rarely invites our kind into his company."

"But you knew him," Evylin said. "The second you saw his face, you knew who he was."

With a slow nod, Auden admitted, "I did."

Evylin frowned. Despite being the crown prince, if the Calders hadn't been even indirectly in his company, it was unlikely they'd ever have the chance to see him. Ephria's crown prince, Caspar, had been wholly unknown to Evylin until their meeting in Banbury. Why should Wauld's be any more common?

"Is his likeness that well-known?" she asked.

Auden adjusted uncomfortably on his horse. "Not particularly. But in the Alliance, they've ensured we all know the greatest threats to our success. Although we were unaware of his immediate plans, we were aware of his interest in the Relics. And as heir to the throne, he was our natural enemy."

"Oh." Evylin couldn't help being disappointed in the mundane answer. She supposed it was smart for the Alliance to pass around sketches of their enemies. Knowing of Blount might have prepared her better for his cruelty in the Keep.

The reminder caused Evylin to frown again. Her jaw, where he'd kicked her, ached with the memory. His villainy had astonished her. Though Evylin had read of evil men and women in her novels, she'd never actually met one until Blount. She hadn't known a person could be so vile. Her skin crawled as she remembered the pleasure he'd taken in torturing Auden with Night magic. Her heart stuttered, thinking of how flippantly he'd pronounced Auden's death.

Evylin found herself frowning again. "'Kill him,'" she murmured Blount's last order aloud.

"What?" Auden said tensely.

Evylin met his narrowed gaze. "'Kill him,' he said," she repeated. "Why not 'kill *them*'?"

Auden's expression pinched as she continued with new understanding. "What did he want with me?" she asked.

Auden sucked in a deep breath. His eyes flickered to the nearing settlement. They were only moments away from the village, and this wasn't a conversation to be had among adversaries.

He slowed his horse, lowering his voice to say, "You're a Warrior, Evylin. A *female* Warrior."

An icy sensation scraped along her scalp.

Auden gave her an apologetically direct look. "Warriors are rare enough," he said darkly. "Being a woman makes you even more special, the discovery of a lifetime for Blount. Something he probably never expected to find. Regardless of your allegiance, he would have undoubtedly forced you to Bond with him."

"I would have refused," she insisted.

"Would you?" he asked. "Even after decades of torture?"

Evylin had no answer to that.

"Or perhaps he would have tried another approach," he offered. "Perhaps he would have attempted to woo you, earning your trust, knowing that once you Bonded, he'd regret whatever evil he'd done to you because he'd grow to love you."

"He's a sadist," she spat. "He couldn't love anyone."

Auden's expression turned sorrowful. "Everyone loves someone, even the most vile of creatures."

In her quiet discomfort, Auden continued, "Don't underestimate the power of magic, Evylin. No matter what he did or would ever do, if he succeeded—if Blount managed to Bond with you—you would come to love him. And whatever cruelty he enacted to make you his, you'd forgive him for it."

Evylin's whole being squirmed. She felt violated at the very thought. If magic could make her forgive such heinous acts, if it could unite her to such a depraved man, she swore she'd kill herself before he ever got the chance to Bond with her.

Neither of them said anything more, riding up to the edge of Dunneshead. The village's gray stone buildings had black slate roofs. Everything was dull and murky like the sky above them. Though slightly larger than Whickam Village, the homes and businesses were more densely packed in the sloping valley. A massive, lazy river skirted the village, almost encircling it.

Officious guards patrolled the uneven dirt streets; their severe gazes fastened to Evylin and Auden as they rode past. Due to the prohibition on weaponry in Wauld, she'd left all but a few hidden daggers behind. She felt naked under the guards' intense glares.

The village was sleepy, with few citizens moving through the main thoroughfares. Evylin wondered if the emptiness was due to the presence of the guards or the poor weather. Or perhaps there just weren't enough people to populate the settlement well.

In the main square of the village, Evylin and Auden dismounted, tying their horses to the post. They scanned the square, readily finding the smith at the far corner to ask for directions to purchase tents. Auden dropped his hood once they were under the awning of the smithy, but Evylin kept hers up to hide her Ephrian features. The smith spoke in some strange dialect that Evylin couldn't begin to understand, and she was suddenly grateful that she'd promised not to say a word on their trip.

"Yes, I understand," Auden replied, evidently able to translate the smith's garbled words into something resembling sense. "But my boss, *he* wouldn't understand." He leaned forward conspiratorially, lowering his voice. "He's not the most reputable man, aye?"

Evylin watched with interest as the smith's eyes twinkled. He rattled off some more words, his fingers twitching at his side.

With a deft hand, Auden slipped the man some coins. "I'd be greatly appreciative," he said.

The smith grunted, scanned Evylin—heavily shrouded in her cloak—and turned to forage through his shop.

Evylin shifted closer to Auden. "What was that about?" she asked.

"We're in a village," he replied. "There are no merchants who sell tents. So he's going to do us a favor for a few extra silvers on the side."

"On the side?"

"Off his tax books," he said. "While he can't provide *all* the materials for us, he has the supplies we need for frames, and his friend at the docks has the canvas and rope we need for the shelter-halfs themselves. He'll give us the frames and a note for his friend, and we'll head to the docks."

"Ah." Evylin nodded. She began to shift away when a stranger ducked under the smith's awning.

"Pard'n," he said to her in a thick Waulden accent.

Though her hood was too low for him to get a good look at her, Evylin drifted to Auden's other side to ensure her anonymity.

The stranger and the smith exchanged rapid, unintelligible words. Then the smith kept on with his work, and the stranger waited patiently.

Broad-shouldered but with a narrow waist, the newcomer carried the distinct Waulden features of numerous freckles and sharp cheekbones that gave his face an especially gaunt look. He was young, perhaps in his mid-twenties, with shaggy white-blond hair. His leather jerkin had a hole by the hem, and his tunic was stained with grease. He scratched his cheek, glancing at Auden. The men exchanged polite smiles but otherwise ignored one another.

But then the man looked at Auden again.

Evylin shifted, sliding her hand to the back of her belt, where she kept a blade hidden. Though this stranger had no apparent weapons on him, she didn't like the way he was studying Auden.

"'Cuse me," the man said in his clipped accent. "Ya look familiar. 'Ave we met?"

Auden gave the stranger a steady scan as though seeing him for the first time. Then he shook his head. "I can't imagine that we have," he said.

The man raised his chin. "Ya from the Moorlands?"

Auden's brow furrowed. "Actually," he said lightly, "I am."

"Yeh, me too," the man said, his gap-toothed smile wide. He held out his hand good-naturedly. "Name's Nev, and I can always spot one of our kin. What're ya doin' this far east?"

"Work," Auden said as they shook hands. "Or, more accurately, paying off a debt, if you know what I mean."

Nev chuckled knowingly. "Aye, that I do." He tapped the side of his nose. "Same for me. Pays to sell, ya know?"

Though Evylin didn't know, it seemed that Auden did. He grinned, joining the man's chuckle.

The smith returned, arms loaded down with several poles of wood, forestalling any further conversation. He rambled in his indecipherable dialect, and Auden paid him readily, accepting the note for the dockworker. The Moorlander, Nev, wished them good travels, then they left the cover of the awning into the misty day.

After securing their purchase to their saddles, they led the horses to the docks. It took several minutes of asking around to find the smith's friend. Auden proceeded to haggle with the dockworker, who had nearly as thick an accent as the smith. Finally, they came away with the three canvases and the plentiful rope they needed to make shelters.

Auden shook his head, frowning at his lightened purse. "We're running through our means faster than we should," he said warily.

Evylin frowned. "I thought Ephren gave us enough to last the whole trip."

"He didn't account for the exchange rate," he said, sighing. "We'll have to be careful if we want to make it through the rest of our travels in Wauld."

"How much longer is our journey here?"

Auden pursed his lips in thought. "Ilain's better at numbers," he said offhandedly. Then he muttered under his breath, counting on his fingers. "Another month?"

"A month?" Evylin couldn't help her disappointment. "Please tell me that it won't rain the whole time."

Auden chuckled. "You Ephrians act as though a little damp will melt you like snow. But no," he assured her. "Soon, we'll head west through the moors. It's not so wet there. And then we'll be at the end of spring, so the rain up north will dry up too."

"Thank Allore," she said.

They passed back through the center of the village, coming to an abrupt halt as a man was thrown, bottom over teakettle, out of a building and into the street in front of them. Evylin, Auden, and their horses scrambled back as the man sprawled in the dirt, bleary-eyed and dazed but no worse for wear. A woman stood in the doorway of the building, railing at the man as a burly guard dusted his hands before slipping back into the noisy interior. As abruptly as the man had been tossed out, the woman ducked inside and slammed the door. The round wood sign above swayed, identifying the building as a tavern.

Evylin turned to Auden. "Is it usual to get drunk before noon in Wauld?" she asked sarcastically.

Auden led his horse around the drunkard, who mumbled a love song as he lay on his back, staring at the sky. "Depends on who you are," he replied blandly, and she realized he was serious.

Pulling a face, Evylin followed him around the drunkard. She glanced back at the tavern door, wondering if that was why the village seemed so deserted. Perhaps all this dreary rain mixed with Blount's oppression led the people to drink.

As she started to turn away, Evylin's eyes caught on the tavern's exterior wall where a noticeboard hung. A smattering of papers ruffled in the breeze, a small canopy failing to protect them from the rain. Most of the pages showed deterioration and wear from the elements, but one crisp sheet stuck out like a beacon in the center.

Evylin stopped in the middle of the street, the drunkard still singing off-key about a lady fair and the knight who tried to save her.

"Auden," she called, his name coming out as a warning.

The highlord turned around, expression concerned. "What is it?"

Evylin didn't bother saying a word. She pointed to the noticeboard, letting him see for himself. The poster bore a clean sketch of Auden, Ilain, and Evylin with the words:

> *Writ of Attachment*
> *for crimes against the Crown,*
> *siblings, Highlord Auden Calder and Highlady Ilain Calder*
> *of the Order of the Flame,*
> *and the fugitive Evylin Deckard,*
> *accompanied by their four accomplices.*
> *Reward per head: 20 gold*
> *Reward for all: 150 gold*
> *Alive; Confirmation Mandatory.*

Evylin and Auden stared in disbelief. Blount must have gotten his father, the king, to issue this writ, labeling them as fugitives. The illustrations were good. Realistic enough that there could be no doubt should anyone spot them.

Auden shifted, tightening his grip on his reins. "We have to get out—"

"I'm afraid it's already too late, mucker," a man said, causing them both to whirl.

Nev stood at the corner of the tavern, his gap-toothed grin cunning. Evylin went for her knife, but the sharp press of a blade to her lower back halted her. Suddenly, she realized the drunkard wasn't singing any longer.

More men crept from around the corner, moving to box Evylin and Auden in.

"I knew I recognized you," Nev said, his accent not quite as uneducated as before. He tapped the stone of the tavern wall. "As I said, it pays to sell. And it pays even better when you check the local tavern first."

Evylin glanced at Auden, confused.

He offered her an apologetic frown. "It's a motto of a sort," he explained. "It pays to sell—it means that you're a sellsword."

With a sharp inhale, Evylin understood. These men were mercenaries.

"Well," she said, meeting his gaze, "I've never met a sellsword who could beat a Mage and Warrior."

Auden opened his mouth to reply, but the twang of bowstrings halted his words. They both looked, seeing four mercenaries holding arrows at the ready.

"Don't bother fighting," Nev said, then motioned to his men.

The mercenaries moved forward, ropes ready to bind them.

Evylin didn't hesitate. She let her senses rise, tapping into her magic. In a fluid motion, she twisted away from the false drunkard with so much speed he could only gape, then she brought her hand down to slap his wrist. He yelped, dropping the blade. She caught it, ready to drive it into his stomach. Then she heard a thump and Auden's groan.

She slashed at the mercenary before her, cutting a red stripe across his chest. She whirled to save Auden, finding a trio of men charging as a wall right in front of her on the narrow street.

The men rammed into her, pushing her back and into the noticeboard. The back of her head smacked against the wood, sending black dots swirling into her vision. She flicked her wrist, and one of the men cried out when she found her mark. He crumpled, freeing her arm enough that she could maneuver it to make another strike. But she wasn't fast enough.

One of her assailants slammed the butt of his dagger into her temple. Her knees buckled, but she held onto consciousness with all she was worth. She jammed her blade forward, hitting another man, and drove her knee up, catching his groin and sending him to the dirt.

Then the mercenary's hilt crashed into her temple again, and Evylin dropped too.

CHAPTER TWENTY-THREE

Deckard watched as Evylin and Auden led their horses toward the road to Dunneshead in the morning fog. His grip strained on the hilt of his sword, fighting down the memories of the last time he'd let the two of them go off together. He couldn't help the nagging fear that he was letting them walk straight into danger once more. But he reminded himself that the last time was a suicide mission, and this was a simple trip into a village.

Forcing his gaze away from their shrinking figures, Deckard turned back to the camp. He'd made the right choice, he knew. This was exactly what Hewitt had told him to do; he'd given Evylin the independence she desired.

Evylin's depression weighed on Deckard. Giving her space, letting her process it without his help, felt wrong. The urge to take her in his arms last evening nearly overcame his resolve.

Knowing his weakness, Deckard had searched the trees, looking for Hewitt's ghost. He'd met the man's eyes, shrouded in the distance, silently begging for clarification. At Hewitt's nod, Deckard found the strength to hold it together and trust her uncle. He left her to her fragile emotions and agreed to her request.

Now, he had to hope it was worth it.

Deckard knew convincing Auden wouldn't be easy. He expected the Mage's reluctance. What he hadn't expected was his enterprising.

At Deckard's appeal last night, Auden was good-natured and understanding. But he was also cunning. "If we let her go, the others will inevitably ask to join in the future," he'd said, using the same argument as Deckard. "We can't have that."

"I'll talk to them," Deckard promised.

"That's not enough." Auden took a step forward, his voice low as they spoke at the edge of camp. "This is dangerous. Evylin will not pass as Waulden, not by any stretch of the imagination. We're trying to stay forgettable. An Ephrian woman accompanying a Waulden man is *highly* memorable."

"What do you want me to do?" Deckard asked desperately. "She needs a break. Otherwise, I fear she'll fall apart in the Keep."

Auden considered him, his lips pinched. He clasped his wrist in a pensive posture. "This is a great favor you're asking," he said with calculation.

Deckard heard the weight behind his inflection. He chose to accept it. "And what would you like in return?"

Auden's reluctant response gave Deckard pause, but he knew he'd agree no matter what it was.

"After we've gathered the Relics," Auden said, "completing this mission . . . I want your word that you'll join the Alliance in whatever capacity they ask of you."

Deckard's heart squeezed. That was more than a favor. It was a life sentence. As a Mage married to a Warrior, they'd want him to Bond with Evylin. He couldn't promise that when neither he nor Evylin wanted it.

But Deckard knew something Auden didn't: His marriage to Evylin wasn't sealed. If it came to it, Deckard could dissolve their marriage, saving them both from that fate. Or, he realized, it could save *her*.

If he made this promise, the Alliance could make him marry and Bond with another Warrior, should they find another willing female.

Despite what it might mean for him, despite that he was allying himself with a governmental regime he knew little about, Deckard said, "Fine. You have my word."

Auden's eyes flashed with surprise, then narrowed in suspicion. "Just like that?"

Deckard didn't hesitate. "Do you doubt me? I will do whatever is best for my wife, no matter the cost."

"This is a cost she'll have to pay as well," Auden warned.

Knowing that wasn't the truth, Deckard lied. "She trusts me. If I tell her this is the right choice, she'll listen."

He could tell Auden was skeptical, but he accepted his victory. And now, he was taking Evylin to Dunneshead with him.

Deckard surveyed the rest of the troop. Ethenn and Rafferty were preparing to go hunting while waiting for Evylin and Auden's return. At the far end of the camp, Ilain sat sketching in her book and talking with Thom conspiratorially. Their relationship, if not romantic, had certainly grown friendly. Ethenn cast a dismayed glance at the pair, then hefted his quiver of freshly repaired arrows.

As the hunter and Rafferty disappeared into the trees, Deckard moved toward the horses. He checked his saddlebags, pretending to repack them. He angled himself so that he faced away from Thom and Ilain. Then he willed Hewitt to appear.

The ghost's bushy eyebrows hung low. "You aren't afraid that they'll see me?" he whispered with a jut of his chin toward the couple.

"After all this time of you lurking in the trees, I *know* they can't," Deckard said quietly. "You've heard what's happened?"

Hewitt snarled. "Are you referring to your magic or your stupidity in letting Evylin go to that village?"

"You nodded in approval."

"I nodded to tell you to trust your instincts. I didn't realize they were idiotic."

Deckard sighed. "You're the one who said I should let her take care of herself."

"I didn't mean you should let her risk her life because she's bored."

"You were there," Deckard said with a frown. "She isn't bored. She's devastated."

Hewitt ignored his argument. "You should have talked with me first."

"Even if we hadn't agreed never to go out alone, I now have Auden constantly at my side, teaching me." Deckard grimaced at the thought. Ilain hadn't exaggerated when she said her brother's tutelage would be monotonous. "The man takes a cruel amount of pleasure in chronicling the antiquity of Mages."

"I've heard," Hewitt growled.

Without the ability to talk with Hewitt, Deckard had taken to keeping him around as of late. He needed the ghost apprised of their situation, even if they couldn't discuss it quite yet. And while Auden's absence freed Deckard from his lessons, it didn't make slipping out of camp any easier.

However, it did allow him to gather more information from Ilain.

Deckard tied off his saddlebag and met Hewitt's steely gaze. "Keep listening," he charged, then joined Thom and Ilain at the heart of the camp. He took a seat across from them, watching thoughtfully as Thom leaned over her shoulder.

"That's all wrong," Thom said, reaching over to tap the page. "I'm far taller than Raff."

Ilain whacked his hand to keep him from touching the paper, but his finger came away with a smudge of charcoal on it anyway. She sighed as though dealing with a child. "You are no more than half a head taller," she said. "And *I'm* the artist."

"So that means you can lie in your artwork?"

Ilain lifted her eyes to the Heavens, then turned to Deckard. "Did you need something, Jonn?" she asked, almost hopefully.

Hewitt hovered near the trio, shadowed in the trees. As Ilain showed no signs of noticing the ghost's presence, Deckard's confidence rose. "I had a question," he began. "And with Auden away . . ."

Ilain grinned knowingly. "Mm-hm. What is it he won't tell you?"

Deckard returned her smile. "It isn't that he *won't*. It's that he's too busy elucidating for me to ask in the first place."

"Shocking," Ilain murmured. "What is it you'd like to know?"

"I'm interested in learning more about the resources," Deckard said, keeping his inquiry broad. "And how they impact a Mage's abilities."

"You mean, you want to know what powers they grant?"

"More or less."

Ilain nodded, and Thom sat back, listening with interest. "First and foremost, magic is varied," she began. "The two clearest distinctions in magic are between Warrior magic and Mage magic. And, of course, every classification and type of Mage is unique as well. However, even amongst two Fire Mages, their magic may manifest differently. The strength of the connection between the resource and the Mage determines how powerful the magic will be. All the resources have their special manifestations, but essentially, they are all founded on the same basic functions: summoning, manipulation, and control."

After a breath, Ilain continued, "Every Mage has some level of ability within those skills, with *all* the resources. The stronger your connection, the stronger your influence. It is easiest to learn how to manipulate a resource, but mastering it is difficult. Whereas summoning and control are harder to learn, but once you do, there's little you can't do with them."

Ilain lifted a hand. "For example," a flame sparked to life above her palm, "I *summoned* this flame. Where there was no fire, I created one from my connection to the resource."

The flame flickered out, a small wisp of smoke dissolving into the air. "With a flame like that, I can manipulate it however I want," she said. "Or I can control it."

"Aren't manipulation and control the same thing?" Thom asked.

Ilain gave him a wry smile. "If I set my hand on your knee," she said, doing just that, "I can manipulate your emotions."

Thom knocked her hand away with a scowl, and Ilain's smile grew. "But," she said, "I *can't* control your response."

Deckard didn't know whether to laugh at his brother's discomfort or frown at the complexity of magic. "And all of this is learned by connecting with the resource?" he asked.

"Well," she said thoughtfully, "it's more about developing a relationship with the resource."

Thom scoffed. "How do you develop a relationship with fire?"

"Carefully," Ilain replied with a smirk. "It's part of magic itself. You wouldn't be magical if you didn't already have a relationship with at least one resource. After all, it's the resources themselves that choose you."

"But they're . . . inanimate," Deckard objected. "Aren't they?"

"Yes, but that doesn't make them any less sentient."

Deckard and Thom stared at her blankly.

Ilain considered how to explain before continuing, "Think of it this way: no, they don't have life, but they are the *source* of life. While they are not alive, they are aware, and they can connect to the ones to whom they give life."

Deckard furrowed his brow, trying to understand. He wasn't sure he ever could. "And how are you supposed to have a relationship with something that's not alive?" he asked.

"Do you not have a relationship with your wedding ring?" Ilain said. "Does it not connect you to your marriage with Evylin? It relates to you and you to it because it matters to you. Whether or not you can converse with it doesn't negate the relationship."

"So," Deckard surmised, "a Mage develops their relationship with a resource by . . . valuing it?"

Ilain opened her mouth, then paused. She pressed her lips together in amused consideration. "Hm. I've never thought of it like that, but yes, I suppose so. And it works both ways. The resource that chose you, making it your primary, valued you enough to grant you power. The more you regard and cherish it, the more it will regard and cherish you, thereby strengthening your connection.

"And," she added, "the more you connect with your resource, the more you understand it and its desires. For example, Auden spent a lot of time studying and developing his relationship with Day magic before he realized he could channel its warmth into a room without ever needing to start a fire or call forth a burst of light. He's designed this . . ." Her hands formed the shape of a square. "He's created this box-thing that will conduct the heat of Day magic. He's still perfecting it, but it could heat a large room all on its own. He calls it a heater, but I've told him to come up with something more creative."

Amazed by the idea, Deckard felt his lips part in awe. "You mean, you could have one of these boxes in your house and never need a fireplace again?"

Ilain nodded. "And that's just the start of his inventions, thanks to his relationship with Day. He may not be as powerful as I am, but with his connection, he's likely to become one of the many Day Mages who live well over five centuries."

"Five—" Deckard stopped himself, wide eyes meeting Thom's. His brother appeared equally baffled.

Deckard turned back to Ilain. "You're saying there are Mages who can live to five hundred years old?"

"Of course," she said casually.

Thom's face screwed up in disbelief. "Do all Mages live that long?" he asked, glancing at Deckard as though he'd grown a third arm.

"Oh, no," Ilain said with a laugh. "Most of us only live two centuries, give or take a decade."

Deckard's heart stalled. "Most? Meaning . . . how many exactly?"

She met his worried gaze with her calm one. "If you're wondering how long you'll live, the answer is: I don't know. Every Mage is different. The average Mage lives to approximately two hundred, while Bonded Mages are purported to live well past that. Day Mages tend to live the longest, due to the fact that Day is a life-giving resource."

Uncertain how to feel about living so long—well past the deaths of his family and friends—Deckard found himself asking somewhat hopefully, "Does that mean that Night Mages die earlier than the rest?"

Ilain frowned. "No. Why would they?"

"I thought—" He fought the urge to frown as well. "Didn't you say that Day and Night are each other's mirror? So if Day is life-giving, Night would give death."

"Oh." Ilain shook her head. "While Night *can* symbolize death, it doesn't affect the Mage's lifespan. After all, Night can symbolize rest and recovery as well. It can be just as restorative as Day, used in the correct manner."

Deckard's eyes flashed to where Hewitt hid in the trees. He leaned forward then, cautiously broaching the subject he'd intended all along. "If . . ." he began timidly. "If Day symbolizes life, can it raise the dead?"

Ilain's pale face somehow blanched to a crisp white. "No, Jonn," she said sharply. "It can't."

"Why not?" Thom asked, scanning her curiously.

"Because that's a violation of life," Ilain said with finality. "Once someone has died, they are separated from life. Day can no longer reach them at that point."

The answer confirmed Deckard's darkest suspicions. "Because Night controls death?"

Ilain's keen jade green eyes fell on him. "If you're looking for a way to bring someone back to life, Jonn, stop. It can't be done."

"I'm not foolish enough to believe it hasn't been tried before," Deckard assured her. "And if it had been successful, I would imagine even Ephren wouldn't have been able to keep that from the legends."

Determined to get answers, he continued by asking the question that plagued him. "But that does lead me to wonder: what about ghosts?"

Thom latched on, his curiosity far more natural than Deckard's. "That's a good point," he said. "People have told ghost stories for . . . well, since the dawn of time, I'd imagine. Does that mean that Night magic can—?"

"Stop," Ilain demanded, her gaze flashing between the two of them. "These are questions that lead to madness. I warned you, Jonn, that should you be a Night Mage, Auden would treat you differently. That's because we have firsthand experience with how Night magic can twist a person into a monster. And questions like these lead to that path."

A chill swept across Deckard's skin. Hewitt's ghost crossed his arms in the shadows.

"But," Deckard said, pressing his luck, "that means it can be done?"

Ilain looked on the verge of anger, her jaw rigid and her eyes dull. "I understand the temptation," she said coolly. "Giving Evylin even a moment more with Hewitt would be . . . Everyone longs for the chance to see their lost loved ones again. But I promise, you and she are better off letting the dead rest."

Deckard dipped his chin in repentance, the motion entirely genuine. By whatever means he'd summoned Hewitt—in whatever way he'd grasped his power before even knowing it was there in the first place—he feared it. This was too great, too dangerous a magic. And no matter the benefit of Hewitt's presence, Deckard worried he'd already started down that path to madness.

"I appreciate your honesty, Ilain," Deckard said, meeting her gaze with humility. "I promise, no matter what kind of Mage I am, I will do my best to heed both your and your brother's advice and training. I don't want to endanger any of us."

Ilain's expression softened. "I know," she said, her usual mirth returning. "And who knows, maybe you'll be a Time Mage. That would be wildly fun."

"How so?" he asked, unable to feel any hope that she was right.

Her eyes twinkled. "They control time itself. You could, if you proved strong enough, turn back small portions of time, potentially preventing fatal accidents or devastating mistakes. For instance, had we known this sooner, you could have turned back time while we were in the Day Keep, stopping Blount from taking the Relic from under our noses."

Or, Deckard realized, *I could have stopped Hewitt from dying at all.*

With a false smile, Deckard pretended to accept the idea. "That would be quite ideal," he decided.

Ilain tipped her head to the side. "Though," she said with reluctance, "Time Mages *are* known for becoming somewhat . . . hm. Flighty."

Thom snorted. "In what way?"

"They can become rather enraptured with Time magic and forget that the rest of the world exists," she admitted. Then she shrugged and gave Deckard an encouraging smile. "I'm sure that wouldn't happen to you. After all, you have Evylin."

"And that would help because . . . ?" Deckard asked.

Ilain raised an eyebrow as though he were being obtuse. "Because you're in love with her," she said matter-of-factly.

Deckard swallowed past the instant dryness in his throat, unable to deny it.

"Even if you didn't Bond," Ilain continued, "you would never be able to abandon her. Not for all the magic in the world."

Hewitt's ghost gave a sharp nod in agreement, and Deckard knew they were right. No matter if Evylin asked to dissolve their marriage or chose to stay with him, he would do whatever it took to secure her happiness. No resource and no magic could change that. Not even Night's madness would change his mind.

"Now," Ilain said, picking up her sketchbook, "leave me alone, both of you. I have a drawing to finish."

With a scoff, Thom turned to Deckard. "Care to spar?" he asked.

Deckard looked around the clearing. "I suppose we don't have anything better to do," he said.

Over the next half hour, the brothers tested their skills against one another. Though Deckard had greatly improved throughout their travel with Hewitt, so had Thom. After their bout over two weeks prior, Thom was now prepared for Deckard's new capabilities.

What he didn't have was Hewitt's ghost advising him as they practiced.

While Deckard didn't win all their matches, he did win most of them. Thom's jaw grew continually more tense until Ethenn and Rafferty returned from hunting and joined the brothers. They began a small contest to see who could win, with Ilain acting as a judge when there was some question of fair play.

The Waulden fog began to dissipate as the sun rose higher. Deckard looked up, calculating the time of Evylin and Auden's absence. He frowned. They'd been gone more than two hours. At a twenty-minute pace to and from the village, plus a generous hour for their shopping, they should have returned nearly half an hour before.

Hewitt's ghost stepped up beside him. "I told you," he growled. "You shouldn't have let her go."

Deckard tried to reassure himself that all was well. They might have gotten caught up . . . Doing what? It was a village. There wouldn't be sights to see or special wares to peruse. They should have returned, which meant something was wrong.

Subconsciously, Deckard shut Hewitt out, the ghost disappearing without a trace.

While Ethenn beat Thom a second time in a row, Deckard moved for his horse. "Loxley," he called.

Ethenn turned, alert.

"We're going to Dunneshead," he ordered.

The whole troop stared at him in surprise.

"Jonn," Ilain said warily. "That's—"

"It's been too long," he interrupted, clasping his cloak around his neck. He unbuckled his sword belt, slipping the scabbard free. Carrying weapons in Wauld without a written permit was a crime punishable by flogging and months in a labor camp. He could only carry concealed weapons into this fight. "Something's wrong."

Though Ilain's expression dropped, her eyes wide with worry, she shook her head. "You—you don't know that."

Deckard met her gaze. "Yes," he said, "I do."

Thom and Rafferty stood around them while Ethenn strapped his own hidden blades on his person, leaving behind his bow and quiver. His hatchet landed with a *thunk* in the band on his belt. While less inconspicuous, he could claim its use was for chopping wood alone.

Deckard's sudden declaration had sent a charge through the camp. They all wore haunted expressions. They'd been in this situation before when the five of them went to save Evylin and Auden in the Water Keep.

Thom stepped up, setting a hand on Deckard's arm. "You don't seriously plan to go in with just you and Ethenn, do you?" he said.

"We can't take a large party," Deckard said.

"That's ridiculous," Thom retorted. "What if it's an ambush? What if there are too many of them? Two people aren't a rescue party."

Deckard pulled away from his brother's grip. "What if you're right?" he returned. "What if this is an ambush? What if we all go in there and find that Blount has them? We'll be giving him the opportunity to take all three of our Relics and eliminate everyone opposing his attempt to gain the others."

Deckard shook his head. "We can't risk that. Ethenn and I will find Evylin and Auden while you and Rafferty protect Ilain, taking her to the next stop. If we don't meet you there, then it's up to *you* to get the rest of the Relics and take them to the Alliance."

Thom glared at him, lips parted incredulously. "Are you insane? You can't do this—"

"Captain Deckard," he said, voice sharp like an officer's.

His brother's shoulders instantly drew back.

Deckard held his fierce stare, then placed a hand on his shoulder. "I need you to protect Ilain and the Relics. This is not a request; it is an order. Do you understand?"

Thom's jaw tightened in the way it used to when they were young. For a heartbeat, Deckard tensed, his mind flashing back to their childhood. Should they have been ten years younger, he would have expected his brother to lash out with his fists.

Now, Thom leaned in, words hissing out between clenched teeth as he said, "I want to help."

"And this is how you help," Deckard insisted.

"No," Thom spat, grabbing a fistful of Deckard's coat. "I want to help you find her."

Deckard saw the possessive flare in his brother's eyes with those words. It was the same look he'd seen when Thom declared that he would do whatever it took to protect Evylin. And Deckard's chest seared with anger now as it had then.

Deckard shoved Thom back, breaking his hold, and reminded him, "She's not your wife."

Before his brother could respond, Deckard turned. "Ilain, what is the next stop?"

The woman's eyes flickered from brother to brother. "Dunbar. Twenty-two miles southeast."

Deckard swung up onto his horse, Ethenn following his lead. "Take Thom and Rafferty there," he instructed the Mage. "We'll find them and meet you as soon as we can."

"Colonel," Rafferty said, hurrying over. He raised a hand, a Relic hanging from his grasp. "Take this with you."

Deckard stared down at the dull amethyst. Night, like his magic. Did Rafferty know, or was it just a coincidence? The Relic would help. Though Deckard had yet to access his magic, if danger arose, surely he could with a Relic in hand. But then Deckard *had* used magic when he'd summoned Hewitt. And he knew, with or without the Relic, he *would* find Evylin and bring her back safely, no matter what.

It was too dangerous a risk. If Blount had captured them . . .

Deckard's jaw grew tense at the thought. If Blount had captured them, Deckard would *need* to be stronger than the Night Mage.

Swallowing the lump in his throat, Deckard swept the Relic from Rafferty's grasp. He tugged open his collar, working the beaming amethyst pendant under his coat. Its cold metal sent an eerie calm sweeping across his skin.

Ilain watched, her chin raised in question, but she didn't speak.

Deckard took it as all the approval he needed. Then he met Thom's angered glare. "Keep her safe," he charged.

Without waiting for a reply, Deckard dug his heels into his horse's flank. He and Ethenn tore out of the forest, riding straight and fast toward Dunneshead.

CHAPTER TWENTY-FOUR

As the dirt road broke through the overhang of trees, they slowed their horses. Deckard's heart beat with the urgency of a ticking clock. He scanned the distant village looking for any sign of disturbance or . . . well, he wasn't quite sure what he expected to see. Some sign of whatever had waylaid Evylin and Auden this long, he supposed. But the village appeared calm, the thinning fog drifting out over the nearby lake.

The horses snorted, grateful to exchange their race for a plodding pace. Deckard's hand twitched on the reins. The tingling of the Night Relic's metal against his bare chest, tucked beneath the layers of his clothes to hide its glow, seemed only to heighten his agitation. He hated being forced to slow down. He wanted to charge into the village, knocking down doors until he found Evylin.

He fought those urges, remaining alert to survey the buildings as they drew near.

"Sir," Ethenn muttered, his unusually shaky tone betraying his unease, "I don't mean to question you, but . . ."

Deckard glanced at him. "But you have a question?"

The young man nodded.

"Go ahead."

Ethenn eyed the village, his keen hunter's gaze picking up things Deckard was sure he'd missed. "I'm concerned that Thom was right," Ethenn said. "This could be a trap, and walking in with only the two of us. . . ."

Deckard let the worried thought hang for only a moment. "Do you know why I chose to bring you with me, Loxley?"

The young soldier considered it. "No."

"Because you're a hunter. You can track, and you have stealth. If there's a need, both will help us rescue Evylin and Auden; hopefully, without a fight."

After a moment of consideration, Ethenn said, "We'd have to be *very* lucky." He paused then and eyed Deckard warily. "I'm worried, sir. If we're walking into a trap, I'm not sure you should be here."

Deckard's brow furrowed. "Why shouldn't I be here?"

"You're a Mage. You're every bit as important as the Calders now. And if we fail here, you could have helped Lady Calder obtain the Relics. Instead, we'll leave only one Mage and two non-magical people to complete our mission. After our time in the other Keeps, I don't see that small of a party succeeding."

Despite the logic in his argument, Deckard felt that it lacked understanding of the situation. "Whatever happens," he said, meeting the man's troubled stare, "I could never leave Evylin without knowing she's safe. One day, when you have a wife, you'll know what that's like."

Ethenn gave him a soldier's nod of acceptance, though his expression remained disquieted.

They passed the first buildings, entering Dunneshead proper. Guards patrolled the streets, scanning them. Deckard kept a firm grip on the reins, trusting that his weapons were well hidden. They'd both left behind their swords, keeping only concealable daggers and throwing knives upon their persons. The village was still, windows were shut, and the streets were empty. A few housewives swept their porches or hung laundry on lines, pausing to watch the strangers warily. There was no ready sign of Evylin or Auden.

"I'm not sure I'll ever marry," Ethenn said under his breath, drawing Deckard's attention back to him.

"Why not?" he asked, rather grateful for the distraction from the heady sensation of the Night Relic, which tugged with gentle pressure at his focus with its subliminal aggression.

With their hoods up, Deckard could hardly see Ethenn's face, but when he caught a glance, he thought he recognized the dejected look there. "I'm not sure I was made for it."

Unable to stop himself, Deckard chuckled. "How old are you, Loxley?"

"Twenty-one."

Deckard let out a bemused puff of air at the eleven-year discrepancy between them. "Trust me, you have plenty of time to meet the right woman."

Ethenn gave another of those agreeable nods, as though accepting his commanding officer's orders regardless of his personal opinion. Then he glanced at Deckard warily. "Sir," he said thinly, "do you—do you think it's acceptable for a man to be younger than his wife?"

After overhearing the conversation between Ethenn and Ilain, Deckard found himself internally grimacing, knowing the intention behind the question. "While it isn't common, I don't see anything wrong with it," he replied hesitantly. "However, I suppose that would depend on the woman in question."

A moment passed as they came to the village's center. Small shops, a smith, and a tavern filled the square. They dismounted, tying their horses to the hitching post. Still no sign of Evylin or Auden.

"Did you know it was Highlady Calder's birthday yesterday?" Ethenn asked quietly.

Intent on the search for his wife, Deckard tried not to find the young man's inquiry annoying. "I did not," he said casually. "Seems it's the week for birthdays. Evylin's is in five days."

Ethenn straightened his cloak to hang flat over his hatchet. "I believe they're the same age," he said. "Twenty-six, or . . . I suppose, twenty-seven with Evylin's birthday coming."

Deckard frowned as he scanned the streets. "It isn't polite to discuss a woman's age, Loxley."

"I'm sorry, sir," Ethenn said inattentively, then took a step toward the tavern. "Sir?"

Following the young man's gaze, Deckard studied the tavern. Its weathered stone walls and aged wooden shutters were worn down like most of the buildings he'd seen across Wauld. It had two stories, and the top floor's windows were all shut up. The bubbled glass of the street-level window showed a warm, orange glow. The hum of music and laughter emanated from the building.

But it was the noticeboard that caught the men's attention.

On the side of the tavern was a writ of attachment, a warrant for the arrest of their troop, along with sketches of Auden, Ilain, and Evylin. Despite the mention of four other companions, the soldiers' names were excluded. Deckard supposed Blount had not yet had the chance to learn them.

Fear coursed through Deckard's veins, his heart beating faster. In all their caution and preparation, they hadn't anticipated this. With a writ on them, there would be no moving freely through the settlements of Wauld anymore.

"I suppose we know what happened to them now," Ethenn remarked dully. "Do you think we're too late?"

Deckard shook his head with determination, forcing himself to move away from the writ to avoid appearing suspicious. "No," he insisted, leading them across the village center. He wasn't sure whom he was reassuring—Ethenn or himself. "No, at most they could have only been taken two hours ago. And we don't know if they were taken at all. They could be hiding from their pursuers."

Eyes on the ground, Ethenn had instinctively begun to track. "There were no signs on the road of a large party leaving the village," he said, even as he scanned the dirt. "Given the way the river encircles this settlement, there'd be no other way in or out. Which means they're still here."

"What if their party was small?" Deckard asked, tugging his hood lower as a damp breeze cut through, signaling another bout of rain.

Ethenn held up a hand to stop him, gaze still cast downward. His brow furrowed in concentration as he spoke. "It would take at least three men to subdue Evylin, and that's only if they have the element of surprise. To take down Auden too . . . No, it had to be a large group."

Deckard was impressed by the man's reasoning. It was the exact reason he'd chosen the hunter's aid. "Did you find something?" he asked at Ethenn's prolonged pause.

The young man's brow furrowed, then he looked up toward the smith's shop. The pounding of a hammer on metal reverberated out to them. "This is going to sound odd," he said. "But I can sense that they visited the smith."

"Sense, how?" Deckard asked skeptically.

With a grimace, Ethenn glanced at him. "Call it hunter's intuition?"

Though Deckard had never heard of such a thing before, he chose to trust the man. As they crossed the muddy street, the first drops of rain began to fall. They ducked under the awning as it intensified. The smith looked up, his thick arms belying his narrow frame.

Adopting his fake Waulden accent, Deckard greeted the smith. "I'm looking for my wife and our comrade," he said cheerfully. "He's about my height with bright red hair, and . . ." He gestured toward the smith's scraggly copper beard and chuckled. "Well, I suppose that describes the lot of us, eh? But my wife is from the border with Ephrian heritage, a few generations back. She has dark hair and eyes and stands about, well—"

Deckard set a hand on Ethenn's shoulder. "She's about her brother's height," he concluded.

Ethenn shifted uncomfortably as the smith eyed him.

"They came into town to get tents for us and our band," Deckard continued. "We wondered if they came here in their search."

The smith turned his critical stare to Deckard. "Wh' din' yeh com' wi' yer wi'f?" he asked.

If Deckard hadn't gone into town with Auden over the last couple of weeks, he wouldn't have understood. Thankfully, his grasp on the Waulden accent was growing stronger. "It was our employer's idea," he said, stating their agreed-upon lie. Every time they went into a settlement, the story was that they worked for a mercenary band, traveling on behalf of a Waulden noble who would prefer his cause to remain unknown. As it turned out, such behavior was common in the country.

After a beat, the smith relaxed. He rattled off a broken string of words that Deckard managed to cobble into an explanation. Yes, they had been there about an hour ago. He gave them poles for the tents, sent them to his friend at the docks for the canvas and rope, and hadn't seen them since.

Handing over a small stack of nanny farthings, Deckard thanked the smith. Then he relayed the explanation to Ethenn as they stepped out into the rain.

"Do we go to the docks then?" Ethenn asked.

"I suppose," Deckard said with a sigh, reverting to his Ephrian elocution. "Though I have a feeling we're going to get the same answer from the dockworker. If they were taken by a group as large as you suspect, I can't imagine they'd do it out in the open."

"What if they ambushed them before they got to the docks?" Ethenn said as they neared the tavern once more. "Could be—"

The hunter stopped in his tracks, frowning.

Deckard paused. "What is it?"

Eyes on the tavern, Ethenn sniffed as a cold breeze cut through the rain. Then he shook his head. "It's nothing," he said. "We should go to the docks."

Though Deckard stared at the tavern for a lingering second, he followed Ethenn down the street. The rain ran over the shoulders of their wool cloaks, turning the dirt to mud under their boots. His anxiety was beginning to rise, his fear that Evylin's captors were getting away while he searched in vain.

Suddenly, Ethenn grabbed Deckard's arm and pulled him down an alleyway.

"Loxley, what—?"

Ethenn shushed him, then surveyed the narrow passage. "All right," he whispered once his inspection was complete, "we're safe. I found them."

Deckard stared at him, baffled. "What?"

Ethenn tossed his hand in the direction of the town center. "They're in the tavern. There must have been a scuffle because . . . Well, listen, you know how I said I have this hunter's intuition?"

"Yes," Deckard said, narrowing his eyes.

With a grimace, Ethenn shrugged. "That wasn't true," he admitted, then scratched the back of his head through his hood. "I kind of . . . caught Evie's scent."

"I'm sorry, what?"

"I know, it's strange," Ethenn said, obviously uncomfortable. "But it's something I learned over the years. You can kind of smell your quarry, and it helps lead you to them. And—well, I know the scent of Evie's sweat from all the times we've trained together.

When the rain was about to start, the wind picked up, and I caught her scent coming from the smithy. When we just passed the tavern, I caught it again, but stronger."

Despite the oddity of the situation, Deckard scanned the young man with interest. "That's the most bizarre thing I've ever heard," he remarked. "You're sure she's there?"

Ethenn hesitated but nodded. "I think we should get a better look at the place," he said and pointed up. "We'll climb onto the roof of this building and see what we can learn."

"I think that's a good idea."

With the assistance of some wooden crates in the alley, they made their way onto the slate roof. They stayed low, crawling to the ridge. The clay tiles were slick under their feet, but the slant wasn't steep, and they easily sprawled across the wet rooftop.

Two buildings away, they surveyed the side and back of the tavern. Though it stood two stories, it wasn't a large establishment. Often, taverns in Ephria doubled as inns in villages as small as this one. Perhaps Evylin and Auden were being held captive in a room on the second floor.

A separate alley wound behind the tavern, and two men stood guard by the back door. Their presence confirmed Ethenn's deduction. There would be no reason to guard the back door of a tavern—unless you had something to protect.

"What do you think the chances are that those are the only guards?" Ethenn said cynically.

Deckard surveyed the shuttered and darkened windows of the second floor. "I'd say the odds aren't in our favor."

"I'll get a better look," Ethenn said, rising on his hands to shift away.

Deckard grabbed his arm. "It's not safe."

"I may not be as good at sneaking around as Raff, but I'm a hunter," he noted. "Stealthy observation is part of the job."

Reluctantly, Deckard nodded. This *was* why he'd brought the lad. "I'll wait here."

With that, Ethenn scampered easily across the tiles to the building on their right. Deckard watched nervously as the young man stopped, surveyed, and moved again until he dropped out of sight. He tried to catch a glimpse of him on the ground but didn't see so much as a flick of his dark cloak.

Turning back to the tavern, Deckard scrutinized every inch of the building. He could make out the rough outline of movement on the bottom floor. A few denizens entered and exited through the front. Aside from the guards at the back, nothing seemed amiss.

After the better part of an hour, Ethenn returned, almost soundlessly dropping back into his place beside Deckard. "There's no way for us to sneak in," he said ruefully. "The only entrances are the front and back doors or those windows up top. But with them shuttered and so high off the ground, our only chance to reach them would be through the back alley, but those guards will prevent that from happening."

"Could we distract them?" Deckard asked, then added reluctantly, "Or take them down?"

Ethenn considered it. "Possibly," he admitted. "But I don't think it would do us much good. From what I can tell, there isn't anything to climb on in the alleyway, and the back door isn't hidden from the rest of the main floor's view. Even if we *could* sneak in, there's a good chance we'd only find ourselves face-to-face with more guards."

"Hm." Deckard gave the building one final inspection. "So we won't be able to get in unseen?"

"I don't think so."

Pressing a hand to his temple, Deckard resigned himself to the one solution he had. A heaviness had settled over his heart in the last hour, spurring a dark mood. This wasn't how the day was supposed to go. Evylin was supposed to come to Dunneshead, have an enjoyable break from the monotony of the road and her overwhelming depression, and return safe and sound.

Instead, he lay hunched on a rooftop, seeking a way to rescue her.

"All right," Deckard said with renewed determination. Whatever else happened, he *would* save his wife. "We've no choice but to go in directly."

Ethenn turned to him in surprise, dark eyes wide. "You mean, go through the front door?"

Deckard began to back off the roof. "That's precisely what I mean."

Ethenn followed. "That's a terrible idea!" he exclaimed in a whisper. "They'll know we're coming."

They dropped into the alleyway once more. "Not if they think we're patrons," Deckard said. "We'll order a drink and blend in, waiting for our opportunity."

"Sir," Ethenn said, his voice thick with agitation, "there have to be at least a dozen men in there. If they could take down Evie and Auden, don't you think we're a little out of our depth?"

Deckard set a hand on his shoulder and smiled. "Never underestimate what a man is willing to do to get his wife back, Loxley," he said. "They're after money. I'm after something I'd die for."

The young man must have seen the violent resolve in Deckard's stare because his chin lifted with confidence. "And you're a Mage," he noted. "I'd wager none of them will be ready for that."

For the first time, Deckard felt a thrill at the mention of his magic, the Night Relic warming against his skin. Yes, he was a Mage. He might still be in training, but he did not doubt that his power would respond readily in defense of Evylin, regardless of whether he had no true understanding of it yet.

They walked back onto the street, casually making their way to the tavern. A pleasant bell chimed as they pushed through the door. The soft strum of a mandolin came from the bard in the corner. Some patrons looked up at their arrival, turning back to their drinks after a few moments of inspection.

Deckard gave a cursory glance at the space, counting seven customers, the musician, and the barkeep. He drew back his hood as he moved to the bar and took a seat. The barkeep, a stout woman with blonde braids and a stained apron, stepped closer. "What'll yeh have?" she asked in a husky Waulden cadence.

Assuming his fake accent, Deckard gave her a teasing grin. "What've you got?"

She returned the smile, adopting a more sultry stance. "Ale," she said. "Blonde, brown, or red?"

"Brown," Deckard said.

"Red," Ethenn mumbled, attempting to cover his Ephrian inflection.

The woman went about her service, giving Deckard a wink as she set a large tankard in front of him. He tipped her generously to keep up the ruse.

Two men at the back of the tavern waved for the barkeep's attention, and she drifted away.

Ethenn tapped the handle of his tankard worriedly. "Are you sure we should drink?" he asked quietly.

"Drink or not," Deckard replied under his breath in his normal tone. "I'm not leaving without her."

Ethenn sighed, lifting his ale. "It's the leaving part I'm worried about."

Laughter from a group at the center of the room caught Deckard's attention. He kept his eyes forward, avoiding notice. He hated to place his back to the room but settled for listening as the men spoke.

"I dunno, Trover," one man said with a slight slur. "You seemed to enjoy that second hit more than the average blighter."

A grunt sounded, presumably from Trover. "It felt a'right," he said, voice like the rusty sign out front. "Was'n so much bringing that hilt down on her lovely brow as it was the feel of her body pressed ag'nst me. Never felt a woman so lean and supple."

Ethenn choked on his ale.

Deckard clenched his jaw, focusing on the words and not the anger rising within him. He had no way to know if these men were discussing Evylin. But to speak of any woman like that . . . Deckard's knuckles grew white on his tankard's handle.

The barkeep returned, checking on them before stepping into the back. The two other patrons she'd attended rose and clomped through the tavern, the bell above the door clattering as they exited.

After the door shut, the voices of the remaining five patrons spoke up more clearly. "Forty gold," another man said with a chuckle. "Can yeh imagine forty gold for them two? That's more than I've seen in my lifetime."

"It ain't like yer gettin' much of it, Arn," said a nasal voice, its tone grating against his broken words. "Far-ty gold divided by the eighteen of us. That's only . . ." The man fell silent, and Deckard imagined him counting the math on his fingers.

"That's nineteen of us, Fourd," the first man corrected.

"Ah, now I've gotta start over," Fourd lamented.

A new voice joined the group, smoother and more authoritative than the rest. "Two gold a piece," he said. "Give or take a bit."

"Who'll be takin', and who'll be givin'?" Trover asked.

"That's for me to decide, isn't it?" the leader replied.

The other four men fell silent.

Deckard forced himself to drink, pretending that he wasn't engrossed in the conversation. The bitter yeast tasted flat. He had confirmation now. Evylin was somewhere in this building, struck twice by this Trover and likely bound. His mind began to torture him with images of all the dark ways they might have harmed her in the past few hours.

A heat rose under his skin.

"Yeh know," said the first man. "Twenty for that tasty morsel seems short, by my reckoning."

"Aye, I'd say 'tis, Maurd," Arn agreed with another wheezy chuckle. "Quite a bit short."

Maurd let out a long, suggestive sigh. "I think she oughta be . . . oh, at least a hundred for that fine face."

"'Nother hundred fer tha' fine ass too."

"Lest you boys forget," Trover added, "the rest of her ain' so bad either. Believe me."

Deckard's blood spiked as Trover continued. "No, no," he said over his comrades' laughter. "A mere two hundred wouldna begin to cover that fine creature's fee."

Ethenn tensed.

"It's near robbery to suggest we let 'er go for less than five," Arn agreed. "We oughta demand proper payment."

"And if the king won't pay," Maurd said, "might be her that needs to."

The men burst out with more laughter.

Deckard ground his teeth, anger rising with a murmur in his ears. He closed his eyes and curled his hands into fists on the bartop, fighting for control. It was all talk, useless vulgar chatter to bolster their male egos. It wouldn't matter what they said once he got Evylin out of there.

"Colonel," Ethenn whispered, worry lining his voice.

The leader spoke again, cutting over his men's laughter. "I don't care what you do to her," he said sharply. "But she'll stay alive and recognizable for the king's men to confirm, got it?"

His men mumbled their understanding.

A squeal of wood against wood marked the scrape of chair legs over the floor. "Good," the leader said. "Make sure you remember that. And Trover, the next time your hit leaves a mark on our guests, it'll be your pay doing the giving."

Heavy footsteps crossed the room, turning the corner before stomping with an unmistakable tread up the stairs.

Deckard worked to slow his breathing. He kept his head dipped, focusing on the sounds around him. With the leader gone and the barkeep in the back, only four men and the bard remained. Their odds had improved here in the tavern, but they didn't know what awaited them upstairs.

Arn piped up again. "What'da'ya think the king wants with 'em?"

The others were silent for a time.

"Maybe he wants the same as us," Maurd suggested. "Wouldna be the first time he's had his fun, the old dog."

"Is'n he a little old for that?" Arn said with a chuckle. "Or maybe he has some magical tonic that helps 'im."

Deckard felt a tremor pass through his arms and into his fists, a subtle thrum working through his skull.

"Colonel," Ethenn whispered again, "you need to calm down."

"I'll tell you what," Trover said, rusty voice amused. "Good ol' Blount can have the bitch after I'm done with her. Then I can say I rutted the king's whore, and he can have my leftovers."

Heat tingled along Deckard's skin, racing up his spine and across his scalp. A buzz settled into his ears, whispering violently. He grasped onto the newly familiar sensation, letting it take hold of him. His eyes flew open, his vision black at the edges.

Ethenn gasped. "Colonel, your hands."

Ignoring the young man's warning, Deckard rose from his stool. A stillness washed over his mind, his emotions steadying with unnatural calm. The room was tinged in sudden shadow, though no one else seemed to notice. It was as though he'd stepped outside himself, separating from the man he was to become the Mage he was supposed to be.

Casually, Deckard approached the men's table. He gave the thugs a friendly smile and clasped his hands behind his back. "Good morning, gentlemen," he said, allowing his clean Ephrian accent to come through.

Instantly, all four of the men at the table went for their weapons. The music stopped.

"What do you want?" the man whose voice he recognized as Trover's growled.

"I'm looking for my wife," Deckard said. "Perhaps you've seen her. She's quite beautiful with dark hair and tan skin, tall for an Ephrian, and strong enough to fight ten men at once. Worth about five hundred gold, some might say."

The thugs' eyes grew bright with greed.

"Ah, yeh?" Maurd asked, rising. "Seems I have seen her."

"Tha's right," Arn said, drawing his sword. "Why don't we take yeh to 'er? Then yeh can watch as we have our fun."

The other men sniggered, taking out their own weapons. The bard set his mandolin aside and drew a long-bladed dagger, ready for a battle.

Deckard smiled dryly. "I have a better idea," he said, then raised his hands. No thought went into his action. He could never explain how any of it happened. He only felt a violent power flow through him as purple-black masses erupted from the floor.

Two sharp crystalline shadows pierced through Arn and Fourd, the men screaming as Maurd recoiled. Trover didn't lose a second, leaping across the table, knife raised.

Deckard swept a hand through the air. One of the shadows slammed into the thug, knocking him across the room.

Ethenn's reaction was instantaneous. He pulled out his throwing knives, sending them flying through the room with precision. Maurd dropped, the small hilt protruding from his eye. The bard was next. Amidst the commotion, the back door slammed open, the two guards bursting in as footsteps raced down the stairs, drawn by the sound.

Deckard gestured to the guards, the purple-black shadows leaping to his command. They pierced into the guards' chests in a swirl of glittering shards. The crystalline shadows ripped through them before they flew back to rest in Deckard's hands.

Two more men appeared at the bottom of the stairs, swords drawn and eyes wide. Deckard could only imagine what they saw. Dead bodies lay strewn across the tavern floor, three of them at his feet, while shadows hovered around him.

Ethenn's hatchet embedded in one man's chest while Deckard's magic sliced through the other.

The barkeep and another man appeared from the back, weapons drawn as they charged Ethenn. They weren't fast enough, and Deckard cut them down readily.

"Colonel!" Ethenn warned, pointing behind him.

Deckard spun just in time as Trover pounced. He ducked as Trover's long dagger *whooshed* over his head, its blade glinting in the lamplight. The massive man growled and swiped again.

Deckard caught his wrist, then kicked, striking his ankle.

Trover cried out as the bone cracked, falling to one knee. "Take her," he cried, letting his dagger clatter to the floor. "No bitch is worth this."

Deckard grabbed hold of the thug's collar, holding him close. The magic whispered in his head, goading him with its fervor, with its eagerness for violence. "She's worth more than you'll ever know," he said, voice steady and calm. Then he swiped a hand through the air.

A crystalline shard sliced Trover's throat, blood splattering.

Deckard dropped the body and stepped away, the magical shadows following his every move. He met Ethenn at the bar and reached over for a towel to wipe the blood from his cheek. The young man's head dipped, but he motioned to a spot that Deckard had missed.

"Thanks," he said, then tossed the towel on the counter.

Ethenn watched him warily, drawing back as Deckard stepped nearer. A fleeting remorse crossed Deckard's mind. He'd just killed that man in cold blood. Trover had surrendered, dropping his weapon. Perhaps Ethenn had a reason to fear him.

Yet, the magic coiled with ardent excitement, and he shoved the guilt aside, moving for the staircase. This wasn't the time to have a conscience. These men had abducted Evylin and Auden for money and further debated the merit of raping her. They were no loss to humanity. If anything, they deserved their deaths.

At the top of the stairs, two more guards waited. Deckard took them down with a flick of his wrists. Beyond their crumpled forms lay a shadowed hallway with four doors. He didn't bother waiting for Ethenn. He moved to the nearest one and kicked it in, the door swinging wide to reveal the empty bedroom.

Deckard moved across the hall as Ethenn arrived. With another kick, he discovered a second vacant room.

Hatchet back in hand, Ethenn reached his side, approaching the third door. Deckard reared back and kicked. It sailed open on rickety hinges to slam against the wall. Inside were five men with swords drawn. Behind them to the left lay Auden's prone form. And straight ahead, the leader of the gang stood with Evylin before him, holding a knife to her throat.

"Stay right there," the leader ordered.

Frozen in the doorway, Deckard's darkened vision drifted from his study of the room to settle on Evylin. Her hands were bound in front of her, and a bloody welt marred her forehead. Otherwise, she appeared unharmed.

The magic jolted within him, and Deckard smiled at the sight of his wife. "Hello, dear."

CHAPTER TWENTY-FIVE

A dull ache woke Evylin as she opened her eyes to darkness. The emergence from unconsciousness clouded her thoughts. She couldn't remember why her head hurt or why the room was so dark. Thin beams of light streamed in through the shutters, and she squinted to make out the shadowed space.

Then her mind cleared. She and Auden had been taken.

Evylin's pulse raced into her ears, her breathing growing staggered. She tried to gasp but only wound up choking on the rag used to gag her. Instinctively, she jerked her hands up to remove the cloth, but they stopped short, ropes digging into her wrists.

With an annoyed groan, Evylin struggled with the ropes. Tears formed at the edges of her eyes as the bonds ripped at her skin. This was her fault. She should have seen those posters the moment they entered the village center. They could have returned to camp, avoiding this whole disaster.

But then, she shouldn't have been in the village in the first place. If she hadn't insisted, if she could have just managed her sorrow, then they wouldn't be in this mess.

Evylin writhed against the ropes, the tears falling freely now. Where was she? Had those sellswords taken them from Dunneshead while she was unconscious? She didn't know how long she'd been out. No more than a few hours, surely. But where could they have taken her within that time?

Closing her eyes again, Evylin succumbed to her fear for only a moment. The room was cold, the floorboards hard against her hips and shoulders. She rested her head, angled uncomfortably to the side.

If only she had allowed Deckard to go with Auden. If only she had been strong enough to deal with her grief.

But, Evylin realized, if Deckard *had* joined Auden, then it would be the two of them in this predicament instead. The sellsword, Nev, recognized Auden, not her. Deckard's presence would have done nothing to stop that, which meant that *he* would have been taken with Auden. More than a dozen men had attacked them. With the element of surprise on their side and the shock of the writ to impede their reactions, even Evylin hadn't been able to protect herself against the attack.

Evylin pulled in a deep breath, accepting her situation. If the choice was between losing Deckard or her, this was the best outcome. Deckard had more to offer their troop, both as a Mage and a leader. Moreover, he had a future, with or without her.

And Evylin . . . she had nothing. No more dreams, no uncle she adored, no hope. And if Deckard were lost, too, she would have nothing to live for at all.

The devastating thought threatened to overcome Evylin. She wanted to give in to the tears and wallow in her agony. She was tired of fighting this losing battle against drowning in her grief. Giving in would be so much easier.

With another stuttering breath, Evylin ground her teeth against the gag. She pushed the thoughts away. She began to work her hands in their bonds again, refusing to entertain such defeatist notions. She was a Warrior. She was Hewitt's niece. If anyone could get out of this situation, it was her.

Auden was captured somewhere too. He needed her. Though she'd failed to protect him before, she still had a chance to redeem herself. She would find her way out of these bonds and then free them both.

The fibers of the ropes cut into her wrists. The room was too dark for her to see anything beyond shadows and shapes. Evylin focused on breathing through her nose, steadying her heartbeat. A soothing calm washed over her, and clarity cooled her mind. The magic within her rose to her aid, heightening her senses.

Listening intently, Evylin heard the softest thump of a heartbeat in the room with her, and two more beating even more quietly on the other side of the door.

Evylin turned her head, catching the rough outline of a figure, prone on the floor just out of her reach. Her vision sharpened enough for the small beams of light to clarify the figure. It was Auden, his breathing shallow but steady. He lay on his side as well, absolutely still. Unconscious either by his body's design or their captors.

Pleased they'd kept the two of them together, Evylin scanned the rest of the room. Motes of dust danced in the thin rays. The room was small, square, and mostly empty. A few crates clustered the corners and lined the walls, everything kept well away from the captives. A supply room, she surmised.

Finding nothing of use, Evylin turned her attention back to her ropes. A short length from her hands led to her waist, and another segment extended to her feet. Contorting her wrists to grab the rope, she tried to pull her feet closer. No matter how she twisted, she couldn't get them near enough to work on the knot binding her ankles. She diverted her attempts and angled to reach up for her gag. The rope between her wrists and waist was too short, and she couldn't dip her head low enough.

Frustrated and sore, Evylin flopped back onto the floor. There would be no way for her to untie herself in this position. She could already feel the missing weight of the blades on her person. They'd searched her thoroughly. Her skin crawled at the thought, but she focused on the task at hand. If *she* couldn't remove her constraints, she'd have to wait until *they* did. Then she'd take the opportunity for all it was worth.

Voices echoed outside the room, drawing Evylin's attention to the door. Footsteps approached. Men spoke. Then the door opened. A group of men filtered into the room, their bulky shapes and jangling sounds marking them all as heavily armed.

Weapons weren't supposed to be allowed in Wauld. Unless these men were friendly with the guard. . . .

One man broke from the group and headed for the far window. He opened the panes and shutters. Though the sky was still a dull, cloudy gray, the sudden brightness flared in Evylin's magically enhanced vision. She squinted, willing her sight to adjust.

The man turned around, a halo of light glinting off his blond head. "My apologies for the disappointing view," Nev said in his friendly tone. "We haven't had a sunny day in months."

Evylin scanned the room a second time in the daylight. The five men who came with Nev, along with the two guarding the door, were all clearly Waulden as well. Angular features, tall and narrow frames, and light skin, hair, and eyes. Most of them appeared to be sellswords, too, but a couple wore the gold and purple patch of the guard on their coats. So *that* was how they were allowed weapons. It appeared corruption was rife in Wauld.

With stock taken of her captors, Evylin turned to check on Auden. At the sight of him, she let out an involuntary gasp, choking on her gag again.

"We drugged him," Nev said upon her reaction. "Without a Mage to dampen his powers, we mercs have to take what help we can get."

Evylin couldn't take her eyes from Auden's. He was bound in the same fashion as her—a variation of how one might tie a hog—but he wasn't as unconscious as she'd thought. Or, at least, he didn't appear to be.

A splotch of dried blood coated the side of his face, a stream of it crusted on an eyelid as well as his lashes. Two drying patches of blood marred his leg and shoulder, presumably where one of the bowmen had struck him, the arrows now removed. Worse, his dark green eyes were open, wide and glassy. Alert but unfocused. His muscles were rigid, and veins protruded fiercely from his neck and temples.

Working to remain calm, Evylin wondered what horrible drug could put a Mage into such a state. Then she questioned why she hadn't been drugged as well. An oversight, she thought, if these men considered her less dangerous than Auden.

Nev dropped down in front of her, resting on his haunches. "You're not a Mage, though, are you?" he said, studying her with interest. "The writ named him and his sister as Mages, but it said you were just an accomplice. So tell me—"

He reached out to grab her arm and pull her up to a seated position. Evylin grunted as the ropes tore into her skin with the motion.

Nev brushed some of her sweat-and-tear-matted hair off her face. "What's a pretty Ephrian girl like you doing with two villainous Mages like them?"

Evylin glared at him but didn't pull away as he slid two fingers across her temple and down her cheek. Despite his unscrupulous job and the actions of his men, he hadn't treated her cruelly. She had no reason to suspect he was going to hurt her—not yet. And Hewitt taught her to be cunning in dangerous situations. Rash behavior would garner no favors from her captor nor aid in her escape.

Nev tucked his fingers under the edge of the gag and pulled it free. His light hazel eyes watched her carefully as the rag slipped out of her mouth, dropping around her neck. He smiled winsomely. "I'm curious," he said.

Evylin swallowed. Her tongue felt thick as she swept it across her dry lips. Nev wasn't altogether unattractive, and he was personable enough to be charming. If she played this right, she might be able to earn his favor. Or perhaps learn some information.

Cautiously, Evylin studied him as though unsure of his intentions, hoping he'd buy her innocent act. "If I tell you," she said, "will you answer a question for me?"

Nev chuckled, his men exchanging looks behind him. He settled his arms on his knees. "You're not really in a position to negotiate, dearie."

Though he was right, she didn't see any reason not to try. "I'm not sure I'd say that," she replied with feigned nervousness. "I may be your captive, but there's no reason for me to answer your questions without something in return. Not when I have nothing to lose."

He considered her, a slight smile on his lips. Then he brushed his forefinger softly along her jaw—the gentle caress a pretext before he gripped her chin fiercely.

Nev jerked her face close to his. "I could just beat it out of you," he threatened.

Evylin's heart pounded, but she forced her fear not to register in her expression. The reason for playacting was gone. She had no love of pain, but a man willing to follow through with threatened abuse would beat her regardless of cooperation. If she had to endure a beating, she might as well get some satisfaction from denying him.

"Feel free to try," she said, not bothering to hide her disdain this time. "I can promise you won't like the results."

A slow smirk worked across Nev's lips. "I like you," he said slyly. "You're not like most women."

"I hear that a lot."

"Mm." Nev drew back, studying her thoughtfully. "I do suppose a woman who carries—what was it? Six blades hidden on her person? I would imagine a woman such as that wouldn't fear much physical harm."

He dipped his head, brow rising. "But there are other options."

Evylin narrowed her gaze at his tone. He wasn't suggesting . . .

As though he heard her doubts, Nev gave her a cruel grin. "I could violate you," he said softly.

Evylin couldn't stop the tremor that seized her muscles.

His eyes lit up. "Ah. There, I've found your fear."

And why shouldn't Evylin fear such a threat? No man had ever touched her beyond Deckard. The lack of intimacy she'd sought was a conscious choice, not a fluke. There had been amorous opportunities aplenty in her youth. Boys in Whickam Village. Men in Trollenston when she was older. She'd never allowed it all for one simple reason: The idea of being so vulnerable and intimate with someone scared her. Despite how much she enjoyed her kisses with Deckard, no matter the way his touch sent a magical current through her, the thought of consummating their marriage *still* made her nervous, even if she did desire it.

This threat from Nev sent terror straight to Evylin's core. Her imagination battered her with visions of how he might assault her. Her body railed against it, a swell of nausea rising in her gut. But she refused to let it frighten her into submission. Like his previous threat, if he followed through with it as a punishment, he would do it regardless of her compliance.

Evylin tightened her jaw, putting all her anger into her stare. "I'm afraid that wouldn't give you the results you'd like either," she said with more confidence than she felt. Then, without knowing why, she added, "And my husband certainly wouldn't take it kindly."

Nev's eyes widened a fraction, curiosity piqued. "Your husband, eh?" he said with a chuckle. He glanced at Auden's prone form. "It isn't him. The writ named a sister, not a wife."

Evylin refused to answer.

"So where is he then, this husband of yours?" Nev asked, his interest gleaming with greed. "With the rest of your companions? I could use a hundred and fifty gold."

Just as he leaned closer, a sudden scream pierced through the floor beneath them.

Evylin, Nev, and the rest of the sellswords jumped as the muffled crash and clamor of a fight broke out.

Evylin smiled as hope soothed her previous tension. Her senses heightened once more, the coolness of magic winding across her skin. She met Nev's worried stare. "I'd say that's him now," she remarked.

The sellsword scowled at her, then turned to his men. "You two," he pointed to the pair at the threshold, "defend the hall. Anyone makes it through that door while you still draw breath, and I'll personally slit your necks."

The door slammed shut as Nev gave orders to the other five men. They drew their swords, standing at the ready.

Nev turned back to Evylin, pulling a knife from his belt. She jerked away from him, but he went for the ropes at her feet instead. He sliced through them, then the loop around her waist. "Your husband is a fool," he said, roughly hoisting her to stand. "We've got nineteen men. What can he have with him, eh? The writ only mentioned seven of you. Five against nineteen? Not odds I'd want to take."

Evylin smirked. "You don't know my husband."

Another scream rent the air, closer this time. The *thump* of two bodies followed, causing Evylin to hesitate with surprise and confusion. That cry was full of horror and panic. A sound that she couldn't fathom Deckard inspiring. Was it truly him out there? Or had Blount come for her?

Her breath caught in a fresh fear. If the Night Mage were here, she would have to escape. She couldn't let him take her alive. Not when that meant he would do worse than Nev could ever threaten.

A loud *crack* slammed to their right—a door crashing open.

Nev grabbed Evylin's arm, twisting her around. He wrapped an arm across her chest, pressing her against him as he raised his knife to her throat. The cold metal stung.

Another *crack*, slightly more distant.

"Don't let them in," Nev commanded.

The order held no authority. Not as the door sailed open, its frame splintered from the force that tore the latch from its set. A man stood in the doorway, shadows of a purple so dark it could be black curling around him. Evylin's lips parted as she took in Deckard. Crimson splatter stained his wool coat. Shimmering forms coalesced and encircled him within the shadows, jagged shards of magic that seemed to emanate from his hands. Her heart stuttered at the violent look in his dark glare.

The five sellswords took a step back at the frightful sight of him.

Nev pressed his knife tightly to Evylin's throat. "Stay right there," he ordered.

Deckard remained still, taking in the room with stoic composure. Then his gaze landed on Evylin. He studied her in the same manner as she studied him, scanning her as though to confirm her identity. Their eyes met, and her veins flared with anticipation. There was a depth and intensity within his stare, his eyes a rich verdant green, darker than she'd ever seen. This was not the man she'd married. And yet, something in her said that the man before her was in the truest form he'd ever taken.

As magic coiled around his entire frame, the expression on his face fierce and controlled, Evylin stared in awe. He was terrifying. Yet, the Warrior inside of her had never found him so attractive. She yearned to tear herself free and run to him. Her heart pounded, and her muscles quaked, ready for action.

Deckard smiled enticingly. "Hello, dear," he said, his voice as deep and captivating as his gaze.

An impulsive instinct drew Evylin to take a step forward, only Nev's grasp and knife halting her. A sharp sting followed by the heat of pain told her the blade had cut through the top layer of skin.

Deckard's eyes narrowed.

Nev tightened his grip on Evylin, steadying the knife. "A step closer and your lovely wife here is dead," he threatened.

Deckard gave him a bland glance. "I already killed all your men downstairs," he said impassively. "You think these few will stop me?"

Nev's hand began to shake, nicking Evylin again. "You may kill the others, yeah. But if you try to kill me, she'll die before you make the first move."

A dry grin pulled on Deckard's lips. "I don't intend to kill you," he said, then tipped his chin toward Evylin. "She'll do that."

The ominous remark had its intended effect. Nev hesitated, and Deckard flicked his wrist.

With a cry of horror, Nev's grip loosened. "I can't see!" he exclaimed.

The world slowed as, with a sudden surge, the magic raging within Evylin's veins took dominance. Each second stretched, giving her the strange ability to take in everything at once. The five sellswords rushed Deckard as he stepped into the room. He raised his hands, the purple-black shadows twisting into razor-shaped crystals. Ethenn swept in behind him, hatchet at the ready. He took down two guards while she watched as Deckard's magic tore through the rest. Awe filled her body, tingling along her skin as the moment passed with magically induced omniscience.

As Nev reached for his magic-blinded eyes, their irises shrouded in deep purple, Evylin lifted her bound wrists, slamming her fists into his hand. He dropped the knife, letting it fall end over end through the air. Her enhanced sight glimpsed a bead of her blood clinging to the edge. As she reached for the weapon, a black, crystalline shard swept across the room, slicing through the ropes to free her hands. The knife's handle dropped into her palm, and Evylin spun, plunging the blade down. It severed through flesh and sinew, and Nev collapsed, the weapon protruding from his neck as he thudded to the ground.

And time resumed its natural course.

Evylin turned, relief flooding through her. She hardly had time to process Deckard's oncoming figure before he was there. She managed a single gasp of air as he took her face in his hands. Then his mouth covered hers.

The lingering remnants of magic snapped taut between them. Her skin tingled under his fingertips. The rush ripped through her like a current, carrying her far out to sea. And all at once, she was more alive than ever before. This was no gentle kiss or tender caress. It was a furious, demanding passion that refused to let either of them go.

Deckard's arms encircled her, pressing her firmly against him. The longing she'd felt upon seeing him took control. Her fingers latched onto the collar of his coat, pulling him into a deeper kiss. She could feel his heart racing under her hand and hear it beating in time with hers. Their breath mingled, neither of them willing to break for a full inhale. His hands wandered with a freedom he'd never allowed, trailing shivers across her skin. She was vaguely aware that he'd pressed her against the wall. A desperation woke within her, a need she'd tried to ignore for far too long.

Every barrier she'd placed between them was gone. She ran her finger through his hair, down his neck, and across his chest. She felt everything with startling clarity. His deep sigh spiraled down into her core, in resonance with her heart. The sharp scent of pine and sweat mingled with the ever-present crispness of *him*. He tasted of over-malted ale. His warmth countered the coolness that coated her skin. She was overcome by the experience of him, and she never wanted it to end.

The sudden clearing of a throat scratched jaggedly through Evylin's magic-heightened ears. She stilled at the shocking realization that Ethenn, Auden, and half a dozen dead men were in the room with them. A wave of embarrassment slammed into her, dousing her in reality.

Evylin jerked back, shoving Deckard away. They both gasped for air as their eyes locked in startled wonder. She'd expected to see the presence of the Mage still, but his eyes had returned to their usual, subdued green-blue. His expression had softened, the fierceness replaced with gentleness. The purple-black shadows had faded entirely. He'd returned to the Deckard she'd met in Whickam Village, the charming, harmless man she'd married.

"Colonel," Ethenn muttered awkwardly, "we should go."

Deckard hadn't yet looked away from Evylin as though surprised to find her there.

His lips remained parted, his chest still heaving for breath. The pinch appeared between his brows. "Yes," he said, then swallowed. "Yes, I know."

Returning to their senses, Evylin and Deckard shifted away from one another.

"Do you—?" He paused, took a breath, and then started again. "Do you know where they took your things?"

Evylin shook her head, afraid to look away from him. Her heart still pounded, her magic urging her to return to his embrace. She couldn't trust either herself or him at the moment.

Finally, Deckard turned away. "See if you can find them," he told Ethenn. "I'll take care of Auden."

"Yes, sir," Ethenn said, giving Evylin a half-glance before hurrying from the room.

Slowly, Deckard faced Evylin once more, head dipped. He scanned her. "Are you all right?" he asked tenderly.

At first, Evylin thought he was asking about her reaction to the kiss. Then she realized he referred to her capture.

The mixed emotions warring in her disrupted her ability to form words. Was she all right? Abduction and threat weren't pleasant experiences, but this had been nothing compared to her meeting with Blount in the Water Keep. And it was a jaunty trip across the countryside next to Hewitt's death.

If Evylin were honest, that kiss had been more traumatic than her time as Nev's prisoner.

"I'm fine," she managed to say.

A relieved sigh escaped Deckard, and he reached out. Likely, he'd only meant to brush the hair from her face, but she sidestepped, moving out of his range.

His hand fell, his expression dejected. "Did they hurt you?" he asked cautiously.

Evylin tried to smile, shrugging off her avoidance. "Nothing that Auden can't patch up."

Reminded of the Mage, Deckard turned to appraise him. He dropped down to untie his bonds. "What did they do to him?" he asked.

"Nev—their leader—he said that they'd drugged him," she explained. "I don't know what they used."

As Deckard finished freeing Auden, Ethenn returned with their cloaks, purse, and Evylin's weapons. "I found this too," the young man said, then proffered a large money pouch.

"Leave it," Deckard said.

Evylin paused in hiding the daggers about her person once more. "It's a lot of money," she said. "Which we're frightfully low on."

Deckard shook his head. "We're not thieves."

She scoffed. "They're dead. It's not like they're going to use it."

Deckard turned to her, jaw tight. She saw anger in his glare, and she latched onto it. The anger was good. It would put distance between them and that magically induced hunger. It would protect them, walling off their feelings and desires.

Instead of replying, Deckard turned to Ethenn. "Help me carry Auden."

Evylin swiped the money pouch from the floor where Ethenn had left it.

Slowly, the men carried the Mage out of the room, down the stairs, and through the tavern. She followed, eyeing each dead body they passed. Eighteen men and one woman, dead. Five had fallen to Ethenn's blades, and only Nev had died at Evylin's hand. The other thirteen showed signs of the vicious slashes of Deckard's magic.

Evylin stared at her husband's back as they waited in the gore-filled tavern. He stripped off his blood-spattered coat, draping it over the countertop as though to rid himself of this crime. Thirteen people he'd killed by himself. All with magic he'd never touched before. And in some dark fascination, it drew her to him.

Ethenn went off to retrieve the horses—his and Deckard's as well as Evylin and Auden's, which he'd discovered in a stable two buildings away during his earlier search. When he returned, they stepped out into the gloomy rain. He and Deckard secured Auden to his horse, draping him across the saddle.

Then Deckard surveyed the tavern. "We should burn it," he said.

"Why?" Evylin asked.

"Blount can't learn of this," he explained. "It'd be best he doesn't know about my . . . condition."

Though Evylin thought it foolish to compare his magic to an illness, she didn't bother arguing that particular point. "He'll just assume that it was Auden," she said.

Deckard shook his head. "Blount will recognize Night magic when he sees it."

Evylin and Ethenn shared a look. Night magic—that's what the purple-black masses of shadow and crystal were. That's why Deckard had acted so differently—so aggressive and terrifying, so ready to kill. He'd connected with the most violent resource, wielding it as though it were breathing.

While Deckard and Ethenn set the tavern ablaze, moving with haste, Evylin waited with the horses. A few villagers appeared at the fringes of the square, peering at the scene. None of them interfered. Whether it was due to indifference or fear, she didn't know. Even when a gray-coated guard wandered by, he immediately turned around to pace away, as though disinterested in getting caught up in the crime.

Scanning the dreary village, Evylin's thoughts rolled through her head like rocks down a hill. Deckard was a Night Mage, connected to the most brutal, vile form of magic.

The sort of magic she should fear above all. Yet, it inspired the deepest ache within her, the strongest desire she'd ever felt. Was she going mad?

No, this wasn't madness. This was magic.

It was her magic that had drawn her to him. It was as intoxicating as the Day Relic, his power and hers melding together, coursing through her veins. Her whole being felt alive.

Smoke began to seep out of the tavern windows and door.

A shuddering breath slipped out of Evylin. This was a longing she couldn't tolerate. This magical pull was more menacing than Blount and all his Mages put together. If it could induce this reaction from her, if it could make her forget everything she'd lost and throw caution to the wind, she had to defend herself against it most of all. Because now that Deckard was a Mage, he was all the more dangerous to her. Now that their hearts could be fused in an unbreakable Bond, she was at risk of more than losing someone she cared for. She was at risk of losing part of her very soul.

CHAPTER TWENTY-SIX

Hours passed in a blur as they tore through the Waulden countryside. Rain bit into their exposed skin as they journeyed toward Ilain's location. Deckard stared at the horizon in a daze. The Night Relic sent coils of power through him, drawing at his magic again and again, but he quelled it with an inner self-fury. His insides quaked with the knowledge of what he'd done, of all those people he'd killed.

What had become of him? He didn't recognize the monster who so ruthlessly took those lives. Even as a soldier on the border of Ephria and Wauld, he'd counted every death at his hand. Twenty-one. That number increased in the fight against Blount and his Night Mages, but only by a fraction.

Now, it'd risen by nearly twice that original number.

And the worst part was: The magic felt good.

The power of it, surging through his whole being, shocked him. He'd felt alive while under the magic's grip. His heart beat steadily, his head cleared, and his body thrummed with control. It provided an illusionary authority, a boldness to do whatever came to mind, regardless of the consequences.

Deckard could finally understand the megalomania of the Mages. He now knew what drove the Mages of Auld to view themselves as deities. It was little wonder they were always cast as the villains. Magic like that couldn't be trusted.

Perhaps that's why he'd been opposed to his magic from the start. Maybe he'd felt the aggression and chaos it spurred within him. Innately, he'd felt a villainous power welling up inside of him and sought to quell it all along.

Ilain was right; the magic was finding its way out. First, with Hewitt's ghost. Now, with this murderous display. He had no control over his power. He never had.

Deckard's gut trembled with discontent. He'd seen the fear and shock on Ethenn and Evylin's faces. He could feel the immediate distance she'd placed between them after that damning kiss.

The horror of his mistakes lanced through him. His rage to save Evylin overrode his good sense. He'd given himself over to the darkness of Night, letting it wield him rather than using it as a tool. He'd lost control. The magic was intoxicating, deluding him with its power. The moment he kicked that door open and his eyes met Evylin's, all hope of containing his feelings had flown out the open window and into the vast gray skies of Wauld. It moved at the speed of lightning, arcing down to strike the terrae. He'd taken the leader's sight with a flick of his wrist, shadowing his vision in pure night. The guards were down next. Then Evylin caught the knife, her magic flaring. He hadn't had time to consider any of it. Suddenly, he was across the room, and she was in his arms with no regard for anything but one another.

Kissing Evylin always caused his body to heat unnaturally and sent his head into insanity. But this time, as magic burned through both of their veins, it increased every sensation tenfold. He didn't think he would have had the presence of mind to stop if she hadn't shoved him away.

And it was that mindless, lustful act that made him feel all the more vile.

Magic made him the worst sort of villain. He'd killed thirteen men without thought. Then he'd forced himself on the woman he loved.

The forests of Wauld thinned as they rode, the bordering mountains looming ahead. Deep gray storm clouds capped the mountains and drifted to block out the gloomy evening sky. Ethenn slowed his horse at the front. They'd attached Auden's horse, where they'd carefully bound the Mage to the saddle, to the young hunter's mare, and he led the two steeds to the side of the road.

"We should be close," Ethenn said, his hood obscuring most of his face. "But we didn't set a meeting point."

Deckard struggled to find his voice or his willingness to command. After his crime, he felt as though the leadership of their troop should be taken from him. "Can you track them?" he asked, the words coming out in a strangled tone.

Ethenn nodded, then untied Auden's horse from his. He handed the reins to Evylin. "I'll be faster on my own."

Evylin took the reins reluctantly, her gaze flashing toward Deckard. He could sense her fear in the look. She didn't want to be alone with him.

The three of them pulled deeper into the small, wooded area, unwilling to risk any potential incursions or questions about the unconscious body on a horse by fellow travelers. Then Ethenn went off to scout for their troop. In the near half hour of his absence, Deckard didn't bother to attempt a conversation with Evylin. He left her to her thoughts as the Night Relic continued to plague his.

He should have given it to Ethenn. But they'd been in such a rush to leave, he hadn't considered parting with it until this moment. His head and stomach roiled, his limbs trembling with the struggle of containing the power within. Was this what it was like for Evylin? No wonder the Day Relic was so intoxicating to her. If its joy and life had filled her with the same urgency as the Night Relic's tug on his dark, twisted thoughts, then he couldn't blame her for wishing to keep it.

Finally, Ethenn returned and led them to the small camp, farther up the road and well into the woods. The sky was black above them now, and the rain had turned into a torrent. When they came upon Thom, Rafferty, and Ilain, the trio was huddled together beneath an indentation in a rock formation. The tiny alcove couldn't be considered a cave, but at least it was dry.

The men hurried to help untie Auden and lower him to the hard ground, Ilain hovering the entire time. A flurry of questions rang out from their friends, but Ilain's were the most pressing. "Is he all right?" she demanded.

Evylin informed her of what the sellswords' leader told her about the drug and pointed out his wounds.

"How did this happen?" Thom asked as Ilain pushed him out of the way to kneel next to her brother.

"Blount put out a writ," Deckard explained. "There's a bounty on our heads now."

Rafferty's white-blond brows rose. "For how much?"

Evylin scoffed. "You can't turn yourself in for gold."

"Gold, eh?"

Ilain looked up from checking Auden's vitals. "He's stable," she said, her tone tender as she cared for her brother. "The wounds aren't fatal by any means, and he should rouse shortly. Though I'd like to string up the Time Mages who concocted this strain."

"Time Mages made this drug?" Ethenn asked.

Carefully, Ilain propped her cloak under Auden's head. "Viastasis," she named the narcotic. "It was originally intended for surgery. It puts you in stasis, locking you in time while the rest of the world goes on. However, this particular strain is specifically designed to torment Mages. It feeds off your magic, keeping it running longer than it should, and there's a dose of Night magic mixed in to give you nightmares."

That explained why Auden's face looked as though he were fighting off inner demons, his pale skin wan and coated with a layer of sweat as his eyes stared blankly ahead.

Ethenn's brow furrowed with concern. "Is there anything we can do to help?"

"No," Ilain said, brushing Auden's damp and stringy hair off his forehead. "We just have to wait while it works out of his system."

The highlady took vigil over her brother, whispering softly and comfortingly as she tended to his injuries with small bursts of Day magic. The rest of the troop gave them space, huddled by the entrance. They spoke quietly so as not to disturb the siblings.

"Do you think he'll be all right?" Thom asked worriedly.

Deckard wondered if it were more for the highlord's condition or the highlady's emotional state. "I'm sure he will," he said. "Ilain wouldn't be so calm if he were in any real danger."

"They needed us alive," Evylin added. "That's what the writ requires: alive for confirmation."

"You were lucky to get out of there unscathed," Rafferty noted, an uncharacteristic seriousness to his tone.

"We sustained injuries of a different sort," Deckard said with remorse. He reached up to remove the Night Relic from around his neck. Handing the Relic to Rafferty, he swallowed his shame to take up his duty as leader. "We can't take any more risks. Until we're back in Ephria, we can't enter any more settlements."

"But," Ethenn frowned, "that would mean we can't restock."

Deckard nodded. "Blount's writ puts us in too much danger. It bore sketches of Evylin, Auden, and Ilain, meaning none of them can enter. I may be able to get by with a subpar accent, but I don't know the customs well enough. It'd be too easy for us to get it wrong."

The other four Ephrians murmured in agreement.

"Can we make it without the extra supplies?" Thom asked.

"We'll have to," Deckard said.

Thom grimaced. "Allore help us if one of these horses throws a shoe."

Evylin ran a hand through her hair. "This is my fault," she muttered.

"No," the brothers said at the same time.

Deckard met Thom's stare, and he backed down.

Turning to Evylin, Deckard forced his comforting hand to remain at his side. "No, the writ is keeping us out of the settlements, not you," he insisted. "I'm the one who suggested purchasing tents. Your presence changed nothing."

Evylin's head hung low, but she didn't argue.

Deckard drew in a deep breath, stilling the guilt inside of him. "We need to take care of the camp. Rafferty, tend to the horses. We can't fit them in here, but I want them as safe from the storm as possible."

"Yes, sir," Rafferty said, eyeing the rain dubiously.

"Thom," he turned to his brother, "did you hunt this afternoon?"

"Yes, I managed to get three rabbits," his brother confirmed. "They're already skinned; they just need cooking."

"Ethenn, could you take care of that?"

"Yes, sir."

Ethenn moved for the small firepit, a magical breeze from Ilain keeping the smoke out of the rocky enclosure. That left the three Deckards alone.

Thom set a hand on Evylin's arm, his eyes going to the wound on her temple. "Are you all right?" he asked.

Evylin gave him a half smile. "Don't be so squeamish. My pride's a little wounded, but that's the worst of the damage. I'll recover before you know it."

"I'm glad to hear that," Thom said. His hand squeezed her arm before falling away.

Deckard narrowed his eyes, finding the action a tinge possessive. He forced the jealous thought away, presuming it to be a lingering effect of the Night Relic. "Thank you," he said to Thom.

His brother's expression was pinched. "For what?"

"For taking care of Ilain and Rafferty. For getting them here safely and securing a camp for us."

Thom shrugged, his eyes downcast. "I'll go help Raff," he said, then hurried off.

Deckard and Evylin stood there, silent. He thought to apologize, to tell her that he recognized the horrendous actions he had taken. But there in the tiny enclosure, he couldn't bring himself to say anything. He didn't want to admit his sins for the whole troop to hear. Not yet.

"I'm going to help Ethenn," Evylin mumbled, then left him.

With nothing else to do, Deckard took a seat against the wall. He remained there for the next two hours, staring first at his hands, then his food, and finally the fire, wondering how long it would take for Night magic to turn him mad. Had it already begun?

They ate in a tight circle, talking softly or not at all. Ilain sat next to her brother in perpetuity. After the meal, Ethenn joined her with a bowl of rainwater and a cloth to press to Auden's cracked lips. Locked in time, the Mage couldn't eat or drink, and it was the one means of getting sustenance into him. Ilain accepted the hunter's help, quietly administering the water to her brother.

It wasn't until they began to bed down for the night that Auden's racking coughs swept through the enclosure.

The troop hurried over, as close as they could in the small space without crowding. Ilain held Auden's hand while Ethenn propped him up. The highlord sputtered, his eyes filled with tears from the body-wrenching coughs. Ilain held the water bowl to his lips, and he attempted to drink before the coughing took over again, spilling some of the liquid across his front and his sister's arm.

Deckard dropped to his knees next to them. "Can we help?" he asked.

Ilain handed him the bowl, but it was Auden who spoke. "No," he said, the single word slurred and barely audible.

It took several minutes for his breathing to ease and the coughing to subside. Then he had Ethenn help him scoot back so he could lean against the rock wall. Ilain tried to fuss, putting her cloak behind his back, but he pushed off her attempts. "I'm fine, Lain," he said weakly.

She huffed, green eyes fierce. "You certainly look it."

He gave her a feeble smile, patting her hand. "Be easy, firebrand."

At the pet name, Ilain softened.

There was a collective sense of relief as the siblings relaxed.

"Do you need something to eat?" Deckard offered.

Auden swallowed laboriously, then turned to face him. His gaze held a flare of anger. "What in the Heavens and hell was *that*?" he demanded.

A tense silence filled the rock enclosure.

Deckard drew back, his brow pinched. "I don't—"

"You were using Night magic," Auden accused, "as though you'd been doing it for decades. How?"

The silence stretched as Deckard tried to find the words to reply.

Rafferty beat him to it. "If you were drugged," he said to the Mage, "how do you know that?"

"The viastasis places your body in a temporary hold," Ilain explained. "But your mind is still at work. While you can't feel anything, your brain still processes it all. After, you're left with the knowledge but no physical experience of the events."

"So you remember everything?" Evylin asked.

Auden nodded, his eyes locked on Deckard. "Did you take the Relic?"

The shame rose to tighten Deckard's throat. "Yes," he admitted.

Auden's hands balled into fists, but he was too weak to show any further displays of irritation. "That makes this situation *slightly* better. You were consumed with it, weren't you?" he asked.

Panic surged through Deckard as the soldiers and Ilain stared at him. "No, of course not," he lied.

"This is dangerous, Jonn," Auden said. "As a Night Mage, *you* are a danger to everyone here. And your power is already too strong."

Worry clouded nearly everyone's expression.

Deckard drew back. "We don't—what if I'm not a Night Mage?" he asked, despite knowing the truth.

Ilain set a hand on her brother's arm. "It was a situation that called for violence," she advised. "And he had the Relic. It makes sense that he would connect with it."

The condemnation in Auden's gaze was telling. "I haven't seen Night magic that strong since—" He spoke in a whisper, his words breaking off as though it pained him too much to keep going.

Ilain's shoulders tensed. "You're sure?"

Auden didn't say anything, but the steady way he held her gaze was confirmation enough that the siblings were thinking the same thing—but whether of a person or event, Deckard wasn't sure.

"Haven't seen Night magic that strong since when?" Rafferty prodded.

The Calders ignored him, turning back to Deckard. "Tell me the truth," Auden demanded. "Were you consumed by it?"

Deckard shrank back, unable to keep himself from glancing at Evylin with guilt surging in his chest. "I was," he said quietly.

Auden cursed, but Ilain's jade green eyes considered Deckard thoughtfully. "Did you control it, or did it control you?" she asked warily.

Auden gave her a disgruntled look, but she brushed him off, waiting for Deckard's answer.

"The magic?" Deckard asked. At her nod, he shrugged. "It listened to me if that's what you're asking."

"So it consumed you, filling your mind and senses," Ilain concluded, "but you were able to control it—telling it what to do and releasing it when you were done?"

Deckard's memories of the experience left him feeling conflicted by the rush and the horror of it all. But he was gratified to remember that he had, in fact, controlled the magic. He remembered the exact moment he'd released the shadows and crystalline shards: once the final threat had fallen. Assured of Evylin's safety, the magic remained, but its manifestations did not. And no matter the urging of the Relic upon his psyche, he'd held it at bay.

Assured of his control, Deckard nodded. "Yes."

Ilain gave Auden a pointed look.

"That doesn't make it any better," he said glumly.

"Night magic isn't evil incarnate, Auden," she argued. "It's dangerous, but it can be channeled without driving a person mad. Look at Obel."

"I don't trust Obel," he grumbled.

Ilain rolled her eyes. She faced Deckard once more. "It appears that you have a strong connection to Night magic. That doesn't necessarily mean you're a Night Mage, but . . . it makes a good case for it. That said, if you can control it, then we shouldn't have to worry about the Deep taking over."

"The Deep?" Thom repeated incredulously. "What the hell is that?"

"It's the name given to the madness that overtakes some Night Mages," Ilain said flippantly. "But as I said, there's no need to worry at this point."

"So long as I control it?" Deckard added, anxiety clouding his mind.

Ilain leaned forward. "You *will* control it, Jonn. This isn't altogether shocking. You are a young Mage with barely any training, and you were carrying a Relic. It could all be a fluke. Auden and I will ensure the rest of your training to protect you from whatever ill effects Night may present. But you need not fear your power. You just have to learn to . . . rein it in a bit."

But Deckard did fear his magic.

And with a look around at the others—Auden running a worried hand along his beard, Rafferty grimacing dramatically, Ethenn avoiding his gaze, Thom frowning warily, and Evylin tugging on her rings—it appeared they did too.

CHAPTER TWENTY-SEVEN

Their entrance into Sutterlund Reach was blessedly uneventful. While Auden and Ilain worked together to shroud themselves and Evylin, entirely subverting the guards and slipping through the gate as quickly as possible, the Ephrian soldiers entered with Deckard and the documents from the Alliance. It was clear the writ had done its job. The guards stopped what few individuals were traveling into the Reach, inspecting them heavily before allowing them passage.

Given Deckard's Waulden appearance and acting skills, Thom's resemblance to his brother, and Rafferty's light coloring, they were able to play off Ethenn's obviously Ephrian heritage without trouble. After a brief search of their persons and horses (and claiming that the extra three were meant to keep fresh mounts for their journey), the guards readily allowed them to pass through.

It took the rest of the day for them to reach the approximate location of the Wind Keep. Near the ocean, as all the Keeps were, they relied on Ilain to guide them when they approached the rocky seaside, her strength not as weakened as her brothers after the shroud. Determined not to allow Blount's Mages to ambush them as they had at the Night Keep, the majority of the troop set up camp while Ethenn went with Ilain to seek out the exact location, ensuring a stealthy approach.

In the bright dawn, Deckard set forth their plan. While Auden and Ilain trained him, Ethenn would lead Thom, Evylin, and Rafferty to the Keep, where the four soldiers would spend the day searching the area to ensure no Mages were camping thereabouts, waiting for their arrival. Though Deckard was remiss in staying behind, none of them questioned the value of his continued training. Not after Dunneshead. Not when they were about to risk their lives in the Wind Keep.

Thom didn't know what to think of his brother's newfound power. At first, he'd been jealous, naturally. It turned out that Deckard wasn't just favored among people; he was favored by magic—by Allore himself, if the Calders were to be believed. It felt like a slight to Thom. One more failing of his to prove he could never measure up.

But the more Thom watched Deckard training, and the more he learned about magic, the more he realized that perhaps this wasn't the blessing the Calders touted.

Ethenn had regaled Thom and Rafferty with the story of Dunneshead the previous day. Though Auden and Ilain made it clear that Night magic could be dangerous, Ethenn's story made it even more evident to Thom. Whatever kind of Mage Deckard was, the magic was changing him.

And that scared Thom more than he cared to admit.

He crouched in the tall marram grass, surveying the coastline. He scanned the dunes and cliffs. The only signs of life were the small blue-beaked seabirds skittering across the variegated black and gray sand. He'd never seen them before, and he wondered at the Waulden fowl. There was a significant difference between the two countries, despite sharing the same continent.

Once they'd arrived in near proximity to the Keep's entrance, the Ephrians decided to split up to cover more ground. Ethenn and Rafferty took the north while Evylin and Thom went south. With the sea to the east, the two teams would work their way back west and meet at dusk before returning to the camp.

"I don't think there are any Mages out here," Thom muttered to Evylin.

At his side, Evylin's keen gaze swept over the shore. He wondered how much more her Warrior eyes saw than he did. Would she have to tap into her magic, or did she naturally have better vision? Or were they one and the same? According to Ilain, magic was a natural part of being a Warrior. To use it was to breathe, even if one didn't realize he or she had the gift.

Evylin swatted a panicle of the beachgrass away from her face. "We've only been searching for an hour," she replied, tone more tense than usual. "Have you grown bored already?"

Thom eyed her cautiously. He knew she was trying to remain her playful, teasing self. But since returning from Dunneshead, she'd been on edge. The nearly constant sense of depression was gone from her, replaced with an agitated atmosphere that made even her smiles pull taut. He couldn't decide whether it was better or worse. He hated to see her in any distress, but was it better that she remain in grief or grab hold of this anxious unease?

"I'm always bored," Thom said, deciding that ignoring her ill mood would be the best course of action. "It's what makes me so foul-tempered all the time."

"Ilain doesn't seem to mind," she noted.

Thom snorted derisively, disappointed that she didn't sound the least bit resentful. "Ilain prefers me when I'm surly. It's why she constantly torments me."

Evylin turned to him, eyebrows raised. "You seem to enjoy her tormenting."

He met her smirk with a frown. "Don't go matchmaking, Evie," he said sourly. "You're no good at it."

"*I'm* not the one flirting with the highlady every second I get," she said, then stood. "Come on. There's nothing here."

As they continued up the shore, careful to remain inconspicuous and out of sight, Thom wondered if he should correct Evylin's presumptions. He might be a wretch for loving his brother's wife, but he wasn't abominable enough to do anything about it. He'd never told Evylin of his feelings, never even hinted at them, because whatever else he was, he wasn't unprincipled enough to have an affair with his sister-in-law. While that didn't stop him from wishing, it did keep his mouth firmly shut.

And thus, Thom didn't know how to make it clear that his flirtations with Ilain were strictly entertainment. Yes, the Mage was beautiful and clever, but despite coming to discover that he rather liked the woman, Thom was more certain now than ever that he could never want her in that way. She was attractive, but he wasn't attracted to her. But how did a man explain that to the woman he *was* attracted to—the woman he *did* want?

Guilt spiked through Thom. He shouldn't think that way. It was only himself that he was hurting by harboring these secret feelings.

Deckard was right—Evylin wasn't Thom's wife. And she never could be. These thoughts, these desires—they could only ever hurt him. The best he could hope for with Evylin was friendship. Unless . . .

Thom grimaced as his darkest thoughts surfaced: He could only hope for friendship with Evylin *unless* Deckard died, leaving her a widow free to pursue true love elsewhere.

Fear and remorse writhed in Thom's stomach. He hated those thoughts. They always made him feel like the basest, most deplorable sort of man. How could he even consider it? He didn't wish his brother dead. Whatever bitterness he held toward Deckard, he loved him. The idea of losing him. . . .

Gritting his teeth, Thom followed Evylin into the thin stand of trees near the beachside. They patrolled the area, looking for any signs of a camp or hiding places. Distractedly, he studied her nearly as much as the world around them. She moved rigidly, though still with her innate athleticism and grace. But he could see in the tightness of her shoulders that something was bothering her.

He had little question as to its cause.

"Evie," Thom said, keeping his voice low, "can I talk to you about something?"

She glanced over her shoulder at him. "We are attempting to move with stealth, Thom," she said in a snarky tone, though that hint of anxiety remained.

Gently, he grabbed her arm. "Then we'll stop for a moment."

Evylin narrowed her gaze, but she halted with him. "Must be rather important."

"It is."

When she motioned for him to continue, Thom sighed. "I'm worried," he admitted. "Ethenn told Raff and me everything. About Dunneshead, I mean."

Evylin shifted from one foot to the other. "Everything?" she repeated nervously.

Thom nodded. "He said—" He swallowed down his discomfort. "He said that Jonn killed a dozen men, showing no remorse until after it was all over. He said that you three even burned the tavern down to cover the evidence."

As he paused to consider the crimes, Evylin chewed on her bottom lip, waiting for him to go on.

He shook his head, unable to reconcile any of the behavior with his brother's character. "That doesn't sound like Jonn," he concluded.

With a curious expression, Evylin regarded him as though expecting him to say more. Once she realized he had nothing more to add, to his surprise, she visibly relaxed. "Oh. No," she said. "No, it doesn't. And I don't think it was."

Thom furrowed his brow. "But—"

"I mean, yes, he was doing those things," she corrected. "But it wasn't *him*. It was the magic—Night—affecting him."

"Doesn't that worry you?" he asked.

Evylin drew in a long breath, then said, "Yes."

"It worries me too," Thom admitted, a tremor going through his chest. "And what Auden said about the madness—the Deep . . . I'm not ashamed to say it, Evie. I'm frightened."

Evylin's eyes widened as she listened.

"What if Jonn goes mad?" Thom scrubbed a hand over his face and ran it into his hair. "That's what's bothering you, too, isn't it? The two of us know Jonn better than anyone else in our camp. While his behavior concerns them, we know: This isn't him."

Evylin turned away to pace.

Thom asked the question that plagued him most of all. "What if the Deep is already taking root?"

"It's not," she insisted. Her immediate defense spoke to her mutual fear.

"Are you sure?" He followed her, cutting off her pacing to meet her gaze. "If what

Ethenn said is true, then this magic has already begun to make him ruthless and violent. Those are two words I would never have used to describe my brother."

"No, you describe him as selfish," she returned sharply.

Thom frowned. Why was she so agitated with *him*? He, too, was worried about Deckard. Why couldn't she see that?

"Evie, for once in my life, I'm not talking as the jealous brother." He set his hands upon her arms, hoping she'd see the truth in his eyes. He could feel his face contort as he did everything possible to convey his fears. "I don't want to lose him."

Evylin flinched as though he'd slapped her. Her muscles tensed under his grasp.

"I'm scared, Evylin," Thom said, the words a frightened whisper. He felt so much like a youth again, watching his brother walk away from Stocburrough—from him—without ever glancing back. "What if this magic destroys him from the inside out? I don't want to watch my brother descend into madness. For all my resentment of him . . . I love him."

She just stared at him, chewing on her bottom lip.

"If this magic can turn Jonn into a murderer," Thom said fiercely, "then we can't lose him to it."

Evylin pulled out of his grasp and pressed a hand to her forehead. "I know," she murmured.

Thom could have dropped to the terrae and wept with relief to hear he wasn't alone in this battle for his brother's sanity. "What are we going to do?" he asked.

"There isn't anything we can do," she returned, letting down his hopes. "Auden and Ilain are helping him get control of it. That's the solution, isn't it?"

"Is it?" Thom doubted it could be so simple. "If he's a Night Mage, doesn't that mean he'll spend his whole life connecting with that resource more and more, getting closer and closer to insanity?"

"Ilain said that—"

"I know what she said," he interrupted. "And sure, maybe some Night Mages can handle their powers, but, Evie, this is *Jonn*. He killed twelve people—"

"Thirteen."

Thom gaped at her.

Evylin sighed. "Ethenn must have miscounted, or he just estimated. It was thirteen, including the woman."

Including the woman.

Deckard would never harm a woman. His scruples wouldn't allow it, even if she threatened his life.

Though in this case, it wasn't Deckard's life she'd threatened . . . It was Evylin's. And Deckard would do anything—absolutely anything—for Evylin.

"That's far worse," Thom said, the full understanding of their situation coming to light.

She shrugged. "In all our travels, I've killed that many and more by now."

"Have you counted every life you've taken?"

"No."

"He has."

"I know."

Thom ran his fingers through his hair. "Don't you understand how that will affect him? If Night magic can make him that merciless in the moment, he will crumble when he comes out from under its hold. You heard what he said: It controlled him. It overrode his judgment, turning him into a cold-blooded killer. Jonn can't live with that."

Evylin began to tug on her wedding rings but didn't speak.

"Even if this 'Deep' doesn't take over," Thom concluded, "he will go mad simply to protect himself from the pain of knowing what the magic made him do."

She tightened her jaw, eyes dropping to the ground.

"There couldn't be a worse person to become a Night Mage."

Evylin tossed her hands to the side, exasperated. "What do you want me to do about it?" she demanded, the words coming out shaky. Tears glistened at the corners of her eyes. "I'm still grieving, Thom. I'm barely holding on, and now—"

Hurrying forward, Thom gripped her arms again, determined not to let her succumb to another panic attack. "I'm not asking you to do anything," he promised.

"Then what do you want?"

Thom opened his mouth, but he didn't know what to say. What did he want? Why had he brought this up in the first place? To find someone to commiserate with? To hear his fears validated? Or did he simply want to know he wasn't alone?

"I want to protect my brother," Thom said.

Evylin stared up at him despondently. "And how can *I* help you with that?"

Reluctantly, Thom whispered, "You're his wife. He loves—"

"Stop," Evylin snapped. She jerked out of his touch, and her rich brown eyes turned cold and impassive. "That has never been part of our relationship, and you know it."

Thom hated the flare of hope that whispered lies to his heart. Though he was sure Deckard loved Evylin, and he'd thought he'd seen her affections growing with the same regard, was there a chance he'd been wrong? He knew her grief drove them apart, but he always imagined they'd grow back together as she healed. But what if . . . ?

Thom forced himself to ignore those thoughts. He ground his teeth but worked out the reply, "Maybe not for you."

"And what?" she shot back. "Would you have me coddle him? Should I tell him that it's not so bad, killing thirteen people like it's a stroll through the market? Perhaps I can absolve him of his guilt—turn him cruel and calculating like me."

"Don't put words in my mouth, Evie," Thom retorted. "I'm not asking you to do anything. I'm simply saying that he would do *anything* for you, even if it takes killing a hundred people to do it."

Evylin's mouth parted in shock. "So you're blaming me for this?"

"No!" Thom didn't know where he'd gone so wrong. Why was she reacting so defensively? This wasn't like the Evylin he knew.

Hoping to repair the damage, Thom took a step closer. "No, Evylin, I'm not—all I'm saying is that he cares about you. And regardless of how you feel about him, he trusts you. He relies on you. Together, you and I can protect him. I believe that."

"Protect him from madness?"

"Yes."

She eyed him. "That could be accomplished if he stopped being a Mage."

Thom furrowed his brow. "We've already established that that's not a possibility. Haven't we?"

"Perhaps. But after all this ends, what is there to keep him living as a Mage? He could put it behind him and go back to being a soldier."

"Doesn't the Alliance have some sort of plans for you two?" Thom asked begrudgingly.

"I don't care what the Alliance wants," Evylin said, firm and resolute. "I'm not Bonding with *him* or anyone else."

"All right." He held up his hands in surrender. "But aren't you worried about him?"

Evylin's expression pinched. "Yes, but . . ." The words came out in a pained whisper. Then she shook her head. "I can't figure this out now, Thom. There's already too much. . . ."

She didn't have to finish the sentence. He knew perfectly well.

Cautiously, Thom reached out. He set a hand on her shoulder, telling himself that it was what a friend would do. He brushed his thumb across the firm musculature there, promising himself that it was a brother's comfort he was offering.

"I know," he said weakly. "And maybe you're right. Maybe we only need to watch Jonn and keep his hands as clean as possible. Then this will all go away once we get these damned Relics out of our lives."

Evylin placed her hand on his, a silent gesture of gratitude.

"Maybe," he gave her a sad smile, "we can go back to how everything was before."

Evylin didn't agree, but neither did she deny what they both knew: Going back was impossible. Hewitt was gone. Deckard was a Mage. Evylin was a Warrior. Nothing could be like it had been for them.

Only Thom remained the same. Only he was stuck in a perpetual unremarkable existence. *He* could return to life as a common soldier. *He* could go back to the drudgery and loneliness of his previous life because he was no more special than anyone else.

Not wanting to consider how inferior he was to his brother anymore, Thom pulled away from Evylin. "We should keep scouting," he said.

At her nod, they moved on. They followed their route back west toward camp. But even as the light began to fade, Thom's worries didn't ease.

Whatever grief plagued Evylin, keeping her idle, Thom held no such impediment. He might not be special. He might never be deserving of people's respect and admiration. He might resent his brother until his dying breath . . .

But he'd be damned if he didn't keep Deckard from madness.

CHAPTER TWENTY-EIGHT

13TH OF CHRONOS, 1574

All around their small camp, the team prepared to enter the Keep. The soldiers belted on their swords and affixed daggers to their persons. Ethenn strapped his quiver and bow across his back. An undercurrent of worry haunted their ranks. Each of them spoke in hushed, anxious tones.

Deckard felt this apprehension keenly, sure that he was the cause of it all. And why shouldn't he be? Even after his work with Auden and Ilain, the thought of touching magic made him queasy. He didn't want to experience the same jolt of power or feel the intense reaction it caused within him.

Over the past two days, the Calders took the time to teach Deckard how to connect with resources other than Night. Though Auden was attempting to teach him something called the Path of Vieran, a meditative manner of focusing on the resource, it wasn't working well, as they were attempting to subvert his primary, and that was really the whole point of the meditation.

Ilain suggested they try a different approach, evidently disapproving of the Path. While she claimed she wasn't bothered by Deckard's dark magic, she did what she could to alleviate his and Auden's worries by teaching the principles of accessing the resources aside from your primary.

"There are two schools of thought amongst Mages," Ilain said practically. "I subscribe to the first method: You should master all the resources at your disposal, granting you varied abilities."

"And I agree with the second," Auden added. "You should master your primary resource only, capturing its essence and harnessing the vastness of its power. Something impossible when you branch out into other resources."

"Both are viable," Ilain said, then smirked. "But mine is better."

"That's debatable," Auden muttered.

"It is not." She raised her brow and motioned to Deckard. "If I followed your example, I wouldn't be able to help Jonn access magic other than Night."

Deckard frowned at the two of them. "So Night is my primary resource, but I can ignore it?"

"Night is *most likely* your primary," Ilain corrected. "Regardless, there is a further hierarchy to the resources for every Mage. Fire is my primary, next comes Wind, then Water, and then Terrae. I'm horrible with Terrae. I can't quite get the slow steadiness of growth down. I think I like to burn things too much."

Without giving either man time to comment, Ilain continued, "In order to connect with other resources, you need to develop your relationship with them. We don't have time to discover your hierarchy, but as Auden is especially connected to Day, we'll focus on that."

And though Deckard tried finding a relationship with Day magic, he found it immeasurably difficult, like grasping at the wind. To all of their chagrin, he managed one burst of dull, muddy-yellow light and nothing more.

"We could give him the Day Relic," Ilain suggested when they determined the resource must be a low connection for Deckard. "That would help."

Auden shook his head. "He's too inexperienced," he said, then turned to Deckard. "Magic takes energy as well as focus. You can have the strongest connection in the world, but if you overexert yourself, your magic will falter. The Relics give you focus and power, but they don't give you energy. I fear putting it in your hands would burn you out too quickly."

"How will I know if my magical energy is waning?" Deckard asked warily.

"The same way you know when you've worked too hard and need a night's rest," he said. "If you push yourself too far, your body will begin to shut down to preserve itself. And blacking out mid-fight is never ideal."

After that lesson, Deckard felt even less prepared.

He couldn't say he'd experienced any signs of exhaustion after their time in Dunneshead, but he hadn't used magic for more than a quarter of an hour. Their time in the Keeps spanned at least eight times that length. Since he didn't know what his threshold for exhaustion was, that led him and the Calders to agree that Deckard shouldn't tap into his magic until absolutely necessary.

Now, as Deckard secured the last of his weapons—sliding a small dagger into his boot—his eyes drifted to the empty trees around them. He hadn't summoned Hewitt's ghost since he'd left for Dunneshead. Not only had he not had the chance to slip away to talk with the man, but he also didn't know what he'd say when he did. How could he explain himself? How could he face the fact that *he* might be the greatest danger to Evylin now?

Thom appeared at his side, a nervous expression on his face. "Could I, uh—" He tipped his head toward the horses at the edge of camp. "Could I talk to you?"

The request placed Deckard instantly on edge. The last time they'd spoken privately, they'd argued. Deckard knew it was partially his fault. His growing irritation toward his brother's relationship with Evylin was causing animosity. An emotion he rigorously quelled, knowing it rose only from his insecurity about the fragile state of his marriage.

The brothers moved to the far side of the clearing. Thom shuffled his feet, eyes downcast as he spoke softly. "Look, I—" he began stiltedly. "I'm worried about you." Deckard's brows pinched together, but he let Thom continue, "With everything that's happened, I—I'm concerned that this magic will hurt you."

Studying his brother, Deckard chose to delay his response. Thom wasn't generally bothered about his well-being. He never asked after him or showed signs of worry—*unless* he wanted something.

"The Calders are working with me," Deckard said at last, attempting to believe the best of his brother.

Thom nodded dismissively. "Yeah, I know," he murmured. "I just—" He broke off then, glancing toward the camp.

Deckard followed his gaze, finding that it landed on Evylin. Instinctively, he tensed.

"If it's none of my business, you can tell me," Thom said, turning back to Deckard. "But as your brother . . . I feel I should ask. Is everything all right? Between you and Evylin, I mean."

A muscle in Deckard's jaw twitched. His baser instincts wanted to tell Thom that, no, it wasn't his business. He chose to take the higher moral road. "It will be," he said hopefully. "The last several weeks haven't been kind to either of us, but we're managing."

Thom nodded again, the movement tighter this time. He stared at the dirt, scuffing his boot against the root of a tree. "Jonn . . ." He paused as his voice betrayed his tension. Then he lifted his gaze, gray-blue stare wary. "Do you love her?"

Deckard's heart squeezed, and his jaw spasmed. The question drew forth the irritation within him once more. Of course, he loved Evylin. Little could be clearer given his actions. How his brother or anyone else could fail to see that was incomprehensible. And after watching Thom grow more and more possessive of Evylin over the course of their relationship, Deckard couldn't shake the indignation that rankled within him.

"She's my wife, Thom," he said sharply. "It's my job to love her, and I take that very seriously."

Head dipped, Thom muttered, "Right," then drew in a sharp breath through his nose. He met Deckard's stare once more, a glimmer of annoyance within his gaze. "Glad to hear it," he said and turned away to join the others.

Deckard stared after Thom, skeptical of the short conversation's purpose. What had Thom intended? Why had he asked after Deckard and Evylin's relationship? Was the fragmentation between them obvious to everyone?

Forcing himself to forget the confusing exchange, Deckard worked to settle his mind. The troop was ready to go. They had a short walk to the Keep's entrance, then they would enter and face another battle for a Relic. Magic required total focus of thought. If he was going to tap into Day at the appropriate time, he couldn't let his roiling emotions distract him.

Under Deckard's command, the troop made its way out of camp toward the coastline. They'd tied the horses within the copse of trees close to the Keep to make their exit from Sutterlund Reach as smooth as possible. Though they were secure in their sweep of the area and no Wind Mages were loitering in the shadows to ambush them, they couldn't remain within the Reach once they retrieved the Relic. After their trek through the Keep was complete, they would hurry back to the camp, mount their horses, and ride until they passed back through the Reach's gates and into Wauld proper.

The amber sunset peered from behind the gray-brown clouds. On the cliffs surrounding the beach, only the faintest wash of slate ocean could be seen in the distance. They followed Ilain's lead down a steep incline before facing a narrow opening in the deep brown stone. Ethenn went first, bow at the ready. Then the rest of them filed into the Wind Keep's antechamber, prepared for whatever the next few hours would bring.

Like all the rest, a hallway of arched windows stretched out before them, smooth stone walls and columns granting the space a sacred air, almost like the kirks of Ephria. Ashy light poured from the windows, swirling patterns in their wrought iron frames. An iron door waited at the end, the same scrollwork etched in its face.

Rafferty stepped forward, Relics in hand. "Fire for the highlady," he said, handing the ruby necklace to Ilain, then the yellow topaz to Auden. "Day for the highlord. And . . ." He paused, proffering the amethyst. "Who gets Night? Colonel? Evie?"

Auden spoke, giving Deckard a guarded look. "You shouldn't carry it."

"I agree," Deckard said.

They all turned to Evylin.

She took a step back, staring at the Relic like it was a viper prepared to strike. Deckard couldn't tell if her hesitation was due to her previous experience with the Day Relic or if it had to do with her recent experience with Night—*his*—magic.

Evylin drew in a bolstering breath and took the Relic from Rafferty's upturned palm. A spike of energy leaped through the air. Bright purple light beamed off the Night sword, now gripped firmly in her grasp.

Deckard drew his sword and stepped under the domed ceiling of the hall. This was no time for his sorrow or guilt. He was a soldier with an assignment. He would fight using sword and dagger, and if he had to, he'd tap into his newly discovered magic to get the job done.

Auden lifted his hand to the iron door. For the first time, Deckard was entering a Keep with the knowledge of his magic. *Will it be different?* he wondered. *Will I feel and sense the same power as the Calders?*

As the door rumbled open, Ilain stepped up to her brother's side. The passage cleared, revealing the Keep beyond them. Silver-gray mist and dove-gray clouds drifted lazily, a fog denser than any in Wauld as far as the eye could see. Only a narrow stone path, covered in the same swirling pattern as the door and windows, stretched ahead of them. It hung suspended with nothing but thin air on all sides.

At Deckard's side, Thom grimaced. "That looks welcoming," he said.

Ilain sent him a wink. "Don't worry, dearest. I may be a Fire Mage, but Wind and I have a special relationship. If you fall, I'll catch you."

Auden ignored his sister's casual attitude. "Everyone, walk carefully," he instructed. "The Shades will be infused with Wind, and I suspect they'll be able to fly."

While the Calders stepped out onto the path, the Ephrians froze in the hall.

"Fly?" Rafferty's face contorted in disbelief. He looked up at Deckard. "I've decided," he said weakly, "I'd like to resign from my post, sir."

Drawing in a stilted breath, Deckard forced his feet forward. "I'll join you."

They followed the Calders into the Keep.

The stone path would only admit their passage one by one. Ethenn took the initiative, following behind Ilain. Thom went next. Both men immediately braced themselves as the fog swirled around them, curling around their forms as though seeking to wrap them in its arms. Rafferty and Evylin went next while Deckard stepped in last. The mist clung to the bridge, instantly coating them with a thin layer of dampness. A biting wind nipped at their faces.

Deckard looked down to ensure his footing, only to realize his mistake as his head spun. Free-floating on the bridge, his stomach revolted at the thought of falling for eternity. He trained his eyes on the horizon from then on.

The door shut with a reverberating *thunk* behind them, sealing them into the Keep. Slowly, they crept along. The wind rose, whistling in their ears. Then the hum of the Shades came, a gentle *whoosh* that sent chills down Deckard's spine.

"They're coming," Ilain called.

They all prepared their weapons—Auden and Ilain raised their hands, Deckard, Evylin, Thom, and Rafferty tightened their grips on their swords, and Ethenn nocked an arrow. Then a fierce rush of wind swept in, bringing the first onslaught of Shades with it.

The humanoid creatures burst from the clouds, magical streams of air holding their clay forms together. Their arms reached out to grapple the troop, the force of the gale causing them all to wobble on their feet. Evylin and Ethenn fared best, holding their footing with practiced agility. She swept her sword in an arc, catching a Shade square in the center of its chest. The hunter's arrow managed to land on the very edge of another's shoulder.

It was a horrible mistake.

The Shades' clay bodies shattered, and a giant blast of air whipped out. Both Evylin and Ethenn lost their footing then. She was knocked back, her heels hanging over the edge of the bridge as she fought to maintain her balance. Deckard's heart lurched, and his hand shot out. He caught her arm, pulling her to his chest and safety. His pulse spiked as he held her against him, a tingle of magic spreading across his skin.

Ethenn wasn't so lucky. He pitched backward, arrows spilling out of the quiver at his back.

Ilain let out a cry of alarm, then thrust her hand forward. The young man froze in midair, his chest pumping furiously. But there were still Shades swirling around them, reaching and grabbing, trying to pull them from the path. Killing them was as ineffective as ignoring them, their deaths sending forth those frightful blasts of wind.

While Ilain used Wind to settle Ethenn back on the stone bridge, the rest of them fought off groups of Shades, clinging to one another as they fought to stay in place.

"Ilain," Thom called when he nearly lost his footing after Auden killed another Shade with a flare of Day magic, "can't you keep them away from us?"

Assured that Ethenn was safe, Ilain gritted her teeth and threw her arms up to the sky. A squall of upward wind knocked the Shades into oblivion. The roar of it all filled Deckard's head like he was trapped underwater.

Freed from the onslaught of Shades, they relaxed for a mere second before bolting down the path.

"I can't do that again," Ilain warned. "So you'd all best be at peak performance if you want to make it out of here."

"I thought you had a special relationship with Wind," Thom sassed.

"I do!" she yelled back at him. "But killing a Guardian takes more power and focus than you could ever imagine. In order to retain enough energy to get us out of here, I need to conserve as much now as possible."

Another gust ripped through, bringing more Shades.

"Stay low," Evylin called.

They all listened, crouching and widening their stance as they defended. Centering their gravity helped to keep them on the path, but it hampered their progress on the bridge. They could defend their onward march this way, Deckard knew, but eventually, they would tire. They still had to get to the Chamber, defeat the Guardian, and return through the Keep with the Relic in tow. Ilain was right; they had to conserve their energy.

A Shade swept in, its arms latching onto Rafferty. It carried him over the side of the bridge, his feet dangling. Evylin caught his arm, but the Shade's force took her with them.

Deckard dived forward. His arm slipped around her waist, keeping her on the path as Rafferty hung over the side. The weasel let his short swords fall into the never-ending fog around them to clasp onto Evylin, his light gray eyes panicked. A blast of wind from another downed Shade whipped around them. Evylin's feet were barely on the path, giving them very little leverage as Rafferty clung to her. She still held the Night sword in one hand, unwilling to let the Relic go.

Deckard fought to maintain his footing as their weight drew them an inch closer to the edge.

"I'm slipping!" Rafferty cried, his hand sliding down Evylin's arm.

The rest of the team was too embroiled in their own battles to assist as more and more torrents of wind whirled around them. Shades flew by, tearing at them, trying to drag them over the side.

Carefully, Deckard let his sword clatter to the bridge. He reached around Evylin, grabbing Rafferty's arm. "We've got to pull him up," he told her, doing his best to ignore the way his body lit up with her closeness.

"I'm aware of that," Evylin called back. "How do you propose—?" A Shade jerked at her arms, and Deckard released Rafferty to slam his tricep into the Shade's head. Evylin cursed as Rafferty slipped farther out of her grasp.

"Lean back," Deckard ordered, setting his feet. Her back pressed into his chest as she did as instructed, placing all her weight on him. With slow, careful steps, he drew them farther onto the path. His muscles ached from the strain. Their weight and strength gave them just enough leverage to pull Rafferty high enough to hoist himself onto the bridge.

Huffing from the exertion, Deckard released his hold on Evylin. A small gap had formed between them and the others. Shades rushed to fill the space around them. Evylin swung her amethyst blade, catching two, while Deckard took his sword back up, joining her defense. With his short swords lost, Rafferty cautiously used his throwing knives, ensuring his aim before losing what precious little weaponry he had left.

Once they'd cleared their way, Evylin pulled her broadsword from the scabbard belted to her waist. "Here," she said to Rafferty. "Don't lose it."

Rushing up the path, they closed the distance between them and their team. Though they'd fought through so much already, Deckard knew they still had hundreds of feet between them and the Chamber's entrance. They had to move faster. Hordes of Shades would keep coming, and they couldn't waste their energy here.

Growing accustomed to the attacks, they began to work efficiently, ducking and huddling together whenever someone knocked a Shade from the air. Sweat dripped down Deckard's forehead, sliding over his brow and into his eyes. The prickle of magic whispered across his skin, urging him to access it.

After too long, the face of a dark gray spire-like tower came into view, wrapped in the fog's embrace. An iron door beckoned them with a promise of safety. They sprinted for it, dozens of Shades flying toward them. Thom and Ethenn caught two right as Auden hit three others with a burst of Day. The onrush of wind hit both of the Ephrian soldiers full in the chest and over the side.

"Thom!" Deckard screamed, fear and panic lancing through him. He was useless to help, with Evylin and Rafferty standing between him and his brother.

With a deep, throaty bellow, Ilain raised her arms. Her face screwed up in concentration and effort. She caught both men with her magic, carrying them back to the platform. Her arms shook as Wind whirled around her, making her fiery hair dance like a flame. Auden defended his sister as she rescued the men, while Deckard, Evylin, and Rafferty took care of the final few Shades.

As soon as Thom and Ethenn's feet hit the stone bridge, she whirled around to follow her brother into the stone tower. The Ephrians all hurried along behind them, piling into the obelisk's staircase. Deckard shut the door behind him and took his first easy breath since they'd entered the Keep.

"Everyone's safe?" Ilain asked.

"Yes," Deckard confirmed.

"Good," she said, then whirled to face Ethenn, stepping up onto the stair in front of her. She grabbed hold of his collar and jerked him until his nose was within inches of hers. "If you fall one more time," she snapped, "I will let you go, do you understand?"

Ethenn's swallow was audible as he nodded. "Sorry," he muttered.

"You're not forgiven," she said, then released him roughly. Something in her expression made Deckard acutely aware of her fear. A fear he felt within himself. His heart felt perpetually lodged in his throat. His eyes caught on Evylin's windswept hair, her braid nearly undone. Twice, he'd almost lost her out there.

And they'd have to traverse that perilous path again.

With Auden and Ilain in the lead, they descended the long, spiral stairs. At the base, it widened into a massive Chamber like the others. But this was worse—far, far worse than the rest. The space held the same design, stretching hundreds of feet between the entrance and the dais on the far side, yet there was no floor. The columns hung in midair, going on forever into the clouds above and below them. The dais hovered as a floating island. Nothing lay between it and the short, arching platform they stood on at the base of the stairs. There was no path, no bridge, only sky and fog for miles.

Rafferty gestured flippantly at the dais. "How are we supposed to get over there?" he asked, incredulous.

Ilain pursed her lips in agitation. She scanned the Chamber, then shrugged. "Maybe we're not supposed to," she said, then raised her hands. With a flick of her wrists, a swirl of Wind rushed toward them.

Nothing happened.

Thom frowned at her. "Was that supposed to accomplish something?"

Ilain gave him a bored glare. "I thought maybe I could summon the Wind to carry the Relic to me," she said. "I suppose that would have been too easy."

An earsplitting cry pierced the air, causing them all to jump in alarm. They raised their weapons. The sound was entirely foreign to Deckard, somewhere between the roar of a bear and the screech of a hawk. His heart thundered as a giant beast descended over the dais, swooping through the air toward them.

"Shoot it, Loxley!" Rafferty shrieked, though they all knew an arrow would do little good against this creature.

The Chamber Guardian flew in on feathered wings that spanned the room's length. Deckard had never seen such a beast. It was a fearsome blend of bird, bull, and bear. Its four giant paws held claws the size of a man. Large horns rested atop its head like a half-moon. Its muscular limbs flexed as it neared, ready to pounce.

Ethenn let loose a torrent of arrows as Auden threw arcs of light at its razor-sharp beak.

"How are we going to get across?" Evylin asked, hands tight on the Night sword and eyes locked on the Guardian.

Thom turned to Ilain. "Can you make a path?"

"Out of what?" Ilain asked skeptically.

Thom floundered, looking around the room. "The columns," he said at last. "You could tear out chunks of stone and make a path with them."

Ilain frowned, her green eyes worried. "I'd have to use Terrae to do that."

"Then do it," he insisted.

"I told you," she set her hands to her chest, "Terrae is my worst resource. It'll use up too much energy—"

"Do you want us to get this Relic or not?" Thom demanded.

Ilain scrunched her nose, a small wrinkle appearing on its bridge. She growled—actually *growled*—at him. "If we die," she said, "I'm blaming you."

"If we die," Thom retorted, "I won't care."

Ignoring his quip, Ilain turned, her dark skirts swirling around her. She pressed her lips together and stepped to the edge of the platform. The Guardian screeched its rage as more arrows and Day hit its gray hide. Closing her eyes, Ilain raised her hands. The wrinkle on her nose deepened as she concentrated.

Deckard, Evylin, Thom, and Rafferty stood by helplessly, only able to watch. Deckard wanted to do something, but he worried about tapping into his magic. What if Ilain used too much power now, and they relied on him to get out?

A sharp *crack* echoed through the Chamber. The columns trembled. Ilain groaned and crumpled her hands into fists. Chunks of stone ripped free of the columns. Slowly drawing her hands together, Ilain arranged the large stones into a gaping path that stretched from the entrance platform to the floating dais.

Before they'd even fully locked in place, Evylin leaped onto the first rock. Deckard called her name worriedly, but she didn't hesitate or look back. She hurried forward, jumping from rock to rock.

Deckard prepared to go after her, but the Guardian flapped its enormous wings furiously, sending a fierce gale through the group. It drove Deckard and the others back as Evylin stumbled on the rocks. She caught herself easily, continuing on her path.

"Jonn," Auden called from the far side of the platform, "we need your help."

Deckard stared after Evylin, afraid to take his eyes off of her. He wasn't ready to access his magic, to feel that overwhelming sensation once more. But if he wanted to ensure Evylin's safety, this was his best means of doing that.

Deckard curled his hands into fists, feeling for the heat that simmered under his skin. It prickled, subtle yet attentive—waiting. He tried to grasp hold of it, urging Day magic forward, visualizing the bursts of Day as Ilain had coached. He thought of the sun, glowing and golden, life-giving and warm. He worked to channel it into a flare of light, bright and luminous. His fingers flexed, willing the power to surface. Instead, the heat receded, the magic pulling away from his grasp.

"No," he muttered. Desperation drove him to release the image of Day. The tingle returned, an almost intrigued sensation across his flesh. He let the magic guide his connection, forming a link to the first resource it found. It crawled over his scalp, tingling and whispering in his head. *At last,* he could almost hear it murmuring.

When he raised his hands, the crystalline shadows were there, dark and glittering.

Despite himself and all of Auden and Ilain's training, Deckard gave in to the darkness. He released the shadows, sending the black shards toward the Guardian. It connected with the creature's left wing, causing it to roar in pain.

Out of the corner of his eye, Deckard saw Thom and Rafferty run for the path of rocks. They followed Evylin, hurrying from stone to stone. His fear spiked, seeing his brother risking his life too. But he kept his focus on the Guardian with Auden and Ethenn. Ilain stood at the head of the platform, concentrating on the floating path.

Halfway across the expanse, Evylin landed on another rock as the Guardian bellowed and charged after her, its claws extended. As it neared, she slashed up with the Night sword, striking its paw. It screeched in pain, then circled the sky to try again.

Deckard sent another streak of black crystal after the Guardian. It grazed the feathers of its wing as it swooped toward Evylin. She ducked as the sharp claws closed around half of the stone chunk. The rock tilted in the beast's grasp, and she began to slide down the side. Without anything to grab onto, Evylin dropped into the clouds.

Thom and Rafferty called out as they scrambled forward, but Deckard screamed her name, his vision turning dark. He charged to the edge of the platform, casting his hand out before him. The crystalline shadows knew his thoughts even better than he did, arcing through the air. They spiraled together, forming a bridge of shimmering, coal-like rock.

Evylin hit the bridge with a *thump*. She nearly rolled over the side before catching herself. She pulled herself up and stared back at Deckard, eyes wide.

"Go!" he ordered.

Without hesitation, she ran, the crystal cloud forming the path as she went. Deckard could feel every step like an imprint in his mind. He focused every ounce of his will to ensure the shadows remained solid.

The Guardian swooped down again, ready to attack, and Deckard felt his attention slip. He pressed his lips together, reinforcing the bridge as he closed his eyes. He would trust her to make it across the expanse. Raising his other hand, he centered his attention on the bridge.

Somehow, Deckard could feel the pulse of the Night sword in Evylin's hand as she ran. He latched onto it, accepting whatever magical connection they shared. He held the bridge until her feet leaped free. He opened his eyes as she landed on the dais. She sprinted across the platform, her fingers closing on the Wind Relic.

When she lifted it from its pedestal, it glowed with swirling silver light. Then it shifted into a double-ended sword.

Deckard's jaw dropped at the same time as Evylin's.

"Evie, look out!" Thom called from the rock path. He and Rafferty were closing in on the dais, but the Guardian was already there.

Auden, Deckard, and Ethenn sent their attacks with renewed focus. Golden light and dark crystals struck the beast, while the arrows merely ricocheted off its hide.

In one fluid motion, Evylin turned the Night sword back into a Relic to hang around her neck and spun with the Wind sword twirling in her grasp. She struck at the Guardian's paws. It flapped its wings as it stomped at her, its claws scraping the dais floor. Evylin rolled away, coming up on her knees as she swiped up.

Thom and Rafferty finally leaped onto the platform, charging with their swords raised.

Ilain instantly sighed, releasing the rock bridge. The chunks fell out of sight. "Auden," she said weakly, "I need help."

In a heartbeat, Auden was there. He grabbed her hands and drew her close. They both closed their eyes, focusing their efforts on defeating the Guardian.

Evylin sliced open one of the Guardian's digits, and it lashed out, screeching in pain. Its violent kicks knocked Thom back. Rafferty caught hold of him, keeping Thom from tumbling into the clouds.

An arrow finally stuck in the Guardian's side. Then Ethenn turned to Deckard. "That's it," he said, motioning to the empty quiver at his back. "I'm out."

Gritting his teeth, Deckard focused on the Guardian. "Defend Auden and Ilain," he said. "If that creature comes for them, we can't leave them unprotected."

Ethenn nodded, drawing his sword as he hurried to the Calders' sides.

"I can't focus," Ilain said, her voice frail.

Auden squeezed her arms. "Come on, Lain," he said encouragingly. "We're almost there."

She shook her head, face taut with effort. "I'm too tired," she murmured.

Deckard sent more shadows to distract the Guardian. It roared in protest, but its injuries could only irritate it. Guardians were defeated by connecting with the resource, not by killing it. The troop's attacks kept it from coming for the Mages alone. Unless Auden and Ilain harnessed a strong enough connection with Wind, the Guardian would remain.

"Jonn," Auden called, "we need help."

"I'm not an Elemental Mage," Deckard said, focus split between protecting Evylin, Thom, and Rafferty and watching out for the Calders and Ethenn.

Auden's pleading gaze locked with Deckard's. The Mages were failing. Ilain had expended too much energy, and she couldn't keep it up any longer. If they didn't end the

Guardian now, she would black out from exertion, and they couldn't carry her unconscious body back through the Keep with Shades attacking from all sides.

Deckard made his decision a second too late.

"Auden," Ilain mumbled just as her knees buckled.

But it wasn't Auden who caught her.

CHAPTER TWENTY-NINE

Ilain's grip dropped from her brother's, her strength gone. She gasped as she began to fall. Auden moved a fraction too slowly, his hands failing to hold her steady.

The clang of metal against marble echoed as Ethenn reached out, his sword clattering to the floor. His hands landed on Ilain's arms as she crumbled into his chest. Then her eyes went wide, and Ethenn sucked in a sharp inhale.

Simultaneously, the Guardian roared, its screeching bellow piercing as it slammed its paws against the dais once more. Then it burst apart in a torrent of wind. It knocked Evylin, Thom, and Rafferty to the floor and drove Deckard and Auden several feet back. But Ethenn stood steadily, Ilain resting in his immovable arms.

The wind died down, and their clothes and hair slowly settled back into place. The Guardian was gone, presumably defeated by Ilain. Their fight was over, though Deckard couldn't fully comprehend how the highlady had suddenly managed the connection.

Ilain tensed, pulling away from Ethenn. "Auden," she murmured even as her eyes remained locked on the young man.

Ethenn tightened his jaw, stepping back.

"Hey!" Rafferty called from the far side of the room. "How are we supposed to get back over there?"

Deckard turned from the confusing scene. He lifted his hands. The glittering shadows formed a path linking the dais to the entrance. With a flick of her wrist, Evylin turned the Wind sword back into a necklace and slipped it over her head to hang next to the Night

Relic. Then she hopped on the bridge readily, though Thom and Rafferty tested it before trusting it with their full weight.

The three of them hurried across, Evylin's gaze meeting Deckard's. "Thank you," she said lightly. "For catching me back there."

Deckard dipped his head, the urge to take her in his arms frightfully severe. He pressed his hands to his sides. "Always," he said.

With Thom and Rafferty back, Deckard released his hold on his magic as Auden had taught him. A small tug at his mind alerted him to the discharge of power. He now understood Auden's lesson on magic taking energy. The thing was that this fatigue felt milder than that of a short jog.

Turning to the Calders, Deckard was surprised to find them both staring at Ethenn in shock while the young man looked everywhere but at them.

"What's going on?" Thom asked warily.

None of them spoke.

Deckard stepped forward, a nagging suspicion coming to his mind.

Then Ilain said, "Give him the Relic."

Ethenn flinched. "That's—that's not necessary," he said.

Following his instincts, Deckard guided Evylin forward. At her confused look, he gave her a nod. She slipped the Wind Relic over her head and held it out to Ethenn.

He shook his head. "I'm not—I don't want—"

"Take it," Ilain commanded.

He met her fierce glare, then wilted. He accepted the Relic reluctantly. Its silver glow brightened, and the necklace shifted form. A beautiful gray birch bow rested in his grasp, twin blades tipping its edges.

They all stared at Ethenn, dumbfounded.

Rafferty let out a low whistle. "Well, well, little Lox," he said. "Looks like you've been holding out on us."

"You're a Warrior," Ilain said it like an accusation.

Ethenn's head drooped as he shrugged. "I guess."

"You guess?" Thom repeated. "Bloody hell, kid. This would've been nice to know a month ago."

"I didn't—" Ethenn cut himself off. He sighed. "I didn't know."

"Until when?" Auden asked, eyeing the young man curiously.

"Until now," Ethenn said.

Auden tipped his head to the side. "You avoided taking the Relic. That suggests you knew, but you didn't want us to."

"I didn't know," Ethenn insisted. Then he slumped. "I only suspected."

"For how long?" Evylin asked.

Absently, Ethenn played with the string on the Wind bow. A silver arrow materialized between his fingers, and he let the string slip in his surprise. The arrow fell to the floor before disappearing in a wisp of fog.

"That's a neat trick," Rafferty commented.

Ethenn grimaced, holding the bow uncomfortably. "I started wondering when—" He hesitated. "When you told us about how it feels when you fight. How your senses heighten and—and everything is easier. That's how I feel when I'm hunting or when I'm fighting. Not as strong, but . . . I didn't have a Warrior uncle training me my entire life."

When Evylin shifted tensely beside him, Deckard had to grip the hilt of his sword to keep from reaching to comfort her. She spoke steadily. "When Deckard asked if we felt it, too, you said no."

"I shrugged," Ethenn corrected. "I wasn't sure then. Over time . . ."

"You're a bloody Warrior," Ilain said again, something like horror in her tone.

Deckard wasn't sure what made the woman's face scrunch like that, but after nearly blacking out, he was worried about her. "Ilain," he said, barely catching her attention as she continued to glare at Ethenn. "Are you all right? Can you safely make it back through the Keep?"

Clamping her jaw, Ilain finally turned from their newly discovered Warrior. "Yes. If it weren't for—" She flexed her hands. "If it weren't for Ethenn, I'd be unconscious right now. When I killed the Guardian, I was able to channel his magic enough to use his energy and not mine. However, that's the extent of my magic. I'm depleted."

"You're sure?" Auden asked worriedly.

Ilain nodded. "I can run out of here, but Allore help us if I need to use more magic."

"What if you carried the Relic?" Ethenn asked, voice thin.

Ilain eyed the Wind bow he proffered toward her. "Relics give power, not strength," she said. "Utilizing its power would drain me faster, and I'd black out more quickly with it than without."

Ethenn dropped the bow to his side.

"Guess you've got a new toy, eh, Loxley?" Rafferty said.

"This—" Auden scoffed as he stared in awe. "This is impossible. Three Warriors and a Mage in a group of six. The odds. . . ."

Deckard met Evylin's skeptical stare. The odds *were* impossible. With the supposed rarity of magical beings, there shouldn't have been more than one with magic in their ranks. Perhaps, there shouldn't have even been that.

But the truth was clear: Hewitt, Evylin, and Ethenn were Warriors. Deckard was a Mage. How had such an impossibility become a reality?

"This is a topic to discuss once we're safely out of the Keep and back on the road," Deckard said to the whole troop, putting a pause on their wondering. "Ethenn, I want you to stay with Ilain—"

The pair, separated by several feet, straightened and glanced at one another dubiously.

Deckard ignored their discomfort. "As a Warrior, you can protect her best. Don't let those Shades get near her."

Ethenn nodded, then looked to Evylin. "You should try using a bow out there," he suggested. "It'll keep them back so the wind won't knock us off."

"I'm not trained with a bow," Evylin said. "And with all that wind, how are we supposed to aim?"

The hunter hesitated, then shrugged. "I think the magic takes care of that."

Suddenly, Deckard realized that during their run across the bridge, Ethenn's arrows had all hit true. A miraculous feat that was, in all actuality, a Warrior's magic.

Evylin took the Night Relic from her neck. It beamed deep purple in her hand, shifting into a recurve bow. Its shiny metal frame was rich amethyst, reflecting light violet in the gray atmosphere. She drew back the string, and a shadow formed into an arrow of the same purple metal.

With these revelations on their minds, the troop headed for the staircase, out of the Chamber. They worked up the stairs slowly, conserving their energy and preparing for another exhausting sprint across the narrow stone path. Deckard took the lead, with Evylin and Thom right behind him. They chose to put Ilain and Ethenn in the middle to ensure the defenseless Mage had the most protection. Auden and Rafferty took the back.

At the top of the staircase, Deckard looked back at them. Their faces were haggard, their bodies tense as they prepared for the treacherous journey. "We run," he told them, hand on the door. "We're too tired to fight these Shades the whole way back. We run, and we get out of this Keep as fast as possible. Got it?"

A wave of grateful nods passed over the group.

With a final deep breath, Deckard drew his sword, opened the door, and tore across the narrow bridge and into the fog.

The hum of the Wind Shades was no longer the gentle *whoosh* from before. It screamed in a torrent around them, bursting forth as Shades assailed the team. They ducked their heads, dodging carefully as they rushed over the path. Deckard's orders were impossible to follow. Even he had to stop and slice down a cluster of Shades as they ripped at his arms, legs, hair, and face. When the cluster disintegrated in a blast of wind, Evylin and Thom held Deckard steady.

They resumed their run, boots pounding on the stone. Evylin and Ethenn picked off dozens of Shades with their bows. While the wind still rolled and blustered around them, the Warriors managed to keep enough Shades back to ease their path.

The fog grew denser, shortening their range of vision. Deckard kept his eyes locked on the path ahead, alert for the appearance of the stone entrance. A Shade swooped over his head, and he ducked, the Wind creature's fingers tugging at his grown-out hair. He grimaced as it ripped at him but jerked away despite the pain. He determined then and there to find a way to cut his hair before the next Keep.

Wind erupted all around them, giant blasts of air slamming into their sides. They struggled to maintain their footing. Ilain let out a cry behind him, but Deckard trusted Ethenn to keep her safe. He kept his eyes ahead, desperate to find the door.

Lungs burning and side aching, Deckard forced his feet faster. Shades screamed in his ear, their hum a deafening howl. Arrows streamed through the clouds, cutting through the creatures. A heavy shadow formed in the fog; the door loomed in the distance.

Deckard called for the others to slow as they barreled closer. The shadow grew darker and more solid. The edges sharpened into the rectangular frame and iron face. Skidding to a stop, Deckard slammed his hand against it. A vibration tingled through his palm and up his arm. The lock disengaged with a *clunk*.

The second the door opened wide enough, Deckard slipped through, turning to pull Evylin with him. A final howl from the Shades ricocheted through the Keep, following them through the door. Thom, Ilain, Ethenn, Auden, and Rafferty piled in. Then the iron door shut, sealing them into the shocking contrast of the hall's silence.

They stood there, catching their breaths and collapsing against the wall.

Deckard dropped his head back against one of the stone arches. They'd made it out of the Keep. They had a fourth Relic. Now, they had to return to camp and ride hard until they left the Reach. A task that would require him to work with Auden to shroud the entire team, horses included.

Despite how well he'd managed his use of magic within the Keep, his body ached. He was tired. Even if he used the Night Relic, he feared he'd fail to hold on long enough to get them out safely.

"Take a few minutes," Deckard told the troop. "Rest. We have a long night ahead of us."

14TH OF CHRONOS, 1574

They emerged from the Wind Keep's antechamber a mere quarter of an hour later, sprinting back to the horses. They needed the cover of night to aid their passage through the checkpoint on the border of Sutterlund Reach and Wauld. The twin moons shone overhead, the ivory one glittering half full and the shadow one a beaming gibbous.

In the depths of the night, they had another five hours at most. It would take them at least half that time to reach the gate at a full gallop. Crossing through under a shroud would require more stealth, which meant more time.

They mounted up, hurrying away from the coastline to the main road. None of them spoke. They were of single-minded purpose, riding through the darkness.

The soft sea breeze tickled Deckard's face beneath his hood. It was gentle, almost comforting compared to the wind of the Keep. It whispered through the trees and over the grass. Crickets chirruped and fireflies twinkled like the stars. The stillness of the night was tranquil and soothing after their harrowing experience.

Warmth spread across Deckard's skin to the base of his skull. He pushed it away, recognizing the signs of magic attempting to grab hold of him. After exiting the Keep, he'd felt the magic ease back. His body relaxed, and his mind grew less alert. He felt shaky without the magic, but he preferred that, knowing it meant he was experiencing humanity.

That was what he'd now come to understand after the Wind Keep. Magic made him less human. Less vulnerable. Less feeling and more apathetic. He lost morality when magic came over him. It gave him clear-minded logic and near-divine abilities, but it took away the man he was at his core.

He hated it.

They had to slow their flight as Ilain's exhaustion caught up with her. At one point, she nearly toppled from her horse. Ethenn rode up to catch her just in time. Thom came forward then, offering for her to ride with him. It would force them to reduce their speed, since the weight of two individuals was too great for his horse to maintain the breakneck pace. Still, they all agreed it would be for the best.

Two hours later, the stone walls between the Reach and the Waulden kingdom peeked over the trees. Deckard slowed his horse even more, ready to guide them off the road so he and Auden could set the shroud in place, a skill he hoped he could achieve. The others reined in their horses, their cloaks turning them into hulking shapes in the night.

Deckard opened his mouth to direct them when, without warning, a giant gust of Wind crashed into them.

The surprise attack threw all but Evylin and Ethenn to the ground. Deckard slammed into the muddy terrae, his horse sidling nervously beside him. He rolled away from its stamping hooves as a mass of dark figures stepped out of the murky forest on both sides to encircle the road.

Evylin and Ethenn, secure on their horses, had their Relic bows already drawn, arrows flying. A host of Wind Mages raised their hands, catching the arrows with magic and sending them off course. Evylin cursed, shifted the Night bow into a sword, and spurred her horse toward the left side.

Deckard scrambled to his feet, reaching for his sword. Roots grew out of the mud, wrapping around the hilt and blade. Instinctively, he knew it was Terrae magic. Another gust of Wind struck Deckard, dragging him back to his knees. The Mages surrounded them, drawing closer. The roots encircled their ankles, trapping them in place. The horses whickered in fright as the terrae worked to imprison them too. The magic kept all but Evylin and Ethenn trapped, but even the Warriors couldn't bear up under dozens of Mages.

Deckard cursed inwardly. They'd expected an ambush at the Keep. They hadn't considered one at the gates into Wauld. Blount had outsmarted them.

Rafferty cried out, hand to his face. A line of blood marred his cheek. Deckard frowned, confused at what had hit the man when, suddenly, he was struck too.

A needle-like pain pierced his shoulder. He gasped as it jerked him back, sending him sprawling into the mud. The distressed cries of his team rang through the night as he realized the Mages were attacking them with sharp bursts of wind, so concentrated they wounded like the slash of a blade.

Deckard heard Evylin's agitated shout and turned, finding her stumbling back as a large group of Mages surrounded her with a whirlwind of magic. She slashed at the roots that tried to pull her down, the mud climbing up her boots. The wind cut at her, tearing holes in her cloak and drawing streaks of blood along her face, arms, torso, and legs.

The rest of the Mages continued their assault on the others. Thom and Auden shielded Ilain from the brunt of the attacks, while Rafferty and Ethenn failed to get any closer to their assailants. Auden sent out an arcing surge of Day magic, managing to knock down a few Mages. But it wasn't enough.

The Wind and Terrae Mages pressed deeper into their ranks. Evylin dropped to her knees, arms covering her head to protect her face. The horses snorted and screamed in protest. Deckard tried to rise, but the Wind and Terrae wouldn't let him. His throat closed. His fingers clawed at the dirt, trying to carry him closer to Evylin.

Ilain grabbed her brother's hand and called out for Ethenn. The Warrior lunged for her, hand outstretched. Ilain's eyes locked with Deckard's, conveying her message. He didn't know whether to protest or accept the weight of responsibility she'd placed upon him in that singular look.

Then she squeezed her eyes shut in a concerted effort. Ethenn and Auden grimaced, their shoulders caving under the pull of Ilain's magic.

Suddenly, the Wind died, and the roots shattered. The world was still. Eerie silence filled the night.

Ilain fell back, unconscious.

Knowing his role, Deckard rose to his feet. The highlady had sacrificed the rest of her energy to give him this chance. He could save them in this momentary reprieve.

Deckard raised his hands, ready to summon the Night and save their lives.

Nothing happened.

Dread spiked through Deckard. He felt no warmth, no power rushing through his veins, no clarity of mind. He stared at his hands, devoid of magic. Panic settled in as realization flooded him. In the assault, he'd lost his focus. His connection to magic was gone, and he couldn't save them. All was lost.

The enemy Mages wasted no time regaining the upper hand. The air swirled around them, violent and gaining speed. The terrae grew up, working to restrain them once again.

However, in the millisecond of her freedom from the whirlwind, Evylin spun. "Jonn," she yelled and threw the Night Relic. It glowed bright amethyst, twinkling in the moonlight.

Deckard lifted his hand. The Relic struck his palm, warm to the touch. It beamed with a brighter luminance, casting a violet haze over the muddy road. Power surged through his arm. Heat radiated across his skin. His heart pounded. The edges of his vision went dark. And his mind stilled.

A slow smile came to Deckard's lips, his whole body filled with renewed life. Relief spread through his veins as Night overtook his mind. The crystalline shadows reformed, coiling around him. He breathed in the crisp air. Then he turned to the Mages surrounding them.

The shards leaped at his unspoken command. They sailed through the air, weaving in and out of the Mages. The magic twisted and sliced. It spun and tore. Mage after Mage dropped to the ground around them.

Ethenn sprang forward, flinging the Wind Relic to Evylin. The ruby of the Fire Relic flared in his hand, elongating into a flaming sword. Thom and Rafferty rose, joining the Warriors as they attacked with their mundane weapons.

It took less than a minute. Not even a full sixty seconds passed as the five of them felled close to fifty Wind and Terrae Mages. Deckard's magic claimed the largest number of victims among them all, though he'd lost count of the true number.

When their attackers lay dead in a circle around them, the team turned to Deckard. He could see the question on their faces. They waited for their next step.

His eyes landed on Evylin. Her expression was clouded as she studied him. Her dark hair was wild, loose strands wispy around her face, streaked with cuts and blood. The double-ended Wind sword shifted back to a Relic in her grasp. Its silver light reflected coolly on her face, revealing her parted lips and shuttered gaze as she watched him.

Deckard's conscience urged him to let go of the magic. He could see the fear in her eyes and the tension in her frame as she stepped back, away from him. She was afraid of him. How many had he just killed without a second's hesitation? How dark, how vile was his magic proving him to be? She *should* fear him.

But Deckard couldn't let go of the darkness.

He tightened his grip on the Relic, the whisper of magic humming in his ears. The power filled him, wrapping with a comforting embrace around his whole being. With the merest thought, he shrouded the whole troop as Auden taught him, along with their horses, their edges turning soft like a mirage. He settled the Relic around his neck and straightened.

"Let's go," he said, his voice unfamiliar to his own ears. It sounded emotionless and void. Flat. Cruel.

He resolved not to let it bother him. Not until they slipped past the guards of Sutterlund Reach, through the gate, and back into Wauld, invisible and silent.

CHAPTER THIRTY

Evylin

Terror gripped Evylin as they raced through the dark forests of Wauld. Her hands shook, and her heart pounded. The sweat that trailed down her chest and arms stung in the cold, foggy morning. The burning cuts from the Wind magic wept thin lines of blood along her temple and cheeks before they dried to crusty patches. Hours passed, the edges of the sky lightening to a soft gray bleeding through with rusty brown and crimson.

Breathless, exhausted, and driven by fear, the team pressed on until they couldn't ride any longer. With Ilain still unconscious and the horses overworked from their sprint through the night, they stopped a mere handful of miles from the Reach. Ethenn scouted ahead, finding a safe place to camp.

Huffing and hanging their heads, the horses came to a grateful stop deep in the woods. However, the adrenaline and anxiety pumping through Evylin remained, causing the world to swirl before her. She watched, body trembling, as Auden and Deckard carefully drew Ilain down, Ethenn handing her over gently from her perch on the front of his horse. Due to their magical strength, the hunter and Evylin were the least worn down of the troop, which had made him the most qualified to ensure Ilain's safety during their dash from the Reach. Thom and Rafferty sprang from their horses as well, hurrying to help clear a place for her to rest.

Evylin was numb; her mind and body were addled by the contradiction of emotion raging within her. Over and over, her eyes sought Deckard, latching on to his every move. Her head spun as she dismounted and tried to regain her composure. Just as in Dunneshead, she felt herself drawn to him, drawn to his dark and mysterious magic.

She'd stared at him in dumbstruck awe after the ambush, amazed by the power he so effortlessly wielded. In that moment, his eyes had met hers, sending a surge of embarrassment coiling through her. Ever-changing, his gaze flickered to a gentle blue in the moonlight before shifting back to a green so dark it could have been black. She was horrified that he'd caught her gawking, mouth ajar in wonder.

Her desire for Deckard was intensifying by the moment, tightening like a vise upon her very soul. The Warrior inside of her had almost gained control as she watched Deckard work magic with the ease she felt with a sword. The power he wielded was deadly, strong, and unfathomable.

And it frightened her—the urge upon her soul that was growing too ardent to ignore, beckoning her to reach out and draw him close.

Evylin's magic wore off during their panicked ride. They'd returned the Relics to Rafferty for safekeeping before they'd ridden away—all except the Night Relic, which Deckard returned to him once they reached their ramshackle camp. Now, a hollowness filled her chest. And every time she looked at Deckard, her heart fluttered, causing her hands to flex.

To complicate her struggle, dread hung over Evylin in the dim gray morning. It wrapped around her like the fog in the trees. She couldn't see clearly. She couldn't think clearly. All she knew was she had to do something. She had to find a way to stop the feeling welling up inside her.

Thom, Rafferty, and Ethenn stood aimlessly to the side while Deckard and Auden laid Ilain amongst the ferns and brush.

Auden pressed a hand to her head, then settled her skirt modestly around her legs with brotherly care. "She's fine," he said, though his voice was unsteady. "Just exhausted."

"She isn't injured?" Ethenn asked in a worried tone.

Auden shook his head. "Her body shut down to protect her. She's in a magically induced stasis. Once the magic ensures her recovery, she'll wake. We can't do anything to help but keep her comfortable and safe."

They all stared at Ilain's prone form, her fiery hair damp from sweat and dew. Evylin clasped her hands to her chest, fighting the jitters that worked through them. Her nerves were frayed from too little sleep, the battle in the Keep, the ambush, and the fear plaguing her every thought.

Auden sighed, his sister's security ensured, and turned to them. "Are any of you injured?"

Scanning the troop, their faces and bodies riddled with sharp cuts from the Wind Mages' attacks, Rafferty raised his brow. "You got enough left in you to fix these?" he asked, gesturing to the scrapes on his cheeks.

"I meant something more life-threatening," Auden said. "I don't have the energy to waste on menial wounds."

"I wouldn't call them menial, but whatever," Rafferty muttered.

When everyone confirmed their overall health, Ethenn and Thom worked together to set up a tent over Ilain. With no idea of how long she'd remain unconscious, they decided it would be best to keep her safe from the elements.

"We're all wiped," Rafferty said as the men worked. "Shouldn't we bunk down too?"

Deckard ran a hand over his jaw, expression tense and haunted. "We can't risk it," he said. "It's almost light. Someone is going to see all those . . . those bodies we left behind on the road. A force of Mages that large couldn't be defeated by ordinary travelers. With Blount's writ, they'll know it was us, and they'll track us."

"But we can't go anywhere," Thom said. "Not until Ilain's recovered."

"No, we can't," Auden agreed, then added, "Not all of us."

Evylin's brow furrowed. They all turned to gape at him, confused.

"What do you mean?" Deckard asked.

Auden mussed his hair, long enough to hang over his collar after their time traveling. He gave a forlorn glance toward Ilain. "The Order of the Wind was clever," he said. "Either by their own means or with Blount's help, they outwitted us, waiting for us to make it out of the Keep and return weakened. They knew we'd make a break for the kingdom's boundary, and they were prepared. The only reason we survived that attack was because of you, Jonn. And while your magic gives us the semblance of an upper hand . . ."

He paused, expression darkening. "I fear it won't be enough next time."

His ominous words hit Evylin like Blount's kick in the Water Keep. Tears sprang to her eyes, and she blinked furiously to drive them away. If Deckard's magic wasn't enough . . . they'd all die the next time.

No, Evylin realized with a frightening start, *not all of us.* She was a female Warrior. Blount would keep her alive to Bond with her. He'd kill the rest of them. She'd lose them all—she'd lose *him*—and be alone for centuries.

Her heart squeezed with panic.

"So what are we supposed to do?" Thom asked with his usual irreverence. "Give up?"

Auden's sharp green eyes narrowed. "No," he insisted. "We will never give up. You see the control Blount has over the Orders, over the whole country. If he gets the Relics . . . No, this is bigger than any of us. We cannot stop. And if we die, we die."

The somber declaration caused the Ephrian soldiers to dip their heads. But it caused Evylin's mind to riot.

She couldn't do it again. She couldn't lose more people. She couldn't be alone.

Evylin clamped her jaw tight. Auden was right; there was no stopping, not when Blount would perpetually hunt them. If Blount was desperate for the power of the Relics— if Bonding could give him even more power—there was no doubt he'd pursue her to the ends of Terraeus as well.

"What do we do then?" Evylin demanded.

Auden sighed reluctantly. "I believe," he said, "we should split up."

"No," Deckard said immediately. "That's too dangerous."

"Staying together is too dangerous," Auden argued. "First, we have to wait for Ilain to recover before moving her. As you said, they won't have any problems tracking us here from the gates. A smaller party would be easier to hide while we wait for her to wake. Second, we're conspicuous as a team of seven. Blount listed our numbers on the writ. That means people are looking for a large party. If we split, we make ourselves harder to find."

Auden drew in a tense breath, his lips quirking down. "Third and most importantly, we'll split the Relics as well. If one party is captured . . ." He shrugged. "Then the other will still have a chance to succeed."

Silence descended as they all took in his reasoning. Evylin chewed on her lip, considering his logic. All his points were valid; they were strong. But the idea of going into the Waulden forests separated from her troop unnerved her. So many things could go wrong. If one team were taken, the other would have no way of knowing, no way of rescuing them. The seven of them together could defend themselves; they'd proven that tonight.

The thought sent Evylin's eyes darting back to Deckard. He'd begun to pace, hand still working over his beard in frustration. Yes, his magic had saved them tonight. But what if Auden was right? What if, next time, Blount's forces were too large? The Keeps were becoming more difficult, and their exhaustion afterward was more severe. What would happen if Blount truly outsmarted them at the next Keep?

Her heart ached at the memory of all she'd lost and the fear of what she still stood to lose.

An idea took root in Evylin. Whether or not they succeeded at the Time Keep, whether or not Blount outwitted them all, she knew one thing: She had to protect herself against the certain death looming nearer each day. She couldn't allow herself to be destroyed when Deckard was taken from her life for good.

After Dunneshead, after the pull of the magic between them, Evylin had to be free of him. She had to break this enchantment that threatened to connect their souls, only to leave her in desolation.

"It makes sense," she said, breaking the silence.

The men looked at her, surprised. Deckard's brow pinched together in that worried way of his. Her heart ached at the sight of it.

She drew her shoulders back, giving confidence to her claim. "It isn't ideal, but it's our best chance."

Ethenn sighed. "I agree," he said, resignedly. "You said it yourself, Colonel. We can't all stay here waiting for Highlady Calder to wake up. But *someone* has to."

Deckard hesitated, his pacing coming to a halt. His eyes flashed between the two of them. "I take it you're both saying this from a strategic position as Warriors?"

Though Evylin assumed it was true for Ethenn, she lied when she said, "It's what Hewitt would do." Instantly, guilt clawed at her heart, having used her uncle's memory to manipulate him like that.

Hand still on his jaw, Deckard's thumb ran along his lower lip as he thought. The movement drew too much of Evylin's attention, spiking her agitation as she remembered the passion of their kiss in Dunneshead.

Blinking to clear her mind, Evylin stared at the ground. Just the thought redoubled her resolve. "We don't have a choice. Someone has to stay with Ilain while the others go on. Splitting up protects the Relics and increases our odds of survival."

Deckard's attentive green-blue gaze met hers. She feared that he'd see through her, divining the truth behind her words. Instead, he sighed, accepting her assertion. "I suppose you're right," he said, then turned to Auden. "How do we go about this?"

Temporary relief assuaged Evylin.

With a bearing of great trepidation and sadness, Auden took a seat next to his sister. "I'll stay with Ilain," he said decisively. "And Ethenn, I'd like you to come with us, if you're willing."

Unsure whose willingness he was asking for—Ethenn's or Deckard's—Evylin didn't particularly care. That did nothing to aid her designs. "No," she said too sharply. They turned to her, wide-eyed. She softened her tone as she excused her reaction. "I need to train Ethenn. We've only just found out he's a Warrior. His magic is completely untested."

Deckard eyed her for a second too long before agreeing. "Besides, if we're splitting the Relics, that means one group will need to take Thom and the other, Rafferty," he said.

The two men looked at one another as they sat side by side.

Rafferty furrowed his brow. "I don't like that," he said. "Who will I make fun of then?"

Thom swatted at his friend, but Rafferty evaded the slap easily.

"Yes," Auden said, ignoring their antics. "You're right, of course. Very well, Thom can stay with us. And we'll keep the Night and Fire Relics, so long as you approve."

Evylin's agitation grew. When Deckard opened his mouth to respond, she cut across him. "That doesn't work either," she insisted. "You have to train Jonn."

Auden frowned as though he'd forgotten about Deckard's dangerous magical predicament. "Mm, you're right." He scratched his temple, working through the problem. "But I can't go with you and leave Ilain to travel with Thom alone."

"'Cause it's improper?" Rafferty asked.

The look on Auden's face said he didn't put stock in Thom and Ilain's flirtations. "Because it's too dangerous," he said.

Wondering how Auden could be so dense, Evylin offered the ready solution. "Then I'll take Ethenn with me, and Jonn will stay with you."

Deckard's eyes flashed up, locking on her face. The rest of the team looked between them, genuine confusion on all the men's faces—except for Thom, who wore a curious, almost worried expression. But Evylin didn't have time to take in her brother-in-law's shocked demeanor. Not while she was trapped under Deckard's knowing stare.

He knew. She could see it in his stoic expression, in the flicker of pain in his ever-changing eyes. He knew her aim. He knew she was trying to get away from him.

Evylin swallowed past the tightness in her throat, turning away from him.

Still too daft to understand, Auden sighed. "That won't work either. It isn't ideal, but Ethenn will be fine without immediate training. He'll go with Thom and Ilain, and I'll come with you, Jonn, and Rafferty."

Evylin curled her hands into fists. "Absolutely not," she insisted. "I won't send Ethenn out untrained. If we want to ensure our survival, he'll need to be as strong as possible. The clearest answer is in front of us."

Auden brushed a hand through the air dismissively. "I won't split a man and his wife."

Evylin ground her teeth. She wanted to shout at Auden for his obtuseness.

"All the more so," he continued, "I won't split a Mage from his Warrior."

"I'm not his Warrior." The words came out clipped and abrupt before Evylin could stop them.

But they made Auden hesitate. It also made Deckard draw back, lips pressing together. Thom, Ethenn, and Rafferty all sat quietly, watching nervously.

"Evylin," Deckard murmured, giving a small shake of his head.

Determined not to back down, Evylin disregarded his warning. "You have no reason not to split us," she told Auden. "It's what's best for everyone."

Shifting in his seat, Auden continued to frown. "Perhaps you haven't Bonded, but as husband and wife, you share a connection that's more powerful than—"

"Are you blind?" Evylin blurted, tone fierce and angry. Her heart pounded in her ears, hysteria threatening her mind. Pressure built in her chest, desperate to find release. "It isn't like that between us."

"Evylin," Deckard said her name like an admonition.

She wouldn't look at him . . . *couldn't*. She refused to be dissuaded, glaring at Auden as she sealed their fate. "Our marriage is convenience alone. I'm no more *connected* to him than I am to you."

The silence that met Evylin's words was deafening.

The early morning light, however gray, was too bright, too revealing for the dark lies she'd spoken. A gentle breeze carried the rainy mist off to another part of the woods, leaving them to the consequences of her rejection. Evylin's throat was raw, and her body felt empty. Had she really said those damning words?

Deckard spoke her name once more, strong and demanding. Her gaze snapped to his of its own volition. She sucked in an instant, choppy breath at the hurt she found there. Instead of the anger he had every right to feel, she saw only disappointment.

Evylin's lips parted in a silent urge to tell him what she'd said wasn't true. They did have a connection. A deep, vibrant connection that made her feel more alive than any adventure she'd ever dreamed of.

She clamped her mouth shut, enclosing those thoughts deep inside her chest. She couldn't give voice to them, not when the world was cruel and would undoubtedly leave them in unending sorrow.

Painful seconds passed as the men scrutinized them. Evylin's face flushed. Why had she made such a scene? Why couldn't she have kept a level head? Now, they knew—they all knew that the marriage between Evylin and Deckard could legally be broken.

Deckard straightened his back, his expression going blank. A vein pulsed in his neck. "We need to talk," he said in a frighteningly calm voice.

Tears threatened, but Evylin wouldn't back down. She was close—so, so close—to being free of him, to breaking the hold he had on her. "Then talk," she replied.

Deckard took in a deep breath, chest rising with tension. "You and I need to talk," he clarified, "*alone.*"

Mouth dry, Evylin knew she couldn't allow that. She couldn't give him the chance to talk her out of this. Being alone with him, being close to him, being honest with him—his very presence could convince her. She couldn't give in.

Evylin shook her head, desperate to remain with the others.

Thom shifted in his seat. "Jonn," he said, sympathy in his tone, "if she doesn't want—"

"I didn't ask for your opinion," Deckard snapped.

Thom glared at him as though he'd been struck by his words.

Deckard turned back to Evylin and took one long stride closer. "I have proven my patience to you time and again, Evylin," he said, the words low and foreboding. "I'd advise you not to test its limits."

The truth caused Evylin to hesitate. Deckard *had* been exceedingly patient with her. His accommodation knew no bounds. Yet, the fierceness in his stare and the firm set of his jaw made it clear: This was no empty threat. If she didn't go willingly, he would forcibly carry her into the woods to have this conversation.

"Fine," Evylin said shakily, grasping onto whatever anger she could muster. "Let's have your talk."

Taking what little control remained to her in the situation, Evylin turned on her heel and marched into the morning fog. She heard Rafferty murmur something but couldn't make it out past the pounding in her head. Her muscles trembled with fatigue and dread. Every step through the trees felt like a battle all its own. She was too tired for this fight. She wanted to lie down, close her eyes, and disappear.

Mud squelched under their feet. The gray fog enveloped them, golden beams of sunlight refracted through its haze. Droplets of water shone on the bushes and budding trees. Its mystic beauty felt hostile to Evylin, mocking her as she made the most painful choice of her life.

She didn't know how long they walked, but it wasn't long enough before Deckard caught her arm. She whirled around to glare at him. Their breath came out in rapid, uneven bursts, frustration, disappointment, and hurt filling the air. Neither spoke as they stared at one another with the weight of her admission and lies between them.

Deckard opened his mouth to speak, then stopped. He shook his head and released her. Then began pacing the woods.

Evylin crossed her arms, struggling to maintain her conviction. "What did you want to discuss?" she asked, fighting to keep her words flat and emotionless.

Raking his hands through his hair, Deckard turned back to her. "Do you know what you've just done?"

Evylin shrugged, unwilling to accept his vague accusation.

"Evylin," his voice was strained, "don't you remember what I told you? If the Alliance finds out about the status of our marriage, they could dissolve it and make us Bond with whomever they want. And you just gave Auden the opportunity to ensure that."

Instantly, regret and worry ate at her, but she refused to give in. "Maybe that's what I want," she said thinly.

Deckard's eyes went wide. "You want to Bond with some other Mage?" he asked, the question breaking with his voice.

"No," she said quickly and vehemently. "No, I won't Bond with any Mage, no matter who. I've made no promises to the Alliance. They can't force me to do anything."

A flare of something—was it disappointment or fear?—crossed his face. "Then it's the dissolution of our marriage," he concluded. "That's what you want?"

Evylin couldn't say the words. She knew she should—she knew it would finally ensure her safety, finally drive him away—but she couldn't state the lie aloud.

Sorrow drew Deckard's face down. He came a step closer, his gaze searching. "I told you months ago," he whispered as though it hurt to speak, "I would do whatever it took to make you happy. If that means dissolving our marriage and letting you go . . . I'll do it."

Evylin felt the sting of tears too late. The first one slipped out of the corner of her eye, burning down her cheek. The brutal truth within caused her heart to ache. "That's the thing, Jonn," she said weakly. "You can't make me happy."

She'd never seen a man look more defeated.

And she chose to hurt him more.

"I didn't marry you because I wanted you," she said around her tears. "You knew that. It was a mutually beneficial arrangement, nothing more. You gave me the chance to leave Whickam Village, and Hewitt gave you the chance to impress your officers. It isn't my fault you failed. Now . . ."

Deckard took a step back as Evylin continued, "Now, I see that nothing I wanted was worth it." She pressed her hands to her chest. "I lost the only thing that mattered, and what did I get in return? Adventure?" She scoffed, the tears coming freely. "What is that but another word for death?"

He looked deeply remorseful, the rising sun catching in his eyes, turning them light blue. Their soft color was eternally imprinted on her brain. "Is there no way for me to fix this? Is there no chance I can help you find what you want now?" he asked.

Evylin shook her head, knowing that so long as he was in her life, she would never be safe. Every day with Jonn Deckard at her side was another day closer to losing what sanity she had left.

"No," she said with finality.

"Why not?" The question came out in a breath, but it struck her like a blow all the same.

She didn't have an answer. Not one she could speak aloud. So she turned away, too frightened to force another lie.

"Is this your decision then?" he asked, a range of emotions filling his voice. "You want an annulment?"

The words caused another uprising of tears. Her heart lurched, an instant clamor bursting forth in her mind. No, of course, she didn't want an annulment. How could she ever? She didn't want anything but him.

The thought made Evylin reel. "Yes," she said, aching deep within.

Deckard didn't speak. He didn't even react. He just stared at her as she felt the sting of her rejection inflicted upon herself.

The silence stretched. Deckard took two long strides, coming within inches of her. She thought to back away, but he stopped short. He didn't reach for her. He only continued to study her face. She didn't know what he was looking for, but she refused to let him know the truth behind her tears.

Tightening her jaw, Evylin raised her chin.

"I need you to know something, Evylin," Deckard whispered, his voice surprisingly gentle and tender. "If we're to be separated, possibly forever, then I have to say it once."

Evylin's heart twisted with hope and fear. Somehow, she knew what he was about to say. She knew the confession rising to his lips.

"Don't," she murmured breathlessly. She couldn't let him say it, no matter how much she ached to hear those words.

"I love you," Deckard said.

Closing her eyes, Evylin savored the words, even as she wished she could push them away. Her breath hitched, and pain lanced through her. "You're not supposed to," she said brokenly.

When she opened her eyes, Deckard stood there, a mournful smile on his handsome face. "I'm not sorry that I do."

Evylin could do nothing but stare up at him. How could such a sentiment fill her with joy and sorrow all at once? How could she hurt so deeply at the wonderful truth of having his love? She wanted to tell him that she didn't mean it—none of it. He *could* make her happy. Day by day, she was growing more convinced than ever that *only* he could accomplish that endeavor. But she couldn't permit herself to endure the devastation that would inevitably follow.

Not when it meant losing her very self to him, as she had done with Ryen and Hewitt.

Deckard lifted his hand, wiping away the last tear that clung to her jaw. She wanted to lean into his touch, to accept his comfort. What a relief it would be to finally give in to him, to return his love.

By sheer force of will, she remained rigid even as her emotions stirred.

"I love you, Evylin," he said again, and the words filled her once more.

Then he stepped back, dropping his hand to his side. "And because I love you, I will keep my promise to you," he said with finality. "When we return to Ephria, whether as members of the Alliance or not, I'll file for an annulment."

Evylin blinked, unable to form a reply. Her mind screamed, her heart ripping in two, and yet she stood there, immovable as stone.

Deckard's head dipped, and his shoulders drooped. "If you would," he said, with as little emotion as though he were addressing a fellow soldier rather than his wife. "Please inform Auden and the others that you and I agree to split up. In the meantime . . . I'd like a moment alone."

Shock and despair clung to every inch of Evylin. Her muscles were leaden, and her limbs were stiff. He wasn't supposed to agree. He wasn't supposed to let her go. He loved her. That meant he should fight to keep her.

The tears came back, and Evylin's feet carried her mindlessly past Deckard, into the woods toward camp. The fog still obscured the trees, oppressively looming and suffocating the light. She walked at a stilted pace, seeing nothing as she moved forward. She didn't fully comprehend what had just happened.

Deckard loved her.

And he was going to end their marriage.

Evylin's knees buckled. Her hand shot out, catching in time to hold her upright against a tree. Her breath came in short gasps. What had she done? Sorrow washed over her, tearing through her gut and bending her over in anguish.

She closed her eyes, pressing her forehead against the tree trunk. This was why she had to end it now. If it hurt this much to leave him without loving him, what sort of unending agony would she endure if she ever truly let herself feel for him?

She'd made the right choice. She'd protected herself.

She didn't love Jonn Deckard. After the irrevocable scarring upon her heart, she couldn't.

So why did it feel as though she'd torn her heart from her own chest?

CHAPTER THIRTY-ONE

Deckard considered himself to be strong and sure, unshakable in the face of adversity or trouble. He prided himself on refusing to give in to fear. From childhood, he strove to emulate heroes like Euon Sergus, men who saw beyond themselves and pressed forward, regardless of the emotions that might rage inside their hearts.

But as Evylin walked away, Deckard recognized his weakness. He was frail—a man broken and devoid of hope in the wake of rejection from the woman he loved.

Deckard kept his eyes set on the forest floor as Evylin left the clearing. He watched each step of her boots, flecked with mud and the gore of fallen Mages. His heart lurched, remembering his part in those deaths. Still, his hand twitched as she passed him, urging him to reach out and stop her. Could he convince her to give him another chance to be the husband she deserved? Should he try? Or would seeking to fulfill his own unrequited affection refute the love he claimed to hold?

Once he was confident in Evylin's departure, Deckard succumbed to his brokenness. Falling to his knees, he dropped his head in his hands. Tears blurred his vision. Isolated as he was, he let them fall readily.

For the past three months, he'd done all he knew to earn Evylin's trust—to earn her love. He gave every part of himself to their marriage. From the moment he met her in Whickam Village, he'd liked her. He'd appreciated her wit and candor, her joy only slightly tainted by her cynicism. She was intelligent and beautiful, friendly and sincere. Everything good, everything desirable. It hadn't been difficult for him to make his wedding vows. Even after three days of knowing her, he'd been ready to pledge his loyalty.

They'd labeled it a marriage for their mutual benefit. Yes, Deckard supposed that was true. Yet, despite losing the bet, he'd always believed he'd come out the unintended victor in the exchange. *She* was meant to have won. All the while, *he* was granted the wife of his dreams.

Perhaps that was why he'd tried so hard to be the perfect husband. From the start, he was ready to love her. Since he was the one who lost the bet, he felt he should pay recompense. So he spent the last three months striving to prove his love, to make her feel she truly had come out on top. He'd attempted to demonstrate his love—*her* prize—through silly means like her wedding ring and new clothing. He'd taken her to Wayford and the lake at Banbury, giving her measly adventures when he couldn't give her grand ones. He'd left notes in his absence each morning. In everything, he'd endeavored to put her first and assure her of his care.

For three months, Deckard had poured his heart and soul into their marriage. Three full months, as of yesterday.

Did she even recognize the date? he wondered. She hadn't remembered when they'd been married a month. Why should she remember it now? Did she know the date of their marriage at all?

The weight of disappointment slammed into Deckard. He'd been warned of this outcome, first by Lawton and then by Hewitt.

"Don't fall in love with her before she falls in love with you."

"Don't pledge your undying love and loyalty to her."

Perhaps it *was* his desire to love her that drove her away. Within all his caring and devotion, she'd felt manipulated rather than cherished. Now, he'd lost her. Good and truly lost her.

What was he going to tell Hewitt?

Deckard stared into the morning fog. He hadn't spoken with the man in days. This was his first opportunity to be alone. And yet, he couldn't bring himself to summon the ghost. How could he admit this failure? Hewitt would never forgive him.

It was his fault, yet another failure. He'd pushed his affection upon Evylin through tokens and deeds, and when that hadn't worked, he'd become a monster of Night magic's design, all in the name of protecting her. No wonder she'd rejected him. He wasn't worthy of her love.

Deckard ran his fingers through his sweat-and-rain-soaked hair. He steeled his heart against further pain, having allowed himself to wallow long enough. A frigid chill hollowed out his bones, numbing his heart and mind. Yet, despite the iciness overtaking him, the barest trace of warmth crept up his spine, as though magic itself was attempting to comfort him.

He shrugged it off, rising. He wiped the mud from his trousers, straightened his coat, and attempted to tame his unruly hair. Though his tears had dried, there was no helping if his eyes had grown puffy or red. If they saw his misery, so be it. The morning was growing late, and they needed to get moving.

The moment to part with his wife had come.

Deckard returned to the camp, finding Auden at his sister's side while the Ephrians huddled together. Evylin and the three soldiers spoke quietly, likely discussing how to split the parties. She didn't look in his direction when he stepped through the trees, nodding at something Thom said instead. No signs of regret or discomfort marred her expression. She carried herself with the same confidence and ease as ever.

Perhaps if he were more impassive—strong and resolute like Hewitt—she would have loved him then. Fighting off a wave of instability, Deckard cast his eyes away from her, moving for Auden. He crouched next to the man and his sleeping sister.

Auden gave him an appraising glance. "Just saying goodbye," he said softly. He held Ilain's hand, her fingers limp in his. "It'll be weeks before I see her again. We've been apart for that long before, but it's been rare. In all our forty-some years, we've spent almost every day together."

Deckard furrowed his brow, realizing for the first time that the Calders were a decade older than his thirty-two years. He ignored his curiosity in the seriousness of the moment. He patted Auden's arm encouragingly.

"What Evylin said before . . ." Auden eyed him warily. "Is it true?"

Deckard avoided grinding his teeth and said, "It is."

"Your marriage isn't real?"

"Legally, yes."

"But not practically."

Deckard dipped his chin in acknowledgment.

Auden sighed and set his sister's hand gently on the blanket beside her. "I still don't like splitting you," he said. "Whether or not you'll admit it, you're stronger together."

It wasn't Deckard who didn't want to admit it.

When he said nothing, Auden continued, "It will be you and I going now," he explained, then tipped his head in the direction of the Ephrians. "They're deciding who we'll take with us—Thom or Rafferty."

With a nod, Deckard rose. "Rafferty," he called.

The soldiers stopped talking. Evylin kept her gaze averted.

"Colonel?" Rafferty said.

Deckard moved for the horses. "You'll be coming with Auden and me," he said. "We need your skills with stealth and tracking."

Rafferty grimaced, then turned to the others. "Guess someone had to be stuck with the short end of the stick," he muttered.

Deckard didn't take offense. "Give the Night and Fire Relics to Thom, then we'll leave."

Auden watched the exchange keenly but didn't object to the command.

While Rafferty dug the Relics from his coat, Deckard called Ethenn to join him. The young man hurried over, his dark eyes alert and his expression pulled down. "Yes, sir?" he asked.

"I have a job for you," Deckard said, dropping his voice to keep the conversation private. He began to secure his saddlebags as he spoke. "I made a promise to Hewitt to protect Evylin, no matter the cost. Since I can't be with her, I'm asking you to do that for me. Will you?"

Ethenn's thick brows furrowed, but he nodded. "Of course."

"Good." He glanced over his shoulder, catching the way Thom stood a little too close to Evylin's side.

Following his stare, Ethenn's jaw tightened. "Regardless of what Evie said, sir," he turned and met Deckard's gaze, "I know it was a lie." Ethenn nudged his chin in the direction of Evylin and Thom. "And I'll protect her from *that* too."

A flare of anger tightened Deckard's expression. Whatever Ethenn meant by that, whatever he knew about Thom's intentions, Deckard pushed away his jealousy. "I have another task for you," he said, then reached into the saddlebag. He held out the small leather pouch. "Evylin's birthday is tomorrow. I'd like you to give this to her."

Ethenn took the gift reverently. "Yes, sir."

Seeing the eager obedience of the young man, Deckard hesitated. At first, he'd judged Ethenn's stoicism and reserved demeanor to be due to youth or insecurity. Over the last three months, he'd begun to perceive the truth. He remembered Thom telling him once that Ethenn was like a long match. Once it burned up, it could become painfully dangerous.

Deckard had come to learn that Ethenn's quietness wasn't a lack of assertiveness or a display of self-doubt. It was a means of control, a way of keeping the fire inside safely contained. In reality, he was as fierce and passionate as the rest of them. He was simply better at hiding it.

"One last thing," Deckard said, and set a hand on Ethenn's shoulder. "Don't lose control. Thom will test you. Evylin will push you. And Ilain . . ."

He paused, and Ethenn shifted uncomfortably.

Deckard let out a small scoff. He slapped Ethenn's arm lightheartedly. "Well, she'll be herself, which is a challenge for a man *without* your regard. Try not to let her get the best of you."

"Sir, respectfully," Ethenn straightened his shoulders, that hidden determination tightening his features, "I'm not a boy. You've given me a job. Trust me to do it."

A smile worked across Deckard's face. He felt oddly proud of the young man. "I do," he said.

Auden joined them then. "Are we ready?" he asked.

"Nearly," Deckard said. "Just let me say my goodbyes."

"Of course," Auden said. "I'll come with you."

Ethenn excused himself to store Evylin's gift as they joined the others.

Deckard forced himself not to stare at his wife as they approached. He gave her a singular glance before addressing Thom and Rafferty. "It's time for us to go," he said.

Thom made the first move, stepping over to pull Deckard into an embrace. "Be careful," he said, a tension in his voice that Deckard knew all too well. It was the same tone he used when apologizing after a fight. The same one that said he knew he was wrong, but he wasn't sorry regardless.

Despite his suspicions of Thom's motives, Deckard returned the hug. He loved his brother no matter the strain between them. "I will," he said, then pulled away. "You do the same."

Auden said a quick farewell to each of them before Ethenn arrived.

Rafferty sighed. "Farewell, kid," he said to the hunter. "You're about to have far more fun than I will." He turned to Evylin and swept her into a hug. "Don't forget me."

Evylin chuckled. "Never."

"Thommy," Rafferty said with a salute to his friend, "don't do anything I wouldn't."

"There won't be much I can't do then," Thom replied with a slap on the weasel's back.

Rafferty stopped and lifted a finger to point directly at Thom's nose. "I'm not joking," he said, with deadly seriousness. "Keep it in line."

"All right," Thom said, holding up his hands. "Geez, what's wrong with you?"

Rafferty rolled his eyes, then smacked Thom lightly on the cheek. "I'll miss you, you idiot," he said, smirking.

Seeing the farewells coming to an end, Deckard gave Ethenn a nod. "Take care," he said, then turned to Evylin.

Not one part of Deckard was ready for what he had to do next. He met Evylin's dark eyes. She shifted from foot to foot, struggling to hold his gaze. Her arms were crossed, shielding herself. The uncertainty between them was palpable. How did he say goodbye to her? Nothing seemed right anymore. He longed to take her in his arms for one last embrace. He wanted to plead with her, begging her to reconsider. His whole being urged him to disregard all her words in the forest and kiss her for what might be the final time.

Deckard took a step closer.

Evylin flinched. "Have a good trip," she said, lips turned up in a feigned smile.

An unamused chuckle escaped Deckard; even to him, the laugh sounded embittered. He wanted to tell her that it wasn't good enough, wishing him well as if he were going on holiday. After everything, he deserved more than that from her.

Emboldened by her indifference, Deckard had nothing left to lose. He reached across the distance to cup her cheek. As his fingers brushed her warm skin, she tensed. He let himself give her a sad smile, showing how deeply her distrust hurt him. Her expression showed reluctance and even fear, but she didn't pull away.

Deckard drew his finger along her jaw, across the rigid cuts left by Wind magic, and up to tuck the wild strands of hair behind her ear. Did he dare press his luck? The pad of his thumb grazed her cheekbone. Would he anger her if he stole a kiss? Did he care?

Retaining control of his senses, he let his hand fall away. Deckard stepped back. "Goodbye, Evylin," he whispered.

He didn't wait for her to respond; he wanted to relieve her of that difficulty. Instead, he turned and walked away, refusing to look back. He stuck his foot in the stirrup of his saddle and swung onto his horse. Auden and Rafferty joined him. They guided their horses away from camp. And all the while, Deckard kept his eyes on the road ahead of him, even as he left his heart behind.

Part III: Moors & Marshes

It was suggested that Rouland Blount I was the most egregiously cunning man. The early records remark on his charm and handsome countenance, while the latter accounts reveal his more diabolical nature. Though he was granted a duchy by King Thourton and given a place on the royal council, it was not enough for the then-duke. Many said Blount wormed his way into Thourton's good graces, seeking to take the place of the king's childless state. Many letters and documents note the relationship between the king and duke, showing their growing friendliness and regard for one another. There is, in fact, an existing will that notes a change in Thourton's lineage, marking Blount as his heir should he never have a son.

Many suspected Blount's intentions, but they were all written off by the king, some even flogged or imprisoned for their sentiments. However, Thourton's affinity for the duke was, as we now know, faulty. Thourton's late marriage to the youthful Carin Doyle produced a child. A month after the announcement, Blount enacted his coup, murdering the king, his wife, and unborn child, and instituting the fifty-seven-year reign of King Rouland Blount I.

Excerpt from** A Complete History of West Auld, **written by Lord Edmaund Fishere, Earl of Mouroc, published posthumously in 1575

BROUNES
RHUNAUR
TINIEN
FELSTON EDGE
AUBINGHAM
FAURMERS
SUTTLIU...
NIRAUS
IDLEVERE
HIGHLOFT MOORS
ORDER OF THE FLAME
DOORSTUNDS REACH
REACH
VAUR...
COUSTON
FAURFIELD
VLAUGMIRA

CHAPTER THIRTY-TWO

It took the rest of the day for Ilain to regain consciousness. She remained in a motionless slumber until sunset while Evylin, Thom, and Ethenn waited cautiously in the woods. The fear of pursuers from Sutterlund Reach and the need to keep watch over Ilain kept them from venturing out of their small encampment. In fact, they hardly spoke, the three of them alert and waiting with bated breath for Ilain's recovery.

It was an unfortunate turn of events for Evylin, as it allowed her far too much time to regret her decision. Throughout the day, she fought back the tears that threatened to overwhelm her. She shoved down her emotions, clinging to reason as her only remaining salvation. She couldn't fall apart. Not now.

Whether spoken or not, she was the inherent leader of their new band. While Thom was the highest-ranking soldier, since Evylin and Ethenn were Warriors, both outranked him in military prowess by default. Ilain would lead their route through the moors of southern Wauld, but she wasn't nearly as strategically minded as the soldiers and would defer to their suggestions. And Ethenn—well, he abdicated all authority handed to him.

Without Deckard, they would naturally look to Evylin. Which meant she couldn't wallow in her self-pity.

Instead, Evylin spent the day quietly working with Ethenn, teaching him to tap into his Warrior senses. It wasn't hard to train him to keep his eyes and ears magically heightened, and they both stood guard around the camp. They took turns on watch, napping to recover from their long night in the Wind Keep. During his shift, Ethenn went out to ensure they hadn't left a trail. A valuable decision, as only an hour later, they heard men searching in the woods around them. They hunkered down, remaining low and silent in the brush as they waited for the patrol to pass.

While they watched, it was Thom's job to take vigil over and care for Ilain when he wasn't catching up on sleep himself. He sat by her side, a strangely contemplative look on his face as he checked her vitals at semi-regular intervals. His gentleness and reflective demeanor gave Evylin pause, and she began to wonder if the flirtations between him and the Fire Mage might have come to mean more than mere playful banter.

When Ilain finally roused from her slumber, it was as though she simply woke from a normal night's rest. She stretched, looked up at Thom, and scrunched her nose. "What a frightfully unwelcome thing to wake up to," she said, then slapped his cheek playfully. "Wipe that furrow from your brow, Thomas. I'm not going to die."

Instead of saying something normal like "I'm happy you're all right," Thom glowered and grumbled, "My name isn't Thomas."

Ilain sat up, her lips curling in a dubious scowl. "You're not serious. Your name is just *Thom*. That's not a name. It's a nickname."

Thom gave her a bland glare. "I just spent the last twelve hours watching you sleep. Do you mind *not* baiting me? Maybe you could even pretend to be grateful."

Ilain's coppery brows rose. "You were watching me sleep? That's creepy, even for you."

"My apologies for wanting to be sure you lived."

"You're forgiven." Ilain rose then, straightening the folds of her skirt. She looked around the clearing, sparing a smile for Evylin and Ethenn before continuing her inspection. "Where are the others?'

Ethenn turned to Evylin.

Swallowing past the tightness in her throat, Evylin motioned toward the road, gesturing well away from their camp. "They left," she said.

Ilain narrowed her eyes. "To go where?"

"The Time Keep," Evylin said, then forced herself to explain the rest. "We decided to split up. They'll go directly across the continent while we loop down through the moors."

It took several seconds before Ilain processed Evylin's words. "Whose stupid idea was that?" she asked.

"Technically, Auden suggested it, but I agreed."

"I did too," Ethenn added.

Ilain's vibrant gaze flicked between the pair. "When did you two decide to go daft on me? What an idiotic plan. What good will splitting up do for us?"

"It lowers the odds of Blount catching us," Evylin said. "And we split the Relics, so if he does catch one group, he won't have all of them."

Ilain rolled her eyes. "This is what happens when I'm left out of decisions. And whose bloody brilliant idea was it to split you and Jonn?"

"Mine," Evylin replied.

That caused Ilain to hesitate. She crossed her arms, eyed Evylin warily, then scoffed. "You and I need to have a conversation," she said flatly. Then she looked around the small camp. "But first, I'm starving. What do we have that we can eat on the road?"

Working to put as much distance between them and Sutterlund Reach as possible, they rode well into the night. The terrain grew flat, and the stands of trees grew thinner and fewer. Thick vegetation spread across the land in large swathes of bushes and grasses. In the darkness, it all bore hues of gray, giving the landscape a decidedly dreary and morbid appearance.

When they finally decided to bed down for the night, Ethenn scouted to find a copse of trees where they wouldn't be seen from the road. Within the shelter of the thin, scraggly trees, they set up their tents. A cool breeze wafted across the flat land, rustling the grasses around them. They sat in the chill of the night, cloaks drawn around them, agreeing that a fire would draw too much attention.

"Not all of the South is like this," Ilain told them. "But most of our journey will take us through the moorlands. Often, you can see for miles."

"We'll have to be careful when we choose where to rest then," Ethenn said. "And hunting will be scarce since I'm out of arrows."

"Not to worry. There are lovely rivers that flow through the moorlands," she said. "They're full of fish, so we won't have to worry about being well-fed."

"I hate fish," Thom said good-humoredly. "Once when I was a child, I caught a fish from the lake—you remember, Evie, the one I took you to?"

Evylin nodded, and he went on, "Well, I caught this fish, and I was so proud. Then I reeled it in, and, wouldn't you know it, it was dead. Half-eaten by the bottom feeders."

Evylin and Ilain scrunched their noses in disgust.

Thom laughed. "I've never been able to stomach trout since."

"Well, you'll have to learn to," Ilain said lightly. "Fish and what little rations we have left are all you'll be offered for the next two weeks."

"That's how long it will take?" Ethenn asked.

"A little more on our route, yes." Ilain braided her curls absentmindedly. "We're going out of our way, but journeying through the south is far safer than up north."

"Even with the open terrain?" Evylin asked.

"Southerners aren't as . . ." Ilain considered her wording before grinning, "political. We're farther from the crown, so we live more freely. There's less nobility here too."

Evylin nodded, noting the similarity to Ephria's southern regions.

"We?" Ethenn caught the word. "You're from this area?"

"Oh, yes." Ilain's smile brightened. "I grew up in the Highloft Moors. We'll pass it, though, from a distance. They make the most depressingly beautiful grayscape you've ever seen. It makes you want to weep and never leave."

"Sounds miserable," Thom teased.

"Sounds poetic," Evylin corrected. "I read a novel once about a woman plagued by the ghost of her first love. She was trapped in a castle, and the way the author described the landscape . . . it sounds just like what you said."

"It could have been inspired by the moors," Ilain suggested.

"What happened to her?" Ethenn asked. "The woman in the story?"

Evylin looked toward the sky, an infinity of stars spread before her. She smiled, remembering the tale. "She was following her lover's ghost through the night," she recounted, "when, suddenly, she was captured by a Mage."

Ilain scoffed. "Mages are always the villains in Ephrian tales."

"Not always," Evylin said. "This Mage—he captured the woman and made her his slave, yes. But then they fell in love, and she was to be his bride. She showed him kindness, and he amended his cruelty. But, feeling betrayed, the ghost of her first love began to haunt her with malice instead of longing. He drove her mad, and she leaped from the castle tower to make it stop."

Thom let out a disbelieving huff. "That's the most depressing story I've ever heard."

"Mm," Evylin agreed. "It was a favorite of my aunt's. She gave it to me with the promise that it would break my heart and make me believe in true love. I didn't shed a tear, and I still fail to see the romance in driving your lost love insane."

"I think your aunt missed the point of the story," Ilain remarked.

"Oh?"

Ilain twisted one of her jeweled rings thoughtfully. "It wasn't about true love at all. It was about loss. If the heroine could have let her first love go—if she had released his ghost and let him rest—perhaps she would have had a happy life with the Mage who lived and loved her in the present. Instead, she held on and let the past kill her."

Evylin's throat was suddenly dry. Ilain's analysis was too astute, too revealing. The woman couldn't know. She'd been asleep during Evylin's outburst decrying her marriage to Deckard. None of them had spoken of it. And none of them knew why Evylin had chosen to push him away.

Refusing to accept the lesson in Ilain's words, Evylin defaulted to the one comfort she still possessed. "I never was much for literary symbolism," she said lightheartedly. "I always preferred sword fights and daring escapes."

"Such a Warrior thing to say," Ilain noted jokingly, though a glint of knowing sparkled in her eyes.

Ready to be out from under the highlady's inspection, Evylin suggested they get their rest. They agreed to stand watch in pairs, the men together during the first period and the women during the second. She and Ilain stretched out under their shelter-half while the men sat up under theirs. But Evylin's attempt to escape the conversation failed to provide any comfort.

As she lay in the heather under the canvas of the tent, Evylin felt lonelier than ever. She wrapped her cloak around her like a blanket, trying not to miss the warmth of Deckard's chest or the weight of his arms. Over the short months of their marriage, his presence became vital to her ability to sleep. She squeezed her eyes shut, attempting to ignore the startling emptiness beside her. Her mind whispered cruelly, reminding her of the sound of his heartbeat and the gentle circles he used to draw on her back.

A burning sensation filled Evylin's chest. She gritted her teeth, barricading her heart against every pang of longing. Yet, the pain only grew. Her lungs spasmed. Once again, she found herself drowning in a well of tears.

Ilain's words chastised Evylin harshly. *"If she had released his ghost and let him rest—perhaps she would have had a happy life."*

Evylin tugged her hood farther over her head, burying her face in the heather. Ilain was wrong. There was no letting go. There was no happiness. Because love only brought pain.

15TH OF CHRONOS, 1574

Evylin woke, groggy and emotionally hollow, to join Ilain on the second watch. They remained in the small cluster of trees, the horses nickering softly in their sleep. With the men sleeping close by, the women didn't bother to converse, making the seconds stretch into hours within hours. Evylin had no heart to speak anyway.

Finally, the sun rose, and they continued their journey.

In the daylight, Evylin had to agree with Ilain; the moors were far superior to the rest of Wauld. Though unvaried, the landscape stretched for miles with a quiet beauty. A gentle fog drifted in the distance, low enough that the western mountains could still be seen above its haze. The soft purple of calluna flowers dotted the ground, with patches of honey-yellow and ivory-white buds interspersed amidst the scrub.

Perhaps most superior of all, the sky above them was a light blue with only patches of clouds dotted overhead. Though Ilain warned them that it could still rain, she promised it would only be light, intermittent showers. The reprieve was a blessing after nearly a month of torrential downpours.

Traveling with a small group felt strange to Evylin. After so much time with such a large number, it was unusually easy to keep everyone engaged in the same conversation. They rode with natural comfort, talking and laughing readily. Ilain and Ethenn took the lead for most of the trek; she gave loose directions as he kept a keen eye on the horizon.

The winding Oulon River spread before them as Ilain predicted, and they stopped to fish. Ethenn and Thom made quick poles from branches they'd procured from the copse of trees they'd spent the night in, using the spare bowstring Ethenn brought for the fishing line. They planned to dry their catch for long-term preservation, ensuring a steady ration for the days ahead. Unsurprisingly, Ethenn caught the better part of their bounty, though Evylin did well herself.

"I didn't know you fished," Thom remarked as she drew in her fifth.

Evylin smiled but hesitated to reply. Keeping her attention on removing the hook they'd fashioned from random bits of metal scraped together from their supplies, she struggled for an answer. It was Hewitt who taught her to fish—her and Ryen. Together, she and her cousin spent much of their youth playing by the creek near Whickam Village. They pretended to be soldiers or pirates, fishing—often, fruitlessly—or basking in the sunshine while they made plans for the future.

Instead of explaining, Evylin handed Thom the fish and said, "There's lots you don't know about me."

The day wore on as they moved at a steady pace. Though they didn't make it across as many miles as usual, thanks to their fishing excursion, they stopped well before sunset, intent on a better night's rest. They rode a mile off the road toward a small rise in the landscape. Though there was no tree coverage, once over the ridge, they were hidden from ready view.

After their arrival and preparation of the camp, setting up the shelter-halfs, and laying out the fish for filleting, Evylin wiped her hands on her trousers. "All right, Ethenn," she said, turning to the young man. "You and I stayed together so that I could train you. So let's get to training."

"Wait," Thom said, looking up from the fish. He motioned toward them with his knife. "We've got scaling to do."

Evylin smirked. "And I'm sure you'll do a lovely job."

Thom's mouth dropped open in disbelief. "You can't take Ethenn. This is what the boy lives for!"

Ethenn scoffed. "I can assure you, it's not."

"You're a hunter."

"Doesn't mean I enjoy the cleaning part."

Ilain sat down next to Thom. "Don't worry, dear," she said placatingly. "I'll help you."

Thom frowned. "You're willing to clean fish? Aren't you too delicate for that?"

"The next time you call me delicate, it'll be you I'm filleting." The highlady held out her hand toward Ethenn. "May I have one of your knives, please?"

Ethenn slipped one of the shorter blades from his belt. "They're daggers," he remarked.

Her brow quirked in amusement. "Knife. Dagger." She shrugged. "Same thing."

Ethenn looked about ready to correct her when Evylin grabbed his arm. "Come on," she said, tugging him toward the horses to retrieve the practice swords.

They walked out across the open moor, looking for a section not overgrown with brush. Several hundred feet away from the camp, they found a wide patch of mossy grass. With spring readily approaching and the terrain flat around them, the sun cast the field in a bright golden glow.

Tossing the training swords down into the scrub, Evylin faced Ethenn. "Ready?" she asked.

He pushed some of his overlong hair from his eyes. Like the rest of the men, his face was now scruffy with a beard, though it was thin and hardly constituted the term. "I guess," he said.

"Don't sound so excited," Evylin remarked.

"Sorry." A small, apologetic smile came to Ethenn's face. It shifted his features, and suddenly, he looked much less serious than usual. "It's just . . . this isn't supposed to be happening—me having magical abilities."

Evylin tipped her chin up, remembering his reluctance in the Wind Keep. His adamant refusal was almost as strong as Deckard's. She considered him. "You didn't want us to know you were a Warrior," she noted. "Why not?"

Ethenn took a deep breath, settling his hands on his thick weapons belt. "Because I don't want to be a Warrior."

She pursed her lips. "And Jonn doesn't want to be a Mage."

"It's—" Ethenn sighed. "It's different for me, I think, though I don't know the colonel's reasons."

Evylin didn't bother to enlighten him. She wasn't so sure she knew Deckard's reasons herself.

"For me, it's . . ." Ethenn paused, then dipped his head as though ashamed. "I don't want to spend my life working for some higher cause, becoming some weapon for someone else's ends. I want a small existence where I can disappear and be insignificant, as suits me."

Frowning, Evylin couldn't fathom such disparaging feelings. "I don't think you're insignificant," she said, hoping to bolster the young man's self-worth.

Ethenn gave her a cynical grin. "You don't really know me, Evie," he said calmly. "Of no fault of your own. I don't let people know me."

"Because you think people don't want to know you?"

"Because I don't like people."

Evylin raised her brow. "You don't like me?" she asked teasingly.

"Well . . ." His neck turned crimson. "No, it—it isn't that I don't like you, but—"

"You don't trust me," she realized, then nodded. "You don't let people know you because you don't trust them. I can relate."

"You can?"

Tapping a finger against the handle of her sword, Evylin decided the conversation was getting too personal—for both of them. "Yes, I can," she said. Then she changed course. "And while I sympathize with your plight, I'm afraid you can't stay untrained. Would you like to get started?"

At Ethenn's nod, Evylin opened her mouth, then closed it. She furrowed her brow, stared at the ground, and let out a "hm."

"Hm?" Ethenn repeated.

Evylin met his dark gaze. "Turns out, I don't know much about how to train a Warrior. I hardly know how to be one myself."

"But you seem to do it so . . . easily."

"I think that's why Ilain says it's innate," Evylin replied. "When the time comes, the magic takes over. I'd guess that's what happened to you, too, in the fighting rings before and in the Keeps now. You just didn't know it. Or . . . you did, but you tried to ignore it."

"I only figured it out recently," Ethenn said. "It was when you mentioned the feeling you get when you fight. Only, I still wasn't sure because . . . well, because it's different for me. Or—maybe not different, but it's . . . compulsory."

Evylin wondered at that term.

"And," Ethenn added, interrupting her thoughts, "not as strong, I don't imagine. Though it's getting stronger."

That made Evylin pause another moment longer. "I know what you mean," she said at last. "My whole life, training with—with Hewitt, I experienced the rush, but not in the same way as now. It wasn't until we saved Prince Ephren that I truly felt it."

Ethenn nodded. "I felt it then too."

"So . . ." Evylin let the word hang as she came to conclusions. "Likely, we never felt it before because we never needed magic to that extent before, which is why Warriors may never realize their magic in the first place. If we aren't put in a true battle, we don't have a true need for it."

Ethenn shifted his weight, head tilting thoughtfully. "So we can only access our magic in life-or-death situations?"

Evylin shook her head. "No, I've now found myself using it many times in daily life," she said, not bothering to mention that Deckard's touch could spur her access to the magic. In fact, her first notable experience with the sensation had been during their kiss in Wayford, well before they rescued the prince.

Ignoring those thoughts and the feelings they stirred, Evylin returned to the topic at hand. "It isn't the dire circumstances that drive us to use our magic," she explained, "it's the focus required of us in those times. In a fight, we have no choice but to concentrate on the moment at hand. We're attuned to our magic because we're open to it. Just like when we watched the camp yesterday. We focused on extending our vision and hearing, and thus, we tapped into our magic."

"Like when I tracked you in Dunneshead," Ethenn murmured.

Evylin furrowed her brow. "You tracked me?"

"Yeah." Ethenn's ears turned pink. "When the colonel and I were looking, I was able to, uh—to pick up your scent. It's something I've always been able to do during a hunt. I just didn't realize it was a Warrior thing until—well, until now."

Despite the oddity of the revelation, Evylin pursed her lips with approval. "I never would have thought of that. But yes, that's a perfect example of what we can do. When we access our magic, our senses become superhuman. It's as though the world becomes brighter, louder, stronger . . . Everything is clearer."

Ethenn nodded enthusiastically. "The world is sharper. You feel connected to it."

"Exactly." Evylin smiled, awed at having someone understand her experience so fully. "Focus is the trick. We have to hone our thoughts, concentrating on our task, to feel that connection."

The lesson reminded Evylin of her youth and training with Hewitt. He'd always taught her that focus was the key to victory. Calming your mind, finding your center—that was how you won a duel. People overcomplicated swordsmanship, he'd said. It wasn't about being the strongest or most cunning. It was knowing the blade itself and trusting your body to do the job. You didn't overthink it. You simply lived as one with the sword.

"How do you practice that?" Ethenn asked, breaking through her memories.

Letting Hewitt's training speak through her, Evylin replied, "By knowing what you want."

Ethenn's eyebrows lowered in confusion.

Evylin chuckled and pulled out a dagger. She was surprised when she looked down and saw that she'd unconsciously drawn the one that had belonged to Deckard. She brushed her thumb along the rosettes on the pommel. Then she tossed it in the air, flipping it end over end. As it began its second rotation, she caught the hilt upside down in her left hand and lunged, pressing the blade to Ethenn's neck. The series of movements occurred in the span of a half-second.

Eyes wide, Ethenn stared at her.

"You don't practice aimlessly, Ethenn," Evylin said, pulling the dagger back. "You know what you want, and you visualize it. Then you do it."

"That's an oversimplification," Ethenn said, though he was smiling.

Evylin raised her brow playfully. "That's being a Warrior. We don't seem to have the constraints normal people have. We focus—we get a picture in our mind, and we act on it."

She slipped the dagger into the sheath on her belt. "The problem comes when focusing isn't easy. From what Auden has told me and what I've observed, it seems that Warriors are predisposed to finding and holding their focus in a fight, but I can tell you from personal experience that you can't rely on that. Once that focus is lost . . ."

Memories of the Water Keep flooded Evylin's mind. The feeling of her feet slipping from under her; water soaking to her bones as she drowned; fear distorting her mind as she faced Blount; anger rising at the revelation that the Calders had lied. And more than all those other things, the grief of losing Hewitt was ever looming at the back of her mind.

"It's hard to recover from that," she murmured.

Blinking away her thoughts, Evylin forced herself to smile at Ethenn. "That's why you need to know your weaknesses," she concluded.

"How's that?" Ethenn asked.

"If you know your weaknesses," she explained, "you can be prepared for any circumstance."

"Wouldn't knowing your strengths be better?"

"Not at all. You're only as strong as your greatest weakness."

Ethenn scratched the back of his neck. "You've lost me."

Evylin smirked. "Think of it this way: You can be the strongest fighter in the world, but if you aren't aware that your armor has a hole in its back, you can't defend yourself properly."

"So you mean that by knowing your greatest weakness, you can become a better fighter?"

Evylin nodded.

"What are your weaknesses then?" he asked.

Evylin could practically hear Hewitt's voice gently admonishing as he taught her to recognize her flaws. Then he'd instructed her on how to overcome them. "I have two," she said. "I'm a woman and a show-off."

Ethenn laughed, crossing his arms. "I would think being a woman is a benefit. People will underestimate you."

"True," she said. "But that benefit only lasts until the first strike, and then they discover how skilled I am."

His eyes gleamed with interest. "How do you overcome those weaknesses?"

"As far as being a show-off goes, I just have to get over my own ego," Evylin said with feigned self-derision. "Doing the job right isn't always fun, nor is it always pretty. But it is the best way, and I have to remind myself of that."

She shrugged. "There isn't much I can do about being a woman. The fact is, I can never be as strong as the average man, and that's a distinct disadvantage. However, that doesn't mean I can't beat him. I have three means of outfighting another's strength: skill, smarts, or speed. The weight of muscle can make a man slow, which means I can be vastly faster. It can also make him think he's invincible. In which case, I can use my knowledge and training to outsmart him. He can rely on his strength to overpower me, but I can use my superior technique to outmaneuver him."

Ethenn nodded along, listening intently.

"However," Evylin concluded, "if my opponent happens to be an intelligent, agile, masterful swordsman with superior strength, then Hewitt says I only have one recourse."

"And what's that?" Ethenn asked.

She smirked. "Run," she said. "And if that fails, kick him where it counts."

Ethenn burst out laughing, and she joined him. It felt good to be free enough to laugh once more, to release deep, rich laughter that came from her gut. When was the last time she'd laughed without a Relic's influence? She couldn't remember.

"Yeah," Ethenn said through his mirth. "That should work."

Evylin scooped up the practice swords. She tossed one to him. "Now, let's figure out your weaknesses, shall we?"

Over the course of the next hour, they sparred, taking careful consideration of Ethenn's weak points and shortcomings. They both worked to channel their magic throughout the training. Ethenn was a natural fighter—they'd known that from the start— and it was hard for Evylin to pick apart his skill. The technical, critical eye was Hewitt's specialty, not hers. And she found it more difficult to pick up on what he was doing wrong than she'd anticipated.

However, she finally struck on some key failings. First, Ethenn was left-handed. Not a fault on its own, but sometimes, it showed in his swordplay. Though he held the sword in his right hand—a standard Hewitt had drilled into him—at times, he grew sloppy, forgetting which arm should bear the brunt of his attacks.

Second, he was slower to make decisions. Evylin thought it came from his training as a hunter and archer, which required sitting still for long periods and perfectly lining up his shot. In a sword fight, you couldn't wait for the perfect moment. Snap decisions were necessary. He'd have to become more decisive.

And thirdly, Ethenn held himself back. Evylin could feel it with every strike and blow—he wasn't putting his full effort into any of it. When she commented on it, he shrugged. "I always do that," he said placidly.

Evylin screwed up her face, nonplussed. "You're not going to hurt me."

"No, it isn't *you*," he said. "I do it with everyone. With every fight."

"Why?"

"Because . . ." He stared at the ground then. He rubbed away the sweat dripping down his nose. "Because I don't like how it feels when I lose control."

Suddenly, Evylin remembered the first time she'd met Ethenn. He'd joined the Third Volunteer Company and become a member of Thom's platoon along with one of his old friends from Trollenston. "Friends" being a loose term, as the other young man had goaded him into a fistfight. One where Ethenn would likely have beaten the boy senseless had Thom not intervened.

Since then, Evylin hadn't seen Ethenn lose his temper. Now, she wondered how hard he'd worked to keep it that way.

"That's why you don't want to be a Warrior," Evylin realized. "It isn't because you lack self-confidence. It's because you're afraid of yourself, of what you could do if you got angry enough."

Ethenn didn't confirm it but stood before her, silent and steady.

"Well," Evylin said with a scoff, "there's your third weakness. You have to stop being scared."

"You don't know what I can do, Evie," he said flatly. "You haven't seen me that way."

She raised her brow. "Because you haven't let me."

"You don't want to."

She stabbed the point of the training sword into the dirt, leaning against it. "Let me guess," she said lightly. "You haven't lost control like that since the attack with . . . Brewer, was it?"

Slowly, Ethenn nodded.

"So you've managed to contain your rage for roughly two to three months now despite numerous battles where your life was at stake."

"If you're trying to convince me that I have control of it," Ethenn held her gaze fiercely, "don't bother. I've gone this long without breaking before. Inevitably, I snap. And then someone dies."

Evylin narrowed her eyes. She couldn't determine if the hunter was being facetious or not. Surely, he hadn't killed someone in cold blood. Should she be concerned by that admission? He seemed regretful of it, and he'd given her no cause to question his morality up until this point.

Seeing the hardness in his gaze, she decided not to press. This was a fear they wouldn't work through in one session. Not if it'd driven him to murder. . . .

Looking up at the fading sun, Evylin lifted her sword again. "We have another thirty minutes of sunlight," she said. "Let's spar until it's gone."

Ethenn held up a hand. "Can I get some water first?"

With a smile, Evylin waved a hand through the air. "Fine," she said, then called as he began to jog toward the camp, "Bring some for me when you come back."

He waved in acknowledgment.

While he was gone, Evylin twirled the training sword at her side. She stared out over the flowers and scraggly bushes. Despite the change in scenery, sometimes she forgot that she was in another country, on the adventure she and Ryen had always dreamed of. The adventure Hewitt had died to give her.

Evylin blinked at the violently bright orange sun as it crept lower and lower on the horizon. Her fingers wrapped tightly around the hilt of the sword, the leather slick under her sweaty palms. The truth was clear to her now. It wasn't worth it, this adventure. She'd kept Ryen's memory alive at the cost of his father. What a horrible price.

"Here," Ethenn said, startling her out of her reverie. He stood at her side, holding out the waterskin.

Evylin caught her breath and thanked him, pretending that the sun's fierce rays were the cause of the tears welling in her eyes. When she took a swig and dropped the skin to the ground, she found Ethenn shuffling his feet uneasily. He held something small in his hands, though she couldn't make out its shape.

"What's that?" she asked curiously.

"It's, uh—" He proffered a small, brown leather pouch. "It's a birthday gift."

Evylin froze, dumbfounded. Was it her birthday? She'd lost count of the days.

Gingerly taking the gift, Evylin eyed him warily. "How'd you know it was my birthday? And why'd you get me a gift?"

"Oh, no." Ethenn shook his head vehemently. "It isn't—it's not from *me*. It's from Colonel Deckard."

Evylin felt her face blanch. "I see," she said hollowly. She dug at the stitching along the edge of the pouch. "You know, we're not soldiers anymore, Ethenn. You can just call him Deckard."

With a dismissive shrug, Ethenn ignored her suggestion. "Would you like to be alone? To open it, I mean."

Though she tightened her grip on the pouch, Evylin had the distinct urge to throw it back at him and flee across the moor in search of a hole in which to hide. "No," she said with an unfelt laugh. "That's not necessary."

To prove her nonchalance, Evylin tugged at the strings tying the pouch together. She lifted the flap, finding a slip of paper sticking out. She removed it, unfolding it awkwardly with one hand. A lump lodged in her throat as she registered the penmanship.

It's been quite some time since I've written a note for you,
but as you kept all the others, I thought you might appreciate one more.
Happy birthday, Evylin.
Yours eternally, Jonn

Evylin chewed on the inside of her lip. How just like Deckard. It was the same as all his other notes: short, direct, and perfect. She couldn't believe he'd noticed her collection of his missives. She'd never meant to save them in the first place. Yet, she had, wrapping them in an old ribbon for safekeeping and placing them on her nightstand in their bedroom in Loclight. A mistake, she now thought.

His valediction worried her most of all. He always signed his notes with that unnecessarily sweet *"Yours."* But the addition of *"eternally"* caused her heart to stutter.

Agitated at the sudden swell of regret and sorrow in her chest, Evylin refolded the note roughly. She stuffed it back into the pouch and tugged out the remaining object. A small, oval frame of walnut wood encased a painting that made her veins cease flowing. Usually, ornamental trinkets like this would rouse her derision. This one elicited her unyielding affection.

The tiny vignette depicted the sparkling frost of an ice-covered lake. She could almost smell the winter chill in the air. Buttercream-yellow grass contrasted with the pines dotting the valley. The intricacy of the work was beautiful; its likeness to the Wayford countryside was uncanny. This was no coincidental bauble Deckard selected for her. It was a memorial of their celebrating one month of marriage, even if it was a marriage of convenience.

And it felt like a slap in the wake of her rejection just a day prior.

Blinking rapidly to avoid the tears that rose, Evylin chose to feel irritated rather than guilty. Hurriedly, she returned the painting to the pouch. "Thank you," she said, giving Ethenn a false smile, hoping he wouldn't see how unsettled she was.

Ethenn kicked at the dirt. "Yeah," he said.

Unsure what to do with the gift, Evylin clutched it to her chest. "We should, uh . . ." She glanced at the training swords, now lying forgotten on the ground. They *should* keep training. She *should* find a way to ignore Deckard's wonderful thoughtfulness.

With a heavy sigh, Evylin picked up the swords. "I'm tired," she said dully. "Let's go back."

Ethenn didn't question her. He walked quietly at her side as she stared ahead sightlessly, her head aching with barely contained emotion. Her fingers tightened around the gift, the leather warm in her hands. She *should* have found a distraction once they returned to camp. Sparring, cleaning, or conversation. Instead, she spent the rest of the evening in a stupor.

And when she lay down in the tent under the stars, she held the pouch close to her heart, wondering if she'd ever recover from this wound that bled slowly inside her chest.

CHAPTER THIRTY-THREE

He'd never witnessed anything so profoundly incredible.

Thom's hands stilled, fish partially filleted before him, as he watched Evylin and Ethenn spar in the distance. Despite the dozens of times he'd seen them duel before, this was different. Now that Ethenn was a Warrior, now that he was intentionally tapping into his magic, the pair moved with speed and agility that no normal human could possess. Their strikes and sweeps passed through the air so fast he could hardly see them. When each bout ended, another started almost immediately.

He was tired just watching it.

"It's impressive, isn't it?" Ilain said wistfully. She sat at his side, the setting sun lighting her hair like a flame. "Warriors at their fullness."

Thom gritted his teeth. A spike of jealousy filled him. He wasn't used to feeling envious of anyone but Deckard. Yet, watching Evylin and Ethenn and hearing Ilain praise them so reverently—it bit at his pride.

"Yeah," he said sourly, returning to his work on the fish. "It's bloody fantastic."

Ilain heard the bitterness in his tone. But instead of pitying him, she chuckled—she actually *chuckled*.

Thom's head snapped up. "What's so funny?" he demanded.

She didn't bother looking at him, deftly deboning the fish before her. "You are. You can't be happy for anyone, can you?"

The barb snagged in his chest, making him feel ashamed as well as jealous. What a pitiful man he was.

Thom carefully laid the filleted fish on the blanket they'd laid out to dry it on. Though the day was waning and the process normally took days, Ilain would use magic to flash-dry the meat. It turned out that having a Mage around *was* rather convenient.

"I'm working on it," Thom muttered.

"Maybe work a little faster," Ilain said. "Watching you sulk is getting old."

Thom looked over at her, perturbed. "My apologies," he said tersely. "I didn't realize my moods were your entertainment."

Again, Ilain laughed wryly. She reached over to set her hand on his, stopping him from continuing to mutilate the fish before him. Thom looked up at her in surprise, her bright green eyes boring into him.

"I have lived a great deal longer than you, Thom," she said, her raspy voice low and impactful. "Trust me when I say, I understand how emotion can manipulate the truth. What you perceive, what you feel—oftentimes it winds up hurting more than helping."

Thom didn't know how to reply to that. He didn't know how to take it. Could Ilain possibly be saying that they were alike? *Were* they? He supposed they were. He felt deeply, and now that he knew her, he could see the same signs in Ilain. They were passionate people, often driven to reckless decisions by the intensity of their emotions. Perhaps Ilain Calder did know a thing or two about him.

Casually moving from under her touch, Thom gave her a lopsided grin. "What? Are you my mother now?" he asked.

Ilain returned his smirk. "I like to think of myself as your conscience."

"Does that make you a figment of my imagination?"

She snapped her fingers.

A flame scorched to life, scalding the back of Thom's hand. "Ow!" he yelped.

With a taunting smile, Ilain shrugged. "Guess not," she said.

Thom inspected his hand, finding it pink but otherwise unharmed. He shook it out. "That was uncalled for."

"Don't get your knickers in a bunch. I wouldn't seriously injure you."

"Oh, but you'd lightly injure me?"

"Depends."

"On what?"

"If you deserved it."

Thom eyed her, sitting back. "I'm starting to think I should be scared of you."

"Took you long enough." She leaned forward to lay out the fillets with precision. "Now, shut up. I need to channel the sunset."

"Why—?"

She sent him a scathing glare, and he closed his mouth.

Ilain closed her eyes then and took a deep breath through her nose. She stretched out her hands to hover over the blanket and the waiting fish. Warily, Thom watched as she remained still as a statue for several seconds. He began to think nothing was going to happen when she said, "Don't look."

Thom began to ask "why not" when a sudden flash of light flared from her hands. He shut his eyes a second too late. Blinded by the Day magic, he grimaced. "You could have warned me sooner," he said, rubbing his eyes.

He thought Ilain waved a dismissive hand toward him, but with his impaired vision, he couldn't be sure. "You knew what I was going to do," she said. "It's your fault you weren't smart enough to think ahead."

"Allore, you really are my conscience," he grumbled. "No one else could be so snide."

Together, they began to wrap the now-dried fish in wax-coated cloths. Thom was amazed at how well her magic had worked. The flaky meat was the perfect mix of tender and dry. It fell off the skin readily, and when he tasted it, he found he didn't mind fish after all.

"I'm reluctant to say," he swallowed the bite and met Ilain's stare, "magic may be my new favorite thing."

She chuckled again, settling the food into a pack. Her gaze drifted to the far side of the camp, however, drawing Thom's attention. He turned, finding Ethenn at the horses, digging through his saddlebag.

Thom glanced at Ilain, who was now pointedly retying the laces on the pack. She didn't bother to look up even when Ethenn stepped over to retrieve a waterskin from the pile near them. He scanned the empty blanket and the pack in front of Ilain.

"Did you finish up already?" Ethenn asked, impressed.

As Ilain continued to ignore the boy, Thom spoke for her. "We did," he said, leaning back on his forearms. "Lainy here has quite the way with a blade."

Ilain sent him a sharp look. "A fact you'll know intimately if you call me that again."

Thom grinned dryly. "Whatever you say, milady."

Shuffling, Ethenn took a step back. "Well, thanks," he said. "Evie and I will take care of it next time."

Thom looked up at the kid. His jaw tightened inexplicably. Maybe that was why Thom felt suddenly jealous of Ethenn—as a Warrior, he was now Evylin's equal. Despite the kid's age and lack of experience, he was suddenly the right hand, all because of his magic. Deckard had even singled him out before they split.

That irked Thom the most. Deckard chose Ethenn over his own brother. What could Deckard have needed from the boy? Had he chosen to impart some knowledge or task upon Ethenn? He'd chosen Rafferty over him too. The thought pricked him with envy like thorns on a bramble. Deckard made a blatant choice when they split, taking Rafferty with his group. Thom had teetered back and forth, wanting to go with Evylin but worried about parting with his brother. It was his responsibility to care for Deckard, to ensure that neither the Deep nor his own guilt overcame him.

And then Deckard had rejected him altogether.

When Ethenn began to leave, Thom found himself speaking. "What did Deckard want with you?" he asked, his voice taut. He attempted to ease his tone, clarifying, "Before they left yesterday."

Ethenn hesitated. He tightened his grip on whatever he'd retrieved from his pack. Thom's eyes narrowed on it, but the kid shrugged.

"Oh, he just asked me to keep an eye on you," Ethenn said casually. His eyes locked with Thom's, accusatory despite his calm demeanor. "You know, to make sure you don't steal his wife."

The blood rushed from Thom's face.

Ilain burst out laughing. "Why, Ethenn," she said, amused. "I do believe your quips are growing more cutting."

Ethenn sketched a bow. "Thank you, Highlady. I'd better get back to Evie."

With one final damning look at Thom, Ethenn turned and jogged back across the plain.

Ilain continued to chortle, the sound suddenly grating. "What a ridiculous notion. Like Evylin would leave Jonn for anyone."

"You don't know what you're talking about," Thom muttered, too low for her to hear. Then, to distract from the truth, he changed subjects. "So what's the plan? You gonna tell the kid how you feel about him?"

That sobered Ilain immediately. "Absolutely not."

Thom raised his brow. The conversation was no longer a distraction but a source of great intrigue. He sat forward, resting his elbows on his knees. "No? He's a Warrior now. I thought that made him everything you want."

"Do you always make things out to be more serious than they are?" Ilain asked tersely. "I said he was attractive, not that I wanted to marry him."

"You said . . ." Thom paused in his correction. "Well, I don't remember precisely. But you made it perfectly clear that the only reason you wanted to dissuade him was because he wasn't a Warrior."

"You misunderstood."

Thom scoffed. "Like hell. I know what I saw when you healed him."

"And what is it you think you saw?"

"You lingered," he accused.

Ilain stiffened. "I did not."

Thom tossed his hands in the air. He leaned back to rest on his arms again. "What's the big deal? You had a thing for the boy, but now that he's available to you, you've decided against him?"

She gave him a ferocious glare. "Have you suddenly turned into a schoolgirl, enchanted with fairy stories and romance?"

The insult made Thom smirk. "Deflect all you like," he taunted. "You'll only convince me more."

"Infantile man," she murmured, then let out a huff. "Yes, his being a Warrior makes our future possible. And yes, I . . . have certain *feelings* for him. No, I won't be saying a word to him about it."

Thom grimaced at the thought of Ilain and Ethenn as a couple. "Bleh." He shivered in disgust, then nudged her arm. "Why not?"

Ilain picked at her skirt, removing grass from its folds. "It's too late."

Thom furrowed his brow. "Seems like the right time to me."

"No—" Ilain heaved a sigh. "I've been dissuading him, remember? This whole time, I've made him think that I like you. Or, at the very least, that I don't have an interest in him."

"Yes, but you made it clear that you wanted a Warrior."

"Exactly," Ilain said, exasperated. "He knew I wanted a Warrior. Yet, instead of informing me that he was one, he chose to wish me luck in finding one who loves me."

"That's because *he*—" Thom cringed at the sentiment, "loves you."

"He *thinks* he loves me," Ilain corrected. "Regardless, I rejected him. How can I expect him to accept me when I say, 'I like you, Ethenn, and I think I could possibly come to love you, but only now that you're a Warrior'?"

Thom stared down at his hands, plucking at the grass.

"Should I expect him to be happy when I tell him I've always liked him but not enough to sacrifice my future?" she asked weakly.

"I see your point."

They fell silent, the mood settling heavily around them.

Thom's eyes drifted to where Ethenn and Evylin stood on the moor. The light dimmed to bronze as they shifted, readying to return. He couldn't understand what Ilain saw in the kid. Perhaps it was a Mage and Warrior thing.

The thought rankled. Thom didn't like to think people with magic were drawn to one another that way—that they were made for each other. Not when he was busy trying to convince himself that Deckard was wrong for Evylin. Not when his hope was renewed with Evylin's denouncement of their connection.

He knew it was wrong of him—hoping she would leave her husband. It didn't matter that Evylin had proclaimed their marriage as a convenience. That didn't mean it was any less lawful or any less binding. Surely, after all this time, they'd finally. . . .

Thom shoved the thought away, accepting the puzzle of Ilain's predicament instead. She was right. Even if she told the unmitigated truth, she couldn't expect Ethenn's favorable response. If Thom were in his shoes, he'd take grand offense at being told, "I like you but not enough. . . ."

For the first time, Thom found himself sympathizing with the kid.

"It's probably for the best," he said lightly, attempting to cheer Ilain before the Warriors reached their camp. "He's too young for you anyway."

Ilain shoved his shoulder. "In the hundreds of years Warriors and Mages live," she replied haughtily, "a twenty-year gap is nothing."

"He could be your kid."

"So could you."

Thom raised his brow. "I'm not a candidate, though, am I?"

A sly tilt crept over her lips. "You were."

His jaw dropped. "I was?"

"There was always a chance you were a Warrior, remember? Or even a Mage. I'm ever aware of opportunities."

Thom found himself laughing. He swept up her hand dramatically. "You are one of a kind, Ilain Calder," he said, then pressed a teasing kiss to her fingers.

Sharp eyes narrowing, Ilain gripped his hand before he could pull away. "And you, Thom Deckard," she said mischievously, "have a surprisingly tender heart."

Uncomfortable with her knowing stare, Thom tried to pull away, but she held fast to his fingers. "One day," she said, jade green gaze boring into him, "you're going to meet a woman, and you won't have to worry about whether she likes you better than your brother or not, because she'll make it clear that *you* are the only one she could ever want."

Thom blinked, and his insides squirmed. She saw him too clearly, too fully. He feared that if she could read his deepest desires so easily, she might also be able to read his darkest thoughts.

But she released him with a smirk. "That woman is not me, by the way," she said, turning toward the horizon. "I'd choose Jonn every time."

Unbidden, a laugh burst out of Thom, stilted and uneasy. "Perhaps you're right to do so," he allowed, wanting to end the conversation.

Gratefully, Evylin and Ethenn arrived, saving him from Ilain.

While the four of them ate fish, barley, and dried fruit, Ilain kept up pleasant conversation by telling them ghost stories of the moors. The evening shadows grew long, and eventually, the women retired to the tent while Thom and Ethenn sat up for their watch. Neither of them spoke much, and Thom found his gaze regularly drifting toward the tent as Ilain's words repeated in his head.

"She'll make it clear that you *are the only one she could ever want."*

Guiltily, Thom's eyes locked on the shadowed form huddled under the canvas, cloak wrapped tightly around her. Evylin slept, and even from a distance, he could see a small shiver shaking her in the night chill. It was odd, seeing her without Deckard stretched at her side. The sight was encouraging.

Was that why she'd done it? Had Evylin denounced her marriage as a means of rejecting Deckard? Was there a chance she wasn't stuck with him after all? Was she trying to tell Thom her true feelings—that *he* was the only one she could ever want?

No.

Thom closed his eyes, turning away from Evylin. Bile coated the back of his throat. He was foul. The wretched and traitorous thoughts burned in his gut. Why was he like this?

"You can't be happy for anyone, can you?"

No, he couldn't. Despite himself, despite how much he wished he could be different, Thom could never be happy for himself or anyone else. Because while they all deserved happiness, he deserved misery. While most people were good and honorable, he was envious and fickle. He couldn't be happy because he couldn't be better.

That was the cruelest truth of them all. No matter how hard he tried, Thom could never measure up. No woman would want him because he could never be enough. He was destined to live in his brother's shadow, wishing for eternity that he might prove worthy of love.

CHAPTER THIRTY-FOUR

16TH OF CHRONOS, 1574

Deckard tried to allow time to take its natural course. The passage of time was required to help anyone process grief. And he was grieving; he could readily admit that. Losing Evylin, truly and decidedly—hearing once and for all that she didn't want him—was an event he needed to mourn. So he'd given himself the space to work through the pain and sorrow clinging to him.

However, he was beginning to think this was a wound that would never close.

Since their separation from the rest of the troop, Deckard had readily distracted himself. Though the first hour of their ride went by in frightfully taut silence, soon Rafferty piped up and hadn't stopped talking since. He'd asked Auden nearly constant questions about their journey, the ins and outs of Waulden culture, and obscure magical lore. The weasel speculated on the Time Keep and what might be inside. Normally, Deckard would have found it annoying, but he came to be thankful for Rafferty's incessant chatter, since it served to keep his mind off Evylin.

When Rafferty *wasn't* distracting them, Auden insisted on working with Deckard on his magic. He was relentless in his lessons. Even on horseback, Auden would take every moment available to guide him in the connection with Day and Time magic to the exclusion of all else.

"Why are you so focused on just those two?" Rafferty asked on the second day of travel. "If he's a Night Mage, wouldn't it be better for him to perfect his connection with Night magic?"

"No," Auden said firmly. "I told you: Night magic is dangerous. Even if it doesn't drive a Mage mad, it taints them, spurring them to violence and malevolence. Jonn needs to learn other ways to use his power."

"Well, what about that fourth existent, the hidden one?" Rafferty asked, then furrowed his brow. He mouthed, "Day, Night, Time." Counting them out on his fingers, he looked to Auden. "What was it again?"

"Space," Auden said. "I can't use it."

"Why not?" Deckard asked.

"Because it's extremely difficult to connect with," he explained. "I know of several Night Mages who can access its power, so maybe you'll manage the connection one day, but it won't be under my tutelage."

Deckard didn't care to think about his continued training after their mission ended.

He remembered Evylin's sharp words in the woods: *I've made no promises to the Alliance.*

But he had.

To allow her to go to Dunneshead, Deckard had promised to join the Alliance in whatever capacity they requested. A foolhardy choice, but one he'd made knowing the possible consequences. He just hadn't thought he'd have to face them alone.

Though the distraction of Auden's training and Rafferty's conversation kept Deckard from dwelling on his regretful circumstances too much, the nights weren't so kind.

They'd fallen into an easy routine within just the last two evenings. Each time they stopped, they'd make camp, eat dinner, and rest. Deckard volunteered to take the second watch, the most undesirable shift. He'd always survived on less sleep than others, his inner strength dedicated to the task at hand. But sitting alone in the dark of the night with only the trees and Rafferty's snores for company, he could no longer escape his thoughts.

After a few short months of marriage, this was the longest he'd been separated from Evylin. Somehow, in three months' time, he'd forgotten the thirty-two years prior. Now, he couldn't remember life before her. He felt unbalanced, like he'd lost a limb. In every conversation, he expected to hear her ready banter, the air hanging dreadfully silent without her voice, light and raspy all at once. Worst of all, he'd forgotten how cold and empty it felt to sleep alone. Where her form used to lie, warm and tucked close to his heart, was now a barren void as though she had been carved from his very flesh.

Was she faring any better than he? Deckard hated to think of her as happy without him, but he hated the thought of her feeling isolated and hurt even more.

Both nights of his watch, Deckard stared out into the thinning forests of Wauld as they made their way toward the marshes. He'd scanned the purple night as it shadowed the world around him. It would only take a thought, an intent of will, to summon Hewitt's ghost. But with Rafferty and Auden sleeping around him, he couldn't risk them waking to his conversation.

Still, Deckard knew it was time. He needed to speak to Hewitt, to confess his failure, and to beg for the ghost's advice. So as they rode the next twenty-three miles under heavy rain clouds, he formed his plan.

"Day after tomorrow we'll enter the marshes," Auden told them as they made camp that evening. "They'll take up the majority of our journey until we enter Vaura Reach."

"I take it there won't be much hunting to be done in the marshes," Deckard noted.

Auden shook his head. "None at all, unless you count the amphibious creatures that fill its swamps."

"In that case," Deckard grabbed a rope from one of his saddlebags, "Rafferty, you and I should hunt. We need to take our last opportunity to ensure we don't go hungry."

Completing the construction of their tent, Rafferty hopped up. "Sounds good to me."

Leaving Auden to prepare what little supplies remained for a meal, the two Ephrians headed off into the trees. Near the South, the temperatures were more moderate and the terrain flatter. But near the marshlands, it was wet and muddy. Insects buzzed and chirruped. Birds swooped low on their return flight north after the winter season.

While they didn't have Ethenn's bow or hunting skills, Rafferty had picked up enough from him to be useful. They moved through the slick terrae, setting up traps with the twine they'd brought on their journey and the branches they'd gathered. Deckard found a particularly thick fallen branch of pine, which he broke apart, keeping the larger end for himself.

The rain grew heavier as they worked, and they drew their hoods more snugly over their heads.

"I don't care what the Calders say," Rafferty grumbled. "This rain isn't natural."

Remembering Auden's lessons informing him that it *wasn't* natural but the effects of the Relics' imprisonment, Deckard wiped his hands on the inside of his cloak. "Whatever the case," he said, "I'm ready to return to Ephria as well."

Rafferty gave a huff of agreement. Then his small eyes narrowed in thought. "What do you think it'll be like? When we get back."

"Before or after the monarchy is overthrown?"

He considered it, tying off another trap. "After," he concluded. "Once we're done with this whole thing."

Knowing that *he* would never be done with it, Deckard chose to play along instead. "I suppose that depends on the Alliance's plans. I'm not privy to their governmental regime, but I hope that it will bring a better world than the one we have now."

Rafferty brushed his hand through the air. "I'm not interested in politics, Colonel. I want to know what will happen to *us*. Will we still be soldiers? Will we continue to work with the Calders?"

Deckard's throat tightened. "I have no way of knowing that, Rafferty," he lied. He knew two things for certain: He would work for the Alliance, and his marriage to Evylin would be annulled. Those things nearly guaranteed that their troop would split, if not disband altogether.

"Don't be a spoilsport," Rafferty pressed. "If you don't have a good guess, tell me what you *want* to happen."

Completely uninterested in baring his soul to the weasel, Deckard kept his eyes on the final trap he was securing. "I don't know," he said sourly. "Maybe we'll remain as soldiers, but from what the Calders have told me, I believe the Alliance is expecting them to work in a more official capacity with the government. Due to that, I doubt we'll have any direct working relationship with them. As far as the rest of us go, they'll probably want Evylin, Ethenn, and me to do some specialized work for the government as well."

"Because you're magical?" Rafferty surmised.

"Yes."

"And what about Thommy and me?"

"Likely, they'll need officers for their army," Deckard said. "I'd imagine they'll grant you whatever position you desire after the service you're doing for them now."

Rafferty pursed his lips. "Nah, I don't think I'd want that."

Deckard looked up at him. "To be an officer or to be in the army?"

"Either," Rafferty said. "I'm sort of done with this whole . . ." He waved a hand through the air at the trees around them. "Thing."

"Really?"

"I mean, it isn't the worst job I've had. But it gets a bit old, you know? Travel hundreds of miles this way. Get a Relic. Travel hundreds of miles that way. Get another Relic. Keep traveling for hundreds of more miles in the pouring rain until you're pretty sure you'll never be dry again. It's monotonous."

Deckard chuckled as he rose. "It is, isn't it?"

Mud squelched under their boots as they moved away from the traps they'd set. Deckard led them to the base of a tree, its roots massive in the wide space of terrae around it. While they could return to camp right away to retrieve their catch later, Auden's meal wouldn't be ready for some time. And Deckard had plans of his own.

Rafferty didn't question Deckard as they sat beneath the tree's budding boughs. Instead, he lounged on one of the large roots, his back against the trunk. "So," he said, the word filled with expectation.

Deckard looked over at him, pulling out a dagger to begin removing the bark from the pine branch he'd found.

Rafferty raised his white-blond eyebrows, a wily lift to his lips. "You and Eve . . ."

Deckard turned away to stare at the branch in his hand, chipping bits away.

Rafferty wasn't dissuaded. "You two never . . . ?"

The innuendo wasn't lost on Deckard.

In typical circumstances, Deckard would have told the man to mind his own business. Discussing the condition of his and Evylin's marriage wasn't a topic he cared to broach with anyone but those he trusted most. Namely, Hewitt. Examining the state of his and Evylin's intimate relationship was even less welcome.

However, Deckard recognized the opportunity for what it was.

Slowly, Deckard raised his eyes from the branch and met Rafferty's expectant, silvery gaze. The moment was exactly what he'd been hoping for when he suggested they hunt together. He could use the man's curiosity, indecorous as it might be, to his advantage.

"I'll tell you what," Deckard said, keeping his voice steady to belie the anticipation within him. "I'll make a deal with you."

"Oh, yeah?" Rafferty asked, a gleam in those cunning eyes.

Deckard gave him a firm nod. "There's something I need to do that involves magic Auden wouldn't approve of. In exchange for your blind eye and silence, I will answer one question."

A wicked grin lifted the corner of Rafferty's mouth. "Our colonel has some Night business to attend to, eh?"

"Is that your question?"

Rafferty raised a finger. "One question seems stingy, by my reckoning. Highlord Calder said Night magic could be dangerous to you and the rest of us. Said it could lead to madness. No, no. I couldn't turn a blind eye to such potentially perilous behavior . . . Not for anything less than five questions, with *honest* answers."

Deckard anticipated the bartering. "Two questions."

"Make it three," Rafferty held out a hand, "and you've got a deal."

Deckard accepted the handshake. "Deal."

Rafferty's smirk was downright malicious. "You and Evie never had sex?"

"Really?" Deckard replied, unsurprised. "That's the best question you can think to ask?"

"Consider me fascinated."

"I'll consider you debauched."

Rafferty shrugged.

Deckard scoffed. "No, we haven't."

"Holy hell!" Rafferty's face screwed up in disbelief. "What's wrong with you? Don't answer—that's not one of my questions. Why not? That's not a real question either. Allore's might, man! I've seen how she is with you, all flirtations and cuddles. How have you not lost your damn mind sleeping next to her? Don't answer that either."

"Do you have a real question for me?" Deckard asked, irritated.

Rafferty tapped a finger to his nose, considering. "Not yet. I need some time to think on it."

Deckard pushed himself up. "Enjoy your thinking. I'll meet you back here in half an hour. Don't follow me."

Sly grin back in place, Rafferty waved him off. "Don't worry, Colonel. I won't risk losing my questions. Because, believe me, I'm not holding back for want of them."

Deckard had no doubt.

Leaving the weasel to ponder whatever hierarchy of inquiries he might have, Deckard moved deeper into the trees. Part of him worried about his sanity, entertaining Rafferty's curiosities this way. Though his time as a soldier had exposed him to indecent and often explicit conversations of his comrades' intimate relations, he'd retained his sensibilities. Such affairs should be between a man and his wife, he believed.

Granted, in this situation, such affairs were nonexistent between Deckard and his wife. So perhaps the point was moot.

Once Deckard had placed an adequate distance between himself and Rafferty, he summoned Hewitt.

The ghost materialized, grizzled and glowering as ever. "What took you so long?" he demanded.

Deckard opened his mouth, but he couldn't bring himself to speak. So much had happened in the six days since he'd last spoken with Hewitt. How did he explain it all? He didn't want to relive it.

"I messed up," Deckard admitted at last.

Hewitt's steely gaze narrowed.

A brutal sigh worked out of Deckard's lungs. "It's over. Evylin's asked for an annulment."

Still, Hewitt stared at him, unresponsive.

Deckard shifted uncomfortably. "I'm sorry, I—"

"She asked for an annulment," Hewitt said, each word slow and measured. He held up a hand, furrowed his brow, and cocked his head. "She *asked* for an annulment?"

Deckard nodded.

"Tell me you weren't stupid enough to give her one."

"Well . . ." Deckard hesitated. He'd expected Hewitt to be angry, to rail and yell and call Deckard a fool. He hadn't expected this flat, contained inquiry. "No, technically not yet. We're still in Wauld, but—"

Hewitt cut him off. "Good. Keep it that way."

"What?"

"I don't give a damn what she asked for," Hewitt said fiercely, the anger Deckard anticipated creeping into his tone. "Don't give it to her."

Deckard pinched the bridge of his nose. This discussion was never going to be easy, but he didn't want to try convincing Hewitt of his reasons.

"I already promised her that I would," Deckard said. "I can't go back on my word."

Hewitt scoffed. "You promised to prize and serve her, to stand by her side through all that life may send," he said, quoting the marriage ceremony of Ephria. "A never-ending promise. Will you go back on *that* word of yours?"

"That's not what this is," Deckard argued. "She's *asking* me to annul the marriage. Once it's complete, those vows are void, as though we never said them in the first place, because we never sealed them. That promise was never fully assured."

"Because you were too scared to assure it," Hewitt said accusingly.

Deckard dipped his head, aggrieved by the man's derisive tone. "Is it wrong that I desired love between us first?" he asked.

"No," Hewitt said, the deep rumble of his voice surprisingly soothing. "It was wrong of you to assume that she *didn't* love you."

An ache filled Deckard with the deepest longing for Hewitt's words to be right. He wished with the most fervent desire that Evylin had come to love him. If she did, he thought he could topple the Waulden and Ephrian monarchies himself if it would make her happy.

"You can't make me happy."

A body-shaking sigh slipped out of him. "I told her that I love her," he whispered.

Hewitt curled his hands into fists but didn't speak.

"I know you told me not to," Deckard said. "But she'd already made her decision, and I . . ."

"You thought it might change her mind," Hewitt concluded when he fell silent.

Deckard nodded.

"And it didn't." It wasn't a question. Hewitt knew his niece well enough to know that Deckard's love would only drive her farther away.

"Why is she like this?" Deckard asked, despondent. "Why can't she accept love as a gift? Why does she feel it to be a burden?"

"I told you," Hewitt gave him a bitter smile, "she's afraid."

"Of me?" Deckard couldn't fathom the concept.

"Of loving you back."

Simultaneous hope and despair rose in Deckard. If she feared loving him, didn't that mean she felt she *could* love him? But what could cause someone to hold such a devastating fear?

The answer stood in front of Deckard as a ghost.

"She's afraid of losing me." The revelation breathed out of Deckard, washing over him like the rain of Wauld. "The same way she lost you and Ryen."

Hewitt gave him a pitying look. "As I said, we never moved on."

Understanding the dynamic at play made everything clearer. Evylin's actions—her intense withdrawal after Hewitt's death—all made sense in this light. Fear was an ever-constant reminder of what she stood to lose. No wonder she'd pushed him away. If she felt for him a fraction of what he'd come to feel for her . . .

"The loss of me would be debilitating," Deckard realized.

Hewitt understood. He stepped forward, gray eyes adamant. "You have to do what I never could, Deckard," he charged. "You have to help her let go of the past. Otherwise, she'll never be able to live."

"How am *I* supposed to do that? If you couldn't—"

"I didn't try," Hewitt admitted. "I didn't want to let go. It's too late for us to get back the last thirteen years of our lives, but it isn't too late to protect her future. You have to help her move on."

"I don't know how," Deckard said. "Not when she's asked me to walk away."

"It's simple," Hewitt said. "Don't walk away."

"Even when it's what she wants?"

"It isn't what she wants. It's what she fears. She's trying to prove to herself that she doesn't need you, that she can bear being without you. Stay by her side. Once she realizes you aren't going anywhere, she'll let herself love you."

Deckard grimaced. "That could be a bit of a problem," he said, then took the time to walk Hewitt through the last several days. He told him everything from Dunneshead to the present, not bothering to leave anything out—not even their kiss.

Hewitt stroked his scraggly beard as he listened, deep in thought. "How long will you be apart?" he asked when Deckard's summary was complete.

"Auden said our journeys will take roughly a fortnight."

With a slow nod, Hewitt stared into the distance. "Mm. Good."

"Good?" Deckard repeated incredulously.

"The distance will serve us," Hewitt said as though solving a puzzle. "She's getting a chance to experience life without you. She'll see just how much she misses you, how lonely she is. It'll lead her back to you."

Deckard hated how hopeful the idea made him. "Are you sure?"

"Do you doubt my knowledge of my niece?"

"No," he admitted.

Hewitt nodded. "This is just what we need. Two weeks. Yes, she'll grow adequately miserable without you, but not so much that she forgets what it's like to have you near."

Deckard didn't like how well Hewitt was taking the situation. "I still promised her an annulment," he reminded him.

Hewitt waved a hand in dismissal. "It won't come to that. Once she sees you again, she'll practically leap into your arms."

"What if she doesn't?" Deckard asked, not as optimistic as the ghost. "What if she sees me, realizes her feelings, and still fears them? What if she requires me to stand by my promise?"

"Convince her not to."

"Oh, I see. Why didn't I think of that?"

Hewitt lifted his eyes to the Heavens. "What do you want me to say, Deckard? If she doesn't figure it out on her own, then you'll have to convince her. Unless you can find a way for me to talk to her, which doesn't seem likely."

Deckard ran a hand over his jaw. "Perhaps not," he said hesitantly. "But . . ."

"But . . . ?"

As the idea sparked in his head, Deckard saw no harm in pursuing it. "Well, as of yet, I'm not a thoroughly trained Mage," he said. "So I would think that certain aspects of my powers are underdeveloped. Such as the ability to summon a ghost."

Hewitt lifted his brow, urging him to continue.

"If I had a better connection to Night magic," Deckard said, "then I would imagine I could summon you more fully. Perhaps enough for someone else to see you."

"I like that idea."

"I thought you might."

An expectant gleam lit Hewitt's gray stare. "*That's* our goal. You work to get stronger and find a way to make me visible to Evylin. If I can talk to her, I can help her."

Deckard stared back toward the camp. He was running out of time. "Auden won't help me with that," he said. "He's afraid of Night magic."

"So get stronger with your other magic," Hewitt suggested. "Surely, that will help."

"Probably."

Hewitt nodded in anticipation. "This is good, Deckard. For the next fortnight, train. Train hard. And when you see Evylin again, let me talk with her. Once she feels how happy she is to be back with you, she won't ever let you go again."

Though it sounded too good to be true, Deckard grasped onto the hope the plan offered with all he was worth. He had to believe that Hewitt was right.

A fortnight.

Deckard would train, he would practice, and he would hope.

He had two weeks to prepare. Two weeks to save his marriage.

CHAPTER THIRTY-FIVE

21ST OF CHRONOS, 1574

The days passed with the same trudging pace. Each morning, they shared a quick, meager breakfast before moving on through the moors. Not much could make riding from dusk 'til dawn, setting up camp, training, sleeping, and starting all over again exciting; however, Evylin found herself grateful for the companionship of her friends.

Together, Evylin, Ethenn, Ilain, and Thom had become an efficient, comfortable team. They filled the hours with easy chatter and friendly banter. Then, at the day's end, Thom and Ilain cared for the camp and the horses while Evylin and Ethenn trained.

As the days progressed, the teaching reversed, and Ethenn began showing Evylin the finer points of hunting, tracking, and using a bow. They brought Thom in on their practice, too, keeping his skills sharp, though he regularly lamented they were impossible to beat. All the while, Ilain watched or sketched from a distance, uninterested in learning swordplay.

The rain was less constant, though the scenery grew less varied as well. As the land began to rise and fall with hills, it lost even the vestige of trees. However, the flowering shrubbery more than made up for the absence of wooden areas. The surprisingly tranquil beauty of the moors enchanted Evylin. Ilain's depiction of its grayness and majesty was quite apt, and Evylin determined that the setting belonged in a novel.

Despite the manifold joys of their travels, it did little to redeem the nights.

As the sun descended, the men took their turn on watch. While the women had several hours to sleep before the second and final shift, Evylin was restless. She'd hoped that a week's passage would help her forget the warmth and comfort of Deckard at her side. *Surely,* she thought, *I won't need his presence to sleep.* But her hopes were proving futile.

Though the weather had tempered during the day, the nights brought cold winds sweeping across the moor. Evylin burrowed deeply beneath her cloak, fighting for the barest morsel of warmth. She'd refused to sleep with the vignette a second night, but she often pictured it, imagining herself stretched out on the blanket in the sunshine of Wayford, reading with Deckard at her side. Though she'd told herself to stop, as such imaginations would do her more harm than good, it was her one means of finally drifting to sleep after hours of shivering and holding back tears in the isolation of night.

Now, Evylin sat in the gloom of the new morning, mind still fuzzy from her fitful rest. A lazy fog drifted across the moors, leaving dew in its wake. Ilain huddled closely at her side, their cloaks clutched around them to keep the damp chill from their bodies.

"How much farther is it to . . . Well, wherever it is we're going?" Evylin whispered so quietly she wasn't even sure Ilain could hear her.

With a cold sniffle, Ilain scooted closer. "Auray and then the Time Keep," she replied, keeping her voice low so as not to disturb the men. "We're roughly halfway. It should only take us another week or so."

One week.

Evylin's muddled thoughts betrayed her as she stared into the haze, which lightened to gray as the sun rose. Only one more week until she could return to Deckard. In eight days, she could sleep soundly once again.

Letting out a long, near-silent breath, Evylin pushed the thought away. It wouldn't be the same when they reunited with the others. It couldn't be. Not after the things she'd said or the choice she'd made.

"They'll arrive before us, though," Ilain continued, unaware of her inner turmoil. "If only by a day or two."

Evylin didn't care to think about Deckard's travel. She didn't want to consider if he was having as hard a time as she was. "And once we get the Time Relic," she murmured, "we'll head back to Ephria?"

"Yes."

Evylin's jaw tightened. Once they returned to Ephria, they'd travel to Estshire for the Terrae Relic and back to Loclight for the Space Relic. It would likely take another month or more for all that travel, but Deckard could annul the marriage the moment he found a magistrate, no matter the settlement. At which point, authority and her future care would fall back to her father. Once Lawton Glaas heard of the annulment, he'd undoubtedly recall her home. Would Deckard wait until the end of their mission for her sake? Or would he take his first opportunity to be free of her?

"I love you, Evylin."

His deep voice, steady and refined, echoed in her memory.

No, Deckard wouldn't annul the marriage until he was sure she could go where she wanted without fear of her father's summons. She knew he would prolong it indefinitely, letting her go to live as she pleased without him if it would make her happy.

Finding herself tugging on her rings, Evylin jerked her hands apart.

Their small party departed an hour later. The day was mild and sunny, a rare gift. Kites and osprey sailed through the powder blue sky, heralding the arrival of spring.

Late in the afternoon, Ilain abruptly stood in her stirrups, raising a hand to shield her forehead.

"Do you see something?" Ethenn asked, alert as ever.

The woman ignored the question, scanning the hilltops. Then she let out a merry chortle of excitement. "Look," she called to them, pointing across the moor.

Following her direction, Evylin, Ethenn, and Thom rode up next to her. There, at the top of a hill, they could see the shadow of a building and horses dotting the surrounding grass.

"What is that?" Thom asked.

"That," Ilain said proudly, "is my childhood home."

They all whirled toward her in surprise.

"I thought you grew up in . . . whatever the Fire Mage Reach is called," Thom said lamely.

Ilain waved him off. "No, no, I moved to Doorstunds Reach when I was ten. I grew up here in Faurna before that. You can't see much of the town from here, but it's just over the ridge. My father breeds and trains horses, as you might be able to tell."

"Your family still lives there?" Evylin asked.

Ilain's curls glimmered in the sunset as she nodded. "My parents do. When Auden and I became Mages, we moved into the Reach, so we have no real home anymore. And our older brother, Vayden, works for the Alliance as well, so while he's meant to take over for Da, he's off Allore and Administration only knows where."

With a final lingering glance, Ilain nudged her horse down the road, but the three Ephrians hesitated.

"Did you . . . ?" Ethenn cleared his throat. "We could stop to see them if you wanted?" He glanced at Evylin as if for approval.

"Yes," Evylin agreed, then considered the writ. "Only if it wouldn't put them in trouble, though."

Ilain didn't stop, so the rest of them guided their horses to follow as she answered. "No, that isn't necessary. I'd be delighted to see them, of course, but it's best if they don't know where we are. Blount will probably be keeping an eye on them in case we come calling."

Understanding, Evylin returned to the previous conversation. "You said your brother works for the Alliance too. Are your parents also members?"

"Oh, yes. My parents joined decades ago. They're quite influential, though they're mostly retired these days."

"How old are your parents?" Thom asked.

Ilain thought for a moment. "Da is sixty-seven, and Mum is sixty-five next month."

Evylin's brow furrowed. "They must have been quite old when they had you," she said.

Ilain looked confused for all of a second. Then she chuckled. "I forgot," she said wryly. "I haven't told you my age. I'm forty-three, dear."

Ethenn choked as he took a sip from his waterskin. Thom slapped him on the back, smirking.

"Mages and Warriors live longer than the average human, thanks to our magic," Ilain explained. "And we look younger because of it."

"Evidently," Evylin muttered, bemused. She shifted uncomfortably in her saddle. "So you and your brothers were born into the Alliance?"

"I suppose you could say that." Ilain twirled a curl around her finger. "Our parents instilled their beliefs into us quite young, but we readily accepted them as our own. They didn't hide the dark truth of Blount's tyranny and the Mages' reigns from us. Even when Auden and I went to live with the Mages, we held onto our faith and our cause dearly."

"Is the Alliance a religious organization?" Ethenn asked skeptically.

Ilain nodded. "Quite religious. Our faith informs much of our policies and decisions."

"Is that what brought your parents to join?" Thom asked. "Religion?"

A long pause drew Evylin to look at Ilain. The woman stared at Thom in consideration. "Do you want to know the real reason?" she asked. "Or the palatable one?"

Thom blanched. "Whichever you're willing to give," he said.

With a tight nod, Ilain turned forward to speak to the horizon. "My mother was the daughter of a duke," she began. "My father's family was well known for their superior stock and training, so Lord Wessam, my grandfather, purchased all his horses from them. When my mother was sixteen, he bought her a gelding. My father delivered it, and that's how they met. Over time, they fell in love."

"I see where this is going," Thom said, amused.

"You don't," Ilain said sharply. "My grandfather didn't approve of his daughter loving a lowly horse breeder, so he forbade them from seeing one another. Being an honorable man of Allorian faith, my father listened, despite my mother's protests. Shortly after, King Blount went on a tour of Wauld. Although his reign had begun nearly a decade earlier, it took some time to stabilize after his coup d'état. Once his monarchy was established, he sought to tighten his hold on the gentry. Those who weren't found loyal and subservient were killed and replaced."

Evylin grimaced, finding the king no better than his son.

"Being a duke, my grandfather's estate was on Blount's route," Ilain continued. "He stayed with the family for a week, and my grandfather did everything in his power to prove his allegiance. He spared no expense and appeased all of Blount's requests, including the use of his daughter."

A sudden silence filled the air as the Ephrians processed the highlady's words. Evylin, Thom, and Ethenn all stared at Ilain, dumbfounded.

"He—" The words couldn't work their way up Evylin's dry throat.

Ilain had no such issue. "He raped her."

Thom and Ethenn slumped as though they were the ones to fail Ilain's mother and not Lord Wessam.

"A month later, it was discovered that my mother was pregnant," Ilain said. "Unwilling to reveal the king's crime, my grandfather shunned my mother and accused my father. When he learned of this, my father didn't hesitate to find my mother and marry her, promising to care for her child as if it were his own. He gave Vayden his name and allowed the world to believe our grandfather's lie.

"But from that moment on, my father swore that he would find a way to dethrone Blount," Ilain said, husky voice thick with passion. "Our parents raised us knowing the truth about Vayden's parentage, though we kept it within our family. They wanted us to know so that we could understand the world we lived in. So that we could know why it needed to change."

Under the weight of the Calders' heavy history, the Ephrians were silent. They exchanged sorrowful, wary glances. The reason for Ilain and Auden's dedication to the Alliance became clear. And Evylin had to wonder how many other families had similar stories.

Thom broke the awkward silence. "I'm—" He paused, brow furrowed. "I'm sorry, but did you say your brother is the king's son?"

Ilain leveled him with a flat glare. "That's what you took away from the story?"

He threw his hands in the air. "Your brother is also Blount's brother," he exclaimed. "We're fighting to bring down your brother's family."

"They aren't his family," Ilain countered. "They don't even know he exists."

Interrupting whatever caustic reply Thom was about to put forth, Ethenn said, "What is he like? Your brother."

After a pause, Ilain's expression softened. "He's wonderful," she said fondly. "Vayden was always the perfect big brother. He's kind, strong, and levelheaded. And while he isn't magical, his smile could be."

A twinge rose in Evylin at the description. Instead of conjuring the image of a redheaded, lanky Calder, it brought her the picture of curly brown hair, tanned and freckled cheeks, and strong arms that gave the best bear hugs.

Forcing the memory away, Evylin turned to Ilain. "Thank you for telling us. About Vayden and your family's past. I think I understand. . . ."

"We don't mind sharing," Ilain promised. "Not even my mother or Vayden will hesitate to talk about it. The more people who understand the cruelty of Blount's reign, the more who will join our cause."

Evylin ran her thumb along the reins. "I know little about King Blount. But after meeting his son . . . Anyone who could have raised a child to become *that* . . . I want to stop him too—to stop both of them."

"My dear Evylin," Ilain said, reaching across to squeeze her hand. "We'd be honored to have your assistance."

A new sense of companionship rose between Evylin and Ilain. Knowing the highlady's story and hearing the motivation behind her affiliation with the Alliance, Evylin knew she would have done the same for her own family. The love of a brother drove the Calders. Her love of Ryen drove her to pursue her dream.

"The Relics," Evylin said, looking at Ilain once more. "You're sure they'll guarantee our success?"

Ilain didn't hesitate. "With the Relics, no monarchy can hope to stop us."

Ethenn and Thom frowned, but Evylin was beginning to lose her skepticism in the Alliance. Ilain and Auden weren't foolhardy or rash. They'd spent years—apparently over forty—preparing for this moment. From the sound of it, the Alliance itself was old. If they'd waited so patiently, forming relationships and working in the shadows, perfecting their plan before making their move, they couldn't be some vapid organization out for glory. They genuinely wanted to see change occur for their countrymen.

"I can't promise I'll become an Alliance member," Evylin said, still holding Ilain's gaze. "But I'd like to see them win this war."

Ilain's lips quirked up in a knowing fashion. "Forget the Relics," she said lightheartedly. "Even if we just had our small band alongside the rest of the Alliance's people, I have no doubt that the victory would be ours."

CHAPTER THIRTY-SIX

25TH OF CHRONOS, 1574

It began to rain again.

The rambling hills of the moors gave way to the towering heights of the Vaulgan Mountains, a thick forest floor growing at their base. Though the fauna wasn't as large and overgrown as in northern Wauld, the trees grew taller and their gnarled roots wider. The road narrowed as they continued, with fewer and fewer travelers taking their route as the days passed.

Ilain informed them that only the mines extended for miles along their path. The meager settlements near the mountain range were either mining or lumber camps. While on this leg of their journey, they wouldn't have to worry about the writ.

"Few enough people who live in this county are literate," Ilain said. "Fewer still bother with the throne's laws."

"Could we enter settlements here then?" Ethenn asked. "To restock our food and weapon supplies."

Thom gave the young man a dubious look. "In what world do you need more weapons?"

"I'm out of arrows," Ethenn said tersely. "I've mangled together some makeshift ones, but I don't have any steel tips for them. They're only good for training and menial hunting at best."

While Evylin thought Ethenn's idea was sound, Ilain shook her head. "Writ or no writ, it isn't safe to enter the settlements," she said.

"Why not?" Evylin asked.

"The Vaulgan people are suspicious and territorial," Ilain explained. "Our mere presence will draw unwanted attention. Should we start making purchases of any size, our money will attract even greater notice. And I don't care to be mugged."

With that pronouncement, the idea was abandoned. Furthermore, Ilain suggested they adhere more strictly to staying together. Though it was unlikely, someone—or worse, a wolf pack—could stumble across their camp. "Best to be safe," she said. "We should always have a companion."

So when Evylin and Ethenn went out to hunt that evening, Thom stayed with Ilain.

After a week and a half of training, Evylin was finally able to put her archery skills to the test. She wasn't as strong as Ethenn, so she struggled to draw the string as smoothly as him, but he let her practice with minimal coaching as they went through the trees in search of dinner. Spring brought the return of furbearers and fowl alike. Even with only the sharpened wooden tips of their arrows, she snagged several hares and a couple of grouse, enough to last them the next few days with Ilain's magical preservation.

While Evylin retrieved and cleaned the arrow from her latest catch, Ethenn prepared to string it up with the others. "Evie," he said, reluctance in his tone, "could I ask you something?"

Handing him the rabbit, Evylin raised her brow. "Depends on what it is, I suppose."

"It has to do with being a Warrior."

"Oh." She smiled. "Well, in that case, of course."

Ethenn took his time tying up the rabbit. His expression remained tight as he finished. "That feeling we get in a fight," he began. "The rush."

Evylin nodded to encourage him.

"Have you ever felt it while *not* in a fight?"

Instantly, Evylin blanched. She could feel her face fall as her mouth went dry.

Ethenn met her gaze, drawn by her silence. "You have, haven't you?"

Evylin most certainly had. But she wasn't interested in explaining it to Ethenn. With forced casualness, she shrugged. "Once or twice."

"With Deckard," Ethenn stated rather than questioned.

The blood that had seeped from her head moments ago came back in a heated rush. "That's—"

"Because he's a Mage," Ethenn added, seeing her attempt to distort the truth.

Evylin just stared at him.

With a slow nod, Ethenn gestured to himself. "I feel it too," he said, "with Ilain."

That caused Evylin's eyes to widen. She'd known—well, they'd *all* known of Ethenn's infatuation, but she didn't think that Ilain returned his regard. And she certainly hadn't thought they'd been kissing.

At her surprised expression, Ethenn hurried to clarify, "It isn't—I'm not comparing it to what you—it isn't like Ilain and I . . ." He grimaced, his entire face pink.

With a heavy sigh, he tried again. "I didn't realize it at first. But whenever we would touch—in passing or—or, you know, just in general—I would feel that spike of what I thought was nerves. With our training, I've gotten more familiar with the feeling, and I've realized . . . it's magic that I feel around her. It's drawing me to her."

Evylin had intimate knowledge of Ethenn's experience. But she had no more explanation for it than he did. "From my understanding, it would happen between any Warrior and Mage," she said, giving what excuse she could to belittle the feeling.

Ethenn accepted it readily. "It isn't like I think fate has called Ilain and me together," he said defensively. "She doesn't want me, even though I am a Warrior. But . . . it makes me wonder: What is it like? Being with a Mage."

Evylin's hand flexed, instinctively wanting to tug on her rings. "Ethenn," she said, slowly and cautiously. "It's not like that between us. I already—"

"I don't believe you," he said brusquely.

Evylin gaped at him.

He stared back at her, expression resolute and serious. "What you said when we split—when you pretended not to love Deckard—" He shook his head. "I don't believe you."

Chest tightening, Evylin clamped her jaw shut. "Your opinion doesn't matter."

Ethenn didn't flinch at her harsh tone. He just kept staring at her with that calm, knowing look of his. "Maybe it should," he said flatly. He flung their strung-up catch over the root of a tree, then faced her again, determination in his dark gaze.

Evylin flinched at his expression. With his distinct Estshire appearance, broad-shouldered, boyish features, and warmly tanned skin, he reminded her too much of the man Ryen might have become. The obstinate tenacity of Ethenn's gaze was too familiar, too similar to Hewitt and Ryen's. Not uncanny but alike enough to cause her heartbeat to falter.

Ethenn stepped forward, pointing to his chest. "I was there, Evie," he said. "In Dunneshead. I helped save you, too, and I saw . . ." Heat curled up his neck once more. "Well, I saw enough."

"It wasn't real," Evylin defended instinctively. "It didn't mean anything."

"Like hell."

She clenched her teeth.

"You can't convince me that you don't love one another," Ethenn said firmly. "Not after seeing that kiss."

Evylin turned away, unable to hold his knowing stare. "You're young, Ethenn. You don't understand."

"I understand just fine," he shot back steadily. "I may be young, but I'm not as innocent as Raff and Thom like to pretend. I fought in an underground fighting ring, remember? You don't think I encountered girls who found that attractive?"

Having never considered it, Evylin now realized he was right. Had she known about the fighting ring in Trollenston, she likely would have gone in search of it. As a young woman, she would have found a skilled young fighter like Ethenn immensely impressive—*and* attractive.

Ethenn gave her a flippant, if bashful, grin. "I've kissed my fair share of girls. Trust me, I know what it's like to kiss for fun. And that's *not* what you and Deckard were doing."

Somewhere between amused, intrigued, and disturbed, Evylin pressed her fingers to her temple. "Why are we discussing this?" she asked irritably.

He gave her an equally frustrated frown. "Because I need to know if I'm doomed to a life of either unhappiness or destruction," he said, a thread of desperation in his voice.

Evylin drew back, startled at the admission.

Ethenn threw his hands in the air, staring into the forest around them as if seeking direction. "I feel lost, Evie. When I was a boy, all I wanted was to be like my parents—to be a hunter, have a small home and a happy family, and never leave Trollenston. Then everything changed."

He didn't give an explanation, and Evylin didn't think she should ask.

"I left the town because of choices I made," he said matter-of-factly. "I told you before: I'm dangerous. My anger gets the better of me, and I lash out violently. I thought maybe if I left, it would get better."

Ethenn's face scrunched with something like disappointment. "Now, I'm *this*. I'm a bloody Warrior—a living weapon, meant only to create death. It makes sense in a cruel way—why I am the way I am." He let out an embittered laugh. "And it seems I'm doomed to two choices: I either accept that fate and find a Mage to marry or live a normal life with a normal woman who can't make me happy."

Evylin frowned, not liking the conversation. "We aren't destined for Mages, Ethenn. You can be happy with whomever you like."

"Can I?" Ethenn asked bluntly. "Whatever you say, whatever lie you like to tell yourself, now that you've experienced what it feels like to be with Deckard, can you honestly imagine loving someone else?"

She couldn't. But not for the reason he thought.

His lips curled in discontent. "Now that you've felt that rush," he continued in a whisper. "Now that you know what it's like to be fully alive . . . Can you truly believe you'd ever be happy with anything less?"

Evylin's pulse thrummed in her ears. Ethenn's panic, his fear, echoed her own. She'd asked herself these very questions many times. Could she live a life not as a Warrior but simply as a woman? Could she forget how her senses heightened in the rush of a fight, making the world purer? Could she be happy without Deckard? Was happiness even an option for her?

When she didn't answer, Ethenn gave his own response. "I can't."

Caught in her indecision, Evylin ran a hand across her forehead. She didn't know how Ethenn came to his conclusion, but she feared that if she followed her thoughts, she'd find the same one at the end. She didn't want to feel that way.

To distract herself, Evylin latched onto Ethenn's predicament. "You said you want to be insignificant. If you're a Warrior, you can't be."

He nodded.

"If you're a Warrior married to a Mage," she added, "you *certainly* can't be."

"I know."

"So what? Are you . . . planning on offering yourself to Ilain?" she asked skeptically.

"No," Ethenn said, his denial almost too quick to be believed. "No, I just know I can't return to who I was before this. And I suppose I wanted to know that pursuing this life isn't something to regret."

"I'm not the person to answer that, Ethenn," she warned. "I regret everything."

"Because of Hewitt?" he asked gently.

"Yes." It was the only answer she had. The only one that mattered.

Evylin regretted everything because her choice, her blind dedication to keeping Ryen alive, had led to her losing Hewitt. If she could go back to the beginning, to that moment when she sat at her cousin's grave and whispered into the cold night, she would tell herself not to make that damning promise. "It isn't worth it," she would say. "Losing him isn't worth what you'll gain."

A sting of bitterness pierced through Evylin's heart. She'd lost Ryen. She'd lost Hewitt. In exchange, she'd simply gained another man she'd inevitably lose.

"Evie?"

Ethenn's voice broke her out of her downward spiral. She looked up, realizing her vision was blurred with tears. He stood there, dark hair hanging in his eyes as he watched her warily.

"I know I'm the kid no one takes seriously," he said with a softness she wasn't used to in his expression. "But trust me, you wouldn't be happier if you could go back."

Evylin raised her chin, wondering how he knew her thoughts.

With a sigh, Ethenn gave her a sad smile. "We left for a reason, you and I," he said. "I'm not sure what yours was, but . . . If Hewitt thought it was reason enough to marry you to Deckard and come out of retirement to travel the country with you, then it had to be important."

Though Ethenn's words held unexpected wisdom, Evylin's mind stuck on his awareness of their arrangement. "How did you—?"

"It wasn't exactly hard to figure out." His smile grew wry. "Rafferty got Thom drunk enough months ago to worm the information out of him. We've known since Stoclund."

Evylin's lips parted in shock. "And you didn't say anything?"

Ethenn laughed. "Why would we? So you got married for convenience? There are worse reasons to get married."

Despite herself, Evylin grinned. She slugged him in the shoulder. "Then you know you're wrong about us."

He scoffed. "And I'm six feet tall."

Pointedly glaring up at his singular inch over her own five foot, six inch frame, Evylin raised her eyebrows.

"See?" he said dryly. "I can lie too."

Now, he reminded Evylin *far* too much of Ryen. "Since when have you been sarcastic?" she asked, a bittersweet amusement filling her.

His smile lit up his face. "I've been spending my days with you. What do you expect?"

"You have a point," she conceded merrily. Then she sighed. "You're right. There is no going back. For good or ill, we chose to leave our homes." She took a step forward and set a hand on his arm. "But that doesn't mean you have to become the Alliance's weapon."

He chewed on the inside of his cheek, his gaze darting toward the camp. "What if that's my only hope of happiness?"

Evylin had no answer for that. She stared at Ethenn, wondering how they were both facing such similar dilemmas. After twenty-seven years of longing for adventure, after holding fast to her vow to Ryen, she found she no longer desired travel and daring exploits. They couldn't make her happy. And she feared that the one thing that could come close would inevitably destroy her.

With a final pat on his arm, Evylin moved away. "Come on," she said, grabbing the brace of grouse and strung up hares. "Thom and Ilain will worry."

Ethenn began to nod, then hesitated. "Evie, one more thing."

She looked back at him, waiting.

He wet his lips. "I think you should be careful with Thom."

Her nose scrunched in confusion. "What are you—?"

"When Raff got him drunk—when he told us about your marriage," Ethenn's swallow was visible along his neck, "he told us some other things too."

"I don't understand."

"He wants to be with you, Evylin."

The statement fell flat, dead in the air. Evylin couldn't fathom it. She couldn't comprehend it. Thom was her friend, and what's more, he was Deckard's brother. Despite the competition and jealousy he felt toward his brother and his accomplishments, she knew Thom loved Deckard. He would never. . . .

Evylin continued to stare at Ethenn, mouth agape.

"Thom told us that he wishes it were *he* you had married."

Evylin's whole body felt as though it'd turned to stone. She'd confided in Thom; she'd trusted him. And he'd encouraged her and advised her in her marriage. Never once had she felt that he was trying to come between her and Deckard.

"That's—I can't—" Evylin stumbled over what to say. "Maybe . . . Maybe he did once feel that way, but—Ethenn, he's not. . . ."

The words dissipated like the morning fog.

Ethenn gave her a sympathetic look. "I thought you should know," he said softly.

Suddenly, Evylin found herself tugging on her rings. It was the last thing she'd expected to worry about. From the start, she'd viewed Thom as a friend. Throughout their travels, she'd come to see him as a brother. Hearing that he might harbor an infatuation with her . . .

The blood drained from Evylin's head. If Ethenn was right, if Thom had feelings for her, then her announcement that her marriage to Deckard wasn't real might seem to be an invitation.

Evylin twisted her rings, the onyx stones rough against her fingertips. She rejected all thoughts of Thom's affections. During the entirety of their relationship, she'd never felt anything but friendship from him. Until he proved otherwise, she wouldn't trust a drunken admission that might have been misinterpreted. Ethenn wasn't privy to Thom's jealousy of Deckard. Perhaps he'd misunderstood altogether.

No, Evylin wouldn't believe one account. But she *would* take Ethenn's advice.

From that moment on, Evylin would be careful with Thom.

CHAPTER THIRTY-SEVEN

28TH OF CHRONOS, 1574

"You've forgotten everything I taught you," Hewitt's ghost said as Deckard's sword dropped into the mud, disarmed by Rafferty.

The weasel's silver eyes twinkled as he spun the long hunting knife. After losing his short swords in the Wind Keep, he'd taken to wielding the blade along with one of the backups he'd brought from Ephria. Though they wouldn't usually spar with real weapons, they didn't have much choice, as Evylin and Ethenn had taken the practice swords with them, and the trees in the marshes were too springy to make good temporary weapons.

"You taking it easy on me, Colonel?" Rafferty said snarkily.

Deckard looked beyond Rafferty's shoulder to meet Hewitt's gaze. "I got distracted," he replied to both of them.

"Thinking about Evylin again?" Rafferty teased, oblivious to the ghost's presence.

"Probably," Hewitt said.

Deckard found himself grinning. "If I were thinking about Evylin, I would have won."

The men ranged across the small island, its long grasses bowing as they traversed and trained. Murky water stretched for miles. Willows and cypress trees towered over them, creating a dense canopy that blocked out the sky. Shafts of sunlight filtered through the treetops, reflecting off the marsh waters.

At the edge of their island, the horses grazed lazily. The marshes were waist-deep on men, but the horses made their trek bearable.

Deckard and Rafferty had left Auden on the small inlet they'd used for their camp in search of enough ground to train. After the first few days of their journey, Rafferty began to complain of boredom. He'd insisted that they should start sparring to keep their skills up. So every day, Deckard would train with Auden during their rides and with Rafferty during the evening.

Sometimes, their marshy camp islands were big enough to spar on. Other times, like today, they had to seek out better ground.

Amidst all his practice and training, Deckard had learned two things. First, he had indeed lost some of the progress he'd made with Hewitt. And second, his control over his magic was rapidly and disturbingly increasing.

Ever since making the plan to summon Hewitt so Evylin could talk with him, Deckard had kept the ghost around permanently. He'd been cautious at first, wary that Auden would discover his deepening connection with Night. When the Mage showed no signs of noticing, Deckard grew more confident.

It felt good to have Hewitt around once again. The ghost coached him through the sparring, giving him much-needed lessons. Hewitt had even given Deckard the idea of training in hand-to-hand combat with Rafferty, bringing those skills up to par. "Mages rely too much on their magic," Hewitt said. "While you lot are busy waving your hands around, an attacker can sneak up on you. You'd best learn to defend yourself without weapons or magic."

Beyond the improvement of his martial skills, Deckard enjoyed having his mentor's company ever at his side. It gave him a false connection to Evylin, despite the hundreds of miles separating them.

Rafferty surveyed Deckard as he reset his stance. "You want to go again?" he asked in surprise.

"Are you getting tired?" Deckard asked. He'd come to understand that conversation with the man was best executed with witty quips. That was the only way to earn Rafferty's good opinion. "By all means, concede."

"You're the old man here," Rafferty said. "I'll still be crowing when you're cold in your grave."

Knowing that Auden held more than a decade on him and Deckard would, in fact, live far longer than Rafferty, he chose not to correct him.

Deckard charged, beginning the next bout. At the start of their training, Deckard found it difficult to keep up with Rafferty's dual-wielded blades. It forced him to be more alert, watching for both sword and knife at once. However, he'd picked up the nuances of the skill faster than he would have with Hewitt standing at his side, offering advice and tidbits to improve all the while.

"You've put too little pressure on his right blade," Hewitt warned. "He'll escape you.

Watch out for his underhand. Don't focus so much on the blades. Keep a watch—he's going to kick your leg out from—oh, you idiot."

Deckard sprawled on the thick grass. Hewitt's guidance had whipped Deckard back into shape, but Rafferty was still too wily at times.

"I've told you." Hewitt crossed his arms. "If your opponent isn't going to fight fair, you can't either."

That was the lesson Deckard struggled to master.

Rafferty held out his hand to help Deckard up, sniggering all the while.

Deckard grabbed the weasel's hand, then swept his leg, dropping Rafferty to the ground next to him. With all the speed he could muster, Deckard rolled to his knees, tapping the point of his sword to Rafferty's chest.

"I win," Deckard said.

Hewitt laughed, and Rafferty smirked. "Now, you're getting it, Colonel," he said. "Takes a weasel to beat a weasel."

Deckard stood and sheathed his sword. He'd have to buff out the nicks later. "I'll try to take that as a compliment."

Rafferty popped up nimbly. "You should. All this time with me has made you less boring. Miraculously, I'm actually rather fond of you now."

"I feel I should be bothered by that sentiment," Deckard remarked. "I've never been friends with a criminal before."

"I'm an entrepreneur," Rafferty corrected. "And whoever said we were friends?"

Deckard raised his brow. "You just—"

"I said I'm fond of you. I didn't say we were friends."

"I assumed the two were synonymous."

Rafferty gave him a wry look. "I assumed the same could be said for marriage and sex. Guess we were both wrong."

Hewitt snorted.

With a disparaging frown toward the ghost, Deckard let the quip go. Rafferty's jokes about his and Evylin's relationship had irritated Deckard the first several days, but he'd quickly learned to let them pass unheeded. The "three" questions Rafferty bartered for easily became twenty as they trained. Then it grew to fifty. Now, Deckard thought they were nearing the hundreds, and while he hadn't answered most of them, he'd grown numb to the indelicate topic.

In fact, Deckard found it somewhat liberating to discuss the situation in abstract terms every now and again.

"We all make foolish assumptions," Deckard said, then moved toward the horses. "Come on. It's time we got back."

Rafferty hopped on his horse while Hewitt appeared farther up the path. The ghost rarely walked. He simply appeared where Deckard wanted to see him.

They guided their horses through the waters and inlets of land. "Really, though," Rafferty said casually, "what was it that kept you from sealing the deal with Evie? It wasn't . . ." His eyes darted over Deckard's person, growing wide. "I mean, you *can*—"

"Yes," Deckard interrupted, heat creeping up his neck. "I chose not to."

"What, 'cause you're a gentleman?" Rafferty asked mockingly.

"No, it was far worse than that."

"Eh?"

"I'd seen what she could do with a sword." Deckard passed Rafferty a flat glare. "I didn't care to test her lenience with unwanted affection."

Rafferty guffawed while Hewitt shook his head. "Liar," the ghost accused.

"So you were afraid of her," Rafferty concluded.

And though Hewitt was right—Deckard was a liar—Rafferty was correct as well.

"In a way," Deckard admitted. "I take the duty of a husband seriously. Beginning our marriage by abusing the role to suit my masculine desires didn't seem advisable. And I didn't want her to hate me."

"Sure," Rafferty said. "I get that. But that was months ago. You'd become quite friendly. You slept all snuggly-like. And, from what I've heard, you spent some quality time snogging too."

Deckard's gaze snapped to Rafferty's face. "Where did you hear that?"

"Most recently? Ethenn."

Deckard turned away, a flush working across his scalp. He'd done his best to forget Ethenn's witness to his and Evylin's kiss in Dunneshead.

"You really did a number on Loxley. The kid was practically shaking in his boots as he told me. He kept that bit from Thommy, though."

Hewitt shook his head, and Deckard shifted uncomfortably in his saddle.

"It was Thom who told me about it in the past," Rafferty said. "The first time, he lamented how Evie confided in him about your prowess after we saved dear ol' Prince Ephren. Good on you, by the way."

Deckard furrowed his brow, confused by the commendation.

"The second time," Rafferty continued, "was back in Loclight. Said he and Hew were just sitting there when you two came barging in, tangled up and tearing at each other. He thought you'd finally worked up the nerve."

"He wasn't the only one," Hewitt remarked.

"Guess that wasn't the case," Rafferty said, waggling his white-blond brows.

Pressing his lips together at the recounting of some of their most intimate moments, Deckard pushed the memories aside. "It wasn't," he muttered.

"I can see how having your brother and her uncle there might kill the mood."

Deckard glanced at Hewitt accusingly. "Indeed."

"But she wanted it, right?" Rafferty asked.

Deckard recoiled. While his sensibilities had relaxed in the past fourteen days spent in Rafferty's company, such a blatant presumption of Evylin's intimate desires caused his moral senses to flare.

Rafferty didn't notice. "I mean, the way Thom talked, she was as eager as you." The weasel gave him a meaningful look. "Something about her tongue—"

"Stop!"

A smug grin remained on the weasel's face as Deckard worked his jaw.

On the nearest embankment, Hewitt scowled. "Tell the fool what he wants to know so he stops asking."

Giving both men an irritated look, Deckard followed the ghost's advice. "I chose to respect her wishes. Whatever that makes me—a coward, an idiot, a gentleman—I don't care. I did what I thought was best for *her*. Because I love her."

Rafferty pursed his lips, listening.

"You weren't there," Deckard said, more to Hewitt than Rafferty. "The night of our marriage, I saw the fear in her eyes. Every time I touched her, even if it was as innocent as a kiss on the hand or a brush of my fingers, she would flinch. I wasn't about to force myself on her. Not when she was so clearly afraid of intimacy."

The twitter of robins filled the marshes around them. In the distance, their small camp awaited with Auden tending a fire. Rafferty drew his horse up short, stopping them. He met Deckard's gaze with the most serious expression he'd ever worn.

"But," the weasel said, "she's not afraid of it now."

A sad smile crept over Deckard's face. He glanced at Hewitt. A familiar tension filled his chest, as though his lungs wouldn't expand to take in air—like his heart refused to beat.

"Yes, she is," he said solemnly.

Rafferty scratched his head, baffled. "But you love her?"

"Yes."

"And she loves you?"

"No."

Hewitt grumbled his dissent, but Deckard ignored him.

Rafferty heaved a large sigh. "May I just say," he set a hand to his chest, "I'm glad I'm not one for monogamous relationships."

"You can say it," Deckard replied. "But it makes you a loveless, deplorable scoundrel."

"I'd rather be a scoundrel than experience the hell you're all going through."

"All of us?" Deckard repeated, sure that he and Evylin didn't constitute that grand a description.

"*All* of you," Rafferty confirmed. "I know you're boring and dull, but no one is blind enough to miss the lovelorn disasters plaguing our band."

"Pretend I am that blind," Deckard said.

Rafferty shrugged casually. "Where do I begin? Well, of course, there are you and Evie. We've all been perfectly aware that you two are besotted with one another, but with Hewitt gone, clearly trouble has found its way into paradise."

Deckard didn't bother correcting Rafferty's presumptions of Evylin's feelings.

"Then," the man continued, "there's poor little Loxley and his adoration for the fiery highlady."

"Ah, yes." Deckard nodded. "He told me about that."

"Did he?" Rafferty raised his brow. "Interesting. The kid never bothered to mention it to Thommy or me, but it's been pretty obvious from the start. Problem is, the lady has it just as bad, but she's wasted too much time making him think she likes Thom, and now Ethenn won't believe she likes him even if she were to hike her skirt—"

"What are you talking about?" Deckard interrupted, uninterested in hearing the conclusion to the euphemism.

"Ethenn likes Ilain," Rafferty said as though explaining to a child. "Ilain likes Ethenn. But as she announced to the whole troop, Ilain needs to marry a Warrior. As Ethenn's magical status wasn't known until a week back, she had to deter him to keep their feelings from developing past infatuation. Thus, her flirtations with Thommy."

Deckard frowned. "But now she knows that Ethenn's a Warrior."

"Doesn't matter," Rafferty said. "Whether or not she likes Thom, she's worked too hard to make sure Ethenn thinks she *doesn't* like him. Now, if she tells him the truth, it'll just sound like she's trying to bag a Warrior. Personally, I wouldn't care so much about that in his shoes. I'd imagine an affair with Ilain Calder would set a man's britches—"

"Rafferty."

"Right." Rafferty leaned against the front of his saddle. "Anyway, the problem now is, Ethenn thinks Ilain likes Thom and that Thommy's stringing the highlady along."

"Children," Hewitt muttered.

Rafferty kept going, unaware of the ghost's complaints. "Over the past month, Ethenn's been getting more and more upset with Thom in defense of his ladylove."

Deckard drew a hand along his jaw, trying to process the complexities of Rafferty's explanation. "If their regard is false, why wouldn't Thom just tell Ethenn?" he asked out of pure curiosity.

"'Cause he's an idiot."

Deckard shook his head. "You've lost me."

Rafferty drew back, studying Deckard with his light gray gaze. His mouth opened, then shut as though judging his next words. "I can't tell if you know or not," he remarked, frowning. "Surely, you know. It's obvious."

A sneaking suspicion tingled at the base of Deckard's skull. "Know what?"

Rafferty tapped his fingers against his saddle. "I could have sworn you knew. What with how testy you two have gotten, I thought you must have figured it out."

"Rafferty, tell me."

"Now, don't kill the messenger, all right? I told him to move on."

"Move on from what?"

"Well, Thom is a talker," Rafferty noted. "Mostly when he's had one too many ales, but also when he's irritable. Which is most of the time. And as I'm the one who's mostly around, I'm the one he's mostly talked to."

"Rafferty." Deckard's prompting took on a hostile tone.

The man tipped his chin up. "So you do know?"

"Just tell me what Thom has told you."

"Thom said he's in love with Evylin."

The candid delivery sparked a blaze hotter than the sun within Deckard's chest. His teeth clenched, and he glared into the forest as though he would see his brother standing there, guilty as charged. Instead, his eyes landed on Hewitt, the ghost returning his glare with a fury that matched his own.

Deckard turned back to Rafferty, enraged. "Does he plan to tell her?" he demanded.

Rafferty lifted his hands placatingly. "I don't know."

"He's my brother," Deckard spat. "She's my wife!"

"Well, yeah," Rafferty replied flippantly. "He knows that."

"Then why would he—?"

"Why are you asking me?" Rafferty interrupted. "Look, I'm not here to defend him. He's an ass. I've told him that. The thing is: He admits it too. He hasn't said anything because he knows how you feel about her, and because . . . Well, he thought you two had—" He made a crude hand gesture, then shrugged.

Regret after regret filled Deckard's mind. He'd known. The whole time, ever since Hewitt's arrangement in Whickam Village, Deckard had suspected his brother's interest. Thom had spent hours trying to convince Deckard not to marry Evylin. He'd begged him, saying that he didn't want Deckard throwing his life away on a woman he'd just met. Even then, Deckard knew the words rang false, the arguments a lie.

Why hadn't Thom told him outright? If he'd had feelings for Evylin, why hadn't he spoken up? Why not ask to marry Evylin himself? Thom had to know that if he'd asked, Deckard would have waited to make the agreement. If Deckard had known of his brother's feelings, he would have hesitated.

So why hadn't Thom been honest?

The answer came to Deckard with something awfully close to shame.

Regardless of Thom's feelings, Deckard would have married Evylin anyway. Despite the short three days of their acquaintance, his infatuation had grown too deep to give her over to his brother. Perhaps he could have relinquished her to another man, one who would take her away, where Deckard would never see her again. But to allow his brother to marry the woman he'd already begun to feel affection for? That would have been too much.

Thom would have known the choice he would make. He didn't speak up because he knew that Deckard wouldn't be selfless enough to let her go.

Suddenly, Deckard remembered all the occasions Thom had advised him during their travels. Despite his feelings, Thom had encouraged Deckard to invest in his marriage, to befriend Evylin, and to try to fall in love with her. However inappropriate Thom's feelings were, he'd not acted on them. Instead, he'd done what he could to support his brother in spite of them.

For the first time, Deckard questioned if *he* was at fault for this misunderstanding. He'd suspected Thom's interest in Evylin, but he hadn't pressed for the truth because he knew if there was a woman between them, the right thing to do would be for both of them to walk away. Since he didn't want to walk away from Evylin, he never asked.

Deckard had used excuse after excuse to justify their marriage. He needed Hewitt to help fulfill his volunteer quota. He wanted to help Evylin achieve her dreams. It was the only way to save his career. It was the right thing to do. Only after their marriage had he been honest with himself: He'd married her because he wanted her.

Evylin Glaas, the village girl with a quick wit, a ready smile, and a deep desire for more from the world, was the first woman he'd ever truly believed could be enough. And he wasn't willing to let such a chance slip through his fingers.

"I did know," Deckard admitted. "I just didn't want to believe it."

Hewitt stood in the trees, glaring at him. "And now," he said in a growl, "*he* knows that your marriage is legally breakable."

Deckard raised his chin, the sharp tingle of worry trickling down his spine. He turned back to Rafferty. "I've sent him away with her. Thom knows that our marriage isn't legitimate, and I've given him the perfect opportunity to make his feelings known."

Rafferty gave him a wry stare. "Why do you think I told him not to do anything I wouldn't?"

Deckard lifted his brow. "Says the man who doesn't believe in monogamous relationships."

"Hey!" Rafferty pointed at his chest. "I may be a scoundrel, but even I wouldn't boff my brother's wife."

The thought sent anger, fear, and heartache through Deckard's chest.

"Besides," Rafferty waved his hand, "Evie wouldn't go for it."

"You aren't my brother."

"No, you dunce, I'm not talking about her and me. Even if Thom plucked up the courage to reveal his feelings to her, she wouldn't go for it."

Doubt crept over Deckard's skin like the mosquitoes of the marshes, sapping his body of its vigor. Evylin had already rejected Deckard, asking for an annulment. She had to know that once he gave it to her, the only thing stopping her father from recalling her home would be marriage to another. Was it possible that she'd accept a marriage proposal from Thom? They'd always been better friends, training and laughing together easily. Rafferty said it himself: Evylin confided in Thom. If she wanted to be free of Deckard, was it possible that it was due to a secret love for his brother?

"She doesn't want him," Hewitt said, breaking into the panicked spiral of Deckard's thoughts. "She wants you."

"You don't know that," Deckard muttered.

"I'm telling you, Colonel," Rafferty replied, believing the response was for him. "You may be too thick to see it, but I'm a smuggler. It's my job to see what others don't. If I fail at that, I lose my neck, understand? I don't miss things. And I've seen how Evie is with you and how she is with Thom. She loves you both but in drastically different ways."

Deckard stared at Rafferty with hopeful interest. "You're sure?"

"Trust me," Rafferty said with a sly grin. "Eve likes to bait you. She's constantly seeking your attention. She doesn't do that with anyone else, especially not with Thom.

"*If* Thom works up the gumption to speak," he continued, "it'll be the worst choice he's ever made. She'll reject him, plain and simple, and it'll ruin their friendship. It's your britches she's interested in, not his."

Deckard couldn't decide whether to feel embarrassed or emboldened by the statement. Still, Evylin's request for an annulment lingered in his mind.

"She's afraid."

"Of me?"

"Of loving you back."

As his silence lingered, Rafferty rolled his eyes. "Look, I don't care if you believe me," he said flippantly. "Quite frankly, I think you're all idiots."

"Agreed," Hewitt said from the trees.

Nudging his horse onward, Rafferty kept up his chatter. "Your petty arguments and insecure romances are my entertainment. This whole trip has been a slog, but watching you lovesick lot bandying about has made for an amusing show. The only thing more interesting would be if you'd get your affairs in order and start locking lips in camp. Now, *that'd* be a show."

Ignoring the weasel's jabbering, Deckard glanced toward Hewitt's ghost. He stood on a small embankment, the marsh water lapping at its edge. His arms were crossed, and his steely gaze was sharp. Through the whole conversation, he'd shown no surprise. The news of Thom's feelings didn't seem to startle him as it should.

Rafferty's revelation wasn't a surprise to the ghost; that much was clear to Deckard.

Lagging behind just long enough to let Rafferty ride ahead, Deckard spurred his horse forward. The water sloshed around its legs. As Deckard passed the embankment, he whispered, "We need to talk."

Hewitt dipped his head in agreement. "We certainly do."

Looking toward the inlet, Deckard saw Auden waiting expectantly by the campfire. After his extended practice with Rafferty, there would be no escaping for the rest of the evening. And Deckard still didn't trust talking with Hewitt while the others slept.

No, he couldn't sneak off tonight, but he wouldn't wait long either.

"Tomorrow," he promised, both to himself and to the ghost.

Tomorrow, Deckard would hear what Hewitt had to say. He would learn why the man had chosen to keep this secret. And he would decide what to do about his brother.

CHAPTER THIRTY-EIGHT

"Can I ask you something?" Thom said to Ilain as they sat in camp.

Evylin and Ethenn were off training again. It had become a point of contention for Thom, since he was rarely able to join their sparring. He felt shunted off to the side, forgotten by two of his closest friends.

He took a breath, rejecting the emotion. Lately, he was attempting to do as Ilain suggested, to be better, to recognize the truth beyond his feelings. It was a harder task than he thought it should be.

Kicking off her boots, Ilain settled onto the grass beside where he lounged. "When have I said no?" she replied.

He averted his gaze as she slipped her stockings from her feet. "Should I have gone with Deckard?" he asked, staring at the rocks around the firepit.

Ilain's toes wiggled in the grass on the edge of his vision. "Why should you have?"

"Because I'm his brother."

"Should Auden have stayed with me then?"

Thom picked at the hem of his coat. Though it was new at the start of their journey through Wauld, the fabric now had rips and a fraying edge. They were moving closer and closer to Vaura Reach, the ultimate destination of the Time Keep, only days away. The path through the mountains was surprisingly well-worn, a result of the mining, Ilain told them.

With their troop's reunion looming closer, Thom had begun to think about his brother more and more. Despite his initial bitterness at Deckard choosing Rafferty to accompany their group, he took equal blame for the choice. If he wanted to protect him, he could have—*should* have volunteered immediately.

Thom tugged a thread loose and threw it into the fire. "I mean because Jonn is a Night Mage," he said, letting the words linger weightily.

"What does that have to do with anything?"

He gave the highlady a bland stare.

"What?" she asked, returning the look dramatically.

"You said Night magic makes people go mad."

"I said Night magic *can* bring the Deep upon its users. It's Auden who believes the whole lot is destined for villainy and insanity."

Her clarification did little to alleviate his concern. "You don't understand. Deckard won't be able to handle it. He's never done well with death. It's part of what makes him a pitiful soldier."

"He's a perfectly good soldier."

"No, he isn't," Thom argued. "He hates the job. He only does it because he thinks it makes him noble. But traveling like this? Recruiting? Fighting? *Killing?* No, he's not a soldier. He's an idealist. And now, he's got this Night magic running wild through him, controlling him, and making him kill everything in sight."

Ilain's prolonged silence drew him to look toward her. The transparent derision of her expression struck him. "You're an absolute idiot," she said bluntly.

Thom gaped at her.

"Have you heard nothing I said?" Ilain reached over to shove his head as Meria might've done when they were children. "Try to get it through your thick skull: Magic isn't evil. Not even Night magic. Yes, sometimes it's violent, and if used improperly, it can bring on madness. But it isn't controlling your brother. He's actually doing a surprisingly good job of controlling *it*. I theorize it has to do with his and Evylin's relationship."

Thom wasn't sure if anyone had told Ilain about Evylin's confession concerning her and Deckard's marriage yet. As he didn't feel compelled to take it upon himself, he ignored it. "You didn't see it," he said, remembering the ambush from the Wind and Terrae Mages. "You passed out before Deckard . . . He killed over forty Mages like it was nothing. That's *not* Deckard. That's the magic taking control of him."

"Do we look dead to you?" Ilain said bluntly.

Thom shook his head, confused. "What?"

She grabbed his wrist, waving his hand in the air between them. "You seem alive enough to me," she quipped. "And as I'm pretty sure I'm still breathing, it seems we made it through just fine."

"I don't—"

"If Jonn lost control of the magic, we would be dead along with those Mages," she concluded.

Thom blinked.

She released him, letting his hand thump back to the terrae. "The magic consumes him in the moment, yes. It makes him appear to be someone he's not, affecting his emotions and actions like a Relic might. But he is controlling it. He tells it what to do, and it listens. Then he lets it go. A man controlled by Night magic would kill everyone in his path, friend or foe."

With a sigh, Thom struggled to take comfort in her explanation. "But Jonn hates killing. Any death caused by his hands will drive him to madness, even if that insanity isn't magically induced."

Ilain hesitated.

"I should have gone with him," Thom said.

"What good would that have done?" she asked.

Thom looked at her, incredulous. "I'm his brother. I could have helped protect him from himself."

Ilain shook her head. "Jonn doesn't need protection from magic. He needs to accept it. It's the only way he *won't* give in to the Deep."

A spike of fear clouded Thom's mind. "What does that mean?" he asked weakly. "What is the Deep?"

Ilain turned away. She stared toward the fire, unseeing. The sharp lines of her face hardened further, giving her a haunted appearance. "It's terrifying," she admitted at last. "Night magic *can* be good. But it can also be the greatest evil."

With a slow breath, Ilain began to explain. "The Deep takes over when a Mage goes too far into the darkness of Night. When they seek to embrace death in its purest form. Some call the practice necromancy, but . . . it's worse than that."

Thom wasn't sure what necromancy was, but he decided not to interrupt.

"When Mages seek to connect with death, their minds warp," she said. "They often begin to see visions—premonitions that frequently come true. It's different than Time magic. Mages who connect with Time can see the future in a linear fashion. They can follow the threads of the future and see what's to come. The premonitions of the Deep aren't so logical, instead giving omens and portents of death. Many begin down this path for the benefit of seeing that future. They claim that if one can see death coming, they can prevent it."

Ilain shrugged sadly. "The problem is, if you prevent one death, you'll only have to face another."

"Is that it?" Thom asked, his worry lifting. Deckard wouldn't have an interest in seeking such visions. "They become oracles of death?"

She gave him a fierce look. "Over time, these premonitions bring mania, resulting in the Deep. But no, that's not the only means by which the Deep comes on a Mage. It can also be the result of experimenting with death, summoning ghosts, and raising the living dead."

A cold sweat broke out across Thom's neck. "I'm sorry, did you say the living dead?"

"It hasn't happened in over five centuries, but yes, there was a Night Mage who summoned a horde of dead to do his bidding. They could only be killed by decapitation or magic."

"Ah." The word choked out of Thom.

"There's a law against it now," Ilain said matter-of-factly, then moved on. "All of these things are what bring on the Deep. How it manifests . . ."

Ilain pulled her legs up, resting her arms on her knees, her chin on her arms. The posture startled Thom. He'd never seen the woman look so young or sorrowful.

"The Deep causes Mages to lose their sense of self," she said darkly. "They become volatile, driven by their visions toward often violent ends. They grow crazed, many muttering to themselves and the dead they see around them. And eventually, they lose themselves to the madness altogether, their visions overcoming their senses and putting them into a comatose state where only their magic keeps them alive."

Thom shivered at the thought. He couldn't fathom something so horrifying. And this was the future Deckard could face.

Comprehending Ilain's dark mood with renewed understanding, Thom's mouth fell ajar. "You've seen it happen?" he said more than he asked.

"I have."

Thom shifted closer, his next question a gentle "Who?"

Ilain took a long, thoughtful breath. "That's not really my story to tell," she whispered.

Thom furrowed his brow, confused at first. Then it became clear. "Auden," he muttered. "That's why he hates it so much. He . . . he lost someone to it?"

It took a long time for Ilain to reply. She raised her head, jade green eyes meeting his with sorrow. "Maura."

Thom waited, breath held in anticipation.

"Twenty-five years ago, Auden was betrothed," Ilain said, the simple start a shock all its own. "Maura was a Night Mage, a magister, like him. They'd fallen in love over their shared interest in using magic to invent practical items for non-magical individuals."

Sympathy welled in Thom, as he could already guess the end of the story. "How—"

He grimaced, wondering if his question would come across as callous. "How is it that Auden found love, yet you didn't?"

Ilain gave him a knowing, if sad, smile. "As a magister, Auden traveled to other Orders," she explained. "They worked together in their studies, which is how he met Maura. As viceMage, I was stuck in the Order of the Flame, training to take the archMage's place as head of the Order upon his retirement."

Thom's eyes went wide. "You were set to run the entire Order of Fire Mages?"

"And Day Mages." Ilain continued with her story, "During the course of their betrothal, Maura's brother—her only family—was killed in the war. She was devastated, and with the influence of her fellow Night Mages, she began to seek out ways to bring him back. She was convinced that restoring the soul to a body was possible. It took her down a dark path."

"And the Deep . . . ?" Thom concluded.

"Yes."

"Did she—" Thom swallowed around the question. "Die?"

Ilain stared at the fire once more. "No. She's locked in the Deep, her mind gone mad while her body lives on in a state of stasis."

Thom drew back. "That's awful."

"It is."

"What—how—I mean, is there some way to heal her?"

A bitter grin pulled on Ilain's lips. "That's what Auden intends to find out."

"I see." Thom scrubbed a hand over his face. What a horrible fate. If that happened to Deckard . . .

Thom shook his head. "Your family has the most tragic past," he said, then set a hand on her elbow. "I'm sorry."

Turning to him, Ilain's smile became genuine. "We've had a happy life too. My parents are well, and they love each other. Vayden found a woman he loves, and they have a daughter, Reyana, who's thirteen and a total spitfire."

Thom laughed with her, imagining a teen version of Ilain getting into all kinds of trouble.

"Reyana lives with my parents," she explained, "as both Vayden and his wife, Isla, work for the Alliance. It keeps them from home a great deal, but Rey understands."

"So what you're saying," Thom leaned closer, his voice lowering conspiratorially, "is that it's just you who's left bereft of love."

Ilain jabbed him in the ribs. "Thank you for the reminder."

Chuckling, Thom draped his arm around Ilain's shoulders as he might with his sister, Meria. "Listen here, Highlady Calder: You've done this to yourself. There's a Warrior out there in the forest who worships the ground those pale feet of yours walk on."

She shuffled her feet under the hem of her skirt.

Thom shook her playfully. "Heavens know what you see in the boy, but if a twenty-year age gap doesn't bother you, why should a simple misunderstanding?"

Ilain shrugged him off. "Ethenn's more mature than you sometimes," she said, then corrected, "*Most* times."

Thom let out a good-natured huff. "Why do you think I like to remind him that he's still a kid?"

Though she continued to smile, she avoided his gaze, remaining silent.

"You could be happy, too, Ilain."

She looked over at him, a curious glint in her eyes. "And what about you? Could you be happy?"

Every part of Thom rebelled at the thought. No. No, he couldn't. Not when he was so inferior. Not when he could never measure up. Not when he was unloved. He couldn't be happy because he wasn't worthy of happiness.

Yet, all his arguments didn't seem to hold the same weight they once did.

A frown tugged at his lips. During his time with Ilain, he'd begun to sense a change in his inner voice. That vile disgust, the chastising insecurity—it had begun to lose its sting. Because with every blow to his self-esteem, he heard her lyrical voice in his head.

"People like you; you're just not willing to see it."

"I'm under no illusions about your worth."

"You, Thom Deckard, have a surprisingly tender heart."

"She'll make it clear that you are the only one she could ever want."

Taking a deep breath, Thom found that things weren't quite as simple as they once felt.

Could he someday have a chance at happiness?

"You know," he replied hopefully, "I think maybe I can. One day."

Ilain reached over to squeeze his hand. "Good."

Thom smiled and returned the gesture. His fingers were still wrapped around Ilain's when Evylin and Ethenn broke through the trees. In the warmer weather, they'd shed their coats for training, and sweat lined their tunics.

"I'm starving. What's for—oh." Evylin stopped. Ethenn also froze at her side.

As one, their gazes dropped to Thom and Ilain's hands.

Immediately, Thom pulled away. "Grouse," he said nervously. "We, uh—yeah, it's the grouse from yesterday. And some barley—the last of the barley, actually. We're kind of out of everything after that."

Ilain sent him a flat look. "Stop being weird," she said, then turned to the Warriors. "It's all ready. The bowls are there."

While Evylin and Ethenn retrieved their meals, they continued to eye Thom and Ilain. Ethenn's jaw was tight, but Evylin's eyes twinkled with something like . . . approval? He didn't like that.

Thom shifted to sit farther away from Ilain. Why was Evylin looking at them like that? She knew the flirtations between them weren't real. And even if she didn't, she shouldn't approve. She should be upset, hurt, maybe even jealous.

"She'll make it clear that you *are the only one she could ever want."*

Thom pushed his jealous thoughts aside for the only one that mattered: Evylin wasn't his. No matter her relationship with Deckard, no matter her reasons for putting distance between them, Ilain was right. If he was ever going to be truly happy with a woman, he had to know without question that she would choose *him* over his brother.

Evylin wasn't that woman.

Ilain wasn't that woman.

The problem was, he didn't know if a woman like that even existed. And he wasn't sure he could live life alone.

Was that the choice? Life alone or life as second best. Either outcome was a brutal reminder of his inferiority. Either was a punch in the gut. Neither was happiness.

Thom looked up from his bowl of roasted grouse and barley cautiously. Ilain had roped the others into a conversation, bringing smiles to both of their faces. Evylin's dimples showed on her cheeks. The last light of day caught in her eyes. Was she happy? Without Deckard, without Hewitt, was it possible that she'd found happiness again?

A treacherous thought crept to the forefront of Thom's mind: Was she happy because she was with *him*?

Thom shook the thought off. Foolish. Vile. Disloyal. He wouldn't entertain the notion any longer. If he intended to follow his new inner voice and become a better man, he couldn't listen to such embittered, covetous thoughts.

"Could you be happy?"

One day, Thom promised himself. One day, he would rise above this deficiency in his soul. He would be a better man, a man worthy of applause and acclaim, a man who held everyone's respect and admiration. And then, on that day, he would be happy.

CHAPTER THIRTY-NINE

29TH OF CHRONOS, 1574

"Two more days," Rafferty said, leaping from his horse. He let out a groan and shook his legs. "Two more days, and then we get a break from this torture."

Deckard grinned, stretching out his own aches and pains from riding for nearly two months straight. Exhaustion like he hadn't experienced since his earliest days in the army worked through his muscles. He was ready for a rest.

Due to their more direct path through the marshes, their trio would arrive in Loches, where they would reunite with the others, with a day or two to spare. That meant they'd get a full day of recovery and rest before journeying the final fourteen miles to the Time Keep. A luxurious prospect that kept the three men determined to maintain their breakneck pace.

Deckard's attention was divided, however, since he was eager to speak with Hewitt. They'd crossed the border into Vaura Reach that morning, easily skirting the guards at the gate with Deckard and Auden's combined power to shroud their small numbers. Within the Reach, there were few travelers and fewer Waulden soldiers, which meant safer travel. And as they were finally free of the marshes' clutches, they could hunt at last.

Prepared with his excuses, Deckard gathered his supplies. "I'll set the traps tonight," he told the men. "You two prepare the camp."

Rafferty let out a sigh of relief. With only their singular tent, caring for the horses, and Auden's sovereignty over the meals, it would mean a leisurely evening for the man. "Sounds good, boss," he said with a salute.

Auden wasn't so easily convinced. "It isn't safe to go out alone," he protested.

"We've discussed this before," Deckard said, keeping his tone calm. "We either leave you alone at the camp, or only one of us goes out to hunt. You told us the Reaches are safer than the kingdom. I'll be fine."

Auden shook his head resolutely, but Deckard cut him off before he could argue. "I won't go far," he promised.

The tension remained in Auden's shoulders, though his expression eased. "You'll stay within earshot?" he asked.

"Yes."

With a sigh, Auden waved him off. But Deckard didn't miss the glint of worry that lingered in his eyes.

Hurrying deeper into the woods surrounding them, Deckard stayed true to his word. He set up the traps quickly, remaining within shouting distance. And once he'd done his duty, he turned to the trees, finding Hewitt already standing before him.

"That Mage gives me a headache with all his bellyaching," Hewitt grumbled.

Deckard sighed. "He's just trying to be cautious. Now," he crossed his arms, glaring at the ghost, "would you mind telling me exactly when you learned that my brother had designs on my wife?"

"That's the least of your concerns," Hewitt said dismissively. "What you should be focused on is how Evylin will respond when he says something to her."

Though he didn't appreciate the redirection, Deckard allowed the momentary distraction. "Rafferty's sure he won't say anything."

"Rafferty's wrong."

"How do you know?"

"Because I know your brother," Hewitt said. "Because I'm also the second son who never measured up."

Deckard's brows pinched together. "You were a military legend."

"I was a screwup." Hewitt raised his bushy eyebrows. "My entire life, I lived in the shadow of my older brother. He was the clever one, the charming one. People always liked him best. *I* was the disaster, the Glaas boy who got into fights and couldn't control his temper. It wasn't until I was conscripted that I excelled at anything."

Deckard wondered if these facets of his history were due to his abilities as a Warrior.

Hewitt took a step forward. "I understand your brother because I *was* your brother. He will say something because he's desperate to prove himself—to himself and you."

"How would—" Deckard shook his head. However Thom justified his actions didn't matter. He chose to ask the question the ghost would care to answer instead. "If you're right, if he says something, what impact do you imagine that will have on my relationship with Evylin?"

Hewitt tugged on his beard, his gaze drifting toward the trees in thought. "There's a chance it will be positive," he mused. "Evylin is afraid of intimacy. Discovering that other men might have designs on her may push her back into your arms."

A swell of hope rose in Deckard, and he immediately quashed it. Wishing for Thom to reveal his feelings only for the sake of forcing Evylin's return to him was almost as dishonorable as Thom making overtures to his sister-in-law in the first place.

"However," Hewitt continued, "the greater odds lie in favor of his profession driving her farther away from you. She won't want to come between the two of you. The guilt of it may further convince her to part with you, no matter her feelings."

Deckard pressed his lips together. "I've worried about that."

"And, of course," Hewitt added, "there's a chance that she'll be so overwhelmed by both your and your brother's attentions that she chooses to abandon this whole quest and run home on her own."

Deckard frowned. "You don't really believe she'll do that, do you?"

Hewitt shrugged, but Deckard could see in the relaxed posture of his mouth that the man wasn't truly worried by that eventuality.

In the fading evening light, Deckard studied Hewitt carefully. His steely eyes held the same brooding slant as Evylin's. They shared the same brown hair, though hers was softer and cooler in tone, whereas Hewitt's was darker and richer. Their dispositions were similar, too: stubborn, clever, and brutally honest. But Hewitt carried a darkness with him, one that harbored secrets. His demeanor was closed off and unfriendly, allowing him to wield people and their vulnerabilities like a weapon.

A man as skilled at manipulation as Hewitt didn't miss a thing. He crafted calculating plans, exploiting others to obtain the ends he needed for success. It was what any good officer learned to do. Identify the desires of your men and utilize them to accomplish the task at hand.

While plotting Evylin's escape from Whickam Village, Hewitt wouldn't have failed to take into account every last opportunity. He would have considered both Deckard and Thom with equity. And just as he'd discerned Deckard's deepest-held secrets and dreams, he would have recognized Thom's as well.

"How long have you known?" Deckard asked, sure of the answer.

Hewitt lifted his chin. "Known what?"

Deckard held his stare, unflinching.

The ghost drew back his shoulder, bearing up to his full, monstrous height. Anyone who hadn't spent so much time in his company might find the posture threatening. Deckard just found it theatrical.

"From the beginning," Hewitt said, confirming Deckard's suspicion. "From the moment I saw you and your brother in my shop. I noticed your attention to her at dinner the previous evening, and I was assured of your regard by the way you spoke to her. It irked me, but unfortunately, it pleased her. A fact your brother didn't fail to recognize either."

Deckard nodded in understanding, but Hewitt kept speaking. "I saw the decision in his eyes then. The moment Evylin smiled at you, when you made her laugh, Thom noticed. And I watched his expression change."

"What do—?"

"Your regard for one another is the only reason Thom felt anything," Hewitt said. "He doesn't love her. He's jealous of your love for one another."

Deckard's brow pinched. "You mean to tell me that his feelings aren't even real? That they're born of competition with me rather than true affection for her?"

"That's precisely what I'm saying."

Deckard ran a hand through his hair.

"It's one of the many reasons I would never have allowed him to marry her," Hewitt said. "While I personally like him better than you, it's only because you remind me of my own brother: perfect, charming, and false."

Though Deckard bristled, Hewitt raised a hand. "I've learned that your intentions are far more honorable than my brother's, but I'll thank you to keep your objections to yourself. You lie—it's your greatest failing and what makes you human. While you pretend to be high, mighty, and unfailingly good, *I* see the truth: You're as selfish as the rest of us."

Taking a deep breath, Deckard held back his arguments. He wasn't selfish. At every turn, he sacrificed for the greater good, and most often, for Evylin's good. He knew that, and he didn't need to convince Hewitt to confirm the truth.

"What were your other reasons?" Deckard asked, returning to the matter at hand.

Hewitt gave a terse grunt. "Most importantly, Evylin didn't want him. A fact I made him aware of when he lamented his woes to me."

A seething anger wrapped around Deckard's chest at the revelation. "He told you?"

"Everything," Hewitt confirmed, then scoffed. "And he had the gall to ask why I didn't choose him."

"What did you tell him?" Deckard asked, sympathy and satisfaction at war within him.

Hewitt hesitated. "I'll be honest, I was weak. As I said, I saw myself in him, and I felt pity for the man I used to be. Thus, I told him the easiest truth to bear: He wasn't the one she wanted."

Deckard stared, open-mouthed and amazed that *that* was the easiest truth.

"Had I been wise enough," Hewitt's thick brow descended heavily, "I would have given him the whole truth. Had Evylin not chosen you, had she been ambivalent or even preferred Thom, I still wouldn't have allowed it."

Deckard took a step back at the ferocity in Hewitt's glare. The ghost pointed at the trees as though accusing Thom from afar. "He's not man enough for my Evie. His self-conceit and arrogance disqualify him. Everything that makes him different from you, every last distinction, is the very reason I would never choose him. He couldn't be the man she wanted; he couldn't be worthy of her love. Because *you* are the only one who can love her the way she deserves—the way she *needs*."

The weight of the sentiment felt equal parts fulfilling and damning. Deckard desperately wished that Hewitt was right. He wanted to be that man for Evylin. Yet, he heard her voice in his head, her declaration, *"You can't make me happy."*

"Had I been strong enough," Hewitt growled, drawing Deckard's attention once again, "I would have told your brother that if he ever tried to take her from you, he would only prove his worthlessness, and I would personally see the rest of his days made a living hell for ruining her happiness."

Deckard flinched. Hearing the rage in Hewitt's voice made his own anger feel small, trivial, and insufficient. Yes, he was hurt. Yes, he wanted to rail at his brother. His basest instincts urged him to return to the days of their youth, when conflicts were resolved with fists. However, in the wake of Hewitt's violent fury, Deckard found his passions tempered. He'd lost the ability to hold resentment toward Thom long ago. This was just one more wound in their long-scarred relationship.

And in truth, Deckard's guilt outweighed his anger. He'd known of his brother's infatuation as Hewitt had, and he'd done nothing to dissuade Thom. He hadn't bothered to confront or resolve the hurt between them. In the end, Thom's pursuit of Evylin was just as much Deckard's fault as his brother's.

"It's good you didn't tell him those things," he said weakly. "It would have only made him try harder to prove himself."

Hewitt narrowed his gaze, but Deckard continued before the ghost could comment on his dejected mood. "What do I do now?" he asked. "We're days away from reuniting, but we've no idea if Thom's said a word or not. How do we prepare for that? What's even the point if Evylin doesn't want—?"

"So this is what you've been doing," a voice interrupted.

Deckard whirled around, finding Auden standing a handful of paces away. His dark brown coat blended with the trees while his red hair shone like a flare in the final, lingering light of dusk. He stepped into the clearing, expression taut. "Dealing with the dead?" he concluded.

Deckard's heart seized.

Hewitt heaved an annoyed sigh. "This ought to be good," he muttered.

"You're going to get us killed," Auden spat, eyes locked on Deckard. "Ilain told me— she warned me that you were interested in ghosts, but she said not to worry. She was so sure you wouldn't go back on your word, yet here you are."

Deckard opened his mouth to apologize but paused. He'd kept Hewitt with him constantly over the last two weeks. Only now, Auden had discovered his duplicity. If Auden hadn't seen Hewitt during their travels, could he now? Did he have any proof aside from Deckard's one-sided conversation?

Choosing to test the boundaries of his magic, Deckard furrowed his brow intentionally. "What are you talking about?" he asked in incredulity.

"Don't play the fool." Auden gestured vaguely in Hewitt's direction. "I can see Hewitt right there."

The ghost stepped around Deckard. "Can you hear me as well?"

Deckard waited for Auden's reply.

There was none.

Hewitt scoffed. "Apparently not."

"Explain yourself," Auden demanded in the prolonged silence hanging between the living men.

Deckard hesitated a moment longer. Auden's inability to hear Hewitt brought into question his claim that he could see him as well. After all, if the ghost was visible, Auden would have seen Hewitt's lips moving as he spoke.

For a moment, Deckard considered continuing to deny the ghost's presence. But by the fury in Auden's glare, he knew the Mage wouldn't let it go.

Raising a placating hand, Deckard tried to play the conversation to his advantage. "All right, I admit it, I summoned Hewitt. But it was long before I made that promise to Ilain. Before I knew I was a Mage at all."

"Before—" Auden gaped at him, terror evident in his dark green gaze. "That's not possible. No one can use magic without knowledge, without training."

That caused a stir of worry within Deckard. From the moment he'd discovered his connection to the Mages' power, its force within him had been stronger than he'd learned should be possible. Summoning a ghost unintentionally, healing rapidly, calling forth those crystalline clouds with barely a thought. None of that was normal, according to the Calders. And it only served to deepen his apprehension toward the path of magic.

Deckard ignored his concerns, focusing on the matter at hand. "I swear, it wasn't intentional. Had I known. . . ."

Auden stepped closer, unwilling to hear him out. "Release him," he ordered.

Without thought, Deckard said, "No."

Shock and fear blended in Auden's expression, causing a spike of anxiety in Deckard too.

"I'm not going anywhere," Hewitt said, his voice a low rumble in Deckard's ears.

Deckard gave the ghost a reassuring glance, unable to promise his agreement any other way. Regardless of Auden's worries or the threat of madness, Deckard couldn't let Hewitt go. Not until Hewitt could speak with Evylin.

"This magic isn't safe, Jonn." A wild look filled Auden's eyes, his voice tremulous. "You're playing with death. Every Mage who's started down this path has lost their mind to the Deep. Often at the expense of innocent lives as well."

The warning sent a chill down Deckard's spine.

"He's bluffing," Hewitt said, pacing behind Deckard. "He doesn't know this magic or you. And I won't let you go mad."

Slowly and calmly, Deckard continued his act for Auden. "I'm sorry, and I'm aware of the risks. It's just that I don't know how I summoned him. I wouldn't begin to know how to release him."

Auden hesitated, clearly unsure of the process himself. "I'll walk you through it," he offered. "But you have to mean it, Jonn."

Deckard tightened his jaw. He couldn't mean it. Not when he didn't want to let Hewitt go.

"Listen to me," Hewitt said. "We can play him. He clearly can't see or hear me. As he hasn't been aware of me this whole time, he evidently can't sense me either."

Auden's gaze flittered from Deckard's face to the space behind him. In the extended silence, it appeared that the Mage had perceived that Deckard was listening to Hewitt. "What is he saying?" he asked nervously.

"Nothing." Deckard shook his head. "He doesn't want to go."

"They never do," Auden said. "Ghosts are unnatural, Jonn. They cling to the living, haunting them. Their presence ushers in the Deep."

Auden continued trying to convince Deckard as Hewitt spoke again. "Let him think that you'll release me," the ghost said. "He won't know the difference."

Deckard hesitated. Though he wanted to keep Hewitt with him, he couldn't deny the impact of Auden's warning. Night magic was too dangerous to play games with. And he'd already proven weak under its allure.

"What if he's right?" Deckard asked the ghost, no longer bothering to hide his presence. "I can't take care of Evylin if I go mad."

Hewitt glared at him. "I won't let you," he pronounced again, every word intense and determined. "I won't let anything come between Evylin and her happiness. And *you* are the only one who can give her that."

"Jonn, don't listen to him," Auden warned, seeing the consideration in Deckard's face. "He'll only lead you deeper into the madness."

Deckard met the Mage's eyes as Hewitt spoke again. "You can't get her back if you send me away."

Swallowing past the tightness of his throat, Deckard dropped his gaze to the dirt. "I know," he said, letting Auden believe he was speaking to him.

"You'll let him go then?" Auden asked.

"Yes," Deckard lied.

"Good," Auden and Hewitt said at the same time.

"Now," Hewitt continued, "convince him."

Deckard took an intentionally shaky breath. "How do I—how do I let him go?" he asked.

Auden reached out to set a hand on his shoulder. "Connect with Night, feel his presence, and release him," he instructed. "But remember, you have to mean it."

With a shake of his head, Deckard grimaced. "He's fighting me. I don't know if I'm strong enough."

Auden nodded as though it was expected. "He can't stop the magic. You are the one with the power. Will it, and he'll be gone."

Deckard closed his eyes, pretending to be forlorn. How easily Auden had fallen for his ruse. How readily he believed Deckard.

Shame welled within him. Hewitt was right; he really was a liar.

With a deep breath in and then out, Deckard raised his chin. "Goodbye, Hewitt," he murmured. "I release you to your rest."

Hewitt snorted. "That's a bit melodramatic, don't you think?"

Auden didn't show any signs of doubt that Deckard was following through with his instructions.

Deckard kept to his role. He tightened his jaw, clenched his fists, sighed, and then reached for the smallest fragment of his magic. Heat crept along his skin, and he grabbed hold, discharging the smallest innocuous swell of power.

He met Auden's stare. "It's done," he said tiredly. "I'm sorry, I. . . ." He let the apology hang, affecting his expression with regret.

Hewitt shook his head, chuckling. "You're a bloody brilliant actor."

Refusing to let the guilt settle, Deckard mentally corrected the statement: He was, unfortunately, just a skilled liar.

And Auden seemed to have bought the ruse. He squeezed Deckard's shoulder. "I can feel it too," he said.

Deckard almost rolled his eyes, the urge informing him that he'd been spending too much time with Rafferty and his flippant behavior.

"You did well," Auden said, dropping his hand. "I know it wasn't easy."

Turning his eyes down once more, Deckard tried to feel remorse for his falsehoods. However, he couldn't find regret within him. Was this the first step toward damnation? Was he slowly walking toward the Deep, all for the sake of securing Evylin's love?

Somehow, he couldn't bring himself to care.

"I'm sorry," he said again, meaning it but not for the reason Auden thought.

Auden gave him an understanding smile. "Let's go back to camp."

Deckard nodded. But as the Mage turned and started the short trek back, Deckard looked to his side. Hewitt stood there, his chin dipped in a proud nod. "We're almost there, Deckard," he said. "Just a few more days, and then I'll talk to our girl."

Despite his untested magic, Deckard silently swore to the ghost that he'd hold up his end of the bargain. Then he followed Auden back to camp.

CHAPTER FORTY

29TH OF CHRONOS, 1574

A restless energy settled over Evylin when she woke that morning. Tomorrow, they would cross the border into Vaura Reach. Two days after that, they'd reunite with their team and head for the Time Keep.

Evylin's breath caught alongside her thoughts every time they drifted to the impending future. Three days. Only three more days until she saw him.

Her stomach churned. What would that reunion look like? Would Deckard be glad to see her? Or in the two weeks they'd been apart, would his heart have hardened from her rejection? Moreover, how would she react to him? Despite her lackluster farewell, her body and mind constantly betrayed her in their time apart. She ached for his presence in a way she never thought she could. Would she be able to hold strong to her convictions? Or would she be so desperate for his embrace that she abandoned all her scruples?

Evylin's ruminations bound her like the sellswords in Dunneshead. As distracted as the thoughts made her, she could hardly carry on a conversation. Her companions noticed, likely presuming it to be her usual distaste for mornings, and they left her to her introspection once they were on the road. She didn't know whether to feel grateful for or irritated by her solitude. The uncontrolled thoughts frightened her, stirring up feelings she wasn't ready to face.

Eventually, Evylin forced herself to join the chatter. The past two weeks had taught her all she needed to know: She was too attached to Deckard. Her present thoughts were proof enough. If she felt this much for him already, she couldn't return to the relationship they'd previously shared. She could no longer entertain yearning and wistful thoughts about their reunion. What came in three days would come. For now, she needed to shore up her resolve.

They rode through the final descent of the mountain pass into the thick forest on the outskirts of Vaura Reach. In the distance, the stone wall of the border stretched like a belt, weaving in and out of the trees. They only saw glimpses of it as they journeyed deeper into the forest. Nearing the northwestern parts of Wauld, the foliage grew thicker once more.

As a band of four, it seemed their plan to split their party had done its job. They'd passed many travelers through the moors and a handful of others through the mountain pass, and yet they hadn't encountered a single obstacle. Evylin wondered how Deckard, Rafferty, and Auden had fared. Was their journey as fortuitous? Then she feared they hadn't made it at all.

The thought prompted Evylin to turn to Ilain. "Do you think the others have made it to their destination yet?" she asked as casually as she could.

Ilain either didn't recognize her anxiety or she chose to ignore it. "No. Though they should only be a day or so away by now."

Thom readily jumped into the conversation. "So you think they crossed the border already?" he asked, his tone reflecting nearly as much agitation as Evylin felt.

"Oh, yes," Ilain said. "They shouldn't have had any problems given Jonn's abilities in conjunction with Auden's."

Evylin and Thom exchanged a look. Though she hadn't allowed herself to admit to sharing his concerns when he'd spoken to her about Deckard's magic, Evylin's heart squeezed at the thought. Thom was right; Deckard would not take well to the death and destruction his magic wrought, and she feared that he would succumb to the Deep simply to relieve his conscience in the end.

Worse, she feared that her rejection might have taken his last vestige of hope, his last reason to cling to sanity.

"I thought you said he might not be a Night Mage," Evylin said to Ilain.

"He might not be," the highlady confirmed, then gave a flippant wave of her hand. "Whatever kind of Mage he is, he *does* have a strong connection to Night." She paused and gave a thoughtful shrug. "Stronger than I've seen in a long time."

That news made Evylin feel worse.

"But you're sure they made it?" Ethenn asked, joining the conversation.

Ilain gave a slow, confident nod. "Absolutely. If they hadn't, I would feel it." She set a hand to her chest. "Here."

Brushing a finger over her rings, Evylin couldn't help wondering if she'd feel it too.

If Deckard were in danger, if his life was threatened or taken, would she know? Or would she arrive at their rendezvous to discover that she'd been right when she'd disparaged their relationship: He was gone, and they'd had no connection at all?

They arrived at their final stop within the Waulden kingdom on the outskirts of a large town roughly twelve miles from the border. To help improve their speed on the following days within Vaura Reach, Evylin suggested she and Ethenn take the evening off from training so they could replenish their stores. Ilain would preserve what they wouldn't eat that night, making dried rations of their catch with Fire and Day.

Evylin chose to stay with Ilain to prepare the camp; her thoughts were too distracted to focus on the task of hunting. The women cared for the horses, pitched both tents, prepared the fire, and readied their tools for butchering the catch. Ilain supplied a ready and easy conversation that helped Evylin momentarily forget her worries. She told her about the many fairy tales the Highloft Moors had inspired, her childhood home filled with legends and ghost stories.

"We have some similar stories in Ephria," Evylin noted. "Though they aren't quite as magical. They're all compiled in a book called *Fables of the Ram*. It's where many of our childhood tales are found."

Ilain nodded. "We have something similar here too. Though we call it *Fables of the Eight*. I believe Ephren altered the tales, replacing the magical influences with animals or elements."

Evylin paused in brushing down her horse. "Really? Huh." She pursed her lips. "What about *The Traveler and the Rook*? Do you know of that?"

"*The Traveler and the Mage*," Ilain corrected. "It's the chronicles of Allund's legends."

Intrigued to hear the Wauldeners grew up with a magical version of her and Ryen's favored tales, Evylin asked, "Does your version include Euon Sergus and Iona the Worthy?"

"Mm-hm." Ilain crossed her arms haughtily. "Warrior and Mage."

Evylin's eyes went wide. "Sergus was a Warrior?"

"And Iona was a Terrae Mage."

"Really?" Evylin repeated with an amused gasp. "Jonn'll be disappointed."

"Why's that?"

"He adores Sergus. It's his grandest desire to be just like him. Turns out, he's Sergus's opposite."

Ilain held up a forestalling finger. "He's Sergus's balance. Or at least, the male equivalent. Technically, *I'm* Sergus's true balance."

Averting her gaze, Evylin went back to brushing her horse. "Because of Bonding?" she asked quietly.

"If you want to know about Bonding," Ilain said calmly, "all you have to do is ask."

Evylin chewed on her lip. Did she want to know? Could it do any good? She wasn't going to stay with Deckard, regardless of how their reunion went. She *couldn't* stay with Deckard. But as a female Warrior, her existence so rare and so important, wouldn't it be wise to learn what made her so valuable? Perhaps the knowledge could help save her from Blount's designs in the future. . . .

The crunch and snap of brush alerted them to Thom and Ethenn's return. The men appeared in the trees, postures tense and demeanors brusque as they whispered furiously at one another. Evylin watched them carefully as Thom gave one final retort and Ethenn jerked the brace of hare from his grip.

Ilain sent Evylin a worried glance, then put away her sketching. Unceremoniously, Ethenn dropped next to the butchering supplies at the opposite end from the highlady. He gruffly went about his work, ignoring all of them, his face flushed a deep crimson.

Thom huffed and took a seat next to Ilain. The woman looked at him keenly. "What have you done to Ethenn?" she asked.

Though his back remained rigid, Thom smirked. He slid his arm around Ilain. "Nothing, milady," he said dramatically. "Little Loxley's just concerned he'll miss his shot." He winked and then added, "You know, in the Time Keep, with all those Shades."

Ilain raised her brow. "He's never been off before."

Thom tugged Ilain closer to his side. "Oh, I don't know," he said slyly. "Seems he has recently."

Evylin frowned, unsure of what precise game Thom was playing. Ethenn kept his head down, though his neck was almost as red as a ruby, and he cut up the rabbit violently, his fury notable but still maintaining his precision.

Ilain gave Thom a disparaging look, then shoved him away, extricating herself from his embrace. She got up and moved to join Ethenn. "Here," she said, holding out a hand. "Let me help."

"I'm fine," Ethenn muttered.

"Yes, I can see that," Ilain retorted. "Now, give me a bloody knife, and let me help."

Ethenn hesitated, then slipped a small dagger from his belt. He handed it to her without a single glance in her direction.

Thom snorted, then stood. He moved to Evylin's side, where she stood next to the horses, gesturing to the brush in her hand. "Want help?" he asked.

Warily, Evylin eyed him. After Ethenn's warning, she'd done as he suggested, handling her relationship with Thom carefully. But after seeing Thom and Ilain holding hands yesterday, she'd been assured that, whatever past interest he'd held, he had clearly moved on. Whether or not the pair's flirtations had begun falsely, it was clear they'd grown to mean more. Perhaps Ethenn had noticed it too. And maybe the young man's jealousy had caused the argument between them.

Evylin remembered Ethenn's warning at the start of their small band's journey. *"I've gone this long without breaking before. Inevitably, I snap."*

She wondered if, after all this time, Ethenn's anger had grown too hot.

Turning back to Thom, Evylin handed him the brush. "Your horse is the only one left," she said. "I'll happily let you care for her yourself."

Thom gave her a half-grin, then shifted to follow her directive.

Evylin glanced at Ilain and Ethenn once more. They worked in silence; she made steady, graceful cuts, while he moved with a feverish, disgruntled pace.

Evylin nudged Thom, then tipped her chin in the pair's direction. "What's that about?" she asked.

Without looking, Thom shrugged. "The kid's sulking."

"About what?"

"What do boys ever pout about, Evie?"

"I wouldn't know."

He gave her a pointed look.

Evylin raised an eyebrow in expectation.

Thom sighed and turned back to brush his horse. "He's jealous of my relationship with Ilain," he said.

Evylin blinked. Had Thom just admitted to having a relationship with Ilain? She wasn't sure whether to smile or frown. "So you argued because he's jealous?" she asked.

Thom's jaw tightened. "Yes."

The way he said it struck Evylin as false, but she couldn't see a reason for him to lie. "I see." She sighed, shifting away from the horses. "Maybe try to patch it up, all right? We don't have time for petty misunderstandings."

Thom continued to stare at his horse's brown coat. "Yeah, all right."

However, the evening didn't improve. Ilain and Evylin carried the entire conversation, speculating on the Time Keep and discussing their return journey to Ephria, the Calders' history with the Alliance, and other empty subjects. While Thom chimed in every so often, Ethenn sat in total silence. Evylin thought she could see the young man attempting to hold in his anger, reeling it back so that he maintained control. She worried about what would happen if he couldn't manage his rage as they went into another battle at the Time Keep.

"Inevitably, I snap."

And then someone dies, he'd added.

Evylin bit her lip as she chewed on her meal. She grimaced at the sharp jab of pain, the faintest tinge of blood seeping into the hare. She sucked on the cut, her mind lost to her thoughts. Could she help Ethenn find a way to channel that temper of his through his magic? Or would his warning come true?

Before dinner ended, Ethenn rose and offered the remainder of his meal to Evylin. She accepted it, and then he turned, muttering about the need for a walk. They all watched as he disappeared into the shadowed trees.

Though Evylin thought she should have either stopped him or gone with him, she couldn't bring herself to intrude. She could see his need for space and sense his desperation to cobble together some semblance of control over the temper simmering within him. She felt a similar need burgeoning within herself.

The moons glimmered in the night, their faces mostly visible. Stars beamed in the amethyst-hued night sky like the facets of the Night Relic. Evylin could almost see the crystalline refraction of Deckard's power in the vastness of its expanse.

Finally, Ethenn returned but remained quiet as he bedded down. Thom sat up with Evylin and Ilain for a short while longer, discussing their plans to slip past the border the next afternoon. With the Night Relic plus the strength of Evylin and Ethenn's magic to assist her, Ilain could shroud all four of them. As long as they moved swiftly and carefully, they would have no problem passing the guards.

"And what will we do if there's another ambush when we leave the Keep?" Thom asked.

Evylin turned to Ilain, worried about the same thing. The highlady stared into the low-burning fire, its golden-orange light warming her pale skin. "We'll be ready this time," she said. "The Time Mages are unlikely to side with Blount, especially after they hear of the slaughter of the Order of the Wind. They prefer to stay neutral, allied to the resource of time alone. I doubt we'll face an attack from them. But that doesn't mean Blount hasn't sent others to take us out.

"We'll do the same as we did in Sutterlund Reach," Ilain continued. "We'll scout the area and ensure there are no ambushes awaiting us. Then we'll get the Time Relic, make our run for the border, and . . ."

Evylin heard the answer in Ilain's hesitance. "We'll take the risk," she said for the Mage, speaking the ominous truth. "No matter what—whether we live or die—we have to risk getting the Relics and hope to be as prepared as we can."

"Will we split up again?" Thom asked. "If they're looking to ambush seven travelers, that will mean we need to confuse them, right?"

Evylin nodded. "I think we should split our numbers even more, at least until we're out of the Reach. Maybe Ilain and Ethenn go together, then Auden and Jonn, and then you, me, and Rafferty."

"Your face is on the writ," Ilain reminded. "You and I can travel together so that I can shroud you. Ethenn can go with the other two."

"Glad to be one of the other two," Thom muttered, then shook his head. "I'll go with Jonn. He's my brother. I—I'll go with him."

"And after," Ilain said in a tone that brooked no arguments, "we will all meet and ride back to Verlund Reach together. I'm done with this separation."

Though Evylin wanted to protest, she, too, felt the exhaustion of being separated from the others. From Deckard.

Thom sighed and bid them both a goodnight, then left the women to the first watch. He lay at the far end of the tent, keeping as much distance between him and Ethenn as possible. Evylin caught the barest shift of Ethenn's form, marking his listening ear during their conversation. She wondered what his thoughts were on their plan. Was he feeling as worried about its failings as she was?

Evylin dropped her gaze, finding her fingers on her rings. She frowned. She hadn't even realized she'd been tugging on them. Her fingertips traced the ivy etched into the simple silver band Hewitt made for her. Then they grazed the onyx stones embedded in the platinum band from Deckard. Her nervous tic, tugging on the rings, had started the day after Deckard had given her his ring. She'd never had a piece of jewelry so fine, and she had an irrational fear that she'd misplace it.

Over time, she found herself worrying at the ring out of habit. Checking to ensure its placement on her finger gave her the strangest sense of comfort. It was as though the mere thought of Deckard's ring could soothe her.

Evylin sucked in her bottom lip. The firelight caught in the onyx stones, glimmering in the facets with a variegated shine. She'd often wondered why Deckard chose it. Most Whickam Village men couldn't afford such fancy rings, procuring the simpler, etched rings from Hewitt or other smiths. The more affluent men in Trollenston bought their fiancées finer rings, like this one, but they always bore bright, sparkling gemstones, like the ones Ilain wore. Evylin never thought she'd want something so gaudy, knowing it would get in the way of her swordplay. But this ring . . .

"It felt right," Deckard had said.

How? He'd known her for mere days when he'd purchased it. They hardly knew how to carry on a conversation. Yet, he'd chosen this elegant, resplendent ring that had proven no more an impediment to her swordplay than Hewitt's. Somehow, Deckard had found the perfect ring based solely on an inner knowing.

Evylin's fingers tightened on the ring, a sudden worry fixed in her mind. She'd asked for an annulment. Their marriage would be dissolved, and this ring would hold no more meaning. Would he expect her to return it? Her heart raced at the thought. She didn't want to give it back. It would make her decision too real, too final.

"Ilain," Evylin whispered without thought.

Beside her, Ilain shifted. "Yes?"

Desperate for some distraction from her thoughts, Evylin turned to the woman. She seized the first topic that came to mind. "If Bonding is so important to you, why haven't you? Bonded with someone, I mean."

Ilain gave her a wry grin, raspy voice nearly silent in the night. "There are many reasons. Most importantly, I haven't found the right man."

"But you said that it wouldn't matter whom you Bonded with." Evylin drew her knees up, embracing her legs. "That the magic would make you fall in love with him."

Ilain gave a thin chuckle. "*Make* is a violent word. No, it doesn't *make* you love each other. Bonding is a connection of souls. You fall in love with your partner because you understand them in the deepest, most intimate way. You feel what they feel. And when you're that intricately tied to someone else, you can't help but love them."

"Oh," Evylin breathed.

Ilain smiled. "It's wise to be selective in choosing such a partner. Just because you share a connected soul doesn't mean you change as an individual. You are still you, and he is still him. Personality differences, internal struggles, insecurities, temperaments, and beliefs—these things don't change. And like a marriage, you want to be sure you can live happily with the one you love."

"I see," Evylin said, and she did. It was one of the many reasons she hadn't married a man from the village or town years ago. Her personality and her desires didn't match those of the men she knew. And she could never be happy in a stifled life.

"I'm lucky, though," Ilain said, "being a woman. Men are more prevalent in magic. I believe I mentioned that to you? And that makes me a commodity. While they all vie for my attention, I have my pick."

"That doesn't make you feel like a prize to be won?"

"Why, Evylin," Ilain set a hand to her chest with a mocking flair, "I *am* a prize. Any man who isn't willing to fight for my heart isn't worth my time."

Evylin couldn't help smiling. "Ah, yes. You have a heart deserving of warfare."

They shared a soft, low laugh.

"Does Jonn make you feel that way?" Ilain asked, her gaze alight with unexpected eagerness. "Does he make you feel prized? As though he would fight an entire nation to win your heart?"

Smile gone, Evylin averted her gaze. She stared into the fire, telling herself the smoke was what caused her vision to blur. "Yes," she whispered. "Yes, he does."

"I thought so," Ilain said. "He's always so aware of you. It's as though you give him purpose."

Evylin didn't like the turn of the conversation. She'd spoken to Ilain to avoid thinking of her husband, not to dwell upon his bountiful merits.

Clearing her throat quietly, Evylin attempted to deflect. "I have to say," she quipped lightly, "there is another man who made me feel even more sought after."

Ilain's nose wrinkled. "Truly?"

"Mm. No man's attention could hope to match that of Prince Ephren's."

Ilain snorted. "Caspar?"

Evylin's gaze snapped to hers. "You know the crown prince of Ephria by name?"

"Oh, indeed," she said, surveying her glittering rings haughtily. "He didn't take much to me, though. I think I made him nervous."

"I think you make most men nervous."

Ilain sighed dramatically. "Such is my lot. But then, I would say the same of you, and you found Jonn, so perhaps there's hope for me yet."

The return to Deckard lodged a lump in Evylin's throat. Her reaction agitated her even more than Ilain's incessant need to bring him up. "It's not like that between us, Ilain," she said firmly. "I know you weren't there, but—"

"But you told the others that you and Jonn married for convenience," Ilain said, completing the recounting for her.

Evylin gaped at her. "How did you—?"

"Auden left me a note."

"Oh."

"Mm-hm. I'm aware of your nonsensical fabrication," she said with a hint of irritation. "And I understand that you're grieving. What I'm confused by is your seeming ignorance of how deeply you two love one another."

"We don't—" Evylin interrupted herself this time. She took a stuttering breath, her body trembling in the cold breeze of the night. "It isn't like that."

"It is," Ilain said flatly. "Why deny it?"

"I don't love him," Evylin whispered vehemently.

"Of course, you do. We can all see it."

"I don't."

"You can't convince me of that," Ilain hissed sharply.

Evylin whirled to face her. "I asked Jonn for an annulment," she admitted. "Do you believe me now?"

Ilain stared at her, emotionless. "I'm sorry," she whispered. "I don't think I understood you."

Evylin held her steady glare. "I think you did."

The woman's mouth dropped open. "Why would you do that? Hold on." She held up a hand. "*Can* you do that? I'm not familiar with Ephrian laws, but in Wauld, an annulment is only possible if the marriage isn't consummated."

"It's the same in Ephria."

Ilain's face contorted in bafflement. "You haven't—?"

"No."

"Well," Ilain sat back, staring into the night wide-eyed, "put me on a mountain and call me a nanny. I could have sworn . . ." She blew out a bemused breath and turned back to Evylin. "Regardless, why would you want to annul your marriage?"

Evylin drew her knees tighter to her chest. "Because I have to."

"Nonsense. There are only two reasons that would be necessary. First, if he were a deplorable wretch. And as this is Colonel Jonn Deckard we're discussing, that's out of the question. Second would be if you didn't love him."

She raised her hand when Evylin began to protest. "You're lying to the wrong person, Evylin."

"Why won't you believe me?" Evylin asked, incredulous.

Ilain wore a firm, perturbed expression. "I am forty-three," she whispered sharply. "I have spent my entire life preparing to help lead a rebellion to success and to take my place in its government afterward. Throughout all that time, I have waited, hoping to find a Warrior who loves me and whom I love in return."

Ilain's fingers curled around her skirt as she leaned closer to Evylin. "I'm looking for one in more than a million," she said. "And by some miracle, you found that. You found your perfect match, a man who's caring, devoted, loving, and a bloody Mage. It's as though he were designed for you. So don't you dare tell me you don't love him. Because you two are the only hope I have left."

A halting breath slipped out of Evylin. She didn't know what to say. A part of her latched onto Ilain's words, heartened by the thought of Deckard being her one-in-a-million match. The other part recoiled, shrinking back like a startled wolf, creeping back into its dark den.

Evylin felt sympathy for Ilain. Their predicament was similar, yes. Yet, it was drastically different in so many other ways.

"I'm sorry," Evylin said, her words entirely genuine. "But you don't understand."

"Then please," Ilain said, her voice taut, "enlighten me."

Meeting Ilain's fierce jade green gaze, Evylin chewed on her lip. Never before had she considered explaining herself. Who could begin to understand the pain that lived in her body, tearing every inch of her heart to pieces? How could she describe the devastation that remained in the wake of her loss? Who would she trust with such vulnerability?

But Evylin was desperate. She'd gone so long without relief, holding back the tide of sorrow and agony that threatened to drown her. Every joke, every sarcastic remark hid the brokenness she felt. She wasn't winning the battle with the tide any longer. She *was* drowning, and she needed someone to grab her hand and pull her back to the surface for a breath of air.

"I was thirteen," Evylin whispered. "And he left me."

Ilain's fierce expression softened, her lips parting in surprise.

Evylin didn't bother fighting the tears. *Let them come,* she thought. Let Ilain see the damage left on her soul, the scars she bore. Let the woman know *why* Evylin couldn't withstand the suffering of another wound upon her heart.

"You have Auden," Evylin said, voice like a wraith, insubstantial and haunting. "I had Ryen."

"Your brother?" Ilain asked gently.

Evylin's head gave the smallest shake. "In all but parentage. He was Hewitt's son."

A fresh understanding dawned in Ilain's gaze.

"Ryen was like the sun," Evylin said with a fractured smile. She could feel the tears on her face, but she wasn't sure when they'd first fallen. "He was clever and funny, and he brought life everywhere he went. I remember . . . I remember days when I felt lonely or left out because the other girls didn't like me. Ryen would always say, 'They don't know what they're missing, Kit.'"

Evylin smiled, remembering the nickname. "He called me Kit because I wrinkled my nose whenever I was annoyed, like a baby badger, he claimed." She let out a thin laugh at the thought. Then she furrowed her brow. "I don't know if I do that anymore."

Ilain shook her head. "I haven't noticed."

"Hm." Evylin stared at her hands. "Anyway, Ryen was always there. We would go out and play in the fields surrounding the village, and he would invent all these wonderful adventures. We'd fight off dragons or save a princess. Sometimes, we'd play in the creek, pretending to sail across the sea. He wanted to be a pirate."

They shared a smile.

Evylin took a deep breath. "Ryen was everything. We had so many dreams together, so many . . . plans. We were going to explore the whole world."

Ilain didn't bother to ask what happened. She simply took Evylin's hand in hers, compassion in her gaze.

"And then he died," Evylin murmured. The words tasted bland and stale, like she'd held them in too long and now they'd lost their life too.

Ilain scooted closer so that their shoulders were touching. She linked arms with Evylin, drawing her close. It reminded Evylin of her sisters and how they comforted one another. She allowed herself to lean into Ilain, grateful for the woman's presence.

"I didn't want to live after that," Evylin admitted. "I intended to die too. But then Hewitt came home, and . . . we became each other's reason to go on. He would live for me and I for him. And somehow, we found a way to be happy together."

She pressed her lips together, knowing that *she'd* destroyed that happiness. "But I'd made a promise to Ryen," she confessed. "I wouldn't let his dream die in Whickam Village. I would do all we'd ever planned, keeping him alive by living out our adventures. No matter the cost."

Ilain rested her head on Evylin's shoulder, both of them staring at the fire while they were meant to be watching the forest.

Evylin rubbed the back of her sleeve against her nose and tear-stained cheeks. "I can't love Jonn," she whispered finally. "Because when Hewitt died, my heart died with him. Now, I have no love left to give."

For a long moment, they were silent. Ilain's warmth seeped into Evylin, their sides pressed together. Evylin's thoughts drifted back to Whickam Village and the sisters she'd left there. Did her family miss her? Had they learned of Hewitt's death? Were they grieving too? Last she knew, Euna's husband hadn't written in five months. A near-assurance of his death. Had the army confirmed it, leaving her eldest sister a widow? And what about Dolia? She was engaged when Evylin left. Had the wedding taken place? She'd missed so much and for what?

Ilain sighed, bringing Evylin back to the Waulden forest. "I must say," she whispered gently, "I don't agree."

They both shifted, straightening to look at one another. Evylin furrowed her brow as Ilain smirked. "I'd venture to say that you love all of us," the highlady noted. "Thom, Ethenn, Rafferty. Even Auden and me."

Evylin sucked in her bottom lip.

"But I won't force you to admit it," Ilain said with a wink. Then she reached up and wiped the last tear from Evylin's face. "Now, shall I tell you a secret?"

"A secret?" Evylin repeated, bemused.

Ilain gave her a nod. "You shared something immensely personal with me. It's only fair I do the same with you."

Hearing the jocular tone in Ilain's voice, Evylin smiled, thankful for the woman's attempt to cheer her. "All right," she said.

With a deep breath, Ilain prepared herself. Her eyes darted to the other side of the camp, and when she spoke, her voice was almost inaudible. "I have feelings for Ethenn," she said, then grimaced. "Which is a problem because I've sort of made him think that I have feelings for Thom."

It took Evylin a second to process the woman's words. Ethenn wasn't the only one who thought Ilain liked Thom. After catching the two of them holding hands, Evylin had been sure that the pair's flirtations had finally taken a serious turn. "I—what?"

Ilain chewed on a nail. "I know," she mumbled. "It's inconvenient."

"Well . . . Yes," she said, disbelieving. "You mean you and Thom—?"

The woman gave a low, disgruntled hum. "It was a ploy," she said. "Obviously, Ethenn has had feelings for me . . . well, he's been attracted to me from the start, I know that. And it didn't take long before I began to return his interest. However, as I thought he wasn't a Warrior—" She said it like an accusation, her jaw tightening. "I couldn't exactly encourage either of us. So Thom agreed to assist me in *dis*couraging him."

Feeling as though she were talking to her little sister, Calyn, through the trials of romance, Evylin blinked. "I don't understand," she whispered. "Do you want . . . to *marry* Ethenn?"

"I can't honestly say," Ilain replied warily. "Maybe? I'm not really sure what love feels like, if I'm being honest. However, I think I've botched that opportunity."

"I doubt that," Evylin said, glancing sidelong at Ethenn's sleeping form.

"He thinks Thom and I are dallying," Ilain argued.

"We all thought you were."

"Tosh." Ilain waved a hand dismissively. "I would never pursue Thom seriously. I like him enormously, but he's not magical, and our life together would be a disaster."

Evylin couldn't help letting out a low snort of amusement. Then she frowned.

She'd seen the way Thom was with Ilain. Their relationship began with so much contention that she never would have imagined that he could be as comfortable and attentive with the Fire Mage as he was now. From morning to night, Thom sought Ilain's company first. They joked frequently, wiled away the hours together, and even ducked their heads in conspiratorial whispers. These days, Evylin expected that he'd begun to confide in Ilain more than her.

Across the low-burning embers, Evylin surveyed the shadowed shapes of the men's sleeping forms. She remembered their earlier argument and Thom's words. *"He's jealous of my relationship with Ilain."*

Evylin's heart felt pulled in two different directions. She supported Thom, of course. He was her brother-in-law and closest friend. But over the past two weeks of relentless travel and daily training, Ethenn had become like a brother as well. Their shared experience as Warriors made him the one person with whom she could truly relate. And now, he *wanted* to marry a Mage, knowing it would prove the most beneficial to his life as a Warrior.

How could she support one man over the other?

Though she supposed it didn't matter what she thought. If Ilain loved Ethenn, then Evylin couldn't hope for Thom's success.

Evylin tilted her head in thought. "Are you asking for my advice?"

"Not necessarily," Ilain said. "I'm exchanging a confidence for a confidence. Though if you have advice, by all means, give it to me."

Evylin scratched her head. "Well . . ." She shot another look at the men's tent. "I'm not really the person to give this sort of advice, Ilain. Romance and I . . . My sisters could tell you that we've never mixed. But if you think you love Ethenn, then I think you should pursue him."

"But he thinks I don't want him," Ilain whispered.

"Then tell him the truth."

Ilain grimaced. "He'll think I only want to be with him because he's a Warrior."

"Is that the reason you want to be with him?"

"No." Ilain said it with such determination, such conviction, that Evylin didn't doubt her sincerity. There was a spark in Ilain's eyes, a crystal clarity that spoke of true feelings. "Warrior or not, he's everything I wanted and more. He's handsome, intelligent, attentive, and strong. Admittedly, he's younger than I expected, but . . . there's something venerable about him despite his age. It's like he knows too much, like his life has forced on him maturity beyond his years. And there's this . . ."

Ilain's gaze drifted across the camp to where Ethenn lay, a wistful look on her face. "This *fire* within him that calls to me the same way magic does."

Evylin shifted uncomfortably. The passion and desire Ilain displayed weren't emotions that Evylin was used to witnessing. Affection was secretive in Ephria, demure and contained. People didn't speak of their significant others with anything remotely as vivacious an expression as Ilain's description. There was blatant want in her tone, and it made Evylin's heart ache for the man she'd separated from two weeks ago.

As if realizing her wanton stare, Ilain blinked rapidly. Her cheeks reddened, and she set a hand to her mouth, hiding a laugh. "Sorry," she murmured. "I got carried away."

"Evidently," Evylin said, sharing her nervous laugh. "So you do love him?"

Her cheeks flushed an even deeper shade. "I think so."

"Then tell him."

Ilain took a long, cautious breath. "I will," she whispered. "But I think I have to work up to it first."

Evylin reached over and took her hand. "And I think," she held her gaze with a serious one, "you need to stop flirting with Thom."

"Mm." Ilain pressed her lips together and gave a single nod. "You're probably right."

They shared a final smile and conspiratorial laugh before returning to their task. Evylin's gaze swept the forest. She took the benefit of Ilain's presence, borrowing her connection to magic to heighten her senses. A gentle breeze swept through the trees. Nocturnal animals rustled in the brush. She listened to Thom and Ethenn's steady breathing. The world was still and calm.

A disappointment settled in Evylin as she considered the men again. Poor Thom. She hated to see his heart broken. Although after hearing Ilain's true feelings for Ethenn, Evylin knew Thom and Ilain could never be happy together. Beyond their magical inequality and temperamental difficulties, Thom deserved a woman who loved him more than anyone else. Still, Evylin didn't want to see him hurt.

In the silence, Evylin's fingers found her rings again. She looked up through the trees at the moons, her thoughts drifting to the Deckard brother whose heart *she'd* broken. Was Deckard on watch too? Was there a chance he was looking up at the sky, thinking of her? Did he ache at the loss of her as much as she ached for him?

"Ilain," she whispered, yearning to share her fear.

"Yes?"

"I think I made a mistake."

Ilain turned to her, listening.

"I think I've lost him."

"Oh, Evylin." Ilain tugged her closer once more. "You could never lose him."

The whole of Evylin's being tried to believe Ilain. She grasped at the words, hoping they would be true. With everything inside of her, she wanted to trust in it. But she didn't.

Because Evylin knew loss was inevitable. Whether she lost Deckard due to her rejection two weeks ago or to his death—be it in the Time Keep, in a decade, or in a century—she would lose him, just as she'd lost Ryen and Hewitt. She'd never recovered from their deaths. She doubted she ever would.

And when she lost Deckard, she worried that she'd cease to exist entirely. Because he wasn't just her husband. He was her balance, the other half of her soul.

CHAPTER FORTY-ONE

30TH OF CHRONOS, 1574

The border crossing went without a hitch. Thom gave Ilain the Night Relic, and she slipped it over her head. "Stay close," she instructed Thom and Ethenn. Evylin rode on the back of Ilain's horse to give her added focus as Ethenn led the empty mare behind his. All their figures were aptly hazy around the edges in a shroud. Thom had grown rather numb to the use of magic around him. Something he wasn't entirely comfortable with but had to admit he appreciated the benefits of.

Once they were safely within Vaura Reach, Evylin returned to her horse, and they sprinted away from the border wall. Ilain dropped the shroud a mile into the Mages' land. She returned the Night Relic to Thom, her usual spark dimmed by the magical exertion. He stashed it with the Fire Relic in the inside pocket of his coat. He didn't care for the responsibility of being a glorified jewelry box. It irked him to have a constant reminder of his non-magical, inferior state. However, he understood the importance of the task and took it seriously.

Their short journey to the border that morning took just over three hours, leaving them with another twenty miles to go until their next stop. They broke for a short meal and to give the horses a rest once they'd progressed farther into the Reach. The mood was a strange blend of jovial and subdued. Evylin and Ilain shared a newfound closeness, sticking near to each other's side. However, Evylin seemed to glance at the road ahead at every opportunity, as though anticipating their final destination. Thom wondered if she was looking forward to the Keep or dreading the troop's reunion.

Ethenn had returned to a somewhat companionable temper as well, though he still wouldn't talk directly to Thom. The reminder of their argument rankled in Thom's mind. It nipped at his conscience, agitating his frayed nerves.

Evylin wasn't the only one anxious about their return. For the past two weeks, Thom had questioned everything about his choices. Despite Ilain's protests, he still felt he should have accompanied Deckard and Auden, supporting his brother. He feared what he would find when they arrived at the Time Keep. After Evylin's rejection and so much death at his hands, would Deckard have succumbed to the magic?

And what about Deckard and Evylin's broken relationship? Thom felt he was beginning to mature. He knew his feelings were foolish, and he couldn't bear to hurt Deckard by taking his wife, even if Thom loved her too. In the last two weeks, he'd worked hard to become a better man. He'd listened to Ilain, heeding her advice and attempting to move on.

Perhaps that was what had angered him so much when Ethenn confronted him yesterday.

"Are you leading Ilain on intentionally?" the boy had asked.

At first, Thom gaped at the unexpected question. Then he laughed. "Trust me," he said. "Ilain's not the one you should be worried about."

Ethenn didn't get the message. "You're going to hurt her."

"You don't know what you're talking about."

"We all know," he said gruffly.

Thom turned around, staring at the kid. "What are you talking about?"

Ethenn glared at him. "You told Raff and me months ago," he said accusingly. "And the colonel knows too."

Panic swept through Thom's veins like poison. "He what?"

"You aren't subtle, Thom." Ethenn's dark brow hung low over his eyes. "I chalk the Calders' ignorance up to them not knowing you well enough."

Thom tried to come up with some sharp retort, but his throat burned with too much fear to speak. He knew exactly what Ethenn was referring to. Since the morning after it happened, he'd regretted his drunken admission back in Nettershire. Rafferty always did know how to weasel information out of others. Thom was too susceptible to his antics.

But Deckard knew too? Why hadn't he said anything?

In Thom's extended silence, Ethenn took a step forward. "You need to stop playing with Ilain's feelings," he charged angrily.

That caused Thom to bristle. "Stop being a jealous prick, Ethenn."

Though Thom turned to walk away from the conversation, Ethenn wouldn't let it go. "Evylin doesn't want you," he called.

Thom froze. The words stung, their truth biting like winter frost. Slowly, he turned around to face the hunter. He gave him a cutting grin. "And Ilain doesn't want you."

Ethenn shifted. "I know."

Thom took a challenging step toward him. "But," he continued, "she *does* want me. So why shouldn't I give her what she wants? Why shouldn't I have some fun of my own?"

A deep rage flickered through Ethenn's gaze, but he remained steady. "You'll hurt her."

A callous smirk lifted Thom's lips. "I don't care."

Even now, Thom didn't know why he'd said it. Despite all his efforts, he'd let Ethenn goad him back into his old, bitter ways. He was just so irritated. The kid was threatening him, spoken outright or not. While he'd spent the last two weeks intentionally holding his tongue and attempting to move on, Ethenn only saw his past offenses.

Let him be wrong. Thom was a better man now. He didn't have to explain himself to the brat.

Those cynical thoughts, along with his embittered actions, had berated Thom through the night. He wasn't a better man. He was the same resentful, impulsive fool he'd always been. It was as though he'd learned nothing, as though Ilain's lessons and admonishments hadn't taught him anything at all.

Why couldn't he be more like Deckard? Why did everything feel like an affront? Why couldn't he be happy on his own?

Now, in the light of a new day, the thoughts lingered.

Thom sighed silently. He had to do better. If he wanted to be worthy, he had to *be* better. So tonight, when they made camp, he would pull Ethenn aside and apologize. He'd admit his faults to the kid and tell him the truth: His relationship with Ilain was a ruse, and he was working to free himself of his feelings for Evylin.

As though a test of his will, Evylin drew her horse alongside Thom's. She smiled playfully, the afternoon sun peeking around the clouds to catch like gold in the wisps of her hair. "I'll bet you two coppers," she said, voice low, "that I can guess what you're thinking."

Thom pressed his lips together. There wasn't a chance she could guess his self-deprecating thoughts. "I'll take that bet."

Evylin tugged back on her reins, drawing her horse to drop back from Ilain and Ethenn ahead. The pair noticed, but Evylin gave Ilain a nod. The woman rolled her eyes but turned to start up a conversation with Ethenn.

Warily, Thom followed Evylin's lead, letting their horses put space between them and their friends. "What are you up to, Evie?" he asked.

"Who says I'm up to anything?"

He gave her a flat stare.

"I'll tell you if you'll play my game with me," she said.

Thom shook his head, amused. "Fine. Guess what I'm thinking then."

Evylin stared ahead with a proud lift to her chin. "You're thinking about Ilain."

Thom snorted. "You owe me two coppers."

"Really? Then what were you thinking about?" Evylin's good-natured smile lit her face like it used to. Somehow, in the past two weeks, her grief had softened. It wasn't gone, but it was less. Or maybe she was just distracted by the loss of Deckard.

Thom adjusted in his saddle. He didn't like that thought or her question. He might be ready to admit his faults to Ethenn but not to her.

Choosing to deflect, Thom shook his head. "I won the bet; now you owe me an explanation. What are you up to?"

Evylin gave him a side-eyed glance. "I'm trying to give Ilain a moment with Ethenn."

Thom frowned. Just a few weeks ago, Evylin was trying to set him up with Ilain. When had she chosen to switch sides? A sprig of inexplicable envy worked through Thom. Why did Evylin suddenly favor Ethenn over him? Was it because of their connection as Warriors? Had she replaced him with the lad?

Shaking off the feeling, Thom forced himself not to care. He cleared his throat and gave her a half-felt smile. "I see. Well, do you still want to know what I was really thinking?"

"I do."

With a ready lie, Thom motioned to the landscape around them. "Say we get all these Relics, and the Alliance has won the war," he raised his brow, "what are you going to do?"

Evylin's grin faltered for only a second. "I haven't really thought about it."

"No?" Thom didn't believe her. "The woman who planned to leave her tiny village for a life of adventure doesn't have plans for the future?"

"No." Her reply came sharply. Then she shook her head as though casting off whatever caused her clipped tone. "Adventure isn't what I thought. Too much horseback riding and sleeping in the rain. Not enough fighting."

"Yes, I know," Thom said, familiar with the sentiment. He gave her elbow a nudge. "You could be a sellsword. I hear they do far more fighting."

Evylin let out an amused scoff. "I'm not sure that Jonn would approve."

Thom turned back to the road. He hadn't expected Deckard and Evylin's marriage to last based on her insistence that they separate. He'd thought she intended the parting to be for good. Now, it seemed he was wrong.

"No, I don't suppose he would," he muttered.

Evylin didn't notice his dejection. "What about you? What will you do?"

His brow furrowed as he realized he hadn't considered it. What would he do? Remain as a soldier? Stay in Deckard's shadow? Run away to the southern continent of Matteire? Start a life of his own?

Thom felt his eyes drift to Ilain and Ethenn. The clouds had obscured the sun once more. A dull gray shadow hung over the terrae. What would Ilain encourage him to do? She was wiser than people gave her credit for—wiser than most women he'd met. And he had no doubt she'd steer him in the right direction.

In his prolonged consideration, Evylin tapped a finger on the front of her saddle. "Thom," she said with something like pity in her tone.

He turned to her, unsure what she had to pity him for.

Evylin's warm brown gaze held his. "You know a life with Ilain isn't possible, don't you?"

Thom's stomach dropped. "Evylin, that's not—"

"I know you've grown close," she said, misinterpreting his denial. "And while I'm sure you share a mutual respect for one another, it wouldn't work between you two."

Muttering a curse under his breath, Thom pinched the bridge of his nose. "Evie, you don't understand."

"I do. I swear."

"No." He gave her a bland glare. "You don't."

Evylin quirked an eyebrow, clearly disbelieving of his claim.

"It isn't like that," Thom said. "Ilain and I aren't—our flirtations are not real. Neither of us has feelings for one another."

However, Thom realized that wasn't altogether true. He did feel something for Ilain. An admiration, a regard, a like-mindedness. They were strikingly similar, and she made him feel understood in a way few others did. It wasn't love—it was, as Evylin herself had said, respect.

Evylin scoffed. "Is that so?"

"Yes."

"Then why, pray tell, were you holding hands the other day?" Despite Thom rolling his eyes, Evylin kept going. "And why is it," she demanded, "that you two are always together?"

"We all agreed not to leave anyone alone," he reminded her. "While you and Ethenn are out having a splendid Warrior time, someone has to stick around to protect the woman."

"*Pshaw*. Ilain can protect herself."

"Then why do we have our rules?"

Evylin smirked. "To protect you, of course. You're carrying the Relics. That makes you our most prized commodity."

"Exactly," Thom said, latching onto her argument. "We can't be alone. That doesn't mean I *want* to spend all my time with Ilain. I just do because I have to."

Evylin eyed him. "So you wouldn't be upset if she were to, say . . ." She paused, clearly pretending to search for an example. "Be with Ethenn?"

Thom scrubbed a hand over his face. He glanced at the pair more than a hundred feet ahead now. Ethenn adjusted awkwardly in his saddle while Ilain continued to talk. For the first time, he worried that the highlady had taken his budding friendship the wrong way. What if Ilain thought he was gaining feelings?

Thom ground his teeth. "Did she put you up to this?" he asked.

"No," Evylin said too quickly.

Thom swore again. "Does *she* think I have feelings for her?"

Evylin dipped her chin, studying him. "Don't you?"

"I've already told you no."

"Then why were you and Ethenn fighting over her yesterday?"

"Evylin, let it go."

"I don't want to see you hurt, Thom," Evylin said, ignoring his dismissal.

Thom couldn't help his caustic laugh. "Ilain Calder can't hurt me."

"Thom—" She reached over and touched his arm comfortingly. His skin burned with guilt under her fingers. "You don't have to be ashamed of feeling something for her. She's a beautiful, wonderful woman. You've gotten close, and it makes sense."

"Evie, stop."

"If you truly don't care," she pressed, "if you have no feelings for her, then why wouldn't you tell Ethenn the truth? Why would his jealousies bother you?"

Heat crept along Thom's neck like a leather strap, choking him. "Just stop," he said weakly.

"Because you do feel something for her," Evylin surmised. "Because despite knowing you have no future, you want it anyway."

Thom hated how true her words were, no matter the misplaced recipient of his affection. It felt cruel, having Evylin reveal his fate to him. For the reality was that his love would perpetually be unrequited. His future was that of broken isolation. All because he couldn't overcome his resentment and failings.

He jerked back on the reins, bringing his horse to a disgruntled stop. He glared at Evylin, daring her to test him. "I don't have feelings for Ilain," he said vehemently.

"Then why are you and Ethenn fighting?"

"Do you really want to know?"

"Yes!" Evylin tossed her arms to the side, her horse sidestepping in agitation.

"Fine." Thom leaned forward until their faces were only a few inches apart. Evylin's expression pinched as he let his gaze soften, locking with hers. "It's because he knows how I feel about you."

A gasp *whooshed* out of Evylin.

Foolishly, Thom set his hand on hers, where it rested on her thigh. "Damn the consequences, Evylin," he whispered. "I love you."

Instantly, Evylin jerked away. "What?" she spat.

Thom felt his expression harden once more. He sat upright, reaping the consequences he expected. "Don't look at me like that," he said harshly. "You knew. You had to know."

"I didn't," Evylin insisted. "I—"

Thom saw it then, the moisture gathering in her eyes. She really hadn't known.

He scoffed, turning away. "Don't worry," he said bitterly. "I'm aware that you don't return my feelings."

"He's your brother," she breathed.

A dagger plunged into Thom's stomach. "I know."

"Why—?" She let the question fall, unasked but still in the air between them.

Thom met her gaze again, forlorn in his deficiency. "Because you're everything I wanted," he admitted. "And once more, Jonn took what should have been mine."

Evylin drew back in contempt.

A self-mocking laugh slipped out of Thom. Yes, she would view him with scorn, as she should. "Do you think I congratulate myself for feeling this way?" he demanded. "Do you think I *want* to feel this way? I've spent my life in his shadow. For once, I'd like to have something—*someone*—of my own. I wish I didn't feel these things, but I do. I love you. I want to be with you."

"Thom, stop."

"It's too late for that."

It was true. It was far too late. He'd admitted his frailty and exposed his misdeeds. Now, it was up to her to absolve or condemn him.

"I didn't dare say anything," Thom prompted his horse to take a step forward, but she sidled hers away, "to him or to you. Not when I thought it wouldn't make any difference."

"And why would it make a difference now?" she asked coldly.

"Because you left him," Thom said, the words a quiet plea. Then he hardened himself once again. "Or I thought you did."

Evylin slumped, her gaze diverting.

"You did," Thom realized. "You left him?"

She confirmed it with her silence.

Thom let out a huff. "Then you've rejected us both."

Evylin sat there, eyes downcast and demeanor morose.

Cautiously, Thom reached out. He brushed back some of the wisps that framed her face. She tensed under his touch. "Whatever the case," he whispered, "I'm glad you know now. And even if you don't want me, I will always want you."

Evylin pulled back sharply, her eyes alight with something like fury. "I could never be with you," she said, the words stinging like the slash of a sword. "Don't you understand that? Every time I look at you, I see *him*."

Thom flinched, the admission of the comparison was everything he feared.

"Every time you smile," she continued, "I see his smile. Every time you laugh, it's his laugh I hear. Any time you touched me or tried to kiss me—it wouldn't be you I'd think of. It would always be *him*."

Cold desolation seared in Thom's veins as her last words hissed out. "You could only ever be a shade of him to me."

Thom clenched his jaw so tight it felt as if it might break. His chest filled with pressure; his eyes welled with emotion. Air struggled to fit into his lungs. But this wasn't heartbreak he felt. It was rage.

"All my life," he managed to eke out, "that's all I've ever been: a shade of my brother. Stronger, more sincere, and far more determined, but still not good enough."

Evylin glared at him, unsympathetic to his plight.

Thom's lips twisted into a snide grin. Her repudiation, her scorn—that was always his fate. He shook his head at the irony. "He could never love you like I could," he said accusingly. "He doesn't have the capacity for it."

Evylin lifted her chin. "I don't want your love."

"No one does," he said, then pulled on the reins. "Don't concern yourself, Evie. I won't bother you with my feelings again."

Leaving her behind, Thom spurred his horse into a canter. He joined Ethenn and Ilain, their conversation stalling with his added presence.

Ethenn eyed him with disdain. "Have a nice chat?" he asked.

Thom's brows pinched together. Was that accusation in Ethenn's voice? Perhaps seeing Thom and Evylin draw back had reignited his anger from the day before. "Quite," he said flatly.

Ilain eyed him warily but returned to her previous conversation. "They say that the ancient Mages sent delegates south on the Veridus Sea," she said to Ethenn. "Some believe they took the missing literature with them, but there's no evidence to support that theory."

"Do you believe it anyway?" Ethenn asked.

Slowly, Evylin approached. Thom blocked out the conversation. His mind reeled over and over, furious with himself and with Evylin. Why had she goaded him? Why couldn't he stand down? He should have let it go. He should have lied, feigning an interest in Ilain.

Thom's fingers tightened on the reins. *What have I done?* Evylin would surely tell Deckard of his indiscretion. Then he'd truly be condemned in his brother's eyes.

A hollow pit opened in Thom's stomach. He glanced at Evylin out of the corner of his eye. She rode straight-backed, ignoring him. It was clear. His rash tongue had caused the loss of both his brother and his closest friend.

Now, he truly was a loveless wretch, destined to spend eternity alone.

What have I done?

CHAPTER FORTY-TWO

The anger dissipated first. It was the embarrassment and regret that plagued Evylin throughout the day.

Why had Thom said those things? He couldn't mean them, could he? In all the time she'd known him, and even though she'd understood his jealousy and resentment toward his brother, she'd never believed that Thom could harbor feelings that were so . . . *wrong*.

A swift breeze cut through the camp, whipping up the smoke from the fire. It whirled, covering Evylin in its acrid stench. She coughed, her eyes stinging as she waved it away.

"Sorry," Ilain said, lifting her hands and using magic to redirect the path of the smoke. Her sketchbook sat open on her lap while the food continued to cook in the pot. "I was distracted."

"It's all right," Evylin promised, returning to her own distracted thoughts. She tugged on her rings, glancing around the rest of the camp. While Ethenn sat on the far log practicing flipping his dagger from one hand to the next in intricate spins, Thom lay under the canvas tent with an arm over his eyes.

He'd been appropriately somber after his admission. Clearly, he regretted it. But whether he regretted the revelation of his secret feelings for the right reasons or for self-focused ones, she couldn't tell.

Evylin drew in a deep breath. How had she not recognized Thom's romantic regard toward her? All this time, Thom's blatant insults toward Deckard's character, his warnings of Deckard's selfishness, and his suggestions that Evylin should move on—all of it held newfound clarity. Thom had been subtly trying to convey his affection to her. And she'd been foolish enough to miss it.

Evylin still couldn't believe it. How could he entertain such desires for his brother's wife? Even if Thom didn't know of Deckard's love for her—which she knew he did—how could he allow himself to foster those feelings?

Her fingers twisted around her rings. And how could he think she'd return them? Perhaps she hadn't been able to return Deckard's love, but she'd never given Thom any encouragement . . . Had she?

Evylin wanted to drop her face into her hands in misery, but she couldn't allow herself to wallow. Not while Ilain and Ethenn were present. Instead, she berated herself silently.

How had this happened? Her brother-in-law was in love with her. Was it her fault? Could she have stopped Thom's affection before it began? Or was she even to blame at all? Could it be possible that Thom's feelings developed from his insecurities alone? She thought back through the entirety of their relationship, back through their travel with the Ephrian Army, to their duel securing her marriage to Deckard, to the first moment she met Thom in Hewitt's smithy. Had there been signs even then of his attraction? She couldn't say.

But then, Evylin had never been good at recognizing a man's interest. She'd completely missed Prince Ephren's revolting attempts at seduction in Banbury. Perhaps it was expected that she'd miss something as plain as Thom's interest as well.

Evylin's heart squeezed. What would Deckard say when he learned of this? He loved Thom, despite everything that had happened between them. He wanted the best for his brother. The discovery that Thom had betrayed him so completely . . . She didn't want to think about how Deckard would respond.

Evylin tried to rationalize Thom's feelings. Perhaps he didn't mean it. He saw life itself as a competition with Deckard. Perhaps his affections were driven solely by his desire to best his brother. It was possible that he'd duped himself into believing he loved Evylin in an effort to overcome the inferiority he felt in the presence of his older brother.

But what if he did mean it? What if he truly loved her? She would be forced to break the hearts of both brothers. She couldn't stay with Deckard, and she wouldn't be with Thom.

Tightening her jaw, Evylin decided to allow her anger to ignite once again. How dare he do this to her? To Deckard? Thom was putting her in an impossible situation and hurting his brother in the process. If Deckard found out about his betrayal, she knew how deep that wound would cut. And she had no doubt it would fester.

Well, she wouldn't be the cause of Deckard and Thom's broken relationship. She wouldn't be the thing that finally drove the two apart. Thom didn't get to make her the villain in this story. He would just have to take responsibility for the disaster himself.

Determined, Evylin rose from her seat. She didn't bother speaking to Ilain or Ethenn, even as they watched her walk across the camp and straight up to the tent where Thom lay.

Evylin kicked the bottom of Thom's boot. He lifted his arm, a look of surprise and worry immediately twisting his expression. "We need to talk," she said quietly.

Thom glanced at the fire where the others sat. Slowly, he rose. He dusted off his pants, not meeting her eyes. "Should we—?"

"Yes," Evylin said shortly, then led the way to the forest edge. She didn't care to walk far from camp; it wouldn't be that long of a conversation. But she stepped behind the trees to keep their argument unseen by the others.

Without giving Thom time to prepare, Evylin began. "This is the final time we will ever discuss this," she told him in hushed, clipped tones. "Do you understand?"

Keeping his chin tucked, Thom nodded. He looked like a little boy, scared and broken by his mistakes.

"Good." Evylin steeled herself with a deep, angered breath. "Everything you said earlier, we're going to forget it."

Thom flinched. "Evie—"

"No, Thom," she cut him off sharply. "I don't care what you think you feel. You are going to forget it all, and I'm going to forget you ever said a word about it. Because when we walk back into that camp, it will be as if it never happened. Got it? You are my friend, and you will feel nothing more for me."

"I understand," he muttered bitterly.

"When this conversation is over, the subject will never be broached again. Not between us . . . or anyone else."

Thom met her eyes then, a strange hopefulness within his gaze.

"I won't tell Jonn," she promised. "Not when I know how this would hurt him. He loves you. He always has. But this . . . I don't know if even *he* can forgive you for this."

Thom swallowed.

"So I won't tell him," Evylin whispered, her voice weakening as her anger returned to regret. "Because I won't be the reason he loses you."

Thom wrung his hands, his breathing sharp and labored. "Evie, I—I appreciate what you're trying to do, but . . . it won't matter. My relationship with Jonn has been broken for years."

"It doesn't have to stay that way," she insisted. "He wants to fix it. He wants to be your friend. You're the one refusing to cooperate."

"It isn't that simple."

"Yes, it is." Evylin glared up at him. "I've listened to both of you. I've heard both sides of the story, and I've watched as time and time again, he tries to love you, and you reject him. This isn't Jonn's fault. It's yours. And once you accept that, then perhaps you'll be able to see past your arrogance and accept his love."

Thom's lips parted in shock as though she'd slapped him.

Evylin's manner remained cold, too hurt by his earlier actions to care. "I'm done coddling you. I will protect Jonn by keeping the truth from him, but I will not protect you from anything anymore."

"I understand," he repeated, his voice flat and his hurt evident. But then he met her gaze. "Are you still going to leave him?"

Evylin's body tensed. She stepped back involuntarily. "Yes," she murmured.

Thom hesitated, his sharp gray-blue eyes studying her. His jaw was tight, his lips pressing into a thin line. Then he sighed. "Look, I understand that I'm a terrible brother. I've betrayed Jonn; there's no way around that. So it may sound a bit disingenuous when I say this, but . . . You are the most nonsensical person I've ever met."

Evylin could only blink in confusion.

He took a step closer, his brow furrowed in a way that reminded her too much of Deckard. "No one—" he began, his voice rough as he spoke, "No one can talk about someone the way you talked about Jonn this afternoon and not love that person. Everything you said about him . . . I wish someone would say those things about me."

Rooted to the ground beneath her feet, Evylin wanted to deny his words. Whatever admiration she held for Deckard, it was simply respect, not love. She wanted to convince Thom of that, just as she tried to convince herself.

Instead, she lifted her chin. "Feelings play no role in this decision, Thom."

"Then what does?" he demanded.

That was a question Evylin couldn't bring herself to answer.

A slow drizzle began, rustling the leaves in a chorus of patters and slaps. In the rising temperatures, neither wore their cloaks. The sudden onslaught of rain began to drench them, but they didn't move, locked in a battle of wills.

Thom glared at her with something resembling frustration. "Do you love him?" he demanded.

"No," she said without giving herself the chance to think.

An embittered smirk came to Thom's face. "You've always been a terrible liar, Evie."

"I'm not lying."

"Fine," he said apathetically. "You don't love him. All the things you said before were the words of some other lovesick sap. You're going to leave Jonn, and you won't be unhappy because you don't care about him. Works for me."

Evylin rolled her eyes. "What do you want from me? Do you want me to be with you or to be with Jonn?"

"*Would* you ever be with me?" he asked, brow raised with a disbelieving arch.

"No."

"I didn't think so." He shook his head. "I don't care what you do, Evylin. Be with him or leave him—whatever you want. But take it from someone who's screwed up everything good he's ever had: You'll regret every moment of your life if you walk away from him."

She stared at him, every argument she could think of caught in her chest next to the wound she'd inflicted on herself when she chose to leave her husband.

Thom dipped his head lower, deliberately meeting her eyes. "There's a reason I resent my brother, Evie. It's because he's the best man this world has, and we can never hope to deserve him." He scoffed cynically. "Who wouldn't be resentful? How is *anyone* supposed to compete with that?"

Evylin turned away, not wanting to hear the truth of what she'd given up.

"Reject me if you like," Thom said in a quiet, self-loathing tone. "I deserve it. But he doesn't."

Then he turned away and left her there.

Evylin stood in the cold rain, her hair and clothes soaked. Droplets trickled down her cheeks like tears. Her fingers twisted her rings absentmindedly. No, Deckard didn't deserve her rejection. And perhaps she should take that into consideration, but . . .

She squeezed her eyes shut around the emotion welling within. She'd cried too much over the past month. Enough tears to fill the whole ocean. Now, her body was hollow, worn ragged under the weight of long-suppressed grief.

No, Deckard didn't deserve her rejection. But neither did he deserve a wife who couldn't love him as well as he deserved. Evylin meant what she'd told Ilain last night. She had no love left to give. Her heart was sundered irrevocably. What could she offer any man when every moment she questioned her very desire to exist?

"The world isn't what I thought it'd be." Evylin's words from months ago drifted back into her mind along with Hewitt's deep, growling voice.

"What are you looking for in the world, Evie?"

"I don't know," she'd admitted. *"But I can't accept that life is as simple and . . . boring as this. There has to be something else out there. Some other reason to live."*

"What would be reason enough to live?"

Evylin didn't have any more answers now than she did then. *"There must be more . . . Life* must be more.*"*

Yet, here she stood in her imagination of "more"—the thrill of adventure—and it felt immeasurably like "less."

Evylin stared at her rings. What would be reason enough to live when everything inevitably ended in death? There was no escaping that unavoidable fact. Hewitt died on a grand adventure. Ryen died in an accidental fire. Nowhere was safe, not out in the world and not back in Whickam Village. She couldn't run from death; she couldn't escape loss. It followed her everywhere she went.

Releasing her rings, Evylin stared into the dimming forest trees.

"What would be reason enough to live?"

Nothing. Because inevitably, those reasons would be taken from her, one life at a time.

CHAPTER FORTY-THREE

32ND OF CHRONOS, 1574

"I've been thinking," Rafferty said, his foot dangling off a branch as he reclined against the tree trunk.

"Of course, you have," Deckard remarked, sitting at the base of the tree, whittling at the chunk of pine he'd found in the woods two weeks ago at the beginning of their trio's journey. It was finally beginning to take shape now, becoming the small toy horse he envisioned. Hewitt stood at his side, watching the road keenly.

Surrounded by mountains, Vaura Reach showcased a hilly, forested terrain. They stood atop one such rise now, overlooking the land surrounding the Keep. Together, Deckard and Auden had discovered the Time Keep's location early the previous day. Deckard had never experienced the low-lying sensation that could only be described as *knowing* that the Calders used to find the Keeps until that moment. With minimal coaching, Auden had helped Deckard find the tug at his core, the pull guiding their steps.

Subsequently, they spent the remainder of the day scouting the area to ensure there were no ambushes lying in wait.

Today, Rafferty and Deckard had taken up the charge again. When they were assured of their safety, they shifted to the role of lookout, watching for their troop on the highest hill they could find. The thick stands of trees mostly obscured the road below. Occasional riders drifted in and out of view, but none had yet matched that of their comrades.

"If the Time Relic gives Mages control over time," Rafferty said, peering down at Deckard, "couldn't we just go back and change it all?"

"Change what exactly?" Deckard asked, leaning against the trunk.

"The war," Rafferty said. "That could be the Alliance's whole plan. Get the Relic and turn back time, stopping the war altogether."

Deckard shook his head. "I don't think so."

"Why, 'cause I suggested it? I'll have you know that I knew Mages were real before the lot of you."

He gave the man a flippant smile. "I'm not Thom. I don't discount people's ideas with offhanded dismissal."

Rafferty snorted at the barb. "What's your theory then?"

Eyes locked on the road, Deckard sighed. He'd become numb to Rafferty's constant questions and chatter. No matter how inane or personal the queries got, Deckard had begun to answer them readily. "The Alliance wouldn't want to turn back time. The Mages of Auld were corrupt; the Calders have said that themselves. The Alliance doesn't support their former regime. They want to create a new world, one where Mages and Warriors bring balance to the world rather than lord their power over it."

Rafferty gave a bored hum, but Hewitt nodded. "Now you're thinking like a leader," the ghost said proudly.

Deckard didn't let the praise go to his head. "Besides," he added, "I don't think there's a Mage alive powerful enough to go back nearly two centuries. The amount of energy and focus that would take. . . ."

"Come to think of it," Rafferty said thoughtfully, "none of them would be alive either. No one's old enough to remember the start of the Centurial War. Why would they care to go back before their lives began?"

"Why indeed," Deckard muttered, watching a small band appear on the road. Three . . . four . . . five riders appeared. He slumped back.

Sharing his disappointment, Rafferty grumbled on the branch above him. "We've been up here for the past three hours. Do you think we've chosen the wrong hill?"

"It's the best vantage of the road we could find," Deckard replied. "They just haven't passed by yet."

"They should be here by now," Rafferty complained.

Hewitt grunted. "I should have beaten the impatience out of him."

Unable to respond, Deckard only grinned dryly. He crossed his arms, settling back against the tree to continue his woodworking project. They'd left Auden at the camp to watch the horses and keep a body around in case the others slipped past Deckard and

Rafferty's notice, arriving at their destination unseen. It was the first time since Auden's discovery of Hewitt's ghost that the Mage had allowed Deckard out of his sight.

Deckard supposed he couldn't blame the man. His connection to Night worried him as well. But he was so close . . .

Despite Auden's caution, he'd continued teaching Deckard, attempting to focus his training on Time and Day magic. All the while, Deckard surreptitiously deepened his relationship with Night too. As a result, he felt stronger than ever, ready to take on the Time Keep and reveal Hewitt's ghost to Evylin.

Though he couldn't deny the selfishness of the act, Deckard intended it as a gift alone. He knew what it would mean for her to see Hewitt again. Even if she couldn't touch him, even if she saw him for just a moment, the ability to have that closure, to say a real goodbye—it would be priceless.

And if, in the end, Evylin still wanted to part ways, giving that gift to her would still be worth it.

Suddenly, Hewitt stepped forward just as Rafferty sat up. "I think I see them," the weasel said, angling to get a better look.

Though Rafferty had made the same pronouncement half a dozen times already, Hewitt's attention caused Deckard's heart rate to spike. He hurried to the edge of the hill, squinting at the thin tan line of the road stretching into the distance. Four horses paced into view, their canter slowing. One rider broke away from the rest.

"That'll be Loxley," Rafferty said excitedly, "coming to find us."

Deckard's breath caught even as he smiled. "I imagine you're right," he said.

Dropping out of the tree, Rafferty landed with acrobatic precision. "Let's go!" he exclaimed, taking off down the hill.

Deckard moved to follow, then hesitated. He turned back to Hewitt. "I can't keep you with me," he whispered. "I know you want to see her, too, but—"

"Go," Hewitt said. "You can't waste your energy maintaining my presence when it could mean her life or death later."

Appreciative of the man's understanding, Deckard let Hewitt lapse back into the ether. Though he'd practiced enough that it took negligible thought and strength to hold Hewitt's ghost in the present, it was still a feat of magic. Upon the rest of their troop's arrival, they would head straight to the Time Keep. With the threat of Blount's writ and Mages looming ever closer, they wanted to spend as little time in Wauld as possible. They would retrieve the Relic, leave Vaura Reach, and abandon the country as fast as their horses would carry them.

Following Rafferty down the hill, Deckard struggled to keep his nerves in check. The steep decline enabled a fast descent, but the roots and rocks could send him tumbling if he missed a step. He was anxious to see Evylin; his whole being was charged with anticipation. Just the thought of being near her again sent his heart spiraling. But he couldn't allow himself to forget the way they'd parted. He couldn't be so overcome with her return that he abandoned her desires.

No, Deckard promised himself that no matter how much he wanted to embrace Evylin, no matter how strong the urge to hold her close and kiss her, he would refrain until she gave him some sign that she wanted it too.

Rafferty beat Deckard to the camp with ease. When Deckard broke through the trees, his companion stood in the alcove, foot tapping impatiently. "They're not here yet," he grumbled.

Auden stood by, anxiously pacing. "Rafferty said you saw them," he said at Deckard's appearance.

"We did," Deckard confirmed, catching his breath. "Ethenn broke away to find us. They should be here any time."

A joyful smile crossed Auden's face. "They're safe, then," he murmured. He looked over their meager camp. "We should prepare. We want to leave immediately."

"We've been apart for two weeks," Deckard objected.

"And we'll have a true reunion once we're safe in Ephria," Auden insisted, beginning to pack his saddlebags.

Deckard and Rafferty exchanged a disgruntled look. "Some celebration," the weasel muttered.

Though Deckard agreed, he moved to help Auden. They tore down the tent, put out the fire, stored the cooking supplies, and packed the last of their personal possessions. And yet, the others still hadn't arrived.

"Shall we clip the grass while we wait?" Rafferty asked, perturbed.

"Shh." Deckard held up a hand, listening. The faintest rumble met his ears. He smiled. "I hear horses."

Deckard turned toward the sound, heart in his throat. The sound grew louder, filling the alcove with its steady beat. The flash of four horses appeared in the trees seconds before they burst into the clearing. Deckard's hands shook, his feet taking him an unconscious step forward.

"Auden!" Ilain called, her horse charging ahead of the others. She practically jumped from the saddle and into her brother's arms. They laughed in relief, clinging to one another.

The three Ephrians showed more decorum, though they all bore large smiles as they dismounted. Rafferty dashed forward to greet his friends. He punched Thom on the arm, slapped Ethenn on the cheek, and swept Evylin into a fierce hug. "Allore, I've missed you three!" he said with a wily grin. "It's been the most boring two weeks of my life."

Deckard's heart filled at the sound of Evylin's laughter. Cautiously, he joined the group. "And here I thought we'd become such good friends," he said to Rafferty.

"We are friends, Colonel," Rafferty said with a flippant wave of his hand. "But even when you're fun, you're not as fun as this lot."

"I believe that," Deckard replied, barely registering his words or the others around him. He was too intent on meeting Evylin's gaze. An indistinguishable expression crossed her face, a guarded smile on her lips as she held his stare. She looked just the same as he remembered. Her dark brown hair draped over her shoulder in a braid, little wisps dancing around her tan cheeks. Her black coat was cropped at the waist, fitting her sculpted figure immaculately. Knives clustered around her belt, the one with rosettes closest to her hip. She was every ounce the Warrior he remembered, every bit as perfect as before.

A long silence hung between them.

Auden and Ilain stepped over. "Good to see you, Jonn," Ilain said cheerily.

The moment broken, Deckard turned to Ilain. "It's good to see you as well. All of you."

"We're glad to be back," Thom replied, a nervous edge to his voice. There was something in his expression, a harried look that made Deckard wonder what had occurred to put it there.

Despite feeling the distance between them and even knowing his brother's offense, Deckard couldn't find it in himself to be angry. He closed the gap between them, pulling Thom into a hug. A reluctance marked the men's embrace. But then Thom relaxed, returning the hug as he hadn't since he was a child.

"I'm sorry I didn't go with you," Thom whispered.

Deckard's brow pinched, and he drew back. He opened his mouth in question, but Thom backed away. He set a hand on Rafferty's shoulder and gave him a shove, moving away from the horses. Ethenn gave Deckard a nod of acknowledgment, then drifted away with the men and the Calders.

Seeing the path cleared, Deckard turned back to Evylin. She hadn't moved, her horse a wall behind her. Her expression remained unreadable, that polite smile and reserved stance defining her demeanor. It wasn't an invitation, but it wasn't a rejection either.

Daring to be brave, Deckard took a step closer.

Evylin flinched, and he paused. "You cut your hair," she noted.

Instinctively, Deckard raised a hand to rub the short bristles at the back of his head. "Yes. It was getting too long for my liking."

"It looks good. How did you manage such a feat?"

The stilted banter reminded him of their earliest conversations in Whickam Village. He couldn't decide whether to find it charming or disheartening. "Rafferty is surprisingly good at cutting hair," he explained.

A small laugh puffed out of Evylin, and she turned to the others. "You know how to cut hair?" she asked Rafferty.

The weasel slipped over to their side. "It isn't all that hard," he said. "If you can skin a rabbit, you can trim a head."

"With that terrifying thought," Thom said, gesturing to Deckard's clean jaw, "I trust you didn't let *him* do the shaving."

Seeing the opportunity of being in Evylin's company disappearing, Deckard didn't feel his smile. "No, I did that myself," he said, then turned back to Evylin. He wanted to ask to speak with her, to greet her properly. Instead, he accepted the lackluster moment for what it was. "How are you?" he asked.

With a slow breath, Evylin glanced at Thom and Rafferty. The men ducked back, moving away once more.

Then Evylin took a step closer to Deckard. "I'm well," she said, looking up at him. "How are you?"

Everything within Deckard begged him to touch her, to hold her, to draw her close, and to never let her go. Instead, he kept his hands at his sides. "Well rested after the last two days," he said, nodding toward the dismantled campsite. "I'd nearly forgotten what it felt like to have a day off."

Evylin's smile softened her whole demeanor. "Aren't you lucky? I haven't felt well-rested in weeks," she said, then drew a sharp inhale as though realizing she'd revealed a secret.

Deckard wondered if that meant she hadn't slept well due to his absence. He tried not to feel hopeful that such was the case. "I'm sorry to hear that," he said.

When she didn't move away or make any attempt to end the conversation, Deckard leaned closer. "I missed you," he confessed.

Evylin's amber gaze flickered between his eyes, an audible sigh slipping past her lips.

And oh, how Deckard had missed her. Seeing her again, being with her, made that absence feel all the more potent. He'd lost two weeks with her, time they would never get back. Yet, it made her presence now even more precious.

Evylin's hand lifted, reaching across the space between them. "I—"

"We should head out," Auden called.

Evylin's hand dropped.

Deckard could have punched the man for interrupting. He pressed his lips together, turning to find Auden at his horse, utterly oblivious to their reunion. The rest of the team stood around, pointedly ignoring the couple.

Gathering himself by letting out a slow, controlled breath, Deckard flexed his hands rather than fisting them. "Just a moment," he said, then turned back to Evylin.

But she'd already stepped away again. With one hand on her saddle, she gave him a soft smile. "I'm glad to be back," she said.

Taking what he knew would be the best greeting he'd receive from her for the moment, Deckard offered her one final smile of his own. Then he moved toward his horse next to Rafferty's. The weasel was already mounted up, smirking knowingly.

"The highlord isn't keen on romantic moments, is he?" Rafferty remarked.

Deckard swung up onto his horse. He gripped the reins, settling into the saddle. "I want to hire you, Rafferty."

"Oh?" Rafferty's blond brows rose high on his forehead, expression expanding with interest.

"As an expert in the art of smuggling," Deckard met his silver-gray stare, "would you have any ideas about how one might slip a dead fish into a Mage's saddlebags?"

Rafferty's grin grew wicked. "I might have one or two."

"Name your price."

CHAPTER FORTY-FOUR

The short journey to the Time Keep brought them through the hills and to the oceanside. The sea spread before them with great cliffs rising on all sides. The afternoon sun lingered overhead, the orb just beginning its lazy descent. The waves lapped against the dark sand, reminding Deckard of their entry into Wauld and the sprint away from the Night Mages across the beach.

He gave another scan around the sand, water, and cliffs, wary of any Mages lurking nearby. Noticing Evylin, Ethenn, Thom, and Rafferty doing the same, he felt confident they wouldn't miss an ambush this time. Not when they were all on edge and extra watchful.

Their plan had been thoroughly discussed on their journey. Though Deckard didn't like it, Evylin and Ilain's plan to split once more made the most sense. At least, it was only for a few short days this time, rather than weeks. They would be able to move more quickly, slipping undetected out of the Reach, up through Wauld, and back into Ephria.

A blend of eagerness and apprehension warred in Deckard as they descended into the Time Keep's antechamber, the setting familiar but no less filled with tension. The heat of his magic rose along his spine, anticipating his touch. His palm tingled on the hilt of his sword. No matter the strength of his control, he intended to only reach for the magic at the last possible opportunity.

Gentle white light flooded the entrance to the Time Keep as they stepped into the hall. The ironwork windows and door bore circles and sharp lines, like the face of a clock. Deckard wondered at the design, realizing Time Mages must have been the originators of the invention.

"Why are each of the Keeps such distinct colors?" Rafferty asked as he handed out the Relics.

"Each resource has its own color," Ilain said, then tapped the ruby of the Fire Relic, which hung around her neck. "Red for Fire, yellow for Day, blue for Water, and so on. When we connect with the resource, our magic takes on the color. You just don't usually notice it because—well, the elements are obvious. And sunlight is yellow, so you wouldn't be surprised by Auden's magic either."

"So," Thom gestured to the windows, "Time is white? What would that even look like?"

Ilain turned to Auden, who sighed. "It's a waste of energy," he said.

"It's a blip," she argued. "You can spare it."

Raising his hand, Auden pointed at Rafferty as he took a step forward. There was the dullest flash of white, and the weasel froze in midair, foot raised mid-step, his expression and posture wooden, locked in time. "That's what it looks like," Auden said, then released the magic. "Albeit a weak version."

Rafferty's body fell forward. He shivered upon regaining control of his muscles. "That was unpleasant," he grumbled.

Ethenn stood at the back of the group, the Wind-Relic-turned-silvery-bow in his hand. "Do we know what to expect beyond that door?" he asked.

Ilain gave him a cheerful grin. "Do we ever?"

"No," he said with disappointment.

Deckard glanced at Evylin, standing at his side. For the moment, things felt as they used to. The distraction of the Keep wouldn't allow for worry about the divide between them or their parting words. She held the Night sword, eyes trained on the iron door.

"Are you ready?" Deckard asked.

A slight smirk brought the dimples to her cheeks. "Probably not," she said lightly.

"We'll be fine," he said, drawing his sword. "We always are."

The Calders spoke their benediction, "Into the fray," and Auden lifted his hand, setting it on the Time Keep's door. It hissed before releasing the lock. Then, slowly, it swung open.

The seven of them rushed into the Keep, ready to dash for the Chamber. White engulfed them in their first steps. At first, Deckard thought they'd entered a snowy tundra. He looked up, expecting snowfall, but all that stretched above them was more white and pillars of alabaster. He furrowed his brow, realizing that all of it was glass. The slick floor under their feet, the never-ending ceiling and walls, the pillars that stretched into eternity—they were formed of milky white crystal.

Stepping farther into the Keep, Deckard tightened his grip on his sword. His magic thrummed within his head like a pulse. He listened carefully for the hum of the Shades, ready for their appearance. His eyes roved over the long glass room, catching sight of another pillar far in the distance with a small black mark on its face—the entrance to the Chamber.

Deckard gestured toward it. "We should run for it," he said.

Silence met him.

Deckard frowned, then turned around. Immediately, he gasped, his mind reeling.

Though he'd only taken a few steps forward, somehow, he was ahead of the rest. Auden and Ilain were staggered, positioned nearer the stairs and in mid-stride, moving as if through water. Thom and Rafferty stood on the top step, completely still. Evylin and Ethenn were missing.

Deckard whirled, panic searing in his chest. Then he found the Warriors, sprinting ahead with inhuman speed. Yet, they, too, were staggered, Evylin slightly ahead of Ethenn.

"Time," Deckard murmured to himself. They were each locked in their own rate of time.

The whisper of a hum hit Deckard's ears. "No," he gasped. The Shades couldn't come yet. Not while they were all isolated like this.

Deckard didn't know what to do; he didn't know how to stop the drag of Time magic on their group. The hum began to fill his ears, a sharp, rhythmic sound like the ticking of a clock.

Deckard took a step forward, but Evylin was too far away. He couldn't reach her fast enough. "Evylin!" he yelled, desperate to get her attention. She was too far, too out of sync with his timeline to hear him.

The hum increased, the vibration shaking him to the core. A horde of Shades would come, and they'd kill them all.

Ahead, Evylin stopped.

She turned, the Night sword a bright amethyst beam in her hand. From across the expanse, Deckard knew instinctively that she was looking at him. She'd heard him.

Suddenly, Evylin moved. With speed like he'd never seen, she was at Ethenn's side. Then they were sprinting back.

Another swell of the hum pressed in on Deckard like a chime of a kirk bell. Evylin and Ethenn were on their way to him, but the army of Shades had arrived. Their clay forms spiraled, white sand swirling around the pieces of their magic-cobbled forms.

Deckard raised his sword, ready to fight. He just had to hold his position long enough for Evylin and Ethenn to reach him.

A hand gripped Deckard's arm, and he jerked away, thinking it was a Shade.

"Jonn!"

Instantly, Deckard's tension calmed at Evylin's voice. He turned to her, sword still at the ready. She gripped his arm tightly as Ethenn kept a hand on her shoulder. "We have to hold onto each other," she explained.

As one, the Shades moved in, each poised to attack.

"Evie," Ethenn said warily, "I kind of need my hand back."

Evylin cursed under her breath as Deckard swiped at the first Shade that came near. With her fingers clutching his arm, his reach wasn't as precise as usual, and he narrowly missed the creature. Evylin struck out with the Night sword, slashing the Shade across the chest. It burst apart in a shower of sand.

The three of them shrank back from the spray. With a flash, Evylin shifted the sword into a Relic, flung it around her neck, and then knocked Ethenn's hand off her arm. She shoved it toward the Wind bow before grabbing the collar of his coat. "Shoot!" she ordered.

Ethenn let off a flurry of arrows, each one a wisp of silver. With deadly accuracy, he killed Shade after Shade, eruptions of sand crashing like waves onto the glass floor.

Lunging with his sword, Deckard fended off each Shade that made it through Ethenn's cover. Sand cascaded at their feet. Hands occupied with keeping their trio on the same timeline, Evylin could only strike with her feet when a Shade came near.

"We have to help the others," Ethenn said as the horde thinned.

Deckard caught a glimpse of the Calders, struggling to defend themselves with slow flares of light and spurts of flame. At the top of the staircase, Thom and Rafferty remained frozen as the Shades dodged the Calders to attack them.

Evylin adjusted her grip on the men. "We run together," she said.

Cautiously, they turned, moving as one. They broke into a sprint, ignoring the press of Shades to get to the Calders faster. A handful of the creatures burst apart at the strike of one of Ilain's flames, white sand and fresh shards of glass spraying into her face. She stumbled back into another Shade. Ethenn let off an arrow, striking straight and true through the Shade's head. It burst apart, and Ilain jerked forward, the sharp spray causing her footing to be off balance.

Evylin locked her ankle around Ethenn's, then reached out to catch Ilain.

Ilain's forward motion yanked Evylin, and subsequently, Deckard, forward with her. However, she caught herself before falling. "What's happening?" she asked immediately.

"We have to keep a physical connection to stay in sync with one another," Evylin explained while Deckard and Ethenn attended to the Shades around them.

Ilain scowled. "I hate Time magic."

Ethenn ducked under a Shade's swipe, and Ilain blasted it with Fire. "We have to get to the others," she said.

"We know," Ethenn replied.

"Ilain," Evylin said, narrowly dodging another attacker. Deckard kicked it back before stabbing it through the gut. "Hold my hand and Ethenn's collar. We'll get to Auden."

As a cluster of limbs with only Deckard and Ethenn capable of defending themselves, they slowly worked back to the entrance. Too slowly. Deckard didn't know how they'd manage to fight their way through the Keep. How could they keep seven people linked and fight wave after wave of Shades? It didn't seem possible.

As they progressed, a Shade tackled Auden, sending him tumbling through the air. Ethenn's arrow struck, the Shade crumbling to dust, leaving only Auden suspended as he languidly began to descend.

Near enough to reach him, Ilain tugged on Evylin's arm, pulling Deckard with them. She drew Evylin's hand to rest on Ethenn's shoulder before releasing her hold. Then she slipped under Evylin's arm, one hand still gripping Ethenn's collar as she reached out to grab Auden's ankle with the other.

"Wait!" Evylin warned too late.

The second Ilain's hand touched Auden, his speed met theirs, and he crashed to the floor, taking the rest of them with him. They fell in a heap of limbs and sand on the glass, Shades scrambling toward them on every side. The singular benefit of the mishap was that they were all touching each other.

Ilain, free of the need to hold onto anyone, threw up her hands. A billowing cloud of fire seared through the air, and the remaining Shades burst into sand and glass.

Freed of the first wave, Deckard scrambled to stand while Ilain explained the situation to Auden. Evylin kept a grip on Deckard's sleeve, but she adjusted her hand into his so that he could help her up, too, the press of her palm warm against his skin. Carefully, the five of them rose to their feet. They placed Auden in the center, one hand on Evylin's shoulder and the other on Ilain's. Deckard and Ethenn maintained the sides. They moved for the staircase where Thom and Rafferty stood, the men slightly off-kilter from the relentless attacks of the army of Shades.

The first up the stairs, Deckard and Ethenn put their hands on their shoulders, ready for them to jump into action.

Nothing happened.

"Thom," Deckard said, tightening his grip. He shook his brother. Still, no response.

"Why aren't they moving?" Ethenn asked.

"They don't have magic," Evylin said behind them.

Deckard looked back at her, realization dawning. Thom and Rafferty couldn't connect with Time magic because they weren't magical. They were stuck, frozen in time.

The hum rose again, harkening the next wave.

"Shades were still attacking them," Ethenn said.

Ilain's eyes went wide. "They'll kill them if we don't take them with us."

"We can't," Evylin said. "We can hardly fight as it is. We can't carry them too."

Deckard grimaced, knowing she was right. He turned back to Thom, his brother's gray-blue eyes staring back at him, unseeing. Fear stung his heart. He wouldn't let him die.

Reaching behind the men, Deckard struck the Keep's iron door. It rolled open.

"What are you doing?" Auden demanded. "We have to keep going."

"Yes," Deckard agreed, then turned to Ethenn. "But they can't come with us."

Ethenn understood. He tightened his grip on Rafferty, and, in time with Deckard, they shoved both men back into the waiting antechamber.

The instant their feet crossed over the threshold, they sprang to life. Unable to catch themselves in time, they landed on their backs, grunting from the fall. Rafferty let out a long string of expletives as Thom scrambled to stand. "What are you doing?" he demanded.

"I'm sorry," Deckard said, then stepped back as the iron door to the Time Keep rumbled closed.

"No!" Thom yelled, but he couldn't get to the door fast enough. It slammed shut between them, leaving the men behind.

The hum increased as Deckard turned, facing their troop's dwindling numbers. He couldn't worry about Thom and Rafferty or their long wait. The five of them had to make it through the Keep alive. And, at the moment, that task was a seemingly impossible feat.

Shades began to form, their hordes dashing for the stairs. Ethenn readily opened fire with his magical arrows, but Evylin turned to Deckard. "What do we do?" she asked. "We can't keep holding onto each other like this. I need to fight."

Staring across the vast distance to the Chamber's entrance, Deckard tightened his jaw. The Shades were growing in number despite Ethenn's efforts. Ilain had adjusted her stance to join his defense. But Evylin was right; they couldn't keep holding onto one another this way. They all needed to use their skills if they wanted to survive this Keep.

Deckard sheathed his sword. "We have to split up," he said. "And I have to use my magic."

"Split up?" Auden asked dubiously.

"Two and three?" Ethenn suggested between his shots. "You and Evie go together. I'll help the Calders."

Deckard gave Evylin the opportunity to object. Instead, she took his hand and pulled the Night Relic from around her neck. It beamed a brilliant purple, a tremor of power threading through her hand and into his as it shifted into a sword.

"We run," Evylin said.

Without another word, Deckard and Evylin rushed down the stairs, slipping past the Calders and Ethenn, stepping immediately into their own timeline together. They charged into the fray of Shades, bolts of Day shining past them. Auden's magic moved at a fraction of a second behind Deckard and Evylin's pace. Fire twisted around them, flying along with silver arrows.

The warmth of magic spread over Deckard's skin, and he grabbed hold of it, sending its power surging through his veins. Hours of training with Auden had honed his connection with the resources. While he still struggled to access Day or Time magic, as the highlord wished he would, he *had* found himself readily accessing the steady and expansive thrum of his primary resource—Night. Now, it whispered in his ears, urging him to access the well of power within him.

Deckard didn't fully grasp *how* he knew how to wield the resource. It wasn't something he thought should be natural. However, he leaned into Hewitt's training so long ago: *"You don't think about it. You do it."*

So without bothering to consider his actions, Deckard let the magic flow through him. The very edges of his vision darkened as he sent a single spiral of crystalline magic into the mass of Shades. The onyx-like shadow swirled and separated, piercing through three Shades at once. Ivory sand tumbled onto the glass floor.

Meeting the army of Shades, Evylin slashed through one and swept the legs out from under another before cutting it down too. She had to bend backward to avoid the attack of a new Shade. Deckard slammed his tricep into the Shade's head, dazing it as Evylin regained her balance and drove the Night sword into the creature's chest in a brilliant arc of violet light.

Deckard returned his focus to his magic, sending individual shadows in a sweep of glittering shards through a whole line of Shades. Each shadow dissipated too quickly. Without the ability to use both of his hands, the gestures felt weak and disjointed, as though he were fighting at half his strength.

Evylin's fingers tightened on his, sending a tingling sensation up his arm. She wielded her sword with choppier thrusts than usual, her movements more erratic than graceful. As much as Deckard couldn't help but enjoy their contact after so long apart, it hampered them both.

"On your left," Evylin said but didn't wait for him to heed her warning. She lifted their hands above her head, spinning under them as though in a dance. Then she lunged in front of him, the Night sword's vibrant purple glow slicing up into the Shade only inches from his side.

Deckard thought to thank her, but all his effort was focused on maintaining the small bursts of his power he was able to send forth into the fray.

"I need both hands," Evylin said, shifting her feet as she struggled to defend.

Unable to assist her, Deckard twisted his free hand, guiding his dampened magic. "So do I."

A Shade leaped at them, and Evylin swiped it down. Sand crashed into them both at its death. "Then we take turns," she said and released his hand.

For a fraction of a second, Deckard moved more slowly than Evylin. Then her hand hit the middle of his back as she stepped behind him.

Time resumed its fast pace, and a fresh wave of focus hit Deckard. Heat coated his body, the magic filling him with its voracity. It murmured in his ears excitedly. The world turned a shade darker, and he raised both hands.

A powerful wave of magic broke forth, creating a wall of shimmering black crystals with a tinge of purple in their facets. A mound of sand was left in its wake.

With the Shades destroyed, Deckard looked for the Calders and Ethenn. They had made it much farther ahead in the Keep, Ethenn standing between the two Mages, sending off flurries of arrows. Fire and Day flashed around them as they made quick time toward the Chamber.

"We've got to catch up," Deckard said.

Evylin's hand dragged across his back and down his arm. "Hold onto me," she ordered.

Forgoing her hand, Deckard placed his hand on her shoulder to allow her as much range of motion as possible. "Go," he said, and they set off at a sprint.

The Night sword's radiant amethyst glow reflected off the stark white glass of the room as she tore through oncoming Shades. Deckard's dark shadows, weaker once more, aided where they could. They shuffled over the sand of fallen opponents, careful not to slide over the slick surface.

The hum of their attackers pounded in Deckard's head, the steady clanging rhythm jarring. He clung to his concentration, letting Evylin's steady presence guide his focus. Darkness severed dozens of Shades as his hand guided the shards through the air.

Halfway through the Keep, Evylin stopped as another wave made its approach. There were too many of them to count, and while Deckard and Evylin defended themselves readily, it halted their progress. Deckard's shadows fended them off as a ranged attack while Evylin's sword caught any that broke through his guard. However, without both of his hands and total attention, too many managed to slip past him.

Sand turned into tiny mountains at their sides. Evylin darted across to Deckard's right, pulling her out of his grasp. His hand began to fall from her shoulder—time slowed—then she caught it—and time sped back up. He regained control of the crystalline shadows as she and her sword danced at his side. More Shades dropped.

Then Evylin spun. "Over," she called.

Deckard didn't even question his instincts. He bent down, and Evylin released his hand. A slow second ticked past. Evylin launched herself up, rolling over his back and landing to cut down a Shade on the other side.

Sand sprayed.

Time slowed.

Deckard's and Evylin's hands met.

They sprinted forward, back in sync with one another.

"Your turn," Evylin said, loosening her grip. Her fingers slid up his arm, sending coils of power along his skin. A renewed strength blossomed within him.

Deckard raised his hands, gesturing ahead and around them. Two new, stronger shadows of the deepest black rose with them, their arcs racing across the Keep. With a thundering surge of energy, his magic ripped through every Shade, blasting them into cascades of creamy-white powder.

Only once more did they have to stop on their way to the Chamber entrance. As they battled across the floor, Deckard and Evylin moved in perfect unison. The magic filled him, and he felt lost to its sway as he had in Dunneshead. Yet, his mind was centered, his actions instinctual, and his body thrummed with an internal heat. His emotions grew cold and calculated, all sense of feeling set aside. All the while, Evylin moved with him, slashing, gliding, spinning, and tearing through Shade after Shade with all the grace of a waltz.

They were nearly to the Chamber when Deckard realized that *this* was what the Calders had spoken of: Warrior and Mage in perfect balance.

They reached the towering pillar with the Chamber's entrance moments after the Calders and Ethenn. The young Warrior shot his silver arrows with precision as Ilain opened the iron door. Rapidly, the three of them darted inside. Evylin took down another Shade before Deckard pushed her to follow Auden. A final Shade lunged, blocking the door, and Deckard lifted his hand. A single shard of black shot through its featureless face as Evylin yanked him into the Chamber. The Shade crumbled to sand, and the door shut behind him.

Gasping for breath, Evylin turned to Deckard, their hands still clasped tightly together. His pulse hammered so hard he could practically feel it in his throat. He leaned against the stone wall in relief.

Ilain set her hand on Evylin's arm. "We can't let go of one another," she warned. "Not even in here."

Deckard nodded, squeezing Evylin's hand. "Of course," he said dryly. "That would make it too easy."

A soft chuckle escaped Evylin. He tried not to let it go to his head.

Between the Calders, Ethenn gestured down the steps. "Whatever Guardian is waiting for us in the Chamber, it won't be good," he noted.

"Not to worry, darling," Ilain said, an unusual twinkle in her verdant gaze. "We've got two Existential Mages to take care of that little problem for us."

Deckard flinched. "I don't know how to defeat a Guardian."

"I'll do most of it," Auden said calmly. "Follow my lead and hone your focus on Time alone."

Deckard ran his free hand through his sweat-dampened hair. "Easy," he mumbled sourly.

"In that case," Evylin said, then loosened her grip on Deckard.

She set his hand on her hip, and Deckard blanched, glancing down at it. He raised his gaze just in time to see her lift the chain of the Night Relic. "You're going to need this more than I," she said, placing it over his head to hang around his neck.

An immediate flare of energy swelled in Deckard, but he tamped it down.

"That won't help him connect with Time," Auden said in an annoyed tone. "It'll just strengthen his focus on Night."

Evylin settled him with a steely gaze that reminded Deckard of Hewitt. "Which would you rather have: a more focused Mage or a less focused one?" she demanded.

Begrudgingly, Auden turned away without a word.

With his hand still resting on Evylin's hip, Deckard thought his focus might be on the wrong thing entirely. He straightened, meeting her gaze. "I don't want you risking yourself," he said. "You're safer with the Relic."

Evylin's fingers closed around his wrist as though holding his hand in place. "I'll be fine," she promised. A flippant smile came to her lips, her amber eyes shining brightly. "So long as *you* take care of the Guardian."

The subtle tease in her voice tugged at Deckard. For all the world, it sounded like she was flirting with him. He didn't dare hope such a case was true. Yet, he couldn't help returning her smirk.

Deckard twisted his hand from her grasp, then threaded his fingers with hers. "I'll see what I can do."

CHAPTER FORTY-FIVE

Evylin knew she shouldn't flirt with Deckard. She shouldn't give him hope that she'd changed her mind. But in that moment, with her senses heightened and the tingle of magic flooding her veins, she didn't care.

Evylin held his gaze—so dark a green it neared black—and dared him with her words. It felt so good to be back in his presence, to fight alongside him. After the battle they'd just waged, she finally understood the truth behind Ilain's words.

"Warriors and Mages are meant to be together."

And while it changed nothing—when they walked out of the Keep, she would still be in great danger of losing him—for a moment, Evylin couldn't care. Here, within the Time Keep's walls, as magic coursed through them, she could pretend the future wasn't uncertain. She could give in to the pull between them. She could let herself believe they *were* meant to be together.

Descending the staircase down to the Chamber, the space held sharpness and clarity. The ivory stone brightened. Their footsteps echoed loudly. She could smell their sweat and taste the salt of it in the air. She even felt the heat radiating off Deckard, pulsing with an energy unlike anything she'd ever felt.

And she knew that was how it was meant to be. A Mage and a Warrior, connected by forces beyond their ken. A united team, working as one with seamless precision. Powerful. Deadly. Balanced.

Auden glanced over his shoulder as they carefully walked down to the Chamber. "Once we're inside," he said, "I'll need you with me, Jonn."

Evylin's grip tightened on Deckard. "Jonn and I are stronger together," she said.

She felt Deckard's fingers twitch between hers.

"Typically," Auden said, "I'd agree with you. However, destroying the Guardian is what matters. That can only be done if we connect to Time itself. While you, Ilain, and Ethenn will distract the creature and head for the Relic, I'll require Jonn's assistance."

Though Evylin didn't like the idea of parting with Deckard, she accepted the plan. It was his job to be a Mage. It was her job as a Warrior to protect him.

The staircase led them down, opening into the wide Chamber, a snowy-white replica of the others. Evylin felt as though she'd been plunged into a vat of the creamiest milk. The glass floor reflected their figures like a mirror. At the far end, the dais glowed like a beacon in the brightness of it all.

Auden shifted near Deckard and Evylin, a hand still on Ethenn's shoulder. "If you three run for the Relic and get it back to us, it'll help us connect more quickly," he suggested.

Ilain frowned at her brother. "I'm not exactly a sprinter, Auden."

"You'll be fine, just—"

A gentle hiss like the sound of rushing water or the rustle of a breeze tore Evylin's attention away from Auden's words. Her gaze jerked up to scan the Chamber rapidly.

"I don't like the sound of that," Ethenn said, raising his bow.

"Me neither," Evylin said.

Ilain stared between them. "What sound?" she asked.

The Warriors exchanged a glance.

Evylin drew the sword hanging at her hip. "We've got company."

At her words, Auden grabbed Deckard's arm and released Ethenn. "Then we'd better get started," he said.

Deckard gave Evylin's hand one last squeeze. "Give it hell," he whispered.

Evylin tossed him a smirk, then dipped her chin in a mock bow. "Anything for you," she said, releasing his hand reluctantly.

Separating from her husband's timeline, Evylin gripped Ethenn's upper arm, his muscles already taut, prepared to draw his bow. "Let's go," she ordered.

Ever at the ready, Ethenn guided Ilain and Evylin forward into the Chamber. The rushing sound grew louder and faster. As it reached a crescendo, the Guardian appeared.

A giant, albino creature with glistening scales slithered into their view. Ivory horns protruded from its diamond-shaped head. Crystal-white slitted eyes slashed across the room. Its tubular body was one massive muscle, weaving into the center of the hall in coils.

Without warning, the creature attacked. Pearly fangs protruded from its giant maw as it struck out toward them on the Chamber floor.

Evylin yanked Ethenn and Ilain back, narrowly dodging the Guardian's bite. Regaining his footing in a flash, Ethenn let out a flurry of arrows. Three hit their mark, embedding firmly in the beast's neck, sand trickling out of the cracks. Evylin stared in awe. Never before had they injured a Guardian so easily.

"The Relics can hurt it," she announced in awe.

"Well, in that case," Ilain said, slipping the Fire Relic from her neck, "take this."

With the ruby sword of Fire in her hand, Evylin released Ethenn and bounded toward the Guardian. Flames heated her back, Ilain's magic whirling around her toward the snake at a slightly slower speed than it normally would. With the delay, the Guardian was able to recoil from the Fire and arrows, hissing angrily. Its white, forked tongue darted between its lips.

Taking Ethenn and Ilain's distraction as her opportunity, Evylin listened to the whisper of her Warrior instincts. She pushed off the glass floor, leaping to climb onto the snake's back. The width and height of the rounded body were almost twice her size. It should have been an impossible leap. But Evylin felt the charge of magic in her muscles, and when she jumped, her body flew through the air.

Evylin landed squarely on the creature's back. Raising her fiery sword, she slashed at the thick scales. They crackled, fissures popping and spreading, but to her frustration, the heat of the flames only turned the sand to glass, effectively resealing the wounds.

She cursed as the serpent's body shifted under her feet, writhing in protest as she attacked. Her footing dislodged, she sprang off its back, tucking and rolling to break her fall. Darting for Ethenn and Ilain, Evylin grabbed the Warrior's arm and proffered the ruby sword.

"I need the Wind Relic," she said.

In one swift move, Ethenn tossed his bow, and she flicked her sword into the air. They caught them simultaneously. In his hands, the Fire Relic transformed into a cherry wood bow with a gold grip and veins of flickering rubies running along its limb. The Wind Relic became a silver, dual-ended sword.

"Go!" Ethenn shoved Evylin away as the Guardian's gaping maw descended. It slammed the glassy floor where they'd just stood.

While Ethenn and Ilain darted toward the dais and the Time Relic, Evylin sprinted straight for the Guardian. She spun the Wind sword in her hand. Its narrow handle was too short for her liking, so she tested the boundaries of her control, imagining the shaft growing longer. The Relic listened.

In her hand, the Wind sword's center hilt lengthened, becoming something between a staff and a sword. Reaching the snake's side, Evylin slashed with the sword, a deep cut splitting its glassy skin. White sand poured from the wound as the Guardian hissed in rage.

Evylin smiled. "All right," she whispered, striking again with both ends of the sword. "Let's dance, shall we?"

A flaming arrow pierced the side of the serpent's head, distracting it. Evylin leaped onto its back once more. Using the staff-like sword, she spun her wrists left and right, over and over, as she paced down the Guardian's back. Stripes gaped along its scales, sand leaking from the wounds.

The snake noticed her nonchalant parade, twisting to strike at her.

Evylin dropped to her stomach, the breath puffing from her lungs as the creature's head sailed over her body. It coiled over itself, and she pushed back to her feet. Holding her balance proved precarious as the Guardian slithered, readjusting to attack again. Another of Ethenn's arrows struck its jaw.

With Auden and Deckard's power combined, Evylin had hoped they'd have killed the creature by now. She glanced their way, realizing suddenly the reason for their delay. The men were on a separate timeline. Out of the five of them, she and Ethenn seemed to move at the fastest speed. Their ability had something to do with being Warriors, she supposed. Deckard and the Calders were much slower to gain ground.

She looked ahead. Ethenn and Ilain were close to the dais. Retrieving that Relic was essential if Deckard and Auden were going to defeat the Guardian.

The serpent's body rolled under Evylin's feet. She didn't have the luxury to watch Ethenn and Ilain's progress. With a fierce jab, Evylin punctured the Guardian's hide with one end of the Wind sword. Ensuring it was firmly embedded, she ran, dragging the blade with her. Her muscles flexed, fighting the drag of the weapon. It tore a long gash, sending a waterfall of sand over its side.

The Guardian let out a garbled cry in pain.

Evylin slid across its back, dodging its strikes. Her feet shifted with its movements, her abdomen flexing to maintain her balance. She spun the sword and sliced another stripe, letting the sand puddle on the ground below them. With every move and swipe, her body listened readily. Her senses were perfectly attuned to the world around her, regulating the brightness, the sounds, and the exertion.

The Guardian drew back to strike again. A line of silver and gold arrows stuck out of its body, neck, and head. Each reflected off the glassy scales. She planted her feet, ready for the Guardian's attack.

When the serpent snapped, Evylin pushed off its back and tucked her knees. Flipping head over heels, she sailed through the air. The Guardian rammed into a nearby column. Evylin landed on the diamond-shaped head, her feet planted right between its long, branching horns. She spun the Wind sword, chopping one of the horns in half.

The beast raised its head, hissing in rage.

Evylin rocked with its thrashing. She crouched and gripped the remaining horn to keep her footing. Ethenn's drawn-out call reached her ears, her name slowed by Time.

She slammed the Wind sword's blade into the serpent's head, holding on as she turned toward the dais. Ilain stood at Ethenn's side, Relic in hand. They were still moving at a slower pace than she was. She watched Ilain hand the glimmering Time Relic to him with what looked like languid movements.

In Ethenn's hand, the Fire bow became a sling. He fitted the Time Relic inside and prepared, his eyes locking with Evylin's.

She gave him a nod, and he reared back, twirling the sling, then released.

The Time Relic sailed through the air.

Evylin steadied herself, watching carefully. Given their varying timelines, she had to pace herself with Ethenn and Ilain. The projectile flew steadily toward her. She took a deep breath, watching its course. Pulling the Wind sword free, she relied even more on the magic within her.

The world slowed down just as it had in Dunneshead. She could see everything in infinitesimal clarity. Ethenn and Ilain watched, wide-eyed and hopeful. Deckard and Auden stood at the back, clasping one another's arms, hearts pounding. Sand flowed from the Guardian's wounds as it slithered and wriggled, trying to displace her from its head.

The Time Relic glided through the air, its path too low for her to catch.

Evylin pressed her lips together and ran. The Wind sword shifted again, becoming a short sword. She jumped off the back of the serpent's head, jamming the sword into its neck, slowing her descent. Sand poured out of the slit over her. She spluttered, shaking her head and spitting out the grit. Then she released the sword, pushing off the Guardian's neck.

Evylin dove, extending her hand as far as she could.

The Time Relic met her palm.

Tucking, she dropped to the ground, her mind focused on keeping the Relic in necklace form as she held it to her chest. She rolled across the glass floor, then clambered to her feet. Suddenly, time resumed its normal pace, the heightened Warrior clarity dropping away. Hastily gathering her presence of mind, she dashed around a pillar to avoid the Guardian's attack. Yet, it followed, its remaining horn scraping a chunk out of the column.

With her free hand, Evylin pulled out a throwing knife. She flung two blades in rapid succession. They both struck the snake's slitted eye nearest to her. The first bounced off, while the second splintered the glassy orb. The Guardian screamed.

Evylin took advantage of the beast's distraction to sprint across the sandy floor. Her darting footsteps were unsteady in her desperation. She felt her focus slipping, her stamina slowly seeping away after so much time under tension. She just had to make it to Deckard.

The sound of slithering came from behind her. The Guardian was making its way toward her. She could sense it looming, feeling the cavernous echo of its maw as it opened its jaws to strike.

She was so close.

In the mirrored floor beneath her, Evylin could see the snake's fangs descending.

So close.

The loose white sand gave way, and Evylin's feet slipped out from under her. She accepted the fall, letting her momentum carry her forward. The Guardian's fangs hit the glass, and Evylin felt a tug on the end of her braid.

Head stinging, Evylin pushed off the floor and sprinted the final distance. She gripped Deckard's arm, tearing it free from Auden's grasp.

"What—?" Auden began to protest, their timelines instantly converging.

"Here!" With no time to explain, Evylin shoved the Time Relic into Auden's open palm, then placed first Deckard's and then her hand on top.

Auden gasped as a simultaneous heat ripped through Evylin's body.

Like an all-consuming fire, it burned in her veins, muscles, sinew, and bones. But the sensation didn't hurt; it just felt like power. Unexplainable, overcoming power. Gooseflesh spread across her skin. Her every sense grew too strong, too aware. She felt, saw, heard, smelled, and tasted everything. The feeling overwhelmed her, and the universe crashed in on her in a single moment.

And then, the feeling was gone, and the magic dissipated.

"What was that?" Evylin asked in a staggered breath.

Auden gave her a surprised look. "That's what our power feels like," he said.

"But on an exponential level," Deckard added, clearly dazed.

With a shrug, Auden agreed. "That's what happens when we destroy a Guardian."

"What? Every time?" Evylin asked, a phantom tingle still tracing her spine.

"Yes," Auden said simply.

Turning, Evylin surveyed the Chamber hall. The Guardian was gone, though mounds of sand still littered the glass floor. Ilain and Ethenn jogged across the expanse. He stooped to pick up the Wind Relic Evylin had dropped. Ilain wore the Fire Relic once more. It flickered brightly against her chest.

Ethenn set a hand on Evylin's arm when they approached. He proffered the Wind Relic to her. "Would you like this back?"

Evylin brushed some of her sweat-slicked hair out of her face. "That's all right. You keep it."

"We have five Relics now," Auden said, holding up the Time Relic. "We can all carry one."

Accepting the new Relic, Evylin took a moment to inspect it. The gold chain and casing resembled the others, although this one bore the same clock-like designs she recognized from the antechamber. A brilliant white diamond glittered in the center. With a surge of energy, Evylin prompted it to transform into a white-bladed broadsword, its hilt made of ivory. While it looked like fragile porcelain, the weight was perfect in her hand, a true work of magic.

Looking back at the others, Evylin smiled. "Well," she said, "shall we be sure Thom and Rafferty haven't lost faith in us and decided to return to Ephria on their own?"

Light laughter spread between the group. Remaining carefully connected, they turned to the staircase. And once more, Evylin allowed herself to take Deckard's hand. Be it a foolish indulgence or not, she reveled in the contact.

For their remaining journey through the Keep, she would feel this connection. She would savor the life that filled her senses because of it. And for one fleeting moment, she would let herself be his Warrior.

CHAPTER FORTY-SIX

They fought their way out as they'd gone in—Evylin and Deckard together; Ethenn with the Calders. With five Relics and ready practice, the journey went by more quickly. Despite the seeming ease of their escape, as they rushed up the steps to the Keep's door, Evylin's tunic clung to her back, and her breathing was greatly labored.

The iron door rumbled open, and Evylin sighed in relief. Exhaustion caused her muscles to ache. She was ready for a *long* night's sleep.

White light greeted them in the antechamber as the door rolled open, Thom and Rafferty immediately bolting upright from their seats on the ground.

"What the hell was that?" Thom demanded, his hands notably shaking. "Why did you leave us here?"

"Calm down, darling," Ilain said, patting his cheek as she walked past. "We were saving your life."

Thom gaped. "My life?"

"What happened in there?" Rafferty asked, his white-blond hair disheveled as though he'd been pulling at it in worry.

"We don't have time to explain," Deckard said, releasing Evylin to move through the arched hall. "It's time for us to make our way back to Ephria."

A hopeful pang went through Evylin. *Back to Ephria.* What a wonderful sentence. Back to sunshine and warmth. Back to rolling hills and ivy-covered homes.

They ascended the stairs to emerge on the Waulden shoreline. Hours had passed since their entrance. A golden sunset glittered along the waves. Fluffy, painted clouds filled the horizon. The gray shoreline was calming after their tiring fight through the Keep.

Evylin took a deep breath of the salty air. She had to admit that Wauld did hold *some* beauty.

As the troop returned up the hillside, a cheerful camaraderie broke forth. After weeks apart, they were finally able to relax together again, if only momentarily. They would split to leave the Reach, but they would enjoy the modicum of time they had left before parting.

Auden and Ilain walked in front, her hand tucked under her brother's arm as they caught up. Their closeness warmed Evylin, making her think of how she'd once been with Ryen. At the back, Rafferty plagued Ethenn with questions about the Time Keep. Thom walked with them, eager for details too.

And all the while, Deckard walked beside Evylin, the two of them remaining silent.

Worry crept along the recesses of Evylin's mind. She was so happy to see him, to be with him. Every part of her longed to take his hand again or to drape his arm across her shoulders so she could press into his side. It was as though being near him wasn't enough. She had to *feel* his nearness physically.

But nothing had changed. Not truly. Her fears hadn't been resolved. She couldn't revoke her request. She couldn't stay with him. So as they passed into the trees, Evylin maintained her distance and stared straight ahead.

Suddenly, Deckard's low chuckle reached her ears. Evylin's gaze flashed to him, finding him smiling to himself.

"What's so funny?" she asked, drawn to the warm timbre of his laughter.

Deckard startled as though he'd forgotten she was there. He scratched the back of his head, his gaze darting guiltily to the side. He was hiding something.

"Nothing," he lied badly. "Just had a funny thought."

"Oh?" Evylin eyed him skeptically.

He *was* hiding something. She knew it. She scanned the trees around them but couldn't figure out what it was.

Prepared to question him further, Evylin paused as rough voices behind them caught her attention.

"Sod off, Thom," Ethenn said irritably.

"What's wrong with you?" Thom demanded, his voice failing an attempt at quietness. "I'm trying to be nice."

"It's a bit late for that."

"Oh, no," Evylin murmured, turning to the three men just behind her.

Thom scoffed. "Why, 'cause your girlfriend likes me better? Sorry, chap. Seems our lovely highlady is smart enough to know a *real* man when she sees him."

Ethenn moved too fast for even Evylin to react. His fist connected with Thom's jaw, the smack of knuckles against bone resounding in the forest. A few paces ahead, Auden and Ilain halted in shock. Rafferty moved out of the way, hands in the air, while Evylin and Deckard jumped into action.

"Stay back," Evylin commanded Deckard as the two men grappled. Their fists flew violently, Ethenn's skills and strength allowing him to land far more damaging blows than Thom.

"Let me—" Deckard began, but she moved faster than he could.

Quickly surveying the situation, Evylin leaped into the fray. She swept Ethenn's leg first, knocking him to his back. Then she grabbed a fistful of Thom's collar, jerking him away. "Stop it!" she commanded, effectively ending the fight.

Thom thrust a finger in Ethenn's direction. "He started it!" he retorted, blood trickling out of his nose. Half of his face was red from the blows, and his lip was split as well.

"And I'm telling you to end it," Evylin returned, then whirled on Ethenn. "And I'm telling you to grow up and control yourself!"

Slowly rising from the dirt, Ethenn ground his teeth, but he didn't respond.

Evylin released Thom with a shove. "What is wrong with you two?"

"I'm tired of his shit," Ethenn said, yanking down the hem of his coat.

Evylin huffed. "Aren't we all? But you're supposed to have better sense."

"He's a boy, Evie," Thom said, then spat out a clot of blood. "One who can't see when he's not wanted."

"Like someone else I know," Ethenn shot back.

Thom stepped forward aggressively, but Evylin blocked his path. "What's that supposed to mean?" he shouted at the young man.

"You know exactly what it means," Ethenn replied, a clear threat in his voice.

Evylin's stomach twisted, and Thom glowered. "You don't know what you're talking about," he snarled.

Ethenn raised his chin. "I heard you."

Evylin slumped. Thom swallowed. Around them, Deckard and the others waited, their attention rapt in the deafening silence.

"I'm a Warrior, remember?" Ethenn said. "Heightened senses and all that. I knew you were up to something, so I listened."

"Ethenn, don't," Evylin whispered.

"You heard nothing," Thom said disdainfully.

Ethenn's eyes glimmered with rage. "I heard you tell Evylin you love her and want to be with her."

A cold breeze rattled the trees. Raggedly, Evylin's breath slipped out. She closed her eyes, feeling Deckard's gaze burning on the back of her skull. This secret was never supposed to be revealed. She'd meant her promise to Thom; Deckard never needed to find out. The brothers' relationship could remain intact. Now, it would be broken beyond repair.

Nearest her, Thom shifted unsteadily. "So what?" he said, though his voice was shaky.

Evylin wanted to move away, feeling as though her proximity made her guilty by association.

A sharp, sardonic chuckle came from behind Evylin. She turned to see Deckard shaking his head in disappointment. "I already knew," he said with frightening calm. "I just didn't think you'd do anything about it."

"Well, I did," Thom said, a look between dread and anger entering his face.

Deckard nodded, his expression cold.

"Don't worry," Thom said sourly. "She told me no."

Deckard's eyes met Evylin's for the merest second before he turned back to his brother. "Why?"

"I'd guess because she doesn't feel the same."

"No, Thom," he said, anger seeping into his voice. "Why did you do it?"

Thom's voice was tense when he shouted back. "Because I'm tired of watching you get what I deserve!"

A long silence stretched over the group as the brothers glared at one another. Rafferty stood to the side, watching with keen interest. Ethenn crossed his arms, scowling. Ilain and Auden shared worried, baffled looks. And Evylin desperately sought a way to bring it to an end, knowing that Thom didn't mean the words he was about to say.

"My whole life," Thom went on, "I've stood behind you in everything. While you're so busy pretending to be perfect, *I'm* the one who's been at her side from the beginning. *I'm* the one taking care of her."

"She's not your responsibility," Deckard said.

"'Cause she's not my wife," Thom retorted. "As you love to remind me. Forgive me for believing that my love for her was more genuine than yours, as I don't see it as a job but a privilege."

Deckard took a challenging step forward. "That's not what I meant."

"But it's what you said."

Every harsh word felt like a blow to Evylin's heart. She hated it, hated watching them crumble. Despite herself, she'd come to care for them both. She couldn't bear them coming apart over her. Thom was her brother. Deckard was her. . . .

"Is this why you've been fighting?" Ilain asked in the lingering silence. She looked at Ethenn, then Thom. "Because it wasn't a joke. Jonn really did ask you to make sure Thom didn't steal his wife?"

Evylin drew in a sharp breath, surprised. Had Deckard charged Ethenn with such a task?

Ethenn swallowed, his eyes on the dirt. "That's part of it," he mumbled.

A cruel laugh slipped out of Thom. "Oh, come on, Loxley. We're all being honest here. It's your turn."

Auden shifted anxiously. "We don't have time for this," he said. "We need to leave the Reach."

Thom didn't listen. "How 'bout it, kid?" He moved past Evylin and shoved Ethenn's shoulder. "Would you like to share the truth?"

"Thom," Evylin called, "stop it."

A red flush covered Ethenn's neck. He didn't back down from Thom's baiting, but neither did he rise to it. "I knew about Thom's feelings for Evylin," he said to Ilain, though he refused to look at her. "So I told him to stop flirting with you."

"That's—" Ilain cut herself off. Because Evylin knew, while there was no truth behind her flirtation with Thom, Ethenn wouldn't understand her motivation.

"The thing is, Loxley," Thom smirked, "our highlady is the last one you needed to worry about."

A sinking feeling churned in Evylin's gut.

"What was between us—" Thom motioned to Ilain and then himself. "It was never real."

Ethenn's expression fell in confusion.

Ilain opened her mouth, but Thom kept going. "She *asked* me to flirt with her. Not because she wanted me."

Evylin hesitated, unsure if Thom was about to reveal Ilain's true feelings or . . .

"Because she *didn't* want you," Thom concluded. "We were never anything. But that's more than you could *ever* be to her."

In a blinding flash, Evylin saw the switch in Ethenn's demeanor, the fire in his eyes, only a millisecond before he acted. *"Inevitably, I snap."*

The Warrior was on Thom again, his deadly blows more accurate and brutal than ever. Within a second, the men were on the ground, Ethenn pummeling Thom's face, again and again. Another second, and there was a grotesque *crack*, then Ethenn's hands curled around Thom's neck. Thom struggled helplessly, his face going from red to purple.

Coming to her senses, Evylin sprang forward to stop Ethenn before it was too late.

"Stop!" Deckard shouted, a depth and volume to his voice that was unnatural. It was loud and fierce and doubled, as if there were two of him. A growl of sound that made Evylin's blood run cold.

Everyone froze, turning to stare at Deckard and the ghost by his side.

With a heave, Ethenn released Thom, who lay on the ground, gasping for air. The young Warrior staggered back as Rafferty stood to the side, mouth gaping. Ilain set a hand to her mouth, and Auden's eyes went wide in rage.

But Evylin's heart fluttered, her eyes filling with tears. "Uncle?" she whispered.

In the fading light, Hewitt stood beside Deckard, looking just as she remembered him, his scraggly beard, bushy eyebrows, massive frame, and commanding presence unchanged. Whole and alive. He wore his gray military coat, with the major's insignia on the left breast pocket. His sword hung, belted at his waist. The hilt of a dagger peeked out from his boot. And his gray eyes pierced her with the intense stare that made her feel so safe, so secure.

"Hello, Evie," Hewitt said, his rumbling voice resonating deep within her soul.

Before she could ask one of the thousand questions pressing to her lips, Auden pushed past Ilain. "I told you to let him go," he yelled at Deckard.

"And I told him not to," Hewitt said with a glare that challenged the highlord to defy him.

Evylin looked at Deckard. His green-blue gaze was locked on her as the Night Relic beamed bright amethyst on his chest. "You did this?" she asked.

"Yes," Deckard said gently.

"What's happening?" Rafferty asked. "How's Hewitt here?"

"I'm a ghost," Hewitt said.

Rafferty laughed nervously. "Good one. But really—how are you here? Did you make a deal too?"

"What?"

"Nothing."

Deckard sighed. "I summoned him."

"I told you not to, Jonn," Ilain said worriedly.

"It was before we spoke," Deckard told her by way of apology.

Evylin didn't care about any of their questions or qualms. She crossed the space between them, staring up into the face of the man she thought she'd never see again. His expression softened, and he gave her a fond smile. The one he never gave to anyone but her.

"Is it really you?" she asked.

Hewitt dipped his chin. "It is."

The truth hit her all at once. Her vision in the Night Keep. Deckard's disappearances into the woods. His deep connection to Night magic.

"I saw you," Evylin said. "In the Night Keep."

"I thought so," Hewitt said. "I didn't dare to hope . . ."

Auden grumbled in the background, but everyone ignored him.

Evylin turned to Deckard. Her eyes dropped to the Relic, understanding dawning. "You summoned him with Night magic?"

"I did," he said, his tone repentant.

Thoughts swirling and heart pounding, Evylin dropped her head into her hands. Her fingers felt like ice against her cheeks. She couldn't understand, couldn't reconcile everything that was happening. After the Time Keep, Thom's confession, and Ethenn's attack, she was too tired, too emotionally wrung out to comprehend that her uncle—her *dead* uncle—was standing in front of her. Her breathing grew shallow as she struggled to keep the tears at bay.

As she hesitated, Auden began to order Deckard to release the ghost. Ilain tried to rationalize with her brother, but he shrugged her off. Rafferty helped Thom up, his face and throat splotched with welts and blood. Ethenn stood to the side, staring at his bloody hands.

Evylin closed her eyes, blocking out everyone else. Her thoughts churned over and over.

Hewitt was dead. But he was here.

Hewitt was a ghost. But he was here.

Hewitt was *here*.

"Would you two *shut up*?" Hewitt shouted at the Calders.

The siblings went silent.

"Thank you." Hewitt scanned the group. "For the first time in a month, I get to talk to someone other than Deckard, and I'm going to use it to my advantage."

The whole troop waited, frozen as they hung on the ghost's words.

Hewitt nodded, pleased with their compliance. "Let's get one thing straight: I'm not here for any of you. I'm here for Evylin. So your petty quarrels and fears of certain types of magic don't matter to me. I'm not benevolent. I'm her uncle."

The smallest smile tugged at Evylin's lips.

"However," Hewitt eyed them each in turn, "your conflicts do interfere with my girl's happiness, which makes them my problem. And if you don't get your acts together, I will come back and haunt each one of you until the end of your days."

"That doesn't sound so bad," Rafferty muttered, and Thom snorted.

The sound drew Hewitt's attention. His sharp stare fell on Thom. "You." He spat the single word like an accusation.

Thom slouched but didn't back away. His nose was notably broken, his face already turning black and blue.

Hewitt moved around Evylin, aggressively bearing down on Thom. "I trusted you," he said accusingly. "And you betrayed me."

"I didn't!" Thom insisted, panic filling his face.

"You tried to take her. You don't call that a betrayal?"

"Not a betrayal of you."

"I chose *him*." Hewitt pointed back to Deckard, then to Thom. "Not *you*."

Thom turned away.

"*She* chose him," Hewitt added, and Evylin's heart squeezed. "If you truly cared for her, then you'd respect that."

Thom kept his gaze down but nodded.

"Humph." Hewitt swung around. "As for the rest of you: I'll state it one more time. Get your acts together. You're not children. Stop acting like it."

Ethenn, Ilain, and Auden studiously avoided Hewitt's gaze.

Rafferty raised his hand. "I'd like to point out," he said, setting the hand to his chest, "*I've* done nothing wrong."

Evylin smiled, and, to her surprise, Deckard laughed.

"Bully for you," Hewitt grumbled. "Now, get out of here, all of you. I want a moment alone with these two."

Auden didn't listen. "We've lingered for too long," he argued. "And this magic is too dangerous—"

Ilain set a hand on his arm. "I'll travel with Ethenn," she announced. "With his power and the Fire Relic, I should be able to shroud us just long enough to cross the border. Auden can take Thom and Rafferty."

"I'll need the Night Relic—"

"Shut up, Auden," Ilain said, passing an encouraging smile to Evylin before pushing her brother toward the dismantled campsite.

As the Calders made their way through the trees, Rafferty put each arm around Thom and Ethenn's shoulders. "Come on, gents," he said merrily. "Let's see if the Day Mage can put your face to rights, Thommy."

Once the Ephrians disappeared beyond the tree line, Hewitt turned to Evylin and Deckard. "I don't miss them," he said flatly.

Evylin let out a gasping laugh. Her head was light with emotion, and her eyes were full of tears.

"Now," Hewitt said, meeting her gaze, "it's your turn."

Taking a deep breath, Evylin stepped closer. "Can I touch you?"

Hewitt frowned. "No. I'm just an image."

Evylin's tears fell. "I don't understand," she whispered. "How are you here?"

"By Night magic, I'm told," Hewitt said with a grin in Deckard's direction.

"But *how*?" It was Deckard she turned to ask then.

Giving her one of his most comforting smiles, Deckard shrugged. "I really don't know. It just happened. One moment, he was here, and I . . . I've kept him with me all this time."

"*All* this time?"

"Since we buried him."

Evylin furrowed her brow. "Why didn't you tell me?"

"At first, I thought I was going crazy," he admitted. "I didn't know it was magic. And when I finally realized what I'd done, I wasn't strong enough to make him visible to you, and I didn't want you to think . . ."

Evylin's fingers found her rings. "You were right. I would have thought you were trying to manipulate me."

Stepping between them, Hewitt drew their attention. "You two can discuss this later. For now, Auden is right. We need to make this reunion quick so you can leave."

Deckard nodded. "I can feel my reserves running out of magic as it is. The Keep drained me."

"Then you'd best give me a minute with her."

With a glance at Evylin, Deckard stepped back. "I'll be just beyond those trees," he told her.

Evylin caught his hand before he could leave, heart in her throat as she whispered his name. He paused, waiting. A regretful smile came to her lips, filled with all the emotion she'd withheld over the last two weeks. "Thank you."

He gave her hand a gentle squeeze, then pulled away.

Evylin and Hewitt watched Deckard go. His long, steady strides carried him through the hazy forest, the sunset casting long shadows around the forest. The last vestiges of light caught in his hair, gilding it to a shade more red than brown.

When he passed into the trees, Evylin let her gaze fall to the rich green grass. She already knew what Hewitt planned to tell her. This was the conversation she'd never hoped to have. They would fight over her decision, and it would turn into a battle of hearts and wills.

Hewitt crossed his arms. "I'm told you defied my direct order," he said.

A sour grin came to her lips. "I know what you're going to say," she said lightly, "what you want me to do. I can't do it."

Hewitt gave her a patronizing smirk. "It's like we've had this conversation before."

"Mm." Evylin reverted to her comfort of humor. "I've always been a slow learner."

"Quite the opposite," Hewitt countered. "You're a fast learner; you're just stubborn."

"I am *your* niece, after all."

Hewitt didn't play her game. "You can't leave him."

"I *can*," she said. "Legally and emotionally."

"Why would you?"

Evylin licked her lips, hesitating. "I want to."

"Liar."

"Maybe you don't know what I want," she shot back.

His steely gaze landed heavily on her. "I know you better than you know yourself."

Evylin didn't bother denying it.

"Why would you leave him?"

"I can't be with him," she said flatly.

"You *can*. Legally, you are. Emotionally . . . That's left to be seen."

"Did you come back simply to verbally spar with me?"

"As I can't physically spar with you, what better way to spend my time?"

A sudden, unexpectedly joyful laugh erupted from Evylin. The tears returned as she stared up at his face, tracing the familiar lines. "I miss you," she said.

His expression softened. "And I miss you, my girl."

Evylin's heart pricked. It was cruel, seeing him and being unable to touch him. She would give the breath from her lungs and the blood from her veins for only one more chance to hug him, to feel the warmth of his embrace.

"Do you love him?" Hewitt asked.

Her throat burned. "No."

His stare bored into her knowingly.

"I can't," she corrected.

"Why not?"

"Because," she gasped, unable to finish the explanation.

"Evylin," he stepped closer, "tell me."

"I—" She shook her head, pulling away. "I just can't."

"Yes, you can. You already do."

"I don't."

"The truth, Evylin."

"I *can't*!"

"*Why?*"

"Because of you!" she exclaimed, her voice breaking, the tears falling in earnest. "Because of Ryen. Because if I love *him*, then the day will come when I have to go through this heartache a third time. And I can't do it again."

Evylin backed away, tugging at her rings. Her chest ached as her tears fell to the forest floor. "I can't love him only to lose him too."

Hewitt didn't even flinch. He watched her in that steady, sure way of his, and she realized he already knew her reasons. "Oh, Evie," he whispered. "My dear girl, I'm so sorry."

His hand lifted before dropping back to his side, unable to comfort her.

It was too much for Evylin. A sob shook her, every part of her exhausted. "I can't do this again," she repeated. "I can't take how much it hurts."

"Evylin," he said gently, "you need to listen to me. Take a breath."

The emotion roiling inside made it hard to obey, but she squeezed her eyes shut and forced air into her lungs. Then she listened to his voice, ever a soothing balm to her ears.

"This is my fault," Hewitt said. "I taught you to run from your grief, to mask it. Together, we shut out the world. It worked for a time, but it wasn't enough. We never healed from our pain. And it didn't hurt any less."

Evylin looked up at him, desolate.

He smiled sadly at her. "You were my happiness, you know? After Irena and Ryen . . . You were the one thing that made life worth living. But I did you a disservice, letting you hold on to him through me. We should have let go together."

Her fingertips caught on the etching and gemstones of her rings. "I don't want to let him go," she whispered. "I don't want to let you go either."

"We're gone, Evylin," Hewitt said in that matter-of-fact way of his. "It doesn't matter if you try to cling to us for eternity. We can't come back."

"But you're back," she murmured.

Hewitt gave her a wry grin. "Not for good."

Disappointment stirred in her gut.

"I am here to help you find happiness, Evie," he said tenderly. "Once I've ensured that, I will go."

"What if I can't be happy without you?" Evylin lifted her chin, daring to use his words against him. "What if *you're* my happiness too?"

Hewitt considered her, a fondness glinting in his eyes just as the final rays of sunlight beamed through the trees. "Perhaps I became that for you in Whickam Village," he said, then tipped his chin toward the direction Deckard had walked. "But you found happiness with him as well. You don't need me anymore."

Evylin stared at the onyx stones under her fingertips, brushing over their fractal cuts.

"You're right," he continued. "Someday, you *will* lose him, one way or another. It's the way of life. But you can't run from that."

Evylin knew it was true. While she'd been trying to prove to herself that she didn't love him, that she could escape the hurt if she lost him now, her heart was breaking anyway. It hurt, every moment spent pushing him away and protecting herself—it all hurt.

"Is that all there is?" Evylin asked brokenly. "A moment of happiness and a lifetime of misery?"

"Yes," Hewitt said. "But generally, it winds up being a lifetime of happiness and only a moment of misery."

A chilling breeze cut through, and a misting of raindrops began to fall. It felt as though Wauld was weeping with Evylin, sharing her grief and fear. She tightened her grip on her rings, her eyes lifting to the trees where Deckard stood waiting. Love him or leave him. Which would hurt less?

"I already love him," Evylin whispered, the admission frightening and liberating all at once.

Hewitt smiled at her. "Tell him. Stay with him."

Evylin shivered, and whether it was from the cold rain or the uncoiling emotion within, she wasn't sure. But something like relief blossomed in her chest. It felt like the ivy of Estshire was growing up to mend the shattered fragments of her heart.

She looked up at Hewitt. "What if he won't take me back?" she asked, knowing it was impossible.

Hewitt scoffed. "Don't be ridiculous. He'll fall at your feet."

A bittersweet laugh slipped from her. She looked up at her uncle, the man she loved and trusted with her whole being. By whatever magic he'd done it, Deckard had given her this chance, this moment to be with Hewitt, to truly process her grief.

"I wish I could touch you," she said. "I would give anything . . ."

"As would I."

A steady rumble met Evylin's ears. She turned toward the tree line, hearing the hooves of the horses approaching from the direction of the camp. "It sounds like it's time to go," she said with a sigh.

"We took too long," Hewitt agreed.

Together, Evylin and Hewitt moved slowly toward the trees. It felt like nothing had ever changed, as though they were walking through the army camp or traveling through the Ephrian countryside with the Calders. She wished they had more time, that they didn't have to rush to leave the Reach. But she wondered how much longer Deckard could have held onto the magic after he'd already been taxed so much. Perhaps soon, he'd be able to summon Hewitt to talk with her again.

The shadows grew longer, with only the moons and stars giving light to the forest now. The rumble of the horses' approach grew louder, and Evylin paused to listen, a frown growing on her face. It was too loud, too thundering for their small, split band of horses. She turned to look at Hewitt, but he was gone.

Deckard burst out of the trees at a sprint. "Evylin! Run!"

Not a second later, the horses broke through. There were dozens of them. Men in dark uniforms rode astride and ran alongside the steeds.

Evylin's heart kicked up with panic. Deckard was nearly to her, only a few feet of forest separating them. She reached out her hand, ready to run.

A rider leaped from his horse, tackling Deckard. They went rolling across the dirt.

"Jonn!" Evylin rushed forward, yanking the Time Relic from her neck. Her worn muscles protested, spasming even at the simplest movement. She prepared to fight anyway, the Relic glimmering into an ivory sword as radiant as moonlight.

Deckard managed to get the upper hand, kicking the man off before rising and incapacitating his opponent in one swift move. Evylin blinked at the speed and accuracy of his blows, impressed despite her panic. She'd never seen him brawl but found that he was surprisingly good at it.

More men pressed in, but Evylin caught up to Deckard. Readily, she cut down two new attackers, defending his back. Deckard knocked another man down. As they did in the Keep, they fought side by side. For a moment, Evylin thought they might be able to take on these unprecedented odds. After all, they were Warrior and Mage: a balanced, unified team. Then she realized that Deckard wasn't using his magic at all.

And neither was she.

Desperate, Evylin reached out and tried to connect with her own magic, waiting for the clarity, the rise, the heightened reality. It wouldn't respond.

One of the swordsmen lunged out, striking her arm. Blood welled from the gash, and the blow caused Evylin to falter. Exhaustion overwhelmed her. But she wouldn't give up.

Evylin kicked out, breaking the man's knee with the force of her strike. A moment later, the glow of the Time sword pulsed in his stomach.

The rain increased, becoming a torrent that seemed to descend in time with the fight. More men pressed in. Deckard grunted in pain. Evylin glanced over her shoulder to see one of their attackers kick Deckard's leg out from under him, driving him to the ground. Two other men tackled him without hesitation.

"He's secure," one said, though Deckard struggled mightily against the three men.

"Get the woman!" a man on horseback ordered.

Deckard bucked against his captors but couldn't budge them.

Evylin continued to fight, the flame of hope struggling to stay ablaze in her heart. Her attacks were becoming sloppy, and she could feel herself weakening. Where were the others? Had these men already captured them? Or had they escaped? She tightened her grip, determined to stand her ground and free Deckard.

They wouldn't lose. They couldn't.

She managed to take down two more men before a heavy weight slammed into her side. Landing in the fresh mud, she gasped, trying to wriggle free of the figure holding her to the forest floor. The slick terrae helped. She began to slip from her captor's grasp. Then three more men were upon her, pressing her deeper and deeper into the mud.

Another man wrenched the sword from her grasp. Disconnected from her power, it shifted to a necklace, its diamond dull and lifeless. "I've got one more," he called.

One more? They had other Relics in their possession?

Frantic, Evylin looked at Deckard. They'd bound his hands, flipping him onto his back. One of them grabbed the chain around his neck, studying the pendant. Evylin's heart lurched in fear. But it wasn't the Night Relic. At the end of the chain hung a plain, tarnished bronze crest Evylin had never seen before.

"This isn't one of them," the man said, letting it fall back to Deckard's chest.

"Evie," Deckard muttered, his eyes dark green in the moonlight.

Evylin sucked in a sharp breath, tasting mud. So he was using magic. Somehow, he was using the final remnants within him to disguise the Night Relic.

A new fear crept into Evylin's mind. *"The Keep drained me."* What if Deckard blacked out? Would the Relic remain hidden?

Eyes locked with her husband's, Evylin fought harder against her captors. They shoved her cheek farther into the dirt, working to bind her wrists behind her. Tears rose as she used the terrae beneath her for leverage. The hard surface wouldn't yield to her. So the men would have to.

She pushed with all her might, determined not to let them stop her. She wouldn't let them take Deckard. Not when she was finally ready to tell him. . . .

With a furious cry of exertion, Evylin strained against the terrae, pushing the men off the ground as they struggled to hold onto her. They loosened their grip, scrambling frantically to subdue her.

"She's the Warrior, you idiots," one man yelled. "Knock her out!"

Two more men leaped into the fray, shoving Evylin down even as her skin tingled with the last dregs of power. Another man stepped forward, a dagger in his hand. The fleeting thought of "not again" passed through Evylin's mind just before he struck. The hilt slammed into her temple, and the world turned to black.

Part IV: The Countess of Keale

Should you succeed, you will have my undying gratitude, and I will see your family line secured in my empire. But know this: I desire that Warrior and will accept no other. Her role is more important than anything—in truth, she is even more important than the Relics. Her future belongs to me.

Gift her to me, and you shall receive more than a bloodline; I shall grant to you eternal life.

Excerpt from a letter from Crown Prince Rouland Blount II to his mistress, Lady Oriane Renaul, Countess of Keale

Order of the Wind
Vaura Reach
Keale
Niraus

CHAPTER FORTY-SEVEN

33RD OF CHRONOS, 1574

Rocks jolted the wagon wheels, sending spikes of pain up Deckard's spine. The attackers left him conscious after he agreed to come willingly. Though everything in him wanted to fight, with Evylin bound and passed out, and his bone-deep exhaustion after the Keep, he knew there was no use. Beyond that, he didn't know what would happen to his disguise of the Night Relic if he weren't awake to stay connected to the magic. He couldn't risk them knocking him out, too, so he complied.

However, the men had gagged him and then prodded him along while one of their other comrades flung Evylin's prone form over his shoulder. One of the riders oversaw the others from horseback. Deckard marked him as their leader. In the darkness of night, his visage was obscured, but his bearing was confident, and his orders were immediately heeded.

They brought Deckard and Evylin back to the camp where they'd kept their horses, prepared to ride out of Vaura Reach. Dozens of men milled around a large prison wagon, iron bars affixed to the wooden bed. The Ephrian soldiers and the Calders were all bound within its confines, though they hadn't bothered to gag the Mages, their eyes glazed over from the effects of viastasis. Their captors were well-armed and well-managed. A small pile of bodies lay to the side, the victims carried back from Evylin's defense.

Deckard didn't know how they'd missed the presence of this band. They'd been thorough in their search of the Keep's grounds, wary of ambush. Yet, they'd seen no sign of them at all. There didn't appear to be any magical individuals among their ranks. Did that mean they were mercenaries? Had they come to cash in on the writ?

"She's the Warrior." The writ hadn't mentioned a Warrior. So how did these men know about his wife's power?

Head down, Deckard kept his eyes and ears open as the men led him to the wagon, hoping to piece together the means of their capture. The iron-barred door creaked open, and the men shoved Deckard forward to the short stairs that led up to the wagon bed. Cautiously, he ascended. The floor of the wagon was covered in hay, and a guard sat on a stool by the door.

All five of their friends were bound to the iron bars that rose above their heads. Auden and Ethenn on one side, Ilain, Thom, and Rafferty on the other. The Mages stared ahead blankly, clearly under the influence of a drug. The Ephrians remained awake, their gazes wide and worried. Ethenn and Thom still bore blood and scrapes from their earlier fight, but Thom's nose was no longer broken, the healing likely thanks to Auden. Mud caked their clothing and hair.

Following orders, Deckard carefully stepped over their feet as he moved to the back to sit next to Ethenn. Two men followed, not caring who or what they stepped on. They bound Deckard to the bars, then reached back for Evylin's unconscious form.

Deckard couldn't tear his gaze from her. Meticulously, the men patted her down, removing every weapon they could find, then did another search to be sure, this time more slowly. He gritted his teeth around the gag, working to keep his breathing steady as they touched her more familiarly than he ever had, and he was thankful she didn't know what liberties they took with her. Her head lolled while they strapped her up next to Rafferty. Already, a welt rose on her temple where they'd hit her. The end of her braid got tangled in the ropes. He wanted to reach out and fix it, knowing it would hurt to yank the strands out later.

Breathing laboriously, he fought to retain the last ounces of strength he had, his eyes steadily fixed on Evylin. From the moment the wagon lurched to a start, through the break of dawn, and into the present moment, Deckard kept watch. His vision blurred as he watched the countryside go by. He refused to sleep, his energy remaining focused on the Relic hanging around his neck. When they'd bound him, the disguised pendant was partially covered by the rope, but it was not obscured enough to give him the confidence to relax. The dull warmth of his magic was barely tangible. His skull felt as though it might split in two, aching from being awake too long and overwhelming fatigue. The whisper of power was barely audible to his straining ears.

In his half-awake daze, visions fluttered past in his unfocused gaze. White glared all around him. Ivory sand shifted around clay, forming the Time Shades.

He blinked to find Evylin's drooped head and a dirt road before him. He fought the drowsiness that tugged at him, attempting to whisk him into sleep. Another flash of an image drifted across his vision, the memory of the white dais pedestal and the glittering diamond pendant of the Relic.

Deckard shook his head. He knew this dream—it was nearly the same one he'd had after the Day and Night Keeps. Could it be a symbol of his status as an Existential Mage? He would have to ask Auden about that . . . if they lived through this.

Along the journey, Deckard's hands had fallen asleep, tingling behind his back. He shifted, attempting to bring them relief. In the open-air wagon, they'd all been soaked to the bone, though the clouds parted to reveal the sun by midmorning. The guard in the corner watched them attentively. Thom and Ethenn stared ahead, dozing on and off. Somehow, Rafferty managed to snore through his gag.

All through the night, Deckard had studied their captors carefully. He'd listened to every word spoken. He'd concluded that they were not the usual band of sellswords but an organized, efficient group of either bounty hunters or some other men-at-arms for employ. They'd been hired to do the job by someone who told them about the Relics and Evylin's magic. If they were simply mercenaries after money, they would have stolen more than the Relics. But they didn't care about the "crest" Deckard wore or his and Evylin's wedding rings.

A thought struck him as the first light of sunrise dawned. It was possible that Blount had hired these men. But if that were the case, then why hadn't the prince accompanied them?

Regardless of the origin of their capture, Deckard knew they *were* being taken to the Night Mage.

The revelation sent his mind reeling. They were carrying five Relics straight to their enemy. Once the prince had them in hand, surely, he'd kill them all.

Desperately, Deckard worked to plan an escape. But his brain refused to cooperate. It screamed in exhaustion, reminding him of how much he'd taxed it. Even if he could think straight, what good would it do him? His magic was depleted, the Calders were drugged, and at least fifty men surrounded them. Perhaps once he, Evylin, and Ethenn had returned to full strength, they could make their move. But with his hands tied behind his back, Deckard doubted his ability to control his magic well enough to rescue them.

Even if Deckard could cut their bonds with the crystalline shards of his magic, what good would it do them? Neither Evylin nor Ethenn had weapons. He would be the only one with a viable offense. No, they had to be patient and intentional when they made their escape. Blount didn't know that he and Ethenn had discovered their powers. He didn't know that another Mage and Warrior were arriving amongst the prisoners. That gave them an advantage. But if they played their hands too soon, they'd lose that edge.

Suddenly, Evylin choked, coughing against her gag as she woke, and Deckard startled out of his planning. He strained against his ropes, wishing he could comfort her as she struggled. He settled for pressing his leg against hers in the confines of the narrow wagon.

As her splutters subsided, Evylin raised her damp eyes to his. Her braid jerked her head down, and she let out a muffled cry. Then she tightened her jaw, yanking it free.

"Hey," the guard called to a nearby rider, "the Warrior woke up."

The rider turned a bored stare at the wagon. "Keep an eye on her," he instructed. "I'll tell Caustin."

As he spurred his horse away, Evylin settled her head against the bars. Her gaze held Deckard's steadily. Her leg pressed against his in acknowledgment.

They studied one another in the ensuing silence, taking clear stock of each other's safety. The cloth gag was so tight it caused her hair to bow around her cheeks, but the angry welt was her only sign of harm. Her breathing steadied, and he could have sworn she was trying to tell him something.

Ropes digging into his chest, arms, and wrists, Deckard tried to adjust his seating. It did little good. Evylin's foot pushed against his thigh. By the occasional glance through the bars, he knew they'd left the rolling hills of Vaura Reach behind, heading through a mountain pass. The presence of pines and moss-covered stones provided a monotonous background to their journey. Shafts of light melted past the clouds, catching in Evylin's amber eyes as they locked with his.

The corner of her mouth lifted.

Deckard furrowed his brow.

Despite her gag, Evylin managed to smirk. Then he felt the toe of her boot slip under his thigh.

Deckard scoffed in amusement. Here they were, captured and on the way to be put to death, and the woman was flirting with him. Blatantly and unabashedly flirting.

Understanding the intention behind her affection, knowing she was attempting to convey her apology for leaving him, Deckard let out a long breath, allowing himself to relax. He softened his expression, resting his boot gently against her leg.

"I know," his stare told her.

The rider returned then. He passed along the message that Caustin had ordered them to keep a cautious eye on Evylin but not to worry about her escape. With a name for the leader, Deckard peered through the bars, trying to perceive which rider he was, but it was impossible to see much from the wagon. He wondered at this Caustin's temperament. He ran an efficient, obedient crew; that much was certain. But through what means? Was he a harsh, violent man who ruled through fear? Or was he reasonable and practical, the sort of man you could reason with?

Periodically throughout the day, the guard took a bucket from a hook on the bars beside them and ladled water over their gags, one by one. It was an effective, if demoralizing, way of slaking their thirst. Once, he'd forced a vial of milky-white liquid down Auden and Ilain's throats. More viastasis, Deckard assumed.

When the sun hung low in the dusky sky, the wagon finally came to a halt, pulling off the road. Nothing had changed in the terrain. They were still moving through the mountain pass, the rock face towering high above them. Deckard had determined by the sun's trajectory as the day passed that they were moving east toward the border between Vaura Reach and Wauld.

Mouth dried out from the gag and his body aching, Deckard watched the men mill about, setting up their camp. The smoke of a campfire singed his nose first, the mouthwatering scent of seasoned meat following shortly after. Only one tent was erected.

A group of men clustered around the wagon as one approached the door. He unlocked it and stepped in. "Time for vittles," he said in a clipped Waulden accent.

The five Ephrians perked up while the Calders remained motionless. The guard stood. "Which one first?" he asked.

Deckard and Evylin shared a look. "First" suggested that their meals would be taken separately. There would be no conversation, no moment to take comfort together.

"Back to front," the man said, then gestured to Deckard.

Together, the men worked their way to the back of the wagon. The newcomer crouched down in front of Deckard. "Here's how this is going to work," he said, reaching for the bindings around his chest. "One at a time, I'm going to let you out. You'll have one minute to relieve yourself, then you'll be given a meal. You have five minutes to eat it. Once that time is up, you'll be brought back here and tied again, and we'll move on down the line. No negotiations, no questions, no fights. Got it?"

The final knot came free. Deckard straightened his shoulders, arching his back away from the bars. He glanced at the Relic, relieved that it remained disguised.

At Deckard's nod of understanding, the guard and his compatriot hauled Deckard up. After the Keep's exertion and no rest since, he stumbled as they guided him out of the wagon. His head spun even with the solid ground beneath him. He looked back at Evylin as they untied his hands and slipped off his gag.

Deckard worked his jaw, his lips raw and chapped.

"No talking," the man ordered, then clamped a hand around Deckard's arm, pulling him toward a small stand of trees.

The man stood resolutely to the side, allowing Deckard to turn his back to relieve himself. He hated to think of how Evylin would be handled when her turn came. Would they give her a semblance of privacy?

Taking the moment given to him, Deckard unbuttoned his coat and slipped the Night

Relic beneath his shirt. He only refastened a handful of the buttons to make it appear that he'd wanted to get more comfortable rather than hide the necklace.

Once his minute was up, his guard led him to a large campfire near the wagon. Dozens of men stood guard around the fire. Two stools awaited, one already taken up by a broad-chested man. His light brown hair was streaked with gray, and his square jaw bore a long, vicious scar. Cold, calculating eyes watched Deckard's every move. He wore the dark purple, military style coat that marked him as a liege officer.

This was the leader: Caustin.

Guided to the empty stool across from the burly man, Deckard took a seat. He kept his expression neutral and his demeanor unthreatening. These men were smart and thorough. Escape was a narrow enough possibility. Signs of defiance would tighten their already restrictive bonds.

"My name is Caustin," the leader said, his accent thick around his gravelly voice. "I run this outfit. I've had my men build this fire close to your wagon so your comrades can hear me when I give my rules."

Deckard accepted the bowl of broth, with the barest flakes of meat and sinew floating in the liquid, handed to him. A crust of bread was tossed to him next. "I'm sure they're listening eagerly," he replied, voice scratchy and thick from disuse. "As am I."

Caustin's gaze narrowed. "As you're the first out, I'll grant you a pardon. First rule: No talking. Not to me, not to my men, and not to one another. Second, no running. We may not be permitted to kill you, but we won't hesitate to sever your hamstring."

Deckard lifted his chin, beginning to understand what sort of leader Caustin was.

"Third," he went on, "no struggling. Should you break any of these rules, there will be unpleasant consequences. Understand?"

Clearing his throat, Deckard gave a singular nod.

"Excellent. You're down to three minutes to finish your meal."

Deckard ate quickly, making sure to clear his bowl entirely. His stomach twisted, the food repugnant since it had been empty for so long. Yet, the meager meal would have to suffice.

Once he was finished, Deckard was led back to the wagon. They gagged him and tied his wrists again, then guided him up the steps to the back of the bed and bound his body to the bars once more. Then they took Evylin.

Deckard sat, tense and anxious, during her short turn. He allowed himself the reprieve of releasing the Night Relic's disguise, and immediately, his body trembled, and his eyes fluttered as he struggled to retain consciousness. It felt as though his desperation and focus were all that kept him awake.

Quickly, he glanced down, assured the Relic's glow couldn't be seen. Still, he didn't relax until Evylin returned. The men tied her in place, then took Rafferty.

Evylin slipped her foot back under Deckard's leg. He met her gaze, satisfied by the calm alertness within.

With his head threatening to tear itself apart, Deckard rested it back against the bars. He closed his eyes at last. He felt Evylin prop her knee on his leg. He smiled. After two weeks, this was not how he'd imagined spending their first night back together.

Disappointment tugged at his heart, but sleep dragged him into its depths as he wondered if he'd ever get to hold Evylin again.

CHAPTER FORTY-EIGHT

34TH OF CHRONOS, 1574

It was his fault. That was the conclusion Thom had come to. If he hadn't been such a monumental ass, none of this would have happened.

But he'd goaded Ethenn, he'd stalled them in the forest, and he'd caused the delay that allowed Caustin and his men to capture them. Now, they rode in the back of a wagon to their certain death, and all he could do was sit in his own filth.

A scout. That was how Caustin's men had discovered them. Thom had realized the origin of their discovery while they were all bound and loaded into the wagon.

"Where are the other two?" Caustin demanded of a small, lithe man—the Waulden version of Rafferty.

The scout led him to Deckard and Evylin then, and Thom knew they'd failed in their surveillance of the Keep's land. They'd looked for a band of Mages or mercenaries. A single man had slipped easily through their nets. And once they'd entered the Keep, the scout returned for his comrades.

Caustin and his men were lying in wait. Sent away by Hewitt's ghost—a fact Thom still couldn't process—Thom, Rafferty, and Ethenn followed the Calders back to the camp where their horses remained. On the walk back, Auden took pity on Thom, healing his broken nose but refusing to fix any of his other injuries. "On principle," he'd said.

Thom hadn't even bothered to roll his eyes. He didn't need reminders of his failings. They were already cutting lines of guilt through his gut.

Then the mercenaries attacked. Or whatever they were. Thom supposed they might be more officious with how efficiently they were run.

Over the past day and a half, Thom had more than enough time to ruminate. He reflected on every action in his life that had brought him to this point. And he officially concluded that, yes, it was all his fault.

Not in a technical capacity, he supposed. It wasn't as though he alone missed the presence of Caustin's scout or allowed Blount to follow them through Ephria, sight unseen. Those things weren't really anyone's fault.

No, the disastrous division within their troop was his fault. All because he couldn't get over his petty jealousy.

That was the crux of it, Thom now realized. With hours and hours to contend with his demons, with a bruised face and aching muscles as tormentors, he could suddenly see with brutal clarity. Everything he thought and everything he felt over the last three months was spurred by envy. None of it was real.

Glancing to the far side of the wagon, Thom caught sight of Deckard and Evylin. They sat across from one another, staring longingly into the other's eyes. Her legs were propped on his as though they were on some splendid holiday ride. Their silent affection was enough to make a man sick.

Yes, it made Thom blisteringly jealous. But not because he wanted Evylin. Because he wanted what they had.

He wanted what *Deckard* had.

Thom stared down at his lap, long hair falling into his eyes. Yes, he *was* jealous of his brother. Yes, he resented his goodness and perfection. But at the core of it all, he knew it was only because, more than anything, Thom wanted to be like his brother. He wanted to be good enough for his brother. He wanted to be worthy of his respect.

And instead of earning it, he'd tried to steal that respect—*making* his brother see his value.

Thom wasn't worthy. He'd always known that. He was less. And what lesser man could ever earn the respect of someone like the flawless, magnanimous Jonn Deckard?

Everything Thom had done had been an attempt to prove himself to his brother. Like some foolish boy, he'd thought that taking what he wanted was the only way of garnering it. Instead of helping Deckard foster his relationship with Evylin, he'd supplanted it. He'd tried to win Evylin's favor, lauding their relationship over Deckard. He'd attempted to secure her affection to show Deckard his value. For if Thom could procure the heart of the woman Deckard loved, his brother would *have* to see his merit then.

What a *fool*.

Thom's wrists burned as he wriggled in his bindings. He tried to sit upright, his back muscles pinched from the great length of time bound against the bars. He used his feet as leverage, scooting back just enough to get a semblance of more comfort.

In the process, his shoulder bumped Ilain's. Jostled, her head drooped, lolling forward at an awkward angle.

Thom muttered a curse through his gag. Ethenn glared at him from across the wagon.

Thom ground his teeth, ignoring the accusatory look. Then he dropped his head, leaning toward Ilain.

"Hey," the guard grunted, "quit that."

Dipping his head farther, Thom pressed his forehead against Ilain's. He struggled against his ropes, slowly nudging her head back.

"I said," the guard rose, "quit that!" He drew a club from beside his stool, advancing on Thom.

Thom growled and kicked out, connecting with the guard's hand. The brute dropped the club, shaking out his hand. Thom took the distraction to complete his task, working Ilain's head back against the bars just long enough for him to guide it to rest on his shoulder.

The guard surveyed them as Thom kept her head in place with his bruised cheek. The pressure sent jabs of pain across his face, but he deserved it. After what he'd done to her. . . .

Deeming Thom's subterfuge to be meaningless, the guard sat back down.

Thom could feel the stares of his comrades around him. He didn't care. He settled in, keeping Ilain's head from drooping again.

Guilt drew a heavy sigh out of him. Why hadn't he let it go? Because of his own torturous disappointment, he'd ruined Ilain's chances with Ethenn.

"We were never anything. But that's more than you could ever be to her."

Ethenn would never believe the truth now. No matter what she said, it would all sound like backtracking. Any excuse she used would come across as a play for his usefulness as a Warrior, not as a genuine interest in him as a man.

All because Thom was hurt.

He wanted to blame Ethenn. After all, the kid had struck first. But in reality, wasn't it Thom who struck the first blow? Be it with words rather than fists, Thom had given Ethenn reason after reason to be angry with him.

Thom had taunted Ethenn about his relationship with Ilain. Ethenn knew of his feelings for Evylin, making him protective of Ilain—as any man should have been. And rather than telling Ethenn the truth, Thom had gotten angry.

It wasn't Ethenn's fault at all.

Everything came back to the same cause: Thom desired his brother's respect, and he had never been man enough to earn it.

"I'm under no illusions about your worth."

Ilain's coppery-red hair tickled Thom's face. He closed his eyes, letting her voice become his new conscience.

"People like you; you're just not willing to see it."

She was right.

Thom didn't want to let go of the bitterness. He didn't want to admit that he had friends and admirers. Because if he did that, then he'd have to accept who he was, and that would mean being less than Deckard for eternity.

No, not less than.

Different.

He didn't want to be different. He wanted to be like his brother. His immaculate, steady, incredible big brother, whom he'd idolized since the first day he could remember. Anything less was . . . *less.* Inferior. Failing. Deficient.

Yet, no one saw Thom that way but himself. He couldn't deny that. Not when he really thought about it.

Hewitt accepted him from the start, inviting him to spar in Whickam Village and handpicking him to train with Evylin, Rafferty, and Ethenn during their travels with the army.

Evylin herself had befriended him readily. She'd confided in him and invited him to do the same with her. Though it'd displeased him at the time, she'd taken him on as a brother.

Even before that, Rafferty had eagerly become his companion. Ever since joining up in Rasnaack, they'd been nearly inseparable, though he'd always assumed that had more to do with Thom's penchant for tomfoolery rather than his true self.

And Ethenn, he put up with Rafferty and Thom's constant teasing, choosing to become their friend despite his quiet nature. The kid, who was really no more a child than Thom, didn't shy away from Thom's volatile temperament or biting comments. He stuck around, laughed along, and proved to be a better man than the two of them put together.

Then there was Deckard, the brother who loved him despite all his failings.

That was the worst of it. Thom knew Deckard loved him, and it rankled within him. He didn't want to be loved for who he was; he wanted to be loved for who he *wanted* to be.

A better man.

"I'm under no illusions about your worth."

Despite the pain in his body, despite the fear that his selfishness had drawn them into great danger, despite regret piled upon regret, Thom found himself smiling into Ilain's hair. She, too, had accepted him, wretch that he was. And he let her words give him hope. Perhaps he didn't need to be a better man. Maybe he simply needed to be himself, and that would somehow be enough.

CHAPTER FORTY-NINE

After another full day of riding, they passed through the border and the mountains. A burst of sunshine met them as they entered the hilly countryside, emerald grass stretching for miles. Deer grazed among copses of trees, curiously watching their party ride by.

They didn't stop until sunset again. Deckard was the first out of the wagon, given the same meal of broth and stale bread around the campfire. Caustin sat as before, watching and timing. Then he was back in the wagon.

Never in his life had Deckard felt so thoroughly uncomfortable. The aches and pains of being tightly trussed up and sitting rigidly for hours on end weren't the worst of it. Other than their minute to relieve themselves in the evening, there was no other break from the strain. The hay absorbed some of the mess, but it did nothing to alleviate the smell. His clothes and hair were coated in grime from when they'd tackled him in the mud, and he felt gritty from the layers of sweat on his skin.

He'd considered asking the guard to dump the bucket of water on him for a reprieve but decided against breaking Caustin's rule of absolute silence.

The men returned Evylin from her meal and gathered Rafferty. He wobbled when they lifted him, then collapsed at Deckard's feet. The guards grumbled, but Rafferty met Deckard's eyes and winked.

Deckard's brow pinched together.

The weasel had *winked* at him.

Then the guards had him back up and carried him out of the wagon. A cold sweat broke across Deckard's back. Rafferty was up to something. He just hoped it wouldn't get them killed.

Escorted to the fire with his bonds removed, Rafferty stretched, giving a pointed look at the wagon. His silvery eyes met Deckard's just before he accepted the bowl from one of the men. Deckard clamped his jaw, his worry increasing. Though he assumed his magic had been restored as his energy returned, he still didn't see their odds of escape being increased anytime soon. They couldn't fight their way out *and* carry the two unconscious Calders with them.

Rafferty took the stool across from Caustin and cleared his throat. "My arse is so numb," he said, smirking, "I can't even feel myself breaking wind anymore."

It only took one second for Caustin to rise. Rafferty's head whipped to the side from the leader's punch. Evylin and Thom flinched at the sound, while Deckard and Ethenn watched in shock.

Caustin towered over Rafferty. "As I said, if you break my rules, there are consequences. Next time you speak, there won't be any quarter given."

Some of Rafferty's soup had spilled on his trousers. He flicked off a speck of coagulated marrow, then grinned up at Caustin. "As *I* said—" He turned and made eye contact with Deckard again. "I can't feel myself break *wind* anymore."

Good to his word, Caustin did not hold back. He hit Rafferty again, harder than before. It drove the man off his stool. Then Caustin stooped, grabbing Rafferty's collar. He punched him again and kicked him, over and over, until the man spat blood.

Evylin and Thom attempted to peer over their shoulders at the scene, worried for their friend. Deckard forced himself to watch it all. Every hit and kick sent a pang of guilt through him. He was their commanding officer. They were his responsibility. He should have protected them.

When they carried Rafferty back, blood streamed from his mouth. One eye was already beginning to swell. Two of his fingers protruded at odd angles; either broken or dislocated, Deckard couldn't tell. They bound his hands anyway, then fixed him to the bars. Rafferty looked barely conscious, but as the guard stepped away, he met Deckard's gaze once more.

Deckard dipped his chin to indicate that he understood. Rafferty was impulsive and flippant, but he wasn't stupid. He'd accepted Caustin's wrath to send Deckard a message.

The problem was, with his brain addled by exhaustion and hunger, Deckard couldn't quite figure out what that message was.

35TH OF CHRONOS, 1574

As the prison wagon rumbled over a rough and jarring road, for the first time in his life, Deckard felt old. Oh, there'd been a time or two since his thirtieth birthday when he'd felt older. There were days when his back tweaked during training or his lack of sleep gave him more trouble than usual. But he'd never truly felt *old*.

The past two days changed that.

An emptiness settled into his gut, and his vision grew bleary. His malnourished body protested in every way it could. He was dirty, hungry, exhausted, and weak. His back ached, his head pounded, his muscles tightened, and his jaw locked.

His one consolation was Evylin, sitting across from him.

During their time as captives, Deckard and Evylin had taken to sitting with their knees bent, planting their feet next to each other in alternating steps. As their only means of contact, it provided comfort despite their dire situation.

Deckard had abandoned all hope of escaping from the liege officers. They were too cautious and too well-run to make freedom viable. Not when the Calders were out of commission. It pained him to admit it, but until they got wherever they were going, they had to have patience.

Evylin's leg brushed Deckard's as she lowered it to the floor. He looked up, refocusing on her face. She was turned away from him, the delicate slope of her nose wrinkled.

Deckard followed her gaze, and his breath caught. They turned off the main road and drove through the gates of a sprawling estate. Verdant manicured lawns stretched endlessly, white flowers dotting their expanse. A shimmering pond reflected the massive mansion at the far end of the pebbled path. Columns and windows lined the edifice, a marvel of architecture. It rivaled the palace in Ephria City.

Caustin was taking them to a noble.

Deckard's hollow stomach dropped. He studied every detail, trying to memorize what he could see of the layout of the grounds. Was it possible that this home belonged to Blount? Would it be any easier for them to escape here than under Caustin's watchful charge?

They rode past a stable and up to the circular path at the entrance to the mansion. Deckard noted a few of Caustin's men leading their seized horses there. A stableman stepped out, eyeing the prison wagon with curiosity. He stuck out amongst all the Waulden men and women Deckard had seen because his skin was deep brown and his stature broad—distinctive Ephrian features.

How had an Ephrian wound up in the service of a Waulden noble?

The wagon rounded the bend, blocking Deckard's view of the stable. He turned to study the mansion instead. More guards awaited them on the terrace and the grand stone staircase. Deckard tried to count them, but their numbers were far too high for his fatigued mind to track.

From the top of the staircase, he watched as five individuals began their descent. Two heavily armed guards, two men wearing long robes—one in deep blue, the other in rich red—and an imperious woman. She walked in front with evident authority. Her black-brown hair was pulled back at the crown, the rest flowing in waves down her back. She wore a silver dress with a high collar, which gave her an official appearance and contrasted with her golden-brown skin. A singular gold and diamond ring shone notably on her right middle finger, her only embellishment.

Deckard immediately deduced that she was the noble's steward or manager of some variety. The formal simplicity of her dress didn't match the grandeur of the estate.

The woman and her companions paused a few steps from the bottom of the staircase as the wagon came to a stop. Caustin's men stepped forward, pulling them from its confines. Deckard's head spun at the sudden change in posture. It took a moment to find his footing, but he managed to stay upright. Caustin dismounted at the base of the stairs, stepping up to the woman. She regarded him icily, then scanned the captives.

The Ephrians all stood, wrists bound and gags in their mouths, while two men carried the Calders over their shoulders.

The woman let out a heavy sigh, then glared at Caustin. "The lady sent you to bring back people, not dogs," she said, the words almost sultry in her foreign accent.

Deckard studied her. So this estate was owned by a noblewoman who employed both an Ephrian and . . . Was this woman Schonese? She matched the description from all of Deckard's studies.

Caustin scoffed. "My job was to bring them back alive, not to give them a holiday. I've done my part; now, I'll present them to the lady and take my pay."

The woman scowled. "They're disgusting. You expect the Countess of Keale to entertain grubby prisoners in her parlor?"

"She said she wanted to see them as soon as they arrived," Caustin said gruffly.

"That was before you turned them into filthy vagrants." The woman turned from him dismissively. She gestured toward the terrace. A troupe of servants stepped forward. "Take the prisoners to their rooms. Clean them up."

Caustin stepped forward. "These people are dangerous," he growled. "They took down twenty of my men even after being weakened by the Keep."

Her dark eyes turned on him haughtily. "We have provisions for that."

Deckard tried swallowing past the lump in his throat, but his mouth was too dry.

Caustin ground his teeth. "Provisions like you."

For the first time, the woman's lips lifted in a grin. "Do you doubt my abilities, Officer?" She took a step down toward him, lifting her hand. "Or would you like a reminder?"

Caustin backed away. "No."

"Good." The woman motioned to the men behind her. "Highlords Braun and Paulson will escort you and your men as you take the Calders to the dungeon."

Deckard blanched.

She gave Caustin a furious glare. "Make sure they are placed in *separate* cells. The highlords will stay with the Calders to ensure there are no daring escapes."

Deckard's pulse rose as the officers carrying the Calders moved to follow orders. What sort of nobility had dungeons in their home? Was there any hope of breaking out their friends once they disappeared down there?

He didn't have long to consider his options as the steward continued to give her commands. "As for the rest of them, Lady Renaul is intrigued to meet these Ephrian rebels. Our people will take care of them."

"What about the Warrior?" Caustin demanded.

The woman followed his gaze to Evylin. She smiled, cold and calculating. "She's coming with me."

Deckard's heart squeezed. Instinctively, he and Evylin tried to step closer to each other. It did no good. They were torn apart in an instant, multiple guards dragging them up the stairs. She kicked and squirmed, trying to wrench free. Then the steward raised her hand.

Evylin immediately went still, choking and gasping behind the gag still over her mouth. Her knees buckled as Deckard strained against the men holding him.

"Don't fight," the woman said—and he recognized her now as a Wind Mage, her silver dress and diamond ring proclaiming her magic. She met Deckard's stare. "It makes me weary."

The guards hauled Evylin to her feet. Deckard met Thom, Ethenn, and Rafferty's angered gazes. He gave them a nod as his captors led him up the stairs. They would fail if they fought now. There were too many eyes, too much attention. They had to wait until a more opportune moment.

Deckard kept his eyes on Evylin even as they entered the mansion. Servants guided the guards up a grand marble staircase with a golden rail. Paintings and mirrors hung on the gold-leafed molding and plaque-decorated walls. The steward walked at the head of the group, leading Evylin's entourage. They went left at the top of the stairs while the men were all led to the right.

Deckard gnawed at the gag in his mouth. He watched his wife disappear down the hall. He'd find a way to get them out of this. He would. He *had* to.

To his surprise, he was led into an opulent guest room. Once inside, the servant accompanying them went about his work under the supervision of two guards. They removed his gag and ropes. Once freed, Deckard rubbed his wrists. He knew that he could take down the three men in the room with him, but could he get the rest of his troop out of the mansion? And what about the other Relics? Where would this countess, Lady Renaul, take them for safekeeping? And how did she know about them in the first place?

There were too many unanswered questions to act in haste. Better to wait and see what this noblewoman wanted with their group.

The servant guided Deckard into a small bathing chamber, a steaming tub already awaiting him. Instantly, he set his focus on turning the Night Relic back into a crest. Within a moment, a soothing whisper of heat traced his skin. The servant moved to strip him, but he requested in a croaky voice to do it himself. The man acquiesced. Deckard left the disguised Relic around his neck, not wanting to risk it being taken away along with his filthy clothes.

Despite his anxiety, the bath was reviving. He scrubbed his skin raw and dunked his head under the water as many times as it took to feel fully free of the grime. After he dried off, the servant came forward with a razor. He refused to give Deckard the blade—a wise precaution, he supposed—and proceeded to slather his jaw with cream before giving him the smoothest shave of his life. The servant trimmed his hair, perfecting Rafferty's previous work.

Then the man helped Deckard into a fresh set of clothes. The fabrics were of the highest quality, soft against his freshly cleaned skin. He ensured the Relic-turned-crest was hidden under the crisp white shirt. In black breeches, shiny black boots, a silken cravat, and a navy velvet coat, he couldn't determine whether he appreciated the finery or found it flippant. He knew little of Waulden customs, but it seemed vulgar to truss up one's prisoners before executing them.

At least, that's what he assumed was the fate that awaited them.

Once the servant walked around Deckard three times to assess his ensemble, he nodded to the guards. Deckard expected them to bind his wrists again. Instead, they took hold of his arms and led him from the room. They walked across the plush purple rugs that lined the halls, down the marble stairs, and into the heart of the mansion. They passed room after room of opulent design. Everything was decorated in stark white, rich purple, and garish gold.

Finally, the guards halted before a pair of double doors. Two servants stood at the side, waiting.

"Don't move," one of Deckard's guards ordered. Then they both released him and stepped away.

Deckard watched cautiously. He wasn't about to make a break for it now. He didn't know where any of his teammates were. And he wouldn't leave them behind.

After several minutes, Deckard wondered what the guards were waiting for. Then Rafferty was escorted in.

Deckard's eyes widened at the sight of the soldier. Not only was he as clean as Deckard, but the bruises he'd obtained from Caustin were gone, and his fingers were notably fixed. The weasel grinned as the guards guided him to Deckard's side.

"I feel like a goose," Rafferty said, running his hands along the burgundy velvet of his coat. "Smooth and scrubbed down just in time for roasting."

Deckard glanced at the guards, expecting Caustin's mandate of silence to hold. As none of the men showed signs of concern, he supposed Lady Renaul didn't mind conversation.

"I kn—" Deckard's voice scratched and broke off, and he had to clear his throat to continue. "I know what you mean," he said, then motioned to his face. "They healed you?"

Rafferty shrugged. "Brought in a Mage in a fancy yellow coat to do it."

"Hm." Deckard wondered at the noblewoman's access to so many Mages.

Ethenn, then Thom, was delivered moments later. Clean-shaven and injury-free, they looked like the men he'd known back in the Third Volunteer Company, though with decidedly nicer coats. Ethenn's was a rich brown, and Thom's a light blue that matched his eyes.

Anticipating Evylin's arrival, the four men hesitated when the servants opened the door the moment they were assembled together. The guards stepped up, ushering them into the room. The opulent decor of the house continued within. The sunset streamed through windows flanked by heavy velvet curtains, tingeing the room with amber. A large table stretched across the space, set with candles, plates, and golden cutlery. Guards lined the walls, spears at the ready and swords on their hips.

A grand fireplace sat on the far wall, crackling with flames. Silhouetted in its glow at the head of the table stood a woman with radiant golden hair. "Good evening," she said, with a distinct poshness to her Waulden accent.

Deckard did a secondary scan of the room, looking for Evylin.

"Where's Evie?" Thom whispered at his side.

He threw his brother a look that said, "How should I know?"

The woman spoke again, stepping around the table. "If you're wondering about your lovely companion. I'm afraid it takes us women longer to prepare for festivities. While I was, of course, aware of our little party, I heard your dear lady had quite the cleaning up to do to make herself presentable. I'm sure she'll be along shortly."

Everything in Deckard urged him to press her to learn more about Evylin's whereabouts and safety, but he determined to remain cautious with the information he revealed. At most, this woman knew what Blount knew. He thought it best to keep it that way.

Deckard assumed the posture befitting a dinner party. He would indulge this noblewoman's strange games and, if possible, play her to his advantage. "Will the Calders be joining us, my lady?" he asked, thankful for the decorum in his voice after so long without use.

A tilt pulled Lady Renaul's lips into a sly smile as she met them at the back of the room. "Oh, no. I'm afraid they won't be lucid for quite some time."

Ethenn and Thom bristled on either side of Deckard. He spoke so they wouldn't. "Then you don't fear the presence of Warriors?"

"Not when they're properly restrained." Renaul's deep green eyes met his. The gold fabric of her gown hugged her frame, hinting at a shapely figure underneath. Her blonde hair was styled in an intricate chignon, with golden beads strung through it. She smiled at Deckard, fine lines crinkling around her eyes, the only tell of her mature age. Deckard wasn't too proud to admit he found her beautiful. But there was a cunning nature and a sensuality in her gaze that made him uncomfortable.

Lady Renaul stepped up to stand directly in front of Deckard. "I take it you're the leader of this little band," she said with a swipe of her finger toward the other three men. "Four Ephrians caught up with two foul Mages and a lady Warrior. My, my, how did that marvel occur?"

Caution foremost in his mind, Deckard returned her suggestive smile with a polite one. "Would you believe me if I said they tricked us into it?"

Renaul laughed. "Four grown men, tricked into finding Relics?" She clicked her tongue. "That hardly seems possible."

"We were equally surprised."

Her laughter expanded, rich as the room around them. "You've got a quick wit." She reached up to tap his cheek with a slender finger. "I like you."

Deckard fought the urge to jerk away and forced his smile to remain. "It's a pity I'm your prisoner then."

Renaul raised her brow in concession, but the click of the latch behind them cut off her reply. "Ah!" She motioned toward the door. "Here she comes."

Deckard and the men whirled on their heels. The white double doors opened, and he held his breath, needing to see Evylin, to know she was safe.

The Wind Mage stepped through first, her dark eyes catching his. In the dimming light of sunset, her silver dress shone in cold contrast against the warmth of the room. She moved aside, revealing Evylin standing in the hall behind her.

Deckard's heart stopped.

Evylin stepped into the room as polished and refreshed as the rest of them. However, their transformations paled in comparison to hers. Her dark hair was smooth and silken, falling in gentle waves to frame her face. Her lightly tanned skin contrasted sharply with the vibrant gown they'd placed her in, the gentle folds an amethyst so saturated it might have been dyed in the very skies of the deepest night. Its full skirt cascaded from her waist to puddle softly on the marble floor. Yet, the bodice featured a distinctive military cut, fitting her every curve with precision. The straps sat off her shoulders, revealing her sculpted neckline, the cut lower than Ephrian society would deem appropriate. Flowing sleeves draped around her toned arms, giving her a regal appearance and leading Deckard's eyes to the iron shackles on her wrists.

Clamping his jaw tight, Deckard met Evylin's gaze then. Neither of them smiled, sharing an instant understanding. This dress was too specific, too appropriate for a Warrior to be anything but intentional. This was no secondhand dress Renaul had cast aside. This was a gown made specifically for Evylin.

Deckard caught his breath and turned back to Renaul. The noblewoman's eyes glimmered with pride as she surveyed Evylin. The lady was no fool. Escaping her would be no easier than escaping Caustin. Already, Deckard understood that her games were intricate and calculated.

And Deckard was afraid they'd never had a chance to win at all.

CHAPTER FIFTY

"Wow!" Rafferty exclaimed, breaking the silence that permeated the dining room like the fog of Wauld.

A wry grin pulled at Evylin's lips as Deckard shot the weasel a disparaging look. Despite her fatigued body, somber mood, and anxious thoughts, her heart beat faster at the sight of her husband. He looked so like the man he'd been when they first met: clean-shaven, immaculately dressed, and decidedly charming. Their circumstances aside, she approved of this presentation.

Based on Deckard's immediate reaction, it appeared he approved of hers as well. His green-blue gaze widened at the sight of her, and his breath caught visibly. Yet, she couldn't quite find the joy in witnessing his attraction to her. They both knew this was no pleasant dinner party. And this was no simple gown.

The double-breasted cut spoke of military design. The revealing neckline displayed her muscular definition with intention. The deep amethyst silk displayed the color of Night magic, its shine glimmering in the evening light.

She'd been placed in the gown of a Night Mage's Warrior. A dress that was intended for *Blount's* Warrior.

Ironically, it could also mark her as Deckard's Warrior. But neither Renaul nor Blount could discover that.

Stepping into the grand dining hall, Evylin chose to claim the gown as a sign of her dedication to Deckard. Even if it could never be, even if their lives were ending just as she was ready to give him her future, she would treat these last few hours or days or however long they had as though they all belonged to Deckard.

Her wistful thoughts dissolved as the woman standing beside her husband stepped forward. "Why, you *are* stunning," she said, eyes locked on Evylin. Her gold dress swished as she drew near. "This color does you justice, my dear."

The woman—Lady Renaul, she presumed—eyed Evylin with a keen gaze. Yet, her beauty was almost off-putting, a disquieting shrewdness in her sharp green stare. "It's an absolute pleasure," she continued, a curious blend of warmth and malice in her accented tone. "I've been told so much about you."

Evylin's throat tightened. "Someone told you about me?" she asked, her voice scratchy from disuse.

"Yes, of course." Renaul gave her a taunting smile. With the tips of her fingers, she lifted Evylin's chin. "Now, let me get a look at you. I was told of your impressive strength, clever tongue, and winsome looks. I can see the beauty and brawn clearly enough. Your wit, I suppose, we'll have to discover through conversation. Though I can already see how taken these four are with you."

Renaul turned to peer at the Ephrian men, a wicked smile on her lips. "Darling, you'll have to teach me that little trick." She turned back to Evylin, and something like jealousy had entered her cruel gaze. "Gaining such admiration . . ."

Evylin clamped her jaw tight, hoping her expression gave nothing away.

The countess's fierce stare swept over Evylin once more. "But, oh!" she gasped. "That's something I wasn't told."

Renaul reached out and lifted Evylin's hands, the chain between her manacles jingling with the motion. "What beautiful rings," the lady remarked. "An Ephrian tradition, isn't it? You're married?"

Conflicted, Evylin's eyes darted past Renaul to Deckard. Whoever had told the noblewoman about her either hadn't known her marital status or didn't consider it a pertinent detail. Increasingly wary of the woman's intentions and with little doubt it was Blount who had given Evylin's description, she had no interest in providing any more information. However, there was little reason to deny such an obvious fact.

"I am," Evylin said flatly.

Renaul's eyes flickered with a strange emotion. "And which of these handsome gentlemen behind me procured such an honor?"

With a flippant tilt of her head, Evylin shrugged. "He isn't here."

"Oh, my dear," Renaul tittered amusedly. Her fingers tightened around Evylin's. "You already gave yourself away."

Evylin clenched her jaw. The lady was too observant, and Evylin knew she had been foolish to look at Deckard upon the mention of their marriage.

"Now, don't tell me." Renaul released her. She clasped her hands with excitement. "I'll guess."

When Renaul turned her back on Evylin to approach the men, the Wind Mage lingering at her side stepped closer as if Evylin would strike when the countess wasn't looking. She'd been a constant guard since their arrival, yet Evylin still hadn't learned her name. The Mage hovered threateningly, her dark gaze cold and alert.

"I love a good game," Renaul announced. "But I want no clues, so tuck those hands away, gentlemen."

The men did as ordered, drawing their hands behind their backs and assuming the soldier's at-ease stance. Evylin almost smirked seeing them obey so quickly, but her amusement died realizing that they were only so accommodating for fear of the noblewoman's retribution.

Renaul paced in front of the men, left to right and back, inspecting Ethenn, Rafferty, Deckard, and Thom. She surveyed them with an astute, sweeping gaze. "While my information on the Calders and our darling Warrior, Mrs. Deckard, is adequate," she said as she appraised the men, "I'm afraid I know next to nothing about you four.

"So, please . . ." She stopped in front of Ethenn, drawing a finger along his shoulder. Heat flushed his neck, but he glared straight ahead, otherwise showing no sign of reaction to her touch. "Tell me your name—given only, as I want no clues—and how you met our darling here."

Frowning, Ethenn glanced down the line. When he received no direction from Deckard or the other two, he sighed. He stated his name and cleared his throat. "I met Evie during my training with the army."

"The army, you say?" Renaul raised her brow, then squeezed his arm. "No wonder you're so muscular."

Thom and Rafferty sniggered as Ethenn flushed a shade darker.

"But be more specific, dearest," the lady said, her endearments too much like Ilain's for Evylin's taste. "I need more information to divine whether your love for the woman in question is amorous or chaste."

Ethenn scowled. "It wasn't anything special if that's what you're looking for. I was invited to join her training squad, that's all."

"Details, love," Renaul pressed. "How did you feel when you met her?"

"Nervous," Ethenn admitted. "She's really impressive, and . . ." His ears were red now. "Pretty."

Despite the gravity of the situation, Evylin couldn't help smiling.

"I'd admired her already," he continued quietly. "Being invited to train with her—to be part of her team . . . I was nervous that I wouldn't measure up."

"Hm." Renaul studied Ethenn a moment longer. "A Warrior would be attracted to a fighter such as yourself. Interesting. We'll come back to you."

The lady stepped forward where Rafferty stood with bright eyes and an eager smile. She didn't even have to prompt him as he readily gave his account. "Name's Rafferty, but you can call me Raff, milady." He gave a wily wink. "I met Eve in the army, too, though I'm more a soldier of fortune than destiny."

Deckard shook his head wearily.

"Found her standing in our camp all lonely-like and decided to take pity on her," Rafferty said. "I flirted a bit, and she did too. She's an accomplished tease, and I'm quite proud of her for that. I've been at her side ever since."

Renaul's wide grin took on a knowing tilt. "No," she said flatly.

"Pardon?" Rafferty replied.

"No," Renaul repeated. "Your story may be true, but you are not her husband."

"Why not?"

"You're all flash."

"Believe me," Rafferty smirked, "I'm plenty substantial."

Renaul laughed boisterously at his innuendo but moved on to Deckard. "And what about you, handsome?" She peered up at him, propping a finger under his chin. Evylin tried not to grit her teeth. "Are you a soldier too?"

"I am," he replied.

"Are you all?"

"We are."

"And your offices?"

Deckard readily gave their ranks as soldiers.

"Well, then," Renaul said. "Is the colonel of our troop the lover of this lady?"

Deckard's lips lifted in the charming smile he wore for magistrates, nobles, and officers—one that warmed people's souls but rarely revealed his true feelings. "Would you like me to answer honestly?" he asked pleasantly. "Or would you like me to play your game?"

"Do play on," Renaul said, her voice throaty and provocative.

With a deferential nod and a glance in Evylin's direction, Deckard proceeded. "My name is Jonn. I was a guest in the home of Mrs. Deckard's family, and we met at dinner. Evylin was . . ." He paused, the corner of his smile twitching fondly. "Notable."

Renaul frowned. "That's all? She was *notable*."

Deckard lifted his shoulder in a casual shrug. "You requested the details of our meeting, not her manifold virtues."

A small, breathy laugh escaped Evylin, but she managed to cover it with a sniff of her nose.

Deckard glanced at her again, though his expression gave nothing away.

Renaul pursed her lips. "Even *I* could come up with a more charming description. Is that really all you have to say?"

"Would it serve your game for me to say I found her to be the perfect woman?" he asked dryly. "Or shall I say that she captivated my very soul?"

Though there was a definitive snark in his tone, Evylin had learned Deckard's manner of teasing well enough to know that he meant both those things. Her heart beat faster as her fingers found her rings, and she watched him closely.

"Mm," Renaul hummed, then waved Deckard off. She stepped forward to stand before Thom. "May I assume by your likeness that you two are brothers?"

Though she addressed Thom, he remained silent.

"We are," Deckard replied, sending a pointed glare to Thom.

Renaul reached up to brush some of Thom's newly shorn dark locks off his forehead. He pulled out of her reach. "I don't care to play your game," he said coldly.

"Nevertheless," her eyes flashed threateningly, her reply swift, "you *will* play."

Evylin met Thom's gaze then, raising her brow. It wasn't the time to test the woman. She held the Calders and the Relics captive, and there was no doubt in Evylin's mind that Renaul was working with Blount. It wasn't worth testing the countess to find out what vile things she was capable of.

Jaw tight, Thom complied. "My name is Thom, and I met Evie at her uncle's smithy. I . . ." He hesitated, meeting her stare. Something like regret passed over his face. "I liked her instantly," he said, addressing Evylin rather than Renaul. "Somehow, I had the good fortune to become her friend. And I can't fathom why she'd be that good to me."

Deckard shifted uncomfortably beside his brother, tension creeping into his shoulders. But Evylin heard the apology in Thom's words. He regretted his actions, and he was repentant. Genuine remorse shone in his eyes, knowing that he'd hurt her.

Evylin offered Thom an absolving smile. Whatever his flaws, Thom Deckard was a good man. Sometimes, it just took him longer to display his goodness. And in the face of death, it was not the time to hold a grudge.

"How sweet," Renaul muttered dully. "Well, I think I have the information I need." She tossed a hand in Ethenn's direction. "Not you."

The hunter visibly relaxed.

"Which puts it down to the brothers," Renaul said dramatically. "Now, pretty Thom," she patted his arm, "I see you have a soft spot for our darling, but I'm afraid friendship *was* its end. There's a foreign quality in the way you say her name. As if you know the sound of it, but you can't quite understand the meaning."

The lady's intense gaze floated up to Deckard's face. "But you, Jonn *Deckard*, speak her name with knowledge," she said, and inexplicably, Evylin's heart filled at her words. "A knowledge that only intimacy can impart."

Though Evylin doubted their marriage shared the sort of intimacy this noblewoman implied, she didn't doubt the truth of her conclusion. Deckard did know her—better than anyone alive. Despite all the barriers Evylin had constructed, he'd discovered her heart. And he'd done so not by force but by attention. He hadn't knocked down her walls; he'd scaled them. He'd accepted the distance she placed between them and perched on the top of those barricades, watching her from afar and learning her better than anyone she'd ever known.

And she loved him for it.

"Have I guessed correctly?" Renaul asked, breaking through Evylin's reverie. Her sharp glare held a hostility Evylin didn't quite understand. "Is Jonn your husband?"

Meeting Deckard's steady and tender gaze, Evylin allowed herself one moment of awe at the truth of it. "He is," she whispered.

The gentlest, most loving smile lifted Deckard's whole expression.

Renaul scoffed. "Tricked into helping the Calders, indeed," she said caustically.

"What better way to trick a man," Deckard said, "than with the woman he loves?"

Evylin couldn't contain her grin. "Incorrigible flirt," she said.

He dipped his chin in a mock bow. "Anything for you."

Renaul let out a considering hum. "Charming," she said, then motioned between the two of them. "If you would, Colonel Deckard, please escort your wife to her seat. I'm sure you all must be starving after your journey with my liege officer. Caustin is not the most hospitable, I know, but he gets the job done."

As Renaul moved out of the way, Evylin and Deckard stared at one another, both hesitant. Neither could quite believe the woman would allow them to be together. But as the lady drifted to speak in hushed tones with the Wind Mage and none of the guards made any move away from the walls, it appeared no one would stop them.

Cautiously, Deckard began to approach, and Evylin met him halfway. His hands came to rest on her arms, pulling her close. "Are you all right?" he whispered, brow pinched together.

Evylin's heart jolted, remembering how he'd asked that same question in Dunneshead, just after their kiss. She wished she could recapture that moment in this one.

Instead, Evylin reached up, the shackles clinking once again as she settled for brushing one hand along his forearm. It felt so good to touch him, to have him near. "I'm fine," she replied with a reassuring smile.

Though the pinch didn't ease, Deckard let out a relieved breath. He offered his arm, and she took it, letting him lead her toward the table.

"Colonel," Renaul said, beckoning, "you'll sit at my right hand, and—oh, sweet Thom—"

Following behind Evylin and Deckard, Thom paused.

"You must sit on my left," she instructed. "After all, the seat next to Evylin is claimed."

As they took their seats at the grand table, Renaul gestured to the Mage at Evylin's side. "Allow me to introduce my steward properly," she said smugly. "This is Highlady Aterian Isla Freye. She's my insurance to keep our precious Warrior in check. Highlady Freye came to me from the Order of the Wind years ago, but we recently learned of the tragic loss of most of her brethren. Isn't it shocking, such a number of dear friends murdered so brutally?"

The comment was accusingly pointed. The deaths of the highlady's Order had been at their troop's hands.

Highlady Freye sat beside Evylin rigidly, the reason for her frosty demeanor all the more clear.

"She's reserved," Renaul continued, "but immensely loyal."

The troop took in the lady's words. Evylin noticed Deckard's hand gripping the seat of his chair fiercely. Undoubtedly, he was remembering his role in the death of those Mages. Evylin wanted to reach out to comfort him, but she remained still, knowing her manacles would alert the whole table to her actions if she tried to touch him.

Renaul signaled the servants, and they opened a side door, ushering in more men and women who bore platters and trays filled with food. The savory, robust scent of roasted meat filled the air, causing Evylin's stomach to twist with anticipation. She'd been deprived of quality meals like this long before their time as captives.

Dish after dish was set before them. Sumptuous venison and smoked pork. Boiled potatoes with dried herbs and butter. A medley of cooked vegetables. A creamy, cheesy soup with crisp, yeasty bread. Fresh-cut apples, pears, and berries adorned the table.

The servants filled their crystal glasses with deep crimson wine as Renaul clapped her hands with gaiety. "Wonderful," she said, passing a superior grin to all of them. "My cooks have outdone themselves, haven't they? As it is to be your last meal, I did want it to be quite the feast."

The casual remark hit Evylin like a blow to the head—an experience with which she'd become frightfully familiar. The Ephrians exchanged worried glances.

"Our *last* meal?" Thom repeated.

"I'm afraid so, pet," Renaul said, golden and bejeweled rings glinting in the firelight as she lifted her glass. "But as a consolation, I will make this evening ever so exciting for you."

"How so?" Rafferty asked, the only one of them intrigued by the proposition.

Renaul sipped her wine languidly. "As a little, mm . . . Let's call it a farewell, shall we? I will answer any question you have with total honesty. But let's not allow this dinner to grow cold, darlings. Tuck in."

Slowly, the men began to fill their plates, all of them silent. However, Evylin latched onto Renaul's offer, the value undeniable.

Evylin caught the noblewoman's gaze. "*Any* question?" she asked.

Renaul stabbed a slice of venison. "Whatever your heart desires."

Appetite all but forgotten, Evylin leaned closer. "Do you work for Blount?"

The men froze while Renaul and Highlady Freye continued to pile their plates high.

"I do hope you aren't referring to His Majesty, the king," Renaul said. "I thought even Ephrians were taught to respect the crown."

"I'm not referring to the king," Evylin said. "I'm asking about his son, who deserves no respect."

Deckard's hand brushed Evylin's in a gentle warning, then returned to his meal. She understood and appreciated his concern, but if they were going to die, she saw little point in caution.

Renaul didn't reveal any offense at the statement. In fact, she grinned. "Rouland said you have cheek," she noted, the remark as good as an admission.

"So you do work for him?" Evylin pressed.

Deckard leaned in to murmur a cautionary "careful" before he began filling her still-empty plate for her.

Renaul popped a berry in her mouth teasingly. "I don't work for anyone, my dear."

"But you are after the reward?" Rafferty said from his seat between Thom and Ethenn.

"I don't need or want the money," Renaul replied flippantly. "You're all my gift to Rouland."

They all paused again. Deckard cleared his throat and finished setting a scoop of potatoes on Evylin's plate. Thom and Ethenn resumed chewing.

Thoughts churning, Evylin tried to remember if the Calders had mentioned whether Blount had a family. She eyed the noblewoman thoughtfully. Renaul was older than she would have expected for the prince, but then the Calders were likely the lady's age themselves. Though she'd imagined the prince to be Deckard's age, there was a good chance he was vastly older.

Working to deduce Renaul's relationship with Blount, Evylin asked, "You're his wife?"

The woman's hearty laugh filled the room. "I am no man's wife," she said, then raised her brow. "I'm the king's mistress."

Caught off guard, Evylin didn't have a response to that. She had read about kept women in a few novels, but as she'd never met one, she almost doubted their existence.

"So," Ethenn said, fork lowering to his plate, "we're your gift to the king?"

"No, no." Renaul brushed the idea away. "King Rouland has no interest in you. It's *Prince* Rouland I'm gifting you to."

Thom screwed up his face in confusion. "You're trying to earn his favor?"

Renaul gave Highlady Freye a bewildered look. "They don't understand at all, do they?" She reached out to pat Thom's hand. "My dear, I'm giving you to Rouland as a token of my affection. I do not need to earn his favor. I'm already his lover."

Evylin felt her lips part in shock and revulsion. Deckard's fork scraped his plate, Ethenn choked on his wine, and Thom gaped.

"Hold on," Rafferty said, a wily smirk gliding over his face. "You're boffing both the king and his son?"

"Rafferty," Deckard hissed, but Renaul laughed uproariously.

"Mostly his son, these days," she confirmed. "The king, being in his eighties, is not as virile as he once was, but he does visit every few months."

The Ephrians fell silent, unsure how to respond to such information. With an aunt like Serene Loore, Evylin had heard much sordid gossip about the behavior of the royals and nobility. But she'd always thought it overdramatized for effect. This sort of unabashed debauchery caused her skin to crawl.

Deckard let out a heavy sigh, at an apparent loss for words.

"Does my lifestyle displease your sensibilities, Colonel?" Renaul asked with an amused smirk.

"I believe my shock is perfectly evident," Deckard replied sharply.

Renaul hummed with marked disdain. "I'd heard that Ephrians were prudish, but with a wife like yours, I'd imagined you would be a bit more open-minded."

Deckard glared at her. "I'd ask you not to insult my wife by suggesting she's anything like you."

As Renaul lounged in her chair with a haughty smile, Evylin slipped her fingers to Deckard's wrist. He'd advised her of caution. It was the least she could do to return the favor.

Her gentle touch brought his eyes to hers. Then he turned his hand, intertwining their fingers together.

"While you may be correct at the present," Renaul said, ignoring their affection, "I'm afraid you won't be for much longer."

"And why is that?" Deckard demanded.

"Because tomorrow, you will be dead, and your wife will be free."

Fear gripped Evylin around the throat. Was it to be just as she'd feared? Just as she'd chosen to let herself love Deckard, he was to be taken from her? She hadn't even had the chance to tell him yet. A crushing wave of emotion threatened to pull her under, drowning her in the expectation of her sorrow.

"You said this was our last dinner," Thom said.

"It is," Renaul said. "You, your brother, and your friends: It's your last dinner. The lovely Mrs. Deckard, however . . ."

Cold dread slid over Evylin, wrapping around her veins. She knew exactly what Renaul was about to say.

"You see," the noblewoman's eyes glimmered with vile glee, "Rouland was quite taken with our beautiful Warrior. And he intends to have her for himself."

Deckard's fingers tightened on Evylin's.

"No, your death would be a waste, dear," Renaul said to her. "And Rouland is never wasteful. He is married to my niece, of course, so you won't have the honor of being his wife. But I hear magical Bonds create a far more powerful connection anyway."

Trembling with repulsion and fear, Evylin scowled at the woman. "I would rather die," she said.

Renaul gave her a truly bemused look. "Nonsense. If you're worried, he's a wonderful lover. Gentle and attentive, in fact. Much better than his father, though not quite as enthusiastic."

Deckard shot a furious glare at her. "He will not touch her," he growled fiercely.

"I appreciate your jealousy," Renaul said in amusement, "but it will do you no good. Rouland will be here in the morning. He will kill the four of you gentlemen, and then he'll likely torture the Calders for their knowledge and kill them after. And as soon as he has all the necessary implements, he'll Bond with Evylin. From there, the Bond will do the work, or so I'm told."

Evylin struggled to breathe, her head reeling. She stared down at her plate, which sat still untouched. Bile rose as she watched the juices and sauces bleed together in the center. Deckard's fingers were painfully tight around hers, but she could hardly feel the pressure. Under no circumstances would she allow herself to be Bonded to Blount. She couldn't bear to fathom the thought of such an end.

Renaul set her empty wine glass down, and a servant sprang forward to refill it. "I must say, you're all far too upset by this. You should be pleased that he's allowing her to live."

"Some lives are worse than death," Thom said with anger. "None of us would subject Evylin to such a cruel fate."

"Pity that you feel that way," Renaul said with a bored inflection. "Well, is that it then? Do you have no more questions for me?"

None of them spoke. Evylin's fear continued to rise, choking her. Left with no other choices lest she be shackled to the whim of a sadistic tyrant, she would have to kill herself. But how? She had no weapons, no means of inflicting bodily harm. If Blount wanted to Bond with her, he wouldn't allow Renaul's men or Highlady Freye to kill her, no matter what she did to provoke them. If she tried to escape or fight, they'd just injure her enough to force her into submission. As Auden had said, Blount would do whatever it took. . . .

No, if she wanted death, there was only one recourse.

Staring down at their joined hands on the table, Evylin drew her thumb along Deckard's. If she wanted to be protected from such a cruel fate, she'd have to convince *him* to do it.

In the prolonged silence, Ethenn cleared his throat. "I have a question," he said.

Renaul gave him a cheery smile. "That's the spirit. Ask away, handsome."

"Where are the Relics?"

They all perked up at that.

"Mm, you are a clever one, aren't you?" Renaul tapped a finger to her chin, considering Ethenn. "I did promise you honesty. They are safely locked away in my vault."

"And where is your vault located?" Ethenn asked.

Her smile grew. "In my bedroom."

The five Ephrians shared thoughtful looks.

"Don't bother planning a heist, dears," Renaul said jovially. "Rouland gave me this vault as a gift. It's magical in design, and only he or I can open it."

"Seeing as how he's intending to throw you over for Eve," Rafferty mused, "what d'ya say to switching sides?"

Hope didn't have a second to grow in any of them as Renaul laughed instantly at the suggestion. "I think not. You cannot offer me what Rouland has. And what would the purpose of all this have been if I simply let you go?"

"An entertaining diversion?" Rafferty suggested.

Renaul sipped her wine dismissively.

"What about the Calders?" Thom asked. "Where are you keeping them?"

"In my dungeon," she said.

"And where is that?"

"In what used to be my family's catacombs." Renaul sat forward, eyes twinkling. "You can't rescue them either."

Thom turned away, not deigning to reply.

"Any further questions?" Renaul asked.

At their prolonged silence, she shrugged. "Very well. I'll admit I'm disappointed. I thought we might have more fun, but alas . . ." She surveyed them coldly. "Now, if you're done with our conversation, I'd advise you to finish your plates. The hour grows late, and you'll want to be at your best in the morning."

Renaul's hospitality withered as her entertainment waned. Uncertainly, the men returned to their meals while Highlady Freye continued to eat with indifference. Evylin couldn't bring herself to move. Not while panic pooled in her gut.

Deckard dipped his head toward her. "Eat," he whispered. "Please."

Holding his calm green-blue gaze, Evylin discovered an unexpected confidence within. Did he still have hope they could escape? The thought of the disguised Night Relic bobbed to the surface of her memory. If Deckard had it, could he slip it to her? But what good would that do? One weapon wouldn't be enough against the numerous guards and Mages in Renaul's employ. Would it? With Deckard and Evylin's powers combined . . . Maybe.

Even if they managed to resist, escape seemed impossible. Deckard's magic was strong, but it wasn't limitless. So far, he'd only used it in quick but powerful bursts. Though their jaunt in the Time Keep was long, he'd entered the battle after two days of rest. They were all weakened by their time with Caustin. If they relied too heavily on Deckard's magic, he could black out as Ilain had after the Wind Keep.

Heeding Deckard's request, Evylin began to eat. Her stomach felt weighted. With each bite she swallowed, the heaviness increased, driving the worry deeper and deeper into her core.

Regardless of whether they could launch an escape attempt and no matter if they succeeded, Evylin was determined to procure Deckard's promise first. If it came down to staying alive to Bond with Blount or dying to be set free, he *had* to kill her. She might not have a weapon, but he always would. The image of his magic at work rose to the surface of her mind. He could summon one of those crystalline shards and pierce her heart, saving her from a dreadful fate.

Deckard would protest, of course. He would rail and insist there was another way. Yet, in the end, he'd see reason. He would end her life to spare her from agony because he loved her.

Emotion constricted Evylin's chest. Deckard loved her, and she loved him. But the chance to tell him was swiftly slipping from her grasp. When the dinner was over, Renaul would separate them, and Evylin would lose her final opportunity. She had to secure his promise and tell him of her love *before* dinner concluded.

The gentle clatter of utensils on porcelain and the crackle of the fire were the only sounds in the room. Evylin lifted her eyes to Rafferty, silently pleading with him to start a conversation so she could speak with Deckard. Somehow, the weasel caught her stare and interpreted its meaning with a subtle nod.

He opened his mouth, but Renaul beat him to it. "Well," she said with a snap that made Evylin jump. The servants stepped forward to clear the table. "This has been a real pleasure. Before we depart, I wanted to thank you all for your help in recovering the Relics. Rouland will be so pleased."

Rafferty cleared his throat, staring pointedly at Deckard. "Happy to be of service," he said significantly.

While Evylin furrowed her brow, Deckard gave the man a barely perceptible nod.

Renaul didn't notice their silent communication. She rose, beckoning the guards forward. "Return them to their rooms," she ordered.

Evylin reached for Deckard, but he was already grabbing her hand. Her panic spiked. She needed to tell him, to convince him. The words were on the tip of her tongue. Her heart pounded in her ears.

Renaul stepped back as the guards came forward. "Make sure you station guards at each door," she told Highlady Freye. "No one is allowed to go in or out until Prince Blount arrives in the morning. If they give you trouble, tie them up, knock them out, or do whatever you think is best."

Highlady Freye stood, her fingers coiling around Evylin's arm.

"Jonn," Evylin whispered, her hands and voice shaking as she clung to him. The shackles jangled as the Mage pulled her out of her seat. Deckard stood with her, pushing one of the guards off to remain with her.

"Please," Renaul said as though they were petulant children, "don't make a scene. It's so unnecessary."

"At least give us a moment to say goodbye," Deckard pleaded, his arm crushing her to his chest. Evylin didn't like how unsteady his voice sounded, like another man's and not the kind, sure captain she'd married.

Renaul gave a flippant wave of her hand. "Oh, you'll have all night for that."

Evylin and Deckard froze.

"What?" Evylin gasped.

Renaul smirked. "I have a soft spot for romance. And I want *you* to remember every second of your last night together." She said the words with a pointed and cruel look in Evylin's direction.

Unconvinced, Deckard held her close, and Evylin pressed herself into his side.

"Rest well, dear ones," Renaul said, then surveyed the other three men. "I'm afraid you'll have to remain alone. Unless . . ." She studied Thom with a wicked eye. "You'd be interested in joining me?"

Thom snarled at her. "I'd sooner let Ilain Calder burn me alive."

"Suit yourself," Renaul said, and with a last flick of her wrist, directed, "Take them away."

CHAPTER FIFTY-ONE

In a grand parade, Highlady Freye and the guards led the five Ephrians back through the shadowed halls of Lady Renaul's mansion. Deckard and Evylin refused to let go of one another, still not secure in the noblewoman's promise. Neither would put it past the lady to play such a cruel joke.

Surrounded by guards on all sides, Thom, Rafferty, and Ethenn trailed behind them. Despite the hours remaining until Blount's arrival in the morning, it felt like a death march. The chill of the night seeped into the mansion, turning its white halls an eerie gray. Servants pulled the curtains as they walked, deepening the darkness. Their footsteps echoed off the marbled floor, each thud reverberating in Evylin's chest to rattle her senses.

They neared the main foyer, where the grand staircases awaited their ascent. Thom pressed forward, closing the gap between them as much as his guards would allow. "If this is it," he said, gaining Deckard's attention, "I want you to know: I'm sorry."

Deckard scanned him, his arm still tightly around Evylin. They turned the corner to begin ascending the staircase. "So am I," he finally said. He hesitated, taking a deep breath. "It isn't said enough between us, so I'm not sure you know it, but . . . I love you."

"Yeah," Thom said, sorrow etching his face and words. "I know it. And . . . I—well, I—"

"I know," Deckard said, granting him mercy. Then he turned to Ethenn and Rafferty. "Thank you both. For everything."

"It was an honor, sir," Ethenn said, his face grim. His dark eyes met Evylin's. "You, too, Evie."

She smiled, but Rafferty glowered. "I'm not saying goodbye," he insisted. "Not until we're dead."

Nearing the top of the stairs, Thom didn't share his friend's scruples. "I'm sorry, Evie," he said desperately. "I shouldn't have—but I did, and I—I'd say I didn't mean it, but that doesn't sound right. But I don't think I did—mean it, that is. I love you but not like that."

The guards jostled them, muscling between them to part their groups. Evylin struggled to hold Thom's gaze as she said, "It's all right, Thom. It's forgotten."

He looked ready to fight through the entire Waulden Army himself to stay with them, but she gave him one final nod, and he let the guards carry him, Ethenn, and Rafferty to the right while Highlady Freye guided Deckard, Evylin, and their sentries to the left. Watching them depart as long as she could, tears welled in Evylin's eyes. She hoped beyond reason that Rafferty's optimism wasn't misplaced. She didn't want to say goodbye to them either. Emotion choked her, a sob rising in her chest.

After all she'd lost—Ryen as a child and Hewitt a mere month ago—after all the careful protection of her heart, she'd come to love these men too. The thought of losing any of them, while not as debilitating as the very suggestion of losing Deckard, was heartbreaking.

The rug in the hall gave gently under Evylin's slippers. Everything in Renaul's home was beyond any opulence Evylin had ever seen aside from the Ephrian palace. She couldn't fathom living in such splendor. It was beautiful and stirring, pulling at all her senses. And it felt like a slap in the face given their circumstances.

The highlady came to a halt, flinging open the door to the room Evylin had been readied in. The guards pushed her and Deckard inside, then took up their posts. The Mage stepped up, a jangling keyring in hand. "Don't get any ideas from the lady's generosity," she said in her sultry foreign accent. She lifted Evylin's wrists, unlocking her shackles. "If you try to escape, you will die. Should you cling to false hope, allow me to clarify your situation: There are seventy-five guards under Lady Renaul's employ. In addition, Officer Caustin and his forty-eight men remain on the estate."

Evylin rubbed her freed wrists as the woman continued, "Should you determine that normal men pose little threat to a Warrior, I'll inform you that there are six other Mages here aside from myself. And I will personally remain outside your door through the night. If you consider jumping out the window, the fall alone would cause devastating injury as well as put you in the direct path of the sentries posted to patrol beneath those windows. Have I made myself clear?"

Her body and mind numb, Evylin allowed Deckard to guide her farther into the room. "Immensely," he replied on their behalf.

"Excellent." Highlady Freye retreated through the door and shut it with a snap. The rasp of the bolt sounded a second later.

Standing motionless in the entry hall to the opulent suite, Evylin struggled to breathe as Deckard's hold on her loosened. Her brain spun, fear winding its cruel grip around her limbs. The odds against them were too high. Even with the hidden Night Relic in their possession, the full potential of Deckard's unknown magic abilities, and her skills, their chances of rescuing their friends and the Calders, retrieving the stolen Relics, and escaping were next to impossible. They *would* die. It was just a matter of whose hand dealt the killing blow.

Deckard released his hold on Evylin altogether and stepped away. Cold air seeped into the space he'd abdicated. Surprised by his abandonment, Evylin turned to find him stepping farther into the room. He scanned the grand space, taking in its amethyst draperies, roaring hearth, painted ceiling, plush settees, and palatial four-poster bed. A fully furnished bathing chamber waited on the other side of the hall, where Evylin had been scrubbed and polished within an inch of her life. They'd poured an expensive-smelling oil all over her skin and hair, dousing her in its rich, musky scent.

With a final scan, Deckard sent her an amused look. "Your room is bigger than mine," he noted.

A surprised laugh caught in Evylin's throat. "Is that so?"

He tapped the back of one of the velvet settees. "Seems as though you've been given a suite."

Usually, Evylin would return his banter with a witty retort. Tonight, she couldn't find the words.

Moving into the room, Evylin bypassed Deckard and went to the windows that lined the back wall. She understood that this opulence was gifted to her as Blount's intended vassal. Dread curled up her spine as she pushed back the heavy curtains to peer out across the lawn. Immaculately cut gardens and drifting shadows met her inspection. Cool moonlight shone like a beacon, the ivory moon large and round, a violet halo softening its edges as the shadow moon's crescent peeked from behind it with a silver glow.

Evylin let the drape fall back to a puddle on the marble tile. Everything in the room spoke of luxury. The silk and velvet fabrics. The gilded walls and furnishings. Even the towering ceiling was beyond the scope of typical elegance with its intricate depiction of the night sky. The heavenly bodies and stars glittered with metallic leafing. Yet, just as the soft dress felt like chains around Evylin's skin, the room's grandiosity felt like the most oppressive dungeon. *You're trapped,* it whispered. *You will be given everything, yet all that truly matters will be taken away.*

The fire popped in the far corner. She glanced at the finely wrought hearth before her eyes drifted back to Deckard, who now sat on the far settee. He'd unbuttoned his navy coat, letting it hang open as he untied the cravat. He dropped the silk tie on the tea table before leaning down to remove his boots.

"What are you doing?" Evylin asked, her heart lurching at the thought that he'd given up.

His gaze flickered up to her as he set the first boot aside. "Getting more comfortable."

She crossed to stand behind the settee opposite him. "Why?"

"Because I'm tired of this frippery." Deckard set the second boot next to its pair, as orderly as ever. He looked up, his brow pinching as he surveyed her. "You look concerned."

"I am," she said, thinking he should be too.

A slow, confident smile came to his face. "You needn't be. We're going to get out of here."

Hope and reality warred within her. She was glad to know he hadn't surrendered to death yet, but she also worried that he wouldn't take her request seriously. Her fingers brushed over her rings. "How?" she asked. "I don't have a weapon, the Calders are drugged in a dungeon, the Relics are in a vault with an unpickable lock, and there are more than one hundred guards between us and escape. Not to mention the Mage waiting outside our door."

Deckard watched her calmly. "Are you finished?"

Evylin gave him an agitated look.

He grinned. "None of that worries me."

"Why not?"

Unfastening the buttons of his collar, Deckard reached beneath the fabric. "Because," he said, pulling the Night Relic free, "you do have a weapon, as do I. Despite Caustin's effort to weaken us, we're both reasonably recovered from our time in the Keep, and we have nothing to lose. Once we retrieve Ethenn, we'll have a second Warrior. And with Rafferty by our side, a second Relic."

Evylin gaped at him. "What? How?"

"I'm not sure how he managed it," Deckard said. "But he's gone to a lot of trouble to tell me something, getting himself beaten bloody in the process. I'm convinced that Ethenn somehow passed Rafferty the Wind Relic when they discovered the danger. Smuggler that he is, Rafferty's managed to keep it hidden."

Hope burgeoned within Evylin. Two Relics, two Warriors, one Mage. Yes, it would seem their odds were rising. "You know which room Raff is in?" she asked.

"As long as they returned them to their original rooms, yes. I know where all three of them are being held."

Evylin stepped around the settee to take a seat. "What about the other Relics? How are we going to retrieve those?"

Deckard hesitated, then looked at the rug beneath his feet. "We may have to leave them."

His downcast tone caused Evylin to go rigid. "And what about the Calders?"

"I fear . . ." He didn't meet her gaze. "We'll have to leave them too."

Evylin's heart dropped. "No," she gasped. "We can't do that."

"I'm not sure we have a choice."

"Jonn, we'd be leaving them to their deaths."

"I know," he murmured, running a hand over his face. "But if it's between letting Blount gain five Relics or three, you know what Auden and Ilain would tell us to do. Yes, the Calders will die if we don't save them, but . . . They'll likely still die if we try to."

Evylin stared into the fire dejectedly, her thoughts plaguing her with visions of Ilain and Auden left to Blount's devices.

"If, however," Deckard continued somberly, "we do make it out with the two Relics we have, we know where the final two are. We can return to Ephria and obtain them before Blount. Then we'll each have four. Even if we have to go into hiding, he won't have succeeded entirely, and we can increase our strength or find the Alliance. Whatever it takes, if we live through this, we can stop him. If we don't. . . ."

He didn't need to finish the alternative. They knew what would happen if they failed to escape Renaul.

Evylin took in a broken breath as she considered their situation. The Calders had dedicated their entire lives to stopping King Blount and his tyranny. Dying at the hands of his son . . . What a brutal injustice that would be. But then, their deaths would secure his ultimate end, and that would be the grandest justice the siblings could hope for.

She wanted to insist on saving them. It would be better for them to live to see that justice meted out by their own hands. If they could only find the Calders, give them the Relics, and let them escape to fight another day, Evylin thought it would be worth it, even if the rest of them lost their lives.

But she knew it would be impossible. The Calders were locked in separate cells, drugged by viastasis. Even if they found them, they'd have to carry them to freedom. Which would be an impossibility if they were to fight their way out.

No, they couldn't save the Calders or the Relics. Their only hope was to make a run for it themselves.

Even still . . .

"I need you to promise me something, Jonn," she whispered, unable to find her full voice.

Deckard looked up, expectant—waiting.

Evylin held his attentive gaze, her heart breaking with her words. "If we don't make it out of here, I want you to kill me."

His expression hardened, his eyes growing wide in refusal, but she continued before he could protest. "I won't be Bonded to Blount," she said, fervor strengthening her voice. "No matter what it takes, I will find a way to kill myself before that happens. But it could take years of torture before I find that opportunity. If it comes to it, if there is no chance of escape and he's about to take your life, I want you to kill me first."

"Evylin, I—"

"Please, Jonn." She let all the terror roiling inside her show, pleading with him through her vulnerability. "I need you to save me from him."

His whole bearing changed then, becoming broken and sorrowful. His head hung, and his shoulders drooped. But he whispered, "I promise, whatever it takes . . . I won't leave you to him."

Evylin didn't know whether to feel relieved or devastated. "Thank you."

"But—" Deckard's gaze rose with a new vehemence in their green-blue depths. "I will pursue every other avenue of escape before I ever lift a hand to you. Be it tomorrow morning or a century from now, I will save your life before taking it."

A soft, if doubtful, smile came to Evylin's lips. "Well, then . . ." She brushed her hands over the skirt of her dress. "I suppose we ought to escape now."

The smallest fraction of a smirk lifted the corner of his mouth as he raised a hand to stall her. "Not yet," he said. "Soon, but . . . We should let the guards relax. If we move too quickly, they'll be alert and ready. If we let them think we've given up, hopefully their defenses will be lowered, and our escape will be easier."

Nerves rattling through her limbs, Evylin fought the urge to twist her rings. Her body needed movement and action. It craved the chance to fight, to run, to do anything that would distract her mind from the waiting. And from the words she couldn't figure out how to say.

Dropping Deckard's gaze, Evylin took a steadying breath. "What should we do in the meantime, then?" she asked.

"We were apart for two weeks," he said thoughtfully, "and forced into silence for four days. I'd say we have some catching up to do."

Evylin turned back to the fire, unable to sit still in the weighty expectation of the moment. "I suppose you're right."

"Shall I tell you about our journey, or would you like to start?" he asked.

"You start."

"All right." Deckard shifted to sit on the edge of the settee, resting his arms on his knees. "I will warn you; Rafferty was right. It was rather boring."

A quiet chuckle slipped out of her at his teasing tone. "Is that so?"

"*I* was dreadfully bored, so I can only imagine how he fared."

"Poor dear."

He raised his brow. "Me or Rafferty?"

She gave him a sideways glance. "Both of you."

Deckard dipped his chin in mock appreciation. "Your concern is too kind." He drew a hand along his smooth jaw before beginning. "Well, there isn't much to tell. Traveling and training took up most of our time. I *can* say that the marshes of Wauld are worse than all the rain in the North."

"Impossible."

"You'd say that until you've been eaten alive by mosquitoes."

Evylin scrunched her nose in disgust. "Heavens forbid."

One of Deckard's brightest smiles relaxed his distressed countenance. At the sight of it, the tension in her muscles eased. Here was the man to whom she'd bound her life—the noble captain who could charm even Hewitt Glaas into spending his afterlife with him. Though she'd thought it due to meager novelty, she'd been drawn to Deckard from the start. It was a subtle sort of attraction, one that snuck up on her rather than sweeping her off her feet. Yet, here in this moment fraught with danger and impending death, she wondered how she ever could have lived without this wonderful man she'd come to call husband.

Despite their dire situation, this was the moment for which they'd both waited. They had returned to one another, and if nothing else, they could enjoy their final hours in each other's company.

The thought pinched in Evylin's chest.

"During our journey," Deckard continued, "I began to keep Hewitt around at all times."

Evylin looked up. "I thought you summoned him after . . . in Ephria."

"I did, but I only saw him occasionally, and it was when I wanted to. While traveling through the marshes, I kept him around constantly."

"But . . . You couldn't talk to him or give any sign he was there. Why would you—?"

"I missed you," he said plainly. "And Hewitt was the closest thing I could get to being with you. Even if we couldn't talk."

A sorrowful joy rose in Evylin. How could she truly appreciate the sentiment when she'd so foolishly been the one to drive him away?

Staring at her hands, Evylin let the discordant feelings rage unhindered. "Auden said he told you to let Hewitt go. He found out?"

"He did, but I didn't listen."

"Mm. Did he see him? Is that how he discovered him?"

Deckard shook his head. "He stumbled upon me talking with Hewitt in the woods. Auden couldn't see or hear him; he just knew I was talking to someone invisible and correctly assumed it was Hewitt's ghost."

Evylin frowned. "No one else saw him? Until after the Time Keep?"

"No."

"But I saw him in the Night Keep."

Deckard shrugged. "I would assume that's because it takes Night magic to summon a ghost, and we were in its Keep. My power was probably stronger there, making him visible."

Evylin considered the memory. "And," she added, "I was holding the Night Relic at the time."

"That probably had its influence as well."

She played with the folds of her skirt. "I understand why you didn't tell me," she said softly. "But I wish you had."

"I do too," he admitted.

"And I wish I had told you that I'd seen him. If we could have made this connection before, I could have talked to him sooner, and we could have avoided . . ."

Deckard didn't respond but held her gaze with a gentle look of understanding. If they had discovered the truth sooner, so much would have changed. Evylin would have let go of her fear. The parties may still have split, but she would have gone with Deckard. These last weeks, they would have been happy and in love, as she knew they should have been all along. And now, they'd lost so much time.

"Anyway," Deckard said, breaking the silence. "That's the end of my story. As dull as I remembered."

The fire crackled, tinting the white walls and floor tiles in its golden red hue. Evylin hesitated, not wanting to relive the days without him. She didn't care to give voice to the memory of Thom's traitorous confession.

"I suppose," she spoke regardless, "it's my turn now."

Sitting up straighter, Evylin took a deep breath. "Our travel wasn't much more exciting than yours, but it was greatly more dramatic."

"So I gathered," Deckard said with a lightness that didn't quite match his expression.

Evylin attempted to ease the growing tension in the atmosphere. "It was like being home with my sisters again. I never thought men could be so emotionally unstable."

She was relieved to see he afforded her a small, amused smile.

With a sigh, she continued, "It didn't start that way, of course. We all got on rather splendidly the first while. Ethenn and I trained together most days, and we became . . .

close, I think. At least, closer. I sort of assume I know what it's like to have a little brother now."

This elicited a chuckle from Deckard. "He's more talkative when you get him alone, isn't he?"

"That he is," she agreed. Then she bit her lip. "He gave me your birthday gift."

Deckard paused, meeting her eyes.

"It was beautiful," she said, her voice weak with affection. "I'm rather disappointed, knowing that it's lost to me forever now."

"It's a painting," Deckard said kindly. "We can find another."

Evylin's chest expanded with tender emotion. "It was so similar . . ."

His smile practically made his eyes sparkle with triumph. "You noticed."

"Of course, I did." She felt her own smile falter. "I'm sorry that it's gone."

"As am I."

The fondness in his gaze caused her hands to twitch. Subconsciously, she slipped to the edge of the couch, her feet all but begging her to go to his side.

Instead, she returned to her story. "Ilain and I grew close as well, and she told me about her family and their lifelong connection to the Alliance. And I've discovered she's one of the better people I've ever met."

Deckard nodded as though he'd already determined that for himself.

"But," Evylin sighed, "Thom and Ethenn began to fight over her. I thought it was because they both had feelings for her when it turned out . . ."

"We don't have to talk about that," Deckard said, a flat edge to his tone.

Evylin met his gaze. "I think we do."

The openness in his expression shuttered itself, his shoulders becoming rigid, but he didn't stop her.

"Jonn," she whispered, "I didn't know."

"It doesn't matter."

"It does." She leaned forward, her fingers gripping the cushions. "You have to know, I never would have befriended him, I never would have confided in him, had I known."

"Evylin," he replied, a severity coming into his stare that she wasn't used to. "This isn't about what you did or didn't do. It's about what Thom did, how *he* behaved."

"But do you believe him?" she asked, daring to hold that hard glare. "His apology tonight, what he said to us before they took him away. Do you believe he means it?"

Deckard was silent. He rubbed his palms together, his thoughts so deep she could see the tension in his hunched form. Whatever arguments raged within, they drove him from his seat. He began to pace across the room, running a hand through his hair. "I don't know," he muttered at last. "Of all men, I understand why he—why any man could love you—*should* love you. But my brother . . . It's hard to believe that anyone could dupe themselves into having feelings simply out of competition."

"Perhaps," Evylin offered, "his feelings were genuine but misinterpreted, as he suggested tonight."

Deckard continued to pace. "You believe he loves you but is not *in* love with you?"

"Exactly." She wanted to rise, to take his hand and make him look at her. But she wasn't ready yet to say the things she needed to, to make her confession. "I think the only reason he pursued those feelings, incorrectly attributing more to them than he truly felt, was because he saw it as a chance to compete with you. He wanted to prove that he could beat you. But I don't believe he ever thought he actually could, and that's why he waited so long, why he even fought me tooth and nail before he ever tried to take me from you."

His pacing faltered as he stepped behind the far settee. He gave a forlorn-sounding chuckle. "I suppose he didn't realize it wouldn't matter. You weren't mine anyway."

"Don't say that," she whispered, her heart breaking at the thought. After two weeks separating them, after the cold and lonely nights, after only finding sleep by dreaming of his presence again . . . After her conversation with Hewitt's ghost, Evylin had come to realize that somehow Jonn Deckard had become the person upon whom she relied. He was her heart, and she never wished to be parted from him again.

Deckard met her stare, silent.

Something in his hesitation, his stoic resignation, emboldened her. He needed to know. If they were going to die tomorrow, she wanted to tell him. She held his gaze firmly as she spoke.

"I could never be anyone but yours."

Deckard's breath caught. Then his eyes fell away. "Evylin, you need to know something."

His unexpected reply caused her to straighten in her seat.

"If we make it out of this alive," he began, "I'm not . . . free. I promised Auden that when our mission with them is through, I will join the Alliance in whatever capacity they ask of me."

Evylin blanched. "When did you make this promise?"

He tapped the back of the settee guiltily. "A little over three weeks ago."

Doing a quick recounting of the time, Evylin realized that it would roughly coincide with the discovery of the writ. Her lips parted in shock. "Was this the price of my joining him in Dunneshead?"

"It doesn't matter."

"Jonn," she said his name like an admonition, "please, tell me you didn't sell your life purely to give me a break from the road."

"You were drowning, Evylin. I had to save you."

Knowing this was another result of her foolish fears, Evylin dropped her head in her hands. She took a deep breath, then looked up, pushing the hair back behind her ears. "So," she concluded, "you made this promise knowing they'd want you to Bond with . . . with me or another Warrior should I . . ."

His lack of response was all the confirmation she needed.

Evylin shook her head, a disbelieving laugh slipping out of her. Auden had taken Deckard at his word because they all knew: Deckard would never break a promise. His nobility and integrity were faultless. It was part of what made him so insufferably wonderful.

"All right," Evylin said.

Deckard's eyes narrowed. "All right?"

She shrugged. "You were a soldier when I married you. Your future was never yours to begin with. Why should it bother me now?"

His grip on the settee tightened. "Because if we remain married, they'll require us to Bond," he said as though it were a death sentence. "I know what Hewitt meant to convince you of. Trust me, we talked about it plenty. But I will still give you an annulment if that's what you want because if you stay with me, our future will be bound to the Alliance and . . . to each other."

Evylin held his gaze unflinchingly. "Our future . . ." she whispered with a sad smile. "I'm afraid we might not have much of one."

Rising from her seat, Evylin walked around the settee. She felt the need for distance, to put physical barricades between them as she worked to pull down the intangible ones she'd erected long ago. She needed the safety of separation before she could risk the fullness of vulnerability.

The rich velvet of the seat back tingled under her fingertips as she faced him once more. "Jonn, I was a fool," she began, her voice soft and slow.

His chin lifted, brow pinched together as he listened intently.

Evylin couldn't help smiling at that quirk of his. She adored that concerned wrinkle. "I convinced myself that I couldn't be with you," she admitted, "because I was afraid of you."

Deckard's lips parted, but he didn't try to speak.

"The truth is," she continued, "you scare me more than anything we've faced. You always have."

Her breath caught as she forced herself to be brave. "I never wanted a normal life. Though I secretly dreamed I'd marry, I never believed I'd find someone who . . ." She paused, thinking of his criteria for a wife. "Who was enough," she said tenderly.

He let out a singular, breathy scoff, turning away. She studied his profile, the angular lines noticeably Waulden now that she knew of his unexpected ancestry. He'd always had a regal bearing, something beyond the down-to-earth quality of Ephrian heritage.

"Then you came along," she continued, "and you shattered everything I ever thought I wanted. You were good, clever, caring, and ambitious. You were handsome, too, though I didn't want to admit it."

He shook his head, though her compliments drew the corner of his mouth up in a smile.

"Beyond that, you were a captain—the very sort of man who could take me on all those adventures I'd dreamed about."

Evylin forced herself to keep speaking as Deckard finally met her gaze again. "It all terrified me. I'd never wanted to be alone, but I'd never wanted someone before either. I—" Her words faltered as he began to walk around the furniture toward her, their gazes locked. It was too soon. She wasn't ready for him to be so close, to see her so wholly exposed.

As she stepped back, hand gliding over the golden rim of the settee's back, he paused, only a few short strides separating them.

Evylin's lungs grew tight in her chest, her breath coming in rapid bursts. "I didn't know what to do," she finally said. "And then Hewitt went and—and got us married."

They both smiled at that.

"He has always given me everything I wanted. Even when I didn't know what that was myself."

Evylin swallowed down the rest of her fear, ready to reveal her whole heart to him. "But even if he hadn't," she said, the words a whisper of sound in the grip of her emotions, "had the circumstances been different . . . Had you asked to write to me, to court me from a distance . . . I would have said yes."

Her grip on the couch tightened, holding herself in place as he took one step closer.

"Had a year—or simply months—passed, and if you'd asked to marry me . . . I would have said yes."

Deckard closed the gap, standing directly in front of her. She lifted her chin to stare up into his eyes, so brilliant and ever-changing. All it would take was a raised hand or the smallest lean in, and the space between them would dissipate.

Evylin marveled at his restraint as her fingers ached to reach for him. She struggled to keep her voice even as she spoke. "Time would have done a lot for us, I think. I might not have been so afraid of you and how—" The words tried to fly away, but she scrambled to capture them like memories nearly forgotten to time. "How you made me feel. No matter what—whether you wrote to me or if we married as we did—I think we always would have ended up together."

She took one last breath before releasing her fear, feeling the tension of it lift from her chest once and for all. "I've known for a while now. I've known just how much I wanted you—how much I . . ." Her words dropped to a whisper that was almost too gentle for her own ears. "How much I love you."

A weighty breath slipped from Deckard's lips.

Tears blurred the edges of Evylin's vision. "And knowing that scared me more than death itself," she admitted. "So I told myself it wasn't true. I lied to myself and to you."

"Evylin," he whispered, his smile so bright and so tender it nearly broke her heart.

Deckard took her face in his hands, severing the final barriers between them. Evylin gripped his arms as his thumbs brushed over her cheeks. "I've loved you for months now, Jonn," she told him, the strength returning to her voice. "I just couldn't bring myself to face it. And now . . . now we're about to die."

Deckard shook his head, leaning closer. "We're not going to die, Evylin."

"I think we are," she said, the words almost a sob as she realized how much time they'd lost, what she'd stolen from them by giving in to her fear.

Yet, he didn't seem to share her reservations or sorrow. He drew her in, his words a whisper against her lips, "I won't let that happen."

Evylin closed her eyes just as Deckard kissed her with a gentle caress so soft and filled with the love they'd once held back so carefully. She'd always enjoyed kissing him, the magic within her veins rising at his touch. But she'd never allowed herself to give her all to the experience. No matter how passionate or desirous she felt in the moment, there was always a piece of her heart she'd kept from him. She'd always clung to her fear that she was making a mistake, that she would lose *herself* if she gave her heart to him.

That fear no longer existed.

Evylin released every worry, bowing to the tide of magic that swept through her. Her senses rose as she returned his kiss with what she hoped he'd know was, at last, unrestrained love. All her heart and every ounce of hope, she poured into affection for him.

His fingers wove into her hair while his other hand dropped to her waist. He drew her closer than he ever had before, sending spikes of energy across her skin. She slid her hands up his arms to settle on his back, relaxing into his embrace.

"Evie," he murmured between kisses.

"Mm?" she sighed against his mouth.

Deckard broke away only far enough to rest his forehead against hers. His hand grazed her bare shoulder, power pulsing through his touch to bound across her skin. The world became brighter in clarity. The weight of his hand on her lower back, the pattern of his heightened breathing, the scent of wine and fragrant oil—it all filled her senses with the promise of their love.

His nose brushed hers as he whispered, "Will you stay with me?"

Evylin smiled as his hand trailed from her shoulder, down her arm, and to her hand. She refused to hesitate, lacing her fingers with his. "Yes."

Something between a sigh of relief and a laugh broke out of him, and he kissed her again. "I love you."

"I love you."

They returned to the kiss, though it was no longer gentle and tame but eager and impassioned. His arm twined farther around her waist as he deepened the kiss. Their embrace went on for untold minutes. Her hands found their way beneath his coat to press against the firm planes of his chest as he caressed her arms, back, and sides. Every touch, every breath enhanced her senses, drawing her magic out.

Eventually, he shrugged out of the coat, and she kicked off her slippers. Deckard took her hand then, drawing her across the cold tiles and plush rugs toward the bed. With the faintest interest, Evylin realized they hadn't shared a bed in weeks. In all that time, she never would have anticipated their first night back together would result in *this*.

Between kisses, affectionate touches, and euphoric laughs, Deckard finally worked free the buttons of her dress as she tugged loose the tails of his shirt. Time slowed into an otherworldly stillness as he lifted her onto the mattress. The downy comforter was cool against her skin and far too soft after weeks of sleeping on the hard forest floors of Wauld. All her perceptions were overpowering—every sight, smell, taste, sound, and touch. And she never wanted it to end.

Yet, despite the blissful new sensations dancing along her skin, the cool stillness of magic steadied her mind, and Evylin's absent-minded musings fell away to nothing as he kissed her, and she kissed him in return. Fear was no longer a word she understood. Everything around her and everything within her settled into Deckard's arms until only one thought remained: Why hadn't they done this months ago?

CHAPTER FIFTY-TWO

36TH OF CHRONOS, 1574

Shock and disbelief clouded Deckard's mind. Evylin lay tucked into his side on the cloud-like bed, their breaths heavy and hearts reeling. The heat of his magic receded into dormancy. Though he hadn't actually grabbed hold of the power that sweltered underneath his skin, he'd felt it awaken with each intimate touch and kiss.

Now, the cool air of the room washed over him, steadying his head.

"Well," Deckard muttered around a shaky exhale. "I've wanted to do that for a while."

With a playful huff, Evylin slapped his chest.

He caught her wrist, grinning down at her as he leaned back against the pillows. "What? It's true, I have."

"If you're hoping for an apology," she said, nestling against him, "I'm afraid I don't have one."

He raised his brow. "And after that, I don't need one."

Though she rolled her eyes, he leaned forward to kiss her. He kept it short and sweet, unsure if his heart could manage anything more.

When he pulled back, Evylin lingered. "It's what you expected then?" she whispered, eyes downcast as though uncertain if she should ask.

Deckard let his fingers trace her spine. "More or less. Mostly more." At her soft smile, he asked, "Was it what you expected?"

Tucking her chin, she betrayed her timidity despite her flirtatious bravado. "No," she said hesitantly. "But I didn't have many expectations."

"No?" he asked, keenly aware of the way her fingers traced circles on his collarbone.

Her shoulder lifted with a small shrug. "It isn't a topic women discuss in polite society. Aunt Serene always enjoyed alluding to 'wifely duties,' and my mother gave me a short sermon before our wedding, but there was little explicit conversation in my life. I knew the general science of it, I knew that it might take a while to get used to, and I knew that if the man loved you, then somehow, he'd be able to make it more enjoyable. All in all, my speculations were rather vague."

"Then tell me . . ." Deckard took her hand and threaded their fingers together. "Did I make it clear that I love you?"

Evylin's cheeks flushed, her dimples appearing with her bashful smile. "More or less," she mimicked. "Mostly more."

They shared a contented chuckle, and he pulled her closer for a succession of soft kisses. She drew back abruptly, a question in her amber eyes. "It was over rather quickly, though, wasn't it?"

Unable to contain himself, Deckard laughed. "Yes, that would fall under the category of things taking a while to get used to."

"It would?"

He teased his fingers along hers. "I'm no expert, but soldiers talk far more explicitly than polite society. I've heard all I need to know that time will take care of that."

Curiosity lit in her gaze. "How does that work?"

With another laugh, Deckard stared at the ceiling, taking a restorative breath. "While I would love to discuss this in painstaking detail with you—" He set his hand on her hip and, with a gentle shove, rolled her over onto her back. "I'm afraid we really ought to get going."

"Jonn, we're prisoners," she said, her fingers curling to the back of his neck to pull him closer. "Where are we going to go?"

"I told you," he kissed her quickly before tearing himself away, "I'm not going to let us die here. Especially not after that."

Evylin's demure giggle tempted him back to the bed, but he remained resolute. "Fighting is going to be a bit difficult in that dress," she said, watching as he hurried to gather their discarded clothing.

"I'd offer to trade," he teased, "but I'm not sure it'll fit me."

"Mm, no," she said, catching the dress when he tossed it to her. "Purple wouldn't suit you anyway."

"A true pity."

She slipped off the bed, and he struggled not to stare at her as he reached under the pillow to retrieve the Night Relic. He'd stashed it, not wanting its pull on his magic to affect his ability to focus on the task at hand. "They didn't leave you with anything else?" he asked, slipping the Relic's chain back around his neck. The cold metal stung against his chest.

"It isn't exactly like they wanted me fighting."

Deckard meant to tell her she made a good point but got distracted watching her dress. When she caught him, he grinned abashedly and pulled his shirt over his head.

"Is this going to be a problem for you?" she asked, fastening her buttons. "Staring at me?"

"Yes, probably," he admitted, tucking the shirt. Her eyes darted down to watch the process, and he raised his brow. "Is it going to be a problem for you?"

Evylin smirked dryly. "No problem. Only a pleasure."

Charmed by her suggestive quip, Deckard stepped forward to pull her back into his arms and kiss her.

A sudden *thump* rattled the bedroom door, stopping him in his tracks.

They turned, staring at the door in the entry hall. "What was that?" Evylin whispered.

He stepped up to her side just as the lock was disengaged.

Evylin grabbed his hand with a sharp gasp. "It isn't morning," she said, a tremble in her voice. "He can't be—"

The door's latch clicked open. Deckard reached into his core, summoning the store of magic within. The Night Relic thrummed against his chest with a ready power. Whether Blount had arrived early or Renaul had changed her mind, he would be prepared.

But when two men stepped around the corner, Deckard hesitated. Both men wore dark coats and trousers, ideal for stealth. That's where the similarities ended. One man stood tall and lean, his pale skin and sharp features distinctly Waulden. The other was the dark-complected Ephrian from the stable.

"Well," the Waulden man said, his gaze swiftly taking in the room, lingering on the rumpled bed. "Looks like someone had a good time."

"They are married, Jarrad," Highlady Freye said, stepping into view.

Evylin's grip tightened on Deckard as he angled in front of her protectively.

"Doesn't mean it was a bad time," the Wauldener, Jarrad, replied.

The Wind Mage muttered something prayerful in a language Deckard had never heard. Then she tossed him a familiar bag—one of the packs they'd purchased in Norhels for their journey through Wauld.

"Ignore him," the highlady advised as though they shouldn't be surprised to see her. "He's a nuisance, but I'm not allowed to get rid of him."

Scanning the trio warily, Deckard stood his ground. "What do you want?" he demanded.

The Mage sighed. "I had hoped you knew, but I suppose Auden and Ilain didn't have the opportunity to tell you." Her stance relaxed in a manner Deckard assumed was supposed to set them at ease. "This is Highlord Aterian Jarrad Hoult, Terrae Mage, and that—" she gestured to the Ephrian stableman, "is Emmaas Caarney, our Warrior."

Evylin sucked in a sharp breath behind Deckard.

"We work for the Alliance."

Gripping the pack tighter, Deckard couldn't quite feel the hope underneath the shock radiating through him.

In their stunned silence, Highlady Freye continued, "If Auden and Ilain had known you were coming, they would have prepared you. I've been stationed here in Keale as Lady Renaul's steward for the past three years to infiltrate Blount's network. A worthy risk, as I am now in the position to save your lives."

"With some help," Jarrad added.

"Isla," the Ephrian, Emmaas, said. Surprisingly, his accent matched that of the Schonese woman. "We're short on time."

Still hesitant to believe the Mage, Deckard drew Evylin closer. "How do we trust you?" he asked.

"You either do, or you don't," Isla Freye said, then gave a pointed nod to the pack in his hands. "However, that might aid your decision."

After a shared glance, Deckard handed Evylin the pack. She pulled out two daggers, a change of clothes for her, including boots, and a black coat for Deckard.

"It isn't much," Isla admitted. "But in the hands of a Warrior, it's a start."

Evylin gave Deckard a casual shrug as if to indicate that trusting the three purported Alliance members gave them a better chance than attempting to escape alone.

"All right," Deckard said, taking the coat. "Go change, Evie."

"Hurry," Isla instructed as Evylin darted for the privacy of the bathing chamber.

Eyes briefly locking with Evylin's before she shut the door, Deckard crossed the room to where his boots waited by the settee. "What's the plan?" he asked.

Isla and Jarrad turned to the Warrior, Emmaas. In the firelight, his bald head glowed with a rich mahogany sheen. "First, we'll rescue your friends," he said, his deep voice mellow like the finest Schonese wine. "They're on the far side of this floor. Isla will enter the hall first, pretending to be on Renaul's orders. With her distraction, we'll take down the guards. Are your comrades good fighters?"

Deckard's heel sank into place in his second boot. "We're all soldiers. Thom and Rafferty are good. Ethenn is . . ." He paused, then decided their success necessitated honesty. "Ethenn is a Warrior too."

"What?" Isla gasped. "Auden and Ilain didn't tell us that."

"We didn't know until recently." Deckard hesitated for a moment more, then shrugged. "I assume that means you also aren't aware that I'm a Mage."

Isla's lips parted in shock as a sly grin took over Jarrad's face. "Well, this makes our lives easier," he remarked.

The bathing chamber door opened, and Evylin reappeared, dressed in black from head to toe. Jarrad's chin lifted in her direction. "A Mage and a Warrior already married? What could be more convenient?"

"Not being prisoners?" Evylin suggested as she took up the knives. "Shall we go?"

Deckard buttoned his coat as the trio led them out of the room. He gave the luxurious space one last glance over his shoulder, finding he held an unexpected fondness for their time in the opulent prison. Perhaps it wasn't the precise location and situation he would have chosen for his and Evylin's first intimate moments together, but it had served quite nicely.

They stepped into the hall where four guards lay unconscious. "Keep quiet," Emmaas warned in a whisper, "and to the shadows. There are patrols about."

Following the Warrior's lead, they walked carefully through the house. The lush rugs kept their footsteps silent. A ticking clock haunted their trek, only the occasional sound of guards muttering or adjusting breaking the silence. When they reached the main landing where the grand staircases opened up, they had to dash for the far hall, hoping to avoid notice as they passed through the flood of light from the massive entry window.

Nearing their friends' rooms, Isla moved ahead while the rest of them waited in the shadows. Her silver dress caught the dim lamplight as she approached the guards. They snapped to attention at the sight of her.

"Can we help you, ma'am?" one man asked.

"Yes," Isla said, her tone flat and emotionless once more. "Lady Renaul requested I bring the pretty one, Thom, to her chambers."

A huff came from another guard while a few more sniggered. "He's in that room," the first guard explained.

"Thank you," Isla replied, moving toward the middle door. She lifted her hand as if to turn the handle, then flicked her wrist. A gale shot forth, sweeping to the left and right to knock all twelve guards off their feet.

Emmaas and Jarrad hurried down the hall ahead of Deckard and Evylin. At the other end of the corridor, Emmaas produced hidden blades from his sleeves, slicing into the guards readily. With a flamboyant air, Jarrad raised his hands, curled them into fists, and then jerked them back. The wood of the baseboards, molding, and wall detailing sprouted new growth. Jagged blade-like branches pierced through more of the guards.

At the front of the hall, Evylin sprinted before dropping to her knees, matching the fallen sentries' height as she slid across the rug. She struck out with the daggers, slashing through two men before leaping to her feet with impossible grace. Deckard kept at her side, ready but not daring to use his magic yet. He wanted to save his strength for whatever disasters might come their way.

With the guards quickly felled, Isla tossed a key to Deckard and then another to Jarrad. "Retrieve the other two," she instructed, lifting a third key. "I'll get this one."

"Wait," Deckard said, reaching out to stop her. "That's my brother."

She put the key in the lock. "You don't think I can handle him?"

Realizing that she could, Deckard still felt the need to warn her. "He'll try to kill you."

"Sounds like fun," she replied, turning the key with a scrape of the metal lock.

Evylin grabbed Deckard's arm, pulling him in the direction of the first room. When they entered, their jaws immediately dropped. The entire room had been turned over in what looked like a furious search. Curtains were ripped down, the mattress was flipped over, paintings were torn from the walls, and in the midst of it all, Ethenn sat on the floor. In his hands, he held a splinter of the bed frame as he used a broken candlestick to whittle its edge to a violent point. Clearly, his hunt for a weapon was fruitless, so he'd determined to fashion one himself.

At their appearance, Ethenn startled and looked up, dark eyes wide and rimmed with exhaustion. His lips parted in shock. "How'd you get free?" he asked in awe.

Evylin laughed as she hurried over and helped him to his feet. "Come on," she said. "We'll show you."

As they stepped back into the hall, a crash echoed from the next room, followed by a furious string of curses. Deckard sighed and hurried in. Thom stood on the far side of the room, arm reared back, ready to throw another expensive decorative piece Isla's way.

"Thom!" Deckard called, skidding to a halt.

Freezing, Thom gaped at him. "Jonn?" He lowered his hand and looked at Isla with renewed interest. "You weren't lying?"

"No," she said, an amused smile on her lips. "I wasn't."

"Sorry," Thom muttered, then chucked the painted vase in his hand over his shoulder. It shattered on impact with the marble floor.

Back in the hallway, they met Evylin, Ethenn, and Jarrad as Emmaas and Rafferty emerged from the far room. The weasel grinned and kissed Evylin's cheek when he drew near. "Am I happy to see you," he said, then his feet backtracked across the floor. "Had to make sure. Wait here."

"What's he doing?" Jarrad asked as Rafferty disappeared into his room.

"Retrieving something, I expect," Deckard said, sharing a smile with Evylin.

Isla frowned. "The orders were to take everything from you upon your arrival."

"Renaul should get better servants," he noted.

"Wait a minute—" Thom stepped forward, staring at the Wind Mage. He pointed at her as if struck by sudden clarity. "Renaul called you Isla."

She blinked, then cocked her head, confused. "That's my name, yes."

Thom's mouth dropped open. "You're married to Ilain's brother, Vayden?"

A small smile came to her lips. "So they did tell you about me," Isla said.

While the rest of them processed the revelation of her identity, Rafferty returned. "Here you go," he said, the Wind Relic dangling from his fist. "Safe and sound, just as I said."

"That isn't exactly what you said," Deckard replied, then stepped back, motioning for him to hand it to the hunter among them. "Ethenn."

Isla, Emmaas, and Jarrad watched in shock as the necklace shifted to a bow in Ethenn's grasp.

"You have a Relic?" Isla gasped.

"It turns into a weapon?" Emmaas asked, a certain measure of awe in his voice.

Evylin passed her knives to Rafferty, and Deckard slipped the Night Relic from around his neck to hand it to her. "We have two, actually," she said as it beamed and morphed into a sword.

"What now?" Thom asked, one of the guards' swords in his hand.

"We're getting the Calders and the Relics, right?" Ethenn said.

Emmaas held up a hand, beckoning them to follow him down the hall. "First," he said, "we need to get moving. We're on a tight schedule, and we've only got another . . ." He paused, glancing down at a small metal trinket in his hand. "Twenty-three minutes."

"That doesn't give us much time, baldy," Jarrad quipped as Isla opened a hidden door at the end of the hall.

Emmaas held the door open as Isla slipped inside. "Through the servant's passage," he instructed, then turned to Evylin and Ethenn. "As impressive as those are, you can put them away. We're going for stealth and speed. If we get into any skirmishes, we won't be making it out."

Evylin and Ethenn did as he suggested, slipping the Relics around their necks, the weapons easily transformed back into pendant form with a mere thought and flick of their wrists. Then, one by one, they slipped into the dimly lit staircase, following Isla's bright skirts and confident strides. "As Emmaas said, we're on a tight timeline," she said in a low voice, "and we cannot recover the Relics. However, we can save Ilain and Auden. We've planned your escape down to the minute—"

"And we're running four minutes behind," Jarrad added helpfully.

Isla ignored his interruption. "Once we retrieve them, we'll head straight for the exit.

We'll make a break for the stables, where Emmaas has your horses prepared. Then we'll escort you to the Alliance."

"To the Alliance?" Evylin repeated at Deckard's side. "Here in Wauld?"

"For the time being," she confirmed. "After this defeat, you'll need to regroup."

Deckard wanted to ask what she meant by "regroup" but figured that was a conversation for after their escape. They wound through the narrow back staircases and halls of the servants' passage, only intermittent oil lamps lighting their way.

Eventually, Isla led them back into the main house. With such a large group, Deckard knew it would be difficult to move through it unseen. However, it appeared that Isla was right; they had everything planned out. She knew the precise timing of every patrol and the location of every guard. They slipped through the house like wraiths, invisible and silent.

The ivy that had once shriveled around his heart regrew. Hope watered it, trusting that they would escape. Moreover, the knowledge that, at last, he had Evylin's love nurtured its growth. What had seemed impossible at the start of the night now gave him life. They would make it to freedom, and she would stay with him forever.

They passed through a door and out into a small courtyard. Finely tended hedges and flowering trellises filled the square garden. In the center, a statue of a hooded and cloaked figure stood sentry, its hands held out, with purple flames burning in lamps above its palms. Deckard had never seen colored flame like that before, and he studied the figure as they entered the space.

At the back of the garden, Isla stopped in front of a large wooden door with half a dozen locks encased in the stone wall. As she began the task of unlocking it, Deckard eyed the sculpture, wondering what or who it was meant to be.

"Obscura," Jarrad said, coming to stand beside him.

Deckard furrowed his brow. "Pardon?"

Jarrad motioned to the statue. "That's Obscura," he said.

"Like the month?" Rafferty asked.

"Indeed," Jarrad confirmed. "Or in Wauld's case, the patron of Night. Many keep statues of the god near their family crypts. He supposedly takes the dead to the moons where they can rest in peace for eternity."

Deckard eyed the stone cloak, coiling lines of shadow etched into the statue. "A Night Mage, then?"

The final lock clicked in place, and Emmaas opened the door while Isla silently shushed them, then motioned for them to follow at a distance. Cautiously, they stepped down the stone staircase into the heavily shadowed hall below. The flickering firelight cast eerie shapes along the weathered walls. A damp chill permeated the air as they descended below ground.

Isla held her hand out to the side, signaling them to stop as she reached the bottom. Since the ceiling was slanted, Deckard heard more than saw two guards snap to attention. Isla exchanged some words with them, seeming to set them at ease just before simultaneous *thunks* sounded below. A second later, she summoned them down.

They descended the final steps and met Isla at the arched entryway to the crypt-turned-dungeon. The guards lay sprawled at her feet.

"How'd you do that?" Thom asked.

Isla lifted a shoulder in a shrug. "I took the air from their lungs."

Deckard's jaw tightened, struggling not to resent how many lives were being taken to buy their freedom.

Rafferty eyed Isla with interest. "Have you ever thought of joining an enterprise of contraband runners?" he asked.

"Not recently," she replied, then turned to Emmaas. "Braun and Paulson are the only ones left down here. I managed to convince Renaul that they'd do the trick against two viastasis-drugged Mages since the greater threat was the Warrior."

"She should have drugged the Warrior too," Jarrad remarked.

Deckard frowned, but it was Evylin who spoke. "If anyone comes near me with that stuff, they'll lose a limb."

"Which would be the reason for drugging you, after all."

"Stop messing with them, Jarrad," Isla ordered, leading them through the frigid corridors. "And be quiet. We're almost there."

"Braun and Paulson, you said?" Jarrad asked in a hushed tone. "Mm. Fire and Water. No problem."

Rafferty nudged Ethenn beside him. "Sounds like we'll have an Elemental showdown," he whispered.

"It won't be a contest," Emmaas replied. "Isla chose Braun and Paulson for a reason."

Rafferty frowned, twirling the knives in his hands. "Did you make this whole escape boring on purpose?"

"Boring is better than dead," Isla hissed. "Now, shut up."

The catacombs were larger than Deckard expected. Dozens of dark alcoves lined the walls, torches bracketing them every few feet. The dead rested in stone caskets, long-wilted flowers and burned-out candles decorating most of the ledges. Spiderwebs and the skitter of insects caused Deckard's skin to crawl. Even if the ominous statue of Obscura had not loomed at the entrance, the crypt was chilling in its own right.

As they neared the back of the tombs, iron bars began to enclose the alcoves. The renovations Renaul had mentioned, Deckard presumed. Isla held up her hand to slow them. "Just around the corner," she mouthed.

With a quick hand signal, Jarrad and Emmaas stepped up to her side. The trio rounded the corner, a Mage on either side of the Warrior. The troop watched as Isla and Jarrad raised their hands, releasing their magic. Wind whipped through the corridor, whirling around the blue-and-red-coated Mages at the end of the hall. The paving stones beneath their feet began to rattle, causing them to lose their balance. A few rocks tore loose from their mortar, pelting the men.

The Mage in blue raised his hands, a jet of water beginning to spout forth. But Emmaas was too fast. With the smoothest flick of his wrists, two small blades flew through the air, embedding squarely in the center of each Mage's forehead. They dropped unceremoniously to the ground.

Evylin and Ethenn gaped, impressed.

"About bloody time," a feminine voice called from one of the alcoves.

In side-by-side cells, the prone figures of Auden and Ilain Calder rose to their feet. Their clothing remained rumpled and stained from their time in the prison wagon. Their matted and greasy hair made their malnourished frames appear even more gaunt than usual. But otherwise, they were whole and well.

Ilain's eyes practically sparkled as she surveyed them. "It's rank in here," she said as Isla hurried to unlock their cells.

"That's probably your own filth, Red," Jarrad said merrily. He tipped his chin up toward Auden. "How's it going, genius?"

"It's not ideal," Auden said, his tone grim despite his smile as Isla approached. "Hello, Ise."

Isla patted his cheek like only a big sister could, then she tugged Ilain close for a fierce hug. She drew back, waving a hand in front of her nose. "Heavens above, you weren't joking about the smell."

"Tell me you can do something about it," Ilain pleaded.

Emmaas stepped up then, offering a canvas sack. "Best we can offer," he said.

"Oh, Major Caarney," Ilain rolled onto the balls of her feet and kissed his cheek, "I could almost marry you."

Ethenn shifted uncomfortably beside Deckard as Emmaas chucked Ilain on the chin. "No, thank you, darling," the Warrior said playfully.

Without any further preamble, Ilain and Auden began to disrobe.

"Whoa, whoa, whoa!" Thom exclaimed, whirling around.

Deckard quite agreed. He, Ethenn, and Evylin immediately followed suit. The Alliance members turned away more casually. Deckard snatched Rafferty by the collar and forced him to turn around as well.

"What's the plan?" Auden asked as they dressed.

Emmaas gave the summary. "We're down to—" He glanced at the metal disk again. Deckard could see it better now, realizing it was a pocket watch. A rare and expensive trinket, due to its intricate workmanship. "Eleven minutes."

"And it took us twelve to get here," Jarrad noted. "Splendid."

"We'll just have to move fast then," Ilain said, appearing at their side. For the first time since their acquaintance, she wore trousers with a man's shirt tucked into the waist, both in dark gray. Auden's outfit matched.

As they began to jog back through the crypt's corridors, Thom let out a low, teasing whistle. "Why, milady," he said, giving Ilain a scan. "You should wear trousers more often. Ouch!" He shook out his hand from where a flame had flared up and scorched him.

Ilain seared him with her glare. "If you want to retain possession of your lashes, you'll keep your eyes off my ass," she threatened, then looked pointedly at Rafferty and Jarrad. "That goes for all of you."

"What about Loxley?" Rafferty asked.

Ilain shrugged. "He can look all he likes."

Ethenn's entire face went bright red. Despite his embarrassment, he managed to speak steadily. "I'm glad you're both safe."

"Same to all of you," Auden said. "We're sorry we couldn't prepare you for Isla's presence. I'm sure you've been greatly worried."

"How exactly are you two lucid?" Thom asked. "I thought that drug took hours to wear off."

"It does," Isla said. "Which is why I faked their final dosage when they arrived. The viastasis should have worn off at least four hours ago."

Ilain let out a dramatic sigh as they exited the crypt. "And let me tell you, four hours of listening to those two waxing poetic about Renaul's fine larder when you haven't had a bite to eat in days is the severest form of torture."

"Aw, buck up, kiddo," Jarrad said as they entered the small courtyard. "We'll have a grand feast when we get home."

While Deckard thought it surprising that Jarrad, who looked no older than Thom, would call Ilain "kiddo" when she was in her forties, he realized he had no way of knowing the man's true age. Or any of the Alliance members' ages, for that matter, since the magic they wielded tended to prolong the aging process considerably.

They passed the statue of Obscura and returned to the dark halls of Renaul's home. "Seven minutes," Emmaas whispered as Isla took the lead once more.

Back in the servants' passages, Auden asked for their exit strategy.

"Front door," Emmaas said simply, clearly too focused to reply in full sentences.

Deckard's brow pinched together. "Won't that be the most heavily guarded?"

"We don't have time for discussion," Isla said. "Faster now."

They wound and twisted through the halls and passages, going out of their way to bypass numerous patrols. "Won't someone have found the guards we left outside our rooms by now?" Ethenn asked.

"That's part of the plan, kid," Jarrad replied, then shoved him into a back corridor. "Emmaas?"

"Two minutes."

"Excellent."

"Exactly what are we counting down to?" Thom asked.

"Our exit strategy," Jarrad said with a cheery lilt.

At the back of the group, Isla shut the door, closing them into a servant's stairwell near the front of the house. "Down," she instructed.

The ten of them wound to the bottom floor, Emmaas now in the lead. He stepped to the entry door, holding up a hand. Cautiously, he opened the door to allow a slit of light through. Deckard peered past him to see roughly a dozen guards patrolling the entryway, spears and swords at the ready. Then Emmaas shut the door without a sound.

The Warrior turned back to the large party, his voice faint as he whispered, "When we get outside, head straight for the stables." He looked pointedly at the Calders and Ephrians. "I made sure your horses were prepared. Saddles and all."

"How?" Evylin asked.

Isla spoke up from the back. "When I learned of Renaul's plan to send Caustin and his men to capture you, I hired Emmaas as our new stablemaster. We've been planning ever since."

Rafferty eyed Jarrad. "Do you work here too?"

"Nah," the Terrae Mage said. "It would have been too boring."

"Couldn't find a job you'd be good at?" Ilain asked.

Emmaas cut off Jarrad's reply. "Thirty seconds," he said.

Silence fell in the passageway. Cramped and anxious, the air grew stifling. The barest muffled conversation could be heard from the guards patrolling outside. Rafferty adjusted behind Deckard, pushing him forward into Evylin. She glanced over her shoulder at him, then smirked, leaning back into his chest.

All at once, a rumble shook the floor beneath their feet. A loud crack ripped through the air. The guards began yelling in panic outside their passageway. Struggling to maintain their footing within the small space, the Alliance members and Ephrians stumbled into one another.

Ethenn bumped into Ilain, and she set her hand on his shoulder. "Steady on, darling," she said, grinning at his wide-eyed expression. "It's only a bomb."

"What the hell is a bomb?" Thom asked.

Rafferty's silver eyes twinkled in the darkness. "It's proof we're on the right side," he said with glee.

Frantic footfalls and gruff orders rumbled from the entry. The guards were distracted, thrown off by the explosion. Yet, Emmaas kept the door closed.

"What are we waiting for?" Deckard asked.

Emmaas held up a hand, eyes locked on his pocket watch. His lips moved slowly, counting. Seven, six, five . . .

Deckard wondered what he was counting down to just as another sharp, crumbling crack reverberated through the building. This one was closer, sending a wave of sound slamming into Deckard's chest. He tightened his grip on Evylin. The only reason any of them remained upright was due to their tight quarters, the walls physically holding them up.

Before the explosion's cacophony fully died out, Emmaas flung the door open. He darted into the entry, the hidden blades back in his hands. They flashed in the moonlight as he sliced down two guards. "Go," he ordered.

Piling out of the passageway, their party sprinted for the front door. Or what should have been the front door. Now, it was simply a gaping hole.

Jarrad took the lead, guiding them. Any guards left alive after the explosion lay on the ground in wounded heaps. Their path to the stables was almost completely clear, and Deckard realized as they ran that the first bomb was a distraction. It had drawn many of the guards away, leaving only a handful for them to fight.

However, after the explosion, those few men were ready. They raised their weapons and charged, calling out for backup. Without time to stop and fight, Deckard flexed his hand, summoning his magic.

Jarrad was already on it. He thrust his hands toward a group of guards. The ground immediately gave way, tearing out from under them and swallowing them whole.

Deckard's crystalline shadows swept through the rest. The black shards glittered in the night as they ripped through the guards' chests, clearing the path to the stables.

"What kind of Mage did you say you were?" Jarrad asked in awe.

"I didn't," Deckard said, the magic fading away into the night.

They reached the stables, Emmaas on their heels. The door was already open, bright light glowing within. Ten horses waited as promised. They mounted up quickly, the horses pounding the ground, ready to run. Deckard did one last sweep to ensure they were all there—Evylin, Thom, Ethenn, Rafferty, Ilain, Auden, Isla, Jarrad, and Emmaas. Then they galloped out of the stable.

The cold night air stung their eyes as they darted down the pebbled path. The gates of Renaul's estate loomed ahead of them, open and unsecured. Deckard's heart thudded with relief. These Alliance members had thought of it all. They were going to make it. They would live to return to Ephria and stop Blount, putting an end to the Centurial War.

Tearing through the darkness, Deckard glanced back at Renaul's mansion. Stone tumbled across the ground, the front of the beautiful edifice now in shambles. A fire raged somewhere at the back of the building. An orange glow reflected off the windows as the diminishing figures of the guards worked to extinguish it. Where was the noblewoman amid this destruction? Did she realize yet that they'd made their escape?

The thought brought a damning realization to Deckard. He'd been blinded by hope and Evylin's love. This wasn't a success. This was a consolation. They were leaving behind three Relics. That meant Blount now had four while they had two. After their struggles in the Wind and Time Keeps, Deckard wondered if they could hope to survive the final two in Ephria.

Their escape wasn't without cost. They might have made it out of Renaul's clutches with their lives, but Deckard wondered if it would be the death of them yet.

CHAPTER FIFTY-THREE

Thom

Under the cover of night, the troop tore through the countryside. They passed the city of Keale, the capital of Lady Renaul's county, about a mile into their ride. Even during the late hours, lights glittered in windows and from the parapets of the city wall. Under the guidance of the Alliance members, they gave the settlement a wide berth.

An hour after clearing the city, they eased their pace to give the horses a rest. And that was when Thom realized the true cost of their escape. In the heat of the moment, adrenaline had kept him going. Now, his head pounded with fatigue. After three days under Caustin's cruel conditions and a sleepless night, his aching body was ready to give up.

Thom looked over his friends, realizing they all looked the same as he felt. Ilain and Auden had fared the worst of them all. The siblings both sagged in their saddles, their pale skin ghostly in the moonlight. Ilain's usually fiery hair looked more like rust, hanging in limp curls around her shoulders. Her head drooped like a wilted flower. He realized that her bravado from before had expended what little energy she retained just before she started to fall.

Cursing under his breath, Thom spurred his horse forward, ready to catch her. Then Ethenn was there, as he always was. The kid—*the young man,* Thom mentally corrected— steadied Ilain with his arm around her back.

Thom pulled up short, arriving at their side just as Ilain quipped, "My hero."

"Yeah, shut up," Ethenn said with a lighthearted tilt. "I'm too tired to be made fun of."

Thom raised his brow. "Have you finally figured out how to banter, Loxley?" he asked. Ethenn gave him a wary glance but didn't reply.

"Here," Thom guided his horse to the other side of Ilain's, "let me help." Together, they got Ilain onto the saddle with Ethenn. She slumped against the hunter's chest, her lids heavy and her limbs trembling.

"You all right there, milady?" Thom asked as he tied her horse off to his.

Resting her head back on Ethenn's shoulder, she closed her eyes and mumbled, "Leave me alone to die in peace."

Thom smiled and gave Ethenn a nod. Ilain would be just fine.

After checking in with Auden to ensure his security, Thom allowed himself to lapse into solitude. None of their band felt much like talking after all they'd endured. At the front of the line, Emmaas and Isla led, with Deckard and Evylin right behind. The rest of them fanned out as they cantered through the hills away from the main road.

After several hours, the sun finally broke on the horizon, turning the sky golden. A light fog drifted near the mountains to the north. They headed for a thick stand of trees, stopping for a short break to let themselves recover as much as the horses. Isla passed out some small rations of dried meat and fruit. It wasn't much, but it would sustain them. Thom gave his portion to Ilain to split with Auden, his hunger somewhat abated by the prior night's feast that Renaul had intended to be their last.

Despite their freedom earned, none of them spoke of it or rejoiced yet. Not only were they too tired, but Thom knew they felt the same way he did. There was no true victory until they were safely away from any hunting party Renaul had undoubtedly sent to find them. Wherever that safety might be found, whether with the Alliance or in Ephria, Thom didn't know.

In the subdued atmosphere of recovery, Thom watched the band carefully. Isla stayed with the Calders, hovering like a mother—or more appropriately, he supposed, like a sister. Ethenn sat nearby, staring dejectedly at nothing while he chewed on a strip of dried venison. Rafferty sprawled under the low-hanging boughs of a hawthorn, promptly passing out. Jarrad and Emmaas stood to the side, strategizing in hushed tones.

Meanwhile, Deckard and Evylin sat against the trunk of a tree away from the rest of the group. Her head rested on his shoulder, neither of them speaking.

Thom's heart squeezed. But not out of jealousy. Out of guilt. How had he not seen it? In all their time together, how could he have been so blind, so bitter? Why couldn't he see what was so plainly before him: They were perfect for one another.

Stepping across the small enclosure of trees, Thom joined Emmaas and Jarrad. They paused their conversation, scanning him curiously. "How long do we intend to break here?" Thom asked.

"Only an hour," Emmaas said. "I'd like us to be out of Nirraus County before lunch."

Though Thom had no idea how large the county was, he nodded. "Great, thanks."

Leaving the men behind, Thom made up his mind. He couldn't put it off any longer. An hour was more than enough. He set his jaw and made his approach.

"Do you have a second?" he asked.

Deckard and Evylin looked up at him.

Realizing he needed to be more specific, Thom turned to his brother. "I'd like to, uh—I'd like to talk with you."

Though Deckard hesitated, Evylin patted his arm encouragingly. "Go on," she said. "I promise to be here when you get back."

With a heavy sigh, Deckard pushed himself off the ground. The shadows seemed to cling to his face, giving him a haggard look. He motioned for Thom to lead the way, and they began to move toward the trees. The space between them could have allowed three men to walk side by side in the gap. Neither bothered with small talk or pleasantries. They were too tired for that. Moreover, they were too aware of the potential for argument in their weary states. The impending conversation was twenty-seven years in the making, and neither wanted to rush into it.

Far enough from the others to speak securely, even should a raised voice be a possibility, Deckard stopped first. He crossed his arms and met Thom's stare. "What did you want to discuss?" he asked calmly.

Too calmly.

Thom tried not to let his hackles rise. "You know, don't you?" he said.

"I assume," Deckard replied. "But I'd rather give you the opportunity to lead this conversation."

Thom shut his eyes. He couldn't look at his brother. Not when he was trying to hold it together. Why did Jonn have to be so damned accommodating all the time? It would be easier if he simply got angry like everyone else. Instead, he threw his goodness in Thom's face, making him feel inferior for having such contentious emotions. Albeit unintentional, it was bloody annoying.

In an attempt to quell his rising irritation, Thom took a steadying breath. "I need you to stop doing that," he said.

Deckard frowned. "Doing what?"

"Being so high and mighty."

Immediately, Deckard bristled.

Thom tossed his hands in the air, already exasperated. "I want to apologize. But I can't promise I won't make this worse if you don't stop acting like I'm a child."

Deckard pinched the bridge of his nose like a long-suffering parent. "You don't have to do this, Thom," he said, then took a step back toward the camp. "You're my brother. I'll always forgive you, even for this."

"Stop it!" Thom exclaimed in a sharp and cutting tone. "I'm not apologizing for you, you stupid git. I'm doing it for myself."

Deckard froze, exhaustion plain on his face. Then he scoffed. "All right, go ahead then. Apologize so that you feel better."

Thom groaned, holding his hands out in desperation. "Why can't you see what you're doing? I'm trying, Jonn. I'm really trying. But you're making this so bloody difficult."

"I'm making it difficult?"

"Yes!"

Deckard glared at him. "I'm not the one who asked my brother's wife to leave him. You can't get much more difficult than that, Thom."

Agitated and too worn out to control his temper, Thom began to pace. "This is unbelievable."

"Oh, I'm sorry my hurt is too confusing for you to believe. Would you like me to explain it to you?"

A thousand words tried to burst out of Thom at once, and he just wound up spluttering indignantly for a few seconds before shouting something that sounded something like, "*Bwah*!"

Deckard sighed with disappointment.

Somehow, that discontented sound brought back Thom's ability to articulate. "I don't understand you, Jonn. I'm trying to tell you that I'm sorry, but you slough it off as though what I did doesn't matter. Of course, you're hurt. She's your wife, and I tried to undermine your relationship with her—multiple times! But I'm trying to explain that I didn't know what I was doing."

"What the hell is that supposed to mean?" Deckard demanded. "You knew exactly what you were doing. You knew I loved her, so you wanted her just like you wanted everything else I ever had. Not because you loved her yourself but because you couldn't stand to see me happy."

"Exactly!" Thom yelled triumphantly. He let out a hysterical laugh, thankful that he didn't have to explain himself. "I *didn't* love her. I never wanted her—not *really*. But I didn't realize that until after it happened."

That surprised Deckard. He stood there, lips parted and brow pinched.

Thom knew why. In all their fights, Thom was careful never to admit his competitive nature. He'd always clung to the pretense he was in some way just as injured as Deckard in their fights. Though he was the instigator, he played the victim. He refused to take responsibility, instead blaming his brother for his resentment.

In Deckard's hesitation, Thom pressed on. "I didn't know what I was doing, Jonn," he repeated somberly. "I didn't realize that all it was—all it had ever been—was me wishing I was you."

Deckard drew back as though Thom had struck him. "What?"

Dropping his eyes to the terrae, Thom struggled with the words again. He felt like a little kid, unable to comprehend the emotions causing his stomach to twist with both awe and discontent. "You were always the perfect big brother," he muttered at last. "I thought . . . Well, I thought you were next to Allore when we were kids. You were so perfect, so good all the time. You always did everything right, and Mother and Father were always so pleased with you. *I* was always so pleased with you."

He shrugged and kept going while the words were there. "It hurt, watching that. Wanting to *be* that and knowing I could never measure up."

Deckard sighed, sadly this time, and took a step forward as if to comfort him.

Thom held up a hand. "Not yet," he muttered. "I'm not done yet."

With Deckard's compliance, Thom took another breath. "I tried, you know? As a kid. I thought if I tried hard enough—if I really, really meant it . . ." He shook his head self-derisively. "I thought that maybe—just maybe—I could manage to make you proud of me. And then I'd be perfect too."

Thom met his brother's gaze, feeling the same awe he'd felt as a boy. "I don't understand how you do it," he confessed. "Being so perfect all the time."

"I'm not perfect, Thom," he said immediately.

"You are to me."

Deckard blinked.

Thom scoffed. "You are to Evylin. To Mother and Father. Hell, our sister named her baby after you."

"That's because Meria is ridiculous."

They shared a thin laugh.

"But Vaan thinks you're incredible too," Thom reminded him. "Everyone you've ever met loves you."

"Hewitt didn't like me," Deckard offered.

"Which was why I liked him," Thom admitted. "And now, he's spending his afterlife with you."

"Not by choice."

Thom raised his brow. "You think Hewitt would waste time talking to you if he didn't like you?"

Deckard didn't bother arguing that point. "You forget General Rand. The man tried to have me killed."

"That man doesn't like his own mother."

Deckard conceded that point as well.

Thom held up his hands again, imploring Deckard to understand. "No matter who it is, whether or not they like you as a person, no one can help but respect you. You can't tell me you don't see that."

"Why are you telling me this?" Deckard asked, shifting uncomfortably. "Are you trying to make me feel bad?"

"No. I'm trying to explain myself. It isn't justification, but it's . . . I don't know—maybe a glimpse of why I . . . why I hate myself so much."

"Thom—"

"No, I do," he insisted, knowing deep down that it was the truth. "I hate myself. I always have."

Deckard looked truly stricken. "You shouldn't."

Thom shrugged flippantly. "But I do."

"Why?"

"Because I'm not you."

The admission hung heavily between them.

Thom sighed, the truth finally revealed. "Like I said, it's not an excuse for my behavior, but . . . I just thought you should know. I was never mad at you. In the whole of our lives, my anger was never truly directed at you. It was directed at myself because I couldn't be like you."

Shaking his head, Thom wished he could turn back time and help his younger self through this understanding. "I'd get so angry as a kid, so hurt that you stayed good and considerate through it all. You apologized before me; you took the blame for me. It was like you didn't care that I was a brat, like you didn't notice how hard I was trying."

"I did notice," Deckard said, compassion in his eyes and voice. The same compassion that had once made Thom feel so frustrated. "That's why I did those things. I could tell you were trying, and that's why I didn't blame you for any of it."

Deckard took one step forward. "I was never perfect, Thom. I was just older. Perhaps I have a more levelheaded disposition, but that doesn't make me a better man. And it certainly didn't make me naturally good at anything either. I have five years of practice on you, five years to learn and grow. You were never inferior to me. You were just younger."

"I understand that now," Thom promised. "But as a child . . . I just felt incapable. And it wounded me, making me feel as though I could never be good enough for you and your grand ideals."

Deckard drew in a sharp breath, and Thom couldn't help his somber grin. "You always wanted the best, Jonn. From our earliest days, I remember how determined you were to do more, to be more. And when I couldn't measure up, I feared that you wouldn't want me."

A long silence hung in the air, the feet separating them feeling like miles. At last, Thom had voiced the insecurities that had plagued his heart for nearly three decades. He felt lighter, emptied of the resentment and bitterness. Yet, he felt isolated as well. Confessing his sins didn't change the distance, time, and actions that had placed a chasm between him and his brother.

Things were not fixed. Not yet, after everything he'd done.

At last, Deckard sighed. "Oh, Thom," he muttered. He crossed the divide then and set his hand on Thom's shoulder. "This is my fault."

"Jonn, no—"

"It's my turn now," he insisted. "You listen to what I have to say, all right?"

Thom pressed his lips together but nodded.

"Good." Deckard held his stare, steady and sure. That look expressed everything Thom had always hoped to see in his brother's gaze—the regard of an equal. "Throughout our lives, I've always known—I knew that you wanted to prove yourself by becoming like me. And I should have told you years ago: I never wanted nor expected that of you. I rather liked the brother I got. He was braver than I and was more willing to take risks and live without fear of the consequences. He had more passion than I did, feeling everything deeply and loving more fiercely. I was never very good at that. I can make people feel seen and heard; I can care for them. But to truly feel something for them? That was hard. Yet, you never had a problem with it. You either love someone, or you don't. And by Allore, do you *love* the people whom you love."

Something in Thom broke at those words. His whole life, he'd attempted to earn Deckard's respect by becoming like him, imitating him in his excellence. Now, he learned that had he just been himself, he would have had his brother's respect all along. The knowledge brought the greatest relief and pain all at once.

Deckard squeezed his shoulder more tightly. "I forgive you, Thom, forever," he said, words thick and impassioned. "Not to be the better person or because it's the right thing to do. I'm forgiving you because after Evylin . . ."

A small, tender smile filled Deckard's face, and Thom could honestly say he'd never felt so cherished in his entire life.

"After Evylin," Deckard concluded, "you're the person I love most in this world."

Thom's heart and breath stuttered. And for once, he realized he actually believed it when his brother said he loved him. *Him.* Not the idea of him, not his efforts, and not out of duty either. Deckard genuinely loved and valued Thom as he was.

And that meant Thom could be enough.

Still, there was the sting of the guilt that lingered for all he'd done and all he'd said.

"Did I—" Thom broke off, voice scratchy with emotion. "Did I ruin it? With Evie. Is she—she told me she didn't want to come between us. Is she going to leave you because . . . because of me?"

An amused grin slipped over Deckard's face. He released Thom and stepped back. "No," he said simply.

Thom's brow ached from how long he'd kept it furrowed. "No, she's not leaving you, or no, it's not because of me?"

"She's not leaving me."

Immediately, a sigh flew out of Thom's lungs. "Thank Allore! I thought I'd ruined everything. And she's staying with you, as in, for good?"

Deckard nodded, a strange expression on his face.

Recognizing the subtext in his brother's averted gaze and reluctant expression, Thom gaped. "Oh," he muttered, then his brow rose. "Oh!"

Deckard gave him a look that said he didn't care to discuss the solidification of his union with Evylin.

Thom didn't particularly care to discuss it himself. "Well . . ." He cleared his throat. "About time."

After a deep breath, he tried to move forward. "I know this didn't fix everything," he promised. "I know I'll have to regain your trust—or gain it in the first place, I suppose. And . . . I am going to try, Jonn. I want to be a better man, and now I know that simply means being a better version of myself. But I think I'll need your help."

Deckard met his gaze, a strong, caring smile on his face. "You'll always have it."

Heart full of burgeoning hope, Thom slapped Deckard's arm. "You're the worst," he said good-naturedly. "Always so good and forgiving. You put the rest of us to shame."

"I didn't feel so forgiving at first," Deckard remarked slyly. "I felt like beating you senseless."

Thom laughed. "You could have tried. You haven't beaten me in a fistfight since we were teens."

"We haven't fought since we were teens," Deckard said, then lifted his brow slyly. "And I've been training with Rafferty."

In mock worry, Thom eyed him. "Don't tell me you've finally learned to fight dirty."

He lifted his shoulder. "I've come to find fair play to be overrated."

"Aha . . ." Thom let out a whistle. "Seems we're both changed men."

CHAPTER FIFTY-FOUR

Upon Deckard and Thom's return to camp, the troop made preparations to move out once again. Emmaas informed them that he hoped to ride through the majority of the day, putting as much distance as possible between them and Keale. "We'll continue riding off the road," he explained. "Though our path will lead us through denser forests, our spies have developed a secure route to ensure our comings and goings remain secret. There are a handful of campsites along our route, so we'll stop at one before heading to our final destination tomorrow morning."

"And where is that destination?" Deckard asked.

"Mouroc," Isla said. "The capital of Wauld."

"Isn't that the most dangerous place for us to go?" Thom asked in surprise.

"No," she said calmly. "It's where the Alliance is headquartered within Wauld, making it the *safest* place you can go."

Evylin's eyes narrowed. "The Alliance chose to put their base of operations in the same place as the Waulden monarchy?"

Jarrad grinned. "Have you ever heard the old Auldan saying, 'Keep your friends close and your enemies closer'?" he asked. "The Alliance takes that saying a bit too much to heart for my taste."

"It helps us keep a close eye on our greatest threats," Isla explained. "And it gives us opportunities to infiltrate the circles of the monarchy's greatest allies. If I hadn't come to the capital years ago, I never would have had the opportunity to work for Renaul."

With the expectations of their destination in mind, they traveled through the thick forests toward the capital of Wauld.

Along the way, Emmaas kept his eyes on the trees. Ethenn—eyes as keen as ever—pointed out the hidden scraps of light gray cloth tied among the branches to Deckard. High among the boughs, each one took Deckard several tries to spot, even with the young hunter's guidance. The Alliance had marked out the route in such a way that only the sharpest trackers or those they'd revealed the markers to could follow. Deckard wondered if it was by a Warrior's design.

Exhausted from the past several days and a lost night of rest, the Ephrians and Calders remained subdued. Still in her weakened state, Ilain had taken to riding with Isla. Their combined weight made for an easier burden on the horses, which they switched every few hours. Jarrad kept to their side, chatting in his strange, direct manner. Though Auden fared better than his sister, he remained close to Emmaas, trusting the Warrior to catch him if he should prove too weak to stay upright.

At the back of the procession, Thom spoke with Evylin. Deckard had happily left them to ride alone, knowing that Thom wanted to offer his apology to her as well.

A warmth spread through Deckard that had nothing to do with his magic. He was truly grateful for this turn of events. While it didn't change Thom's past behavior, it did give Deckard the most profound hope for their future. His brother was changing. He was growing. And Deckard thought they stood a chance of finally attaining the relationship for which he'd always yearned.

Though Thom undoubtedly expressed all his regrets hours ago, he and Evylin still rode together, laughing and talking like they once had. But Deckard no longer felt any prick of jealousy or concern. Even if he and Evylin hadn't confirmed their love, he could see it in Thom's manner—he loved Evylin not as a woman but as a sister. She was his friend, their relationship easy and lighthearted, and that made Deckard happier than he had any right to be under their present circumstances.

Surprisingly, Rafferty didn't join their antics, choosing to ride in front of Deckard and Ethenn toward the middle of the pack. The pairings suited Deckard just fine. Though Ethenn made occasional remarks, he otherwise left Deckard to his solitude. A courtesy that was a great boon, given the state of his pounding head.

When Emmaas finally allowed them to break for the evening, he offered for their troop's members to rest while their rescuers set up camp. Though Ilain, Auden, and Rafferty readily took the repose, the rest of them offered their help anyway.

The rocky clearing they'd stopped in was, evidently, the Alliance-procured "safe location." Hidden in the brush was a trunk stashed in a dug-out portion of the terrae. It h eld non-perishable items, such as clay jugs of fresh water, sacks of barley, and supplies for hunting, including two bows with a plentiful supply of arrows. Thrilled, Ethenn offered to hunt, and Evylin readily volunteered to join him.

While Ethenn gathered the hunting supplies, Evylin drew Deckard aside. "Here," she said softly, slipping her hand under the loose collar of her shirt. "I think you should keep this."

The Night Relic hung from her grasp, its amethyst glow contrasting with the late-evening amber of the sunset.

Deckard clenched his jaw, considering. "If we've learned anything from our travels in Wauld, it's that it isn't a good idea to wear Relics for long periods," he said cautiously.

Evylin gave him a cunning grin. "You carried it the past four days without using magic to do anything but hide it," she noted. "I think you'll be just fine."

Deckard opened his mouth, then paused. Strangely, she was right, and he hadn't considered it until she pointed it out. Over the past weeks, since learning that he was a Mage, any time he'd held the Night Relic—which was admittedly the only Relic he'd had much contact with—he felt very little. Though there was a perceptible emotional shift, its influence making him more coldly calculating, the rippling of power under his skin was containable. And over the last four days, even that detachment hadn't made him unduly violent. It didn't make sense. His experience was nothing at all resembling Evylin's with the Day Relic. Even Auden and Ilain admitted to having their feelings intensely altered by the Relics.

"I know what it's like to hold this Relic, Jonn," Evylin said, the chain still dangling from her fingers. "It's heavy, like death and resurrection all at once, fear and peace. It inspires violence and protection, demanding action. It changes you. I've felt that draw for the last several hours. Yet, for the last four days, you remained the same."

Wetting his lips, Deckard stared at the gemstone. "Perhaps it's because I'm a Night Mage."

"Shouldn't that make you more vulnerable to it?"

"I don't know."

Evylin sighed, holding the Relic closer to him. "You should carry it."

"It's dangerous," he warned.

"Perhaps," she said, then smiled. "But I trust you."

Deckard's muscles relaxed as he held her gaze. How long had he waited to hear her say that?

"Or maybe," her dimples appeared as her eyes twinkled with mirth, "I just want you to let me see Hewitt again."

Taking the Relic, Deckard couldn't help returning her playful grin. "At the soonest opportunity," he promised.

"I'll hold you to that," she said, then turned to accompany Ethenn into the forest.

Remaining behind, Deckard and Thom helped Emmaas, Isla, and Jarrad with the rest of the work. In a separate hidden trunk, they found canvas shelter-halfs. Along with the three they'd purchased on their journey, which had been affixed to their saddles when they fled Renaul's, they pitched them at various distances around the clearing. Deckard made sure to put his and Evylin's as far from the others as feasible. Not that he intended to pursue any marital advantages in an open-air tent, and certainly not around so many people. He simply wanted to enjoy having his wife back in his arms without thinking about the observations of the eight others in their company.

Once the tents were pitched and the fire started, Deckard helped Thom and Emmaas care for the horses. They removed their saddles, then gave them water and brushed down their coats. When the work was done, Deckard knelt next to his saddle, checking the bags. Everything remained. His personal items, money, and extra supplies—they were all there. All things that didn't matter while they'd left behind the Relics.

While he sorted and repacked his belongings, Evylin and Ethenn returned. They moved to begin cleaning their catch, Emmaas and Thom joining them.

His work completed, Deckard stood to survey the campsite. The Calders, Isla, and Jarrad sat talking while the others worked. And on the far side of the camp, Rafferty sat on a felled log, chewing on a strand of grass, his silver eyes shifting constantly from one member to the next.

With nothing left to do, Deckard joined him.

Rafferty didn't look his way but said, "Thought you and Thommy might come back with bloodied noses this morning."

A small grin tugged up the corner of Deckard's lips. "So did I."

"All's forgiven then?"

"All's forgiven," he confirmed, then tipped his head closer. "Now, why are you sitting over here by yourself?"

Rafferty spat the mutilated grass back on the dirt. "I'm not by myself. You're here."

Deckard raised his brow at the evasive behavior.

Plucking more grass, Rafferty fidgeted with it, eyes locked on the camp. "I don't like these Alliance people."

Now, Deckard frowned. If *Rafferty* didn't get a good feeling about people, then surely, something was off. "Why not?" he asked.

"They're new."

The tension that had sprung to Deckard's shoulders immediately relaxed. "I would have thought you'd like new people, that you'd think they were entertaining."

"Yeah, well, I don't." Rafferty rested his elbows on his knees. "I was happy with the seven of us. Course, it would have been better if Hewitt were still around, but we were doing all right. Then we split, and now *these* people have shown up. It's like we've been infiltrated."

Deckard chuckled lightly. "It's only for a time. They'll take us to the Alliance, then we'll restock, finalize our plans, and head back to Ephria. There's a chance we'll never see them again."

"I'm not so sure," he muttered sourly. "The winds of change are about. And I'm not just talking about Isla's magic."

"What *are* you talking about, then?"

His silver eyes narrowed, still flicking around the camp. "I've told you—I see things others don't. And I've been watching all day."

"What is it you've seen?"

"Auden is acting strangely."

Deckard felt his brow pinch together. "How so?"

Rafferty opened his mouth to speak, but their attention was diverted as Evylin joined them. She'd tied her hair back in a braid again, the plait draped over her shoulder. Her lips were tipped up in an amused smile. "What's this about?" she asked, brushing a finger along the crease between Deckard's brows.

Deckard forced his expression to relax. "Nothing. Rafferty's just being paranoid."

"I'm not paranoid," Rafferty insisted. "I'm onto something."

Evylin slapped the man's shoulder gently. "Well, go be onto something elsewhere. I want to sit there."

With a huff, the weasel grumbled his way to the nearby patch of ground. "Couples are insufferable."

"Don't sulk," Evylin said, taking his abandoned seat. "I'll listen to your theory if you'd care to share it."

"It isn't a theory. It's an observation."

"What have you observed, then?" she asked, her hand resting half on Deckard's on the log between them. She angled her legs, blocking their hands from view. He spread his fingers so hers would fall into the space left behind. Her thumb traced circles along the back of his hand.

Rafferty's constantly moving gaze drifted around the camp. He leaned toward them, voice low. "The thing is, Auden's been acting off. At first, I thought it might have to do with that viastasis stuff. But Ilain's behaving perfectly normal—even if she is brazenly flirting with Loxley instead of Thommy."

"What about Auden's behavior seems off to you?" Deckard asked. He flipped his hand, properly interlocking their fingers. "I haven't noticed anything."

"Me neither," Evylin agreed. Her grip loosened on Deckard's, her fingers slowly teasing through his. He'd never known how potently seductive holding hands could be until that very moment.

Rafferty raised his white-blond brows. "How could you not? He isn't talking to us. At least, not the way he used to. The Calders have always been friendly, but now, Auden is practically ignoring us."

Deckard considered the assessment. He supposed it was true. Ever since they'd left Renaul's, Auden had said little, and what he had said had been directed toward the Alliance members. The change in his demeanor hadn't given Deckard pause because the Mage was naturally reserved, and they were all tired. He had assumed that any oddity stemmed from the exhaustion.

But now that he considered it, Auden had given them all wary glares and abrupt replies since they'd left the catacombs.

"Still," Deckard said, wanting to give the highlord the benefit of the doubt. He angled his hand to press against Evylin's thigh. "We've been through quite an ordeal. He and his sister experienced the worst of us all. There's a chance he just needs a good night's sleep."

"Would you believe me if he were glaring at us now?" Rafferty asked.

Evylin rolled her eyes, casually glancing toward the camp. "He's right," she said quietly. Her fingers shifted, playing with his wedding band. "Auden looked away right after I caught him."

"Could he tell you were checking?" Deckard asked, rubbing his finger along the side of her leg.

Her eyes were dusky as she held his gaze. "I don't think so."

"What are you doing?" Rafferty asked, frowning at them.

Deckard and Evylin turned to him, the movements of their hands going still.

"What are you talking about?" Evylin asked.

Rafferty quirked his brow. His chin jerked in their direction. "Your hands. They're rather active."

Breaking all contact with one another, Deckard drew his hand to his side while Evylin set hers in her lap. "I don't know what you're talking about," she said flatly.

As much as he tried, Deckard couldn't help the smirk that tugged at the corner of his lips.

Rafferty caught it. "Colonel?"

"Leave it be, Rafferty," he said, then edged closer to Evylin. There was no reason to hide their renewed relationship. No one knew the danger it had been in only a few days ago. At most, they'd assumed that, due to Hewitt's death and Evylin's grief, they were going through a rough patch. Reunited, they could behave as they once had, as any married couple would.

Evylin seemed to be of the same mind, passing him a playful grin. She bumped her knee against his.

Rafferty scoffed. "You're flirting with one another," he noted. "That's cute."

"Shut up, Raff," Evylin said, then leaned into Deckard's side anyway.

Just as Deckard began to rest his arm behind her back, Auden arrived at their side. "I need a word," he said, voice thick with agitation.

Rafferty muttered something about "told you so," while Deckard and Evylin tensed.

Without waiting for a response, Auden continued, "You need to give the Relic back to Rafferty."

Deckard drew in a long breath through his nose. He should have expected this.

"Now," Auden concluded.

Before Deckard could get a word out, Evylin answered for him. "No."

Auden's rich green eyes flared. "No?"

"After everything we just faced," she replied steadily, "it's wiser that Jonn continues to carry it."

"Wiser?" Auden repeated, nearly shouting the word.

Everyone in the camp froze. Sitting together, Ilain, Isla, and Jarrad's expressions showed varying levels of confusion and surprise. At the fire, Ethenn and Emmaas stopped talking while Thom paused in attending to the roasting meat. Rafferty let out a low whistle.

"After *everything*," Auden retorted, "I should think *you'd* want him to give it up most of all. But I suppose you've changed your mind now that he can give you what you want."

Deckard bristled at the suggestion in the man's tone. He set his hand on Evylin's hip protectively. "That's uncalled for," he said, speaking as he might to an unruly soldier in need of reprimand. "I understand you don't trust my magic, but—"

"Of course, I don't trust it," Auden interrupted, towering over them. "We established its danger weeks ago. Yet, time and time again, you insist on using it for your own selfish gain."

Deckard prepared to refute his claims, but Auden kept talking over him. "You don't care if it kills us all, do you? Not if it results in—" His hand thrust in the direction of Deckard and Evylin. "Whatever the hell this is!"

Everyone continued to stare back and forth between Auden and the couple. Deckard shifted uncomfortably, feeling as though he were a youth caught romancing his sweetheart. Evylin's temples went pink, suggesting she felt the same. She began to shift away, but he tightened his grip, keeping her close.

In the momentary lull, Jarrad turned to Isla. "I thought you said they were married," he commented.

"They are," Isla said defensively. Then her brow furrowed, and she turned to Ilain. "Aren't they?"

"We are," Deckard confirmed, temper rising.

"Right," Auden said as though Deckard had just condemned himself. "Which is profoundly convenient when just weeks ago we split up because she didn't want you anymore."

"That's not—"

He cut Evylin's defense off. "We lost three Relics. We practically handed them over to Blount. All because you—" he pointed at Deckard, "were desperate to convince her—" he pointed at Evylin, "not to annul your marriage. So you summoned her uncle to keep her at your side, damning the consequences for the rest of us. Don't you understand that your connection to Night is going to get us killed?"

Deckard didn't know whether to rise and punch the man or ignore him altogether. However, a niggling doubt wormed its way through the ivy of hope around his heart. Auden wasn't wrong. Deckard *had* chosen to keep Hewitt around despite the threat to their safety, all to make Evylin happy. And he'd had little doubt that it *would* convince Evylin to stay married to him.

"Hang on," Jarrad piped up from the far side. "I'm confused: What's happening?"

"I don't think it's our concern, Jarrad," Isla said.

"I'll explain it," Evylin said, her voice as tight as her rigid back. "Auden is upset because Jonn is carrying the Night Relic, and he's afraid of Jonn's power."

"There's more to it than that," Auden objected. "We lost the Relics because of you two. If you had listened to me and released that ghost, we would be back in Ephria with five Relics by now."

"Oh, Auden," Ilain chimed in, rolling her eyes. "That's not true, and you know it. Caustin was smart; he would have captured us regardless of Jonn and Evylin's situation."

"Well . . ." Ethenn began, then stopped.

"What?" Evylin asked, gaping at him.

Ethenn shrugged, prodding the fire with a long stick. "I sort of saw the scout on our way back to the camp but was too, uh—distracted to process what he was doing there until it was too late."

Rafferty sniggered. "That's because your head was up your ass about . . ." He gestured between Thom and Ilain.

Ethenn shot him an annoyed look. "Anyway," he grumbled, then looked to Deckard apologetically. "I saw him, but then everything happened with—with Thom and me and then with Hewitt too. I don't know that it would have changed much, but I was getting ready to warn you when Thom egged me on."

"I didn't—" Thom cut himself off, holding up a hand. "Never mind. It doesn't matter."

Deckard almost smiled at his brother's obvious attempt to be a better man but felt too off-kilter after Auden's agitation and this new revelation. He sighed, giving Ethenn a forgiving nod. "I understand," he said peaceably. "The truth is, I doubt it would have made a difference. We were all too tired to do much good at that point. Our chances of escape weren't high. Given the circumstances, I'd say this is the best outcome we could have hoped for."

"The best—" Auden let out an angered huff. "Blount has four Relics now!"

"And don't you think it's a miracle that Jonn managed to keep the Night Relic from him too?" Ilain said, coppery brow raised.

"Excuse me," Jarrad said, lifting a hand in a little wave.

The Calders turned to stare long-sufferingly at him. Emmaas gave a resigned sigh as he continued to sharpen the collection of daggers he'd pulled from his person.

"A few questions for you—" Jarrad began ticking them off as he spoke. "First, you said the Warrior—Evylin? Yes. Evylin didn't want her husband, the Mage. Jonn or Deckard? I'm losing track of the names."

Isla glared at him. "His name is Jonn Deckard."

Jarrad gave her a baffled look. "Then why does his brother call him by his last name?"

"I don't always," Thom defended.

Deckard pinched the bridge of his nose. "Just call me Deckard."

"Right." Jarrad snapped his fingers and went back to his question. "So Mrs. Warrior didn't want Mr. Mage because . . . grief? But then something about a ghost convincing her not to annul their marriage? How does that work?"

Isla pressed her fingers to her temples as though staving off a headache. "You are the worst," she mumbled.

"All in a day's work, love," Jarrad said, patting her shoulder. When nobody attempted to answer him, he tried again. "I can restate the question if you'd prefer."

"There isn't really anything to say," Deckard replied. "Evylin was dealing with the loss of her uncle, and it took some time for us to work through it together. Unknowingly, I summoned her uncle's ghost, which is why Auden is angry."

"That's not the reason I'm angry," Auden argued.

"Let's stay on track here," Jarrad interjected, then turned back to Deckard and Evylin. "Why would Auden think you'd be annulling your marriage?"

Deckard rubbed his hands together while Evylin chewed on her bottom lip, neither of them willing to admit the truth.

Ilain grimaced. "That might be because I told him they were."

"Ilain!" Evylin gasped.

"I'm sorry!" Ilain's shoulders nearly brushed her ears with the exaggeration of her shrug. "I tell him everything. I didn't think he'd go announcing it."

"Well, I don't know what the Ephrian laws are," Jarrad remarked, "but they sure as hell can't get an annulment here."

Silence met the statement as the group struggled to understand his meaning. Deckard dropped his head in his hands. While he hadn't exactly been opposed to the troop finding out about their reconciliation, he hadn't anticipated revealing *that* part of their resolution.

At the man's words, Rafferty collapsed into a fit of laughter. Jarrad, Isla, and Emmaas watched the man's hysterics with confusion. Thom stared pointedly at the fire. Ethenn stared at his friend, puzzled. Auden blanched, and Ilain said with strange excitement, "Really?"

Evylin wrapped her arms around herself as though trying to hide. "Can we please move on?" she asked irritably.

"Well, I have another question," Jarrad offered.

"I don't think I want to hear it," Evylin shot back.

Jarrad waved her off. "It's not about that," he promised. "You said something about a ghost . . . Where is it?"

Everyone turned to Deckard.

Deckard sighed. "I can summon him if you'd like," he offered. "I'm tired, but with the Night Relic, I think I could make him visible to everyone."

"Yes, please," Jarrad said with obvious enthusiasm. He gave Isla a pleased look. "I've always wanted to meet a ghost."

With a glance at Evylin to ensure she was prepared, Deckard gathered his focus and willed Hewitt to appear. A flush of warmth spread up his spine, then receded, leaving behind a dull ache. He was getting dangerously tired again. While he hadn't expended much magic over the last several days, his weak and worn-out body wasn't able to support the surge much longer.

But Hewitt was there, standing at his side as big, burly, and stoic as ever. "Where the hell have you been?" he demanded.

"Wow," Jarrad remarked lightly. "He looks so real."

Hewitt turned, taking in the rest of the camp. "And who are these lot?"

"Alliance members," Deckard explained. "They saved us, and now we're traveling to their headquarters."

"Mm." Hewitt crossed his arms. The evening waned, only his figure unable to cast a shadow in the vibrant remains of sunset. He looked beyond Deckard to smile at Evylin. "Are you well?"

"Yes," she promised.

"This is the uncle?" Jarrad asked.

Hewitt stared at him skeptically. "Who are you?"

"Name's Jarrad Hoult," he said casually. "And you are?"

"Hewitt Glaas."

"Pleasure."

Hewitt turned away. "What am I doing here?"

"Well, that was on my request," Jarrad said. "I was curious: What's your purpose here?"

Deckard blinked, surprised at the Terrae Mage's decisive interest. Isla perked up even as Auden scowled. "That's irrelevant," the highlord grumbled.

"It's not," Isla said, kindly contradicting him. "Obel said that so long as the purpose is honorable, the risk to the Mage is greatly lessened."

"I don't trust Obel," Auden said, and Deckard realized he recognized the name. He couldn't remember from where, but he'd heard it—and possibly that exact sentence—before.

Isla gave him a small smile. "Vayden does," she said. "So do I."

Agitated, Hewitt spoke before the rest of them could. "I'm here for one reason, and one reason alone: to ensure Evylin is happy and cared for." He took in the way Evylin sat comfortably with Deckard's arm around her and nodded. "As I find that to be the case, I'm ready to go."

"What?" Deckard and Evylin said together.

Hewitt settled them with a gentle but serious stare. "Back in Whickam Village, I would have sworn an afterlife was merely rhetoric to make people feel good about death, but . . ." His eyes rose to scan the camp. "After Mages, Warriors, ghosts, and Relics, I'm rather certain there's more to life than anything I could dream up. And if there's a chance that I can get back to my Irena and Ryen, I'm taking it."

Deckard drew in a long breath as Evylin slumped against his side. "You want me to release you?" he asked, sorrow etching his voice. After all this time, he couldn't fathom letting the man go.

"I do," Hewitt said with determination.

Reluctantly, Deckard nodded. "Very well, but . . ." He turned to Auden. "I don't know how."

While Auden considered the question, Isla spoke up. "None of us can teach you that," she said. "However, where we're going, we have just the man for that job."

Auden scowled again but didn't argue the point.

"When we arrive tomorrow," Isla continued, "I'll make a request for you to meet with Highlord Obel. I guarantee he'll be able to help you. And if you summoned a ghost unintentionally," she shrugged, "it sounds like you could use his training too."

Deckard didn't know whether to be grateful or afraid of what that meant. More training meant a deeper connection to Night. And despite his determination to keep Hewitt around, he had to admit that Auden's warnings concerned him. What if he were predisposed to this Deep they'd talked about? If he could accidentally summon a ghost, what else could he do?

Running a hand through his hair, Deckard's exhaustion hit him full force. He looked up at Hewitt. "I don't have the strength to keep you here anymore."

The ghost's gray eyes flicked to Evylin's, then he nodded.

Deckard let him lapse away, easing the strain on his mind. He addressed Auden. "I'm not giving the Night Relic to Rafferty," he said, hurrying to continue before Auden could protest. "I won't use it, but it's safer with me. I know it's hard for you but try to trust my nature more than you distrust Night's. The Relic doesn't affect me the way it affects others."

Jarrad tapped his fingers thoughtfully along his knee but remained silent.

Auden sighed. "All right . . ." He flexed his hands as though trying not to fist them. "But once we get back to Ephria—"

"I'll happily give it up," Deckard promised.

With a final nod of acceptance, Auden backed away. An awkward silence remained as everyone attempted to return to their business. Thom took it upon himself to bring an end to the discomfort by announcing that the meal was ready.

Deckard watched knowingly as his brother helped everyone fill their bowls before he took his own meal. It was clear that he was already working to become a new man, while at the same time being more Thom than he had ever been before. It made Deckard proud.

The dinner helped them all to slip back into easy conversation. They learned more about Emmaas and Jarrad, discovering they had families in Wauld too. While Emmaas was an Ephrian by blood, he was born and raised in Schon, as his many-times great-grandfather had crossed the sea during the Auldan Mages' eradication of the Warriors in the late 1100s. It became quickly evident that he was far older than he looked when he told them about his family, most of whom remained in the Schonese Empire. He was a widower with three grown daughters who had families and grandchildren of their own. Only two of Emmaas's grandchildren had relocated to Wauld with him when he'd chosen to join the Alliance, thanks to one of their agents who worked in Schon to recruit the Warriors who had escaped to its shelter, as well as the few Mages born there.

Jarrad's story was far simpler. He was a northern Wauldener who'd discovered his connection to Terrae as a child. At which time, he was taken to Sutterlund Reach to train at the Order of the Wind (since the Order of the Terrae, originally in Ephria, was destroyed during Ephren's uprising). That was where he met Isla after she'd come to join the Order a few decades later. Despite their bickering, it seemed they were good friends, and she'd convinced him to join the Alliance. Afterward, he met his wife. They'd had their first child two years prior. However, like Isla, Jarrad was an aterian, with a position as a guard and steward for a member of the nobility in Mouroc, which took him away from his family for the time being.

"Isn't that hard?" Deckard asked. "Being away from your wife and child?"

"Of course," Jarrad said. "But it's worth it, knowing I'm making a better future for my son."

As interested as Deckard was in learning more about the Alliance and the members who had saved their lives, the moment he finished his meal, he excused himself. He was worn out in ways he'd never experienced. If given the opportunity, he thought he might be able to sleep for a full day. Maybe two.

Though he hadn't requested Evylin to retire with him, she followed behind readily. He glanced over his shoulder, noticing most of the camp doing the same. Emmaas and Ethenn sat up together, agreeing to take the first watch.

Far from the others, Deckard still kept his voice low as Evylin sat down next to him on their bedroll. "My head feels like it's about to tear in two," he said as he removed his boots. "I'm getting too old for this."

Evylin laughed, her arm brushing his as she worked off her coat. "I hate to remind you," she said playfully, "but you've got a minimum of another century to your life if Ilain is to be believed. You're not too old for anything."

"Oh, I forgot about that." Deckard sighed and lay back. The thought truly was daunting. One lifetime was enough to consider. He'd expected to live into his eighties, perhaps his nineties if life was kind, watching his children and grandchildren grow. He hadn't once thought that he might outlive them.

The thought sent a jolt of panic through his chest.

Deckard watched Evylin lie down next to him, his arm coming around her as naturally as breathing. "Do you know if Warriors live as long as Mages?" he asked warily.

Evylin scooted closer. "You can't get rid of me that easily," she teased. "According to Ilain, I'll live just as long as you. If not longer."

"How disappointing," he said, then kissed her temple.

Holding her in his arms again, it felt like they'd never been apart. And yet, somehow, it felt wholly different as well. She pressed into his side with far more comfort and intimacy than ever. He didn't fear making her uneasy with his affection or touch. They were as they were always meant to be.

Evylin rolled into him, resting her chin on his shoulder to meet his gaze. The distant fire cast the very edges of her figure in rusty red light. It caught in her eyes, highlighting an unexpected somberness within. "Jonn," she murmured, "I'm sorry—for everything."

Reaching up, Deckard cupped her face. "There's no need."

"But there is," she said. "Auden was right—well, not about our time with Renaul, but the rest of it. It's my fault. If I hadn't insisted on splitting up—"

"That was Auden's suggestion."

"But I pushed for it," she argued. "All because I was afraid of how I felt about you."

Brushing his thumb along her cheekbone, Deckard gave her an understanding smile. "And do you really think staying together would have helped you overcome that fear any sooner?"

Evylin hesitated. "Well . . . No."

He chuckled and leaned forward just enough to kiss the tip of her nose. "Then there's no reason to worry about it."

"But it didn't matter," she lamented. "We weren't attacked; we weren't followed. There was no reason to split at all."

"We don't know that. It's possible that our splitting is what kept those things from happening."

She raised her brow with a dry tilt. "Jonn, I'm trying to take responsibility for my actions. It would be nice if you'd let me."

Her words—albeit teasing—reminded Deckard of what Thom had said to him earlier. *"I'm trying to tell you that I'm sorry, but you slough it off as though what I did doesn't matter."* Was this a fault of his—being too apt to reject others' apologies in an attempt to absolve them?

He held Evylin's adamant stare. She was trying to apologize, and he'd immediately shut her down to make her feel better. Instead, he belittled her sincerity.

Deckard drew his hand down her back. "You're right," he whispered. "It appears that splitting may have been of no use. And yes, you impeded our happiness because you were too afraid to love me sooner. But I don't blame you for any of it. Not when I know the reason for the fear that drove you away from me."

She chewed on her bottom lip, her gaze dropping. Her thoughts muddled her expression, and Deckard wondered if she was thinking about Hewitt or Ryen.

"I owe you the truth," she said softly.

"About what?"

Her eyes met his. "About my past. About what I lost."

Deckard gave her a gentle smile, then drew her to lie fully beside him. He brushed the wisps of hair off her cheeks, grateful to be this close to her once again. "I would very much like to hear whatever you want to tell me," he promised, then let his lips lift in a sly grin. "But perhaps we can have this discussion at a later time when my body doesn't feel like it's been trampled by a dozen horses."

She returned his good humor with a melodramatic sigh. "If we must."

"Good."

She slipped her arm around him, letting it drape over his chest. He rested a hand on her arm, pressed a kiss to her forehead, then settled into her comfort. The gentlest warmth spread through Deckard. His magic rose, not urging but soothing. It was a tether between him and Evylin.

Past the canvas tent, he stared up at the depth of the night sky. The ivory and shadow moons beamed as bright as ever. The stars twinkled golden and silver. The heavens lay above them as the future lay before them, infinite and unknowable. Deckard was strangely content at the thought. His fingers began to draw little circles along Evylin's back, eyes locked on the rich black expanse shining deep purple around the celestial bodies. His lids grew heavy as peace soothed his exhaustion.

Evylin's nose tipped up, brushing his chin. "Jonn," she whispered.

"Hm?"

Her lips pressed against his neck, gentle and teasing. "I wish we were alone." The whisper of her breath raced across his skin in a heated tingle. His chest contracted in a silent laugh.

"I do too," he mumbled in reply, turning his face into her hair.

Evylin burrowed deeper into him. "I love you."

Deckard closed his eyes, giving in to sleep as the words slipped out. "I love you."

Also Available from V.K. Dixon

WARRIORS & MAGES
Fire & Night
Sword & Shadow
Relics & Thrones

ARCHIVES OF THE WARDEN
Lake of Glass
Vault of Stone
The Raven's Cry
Veil of Mist
The Wolf's Howl
Of Spirit & Ether (Coming Spring 2026)
Book Seven (Coming Fall 2026)

Acknowledgments

The sequel is inevitably the most difficult to write, it seems. This story took more than I expected—more heart, more thinking, more patience, and more determination. But I am thrilled to say I love what it's become.

My eternal gratitude to you, my readers. You have made this journey so much more beautiful and fulfilling than I ever imagined!

As always, Josh, you are the reason this story exists. Your encouragement and support over the last five years have breathed life into me. Every adventure you promised, you have fulfilled and more!

Thank you to all my family and friends. Thank you to my sweet Sam, whom I can't wait to introduce to this story once you're old enough.

Once again, to my editor, Brittany: Working with you has given me the skill to tell this tale. Without your guidance and help, I never would have been writer enough for this task.

Thank you to my Substack paid subscribers who have helped see me through this journey.

Thank you, God, for meeting me on this journey and taking me farther than I ever imagined I could go!

About the Author

V.K. Dixon writes fantasy and romance novels filled with found family, lasting love, and unique magic. She believes that the extraordinary gives us a deeper desire for the things beyond us—the things of God.